Alexander gathered Jane up in his arms and placed her gently on his bed.

"Will I be the first, or has the ghost won that contest as well?" he said.

"No," Jane whispered, with a mixture of shyness and sorrow. "Ye are the first."

"Ah," he said softly. "Then perhaps I have a chance."

Jane closed her eyes until she felt the length of his body next to hers. She waited a moment for him to make his claim on her, but all was silent. After an interlude, she fluttered open her lids to see him smiling at her.

"The Duchess of Gordon," he said quietly, tracing his slender finger lightly down her cheek, to her throat. "That's what you are, my love . . . that's what I want this night to mean. The past is finished. We are the House of Gordon."

Jane rose up on one elbow in order to look him fully in the face. She had no doubt, now, this complicated man was in love with her. Perhaps she could one day feel the same blinding commitment she had felt toward—

Jane clamped her eyes shut, willing the very name of Thomas Fraser banished from her mind.

"Help me!" she whispered into Alexander's ear, nuzzling his lobe as he had hers. "Help me banish all the ghosts, Alex, so we can truly be . . . the House of Gordon. . . ."

Island of the Swans

Ciji Ware

BANTAM BOOKS
TORONTO • NEW YORK • LONDON • SYDNEY • AUCKLAND

For
Anthony Pattison Cook
who always takes the high road

ISLAND OF THE SWANS

A Bantam Book / March 1989

ISBN 0-553-27598-4

Published simultaneously in the United States and Canada

Bantam Books are published by Bantam Books, a division of Bantam Doubleday Dell Publishing Group, Inc. Its trademark, consisting of the words ''Bantam Books'' and the portrayal of a rooster, is Registered in U.S. Patent and Trademark Office and in other countries. Marca Registrada. Bantam Books, 666 Fifth Avenue, New York, New York 10103.

PRINTED IN THE UNITED STATES OF AMERICA

O   0 9 8 7 6 5 4 3 2 1

Author's Note

The life of Jane Maxwell, on which the novel *Island Of the Swans* is based, has never been examined in depth by any serious scholar. This fact says more about the selection process employed by twentieth-century academics than it does about this fascinating eighteenth-century Scottish "Woman of Fashion" whom fate decreed would be beloved by two men—and would become a confidante of kings.

Most of what we do know about Jane Maxwell comes from passing references made by some of her contemporaries, including the Prince of Wales, Sir Walter Scott, Robert Burns, William Pitt (the Younger), Henry Dundas, Horace Walpole, Henry Erskine, Nathanial Wraxall, Dr. Samuel Johnson, and Sir Joshua Reynolds. Enticing clues to Jane's story can be found in newspaper and magazine accounts of her day that chronicle the events of the eighteenth-century Enlightenment, a glittering period of great cultural and political ferment. Records of the behind-the-scenes maneuvering during the tumultuous times of Scottish involvement in the American Revolution, the Prince of Wales's Debt Crisis, and the five-month Madness Crisis of George III in 1787–1788 describe events in which Jane Maxwell figured prominently. Also related to the story are the packets of letters, documents, and family papers stored in the National Library of Scotland, the Edinburgh City Library, and King's College Library in Aberdeen, among other archives.

The Huntington Library in San Marino, California, possesses a small number of letters relating directly to Jane and members of her family, as well as an enormous treasure trove of books, manuscripts, maps, and ephemera concerning Scotland, England, and America during the period this story takes place: 1760 to 1797.

My goal has been to combine the facts that are known from the written record about Jane Maxwell, with intelligent supposition about what is *not* known. This biographical novel spins a tale about love and the vagaries of fortune that shaped the life of a woman of great achievement in an age that, in many surprising ways, set the stage for our own.

Although great effort has been invested in weaving accurate research into the novel concerning the linkages between the Gordon and Fraser clans, Jane Maxwell, and the period in which she lived, several minor chronological shifts and time condensations were made for dramatic purposes within this work of fiction. None, I trust, distorts the overall sense of the story as I have been able to unravel it.

Many of the wits and writers of the eighteenth and early nineteenth centuries castigated Jane Maxwell for the unusual role she played in the social and political events of her day; others worshipped her. I choose to let the reader decide the truth.

> Ciji Ware,
> Beverly Hills, California

The Gordons boldly did advance
The Frasers fought with sword and lance

Anonymous

The Maxwells of Monreith

Sir William Maxwell m.1747 Magdalene Blair of Blair
3rd Baronet b.   d.1771   b.   d. 1807

Sir Wm., 4th Baronet   Hamilton   Catherine
b.   d. 1812   b. 1746(?)d. 1794   b.1747 m.1767
m. Katherine Blair   in India   John Fordyce
    of Ayton

The Dukedom of Gordon

Alexander, 2nd Duke m. 1706 Henrietta Fraser
b. 1678   Mordaunt

Cosimo George,   m.1741 Katherine Gordon (Haddo)
3rd Duke   b. 1718 d.1779
b. 1721 d. 1752

The Frasers of Lovat

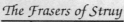

Simon the Fox m.1. Margaret Grant
11th Lord Lovat   m.2. Primrose Campbell
Executed 1747   Archibald

Master Simon m. Miss Bristo
b. 1727 (?) d. 1782
(Godfather to Thomas Fraser of Struy)
Estates Restored 1774

The Frasers of Struy

Sir Thomas m. Marguerite
b.   d. 1747   b.   d.1747

Thomas Fraser
b. 1747 d.

James Maxwell m. Elizabeth Maxwell of Ardwell   others

6 sons (including Montgomery); 3 daughters

Jane Maxwell
b. 1749 d. 1812
m. 1767 Alexander
4th Duke of Gordon
(see below)

Eglantine
b. 1751 d. 1803
m. 1772 Sir (!) Thomas
Dunlop Wallace

Dunbar
b.   d.1775

Charles
b.   d. 1780

Lewis
b.   d.1754
(Jacobite)

Adam
b.   d.1801

others

Alexander, 4th Duke
b. 1743 d. 1827
m. 1767 Jane Maxwell
(see above)

William
b.
d.1831

George   sisters
b.
d.1793
(Gordon Riots)

Charlotte m. Charles Lennox
b.1768   4th Duke of Richmond
d.1842   b.1764 d.1819

George, 5th Duke
(Lord Huntly)
b.1770 d.1836

Madelina m. Sir Robert
b.1772   Sinclair
d.1849

Susan m. Wm. Montague
b.1774   5th Duke of Manchester
d.1828   b.1771 d.1843

Louisa m. Marquis
b.1776   Cornwallis
d.1850   b.1774 d.1823

Georgina m. John Russell
b.1781   6th Duke of Bedford
d.1853   b.1766 d.1839

Alexander
b.1785
d.1808

Design by
Marilyn McCracken

1

1760–1767

Here lived the lovely Jane
who best combined
A beauteous form to a
superior mind

Sir John Sinclair

1

Edinburgh, October 1760

Perched uncomfortably on a low stool in the drafty sitting room, the young girl stared miserably at the wrinkled scrap of embroidery lying forlornly on her lap. Refusing to look at her mother, Jane Maxwell angrily stabbed her needle into the clumsily stitched letters that proclaimed She Is A Joy Who Doth Obey.

"Jane!" said Lady Maxwell crossly, pointing to the threads that ran at decidedly odd angles across the soiled fabric. " 'Tis impossible to sew properly if ye dinna stretch the piece upon yer frame. Ye'll take out every *word*, missy," she said in an exasperated tone, "until ye do it *perfectly*!"

Voicing her reproach at her ten-year-old daughter's failure to master yet another of the feminine arts, Lady Maxwell retrieved Jane's crumpled sampler and sighed audibly as she examined it more closely.

"Ye haven't made a bit of progress since yesterday, lass. In fact, 'tis *worse*! Were ye up to no good with Thomas again when ye should have been at yer needlework?"

Jane's silence confirmed her guilt.

"Every daughter of mine will show prospective suitors she has mastered the art of being a *lady*!"

"But, Mama—surely I shan't have to marry someone as dreadful as Daddie for years and years!" Jane retorted vehemently.

"Impudent chit!" Lady Maxwell snapped. "A mother has only to *blink* and she has a spinsterish lass on her hands. Now, I want ye to sit on this stool till ye've restitched the entire line!"

A rebellious flush flooded Jane's cheeks as she bent over her embroidery, her hands clenched.

"I *hate* it and I winna *do* it!" she muttered under her breath.

"*What* did ye say?" Lady Maxwell inquired, her eyes growing hard.

Looking up at her mother's glowering features, Jane swallowed her pique.

3

"I've no talent with a needle, Mama," she corrected herself carefully, "and 'tis so hard on ye to be bothering with such a hopeless seamstress as I."

"Ye've only been trying with half a heart," her mother replied, unmoved by Jane's entreaties. "By the time I return from my morning calls I expect ye to be finished with it, do ye hear me?"

Lady Maxwell stalked out of the chilly room before Jane could protest any further. In the three years since baronet Sir William Maxwell had deserted his wife and daughters in favor of his ramshackle holdings and estate-bottled whiskey in Monreith, south of Edinburgh, Magdalene had attempted to rule her middle daughter with a firmer hand. She had launched a campaign—fruitless, so far—to mold the mutinous lass into a highly desirable young lady capable, one day, of catching the fancy of a suitable gentleman of means. It was the only route open to her as a respectable, albeit lowly and impecunious member of the Scottish aristocracy.

Lady Maxwell's eldest daughter, Catherine, was sweet but plain, as anyone with eyes could see, and there wasn't time to wait to see how wee Eglantine would mature. Yes, a proper match for Jane as soon as was seemly could rescue them *all* from the wretched, genteel poverty in which they now lived, a poverty surely deepening with each passing year.,

By the time she's sixteen, Jane will marry well! Lady Maxwell vowed to herself. *I will show that drunken sot of a husband he canna ruin Magdalene Blair of Blair!*

She attempted to calm the throbbing in her temples—a sensation that plagued her whenever she contemplated the abusive treatment and shocking lack of funds she had endured at the hands of that cursed man. However, all was not lost. Jane, thank heavens, showed unmistakable signs of becoming a beauty!

Sweeping her threadbare skirts past the front door and into the dark, narrow alley called Hyndford Close, Lady Maxwell offered her hand to the strapping bearers poised to assist her into her hired sedan chair. The household might go without meat for days at a time, but nothing would stay her from making her morning calls in a suitable conveyance. Magdalene relaxed against the worn upholstery, as she was borne in and out of the traffic clogging Edinburgh's High Street, and closed her weary eyes.

Suddenly, she was startled by the cacophonous sounds of clanging church bells and cannon fire rumbling eerily through a maze of narrow streets and alleyways that fanned out from the entrance gates of Edinburgh Castle, high above the city.

"Not to worry, madam," cried one of the sedan chair bearers over his shoulder. " 'Tis the six guns of the Argyle Battery! Have ye ever heard such thunder in yer life?"

"I'll wager George the Third can hear this clamor all the way to London town!" muttered Lady Maxwell sourly. For her, the noisy commemoration of the twenty-two-year-old king's unanticipated ascension to the throne of England, Ireland, Scotland, and Wales held absolutely no excitement as her own domestic troubles claimed her complete attention.

Lady Maxwell stared absently at the clear autumn sky. She sought solace in the fact that Jane continued to show signs of developing into an appealing wench, even if her manners were atrocious. She realized that her hoydenish daughter would rather climb the back fences of Edinburgh or browse among the bookstalls on the High Street with that neighborhood waif, Thomas Fraser, than acquire any of the feminine charms that would eventually provide a secure future for her. However, Lady Maxwell had a plan to remedy the problem. She tapped her fan against the stained velvet curtain that shielded her from the riffraff traveling along the busy thoroughfare. She would soon put an end to her daughter's devotion to that pleasant but penniless orphan.

A small stab of guilt pricked Lady Maxwell's conscience, as memories of Thomas's brotherly kindnesses toward Jane and her sisters during these difficult years floated through her mind. However, a mother had her duty, and unless something drastic was done, the task of keeping Jane and Thomas apart would soon be nigh impossible. Thomas was plainly fondest of Jane, and her middle daughter had utterly ignored all of her mother's pointed instructions as to the appropriate behavior of young ladies.

In fact, Jane's near legendary willfulness was the subject that preoccupied Lady Maxwell as the sounds of cannon faded and the normal clatter of town activity resumed. Feeling utterly overwhelmed by unpaid bills owed the fishmonger, the pub master, the seamstress—just to name a few of her most pressing creditors—Magdalene Maxwell turned over the few possibilities open to her as her sedan chair bearers threaded their way among the foot and wheeled traffic. Plastering a grim smile on her lips, she prepared for the first of several duty calls on aristocratic

mothers of eligible sons who might one day trade their titles and
wealth for Jane Maxwell's fair hand.

At the bottom of the stone stairs, Catherine Maxwell stared at
her younger sister with a mixture of apprehension and awe.

"I think we should go back, Jane," she ventured nervously as
thirteen-year-old Thomas Fraser hailed them from the far end of
the cobbled alley behind their five-story dwelling in Hyndford
Close. "Mama will lock you in the attic if ye dinna finish that
line on yer sampler."

"Pooh!" Jane dismissed her with a wave of her dainty hand.
"Mama will be hours making her rounds. Hullo, Thomas, what's
that in yer hand?"

"A little souvenir of today's coronation," he replied slyly,
waving a torn piece of parchment. "Want one for yerself?"

"Aye . . . let's show that King Geordie what we think of 'im
in Scotland!" Jane declared, ripping down several pieces of an
official-looking placard from the stone wall above her head, and
dancing a jig on them with her scuffed brogues.

She looked triumphantly at Thomas Fraser, her companion in
crime, who grinned his approval, while Jane's two sisters stared,
open-mouthed, at the young vandals' daring.

The three Maxwell sisters and the spare, hollow-cheeked boy
trod stealthily along the stone wall nearest them and peered out
from the dark shadows of Blackfriars Wynd at the retreating
figure of Edinburgh's Chief Constable Munro. They watched the
officer stroll down the walled city's principal road, carrying a
sheaf of newly printed broadsides under his arm. The posters he
had been distributing throughout the city proclaimed the coronation, this twenty-fifth day of October 1760, of George III, King
of All Britons.

Jane, her brown eyes glinting with mischief, looked around
Blackfriars Wynd cautiously. Standing on tiptoe, the youngster
grabbed another of the elaborately lettered coronation notices off
the granite wall that faced the worn stone stairs leading to the
local wigmaker's shop. She thrust the detested parchment into
the hands of her young male companion, who promptly tore it to
shreds. Together, Jane and Thomas stamped furiously on the
remains until they had trampled the proclamation to bits.

"Och, Jane! The constable nearly turned around!" gulped
Catherine Maxwell, the eldest and invariably the most cautious
of the quartet. "I thought sure he'd spy ye this time!"

"And what if he should?" Jane demanded. "He probably

feels the same as we do! Thomas says that fat Hanoverian's no king to us Scots. Charlie's our true sovereign—'tis so, Thomas Fraser, now, 'tisn't it?''

The gaunt, shabbily dressed lad merely frowned at Catherine and leaned against the stone-paved arch. As far as most northern Scots such as young Thomas Fraser were concerned, the late George II was a brute and his recent demise was suitably ignominious: he had collapsed in his water closet earlier in the week from a stroke brought about by his fierce exertions in that most private of chambers. Few Highlander families such as the Frasers, who had failed in an attempt fifteen years earlier to restore the Stuart dynasty to the throne, mourned his passing, nor did they look forward to the coming reign of his baby-faced grandson, George III.

A shaft of sunlight filtering through the shadowy passageway transformed Thomas Fraser's distinctive dark red hair into the color of aged burgundy. His ruddy skin was free of freckles, thanks to the legacy of a Roman ancestor. And if the boy hadn't been so thin and undernourished, his prominent cheekbones and gray-green eyes would have made his young face quite handsome.

" 'Tis not child's play, what we're about!'' Thomas said ferociously to his female audience. To dramatize his point, he yanked down another placard affixed to the wool merchant's shop. " 'Tis an action 'gainst that English swine who dares call himself king!''

Suddenly, Jane clapped her hands excitedly.

"Ye've just given me a grand idea!'' she said, a wicked gleam in her eye. "A *pig* race! Let's have a pig race!'' she exclaimed. "We havena had one in *such* a long time—and 'twill be a fitting *tribute* to our new king, dinna ye think, Thomas?'' she added impishly, tugging on his sleeve as she composed her expressive features into a look of feigned respect.

"Nay, Jenny!'' interrupted Catherine, using their pet name for Jane, and shaking her head vehemently. "We mustna race the pigs! Mama was *furious* the last time. She said if ye disgraced the Maxwells like that again, she'd give ye a thumping ye'd ne'er forget!''

Ignoring Catherine's protests, Jane signaled the others to follow her as she scampered along the High Street, ducking down another narrow passageway. Just before the alleyway dead-ended into a stone wall, the youngsters dashed through an archway and emerged behind the five-storied tenement that included their own lodgings. Jane and Thomas led the pack, running swiftly across the communal backyard toward a pig enclosure at the far side of the small, green pasture tucked behind the tall buildings. To the south of this clearing lay the stone boundary wall of the city, and below it, a sheer, four hundred-foot granite drop. The volcanic outcropping on which Edinburgh was built had protected it from its enemies for eight hundred years.

"Quickly, before old Hector sees us!" Jane cried, motioning to her companions. She prayed that the stableman at the Red Lion Inn, who also looked after the Maxwells' pigs, would not catch the four conspirators and enforce Lady Maxwell's stern strictures regarding Jane and any future pig contests.

In the dim light of the pig pen, the three Maxwell sisters appeared quite alike, with their chestnut hair and slender bodies. But Jane had a more finely etched brow than either Catherine or Eglantine and a nose of aristocratic shape, slightly Roman in cast. Her mouth, quick to smile, framed small, even teeth. Even at age ten, her features had that special stamp of a Maxwell: strong and stubborn. At the moment, however, her expression belied that. Jane was grinning happily at her companions as she settled her weight gingerly on the broad back of an enormous sow. She threw a challenging look toward her more sedate older sister, Catherine, who adamantly refused to join the competition.

"Let *me* race on Tattie! Oh, please, Jane—*please*!" begged Eglantine who, until she'd reached her ninth birthday, had been routinely excluded from Jane and Thomas's mischief making.

Jane glanced over at the younger version of herself, hopping up and down excitedly in anticipation of her very first pig race. Eglantine looked eagerly for her approval as Jane, plagued by a momentary sense of guilt, noticed that the hem of her threadbare day dress was already streaked with filth. With a characteristic act of will, she quickly purged the thought of her mother's displeasure from her mind and nodded to Eglantine her permission to take part in the competition.

Jane surveyed Thomas's ragged breeches and frayed linen shirt as he lifted Eglantine on the back of a second sow, which twitched nervously in its pen. The lad was in an even poorer state than the Maxwells; the Frasers had been stripped of their land and hereditary titles when they supported Bonnie Prince Charlie against the Hanovarians who held the British throne. Clan Fraser had gambled everything on the Stuart Cause—and lost. And Thomas had never even known his parents, who had died amid terrible suffering.

Jane gazed at Thomas Fraser with a fierce sense of loyalty

forged by a friendship with the lad who'd been her closest companion all her young life. His hurt was her hurt. His family's loss of their estates and titles felt like her loss as well. She vowed she would always follow him, protect him and love him as if he were a Maxwell, not a Fraser. Briefly, Jane thought of her brothers William, Hamilton, and Dunbar living in Monreith with her Da, whom she hadn't seen in three years. Before the gnawing sadness could take hold of her, she quickly pushed their shadowy images from her mind.

Thomas fumbled with the catch on the wooden gate that led into the hidden square of open green space, just off St. Mary's Wynd.

"*Ready*, Eglantine?" Jane cried impatiently. She looked back at her younger sister, who seemed thrilled to be allowed a part in Jane's favorite game: turning the dignified High Street into a racing course for swine.

Jane tensed every muscle in her body, anticipating the start of the contest. Thomas yanked open the gate of the pig pen, scraping the worn wood planking through the sucking mud. Jane repeatedly thrashed her mount's sides in an attempt to urge the pig through the opening ahead of her sister.

"Shoo! Shoo!" shouted Jane irritably. "Give her a whack with the broom handle, laddie!"

"All right, minxes," cried Thomas, addressing the riders as well as their recalcitrant porkers, "Out—out! Get along—shoo, shoo!"

He gave both pigs lightning whacks on their rears and roared with delight as Jane's mount emitted an enraged grunt. She reached for a firm grip on the old sow's ears. *This* time, she thought to herself excitedly, she was bound to win. The pig continued to make protesting squeals as it waddled hurriedly into St. Mary's Wynd. The two sisters' high-pitched shrieks echoed along the steep-sided alley as Thomas gave Eglantine's slower beast another slap.

"The first one who passes Fountain Well wins the race!" he shouted so Jane might hear. "On with ye, ye filthy piggies!" he barked.

At the sound of the noisy contest, windows flew open on both sides of the alley and across the cobbled High Street. Peals of laughter reverberated merrily down St. Mary's Wynd.

"Those Maxwell snippets are at it again," chuckled Peter Ramsay as he stood in the door of the Red Lion Inn. His plump wife wiped her rough, chapped hands on her apron.

The innkeeper's gaze followed the erratic path taken by the two pig riders whose mounts waddled toward the mainstream of city traffic. The strolling fishmongers and hawkers called out their wares to residents of the five- and seven-storied tenements rising up on all sides. Carts and wheelbarrows from the farms outside the city walls rattled alongside the elegant carriages of the gentry and the occasional sedan chair borne on the shoulders of burly Highlanders, for whom such menial labor was all that was left to them since the failed Rebellion fifteen years earlier.

From her perch on the sow's broad back, Jane gave a jaunty salute to the couple standing in the doorway of the Red Lion Inn. Ramsay and his wife chuckled and waved back. Jane glanced over at Thomas, who was thumping Eglantine's uncooperative sow with the broom handle.

"Not fair, Thomas!" Jane shouted as Eglantine's pig bolted unexpectedly close to Old Swill.

"I'm looking forward to seeing ye get yer comeuppance, lassie," he joked.

With a few quick strides, Thomas passed the girls as they bounced along, screeching commands to their pigs to move faster, kicking them wildly and cajoling them toward Fountain Well, a hundred yards distant. By now, a crowd had gathered and veteran observers were shouting to the carts and carriages on Edinburgh's bustling thoroughfare: "Make way for the swine—make way for the swine!"

As the race proceeded, both girls kicked and shouted at their rebellious pigs.

"On there, Eglantine!" shouted old Duncan McClellan, pausing to cheer the saucy young challenger as he clutched a basket of unsold fish in his arms.

"Jane, lassie, yer winnin'!" countered Matilda Sinclair, a bride of three months whose surly husband looked down on the proceedings from a second-floor window, his face puckered in a scowl.

Jock Sinclair, who worked long hours at the tannery built on the banks of North Loch at the foot of Castle Rock, was clearly upset. He resented having to wait for his morning tea, especially when the delay was caused by a lass whose pig racing had not long ago landed Jock unceremoniously in the mud. His mouth set in a hard line as he watched his new wife set down her wooden bucket of water pumped from Fountain Well and shout encouragement to her friend Jane. When the pig had run Jock down, Matilda had *laughed* at his indignity—and so had that

Maxwell brat! To his way of thinking, both females needed to be taught a lesson.

"Matilda! Draw yer water and make me m'tea, bitch!" he shouted through the casement window.

"I'll be comin' in a moment, Jock," she shouted back defiantly, though it might earn her a beating later. "Ye're safe enough on the second story, I'll be bound!"

Soon scores of spectators appeared to view the contest from windows and shop doors. A handsome carriage with a ducal crest on its shining black door drew near where Thomas was posted at the finish line at Fountain Well.

As he watched the carriage curtains being quickly drawn aside, Thomas was caught off guard by the appearance of the widowed Dowager Duchess of Gordon and her three sons, Alexander and his younger brothers, George and William. Thomas's jaw clenched at the sight of the quartet staring out at the unusual proceedings through the open window of their elegant coach. How he *hated* Clan Gordon!

"Ah, the famous Jane Maxwell," commented Alexander, the seventeen-year-old 4th Duke of Gordon, as the carriage came to a halt. "I have heard of her little competitions on the High Street." He stared in amusement at the two riders whose mounts were stubbornly refusing to head in the same direction, despite frantic kicks from their pint-size jockeys. Thomas disdained even to nod at young Gordon. Alexander narrowed his eyes as he stared critically at Thomas.

"Are you not one of Simon Fraser's young pups?" he asked with barely concealed scorn. "Master of the Swine Course, I presume?"

Thomas nodded stiffly and drew himself up in an attempt to look taller. His godfather had never forgiven this duke's deceased father, Cosimo George, the 3rd Duke of Gordon, for refusing to come out in favor of the Stuart Cause in 1745. Gordon lands lay hard by Fraser territory. It might have made the difference at the Battle of Culloden Moor if the Cock O' the North, as all Dukes of Gordon were called, had thrown in his lot with Prince Charlie's men.

"I am Thomas Fraser of Struy, Yer Grace," he said with as much hauteur as he could muster, "godson to Simon Fraser, *Master* of Lovat."

Thomas stared insolently at the passengers in the carriage, remembering the grisly outcome of such Gordon treachery. From babyhood, Thomas had heard the stories of how, after the defeat at Culloden, Master Simon's father, the old gout-ridden chief of Clan Fraser, the 11th Lord Lovat, known as Simon, the Fox, had paused during his hasty retreat and witnessed the king's men burning to the ground the Fraser family seat at Dounie Castle.

"Ah, yes—Colonel Simon Fraser," the duchess said derisively. "I had heard that after his father was executed in the Tower, the son was eventually released from prison and permitted to form a regiment of ruffians to fight the savages in the New World. How perfectly appropriate."

The orphaned lad stared contemptuously at the countenance of the 3rd Duchess of Gordon.

"Master Simon Fraser is your Highland *neighbor*, madam, and serves *yer king*!" he said in a barely civil tone. His adolescent voice cracked slightly and he flushed to the roots of his claret-colored mane. He *despised* these Gordons and their sneers!

Suddenly, the duke's younger brother George emitted a shrill titter and pointed a slender white finger toward Eglantine's and Jane's sows, who were butting heads in the middle of the High Street. Thomas stared at the braying brat with disdain, recalling rumors that the odd-looking Lord George had a touch of the famous Gordon Madness—a malady that Thomas supposed must have resulted from too many Gordon cousins intermarrying. He jutted his chin in the air and met Alexander Gordon's steady gaze.

Attempting to salvage some shred of dignity, Thomas added with feigned solicitude toward the 4th Duke's odd sibling, "Sink me—is he *ill*?"

Ignoring Thomas's barb as well as the strange behavior of his peculiar younger brother, the aristocrat turned to gaze at Eglantine and Jane. The Maxwell sisters were still kicking and thumping their animals in an attempt to get them across an imaginary finish line near Fountain Well.

Refusing to accept Alex's apparent dismissal, Thomas said challengingly, "Ye've finished at Eton, m'lord?"

"Of course," the young duke replied airily. "However, my sainted mama is preparing to ship young William and me off next spring on an obligatory Grand Tour of the Continent before our studies at Cambridge commence," he added with a sardonic look aimed at his imperious mother. " 'Tis a vain attempt to civilize us, I suppose."

Apparently his youngest brother, the giggling Lord George Gordon, was either too stupid or too high-strung to benefit from such travel.

Thomas noted the young duke's English accent. It was free of any Highland inflection, insuring that the Duke of Gordon, to say nothing of his pudgy brother, would be welcome in the drawing rooms of London and courts of Europe. Their futures were assured in every way, while Thomas's remained bleak and uncertain.

"The wagers!" Jane shouted at Thomas, interrupting his verbal sparring match with the Duke of Gordon. "Dinna forget to collect the wagers!"

She kicked her sow's sides sharply, but made little progress toward Fountain Well.

"I'll put a farthing on the challenger!" announced the fishmonger, Duncan McClellan, who handed Thomas a thin coin.

"Then let me put a sovereign on her sister Jane," the young Duke of Gordon said suddenly, pulling out a coin from a pocket in his richly embroidered silk waistcoat.

"We've no need of yer English siller, sir!" Thomas retorted scathingly. "We're *Scotsmen* here."

The intended insult hit its mark. Alexander glared through the window, speechless at Thomas's effrontery. Just at that moment, the attention of the young men, the dowager duchess, and the rest of the crowd was drawn to the shrieking Eglantine, whose sow had discovered a puddle of water seeping out from the base of Fountain Well. The pig was snorting at the muddy water with single-minded fervor while its exasperated rider wheedled and whacked the animal with all her might. Jane's pig suddenly spotted the mud puddle near the fountain and veered over to investigate. At the same time, Eglantine's mount settled itself comfortably into the ooze. As Eglantine, her skirts and leggings slathered with mud, gripped her pig's neck, the sow's curlicued tail brushed against the far side of the base of Fountain Well.

Without so much as a fare-thee-well to the passengers in the black coach, Thomas raced over to where the swine had wallowed to a halt. Noting that the pig's quivering tail had, indeed, crossed the finish line, he rendered his judgment.

"Eglantine Maxwell," he bellowed, "competing for the first time in the Grand Championship Swine Course, is hereby and *officially* declared the true and honest winner!"

He opened his palm flat and presented the youngest Maxwell sister with the few coins wagered by the applauding spectators. Jane's mount, startled by the cheers from an appreciative crowd, suddenly spun around and dashed over the finish line where the pig promptly tossed Jane into the mud beside Eglantine, who was already basking in the glow of victory.

"Damn, damn, damn!" screeched Jane in a fit of temper, using an expletive her mother abhorred.

Jane closed her eyes and clenched her fists, gritting her teeth in a fit of pique. When she opened them, she glared over at her sister and took stock of Eglantine's disarray. Eglantine, in turn, stared back at Jane, caked with mud, and both girls began to howl, laughing along with the crowd. Matilda Sinclair volunteered her water bucket to wash off the worst of the muck, and Jane plunged her hands and arms into its coolness, splashing her flushed face and smiling her thanks to the affable young goodwife.

"His Grace, the Duke of Gordon, offers this linen in hopes it will assist ye," said the duke's footman, extending a frock-coated arm bearing a large embroidered handkerchief, monogrammed with the familiar Gordon stag's head crest.

Thomas was about to dismiss the duke's unwelcome emissary, but Jane snatched the linen from the servant and patted her face and arms with it. Thomas watched stonily as she waved the cloth in acknowledgment above her head. She made a mock, unbalanced curtsy in the direction of the black coach without even focusing on the faces in the carriage window.

The dowager duchess frowned, but Alexander, the 4th Duke of Gordon, glanced back at Jane Maxwell for a long moment. Thomas could swear that their eyes met briefly and then, suddenly, the two young people grinned at each other across the milling throng. Abruptly, the carriage curtains closed, and the aristocratic passengers disappeared from view.

"Ye certainly paid yer public respects to that Anglified fop!" Thomas exclaimed angrily.

"Gadzooks, Thomas, the laddie was merely performing a common kindness! What's ailing ye, for heaven sakes?"

When he failed to reply, Jane shrugged and turned to watch the splendid coach move down the High Street. Then she proffered the damp linen to Eglantine to wipe the brackish water dripping from her arms and face.

Thomas struggled to regain his good humor.

"Well, my lovelies, have ye had enough sport for one day?" he asked, and ordered two stable boys to lead the sows back to the small yard behind the Maxwell's townhouse.

"I've had my fill of yer *judging*, Thomas Fraser!" Jane retorted, turning to chat with Matilda Sinclair, and pointedly ignoring him.

Catherine had remained on the sidelines at the start of the race, cheering both her sisters under her breath in spite of her resolve to show them how much she disapproved of their antics. As Eglantine handed the duke's linen to Jane, Catherine urged her sisters to hurry back to Hyndford Close.

"We'd best be getting home, and ye both changed before Mama sees us," she pleaded, glancing nervously up the street.

"Go along, hinny," called Jane, catching sight of a cart rattling downhill toward Grassmarket Square virtually overflowing with juicy red apples. "For such a miserable ending to a fine race, I intend to restore Thomas's spirits and mine with a reward!"

Before Thomas or Catherine could stop her, Jane was running alongside the lumbering wooden cart, with Eglantine scampering twenty paces behind her. She hooked her right slipper on the base of the platform that supported the mound of shining fruit and hopped a few times on her left foot as her hands felt for the wooden slats on the back of the cart. Hoisting herself up, Jane grabbed an apple with her free hand. She was about to reach for a second when both driver and horse, unaware of the nobly born thief in their midst, responded with a start to the shift in weight. The whoops and cheers from the remaining throng applauding Mistress Jane's latest antics only added to the confusion, and the cart horse flattened its ears and bolted in fright. As the driver attempted to recover the reins, the horse reared up with an angry whinny and leapt forward with a jerk.

Jane felt her arms nearly pull out of their sockets. Her right hand was riveted by a searing pain as she tried to grab hold of the wooden slats. Apples tumbled to the ground on all sides of her as the cart bolted forward again. Falling backwards, she landed with a heavy thud in the middle of the busy thoroughfare. Eglantine began to wail at the sight of her sister lying motionless in the road, and a crowd began to gather once again. Catherine, hearing screams, turned from the entrance to Hyndford Close.

"Oh, dear God!" Catherine shouted across the road to Thomas. "*Jane*!" she cried, pointing a hundred yards down the road. "She's hurt!"

They both ran toward the small heap that lay in the road. Jane was moaning in pain, her right hand clamped between her legs, her body curled up in agony. Thomas reached her first, stumbling over the apples, which had scattered in every direction.

Cradling her head in his lap, he crooned, "Jenny, lass . . . Jenny, I'm here," and unfastened the duke's handkerchief from her waistband where she had stuffed it for safekeeping.

Thomas directed Jane's terror-stricken sisters to run back to the well with the linen to make a compress and to bring him a bucket of fresh water. Then he gently felt Jane's body for broken bones, continuing to talk to her in a melodic, loving voice.

"Jenny lassie, what hurts the most?" asked Thomas anxiously, cursing himself for failing to prevent such a dangerous misadventure.

"My hand . . . my hand . . ." moaned Jane, keeping her legs clamped rigidly together with her right hand pinioned between her thighs.

Catherine and Eglantine dashed up with Matilda Sinclair carrying the heavy bucket of water between them. The Duke of Gordon's linen handkerchief floated on its surface like a cloud. Thomas directed Matilda to get the cloth as clean as possible and wring it dry.

"Let me see, dearheart," he said gently, trying to pry her knees apart so he could have a look at her hand. "Let me see what ye've done to yerself."

"Oh, Thomas, it hurts so much!" Jane cried pitifully, her eyes shut and her body rigid with the pain.

"Please, pet, let me help ye—let me have a look," he pleaded, gently pulling at her right forearm.

Jane suddenly went limp.

"She's dead!" wailed Eglantine, clutching at Catherine's arm.

"She's swooned, Thomas," Matilda said with alarm, while noting that Jane was still breathing.

"Well, that's a blessing," he replied grimly, motioning for Matilda to take his place cradling her head.

Moving down the side of Jane's still body, he carefully pulled her hand from between her thighs. There, lying among the folds of Jane's bloody skirts, was a delicate, freshly washed forefinger held to her right hand by only a thin shred of skin. The bolting of the cart had sheared it right off.

"Dinna look, lasses," Thomas said roughly. "She's torn off a finger and we've got to stop the bleeding."

Eglantine gulped aloud and looked as if she were going to be sick. Catherine, too, had to look away, but Matilda bravely cradled Jane's injured hand as Thomas ripped the duke's handkerchief in wide strips. He firmly bound the linen around the hand with the severed finger. Saving the last strip, he tied the cloth tightly above her wrist to help staunch the flow of blood.

With some difficulty, Matilda helped Thomas lift Jane's unconscious body against his own. They were nearly equal in height and Jane's dead weight meant that carrying her up the High Street was no easy task.

"Here, let me help ye, laddie," Matilda volunteered, knowing, however, that her tardiness would most likely inflame Jock more.

Catherine and Eglantine ran ahead to fetch the physic who lived nearby while Matilda Sinclair and Thomas carried Jane as gently as they could toward her lodgings.

Lady Magdalene Maxwell's sedan chair was just arriving at Hyndford Close when the rescuers reached the entranceway. Hearing Thomas's shouts, her ladyship drew open her curtains in alarm, her hand flying to her mouth in horror when she saw the pair carrying her daughter.

"The lass will be all right, yer ladyship, but she has hurt herself and should be put to bed immediately. Kitty and Eglantine have gone for Dr. McIntyre."

"Oh, dear God! Look at her! There's blood everywhere—come quickly!"

Lady Maxwell stepped briskly out of her sedan chair, instructing the bearers to call for their wages later in the day, and hurried toward the door. Having heard the commotion through the open second-floor window, Fiona McFarland, the Maxwells' disheveled housemaid, flung open the door as Thomas and Matilda struggled with their burden up the narrow stone staircase to the family's private quarters.

"In here," directed Lady Maxwell urgently, turning into a room with a low, timbered ceiling. "Put her on that bed. Fiona, bring up some hot water right away and have Cook heat another kettle."

Thomas and Matilda gently lowered Jane's body on the worn and patched linen counterpane. Lady Maxwell's fear for her child and anger over this mishap were clearly discernible on her flushed face.

"I'll be going now, yer ladyship," Matilda said swiftly, bobbing a curtsy. "I'm sure she'll be all right soon."

"Thank ye, Matilda," Lady Maxwell said, tight-lipped, as the young woman sped out the door, anxious to return to her husband before *his* anger translated into more than a shove or a slap.

"Would ye do me the courtesy, Thomas, of explaining exactly what ye've gotten Jane into *this* time?" Lady Maxwell demanded, barely keeping her emotions under control. Wringing her hands and shaking her head, she complained bitterly, "How do you and the lass find the Devil's own trouble? I warned ye

both to take care after she twisted her ankle when ye two jumped
from the hay byre in the stable yard last winter! She's going to
damage that pretty *face* of hers one day and *then* where will she
be?''

Thomas was fearful of interrupting her tirade in order to tell
her how seriously Jane's hand had been injured.

Jane's eyes fluttered slightly and she began to whimper. Lady
Maxwell's fervent relief that her child was conscious soon gave
way to exasperation.

''What the neighbors must *think* of us,'' she muttered.

She studied Thomas's profile as he gazed worriedly down at
Jane who was moaning softly. *'Twas a pity he'd never be called
Sir, like his dead da, and hadn't two farthings of his own to rub
together*. She noted how tenderly his gaze lingered on her daugh-
ter's still form. At ten, Jane was still only a madcap child. *But
Thomas was nearly fourteen . . . Thomas would soon . . .*

Jane groaned loudly and tried to raise her hand, bound in a
ball of linen stained a reddish hue. Lady Maxwell began to pull
absently at Jane's filthy linen petticoat, when she suddenly realized that Thomas, who had always seemed to her simply like
another of her boisterous sons, was gazing at her partially clad
daughter. Her eyes narrowed. The pair's childhood camaraderie
must be ended forthwith and Thomas be made aware that her
plans for Jane stretched far beyond the hopeless dreams of a
landless, titleless orphan who had a penchant for causing mischief such as this current calamity.

Lady Maxwell called to her maid with irritation.

''*Will* ye hurry, Fiona! Where's that water? Thomas,'' she
added crisply, ''I've not time to deal with yer part in this, but I
will instruct ye to desist from such folly in future, 'Tis no longer
suitable, lad, that ye should engage in such pranks with my
daughters. They're proper young ladies now, and I shall not
permit them to roam the city like urchins. Especially Jane. Now
please go and see what's become of Fiona and then wait for the
physic downstairs,'' she finished, dismissing him with a wave of
her hand.

Shocked at the harshness of her words, Thomas manfully
attempted to mask his hurt. He turned to leave. A faint voice
halted his progress to the door.

''Thomas?''

It was Jane, sounding weak with fear. He had almost never
seen her cry since she was a toddler and her brother Hamilton
would torment her by depriving her of some toy or frippery. But

real tears now swelled silently over Jane's dark eyelashes and rolled down her cheeks.

"Where's Thomas?" she whispered hoarsely.

"He's just going to find Fiona," her mother said impatiently.

"Thomas!" Jane cried out.

Lady Maxwell nodded to the lad, reluctantly granting him permission to return to Jane's bedside.

"Jenny, lass, yer safe in yer mother's house now—not to worry, pet," he said. He suddenly felt painfully self-conscious in Lady Maxwell's presence.

"My hand . . . Thomas . . . my hand hurts so much!"

"I know, Jenny girl. . . . I know. But the physic is coming to help, and ye'll be fine, lassie . . . I know ye will."

"Hold my good hand," Jane gulped between uneven breaths.

With that, he gave her unbandaged left hand a soft squeeze, transferring it gently to Lady Maxwell's waiting grasp and quietly left the room.

"Dinna go," Jane said in a whisper only her mother could hear. "Please, Thomas, dinna leave me."

2

September 1763

Simon Fraser shifted his massive bulk uncomfortably in his favorite chair. He was unaccustomed to entertaining female visitors in his Edinburgh townhouse, save for the occasional wench whom he spirited up the servants' stairs to his private bedchamber. In any event, he was certainly not used to serving tea.

"A drop of brandy, perhaps, to ward off the chill, your ladyship?" he inquired hopefully.

"I find it quite warm for a September morn, Master Simon," Magdalene Maxwell replied evenly. Her estranged husband's perpetual drunkenness had given her a horror of spirits, and she nodded in the direction of a chipped teapot and cracked cup that sat on a scratched silver tray. "A bit of that tea would serve splendidly. Ye are so kind to let me impose upon ye this way."

She settled as comfortably as she could on the frayed, wing-

backed chair provided her by her host. A brief survey of the
other tattered furnishings in Colonel Fraser's abode told her that
the Master of Lovat was as strapped for funds as she was.

"Now that ye have returned to us from the campaign against
those wicked Frenchmen who are stirring up such trouble among
the savages in America," she commented, flashing her most
charming smile, "I'm sure ye agree with my earlier missive to
ye that we must attend to a tempest brewing right here in our
own midst."

Simon Fraser nursed his brandy and considered his guest
closely. He'd tossed aside her ladyship's letter hinting at her
concern over the close friendship that had developed between his
ward Thomas Fraser and that madcap Jane Maxwell. However,
in the wilds of Canada, he'd been worried about saving his own
scalp, not some Scottish chit's hymen. That the brat had lost a
finger through her own folly was none of his affair, and under no
circumstances was Thomas ever going to be permitted to seek
the saucebox's disfigured hand in marriage.

Observing Lady Maxwell's vague discomfort in his dilapi-
dated sitting room, he could sense his visitor was groping for a
delicate way of phrasing her next words. Her eyes focused above
his head on the paint peeling from the parlor walls.

"I have been quite firm with Jane these last years, but I am
sure ye agree that we must now execute our duty as guardians,"
she averred, "and call a complete halt to the free and childish
association that's prevailed between Thomas and Jane."

Simon noted she had the decency to blush slightly as she
continued.

"They are approaching an age when the merest misstep could
be disastrous . . . and could lead to . . . complications, which
neither of us would welcome."

Simon remained silent, pouring himself another two fingers of
the bracing amber liquid he much preferred to lesser stimulants.
As he settled back in his chair, the epaulets of his uniform nearly
touched the plump lobes of his oversized ears. He looked at his
visitor steadily for a moment longer and began to speak.

"My dear Lady Maxwell," he said, "I am but a rough,
unmannered soldier, late of the wilds of Canada and the Seventy-
eighth Fraser Highlanders. I am unused to such sitting room
niceties. Let us, pray, be frank with one another."

Lady Maxwell looked at him warily, but didn't interrupt.

"I am well aware that ye are a woman of shrewd judgment
and tenacity, so let us put our cards on the table, shall we?"

Magdalene Maxwell nodded, her dark eyes narrowing.

"We each have in our care young wards whose futures we feel duty bound to protect," Simon Fraser continued. "Both Thomas and Jane are bairns pleasing to the eye, with wit and spirit. Sadly, the fates thus far have provided them little else for their comfort and future prospects. In other circumstances, a union between our two families might well be thought advantageous."

He noted with satisfaction that Lady Maxwell nodded in polite agreement.

"It is, therefore, imperative," he continued, "if the ample gifts Jane and Thomas *do* possess are to be realized to the benefit both of themselves and of us, who have nurtured them so long, that steps be taken to prevent the natural order of things from reaching fruition."

The veteran campaigner paused for breath and cocked his head to one side.

"Are we in agreement thus far?" he asked.

"Thus far," affirmed Lady Maxwell, a relieved and knowing smile forming at the corners of her mouth. "Pray continue. What action do ye recommend?"

"Ah. . . ." Simon said, sipping his brandy slowly, pleased that he had accurately guessed the purpose behind Lady Maxwell's uncharacteristic neighborliness. Although Thomas and Jane were mere striplings, he, too, had noted that since his recent return from the French and Indian campaigns, the two kept constant company whenever Lady Maxwell's back was turned. For his part, Simon was equally anxious to prevent such adolescent attachment from one day blossoming into an unsuitable match, or worse, a bairn in the lass's belly, which would then force his hand. *Sir William Maxwell's brat will be lucky if she has thruppence for a dowry,* he mused.

Simon set down his brandy snifter and licked his lips. He would certainly see to it that Thomas and the other young Fraser bucks would repay his many kindnesses by selecting brides whose purses would advance the Fraser cause at court. Thus, one day, the lads would be awarded the honors due them as men in the inner circle of Simon Fraser, *Baron* Lovat.

I will have my lands and titles restored! he thought to himself with grim determination. *And so may Thomas, if he marries properly!*

It might take five years for George III to right the wrong perpetrated by the king's grandfather against Simon the Fox and

Sir Thomas Fraser of Struy . . . it might take ten. Simon could wait.

"I think, m'lady," Simon continued aloud, "I should acquaint ye with plans already underway to remove my ward to the Highlands very soon. He shall there assist my herdsman while learning to be handy with sword and firearms to ready him for army life when he comes of age. 'Tis the only route to advancement open to the poor boy, since God knows I have barely the means to keep this shabby abode in Edinburgh and to till the few acres left to me in the Highlands."

"To be sure," murmured Lady Maxwell in a patently false display of sympathy for the failed Stuart Cause, which Simon knew full well the Protestant Lowlander had always disdained. "And I support yer hopes the lad will make a dashing officer someday—all the more likely to snare an heiress with his good looks and kind heart."

Simon was surprised by Lady Maxwell's boldness. Her words proved, however, that she understood his current plans for Thomas, which were quite similar, he supposed, to those she had plotted for that little polecat, Jane. Well, good luck to the lad who fell into this maternal trap.

"I thought, sir," Lady Maxwell said with characteristic Lowland candor, "that Clan Fraser and all others who joined the Rebellion of Forty-five were still forbidden to own or carry arms, or even play the bagpipes. How will ye advance young Thomas in these arts, given these restrictions?"

"These skills will be acquired *discreetly*, madam," he replied testily, "and, as I am sure ye understand full well, it may be some time before I can afford to purchase the lad a fair Commission in another regiment, as the Fraser Highlanders were disbanded after the Peace. Thomas will remain in the north till this be accomplished, however . . . ye have my word on that!"

"A most sensible plan," Lady Maxwell replied soothingly, calculating that Simon's scheme would take at least a year or two to complete, by which time Jane would be fifteen and, she hoped, betrothed to the richest man in Edinburgh—whoever that might be. "And generous it 'tis," she added for good measure, "to provide for the lad out of the portion left to ye."

She set down her teacup to signify their interview was over. Relief filled her heart. *There were no heights a beautiful woman could not scale, if she made the correct choices in life*, thought Magdalene, seeing before her Jane's perfect oval face with its gently arched brows and high cheek bones. *Who had learned that lesson better than Magdalene herself?* she reflected bitterly. She recalled the day so many years earlier when she had succumbed to the charms of a hot-blooded, but ineffectual baronet with nothing but unproductive, marshy lands in Galloway and a disagreeable penchant for strong spirits.

" 'Tis settled, then, to both our good accounts," she said briskly, offering her hand at the door to the stocky soldier who seemed at a loss as to what to do with it.

"Aye, m'lady," answered Simon, bowing awkwardly in the direction of the soft, white flesh extended toward his lips. " 'Tis settled, to be sure."

The narrow path paralleled the River Farrar, which separated Erchless from Struy Forest. Rising on a gentle slope to the right of Simon and Thomas was Culligran Wood, and behind it, the forbidding peaks of Carn Ban and Corry Deanie. The mountains were still capped in winter snow, although the river banks were inundated with icy water from the heavy spring thaw.

"To yer left, laddie, as far as the eye can behold, was yer land . . . Fraser of Struy territory," Simon said quietly, pulling on his horse's reins while gesturing to the south.

Thomas gazed pensively toward the thickly forested ridge that eventually tapered off into stark, steep, treeless mountains on the other side of the valley. Their summits, too, were blanketed in snow. Despite its being May, there was a biting wind, made even colder by dark, rain-filled clouds hovering overhead. A forlorn feeling permeated the entire region, intensified by the sight of the pinched, hungry faces Thomas and Simon had encountered when they rode through the village of Struy earlier in the day. Thomas had had his first glimpse of the fine manor house, just down the road, that his parents had called home before the Rebellion of '45. Now it stood on a weed-strewn hill, windowless and bereft of any sign of life. The garden and orchards were likewise overrun as the result of years of neglect.

The past year and a half had been filled with many such desolate sights. Thomas had been given an extensive tour of the Highlands by his godfather, who pointed out scene after scene of ruined cottages and manor houses, burnt to the ground by the Duke of Cumberland's men following the Crown's triumph at the Battle of Culloden. Since that day, for these eighteen years, the kilt was forbidden—unless worn in a Kings regiment—the pipes were banned as a "weapon of war," and no Highlander could carry arms, not even a dirk, by order of the Crown.

But, for a year now, Simon had been secretly drilling his godson in the manly arts of firearms at sessions held high in the hills, far from prying eyes that might report such illegal activities to Crown authorities. He sent Thomas with his most trusted men high on the moors for several months to master the skill of sheepherding. Out of earshot, Thomas was allowed to practice with a genuine set of bagpipes whose sheepskin airbag was clothed in the outlawed bark brown Fraser hunting tartan. The young man, who had grown nine inches in eighteen months, reveled in being allowed to participate in such forbidden activities at the behest of his elders, and he often thought how much Jane Maxwell would enjoy being part of such clandestine occupations.

His meandering recollections of his time spent in the Highlands were interrupted when Simon pointed toward yet another barren peak dusted with a thick mantel of snow.

"We're not far from the cave that sheltered the Bonnie Prince before his final rendezvous at Loch nan Uamh with *L'Heureux*, which took him back to France," his godfather added solemnly.

"And where did my parents live after my father was released from prison?" Thomas asked carefully, his glance still fixed on the brooding forest stretching in a dark green line across Strathglass.

"That's what I've come here to show ye," Simon said gruffly, digging his boot into the scrawny sides of his Highland pony.

The exhausted horses soon forded the stream and skirted Culligran Falls. For another half hour, their mounts stumbled over rocks and around boulders until the two riders crossed a spongy moor that brought them to a one-room crofter's cottage, which lacked even a thatched roof and stood out starkly against the landscape. Simon dismounted and gestured for Thomas to do the same. The lad's newly attained six-foot stature forced him to duck in order to pass through the low door that led into the stone hut. There was a startled rustle of wings as a grouse scurried to the window ledge of the gloomy chamber and escaped outside.

There was nothing to see, really, for the miserable cottage had long been stripped of anything of value, if anything of value had ever been housed within its thick stone walls to begin with.

"They both died on a bed that was pushed against that wall," Simon said somberly, pointing toward a corner of the room graced only with a dirt floor. "First Sir Thomas, a few weeks before ye were born, and then yer mother, Marguerite, right after . . . froze to death or starved, they told me. I found ye in her arms over there, barely mewing, ye were." Simon turned his back to Thomas and his voice sounded hoarse. "Ye come from fine stock, laddie. Yer da was the best friend a man could have, and yer mother, a rare beauty, with her wine-colored tresses and loving ways."

Thomas felt his eyes grow moist and his throat began to ache.

"Ye owe it to their memory to reclaim these lands . . . not just for them, or Clan Fraser, but for the villagers as well." Simon turned back to face Thomas, and he squinted in the dim light. "The Frasers of Struy did their duty to their tenants and the villagers for generations. Without a working manor, the entire region has become as derelict as Struy House itself. If something isna done in the next ten years, the people will leave the land for the south, or worse, for America. 'Tis yer destiny to bring it all back to life, Thomas Fraser! To help restore our *way* of life here in the Highlands!"

Thomas glanced around the hovel and felt his heart sink. He thought of the hulking mansion in the valley below, with its caved in roof and weed-choked gardens.

"Godfather . . . how can we hope to—"

The master of Lovat's gaze grew hard.

"Ye'll get yer Commission in the Black Watch somehow . . . then, mayhap, the Crown will need good fightin' men in those insolent Colonies and we'll raise another Fraser regiment . . . but ye'll get yer lands back by dint of yer fighting arm! Dinna let *anything* stand in the way of yer duty to yer heritage, lad, do ye hear me? I've done my best by ye all these years, just so ye can salvage what yer da and m'lady Marguerite paid for with their blood!"

Thomas stared, aghast to see his godfather's cheeks suddenly bathed with tears to match his own. The elder man abruptly spun on his heel and strode out of the dim chamber. By the time Thomas had remounted his pony, Simon's horse had thundered across the rain-spattered moor. Soon, man and rider were swallowed up by the emerald wood.

3

October 1765

The sounds of the waking city drifted up to Jane's fourth-story window. Outside, denizens of the neighborhood's teeming jumble of flats and shops were already up, taking advantage of the unusually warm October weather to move about the city in lightweight attire before the onset of another of Edinburgh's treacherous winters.

Still half-asleep, Jane listened to the symphony of noises along the cobbled High Street. She could even hear traffic noises in the distance, clattering down St. Mary's Wynd. The steady drone punctuated from time to time the shrill, singsong calls of the hawkers selling their wares.

Suddenly, Jane felt such a longing to see her friend Thomas Fraser that her throat tightened. The vibrant city that once held such joy and enchantment for the two intrepid explorers, now seemed almost forlorn during his long absence. Jane stared up at the ceiling, feeling dreadfully lonely, despite a house crowded with her kin.

It was wonderful having a semblance of a normal family life once again, Jane thought, attempting to cheer herself out of her gloomy musings. Uncle James, her father's brother, was a career captain in the Black Watch regiment. He was always welcome at Hyndford Close, not only because he insisted on helping with expenses when his brood visited Edinburgh between army assignments, but because the three Maxwell sisters thrived in the warm affection he and his wife Elizabeth expressed toward each other, their children, and their nieces and nephews. Their two boys, Murray and John, provided companionship for Eglantine, as they were just her age, and Jane, for the first time in years, had found in her Aunt Elizabeth someone in whom she could confide.

Aunt Elizabeth had wanted the lying-in for her new baby to take place in Edinburgh. Their old family friend and doctor, Sir Algernon Dick, president of the Royal College of Surgeons, would see that she got the best of care. Jane had watched her aunt's belly grow round and hard over the weeks, and Aunt Elizabeth calmly answered her persistent questions about the mysteries of how babies were created and came into the world.

The door to Jane's low-ceilinged bedchamber opened abruptly, and through half-shuttered eyes, Jane observed her mother in the entranceway.

"I want ye three lasses up and dressed and down to breakfast *right now*!"

Lady Maxwell's crisp tone carried unusual urgency. Jane sat bolt upright in bed. Almost sixteen, she'd grown so tall, she nearly tumbled fourteen-year-old Eglantine, who had been sleeping dangerously close to the edge of the mattress, onto the floor. At the same time, Jane thought she heard a muffled moan coming from the direction of the hallway past her mother.

"Is the bairn on the way?" Jane asked excitedly.

Lady Maxwell looked at her sharply. She had not heard any of the talk between Jane and her sister-in-law concerning pregnancy.

"That's none of yer affair, missy," she replied, looking crossly at the three patched linen shifts hanging on the walls on wooden pegs. She wondered how she would ever outfit her pretty daughters to make the good matches they deserved, let alone provide dowries for them.

"As soon as ye've dressed and had some porridge, I have a number of errands I want ye three little maids to do in town. Fiona will go with ye."

"But I've promised to help Hector in the garden!" Jane protested. She had so looked forward to pulling up the last of the autumn vegetables and gathering in the remaining herbs, their pungent and spicy odors tickling her nose.

"Hector Chisholm has dug turnips for seventy-odd years, my dear," her mother responded acidly. "He will accomplish his tasks on his own today, just as ye'll complete the ones I've planned for ye three. Now quickly—all of ye! Dress and join me downstairs. And I want no nonsense today from *ye*, Mistress Jane!"

With that, Lady Maxwell turned on her heel and quickly shut their door, but not before Jane was positive she had heard the guttural sounds of someone in great pain wafting toward her from the far end of the hallway.

"She *is* having the baby!" Jane exclaimed excitedly.

"It must hurt something terrible . . . listen!" Eglantine whispered fearfully. "Aunt Elizabeth sounds like—"

"An injured animal," Jane completed her sentence for her.

"She said that women make those sounds to help them bear the agony, but that the pain comes in waves, with little rests in between as the body pushes the baby out. Thomas told me sheep do the same thing."

"Ye spoke of this subject with Thomas?" Catherine asked incredulously, patting her face dry with a rough linen towel hanging next to the basin.

Jane shrugged and began dressing.

"It was a long time ago . . . before he left."

Jane involuntarily glanced down at the remnants of the forefinger on her right hand. The small red stump still pained her when the bitter weather set in, and she never looked at her hand without feeling the loss anew. First, she'd lost her finger and then she'd lost her best friend. After Thomas had departed for the north at the behest of his godfather, Simon Fraser, the tight-knit community around Hyndford Close had done its best to cheer her up. Jane had wandered her Edinburgh haunts alone, refusing to speak to anyone for weeks.

Pulling her linen shift over her head this surprisingly balmy October morn, Jane counted on the fingers of her good hand. It had been just two years since she'd seen Thomas, and five years since her accident during the final pig race down the Royal Mile. Grasping the bedpost while Catherine laced up her stays, Jane smiled to herself over the news imparted to her by Hector just the previous day that the few servants left at Master Simon's flat had been instructed by post to remove the dust covers from the furniture and air out the upper rooms in preparation for his arrival any day. Perhaps, thought Jane excitedly, I can pry some word of Thomas from the old goat—or at least from the kitchenmaid, who was rumored to be more familiar with Master Simon than her below-stairs duties would require.

"Aren't ye ready yet, Jane?" Lady Maxwell asked impatiently, reappearing suddenly at the bedroom door as her two other daughters obediently filed out of the chamber.

"Yes, Mama," Jane replied, quickly donning the linen stomacher that was far too tight for her budding torso.

It wasn't that her breasts were so terribly large, she thought ruefully, it was just that their definite roundness couldn't be contained in the bodice of a dress she had inherited from Catherine two years before. After all, Jane realized, she would be sixteen on the last day of this year.

*   *   *

"Here, Fiona," Jane announced, handing the results of their morning shopping efforts to the Maxwells' housemaid. "Take these back to Hyndford Close. If Mama demands we stay away till tea time, we might as well enjoy this fine weather. Come on, m'dears . . . let's stroll around Nor' Loch and watch them work the tanning pits."

"Och!" cried Catherine shuddering. "The smell's enough to make a person sick! The boilin' tannin, and the stink from the loch itself. 'Tis the town's cesspool, that's what it is, pure and simple."

"Oh, 'tisn't *that* bad," protested Jane, who loved the bustle and excitement around the tannery and slaughter houses.

The foul odors were a necessary part of curing hides, Jane thought matter-of-factly. Besides, this brae overlooking the road heading north to the Highlands provided an excellent lookout post for spotting travelers entering town.

Jane didn't particularly relish an encounter with Simon Fraser, who had always gazed at her with a hard look, more suitable for a soldier about to smite his adversary. Still, she might glean some word of Thomas's welfare. She bit her lip. What if Thomas thought her childish and uninteresting, now that he'd learned the manly arts of swordsplay and musketry? Well, thought Jane, jutting her chin in the air, *she* could read French fairly well, and do her sums. *I'm not a completely ignorant dolt, like most lasses*, she thought smugly. As Jane gazed down at the loch's turgid waters, she wrinkled her nose.

"Just think of it," she mused aloud. "Swans swam here during Queen Mary's time."

"Well, eels swim there *now*," replied Catherine, grimacing. "This time of year, with the waters so low, the dead ones will be everywhere. I canna think why ye like going there, Jenny!"

"I heard from old Mr. McClellan, the fishmonger, that years ago the water bailiff discovered a trunk just below the surface on the east end," Jane noted casually, hoping to pique her sisters' curiosity and thus stimulate an expedition down Ramsay Lane to the water's edge.

"What was in it?" shivered Eglantine with excitement.

She was a child born with a sense of drama and was forever begging Jane to act in little theatricals she had fashioned from her vivid imagination.

"The skeletons of a man and woman . . ." Jane whispered melodramatically. " 'Tis said they were brother and sister and had

committed incest. They were drowned for their sins on order of the Kirk Elders.''

''What's incest?'' inquired Eglantine with a puzzled frown.

''Jane, really!'' Catherine protested with all the dignity of her eighteen years. ''All right,'' she added quickly, veering away from such an unsavory topic, ''let's go down to the loch bank, if ye promise we'll stay far enough away to avoid the smell.''

The three Maxwell girls left Fiona in the Lawnmarket district, struggling with packages they'd piled high in her arms. They proceeded down the steep descent from Castle Hill along the brae, which overlooked what remained of North Loch.

In times past, the waters had been considered picturesque, lying in the shadow of Edinburgh Castle, which had been built on the sheer granite cliff, hundreds of feet above the loch's dark, flat surface. For centuries, the loch—a large pond, really—had served as a place of punishment even more forbidding than the a gallows. Women suspected of being witches had been bound hand and foot and thrown into its murky waters.

Catherine sniffed the air suspiciously as the three sisters approached a sharp rise overlooking a series of long, rectangular tanning pits that had been erected at water's edge. After two to four days of soaking the leather hides to soften and swell them, the fleshy residue was then removed with sharp-edged scrapers. The skins were then suspended in boiling caldrons filled with a tanning solution made from powdered chestnut bark and removed methodically from one vat to another, with each pit holding a stronger solution than the one before to achieve the desired color for the hide.

''Look!'' cried Eglantine excitedly, pointing to a knot of men gathered near the spot where the finishing process was completed. ''Ooh—there's going to be a *dunking*!''

Jane and Catherine stared down at the throng, which was growing larger by the minute as workers from other parts of the tannery circled round a man and woman arguing.

''Dinna that look like the Sinclairs?'' Catherine asked in an alarmed voice.

Jane confirmed that the man jerking a rope around the woman's waist was, indeed, Jock Sinclair. Their surly neighbor from the High Street was renowned for his unpredictable temper as well as his ability to pound rough hides into soft leather by vigorously rubbing them with oils, a process known as currying. Jane had always believed he'd have tanned *her* hide for running into him with her pig so long ago if he'd ever had the chance.

"He's *not* going to throw Matilda into the *loch*!" Catherine cried, revolted by the thought of this ancient Edinburgh ritual for punishing disobedient wives.

Jock was yanking on the rope around his wife's waist in an effort to get her closer to the excrementious pool. They could hear her screams all the way up the hill.

"Ye've given me the pox, ye bastard! Yer own true wife!" shouted Matilda as she fought like a wildcat against the rope.

The woman dug her heels into the slimy bog that skirted the waters at the end of the loch. Her face was flushed a vibrant hue, and tears coursed down her cheeks, now prematurely lined from the strain of producing four bairns in five years. If Jane was not mistaken, her belly was swollen beneath the thick band of hemp that held it fast. Not only had the twenty-five-year-old matron contracted syphillis from the philandering Jock, but she was also apparently with child, yet again.

Jane suddenly recalled a vision of Matilda Sinclair as the young, cheerful bride she had seen on the fateful day the apple cart had overturned. It had been Matilda who, with Thomas, had carried her home after her accident with the apple cart.

"We have to help Matilda!" Jane cried, suddenly raging with fury that the tanners could condone such shocking abuse of a woman.

All three sisters were well acquainted with the tales of Edinburgh housewives who, deemed undutiful by their husbands, were dunked six or seven times in the noxious waters as punishment. Women were simply property, like tin cups or cows, to be used or dispensed with as men saw fit.

Matilda's screams were reaching a crescendo.

"Murder me—gang on, murder me! Ye've murdered the bairn, you skelly-eyed son-of-a-whore!"

With a growl, Jock picked up his wife. Raising her over his head with powerful arms that bulged from years of stripping gristle off cattlehide, he pitched her, head first, into the loch's fetid waters.

A cheer went up from the multitude and Jock, preening at the mob's approval, began to run along the bank of the loch, dragging his wife through its filthy eddies.

"That'll teach the wench to fash ye, laddie!" cried a tanner clad in an apron, his face nearly purple with Jock's contagious rage. "She shouldna brought such unwelcome news t'ye so *public like*!"

"Drag the bitch to the slaughter house and back, Jock!"

shouted another who ran beside the barrel-chested Sinclair. "Show 'em *all* a lesson they winna forget!"

Jane felt the bile rise to her throat. Eglantine began to weep. Catherine tried to shield and comfort their younger sister. Then something in the marshes caught Jane's eye.

"Oh, God . . . *no*! Jane, come back!" screamed Catherine as she observed her sister racing down the steep incline toward a small dinghy moored in a patch of reeds.

The crowd was now moving as one along the bank, following Jock. He had dragged Matilda some hundred yards, and Jane could see only the top of the woman's feet in the water. As Jane approached the shore she could see that the cheeks of the red-faced tanner were covered with ugly, running sores. He was panting from exertion and his eyes were bulging, but he continued to run along the bankside, clutching the rope as if determined to win this tug-of-war. His wife's water-logged clothing served as an anchor beneath the surface of the loch.

Jane frantically reached through a clump of razor-sharp reeds to grip the bow of the small boat, and her thin leather slipper touched the back of a dead eel. Stifling a scream, she bolted into the craft and grabbed the single paddle, attempting to find a comfortable grip as her arms arched over the stiff hoops supporting her skirt.

"God's wounds!" she hissed under her breath.

Her progress toward the spot where Jock's rope disappeared into the water was painfully slow. She could hear the murmur of the tanners as they caught sight of her and guessed her intentions. She glanced up the hill behind the mob and saw Catherine and Eglantine huddled together, their arms clasped tightly around one another. She hardly noticed a tall rider whose roan-colored horse had paused on Ramsay Lane, not fifty yards from her agitated siblings.

Blotting out her surroundings, she concentrated on each stroke of the oar, pulling the little skiff closer to the faint splashes several yards away from her.

Jock stepped up his pace, enraged to see Jane Maxwell, of all people, attempting to rescue his wife. A man of fifty, his sides were heaving and his eyes were virtually popping out of his head.

"Stay back . . . stay back, bitch!" he screamed at Jane.

Jock yanked even harder on the rope, but then, he suddenly gave a strangled cry. He dropped the line and violently clutched at his left arm.

Jane ignored the sight of the stricken man suddenly writhing on the ground, screeching in pain. She kept her eyes on the brackish surface of the loch and the spot where bubbles had now ceased to percolate. Matilda was floating close to the surface. Her hair drifted loosely around her head like auburn seaweed. Jane raised the young woman's mouth out of the water, but Matilda appeared unconscious. Desperately, she pulled Matilda's body partway into the dinghy, ripping at the closings of her heavy, water-logged skirt that made lifting her almost impossible. Finally, Jane was able to heave the lifeless form to the bottom of the craft, gasping at her brief glimpse of the crimson bloodstains streaking down Matilda's inner thighs. She quickly turned her head away from the angry boils blistering the woman's gently rounded pelvis.

Jane glanced up to see Jock's bulky form, still and gray on a low rise sloping up from the bank. A balding man leaned down to press his ear to Jock's chest.

" 'E's dead," he announced to several tanners standing nearby. " 'Tis his heart, I'll wager, from the looks o' 'im."

"Who's that tarted-up wench what's interfered with Jock's business?" growled one of Sinclair's cronies. "We'll do the same to her, soon's we get our hands on the saucebox!"

Hearing this, Jane began paddling frantically toward the far shore. She had no time to wonder what she would do, once she arrived there, but simply put her head down and pulled on the oar with every ounce of strength she had remaining.

"Stay where ye *are*!" shouted a deep voice from the opposite shore. "Dinna come closer to the bank, Jenny lass!"

Jane raised her eyes and gazed toward the rim of the narrow loch. In the distance she thought she could discern the hulking form of Simon Fraser. Closer-by, a tall figure with hair the shade of his own roan gelding was poised on horseback at the water's edge. He was unarmed, and the mob was advancing around to the north side of the loch toward him.

"*Thomas*!" she screamed, her suppressed terror surfacing in her cry.

"Keep to the center, love," he shouted. "Catherine's gone for the constable."

"*Go*, Thomas! Ride away!" she cried, noticing for the first time that the tanners were heading toward her old friend, brandishing scraping knives and cudgels.

"I will. . . . I will . . . but turn the wee craft back toward Castle Hill, Jenny lass, and keep yer eyes on me. When the mob gets t'where I'm standin', give 'em the slip by rowing back to where ye came. I'll be there. Now *turn*!''

Jane's upper arms began to cramp, but she forced herself quietly to reverse her craft's direction.

Thomas waited on the shore until the last possible moment. Then he dug his heels into his horse's flank and galloped beyond the reach of three or four dozen men who were howling for revenge.

Gasping for breath, she charted the progress of a brigade of town watchmen proceeding down Ramsay Lane from behind Castle Rock toward the loch. She watched the tiny specks that she knew were Thomas Fraser and his godfather, Simon, gallop at top speed the long way around North Loch, a distance of about half a mile. She was only a score of yards from the shore when the constable and his men arrived at the bank.

The figure of Thomas loomed larger and larger as Jane struggled with the oar to pole her way in. He was now over six feet tall, and his broad shoulders and slim waist erased forever her memory of the pathetically thin figure of her childhood. Only his face, with its slightly gaunt features, was familiar. That most-cherished face, its tanned, unfreckled skin barely camouflaging the high Celtic color of his cheeks and his hair! As the dinghy's prow nosed into the muck clinging to the bank, Jane's hands reached out toward his dark, garnet mane. Thomas roughly clasped her to his chest.

As soon as he had lifted her out of the boat, Jane started to tremble uncontrollably.

''Matilda?'' she cried, shuddering despite the warmth of the afternoon sun.

''Drowned,'' said Simon Fraser, matter-of-factly. He reined in his horse and surveyed the scene. ''Yer interference dinna make a bit o' difference, now, did it, lass?'' he added. ''Mayhap there's a lesson to be learned in that, missy.''

Jane was too numb to take much notice of his critical tone. Unable to stifle her tears, she wept out of anguish for what fate had befallen her friend, as well as sheer relief at being rescued and seeing Thomas again.

Mercifully, someone had already placed a cloak over Matilda's body. A few yards away, her late husband, Jock, lay stiff and gray on a small rise where his friends had dragged him after the heart seizure struck.

''The bairn . . .'' Jane whispered in tears. ''The babe's died too,'' she choked, taking refuge in Thomas's sheltering arms.

"I'm taking Mistress Maxwell home, Godfather," Thomas said quietly to Simon.

The older man looked as if he were about to raise an objection, but held his peace. Jane's eyes, brimming with tears, drifted back to the boat and the lifeless form beneath the cloak. She felt herself lifted up and placed sidesaddle on Thomas's mount.

"Looks like that gang went back to work, once they spied us comin' " she heard Constable Munro say.

"They've had their bit of amusement for the day," Simon commented dryly. "Always did think 'ol Jock's temper would do him in one day. Done his wife in too, it appears."

"Pity 'bout her four bairns," replied the constable.

"Her mother'll look after the brats, I expect," answered Simon flatly.

"Thomas?" Jane murmured, relieved to feel the horse begin walking up the slope of Ramsay Lane. Now she wouldn't have to listen to the sound of Simon's harsh voice.

"Yes, Jenny?" Thomas replied softly, nuzzling his chin in her matted hair, which was moist from sweat and the foul waters of the loch.

"I hope my Aunt Elizabeth had her bairn today," she said, tightening her arms around his waist and patting the solid expanse of his back. "She moaned just like a sheep. That's *good*, 'tisn't it?"

"Aye . . . 'tis a good sign the wee one's on its way."

The horse plodded uphill in silence.

A few minutes elapsed before Jane asked another question. Her eyes were still closed and her body remained relaxed as she sank into the slow rhythm of the gelding's even pace.

"Thomas, d'ye think Constable Munro ever guessed 'twas the two of us who ripped down those coronation proclamations five years ago?"

"No. I believe our secret's safe, pet."

His voice told her he was smiling.

The roan carefully picked its way up the path to Castle Hill and Jane felt Thomas's arms tighten around her body as the incline grew steeper. Suddenly she spoke again.

"I'm so glad yer back, Thomas."

"I'm glad to see ye haven't changed, Mistress Maxwell . . . yer spirit, that is—"

"*Ye've* changed . . . a lot."

"Aye . . . on the outside. So have ye, Jenny, lass."

She sighed and clutched the arm encircling her tightly as she heard the horse's hooves move from turf to cobblestones.

"Dinna kiss my head, Thomas. 'Tis foul smelling," she said softly.

"I wouldna dream of it, lass," Thomas replied, his nose twitching slightly from the rank odors that gave proof of her recent ordeal. "At least, not at the moment."

4

November 1765

Hamilton Maxwell was unable to make out what was being said behind closed doors at the top of the stairs, but he knew from experience his parents were having an argument. Sir William's drunken tirade was soon met by Lady Magdalene's increasingly angry responses, and as the voices grew more strident, Hamilton and his three sisters exchanged discomfited looks.

" 'Tis bound to be about *ye*, Jane," speculated Hamilton, who, at nineteen, liked to assume superior knowledge about family matters in contrast to his younger siblings.

Hamilton certainly had more than an inkling of his father's mood on this particular morning. After all, he had witnessed Sir William's reaction to receiving a letter from Lady Maxwell two days earlier, a letter proposing a ball to celebrate Jane's upcoming sixteenth birthday.

"That woman must be demented!" his father had exploded, pounding the table in the unkempt drawing room at Monreith House while reading Lady Maxwell's words. "I've all I can do keeping two households going as it is, and now she wants to waste good siller on a grand party for a lass who's been naught but trouble since the day she first came squallin' into this woeful world!"

He had shaken his head morosely before gulping down yet another glass of whiskey.

Hamilton had come to realize that Sir William had no fondness for daughters. It was obvious that the disgruntled baronet had never really forgiven his wife for the accident to Jane's right hand five years earlier. He became apoplectic at news of her misadventures on North Loch.

"Odds fish, Ham! What decent gentleman will want to marry a strumpet like yer sister Jane with a hand missin' a forefinger and her meddlin' ways?" he had complained peevishly as they approached the city gates of Edinburgh. "I'll be blessed indeed if me prettiest daughter dinna end up spinsterish, mark me words," he groused, slouched in his saddle. "I'll not keep the baggage in silks and lace, I'll tell ye that, Ham! 'Tis her mother's concern."

Hamilton Maxwell had long since stopped trying to understand the ongoing warfare between his mother and father—a couple who, despite their clear incompatibility, had managed to produce six healthy offspring. For as long as Hamilton could recall, his father had always preferred the clean air and country ways of the Scottish Lowlands—and the right to drink in peace; his mother preferred the excitement and activity of the city—free of her bibulous spouse.

Hamilton glanced around the shabby Edinburgh sitting room at his three sisters, who had each matured noticeably since last he'd seen them. One thing was certain, running two households full tilt all year round put a crimp in the family's meager finances. Presumably, this was the subject of the rantings and ravings now going on behind closed doors.

"Oh, I wish they'd *stop*!" cried Jane, running to the leaded glass windows overlooking the city streets below. "I dinna care about the stupid ball, and I *hate* all this skirling."

Hamilton observed Jane closely as she rested her chin against the frosted window pane. Her skin was flawless and her profile patrician. Clearly, this erstwhile wee duckling had turned into a deuced *swan*!

"Well, *I* hope they have it," announced Eglantine suddenly, interrupting Hamilton's train of thought.

"Have what?" Jane asked vaguely.

"Yer birthday *ball*!" her younger sister cried in an exasperated tone. "I canna think why Da should object, since Sir Algernon has offered to sponsor ye, and 'tis he who'll be paying for the ceilidh he gives every year anyway. I've never *been* to a ball!" she complained, plaintively voicing her desire to attend Sir Algernon Dick's Hogmanay Ball that the physician had hosted each New Year's Eve for as long as any Maxwell could remember.

"And ye probably winna go to this one either," Catherine said primly. "I had to wait till I turned sixteen."

"Da's thinkin' of the fine new clothes ye'll need, dinna ye ken," Hamilton pronounced. "He despises spending siller on ye three, and that's a fact. But he hates charity more, and doesna think too much of Sir Algernon Dick. After all, they were rivals for mama's hand, once upon a time."

"Pooh!" scoffed Eglantine. "*That's* no reason to refuse the doctor's offer. Da doesn't give a fig what Mama does anymore."

"*Eglantine!*" Catherine said sternly. "Not another word from ye, ye naughty lass!"

The eldest Maxwell daughter walked over to Jane, who continued to stare moodily out the window into the foggy November morning.

"Dinna worry, sweeting," Catherine said softly, for once abandoning her pose as the surrogate for Lady Maxwell. "Fighting is the only way Mama and Da know to converse."

"Oh, I dinna care about their fighting," Jane responded, pressing her forehead against the coolness of the leaded panes. " 'Tis just the way Daddie swoops down on us to say Mama canna do something after he's been sitting in Monreith all summer, never bothering to visit or write. He does what *he* likes and spends what *he* wants . . . and he acts just as he wishes, drunk or sober! 'Tisn't fair!"

Hamilton had caught the last of Jane's outburst and walked over wearing a mischievous grin on his face.

"Jenny, dear girl, haven't ye realized that most moppets yer age dinna question their elders and are forbidden to run wild around the city like stable boys? If only ye'd learn to behave yerself like a proper young lady, ye wouldna find yerself minus a finger with which to hold a fan!"

"Why, ye . . ." Jane whirled around from the window and flew at her older brother in a rage, determined to wipe the smirk off his face.

"I'll show ye what *nine* fingers can do . . ." she shrieked, leaping toward Hamilton's six-foot frame. She was mortified that her favorite brother should tease her about the injury that still pained her so much.

"Stop it! *Stop* it, ye two," Catherine cried, jumping between them while Eglantine stood and stared, her mouth agape.

Hamilton easily held Jane, who was now kicking and shouting, at arm's length. He felt a bit embarrassed about his casual cruelty toward the sister he'd always found fun and amusing.

"Och! Jenny," Hamilton began, "I dinna mean to hurt yer feelings—"

"I *hate* ye and I hate *Da*, and I *hate*—"

But before the rest of her family could hear anymore, Jane bounded out of the room, down the back stairs, and ran through the alley to the stable yard.

The early morning mists still clung to the rows of herbs planted off the stable area, but Jane took no notice of the light wisps that swirled around the rosemary and thyme borders and the small arbor of fruit trees.

As she raced through the green open space, past the pigpen and around the corner of the stable, she ran headlong into Thomas. He had a pouch of heavy books on military theory slung over the hitching post, and was just tying up his horse, preparing to unsaddle the roan gelding.

"Whoa, there, Jenny . . ." Thomas laughed, reaching out his arms to steady her. Then he saw the tears brimming in her eyes. "What's the matter, lass? What's happened?"

Jane looked up at her friend to whom her mother had practically forbidden her to speak. She took a breath to begin her tale of woe, and then sighed.

"Oh, ye know how it 'tis at my house, Thomas," she replied dejectedly. "Mama wants one thing and Da disagrees and starts drinking. Then they blather back and forth till yer head hurts."

Jane reached out to touch the leather straps from the bridle of Thomas's horse and twisted them absentmindedly in her fingers. No sooner had she done so, than she became self-conscious at the sight of the red stub on her right hand and dropped the reins with a jerk. Thomas reached for her wrist and folded his other hand over her injured finger.

"Try not to fret about yer hand, lass," he said softly. "Yer still a beauty, ye should know, and dinna let it make ye think less of yerself."

For the second time since Thomas had returned to Edinburgh, Jane began to cry. Great, heaving sobs seemed to come from a place inside her he didn't know existed. Failing to understand why she had dissolved in response to words he meant to be kind, he pulled her close to him and folded his long arms around her for comfort.

"Everything's changing, Thomas," she cried miserably. "My family's cut in two—the boys against the girls—my Mama against my Da. We dinna live in one place anymore. There's always fighting about money. Da's always with the spirits now, and mama says I'm to stay indoors and not spend time with you and do tatting and embroidery and I *hate* 'em *both*, and now yer probably going to leave as well, and—''

Thomas held her away from him for a moment in order to search her tear-streaked face, halting her in midsentence. She stared at him earnestly, then lowered her eyes.

''Well, I just *know* either yer godfather or the army will send ye away again!'' she sniffled, ''and then *who* will be my friend?''

''I'll always be yer friend, Jenny . . . never fear for that, but I want ye to be happy about my Commission. When it finally comes through, I winna be beholden to my godfather any longer. I can begin to make my own way . . . help him salvage something of the life we knew.''

''What life?'' Jane asked quickly. ''Clan Fraser died with old Simon the Fox, before ye were born. Master Simon's filled ye with fairy tales, Thomas. Ye'll break yer heart if ye think ye or Simon, or any other Highlander can win against the Crown. Men with the power hold on to their power. That's the one sensible thing my Da ever told me.''

Jane watched his gray-green eyes narrow and heard the anger tinging his voice.

''Och, Jenny, if ye could *see* the way of life up North. There's nothin' and no one to cling to. Half my mother's kin are nearly starved and living in caves! I've *got* to do something to change that . . . Simon's plan is to do what Scots do best—supply the best damn fighting men for King Geordie's empire. That way the bastard's bound to give us back our lands and titles.''

''Ye mean give *Simon* back his lands and titles,'' Jane retorted. ''Dinna think we'll be calling ye Sir Thomas any time soon, if 'tis left to Simon Fraser,'' she scoffed. ''And if Simon uses the likes of ye for cannon fodder to get his heart's desire, more's the pity!'' she added bitterly.

''Simon's not just actin' for himself, Jenny,'' Thomas said quietly of the newly promoted brigadier general. ''He's a willful, arrogant man, to be sure, but he saw men like my father . . . good men, and their families and their holdings, large and small . . . wiped out. If ye saw with yer own eyes, ye'd *understand*!'' His voice betrayed his anguish over the suffering he had seen. ''There's hardly a wisp left of an entire way of life! I canna just stand by and let it die!''

'' 'Tis *dead*, Thomas! The old ways are gone!'' Jane cried. ''My Da's startin' to run sheep where his crofters used to till and plant the soil, and he dinna have King Geordie as his excuse to throw them off the land. *Ye* were up with the herdsmen! Surely, ye've heard the talk! The few that *own* the land will keep it for themselves to run sheep instead of shelter people, and all yer brave deeds on the battlefield will help no one but the Sir William Maxwells and Master Simon Frasers of the world, who want it only for themselves! Yer a fool if ye dinna see what's in store!''

''For a wee lass of not yet sixteen, ye're mighty acquainted with estate business, aren't ye now?'' he said sharply.

''I've got *eyes* and *ears*, Thomas, even if I am a lass,'' she retorted, stung. ''At least we Maxwells *have* an estate and our titles!''

No sooner had the words escaped her lips than she considered how deeply they would wound her friend.

''Not that Monreith will mean much to *ye*, Mistress Maxwell,'' Thomas responded angrily, smarting at her unfeminine presumption to lecture *him* about a place she had never been. A place reeling from a disaster, the proportions of which no one—man or woman—could conceive, if they had not witnessed it for themselves.

For a moment, the silence hung heavily between them. Then Jane spun around abruptly and ran.

''Jenny, lass . . . wait!'' Thomas called after her, but Jane had disappeared into the stable. When he peered through the gloom, he could see nothing but piles of hay and a mound of horse manure awaiting the wheelbarrow of Hector Chisholm, Peter Ramsay's stableman who also kept the Maxwells' pigs and looked after the Fraser's mounts.

''Jenny . . . Jenny . . . please! Where are ye?'' he called into the shuttered light. ''I want to talk to ye, lass. Please, Jenny,'' he pleaded.

He heard a faint rustling in the corner of the hay loft and quickly scaled the rickety ladder, then threw himself on the straw. He dropped to his hands and knees and crawled toward a spot where he heard a rustling sound.

''There ye are, minx!'' he cried, grabbing her arm to flip her on her back as she tried to escape. ''Oh, no . . . ye're not going an *inch* further!'' Taking both her shoulders in his hand he thumped her down on the mound of hay and straddled her waist with his legs, pinning her fast. ''Now look here, ye saucebox! I'm sorry for my daft words, if ye are as well. . . .''

Jane stared up at him sullenly and remained silent. Thomas heaved a sigh and smiled slightly.

''I'm not unaware, Jenny, that Simon uses whomever and

whatever he has to fight for what was lost. And yes, he'd use *me*, just as soon as anyone else. But what the two of us want is not too dissimilar, if ye think on it. I *want* to find a niche in the scheme of things, Jen . . . and there aren't a lot of choices presentin' themselves t' me at the moment, in case ye hadna noticed. And, yes, Simon wants the land and power and his title returned to him . . . and so do I. *And* he wants a homeland for his people, as well as his sheep. Dinna ye see, Jenny . . . once I have my Commission, *I'll be my own man!* I can decide things for myself!''

''A Fraser Highlander is always *MacShimi*'s man,'' Jane said in a low voice, using the Gaelic word for ''son of Simon.'' ''And *MacShimi*'s men obey.''

Thomas stared down at the little mole at the base of Jane's slender throat. He had an uneasy feeling that much of what this girl, poised on the brink of womanhood, said was true.

''Well, one thing I've already decided,'' he said with a smile, veering away from the volatile subject of Simon Fraser, Master of Lovat, ''and that is, I missed ye something terrible when I was away!''

There. He'd said it. Thomas *had* missed her sorely—and not as his lifelong playmate. He had missed her as a woman. He and Jane were children no longer, and Thomas suspected that Lady Maxwell had long been calculating the worth of her comely progeny.

As Thomas stared down at Jane's lovely face, he wondered if she were aware that she faced a stormy future. Lady Maxwell had treated him coldly from the day he had carried the injured girl back to Hyndford Close after her accident with the apple cart. And Simon's gruff manner whenever the name Jane Maxwell was mentioned indicated to Thomas that the daughter of an impecunious dissipated baronet was far from the matrimonial prize the ambitious brigadier had in mind for his ward. Yet, Thomas found himself drawn to Jane like a horseshoe to a magnet since his return from the Highlands. Despite his earlier reaction to her outspoken views, he realized now as he gazed into her blazing brown eyes, that his feelings of fierce loyalty and friendship had changed to something even stronger.

Thomas let the silence settle between them. He recalled how often he had thought of Jane during the years he was away from Edinburgh. She would come to mind during those lingering Highland evenings when, after days of riding deep into the green and mauve hills above the ancient Fraser seat of Beauly and his home village of Struy, he'd slept on the ground with the sheep and cattle, subsisting on bannocks and wild berries. She was there in a quiet corner of his mind, comforting him, especially whenever he caught a glimpse of his former home, perched broken and abandoned at the end of an overgrown lane, its windows shattered like his father's dreams.

Looking at her now, pinned beneath him, he ached to hold her in his arms. On New Year's Eve she'd be sixteen. Lasses married at sixteen, and even younger, in the Highlands. His mind drifted back to a memory of the wild, wailing sounds made by Simon's own piper as they echoed through Glencannich. Thomas's throat would close with emotion as the shrill, plaintive notes clung to the fading northern sun. It was the same, heart-stopping feeling that was invading his chest this misty morning as he gripped Jane's waist with his thighs and gazed down at her, half-buried in the straw.

Jane stared up at him, wide-eyed. He could see she was also sensing something akin to the giddiness coursing through his body. Paralyzed by the clash of feelings welling up in him, he continued to meet her quizzical stare.

"Thomas?"

It wasn't really a question, it was confirmation.

Slowly, carefully, so as not to frighten her, he settled his weight slightly to the left of her and lowered himself onto his elbow, his right hand toying with a loose piece of straw. He smiled at her, tentatively at first, and then broadly, tracing the bridge of her nose and the lines of her lips with the prickly chaff.

"Aye, Jenny, lass," he said quietly, lightly stroking her soft, luxuriant hair. "Everything *is* different now, 'tisn't it? Different . . . and yet the same."

With a swift movement, Jane's arms broke from the layers of straw and came up around his back, knocking him off balance. He felt her clasp his body fiercely as it fell against her own. It had been so long since a woman had held him close. The few whose charms he'd sampled felt nothing like Jane. Her arms clamped tight around him, half child's grip, half woman's embrace, as she buried her head under his chin, snuggling beneath him and pushing her body instinctively toward his.

"Please dinna let Simon rule yer life," she whispered, her voice cracking with emotion. "He'll send ye where it pleases him . . . where it suits his grand plan for the Frasers."

"Jenny . . . ah, Jenny, love," Thomas murmured in her hair,

"no one's going to keep us apart. Not even Simon Fraser . . . not even yer ma. . . ."

His bold words surprised even himself, but he knew with a certainty forged through the years of their shared childhood that there would never be another woman for him like Jane Maxwell. Somewhere deep inside he had known it when she was just six. Now that she was nearly sixteen, and he, a man, he felt like shouting it to all of Edinburgh. He bent down and kissed her with a tenderness and deliberation that sent shock waves through them both.

"I know 'tis a wee bit sudden, Mistress Maxwell," he said huskily, "but will ye one day do me the honor of becoming my bride?"

Jane reached up, tracing the line of his cheekbone with the back of her hand.

" 'Tis not sudden, Thomas," she said, her brown eyes boring into his. "I've loved ye one way or t'other since we were bairns. *'Tis* different now, though . . . the feelings that come over me when I see yer dear face, or ye take me in yer arms—" She fell silent, continuing to stare at him as if she expected him suddenly to vanish. "I'll be a soldier's wife, or live in a cave in Struy Forest, but I'll do what I have to, to have ye, Thomas Fraser!" she whispered fiercely.

"Ye might even one day be called Lady Jane if I get back what's rightly mine," Thomas said half-mockingly.

"Dinna waste yer dreams on that," Jane said flatly. "I just want *ye,* title or not, and I dinna care *who* tries to keep us apart!"

"We shall have to be discreet, Jenny," he said thoughtfully, "until my Commission comes through and Simon canna call the tune."

"Outfox Simon?" she asked gloomily. "I dinna think him so simple a fool."

"He's not, to be sure," Thomas replied, "but we mustna arouse his or yer mother's suspicions that we plan to marry until I take my training and am given my lieutenancy. Do ye think we can keep a secret for that long, dearheart?"

Jane looked as if she wanted to challenge the plan he had outlined, but, instead, she put her arms around him and pulled his body down along the length of hers. For a long moment they clung to each other, savoring the feeling of safety and warmth. A slight shuddering passed through them both as he nuzzled her soft pink ear lobe. Jane turned her head slightly, brushing his lips lightly with hers with the same curious wonderment they had felt as children discovering a nest of newborn sparrows in the arbor.

At exactly the same moment, Thomas and Jane became aware of a new sensation growing between them. It was Thomas's turn to become wide-eyed and he stared at her, embarrassed.

"Thomas," Jane smiled gently, "I *do* know . . . about what happens to men who take a fancy to a certain lass, ye may be surprised to learn. . . . Aunt Elizabeth explained everything." Teasing him lightly with her hips, she added in a saucy whisper, "and I did sneak out one early morn to watch when Da brought the McCullough stud to court Catherine's pony at Monreith . . . so what's happening to you now is not such a mystery to me as you might suppose—"

Thomas kissed her again slowly, experimenting with the amount of pressure he put to her lips. Jane responded immediately, sensing what moves he would make and falling in stride with him. The straw, the stable, the world enveloping them both seemed to fall away and Thomas was only aware of an overwhelming desire to press his lips to the tiny mole at the base of her throat, to touch her soft breasts beneath her gown and to meld his body into hers.

"Jenny, Jenny, darlin' girl . . ." he whispered, trailing kisses down to pillows of flesh straining against her disheveled linen bodice.

"Thomas . . ." Jane moaned, shifting her weight in needy response to his caresses.

The first of her hesitant, feathery touches to his groin sent waves of pleasure cascading down his thighs. The hardness expanding under his woolen riding breeches filled them both with wonder and delight as she continued to stroke her fingers shyly across his midsection. Gently, he pulled down the cloth covering her breasts, and she responded by arching her body to his exploring lips, while her breath blew into his ear in warm, startled gasps.

Suddenly, penetrating the fog of passion swirling around them both, came the creak, creak, creak of Hector Chisholm's wheelbarrow rolling across the yard into the stable stall. Agonized, Thomas pulled away from Jane, forcing himself to listen intently.

"Shh!" he whispered fiercely, putting a finger to his lips.

Jane's puzzled look changed instantly to one of recognition and she reacted quickly, throwing handfuls of straw over the two of them lying in the loft. They both froze in place, trying not to sneeze or even breathe. Thomas and Jane could hear, but not see, old Hector carefully piling the horse leavings into his wheel-barrow. Jane cast a desperate glance at Thomas, whose weight was becoming oppressive against her slender frame. At last, Hector put his rake in the wheelbarrow and departed, muttering about "young lads who dinna unsaddle their ponies straightaway."

Brushing the straw from their clothes in the dim light of the stable, Thomas and Jane knelt before one another, seeing themselves reflected in the other's eyes for the first time.

"I wanted . . . I wanted to . . .": Thomas faltered as he pulled the last piece of straw from Jane's dark tresses.

Her hand grazed the soft copper hair peeking through the laces of his linen shirt as she flicked the remnants of hay off his chest.

"I wanted to, too," she said simply. Then she smiled, adding with a wry smile. "I probably owe my virtue to old Hector." She looked away briefly and then asked with uncharacteristic diffidence, " 'Tis it proper to consider myself a lass who's betrothed?"

"Aye . . . consider yerself as good as my wife, my Jenny of Monreith," he replied tenderly, wondering silently what Simon Fraser and Lady Maxwell would do if they knew of how he and Jane had plighted their troth in this dark, gloomy byre. To Simon, he owed his life. The question was, how high a price would his godfather demand for it?

5

December 1765

Simon Fraser, Master of Lovat, looked forward to making his appearance at Sir Algernon Dick's Hogmanay Ball at Prestonfield House as a newly promoted Brigadier General in the British Army. It was no mean achievement for a man whose father had been beheaded in the Tower of London by order of King George II.

Standing in the candlelight on this, the last evening of 1765, clad in his Scottish regimental uniform, he admired his reflection with uncharacteristic vanity. With unaccustomed delicacy, he fingered the lacy jabot that frothed at his massive neck and admired his new kilt, all the while musing on the market value of a daughter of an inconsequential baronet.

In the weeks since he and Thomas had returned to Edinburgh from what was left of his Highland estates, Simon had made it his business to ascertain that the lad spent every free minute with that strumpet from down the road.

What a wonderful irony, Simon reflected, that the lass's *own* uncle would provide him the means of removing Thomas from Miss Maxwell's clutches. Indeed, Simon took pleasure in the fact that James Maxwell—a captain in the 42nd Regiment—was using his influence to secure a place for Simon's ward in the Black Watch. 'Twas a pity, Simon mused, that his own Fraser Highlanders had been disbanded following the Peace of Paris in 1763 ending the Seven Years' War, but the Forty-second would do nicely for Thomas—for the present. Such a lieutenancy would, most likely, result in a post for the lad in the Colonies. *The sooner Thomas was removed a safe distance from that penniless and unpredictable wench, the better*, he thought grimly.

Yes, he mused, with a sardonic smile at his own reflection, a couple of years' seasoning in the Black Watch in North America, and young Thomas would be ready to take his place alongside Simon's younger half brother Archibald and the other young lads as a member of *MacShimi*'s men—Fraser kith and kin loyal only to *him*! The next time a prime minister asked Simon to raise a regiment, he would do it—for a price—and most of Inverness-shire would be Fraser land once again.

Keeping time with the tip of his heavy black buckled shoe, Simon experimented with the first steps of "Miss Cahoon's Reel." He looked up just as young Thomas entered his dressing room.

"Well, aren't ye the fine peacock, m'lad," he said, eyeing his ward's new suit of buff-colored breeches and coat of brocade rust satin—all of which had cost Simon a pretty farthing. "I'll wager all the young ladies will be praying to St. Ninian that ye'll be askin' 'em to dance!"

"Thank ye, sir," replied Thomas, flushing slightly. "And thank ye for the gift of the new clothes."

"The better to snare an heiress, eh lad!" Simon boomed. "There's nothing to be lost if a man *looks* prosperous!"

"Aye, sir . . ." Thomas replied, vaguely disturbed by the implication of his godfather's words. "May I say, ye're looking quite magnificent in yer dress regimentals,'" he added, trying to steer Simon away from any specific instructions on how he was to spend his evening.

"Well, lad, there's no finer sight than a man in a kilt, and that's the truth, wouldna ye say?" Simon declared as the pair descended the stairway to the waiting coach. "Soon ye'll be dressed in one of yer own when ye join the army."

Thomas merely nodded as the two climbed into Simon's newly purchased landau, its matched pair of black horses prancing skittishly in the cold night air. For the first time in years, Simon felt almost at ease. *Promotions and pay raises could do that for a man*, he supposed.

Prestonfield House, glowing like a welcoming beacon at the end of the drive, loomed larger and larger through the coach window. The driver reined in the horses as the Maxwells' rented livery approached a smartly accoutred black barouche that had drawn to a halt in front of them.

A satin-coated footman threw open their carriage door and Hamilton leapt out to assist Lady Maxwell, whose wide-hooped ball gown barely squeezed through the narrow opening. Jane paused on the small step of the coach as she gazed over the heads of the arriving guests and caught sight of a tall, scarlet-coated gentleman with a white wig. He was just emerging from another black barouche that bore a stag's head crest on its shining enameled door.

Despite his pyramid of hair, the man was young, of medium height, with strikingly patrician good looks. His nose was slightly aquiline in shape and his hazel eyes were wide set beneath arching eyebrows, which instantly signaled approval or disdain.

The youthful 4th Duke of Gordon paused and cast his eyes on Jane's face. The young man's gaze traveled down to her velvet cloak that was parted at her throat, revealing the deeply cut neckline of the pale blue ball gown beneath. The slim sleeves of the satin gown ended at her elbow and cobwebs of lace swirled down to her delicate wrists. For the longest moment, the gentleman stared at her with practiced aplomb before finally stepping onto the crimson carpet that led the way into Prestonfield House.

Jane remained frozen on the carriage's narrow running step. The duke's imperious mother emerged next from the coach and cast a curious glance in Jane's direction. The final passenger in the coach to set foot on the scarlet carpet was a man at least ten years the dowager duchess's junior. Staats Morris, Katherine Gordon's second husband, took his wife's plump arm and guided her up the steps and into the house.

"Jenny!"

Thomas Fraser approached Jane's coach with a scowl, having just emerged from his godfather's smart new landau.

"Must ye stare at that blighter who practically undressed ye with his eyes!"

Startled from her reverie, Jane glanced down at Thomas and Simon Fraser, who had joined his ward on the gravel drive.

" 'Twas just that he looked so familiar," she mused. "I think he was trying to place me as well."

"I think the Duke of Gordon was trying to place ye where ye have no business being!" Thomas retorted heatedly.

"My, my, Thomas," Jane twitted him, glad to have the man positively identified. "His Grace certainly ruffles yer feathers, dinna he?"

"Thomas is right," Simon growled, heading for the ornate entrance. "Ye shouldna be so brazen just because the flamin' Duke of Gordon looks at ye cross-eyed, lassie."

Jane shot the brigadier a murderous look, which he took in, unblinkingly. Then she grasped Thomas's arm, leaving Simon to escort Lady Maxwell up the stairs following the path taken by the duke and his family.

All right, lass, Brigadier General Simon Fraser thought, grimly staring at Jane's velvet-cloaked back. *So ye, too, acknowledge we are enemies. Let the battle begin!*

In December, dusk fell by three o'clock in the afternoon. Hogmanay guests had been invited for nine and, thus, Prestonfield House was ablaze with a thousand candles. Light poured from the open entrance as the magnificently adorned ladies and handsomely tailored gentlemen mounted the front stairs in succeeding waves. The night air had taken on a crystalline quality, transforming the lighthearted chatter exchanged by arriving guests into puffs of white smoke.

During the long years of friendship between the Maxwells and Sir Algernon Dick and his family, Jane had visited Prestonfield House countless times. Never had she seen the mansion look so beautiful as it did this New Year's Eve. As the housemaids scurried to relieve the Maxwell party of their cloaks, Jane caught sight of the red-coated figure from the drive. He was striding in the direction of a small library off the far end of the hall. Turning abruptly toward Thomas, who looked subdued as he watched the elegantly attired nobleman disappear from view, she asked softly, "Do ye think we could find a quiet place where we could review the minuet just one more time?"

It was the only part of the evening that truly terrified her—the moment, just before midnight, when she would be expected, as part of the ritual of her sixteenth birthday and her first ball, to dance with a partner alone on the floor. It would be a demonstration of her attainment of womanhood, carried off under the critical gaze of the parents and friends of the other youthful ladies coming of age that season.

"The minuet is yer best dance," Thomas said absently, his eyes still focused on the library door, which had closed after the duke entered. "What ye need to practice is 'The Waterman's Rant.' Sir Algernon, at his age, has surely never heard of it."

Sir Algernon was scheduled to assume the duties of Jane's father this night. Neither she nor Thomas spoke of Sir William Maxwell's adamant refusal that morning to attend his daughter's birthday celebration. Nor did they allude to his angry departure for the ramshackle estate of Monreith later in the day.

Jane found herself wondering silently, as they were about to be formally announced by Prestonfield's majordomo, *why* the Duke of Gordon should be closeted in the library, just as the ball was about to commence. Despite the intervening five years, she had noted how his boyish features had matured into a handsome face with well-defined, sensual lips that seemed to mask a faintly mocking smile.

Glancing self-consciously down at Thomas's Christmas gift, a lace handkerchief which she had draped artfully over her injured hand, Jane's mind flashed back suddenly to the day of her accident and the strip of pristine linen with the stag's head crest embroidered on one corner, which had, according to Thomas, staunched the flow of blood gushing from her wounded finger. Unbidden, a vision of the young duke's frank appraising stare tonight loomed in her mind. It was a far cry from his open, friendly gaze that memorable day of the last pig race in the High Street. She wondered what had caused such a change in his boyish countenance since they last met.

Sir Algernon Dick quietly shut the door of the library, muting the sound of the fiddler's reel wafting in from the noisy ballroom. He was pleased that the party had gotten off to such a rousing start and that Jane, his special pet among all of Magdalene's brood, was managing to hold her own to great effect on the dance floor.

"Yer Grace . . . forgive me for not coming sooner," said the elderly doctor to his visitor. "I've only just been apprised of yer arrival. How good it is to see ye again. Yer mother and stepfather appear to be in the pink.''

The young man in the scarlet coat had been staring out the window at the moonlight that illuminated the east end of the book-lined library. He absently tapped his pair of white kid gloves against the frosty glass panes.

"Ah, Sir Algernon, how kind of you to leave your guests," said the Duke of Gordon, his years at Eton and Cambridge reflected in the elegance of his speech. He had turned around to greet his host and slapped his gloves on a small side table, almost as if the gesture spoke of his eagerness to dispense with pleasantries. "I appreciate your granting my request for a few words with you in private. I hope 'tis not too much of an imposition.''

The doctor, thin and stooped from advancing age, offered his visitor a flask of vintage port, and the two men sat down before the fire burning brightly in the grate.

"Yer Grace has provided just the excuse I needed to escape the din," Sir Algernon assured his guest, "although, I must say I am looking forward to the debut of Mistress Jane Maxwell later this evening. Ye know the lass?''

Sir Algernon poured the wine from a heavy crystal decanter into stemmed glasses.

"I certainly know *of* the minx," Alexander chuckled, "and I see from the brief glimpse I caught of her as I arrived, she's grown into a beauty . . . but no, we've never actually been introduced.''

The doctor surreptitiously studied the young duke above the rim of his glass as he slowly savored the ruby liquid. "How have ye been faring, Yer Grace?" Sir Algernon inquired. He was curious to hear why the twenty-two-year-old duke had requested an impromptu audience. "I trust that my prescriptions for that dreadful ague ye contracted in France in sixty-four have had good effect?''

"They did, sir," the duke replied, "though there were moments that summer when I wondered if that fever wasn't an excessive price to pay for a young man's tour of the Continent.''

In his role as family physician to the ducal Gordons, Sir Algernon had intervened discreetly in several family matters during the years since the death of Alexander's father, Cosimo, who had succumbed to a similar malady when his son was only nine. Alexander's mother, Katherine Gordon, was left with six young children after her husband's demise, and the lusty young widow had quickly wed Staats Morris, a brash, ambitious army captain from the Colonies—New York or New Jersey, Sir Algernon thought—a decade younger than she. In the early years of their odd marriage, the couple spent lavishly from young Alexander's estate, both in Europe and London, in an effort to advance their own fortunes at the Court of St. James.

"Tell me, Yer Grace, how fares the Dowager Duchess and Colonel Morris this holiday season?" Sir Algernon inquired. "I saw them only briefly when they were announced upstairs." He was curious to learn of Alexander's relationship with Lady Katherine and her husband, now that the family was reunited and the lad had reached his majority.

"My mother and her husband have a most comfortable living at Huntly Lodge," Alexander replied evenly, "and seem to enjoy it, *especially* when it is laid on someone else's expense."

Sir Algernon speculated that Alexander's caustic tone indicated a high degree of irritation about the spendthrift habits of his mother and stepfather. The Gordon estates had prospered of late, but it would be a decade, at least, before the coffers were replenished to their former abundance.

"Ah, well," replied Sir Algernon, refilling his glass of port. "It's good to see ye looking so fit. Ye know, lad, I've never encountered such a nasty variety of ague in my thirty years of practice. Ye were quite delirious by the time they brought ye to me."

"I don't remember much of the sea voyage, or anything, really . . . only of waking up in your upstairs guest chamber," Alexander acknowledged quietly, pausing to sip from his crystal glass.

The duke's words brought to mind that during the lad's convalescence eighteen months previously at Prestonfield House, Sir Algernon had heard vicious gossip in Edinburgh that the Gordon Madness had infected the young heir, as it had so many Gordons before him. If anyone was mad in the current generation of Gordons, it was Alexander's younger brother George—by far the most peculiar of the lot. Unfortunately, however, several of Sir Algernon's servants had witnessed Alexander during his illness, at times unconscious from the fever, crying out at unseen terrors and weeping as if he were a small, abandoned boy. To those inclined to tittle-tattle, it had certainly caused talk. Such slander, alluding to the "Madness"—which indeed had surfaced in countless noble families where close family members often married—could taint the young man's future at Court, to say nothing of his future as a husband.

"Pray, tell me, Yer Grace," inquired the older man, smiling encouragingly, "how can I be of help on this New Year's eve?"

" 'Tis a delicate matter, Sir Algernon, and one I must beg you to keep in strictest confidence."

The young duke rose from his chair and began to pace slowly in front of the fire. A look of barely concealed distress darkened his features.

"I recall that when I recovered somewhat from that infernal disease last year, you told me there might be some permanent disability from—"

Sir Algernon interrupted him.

"Yer body endured prolonged fits of feverishness and chills. I said it was *possible* ye might suffer some long-lasting side effects. However, I didn't *promise* them," he said reassuringly.

"Well . . . yes," the young duke responded uncertainly.

He approached the older man and sat down again, leaning forward earnestly, his broad forehead creased with worry.

"One thing you warned me about has potentially a very important impact on my life at the moment," he said, looking directly at Sir Algernon. "A young woman of whom I am quite fond . . . in fact she was assigned by Mother to nurse me at Gordon Castle when I returned there to recuperate in September a year ago . . . well, this young woman . . . her name is Bathia Largue . . . she tells me she is carrying my child."

Alexander turned to stare once again into the fire, trying to avoid Sir Algernon's piercing gaze. The old doctor noted the look of pain that had welled up in the young man's eyes.

In an almost inaudible voice the duke continued, "You had told me there was a chance that the long duration of my fever could have affected my . . . could have made it impossible for me to father children."

Ah, thought Sir Algernon, relaxing his grip on his port. *Insanity* was not the question here, but rather, *virility*. The duke feared he was sterile and the lass was playing him false.

"Do ye have any reason to suspect ye are not the only man to have been on intimate terms with this woman since yer return to Fochabers?" Sir Algernon asked.

"I took her virginity," the duke replied softly, "and I have been with her ever since." His eyes locked on the thick pile of embers glowing beneath the enormous yule log burning in the fireplace. "I believe I am the only man who has lain with her, but of course, one has no way of being absolutely sure she has not also . . . kept company with someone else during this time."

"Have ye found that she has been truthful about other things since ye have been . . . intimate?" Sir Algernon asked. Alexander nodded affirmatively.

"Sterility is always a possibility when one endures such a long and intense fever, and, as yer physician, I felt it my duty then to inform ye of potential aftereffects of yer illness. However, 'tis a rather rare occurrence." A kindly smile played across the old man's bony face. Sir Algernon raised his glass in a rakish toast and laughed heartily. "Only the visage of the bairn itself will confirm my present theories to yer complete satisfaction," he added merrily. "However, I am willing to stake my medical reputation that, given yer description of the lass, ye're certainly the lusty young buck ye appear to be! Congratulations!"

Alexander raised his port in a mock salute, a look of incredulous relief shining from his hazel eyes.

"Does the dowager duchess know of the situation, Yer Grace?" Sir Algernon asked bluntly.

"She does not know of Bathia's present condition, but she has heard of our liaison and is displeased, of course," he revealed stiffly. "As a consequence, she and my stepfather have insisted on accompanying me to Edinburgh for the season to look over this year's 'crop' of debutantes."

"And what do *ye* think would be a sensible approach to the situation?" Sir Algernon asked.

"I realize, now that I'm reasonably confident I can produce heirs, that eventually I must marry someone of my station—but, for the first time ever, Sir Algernon, I find I am—pleased with my life."

He faltered, suddenly shy in the nakedness of his own frank admissions.

"It feels strange to say it, but I'm—happy—content, I think, is a better description. I have found since I've been back at Gordon Castle, having recovered my health, that I merely want to ride my lands, talk about sheep and husbandry with my factors, write a bit of verse . . . and be with Bathia."

"And ye feared suddenly the trust ye'd placed in her affections was misbegotten?" Sir Algernon pressed.

"Aye . . . that I did," Alex answered softly. "Ye see, so few people have ever seemed to like me for myself. . . ."

His words drifted off. Sir Algernon could see the lad felt dreadfully self-conscious to have bared his soul, even to his own doctor.

"Well," the older man said cheerfully, "yer current course of activities sounds like just the prescription I would recommend for a lad recovering from a wicked foreign ailment," Sir Algernon replied with a twinkle.

The doctor was pleased that the lad's aversion and distrust of his mother had not distorted his appreciation of women in general, and one woman in particular. However, the physician grew uneasy at a sudden thought. *'Twould be quite difficult for any future Duchess of Gordon, whoever she might turn out to be, if her husband truly loved his mistress even before the marriage vows were said.* Never mind, Sir Algernon reassured himself. This Bathia Largue was Alex's first real passion. She probably represented mere lust masquerading as love—a condition notoriously short-lived in young men, in his experience.

"You've been terribly kind, Sir Algernon—" the duke began.

The doctor reached past the glasses poised on the table between them and lightly patted Alexander's hand in fatherly fashion.

"Not at all, dear boy," the old Jacobite said kindly. Sir Algernon had been one of the few partisans of Prince Charles not to suffer exile or have his property confiscated. Perhaps the Duke of Cumberland had simply not gotten wind of the clandestine meetings held within these very walls so many years before. "This weary country needs young lads like ye to help bind her wounds," the doctor added in a heavy voice. "The last twenty years have been trying for us all."

An old order has passed away, the elderly gentleman thought to himself, *and I am one of the few relics left*. Sir Algernon had accepted long ago that the Catholic Stuart Cause would never be revived, and with that failure, Scotland had lost all chance to be a free and separate country from her neighbor to the south. The economy and an entire way of life were changing, and Sir Algernon Dick knew he would not live to see what this transformation would produce.

With a faint smile, the doctor raised a frail hand toward the sound of music permeating the library walls and stood up. The mood of sweet melancholy that hung in the air was broken.

"Would ye like to join me for the buffet and take a quick look at this year's female offerings?" he asked. "I'd be more than happy to make ye officially acquainted with the stunning Mistress Maxwell," he added, wondering almost immediately if such a suggestion were wise.

"Thank you very much, Sir Algernon," Alexander responded, "I could do with a bite of food."

Sir Algernon's second wife, to whom he had been married

two-and-a-half years, poked her head through the open door,
extending a welcoming hand.

"Algernon, darling, do come for supper." Recognizing the
duke, she added delightedly, "And I pray our distinguished
visitor will join us for the buffet and a cup of Het Pint."

Kettles of the Hogmanay wassail were dispensed traditionally
at such Scottish New Year's gatherings, along with rich food and
savories.

"Aye, Lady Mary," the young duke said, brushing his lips to
her hand gallantly, "and you're too kind to let me monopolize
your husband like this."

"Yer Grace is always welcome at Prestonfield," Lady Mary
replied graciously, "and I'm pleased to see ye're beginning the
new year in such good health."

Offering her his arm, Sir Algernon led his wife out of the
library. They were followed closely by the Duke of Gordon, who
strolled with a light step through the hall.

He was going to be a father!

He could hardly wait to see Bathia again. He was ashamed,
now, of the cancerous doubts he'd secretly harbored that she had
been unfaithful to him. That dark fear, and the gnawing thought
he might be sterile, had driven him to seek this interview, but
how glorious had been its outcome!

His eyes narrowed with interest as he spotted a strikingly
handsome young couple slip, surreptitiously, into the library that
he and Sir Algernon had just vacated. Jane Maxwell, looking
ravishing in a gown whose square-cut neckline did nothing to
still the imagination, clung to the arm of that young rogue who
had served as Master of the Swine Course the autumn before his
Grand Tour of the Continent. What a lifetime away that seemed!
True, the memory of the redheaded lad's insulting and insolent
manner still rankled after five years. Obviously, Alexander thought
to himself, the lass and Thomas Fraser had continued their
childhood friendship, which now looked to be blossoming into a
more mature attachment. The duke's eyes darkened. That Fraser
chap deserved a little healthy, if feigned, competition.

The host and hostess of Prestonfield House had been swallowed up by the crowd of guests milling around the buffet
sumptuously set before them. The 4th Duke of Gordon hesitated
only a moment. Then, with a devilish grin, he retraced his steps
toward Sir Algernon's book-lined library.

6

"Odds fish, ye *are* a wicked wench!" Thomas declared, closing the library door and taking Jane in his arms. "*Finally* I've gotten rid of the confounded competition," he laughed.

"Ye dinna seem to mind talking to Simon and Uncle James about the army," she said tartly. Then she smiled mischievously, putting her arms around his neck and kissing him firmly on the mouth.

"Ahem . . ."

A polite cough and discreet knock at the partially opened door disrupted their embrace and the pair leapt apart, hearts racing.

"Would you be so kind as to allow me to retrieve a pair of white gloves I left on the side table over there?" inquired a muffled voice from behind the door.

"Why, yes, of course," replied Thomas a bit hoarsely. He attempted to regain his composure as Jane dashed over to the other side of the room to fetch the gloves.

"Good evening," the Duke of Gordon said, addressing Jane through the six-inch crack in the door.

"Good evening, sir," replied Jane stiffly, at a loss for anything else to say as she handed him his gloves.

"Aha! I *thought* I beheld the daring Mistress Maxwell," he teased, pushing the door slightly more ajar.

"Aye," Jane repeated shortly, embarrassed that she should be discovered during such an intimate moment.

"May I present my compliments for the New Year," the duke persisted, his eyes filled with good cheer, "and my congratulations, Mistress Maxwell, upon your debut?"

"Thank ye, Yer Grace," Jane answered, her demure words cloaking her curiosity about the young aristocrat she'd seen so fleetingly on that fateful day of her accident, five years before.

"I hope to claim a dance—" he said, smiling, his hazel eyes reflecting an appreciative glint, "perhaps later in the evening. That is, if your escort will permit it."

Jane cast a quick glance behind her. Thomas was glowering at the partially opened door that separated her from the duke. She

57

turned back to Alexander, hoping to send him on his way before
Thomas did anything foolish.

"I'm most honored by yer invitation, Yer Grace," she murmured noncommittally.

"Very good," the duke replied, with the barest hint of a
wink. "Enjoy yourself, lassie!"

And with that, he departed.

"Ye'd actually *dance* with that peacock?" Thomas exploded,
crossing to her side in a few brief strides.

"I dinna promise," she protested. " 'Twas just a ploy to send
him on his way."

"I'd like to call out that Anglicized fop!" Thomas retorted,
pacing before the fire. "I hope to claim a *dance . . .*" he said,
mimicking the duke mincingly. Then, changing his tone, he
declared, "I swear I'll claim some Gordon *land* in return for that
blackguard's treachery."

Jane rested her hand on Thomas's arm and said soothingly,
"Ye mustna blame the duke for the shortcomings of his da. 'Tis
true, the Third duke played spaniel to the Crown," she added
gently, "but the uncle, Lewis Gordon, came out in the Forty-five
as everyone knows. Ye've told me yerself of his brave deeds at
Culloden!"

Thomas remained silent, staring moodily into the embers smoldering on the hearth. Then in a low voice, laden with the
bitterness of the life he had known as an orphan, he said, "If all
the Gordons had been as loyal as Lewis, the tables would be
turned, and I, a *Fraser*, would have the wealth and honors due
my name. Instead, many of my clan face starvation or extinc-
tion. This arrogant young *duke* feels he is entitled to anything he
chooses, by virtue of his position. 'Twas plain by the way he
spoke to ye."

"Thomas . . . dear Thomas," Jane said quietly, bidding him
to sit next to her by the fire. She sensed his sudden melancholy,
as she had on several occasions since his return to Edinburgh.
"We have our whole future before us. The good fortune of the
Duke of Gordon matters little to us, darling."

The tightness in Thomas's jaw relaxed a bit and he leaned
over and kissed her forehead. Jane immediately threw her arms
around his chest, tucking her head under his chin. For several
moments, they did not speak. The only sound was the fire
crackling on the hearth.

Finally, Thomas drew back and took her hands in his, looking
somberly into her dark eyes.

"Jenny—" he said hesitantly. "Simon has had word that my Commission has come through."

Jane stared at him wordlessly, her lips parted, as if to cry "No!"

"In fact, he spoke tonight with yer uncle James about it. There's a company of Black Watch being formed as replacements for patrols at Fort Pitt in the Colonies. Pennsylvania, he said, 'Tis a two-year tour of duty." Jane looked stunned. "Jenny darling . . . this is why we must talk. I wanted ye to know what lies ahead."

She rose from the settle and walked slowly toward the window. The world outside suddenly looked bleak and cold. Thomas was leaving.

"Dinna ye think ye've done yer duty to Simon?" she said finally, her voice a mere whisper. "Ye've tended his sheep . . . ye've followed his orders. Dinna ye see? 'Tis time to do what ye want to do and be what ye want to be!"

"Jenny . . ." Thomas interrupted, shaking his head. "Ye know as well as I that yer da canna be counted on for a farthing where ye lasses are concerned, and besides, *look* at ye!" Jane turned to face him. Thomas's features were etched with worry. "The life of a poor crofter's wife isna what ye've been groomed for . . . nor me, either, if the truth be told," he said candidly. "We're creatures of the city, and when we go to the country, we want to warm ourselves beside a drawing room fire and live in relative comfort, not in a hovel with a thatched roof and dirt floor! A soldier's life and an officer's pay can earn us the place we both want, pet . . . in only a few years."

Jane looked at him searchingly. She saw the determination smoldering in his eyes. *He wants to go,* she acknowledged to herself, *he wants so badly to recover what was once his by right.* Jane's heart sank. She realized Thomas was a man obsessed. He wanted her, to be sure, but he wanted his patrimony with equal fervor.

"I'll do anything I must, to have ye in my life," she said finally. "I've always loved ye, Thomas, and now I love ye as a wife does."

He crushed her in his embrace and held her tightly, but disappointment so deep seemed to be tearing at her inside.

"Jenny . . ." Thomas murmured, kissing her ear and then trailing his lips down her neck, finally resting his cheek against the smoothness of one breast. "Ye're the one thing that hasna been lost to me . . . dinna think the next two years will be easy for either of us. . . .''

Jane arched her body toward him, pressing through the unwanted layers of her boned bodice and voluminous skirts.

"Thomas, please don't go!" she cried. "Tell Simon we'll live in Monreith or—"

"Jenny, lass," Thomas interrupted, rocking her gently in his arms. "Ye know that's not the kind of life we want . . . and besides," he whispered into the soft strands of her hair, "soldiering suits me, I think."

Jane pulled away from him and stared.

" 'Tis what my father was," Thomas said slowly, "and 'tis the only chance left to me to make my way—*our* way." He kissed the top of her head, murmuring, "I want so much for us, lass. . . ." His voice began to throb with intensity. "I want us to be able to walk our *own* land when we go to the Highlands. I want to rebuild Struy House . . . to create a life we can share with those poor souls who are still wanderers in their own homeland. . . ."

Jane looked away, feeling frightened by something she couldn't identify, but that filled her with a dread she couldn't seem to put into words. Until now, the stories her uncle James had told her of the savagery of the Indians across the sea had only been exquisitely frightening entertainments. Suddenly, a vision of Thomas, covered in blood and lying motionless, swam before her eyes.

"I'm so afraid ye'll be lost to me if you go to the Colonies," she whispered brokenly. "*Two whole years!* I dinna ken if I can stand the wondering and worrying. . . ."

Thomas took her chin in his hands, forcing her to meet his eyes.

"Dinna worry for my safety, pet," he said softly. "Yer my own lucky talisman . . . ye've always been, ye know."

"But Thomas," she persisted, "how are we to persuade Simon and Mama to agree to our marriage? There's so little time left!" Brightening, she exclaimed, "We could *elope* to Gretna Green! 'Tis only a half-day's journey south, and . . ."

Her voice trailed off as she stared at Thomas, slowly shaking his head.

"I canna marry ye afore I go, Jenny," he said with finality. " 'Tis not just Simon . . . 'twouldna be fair to ye, lass—"

"But—"

Thomas interrupted before Jane could protest further. He took her hands, kissing each gently.

"Ye're just a lass yet, Jenny, darling. Just sixteen today! Ye havna begun to taste of life. If I made ye my bride and then left ye, yer mama'd punish ye greatly, I fear. Ye'd be shut up like a nun for two years, at the moment yer about to bloom like Highland heather. Ye wouldna be a wife and ye wouldna be a maid." He kissed her softly on the lips. "Ye'd grow to think badly of the lad who'd caged ye up and left ye a prisoner in the prime of yer youth."

Jane stared into his eyes and saw a finality in their depths. She withdrew her hands from his. Her chin tilted up slightly in a pose of characteristic stubbornness.

"I think 'tis more to do with yer not wanting Simon's wrath upon yer head!" she said, fighting her disappointment. "He might not lay down the siller for yer Commission, would he now, if he thought ye were betrothed to *me*!"

"Aye, 'tis true," Thomas said evenly. "And that would defeat our ultimate plan to be free of Simon, wouldna it?"

"Mayhap by then ye'll feel differently about taking me as your wife," she replied cuttingly, turning quickly to avoid his gaze. "I suppose ye'd like to keep several arrows in yer quiver."

"Jenny!" he said heatedly, " 'twill only be two years. Surely ye have stronger faith in our love than yer showing me here!"

"Perhaps ye fear I winna be *suitable* when ye someday recover yer lands and yer title," she persisted, driven, by some force she scarcely comprehended, to deliberately misunderstand him. "Ye'll need an heiress's purse to repair and restore yer estate, and ye know, better than most, that I have none."

Thomas approached her solitary figure and rested his hands on her shoulders.

"We canna lose what we *have*, Jenny," he said simply, his voice low and intense. "No matter where I go, or whatever happens, always remember that: we cannot *lose* this precious thing that has been given us."

Her eyes brimmed with tears. She stared at him, unable to speak. Thomas always understood her, always knew somehow what words would make her feel like herself again. She closed her eyes and felt him brush away with the back of his hand the moisture that had spilled down her cheeks.

A soft knock, followed by the sound of a deep voice booming outside the library door, startled them both.

"There they are!" said a young man not much older than Thomas, as he burst into the room with Jane's elder sister in tow. "Not to worry, Kitty," Catherine Maxwell's escort exclaimed, and he strode toward Jane and Thomas, who were struggling to look composed. "I told ye we could find them in a quiet corner," the stranger said jovially.

"Mama's been asking where ye were—'tis time for the buffet," Catherine said to Jane reprovingly. Turning to Thomas, she announced gently, "Simon wanted to know if I'd seen *ye*, Thomas. He said he and Uncle James wanted to talk to ye straightaway."

Catherine stepped forward to introduce the ebullient young man who'd led her to the library.

"Jane, may I present John Fordyce? Mr. Fordyce, this is my sister Jane and our friend Thomas Fraser."

At that, Catherine led her sister out of the library, trailed by the gents. The dining room was still crowded with ravenous guests helping themselves to roast pheasant and joints of beef. The diners scooped up ample spoonfuls of haggis bulging from casings made of sheep's stomachs, and piled their plates with boiled turnips. Young Fordyce assisted Catherine in selecting the tenderest morsels, and it was obvious to Jane that her sister's swain was taking a proprietary interest in everything Catherine said or did. Fordyce had a solid, respectable look about him, and yet he didn't seem pompous at all. What's more, he seemed to treat his newfound prize with kindness and respect.

Well, well, thought Jane with a mischievous glance at her sister. *Catherine may just have landed the perfect catch for the New Year!*

The New Year. *What would it bring?* Jane wondered. As she and her group passed back through the center hall, Sir Algernon called to them from the Italian Room, the old physician's favorite spot at Prestonfield.

"Come, come, children . . . winna ye join us while ye enjoy yer supper?" he invited.

Seated at small tables set up for the evening were Sir Algernon and his wife, Mary, and Lady Maxwell, still squired by Simon Fraser. As Thomas and Jane entered, it appeared her mother and Simon had been deep in conversation.

"I saw that nice young Jamie Ferguson and ye dancing several times," Magdalene said with a disapproving glance at Thomas as Jane took her seat. "No doubt that fine lad will take up the responsibility of the family estates in Tobago."

"Where's Tobago?" Jane asked politely, struggling to eavesdrop on the conversation Simon had quickly initiated with Thomas. As far as she could make out, Simon was describing a battle called Bushy Run—a clash between a company of Black Watch and those dreadful Indians in North America. All of Edinburgh knew of Bushy Run, and Jane shuddered silently, recalling what she had heard about the bitter battle in 1763 where two companies of Black Watch fought furiously against the Indians deep in the Pennsylvania wilderness. Reports of the scalping and horrifying carnage had been the talk of the town when the first reports filtered back to Britain.

"Why not *ask* Mr. Ferguson about Tobago, Jane dear?" her mother replied to the question that Jane nearly had forgotten she'd asked. "He's quite the expert on the sugar trade, ye know, since the family is so prominent out there, with vast plantations all over the Caribbean."

Jane fell silent, straining to overhear more of Thomas and Simon's conversation.

"Have ye been apprised of my rank, sir?" Thomas was asking eagerly.

Jane nearly gagged on a bite of pheasant. She tried to breathe evenly to regain her composure, but waves of anger and fear swept over her.

Tell Simon ye won't go! she railed at Thomas silently. *They'll send ye to Bushy Run, or some other godforsaken place, and an Indian will have yer scalp and ye'll never come back to me . . . Thomas . . . Thomas . . .*

Jane's plate full of untouched food swam before her eyes. Mumbling a brusque apology, she swiftly left the room. She had a chilling thought as she sped up the stairway toward the ballroom. Thomas seemed happy enough to be off on his world adventures. Perhaps, now, he was actually *ambivalent* about marrying her and *that* was why he had urged her to remain silent and be patient! Despite his distinguished ancestry, as things stood presently, Thomas had no real future, save for kindnesses doled out by the likes of Simon Fraser. One thought kept plaguing her: Who would Thomas choose? His godfather or her?

I'm someone worth having! she thought fiercely, stepping across the threshold into the glittering ballroom. *Thomas Fraser of Struy, ye had better realize that and marry me before ye leave for America!*

She cast her eyes around the room and immediately spotted the Duke of Gordon chatting with Marietta Buchanan whom Jane recognized from dancing assembly. The pudgy girl's overripe breasts were nearly spilling out of a stiff yellow gown. What a pudding she is, Jane thought contemptuously. Look how she gazes at the duke with those stupid cow's eyes.

Jane glanced nonchalantly toward the pair. A plan had begun to formulate in her mind. She and Thomas could *still* elope to Gretna Green, if they left tonight! The little border town was famous for waiving bridal formalities when a couple was in a hurry to marry. If Jane were going to galvanize Thomas into taking immediate action to make her his bride before sailing to North America, the Cock O' the North would suit her purpose admirably, she thought grimly.

Walking briskly, she glanced in Alexander's direction with precision, locking eyes briefly as she flashed him her most winning smile. She stood among a clutch of acquaintances only a moment before the Duke of Gordon—as she knew he would—strode up and greeted her with an amused look on his face. The abandoned Marietta turned to speak with an elderly relative and glanced over at Jane with a murderous look in her eyes. The scarlet-coated nobleman bowed, a smile pulling at the corners of his mouth.

"I must admit, from my brief observations this evening, I never thought Mistress Maxwell free to spare a dance for a stranger. But would you do me the honor? 'Tis the 'Wives of Kilwinnon,' " he said, extending his arm.

"Well, unpracticed as I am as anyone's wife, I accept, if ye will only tell me how the first pattern goes," Jane replied, summoning her sweetest smile to her lips.

As the duke talked her through the opening steps, Jane noticed his eyes lingering, as had those of so many men this evening, on her low-cut gown. She noted with satisfaction that the young aristocrat seemed far more appreciative of her slender form than of the milkmaid proportions of Marietta Buchanan.

Jane and Alexander joined a set of dancers just as Thomas appeared at the ballroom door, looking for her. With an urgent wave of his hand, he signaled for her to join him, but she smiled faintly and shook her head as if she were powerless to obey.

Jane was forced to concentrate on the complicated steps of the dance, which she had only sketchily learned a few weeks earlier from her dancing master, the eminent and exacting Davie Strange. She could almost feel Thomas's eyes bore into her back as she flashed discreetly flirtatious glances at her male partners—including the strikingly handsome Duke of Gordon—as she progressed up and down the line of dancers.

Briefly, she caught a glimpse of Simon conferring with Thomas as she threw herself into the lively rhythms of the reel and glided around the parquet floor among more than a hundred dancers.

As the duke and she stepped forward to take their turn as the lead couple, all eyes in the room feasted on them. Jane noted Thomas standing stonily on the sidelines. His jaw tightened and, abruptly, he spun on his heel, melting into the crowd. When, at last, the prolonged chord signaled the end of the dance, Jane could feel beads of perspiration trickling down between her breasts. She made the traditional deep curtsy, thanking Alexander for being her partner. Her eyes quickly searched the room for Thomas, who was nowhere to be seen.

Suddenly, from the far end of the chamber, voices called for quiet. Sir Algernon was stepping forward in front of the silent orchestra to ask his guests to partake of the traditional birthday ritual.

"Will ye join me in wishing Mistress Jane Maxwell, daughter of Sir William and Lady Maxwell of Monreith, the happiest of sixteenth birthdays!"

Cries of "Hear! Hear!" and loud clapping startled Jane into another deep curtsy to the throng.

"And now, as is our custom at Prestonfield House, Jane, lassie," Sir Algernon announced in a booming voice over the murmurs of the crowd, "would ye do me the honor of dancing with me that elegant confection imported from France, the minuet?"

The Duke of Gordon gallantly passed her hand to Sir Algernon as Jane glanced frantically around the room for a glimpse of Thomas. The tall clock against the wall opposite the orchestra began to toll twelve, its deep tones reverberating throughout the room. Cries acknowledging the new year—1766—spread throughout the throng, as Sir Algernon and Jane walked slowly toward the center of the ballroom. He bowed low and whispered, "Better be on yer toes, lassie! This is to be no ordinary debut dance."

Before Jane could protest, the elderly man guided her across the floor to a smattering of applause. Jane was excruciatingly aware of the hundreds of pairs of eyes staring at her from the human ring surrounding them. She nearly flinched under the critical gaze of the Dowager Duchess of Gordon, whose husband had engaged the attentions of a pretty blond guest who appeared younger even than Jane.

A line of men congregated at the far end of the room, but there was no sign of Thomas. At a signal from Sir Algernon, the gentlemen one by one clasped Jane's hand and danced a few phrases of the minuet with her, passing her on to the next swain waiting eagerly in line.

She could hear an undercurrent of whispering from the surrounding spectators as she spun from partner to partner in a dizzy whirl. She attempted her most dignified turn beneath the arm of Jamie Ferguson of Tobago fame, whose worshipful gaze and slightly bucked teeth unnerved her greatly. Suddenly, Thomas materialized as if by magic. He handed a bystander his woolen cloak. Unceremoniously, he cut in line ahead of the Duke of Gordon, who was, at that very moment, approaching to take Jane's hand.

"I believe, sir," the duke said to Thomas between clenched teeth, "that your opportunity to dance with the fair Mistress Maxwell is yet to come."

"My claim to Mistress Maxwell's attentions takes precedence— by previous arrangement," Thomas interposed rudely, his voice nearly a snarl.

The crowd standing near them could be heard to gasp at Thomas's insolence toward the duke who far surpassed him in rank, with or without the senior Sir Thomas Fraser's forfeited title. The musicians had ceased playing and simply stared at the unfolding drama, bows in hand.

"Can ye imagine the cheek of the lad!" Marietta Buchanan whispered loudly to the Duke of Gordon's mother who was perched nearby on a gilt chair. " 'Tis shocking!"

Jane stood between Thomas and Alexander, completely at a loss as to how to proceed. The duke and Thomas stared at each other unflinchingly.

"If I may interrupt," said a voice behind the tense little group. It was Sir Algernon. "My good man," he said to Thomas pleasantly, "would ye be so kind as to assist the Lady Mary to form a set on the far side of the room for the upcoming 'Captain MacBean's Reel'?"

"I'm afraid I canna comply with yer request, sir," Thomas replied stiffly. "I've come only to bid adieu to Jane, as promised. I'm off to Perth Barracks where I'm to take up my new Commission in the Black Watch immediately. I have just learned that I must depart the White Horse Inn before dawn."

Sir Algernon looked uncertainly from Thomas to the Duke of Gordon.

"But, of course, then, I must defer the pleasure of this dance to another time," Alexander said coolly to Jane. His glance rested fleetingly on Thomas. "Good night . . . *lieutenant*, is it to be?" he added mockingly.

But before Thomas could reply, the 4th Duke of Gordon had gracefully edged his way toward a clutch of gilt chairs and extended his hand to the plump Marietta, who preened with pleasure as she accepted the young aristocrat's attentions. The buxom miss tossed a triumphant glance in Jane's direction.

Thomas and Jane stared at each other wordlessly as Sir Algernon, with an abrupt wave of his arm, directed the musicians to strike up a tune.

"We canna tarry, lad," boomed Simon Fraser, striding over to them with Lady Maxwell and the toothy Jamie Ferguson at his sides. "We must be off, boy. Ye've not much o' the night left to be packin' yer kit!"

"Our prayers and good wishes go with ye, Thomas," Lady Maxwell cut in quickly. "A safe journey to ye to Perth, and to America, when ye sail this spring, m'lad. Come, Jane, dear," she added, grasping Jane's arm firmly. "We mustna delay Thomas another instant."

Jane yanked her arm from her mother's grasp and whirled around to face her.

"Dinna think I am so daft as not to know yer scheme!" she spat in a low voice.

"Jane!" Lady Maxwell recoiled. "Ye will cease this insulting display *instantly*!"

"I will say the truth, and nothing less, Mama *dear*!" she retorted. "Ye and Simon have mixed this poisonous brew this night, and *ye*, Thomas, have drunk it to the dregs! What manner of man are ye, that ye're lead around by the nose on yer face and dinna even know it!"

Thomas stared back at her, stunned by her insult. Jane turned to the flustered Jamie Ferguson and forced her most seductive smile to her lips. She offered him her hand.

"Would ye be so kind, dear sir, to remove me from this stifling atmosphere? A glass of punch, perhaps? I so long to learn more about Tobago. Are the natives there as uncivilized as the savages in North America?"

And with an angry toss of her head, she turned her back on her mother, Simon, and Thomas, urging the bewildered Mr. Ferguson to escort her out of the candlelit ballroom.

The Duke of Gordon paused to survey the tableau of shocked

bystanders who had witnessed Jane's dramatic departure. Much
to Marietta Buchanan's chagrin, she detected a ghost of an
admiring smile lingering on his aristocratic lips. Soon, the crowd
resumed its chatter, speculating who would be the "first-foot,"
the first person to cross the threshold of a home after midnight
and thus determine the luck that household could expect throughout the coming year. A well-favored visitor bearing a pint o'
whisky brought good fortune, indeed, 'twas said.

Alexander inclined his head politely to the guests nearest him
and casually walked through the door to the small room where
the Hogmanay punch was being dispensed to the fiery Miss
Maxwell. The future Lieutenant Thomas Fraser of Struy glared
at the Duke of Gordon's retreating scarlet coat and stormed out
of the ballroom in the opposite direction. Simon Fraser and Lady
Maxwell were left, amid the swirling dancers and inquisitive
onlookers, to gaze at each other, open-mouthed.

7

March 1766

Jane pulled the counterpane up around her shoulders and sank
deeper into the bed linen, ignoring the shaft of morning sunshine
that sliced across her four-poster. Suddenly, Eglantine's voice
and the sound of her footsteps taking the stairs two at a time
shattered the stillness in the room.

"Jane! Jane . . . 'tis from Thomas!" came her muffled cries.
Her younger sister burst through the doorway waving a piece of
parchment, followed by Catherine, who appeared out of breath.
It was the first word Jane had had from him since their angry
parting on New Year's Eve.

"Uncle James brought it," she continued excitedly. "He's
sailing to America with Thomas! He and Aunt Elizabeth arrived
late last night from Perth Barracks and then he and Thomas
departed immediately for the Port of Leith. Aunt and the boys
are going to live with us again while Uncle James is at Fort Pitt!
'Tisn't it grand?"

But Jane wasn't listening. She snatched Thomas's missive out of her sister's hand and tore it open. It said only

Jenny,
I sail from Leith on the evening tide. So much to say . . .
  Tho.

Jane sagged against the bedpost. Tears began welling in her eyes. Incapable of stifling the sobs rising within her, she gave way to them. The weeks of pent-up anxiety and anticipation over Thomas's departure only served to darken her despair.

Jane had soon been filled with remorse over her fiery display of temper toward Thomas at the birthday ball. Lady Maxwell had forbidden her to write to him and had watched her every move since that night, like a jailer.

As her sisters watched helplessly, Jane pounded her fist against the wooden four-poster, the note crumpled in her injured hand.

"Jenny . . . please . . . dinna carry on so—" Catherine began, awkwardly putting her arms around her sister's heaving shoulders. Eglantine stared at both her sisters, agog at the drama her little announcement had created.

"Winna ye leave me alone!" Jane cried. "What does this matter to ye, Kitty? Ye have Mr. Fordyce, safe among his ledgers! What care have ye for my concerns?"

Immediately, Jane was contrite. She turned her tear-streaked face toward her older sister who had shown seeming sympathy for her unhappiness in recent weeks.

"I—I'm sorry, Kitty," she sighed, lamely, trying to regain her composure. " 'Tis just . . . I *so* wanted to see Thomas before he left, and now—"

Fresh tears coursed down her cheeks. Catherine and Eglantine looked at each other in distress. They were at a complete loss as to what to say or do.

"James and I said our good-byes before dawn, Jane dear," Aunt Elizabeth said firmly to her niece an hour later as they sat opposite each other at breakfast. The young matron, her pale blond hair pulled neatly to the nape of her neck, appeared composed, though there were dark circles under her eyes. The journey from Perth with the children after parting from her husband at dawn had taken its toll. "He's probably aboard ship by now. Our going to Leith is absolutely out of the question."

Barely able to swallow her disappointment, Jane stared at her hands twisting the edge of the tablecloth in her lap. Her eyes fixed on her amputated finger. What if she had driven Thomas away for good? She felt a wave of apprehension sweep over her. How could she have taunted him so cruelly, flirting with the very man whose family had been a factor in the downfall of Clan Fraser? Thomas must be *furious*—if he still had any feelings for her at all. The weeks of misery since the birthday ball had taught her how empty life felt without the certainty of his love. She *had* to see him before he sailed!

Jane raised her tearstained eyes toward her aunt. Elizabeth Maxwell represented her only hope of seeing Thomas one last time.

"I dinna have an opportunity to wish Uncle farewell or Godspeed," Jane said softly.

Elizabeth Maxwell looked sharply at her red-eyed niece sitting across from her at the breakfast table. She took Jane's hand gently in her own as a sign of sympathy. She could plainly see that Jane was in love with that fine young lieutenant, and, after all, not everyone could marry a title. Look at Magdalene Maxwell herself, thought Elizabeth. She hooked a baronet and what did it profit her? A life of cares and misery. Elizabeth felt blessed every day that she was happily married to the second son in the Maxwell dynasty, title or no title.

Two whole years without James! Her husband's reassignment to North America had come about without warning. The sudden decision to replace regimental captains at Fort Pitt in Pennsylvania had thrown her into a whirlwind of activity. And what of the new baby she sensed was forming inside her, a short six months after the birth of her last child? To face the dangers of childbirth alone, without the calm, loving support of her husband. Her own misery at the thought of their long separation was matched in her niece's devastated expression.

"Oh, Aunt Elizabeth," Jane sighed, her lip quivering, thanks to her aunt's display of affection and understanding. "They're both *so near* . . . couldna we . . ."

"Jane . . . I am so sorry . . ." Elizabeth began, reaching across the table to smooth back a few wayward strands of Jane's dark tresses, "really I am—but ye canna imagine how rude the waterfront of Leith is . . . how unsuitable a place the docks are for ladies."

"I dinna *care*!" Jane responded hotly, a blazing gleam beginning to glow in her eye. "If ye winna help me, I'll ride Thomas's horse there myself, or take the hourly coach!"

"And ruin yer reputation in the bargain? Not to mention what could happen to yer *person* with such folly!" Elizabeth replied with alarm.

"I *will* go! I will see Thomas before he leaves!" Jane cried, holding back her tears. Her willful tone alarmed Elizabeth more than her words. "Please, *please*, Aunt . . . come with me," Jane pleaded. "It will be yer last chance to see Uncle James . . . to *surprise* him . . . and my last chance, too. *Please*, Aunt Elizabeth!"

Elizabeth gripped the dining table with both hands and remained perfectly still. She thought she had felt a flutter in her low abdomen. She waited for it again: the first sign of life in the babe that would be born while James was away.

The previous night, Elizabeth had revealed to James her growing concern that she had not felt any movement, despite her conviction she had conceived the child four months earlier. The tiny flutter of butterfly wings in her womb filled her with sudden pleasure and relief. But what would she be able to tell this bairn of its father? That he had been drowned at sea? Shot by a French colonist? Scalped by a savage? Would James ever return to see this child who was little more than a prayer the day he departed?

Her niece began to stare at her, puzzled, as Elizabeth sucked in her breath sharply. *She did feel flutters . . . a definite brush of butterfly wings!* Elizabeth looked at Jane and smiled absently.

Oh, James—she thought joyfully, *'tis alive!*

He would be so happy to know all was well, even if he'd be angry at her for subjecting herself to the bumpy coach ride and her niece to the turmoil at dockside.

"All right, Jane," Elizabeth said quietly. "Hector Chisholm can drive us and I'll escort ye to Leith to make yer farewells. There's no need to bother yer mother about this," she added pointedly, " 'Twill be just an outing to visit old friends, which isna really a lie. But ye *must* promise me, Jane, ye'll do just as I say and not create any nuisance."

The shrill curses of the coachman and the crack of his whip roused Jane from a fitful slumber. Her neck was stiff from the nine-mile ride jammed into a corner of the hired livery Aunt Elizabeth had engaged for the hour-long journey. *Oh, please let him be there*, she prayed silently, as Hector cracked the whip over the sloping backs of the nags pulling their rented coach.

By the time she and Elizabeth Maxwell reached the docks by the bay, the area was bustling with afternoon activity. Jane craned her neck to try to determine which ship was the *Providence*. She grew increasingly frustrated at the sight of the forest of ships' masts stretching like a thicket of tall reeds across the harbor. She sat up abruptly to stare at the porters laboring under twice their weight, bearing boxes of coal, barrels of rum, and baskets of glistening salmon. The laborers trudged from dockside to a low-roofed warehouse where they disappeared with their back-breaking loads.

"The *Providence* is a brig," Aunt Elizabeth said, "which means that if she hasna sailed yet, she'll be anchored quite far out, because of her size."

Attempting to keep Jane occupied, Aunt Elizabeth pointed to a man in a worn navy frock coat who was walking along the crescent of the quay.

"That's the Bellman of Leith," she declared wryly. "The locals give him a few pence just to keep him from spending all his working hours in the pubs."

Jane surveyed this bleary-eyed, red-nosed figment of humanity as he rang a large brass bell, and, in a nonstop singsong, slurred the names of people for whom he apparently carried messages.

The two women began to smooth their hair and adjust their clothes in anticipation of their arrival at the waterfront hotel. Jane pulled nervously on the jacket of Catherine's dark green velvet traveling costume. She had borrowed it in haste soon after her mother had retired to do the morning accounts.

The road along the waterfront was jammed with foot traffic of every description, forcing the coach to slow to a snail's pace.

"Will ye *hurry*, Hector," Jane cried through the window.

Hector scowled and began once again to swear to the Almighty while shouting at the pedestrians from atop the coach.

"Make way . . . make way!" he yelled at the milling throng.

Soon the carriage pulled up to a stone building labeled Number 28, which faced the harbor. Its weathered facade and fanned windows seemed to Jane to have a reassuring look about them, as did the carved wooden sign, which swung from a wrought-iron elbow.

"Welcome . . . welcome, ladies, to the Old Ship Hotel," declared a jovial man who had rushed out of the entranceway to greet them. He executed a courtly bow and quickly offered an arm to both Elizabeth and Jane, steering them around the jumble of sea captain's trunks stacked near the entrance awaiting transfer to the fleet.

As the rotund proprietor ushered them inside, Jane stared in wonder at the huge staircase and the shiny black panels and wainscoting of the main public room.

"We are here to see my husband, Captain James Maxwell, who is setting sail aboard the *Providence* on the evening tide," Aunt Elizabeth told their host primly.

"Captain Maxwell . . . Captain Maxwell . . ." mused the hotel owner, rubbing his chin. "Why, I believe he and a young lieutenant arrived early this morning and have let rooms for the day!"

Jane's heart began to race as the innkeeper reached for a large ledger covered with lines of elegant script.

"With more than a thousand vessels comin' in and out of the port each year, dear ladies, we have numerous captains with us at the Old Ship Hotel."

"My husband is not a sea captain, sir," Elizabeth said, bending over his shoulder to take a look at the list herself. "He's a captain in the Black Watch regiment." Pointing midway down the ledger, she said, "That's him, I believe," indicating a notation that read: Capt. Ja. Maxwell & Lt. Tho. Fraser—#23.

"Ah . . . certainly, m'lady . . . that's the very one I was thinking of . . . the middle-aged gentleman accompanied by the copper-haired lad. He and Lieutenant Fraser wished to catch forty winks before boarding their vessel."

"Would you be so kind as to send up someone to inform Captain Maxwell that his wife and niece are here?" Elizabeth asked.

"I fear that 'twill be impossible, mum," the hotelier said, shaking his head. Gesturing to the dimly lit public room they'd passed as they entered the foyer of the inn, he declared, "The two gentlemen had a wee dram in there an hour or so ago, and then they left."

Aunt Elizabeth paled visibly. Jane sensed her aunt was already having second thoughts about the wisdom of their afternoon's journey to Leith. The woman's shoulders sagged and she turned to leave.

"Wait, Aunt!" Jane exclaimed excitedly. "What about the Bellman of Leith? Perhaps he could find them!"

"If they've left the inn,'" Elizabeth replied, shaking her head, " 'tis probably because they're setting sail."

"But the note from Thomas said, 'We sail on the *evening*

tide,' and there's at least a good three hours before sunset, Aunt
Elizabeth! Let's engage the Bellman!'

An intermittent clanging could be heard just outside the door
of the inn. Jane, without waiting for her aunt's permission,
whirled around from the desk and ran for the door.

"Sir! Sir!" she cried, at the man they'd seen on their arrival
in Leith. He was lackadaisically clanging his brass handbell
as he ambled down the street calling, "Captain Jennens! Message for ye . . . Captain Jennens!"

Jane dashed across the threshold of the Old Ship Hotel and
caught his sleeve. The Bellman of Leith stopped midsentence,
apparently startled at being accosted by a lady of quality.

"Please, sir," Jane pleaded breathlessly, "My aunt and I are
trying to locate my uncle Captain James Maxwell. He's due to
sail on the *Providence* tonight, but he may still be somewhere
along the quay. Can ye help us find him?"

Without waiting for his answer, Jane dug into her reticule for
a few pence. The leather-skinned old man took her few coins eagerly, licking his lips as if he already tasted the ale they would
purchase and flashing her a smile that revealed the gaps from his
missing teeth.

"Captain Maxwell, is it now?" he said, tucking the money
into his tattered coat pocket. "I'll do me best, lass, that's all I
ken promise. I'll do me best."

And without another word to her, he tipped his battered
tricornered hat and wove unsteadily down the road, clanging his
bell and continuing his chant: "Captain Jennens o' the *Glory*!
Captain Maxwell o' the *Providence*! Captain Jennens! Captain
Maxwell!"

The old man was about to turn the corner, heading, Jane feared,
for the nearest local tavern. She called after him.

"There might be a tall, redheaded lad with Captain Maxwell!
His name is Thomas Fraser!" she shouted as he disappeared
from view.

"Jane! Really!" her aunt chided as she emerged from the
hotel's entrance. "Mr. Hyde here says they took their traveling
trunks with them."

"Yes Miss," the innkeeper agreed, "and I fear our Bellman
takes any assignment, whether or not he makes full rounds of the
docks before nipping into the pub. Mayhap ye've paid good
siller for naught."

"Please, Aunt," Jane pleaded, nearly in tears. "Canna we
wait a while to see if they answer the summons?"

Elizabeth sighed, her face etched with fatigue from the journey as well as her own disappointment.

"At least Mr. Hyde could provide us with a bit of refreshment before our return journey," Jane added quickly.

"All right," Elizabeth concurred wanly. " 'Twas probably folly to have come at all, but now that we're here, I could do with a bit o' barley broth."

Mr. Hyde led Jane and her aunt to the ladies lounge whose deep-set windows provided a sweeping view of the entire harbor.

The minutes ticked by. After their meal, the plates were cleared by a young servant who stared at them when he thought they weren't looking. A strange sensation passed through Jane's chest, fluttering down to her abdomen. It had been so long since she had felt Thomas's arms around her. For her part, Aunt Elizabeth, her hands calmly resting in her lap, appeared to be absorbed by her own thoughts, as Jane tried to quiet the throbbing in her breast.

"*Elizabeth!* What the Devil!"

Uncle James's loud exclamation took them both by surprise and the two women bolted simultaneously as the tall soldier strode into the room.

"What are ye *doing* here, wife!" he demanded. Then, with a glance at his spouse's pale cheeks, he added in a softer tone, "Elizabeth . . . is anything amiss?"

"I will explain everything, James . . . but, please bid hello to Jane who also made this very uncomfortable journey. She was desperately sorry to have missed ye last evening."

Dumbfounded, Uncle James took his wife's outstretched hands in his own in an unconscious gesture and looked over at his niece.

"Ye brought *Jane* down to this bedlam!" he cried in exasperation. "Really, Elizabeth, surely ye—of all people—have more good sense! When I heard my name called out by the Bellman, I already had one foot in the launch. I was sure someone had died."

"I have a great *deal* of good sense, James," she replied calmly, "and ye'll come to understand my reasons for coming to Leith to bid ye a final farewell. Where *is* young Thomas Fraser, may I ask?"

"Right here, Mistress Maxwell," said a deep voice behind them.

Jane jumped up from her chair and whirled around to gaze at the tall, handsome figure who strode into the room. She gazed at

Thomas wordlessly, her eyes drifting down to his strong, muscular legs in their red and white checkered stockings, fastened at the knees with broad red garters. A thick woolen kilt with the familiar Black Watch green and black tartan hung trimly on his slim hips, secured by an ox-leather belt with a silver buckle. Her eyes took in the large sporran made of otter skin that hung over that mysterious region below Thomas's waist. She savored the sight of his scarlet waistcoat and his handsomely tailored short scarlet jacket with its buff facings and white lace trimmings. His blue pancake bonnet with its border of red around the band sat at a jaunty angle on his dark russet locks, completing the picture of quite the handsomest soldier Jane thought she'd ever seen.

"Oh . . . Thomas . . ." she breathed, unable to say another word.

When he merely continued to stare back at her with a shocked expression on his face, she crossed the three feet that separated them and flung her arms around his neck. She hugged him tightly to her, ignoring the bemused looks of her aunt and uncle.

"Thomas, I was so afraid I would never see ye again!" she breathed into his ear. "Thank God we got here before ye departed! If Aunt Elizabeth hadna brought me to Leith, I—"

"Yer darling aunt has been very naughty to have disobeyed a standing order on that score," boomed Uncle James. "But I'm deuced glad she did!"

Jane disentangled herself from Thomas's arms and glanced at Elizabeth long enough to see she was locked in her husband's embrace. Jane faced Thomas once again and drew him aside. Ill at ease, she cast about for a way to apologize for using the duke to make him jealous, while conveying to him her distress over the way he had permitted Master Simon to order him about.

Reaching for her, Thomas put his hands on her small shoulders.

"I can actually touch ye and not be dreamin'," he said in a soft whisper, glancing over at Elizabeth and James who were now seated in front of the fire, enjoying an intimate conversation.

Soothed by the warmth of his hands on her shoulders, Jane uncertainly began to speak.

"Thomas, *please* forgive me for dancing with the Duke of Gordon instead of ye at Hogmanay." She gazed into his eyes earnestly. " 'Twas just my terrible temper . . . ye know that. . . ."

"I'd like to skewer that dandy with the point of my sword!" Thomas growled. "It looked to me as if ye were enjoying yerself mightily when I saw ye dancing with the fop!"

"I only acted that way to make ye jealous so ye'd elope with me . . . but ye seemed so *pleased* about yer Commission, and leaving Edinburgh . . . and it angered me.''

"I *was* pleased my Commission came through," Thomas replied thoughtfully. "But that dinna mean I'm happy to be leaving *ye*." He demanded to know if she had received any of his letters. "Or did ye choose not to be writing a poor lieutenant, what with a duke coming to call?''

"Dinna be daft, Thomas," Jane replied tartly, secretly pleased to learn he still cared enough about her to write, although she was angry with her mother who, just as she'd suspected, had intercepted his missives, save for the one sent through Uncle James this morning. "I received not a word from ye since that night. And as far as the duke . . . 'tis said he has a mistress at Gordon Castle, and is about to become a father in the bargain. No one's seen a trace of him since the night of the ball.''

"Such news must be disappointin' to ye, lass," Thomas commented sourly.

Jane remained silent for a moment.

"Pray let us stop dissembling," she replied quietly. "I came all this way to apologize for what happened at Prestonfield, and to tell ye that I still wish to be yer wife someday—that is, if ye feel the same as ye did before.''

Thomas's jawline softened. A look of tenderness came into his eyes, telling her instantly all was well between them again.

"The point is, we're together—isn't it?" he said softly. "Ye're *here*, though I canna hardly believe ye're real. . . .''

Thomas moved his hands down Jane's velvet sleeves to grasp her gloved hands tightly in his own.

"I'm real, to be sure," Jane agreed teasingly, smiling up at him. "But aren't *ye* the wonder!" she laughed, stepping out of the circle of his arms to take in the full magnificence of his military attire. "Will ye look at ye, now! Aunt Elizabeth says Uncle James counts ye among his best men. 'Tis proud I am of ye, Thomas," she finished sincerely, discreetly glancing at her aunt and uncle. Uncle James had a look of pure joy on his face and bent forward to kiss his wife directly on the lips.

Jane beckoned Thomas to lean down so she could whisper into his ear.

"From the looks of things, I think she must have told him about the new bairn coming," she said softly, her lips just grazing his ear's smooth pink shell. His clean male smell was heady to her nostrils and she felt slightly dizzy. She clung to his forearms to steady herself.

Thomas folded his arm around Jane once again, sheltering her in the crook of his elbow.

"Someday ye will tell me ye feel *our* baby movin' inside ye," Thomas whispered fiercely. "In two years time, 'twill be Lieutenant and *Mrs.* Fraser."

"We'll elope to Gretna Green and take Uncle James and Aunt Elizabeth as our witnesses!" she whispered gaily, her spirits soaring for the first time in months. Thomas kissed her tenderly on the lips.

"I promise ye, Jenny, when I return in Sixty-eight, there'll be naught to prevent us from becomin' husband and wife!" His eyes gleamed ominously as he added, "And if Gordon ever so much as *looks* at ye with that mocking stare of his, I *swear* by St. Ninian—I'll run him through with my sword when first I set foot on Scottish soil!"

His voice cracked with anger. Jane wondered, though, if Thomas recognized, even now, who was the real threat to their future plans. Jane knew she would simply defy her mother, but had it finally penetrated his consciousness that his godfather would use him for whatever purpose suited Simon Fraser's far-reaching ambitions, regardless of its impact on Thomas's happiness? Suddenly, Uncle James cleared his throat, crossed the wide expanse of the hotel's lounge with Aunt Elizabeth on his arm, and took command.

"We are already late, m'dear, for our meal aboard the *Providence* with Captain Milner," he said to his wife. "I dinna suppose the good Captain would object to two lovely lassies joining us for supper on the occasion of our departure for such exotic lands as Maryland and Pennsylvania, do ye Thomas?" James joked.

Relief brightening his features, Thomas squared his shoulders and replied with a snappy, "No, *sir!*"

"That's splendid then," James replied. "Let's be on our way, little mother . . . I expect Mr. Johnstone's still waiting with the launch, wondering if we've jumped ship!"

A light chop rippled across Leith Harbor in the stiff spring breeze as the small skiff ferrying the Maxwell party to the *Providence* ploughed through the whitecapped water. Squeezed next to Thomas in the bow, Jane closed her eyes for a few moments and tilted her head back to capture the warmth of the sunshine against her face. The raucous caws of the seagulls overhead punctuated the comfortable silence floating between her and Thomas.

"Ye look so peaceful, Jenny lass." Thomas smiled at her, adding softly, "I think I'll remember ye exactly the way ye looked a moment ago . . . yer eyes closed as if ye were asleep beside me."

She reached across and tucked a lock of his garnet hair beneath the band of his hat, teasing him lightly.

"How could I forget a redheaded lad in such a handsome blue bonnet!"

The oarsman shouted for a line as the skiff approached the sleek brig, a two-masted square-rigged ship that, given favorable winds and currents, would carry Thomas to Annapolis in two to three months at sea. Uncle James caught the line cast down to them and secured it to their bow. A large-boned man with tufts of gray hair shooting out at odd angles from his temples and over his heavy-set brow strode forward to greet them. His uniform and commanding demeanor told Jane immediately that this was Captain Milner, master of the *Providence*. Uncle James hastened to explain the presence of the two ladies.

"I hope I've not presumed too greatly on yer hospitality, Captain, to have included my wife, Elizabeth, and my niece Jane Maxwell in yer invitation to sup?" James glanced at Jane with a hint of the same disapproval he had voiced at the hotel. "These two minxes thought to *surprise* us, coming all the way from Edinburgh for a final farewell."

Captain Milner boldly appraised both women from head to toe and then nodded a short welcome.

"Aye, Captain Maxwell. Predictin' what lassies'll do is like predictin' the weather; 'tis a foolhardy occupation. We'll fit 'em in somehow," he said gruffly.

The group settled down in Captain Milner's private quarters to partake of a simple meal of sole and boiled potatoes. Jane gauged the passage of the minutes by the fading of light in the cramped cabin, while a white-coated cabin boy served their midday repast.

"No doubt ye must have many details to attend to, Captain, before we sail," Uncle James announced, setting down his empty glass of port. "May we offer the lasses a brief tour of the ship before sending them ashore?"

Nodding his agreement, their host bid the foursome adieu. Jane followed behind Thomas's broad shoulders down the narrow passageway and into the dazzling afternoon sunshine.

"I'm taking Elizabeth forward where there's a fresh breeze," James said, guiding his wife toward the ship's prow without further discussion.

Sensing a moment of privacy had finally arrived, Jane and Thomas turned and headed in the opposite direction toward the stern.

"I want to see yer cabin," Jane said suddenly, once they'd reached the afterdeck where the ship's standard snapped in the breeze on its flagpole. "I want to picture in my mind where ye'll be these next months before ye disappear into the wilderness."

Thomas smiled wickedly and took her arm.

"Do let me show ye where the guns are placed, Mistress Maxwell," he smirked. Glancing quickly around the deck as they passed a set of stairs, Thomas grabbed her hand. "Shh . . . here's the ladder. Follow me, I think I can find it!"

He quickly led her down a flight of wooden steps, and abruptly turned left into a passageway. Ignoring the rows of cannon that poked their iron snouts through holes in the side of the ship, Thomas hurried her through another long passageway and turned yet another corner. Thoroughly disoriented, Jane wrinkled her nose at the smell of pitch and tar that permeated the bowels of the ship. Nearly tripping over a pile of hemp line, Thomas suddenly pulled her into a small cabin with his and another name scrawled on a scrap of parchment tacked to the door.

"My loyal bunkmate isn't here, thank God!" Thomas breathed, locking the door and pulling Jane to him almost roughly.

Jane inhaled once again the slightly spicy smell of his skin and felt the rough texture of his woolen jacket against her cheek. The sweep of her billowing velvet traveling gown nearly filled the tiny cabin. The bunks, spartan even for officers, were hard and uninviting, but Thomas sat them both down on the canvas cover and began kissing Jane's lips and throat, heedlessly plunging both his hands into her carefully coiffed hair.

Jane sank back and stretched out on the flat, unyielding surface, pulling Thomas's weight against her body. The layers of petticoats and velvet swirling about them seemed to conspire against her overwhelming desire to be close to him, to feel the smooth expanse of his chest cushioned against her breasts, to extend the length of her legs along the longer, more muscular length of his.

She wondered if anyone had seen them steal below deck or enter Thomas's cabin. Despite her rising tide of passion, she nervously listened for the click of the door latch, signaling that Thomas's fellow officer had returned.

Her nagging apprehension was soon blotted out by the insistent probing of Thomas's tongue against her parted lips. His hands gently kneaded her breasts while the sensation of his powerful thighs, entrapping her own, pushed all thoughts from her mind except getting closer . . . closer . . .

"Jenny, darling . . ."

Thomas's whispers filtered through the haze of feeling and need that had enveloped her. Jane opened her eyes and found herself looking directly into his. She glanced down at their bodies—his green and black tartan blended at the hips with her darker forest green velvet skirt. Thomas's sporran had swung to the right and lay slightly askew on the narrow strip of bedding that lay between them. His kilt had separated at the waist, exposing a lean stretch of naked thigh.

"I seem to be far more accessible than ye are," he joked, his voice low with a passion she had never heard before. Slowly, with calm deliberation, he drew her left hand below his waist to the place his sporran no longer camouflaged.

"If ye ever doubted my longing for ye these last months, ye have this proof," he whispered in her ear, pushing his pelvis lightly against hers, his breath sending tremors down her spine. "I went nearly mad that night at the thought . . ."

Jane's fingers slipped around the last woolen layer of his kilt and she heard Thomas moan as he nuzzled her neck.

"Oh God, Jenny!" he cried before burying his lips in her hair. "I want ye so much!"

Roughly, Thomas rolled over on his side and reached down to the tangled hem of Jane's gown. He slid the warm palm of his hand the length of her silk stockings to the bare flesh above her satin garters. Jane sucked in her breath and tensed her body as he traced his fingers deliberately across her skin.

"Do ye *feel* the ache?" he demanded hoarsely, strafing his fingers lightly against the crease where her thigh joined her torso. "Do ye *feel* what *I* feel?"

Thomas seemed almost angry. He kept up a steady, maddening rhythm of feathery strokes along the tops of her thighs. Jane felt as if lightning struck whenever his fingers strayed past the last layer of cloth and sank into the dark matte between her legs. No one had ever touched her there before and she felt both shy and brazen, wanton and afraid. Soon she was nearly frantic with the waves of pleasure and longing that suddenly exploded within

her. She gave a low moan and began to pull at the brass buttons
of Thomas's jacket, their shiny polished surfaces clouding over
from her hot, moist breath.

Thomas shifted his weight again and began pressing down on
her, his breathing ragged.

"I dinna want it to happen this way," he groaned. "I wanted
it to be—"

Jane stopped his words with a kiss, pulling him on top of her
as the heavy folds of her traveling costume surrounded them in a
sea of green velvet. Her hands sought the silver buckle on the
wide belt that encompassed his kilt.

Smiling at her almost sadly, Thomas fumbled at the cloth-
covered buttons that stretched along the front of her dress from
the base of her throat to below her waist.

Suddenly, a high piercing two-tone bos'n's whistle penetrated
the tiny cabin, signaling a shift in the watch, and slicing the
silence of their desperate embrace.

Thomas slumped against her as if suddenly defeated. Slowly
he pulled himself off the bunk, and stepped silently toward the
small porthole that framed, in miniature, a distant view of Leith.
He pressed his forehead against a massive beam on the low-slung
ceiling. She could hear footsteps on the deck directly above
them.

"I want ye so much, Jenny, but I canna take ye like this," he
said in a muffled voice. "Not the first time, in a narrow bunk
. . . not in a hurry."

Jane swung her legs over the side of the cot and stood up,
smoothing her disheveled skirts into neat folds and rebuttoning
her bodice. She crossed the cabin and stood behind him. Pressing her breasts to his back, she put her arms around his waist and
rested her cheek in the hollow between his shoulder blades.

"No one can say for sure what can happen to people in two
years . . ." she heard him say, his sentence drifting off. "But
know this for a fact, Jane Maxwell," he said vehemently, abruptly
turning to face her. "I claim you as my wife and I'll be back to
wed ye, if ye'll be true to our promise!"

"No matter where ye go, or whatever happens," she whispered, "I'll always love ye, Thomas Fraser . . . always, always.
I'll be here when ye come back again. We canna *lose* what
we have."

He drew closer within the circle of her arms, the jut of his
chin resting lightly on the top of her head.

"Ye remember what I said to ye that night . . . before Gordon swept ye away,'' he murmured, stroking her hair softly. Then, holding her an arm's length from him as the calls to quarters thundered overhead, Thomas said the words they'd both been dreading. ''I think we'd best be going. . . .''

As the two quietly emerged on the top deck, the fading afternoon sunshine suffused the ship with an amber light. It gave a strange, burnished glow to the mellow woods and polished brass which surrounded them. The deck was crowded with seamen who watched them pass by.

Jane forced herself to concentrate on the warmth of Thomas's hand. As they slowly walked forward together, they saw James and Elizabeth standing close to one another, talking softly. Off the port side, Jane could see the oarsman waiting in the skiff that would soon be returning them to shore. Her aunt and uncle waited at the quarterdeck where a rope and wooden ladder hung over the ship's side. Elizabeth kissed her husband lightly, brushing her lips beyond his mouth to his ear, clutching him briefly to her.

''Careful, now, darling,'' James cautioned, helping his wife make the awkward descent into the unsteady boat.

Jane turned to look at Thomas and could say nothing. She saw her own tears reflected in his glistening eyes. Slowly, they permitted themselves one last embrace. They didn't kiss, but stood in silence, arms around each other, bathed in the topaz light of the setting sun.

Thomas released her. Ducking her head to avoid his gaze, Jane threw her arms around Uncle James, barely able to stem the sobs she had held in check just moments before.

''Take care of yer aunt, lassie, winna ye, now?'' her uncle said, his voice cracking.

''I promise, Uncle James,'' Jane whispered hoarsely, hugging him tightly once again. ''And thank ye . . .'' she said as the tears started to spill down her cheeks.

Without looking back at either man, Jane quickly gathered her voluminous skirts and climbed unassisted over the side onto the ladder. Carefully she stepped backward, down the steps, and lowered herself into the prow of the small launch, and sat opposite her aunt. The sailor untied the line that was her last link to Thomas and, pushing hard against the rough wooden planking, used his oar to propel his small craft away from the mother ship.

Elizabeth, knowing she was out of earshot of her beloved husband, began to weep quietly. Jane fixed her gaze on the oars, which pulled heavily against the evening tide running swiftly out of the harbor. The skiff skimmed over the water with surprising speed as the sailor found his rhythm and pulled smoothly on the long wooden oars. When, finally, Jane looked back at the ship, all she could see aboard the *Providence* was the silhouette of two men in kilts standing at the railing in the fading light.

Soon, one of the men turned and disappeared, but the taller of the two stayed rooted to the deck until, at length, the descending darkness obscured from Jane's view the solitary figure of Lieutenant Thomas Fraser of Struy.

8

September 1766

Catherine and the housemaid, Fiona, gazed across the upstairs bedchamber openmouthedly as Jane slipped, corsetless, into a diamond-quilted white stomacher and matching quilted petticoat that she wore beneath a split overskirt and bodice of ruby red silk. A white cambric fichu around her shoulders discreetly veiled her alluring bosom. Double sleeve ruffles at her elbows completed her sporty outfit, perfect for an afternoon golfing party at Musselburgh Links on this crisp September day.

"I wonder if anyone will suspect my secret when I earn a low score!" Jane laughed, twisting her body, free of her corset's confining stays, and taking an expert swing with an imaginary club.

"Her ladyship told me to lace ye up tight and to say ye wasna to play golf with the lads!" Fiona said reprovingly.

"Well, if ye dinna inform her, her ladyship will never *know* whether I wear a bloody corset or not, or whether I play golf, will she, now?" said Jane in a threatening tone.

Fiona was cowed into silence. Noting Catherine's worried expression, Jane realized that her placid, obedient sister would never understand what so appealed to her about the Scottish national passion.

Golf was one of the few social institutions in the country where all distinctions of rank were ignored. At least as early as the fifteenth century in Scotland, when Dutch traders introduced the sport, even young children were trained to hit the little wooden ball with a long-handled club. Every Scottish youngster was aware that Mary, Queen of Scots had *adored* the game. The fact that she had played a round of golf in 1567 only two days after her husband's violent death was used in evidence against her at her trial. These days, sadly, male golfers customarily avoided mingling with lady golfers on the links. To be sure, the Fishwives of Musselburgh were allowed their tournament in the dead of winter when few gentlemen frequented the course, but rarely did a woman venture on the greens at midday in good weather. However, over the years, Jane's uncle James had often proposed an early morning round with his favorite niece and young Thomas, and, with practice, Jane had learned to be proficient in the game.

Jane sighed, and tugged at the corner of her stomacher once again. A familiar surge of longing swept over her at the memory of Thomas as a small lad, sharing an unwieldy wooden golf club on a mist-shrouded green.

"Fiona, dinna just stand there like a stick!" Jane said crossly, shaking free from her reverie. "Help me fasten these closings on my gown!"

Fiona obediently hooked the fastenings at the back of the dress while Jane smoothed the bodice over her suddenly softer, more natural silhouette. Twirling around in place, she laughed out loud.

"Now let them puzzle over the reason this lady's golf swing is so deadly!"

Jamie Ferguson opened the door to the coach as it came to a halt next to the smooth green fairway of the Musselburgh Links. The heir to estates in Tobago had been Jane's constant caller since the Hogmanay Ball.

"Jane! Jane . . . how good it is to see ye again!" he cried, with a wide, tooth-filled smile, looking like one of the industrious beavers who dwelt along the banks of the Killantrea near Monreith. As she stepped from the carriage, Jane could see over the young barrister's powdered wig to the River Esk, which wound its way to the sea sparkling in the distance. "We've just laid out supper from our hampers over there," he said eagerly, taking her arm after a hasty greeting to Catherine and her acknowledged suitor, John Fordyce, who trailed along behind. "Come . . . come, everyone! Jane's arrived . . . now we can begin!"

A small gathering of well-dressed young people lounged beneath a graceful willow tree that arched over the river. Servants unpacked two large wicker hampers bursting with Scotch hare and wheels of Stilton and Gouda cheese. There were plates of codfish, cold salmon, and orange-colored crayfish competing for attention with roasted chicken and smoked pheasant.

"When is the golfing to begin?" Jane inquired with a smile as Jamie spread out another large square of knitted wool on the ground for the new arrivals.

"So *competitive,* Jane dear," said Marietta Buchanan, sitting stiff and formal on a small chair that some nameless soul had thoughtfully provided for this overweight, overdressed young woman. "Ye've only just graced us with yer presence, yet ye wish to embarrass us all with yer skill. I canna imagine anyone clever enough to play such a game with one less finger than is customary."

Jane gazed coldly at Marietta, who took obvious pleasure in seeing her rival flinch. It was well known in their set that she, a Buchanan, had a reasonable chance to be mistress of Jamie Ferguson's Pitfour House and Jane was proving to be an annoying hindrance. It had been the same story at the Hogmanay Ball when Marietta had captured the attention of the Duke of Gordon, only to have him snatched away by one provocative glance from the impudent chit!

Jane arched her brows slightly and summoned a bright, hard smile to her lips.

"Golf can be a difficult game to play under any circumstances, Marietta, my sweet, but, in the Game of Life, 'tis better, I think, to be missing a finger than to be carrying more than the usual number of *chins*!" Marietta emitted an audible gasp at the insult. Jane gestured toward the other members of the golfing party. "I'm so glad we're eating *first,* before we play," Jane added wickedly. "I dinna want to miss the spectacle of watching ye tuck into this lovely meal, Marietta."

Stifled laughter erupted around the two women as Jamie's servants began passing plates to the famished group with samples of the various delicacies. As the general conversation drifted to the summer's past events, Marietta resumed eating a leg of rabbit dripping with rich red currant sauce.

"Have ye heard the latest from Gordon Castle?" a young man named Malcolm McKay said quietly to his host.

"I havna seen Alexander in months," Ferguson responded, helping himself to a chunk of mutton laced with turnips.

"Well," said Malcolm, his voice rising with excitement, "My man was told by one of three servants who stood witness, that on the thirtieth of July, a wee bairn named George Gordon was baptised at Gordon Castle."

By this time, McKay's conversation had attracted the attention of several nearby listeners.

"I have it on good authority that the mother, Bathia Largue, was employed as a nurse, and the father"—Malcolm paused for dramatic effect—"the father is none other than Alexander, the Fourth Duke!"

The noisy chatter around the picnic blanket suddenly halted and Malcolm McKay's words blared across the rolling links.

"Well," said Marietta, licking jellied aspic off her fingers, "His Grace may be mad, but apparently he's not *impotent*." Her remark was greeted with shocked silence from the women and snickers from the men. Basking in the stir she'd created, Marietta looked around at her audience importantly. "For my part, I have reliable intelligence that the mother of the babe has mysteriously *died*!"

As the guests murmured to each other, Jane noticed the hard line settling on Jamie Ferguson's lips. As the host, he presumably felt he could not chastise Marietta, although Jane guessed he was certainly anxious to do so.

"I, for one, have only briefly met the duke," Jane intervened loudly over the mutterings and whispers of the group, "but I should think when a family is enduring private tribulations—especially a family far grander than yers or mine, my dear Marietta—it deserves our affection and loyalty, until such time as the truth is winnowed from the vicious gossip."

"Hear! Hear!" said a hearty voice from across the woolen picnic rug. "As the duke's business agent in Edinburgh—and his cousin—I beg each of ye not to indulge in such idle speculation and inflamatory innuendo. I can assure ye, the poor lass died of birthin' fever and the duke has behaved as a gentleman!"

Jane's attention was drawn to the conservatively tailored young gent wearing a bark brown woolen broadcloth coat with matching breeches.

"Ye say ye're not well acquainted with His Grace," he said to Jane, lounging casually on one elbow, "yet ye defend him."

"I defend his right to fair treatment among supposed friends," she replied, aware that a hush had fallen over the party. "And I know that Sir Algernon Dick thinks very highly of him. That's sufficient praise for me."

"Yer praise is well founded, Mistress Maxwell," replied the gentleman in the brown suit who seemed privy to the drama unfolding in the House of Gordon. "His Grace has closeted himself in Gordon Castle since the death of Bathia Largue. He's sorely grieved still, 'tis plain to see," he added with a glance in Marietta's direction. "He has told me he intends to bring up the wee bairn at Gordon Castle with all honor and advantages, though, naturally, the lad cannot inherit."

"A love child, to be sure," murmured Jane.

"The dowager duchess does not mourn the mother's death, I'll wager," Marietta snickered. "Duchess Katherine has high ambitions for her first born, I'm told."

" *'Tis* a difficult situation for any *future* duchess, I should think," ventured Jamie Ferguson hesitantly. "A natural son, brought up side by side with any future heirs. . . . ."

"Especially if the bairn is touched with the Gordon Madness, as some say the father may be," Marietta added viciously.

"God's wounds!" Jane snapped. "Sir Algernon told me all that twaddle about his supposed madness was merely a wicked ague. Ye've had it yerselves . . . all of ye! At least the duke shows some feeling for the poor lass who died," she said, addressing Marietta with fire in her eye.

"Well, *I* certainly wouldna like to be greeted by a bastard in the nursery after *my* honeymoon, I can tell ye that!" Marietta announced.

"I would wager ye're not in the slightest danger of that," Jane retorted acidly. "The duke's bride, whoever she will be, will have no cause to begrudge what transpired before they struck their contract," Jane added, "because, my dear Marietta, 'tis what most marriages are about, alas. It speaks well of the duke if he dinna abandon his child."

"A sensible approach to such matters, Mistress Maxwell," said the stranger, smiling in her direction.

Oddly, Jane felt a kinship with the young Duke of Gordon. She reflected briefly on the vehement opposition her mother had voiced when Jane revealed that Thomas had proposed marriage before he left. Lady Maxwell had made it abundantly clear that, if a better offer came her daughter's way in the next two years, she intended Jane to accept it.

"What I've said may be sensible regarding His Grace, the Duke of Gordon, sir," Jane replied to the stranger dressed in brown, "but I dinna wish ye to think I blindly support marriage bonds forged by bald ambition or merely in the name of family necessity.'' A tremendous flood of anger swept through her when she considered the way both Lady Maxwell and Simon Fraser had shrewdly manipulated Thomas and her in recent years to achieve their own ends. Thomas was a good man, from a distinguished ancient family—one far more illustrious than the Maxwells, if the truth be known. He loved her, and she, with all her soul, loved him! *Once Thomas returns from America,* she thought grimly, *nothing short of banishment or prison shall prevent us from eloping to Gretna Green!* ''Enough of this idle chitchat,'' she finished, anxious to turn the general conversation in a more pleasant direction. ''What of our golf?''

''Surely ye dinna intend to play with the *men*?'' interjected Marietta sarcastically, stung by the public dressing down delivered by her rival.

''This is merely a friendly outing, is it not, Jamie?'' Jane asked innocently of their host, turning her back on the pouting Marietta. ''We're here to have an enjoyable afternoon and to take the air. If several of us wish to swing a club or two, no one would think ill of it, surely?''

''I, for one, would be honored to accompany ye on the green, Mistress Maxwell,'' said the mysterious visitor linked to the duke.

''As would I!'' chimed in Jamie, who had jumped to his feet.

At that, the group, including Jane, stood and stretched. Jamie formally introduced her to their other golfing partner.

''Meet Charles Gordon, a kinsman of the duke and his man of business here in Edinburgh,'' said Jamie with a slight bow. ''Charles, ye must have gathered, has His Grace's full confidence,'' he added.

''And his loyalty, I shouldna doubt,'' said Jane, linking arms with both men. ''Wonderful! I shall have at least two worthy opponents in Jamie and ye.'' Jane glanced over at Marietta, still sitting within reach of the potted hare and sweetmeats. ''Marietta, *dear* . . .'' she called, ''ye winna make it a foursome? No? Well, not to worry. But *do* save us some of those berry tarts, if ye're able, lass. I'm sure we'll be famished by the time we've finished this round!''

Marietta's mouth was stuffed to its absolute limit, precluding any reply to this latest barb. Chewing sullenly, she watched in silent fury as Jane and her two sporting companions took turns stepping up to the little wooden ball, and, one by one, driving it down the field of play. Soon, a cheer resounded from a knot of guests who strolled along the course and had watched Jane Maxwell tee off for the second time.

"Gadzooks!" exclaimed Malcolm McKay admiringly to anyone within earshot. " 'Tis incredible! The lass just hit a hole-in-one!"

Lady Maxwell looked up from her accounts book, startled by the sound of a soft knock at her chamber door. The clock had not struck three, but the December dusk would envelop her bedchamber in less than an hour.

"Beggin' yer pardon, mum," apologized Fiona, thrusting a small silver tray with two crumpled and watermarked letters into her mistress's hand, "but I knew ye'd want these brought to ye straightaway."

Lady Maxwell's pulse beat a shade faster as she saw they had both been posted from Baltimore, Maryland.

"Thank ye, Fiona," she replied evenly. "Please light the tapers, will ye . . . and not a word about these missives—even to yer cousin Meg in the kitchen."

"Ooh, n-no, mum," Fiona stuttered. "Nary a whisper."

"And I'd like my tea served here today," Lady Maxwell added sternly. "Please send it up immediately."

"Yes, yer ladyship . . . right away."

As soon as the door closed behind Fiona, Lady Maxwell smoothed one of the letters on the desk and filed it between the pages of a leather-bound book, saving it for her sister-in-law to whom she could deliver it privately. She stared thoughtfully at the second folded piece of parchment for a few moments, noting the clear, bold strokes forming the letters of Jane's name. It was the third communication Thomas Fraser had sent to Jane since his departure months before—or at least, the third to reach its destination, since heaven knew *what* untoward conditions faced the young soldier as his company headed off for Fort Pitt in western Pennsylvania.

Lady Maxwell was reluctant to admit to herself how much she had enjoyed reading the young man's earlier description of his harrowing ocean crossing and the tumultuous greeting the *Providence* had received as the ship put in at Annapolis. It was, he'd written, the very day, May 22, 1766, that word had reached Maryland of the repeal of the notorious Stamp Act. According to Thomas, the general relief that war between Britain and the Colonies had been avoided was so extreme that the young lieutenant and Captain Maxwell had been wined and dined in an orgy of celebration, including a dinner at the manor of Charles Carroll of Carrollton, a prominent member of one of Maryland's most distinguished families. His second letter had told of Governor Sharpe's request that a small company of Black Watch serve as bodyguards to an expedition led by two gentlemen from England named Mason and Dixon. These surveyor-astronomers and their party were hacking a path westward in an attempt to settle officially the boundary dispute between Pennsylvania and Maryland. Thomas noted that he and his men should reach Fort Pitt sometime in October.

Ripping open this third missive in the chilly December twilight, Lady Maxwell actually looked forward to hearing more about the uncharted wilderness Thomas had traversed, though she had absolutely no intention of letting Jane know the lad meant to keep his promise as her betrothed.

September 15, 1766

Dearest,

A sudden cloudburst has foiled our efforts to set another stone marking the continuation of the Mason-Dixon line, and Jeremiah Dixon—not to mention his fellow surveyor, Charles Mason—are drowning their disappointment with some undrinkable whiskey acquired at the last outpost we passed several weeks ago.

The dark, forbidding gloom of this mid-September storm has descended on our camp, and upon my heart as well. Sweet Jenny, . . . how dear ye are to me and how I long to hold ye in my arms again. It seems so long since we bid adieu. I wish now I had not played the Gentleman so well . . . if by some miracle, should ye somehow appear before me, I should not be so trusty a friend to yer innocence . . .

Well, thought Lady Maxwell, with a look of satisfaction, *at least the lass is still a virgin!* Clearly, that wouldn't have remained the case if she and Simon had not taken firm steps to separate the two. She held Thomas's letter toward the fading afternoon light filtering through the window, and continued scanning the parchment. Several pages vividly painted the beautiful but hostile Pennsylvania landscape. Suddenly, she paused and reread the top of the fourth page.

I pray this part of my letter, buried amongst the inconsequential descriptions of what I've seen, and where I've been, will escape certain scrutinies. I dream of ye, lass, and sometimes, as today, I wonder if ye'll ever be truly mine.

Ah, well . . . enough of these dark musings. We soon leave Mason and Dixon to fend for themselves and proceed North, deeper into Pennyslvania land . . . to Unionville and Fort Redstone, where we hope to find a galley bateau to take us up river to Fort Duquesne—or, Fort Pitt, as 'tis called, now that it's been rebuilt in honor of the Prime Minister.

Although we have, thus far, met only friendly savages, anxious but for a handout of food (and especially spirits), we hear of occasional violence against white settlers. Our guide, Captain Shelby, says the Indians believed that once Britain triumphed over France in this wilderness, the white man would withdraw and leave the braves to their hunting grounds. Yet more and more settlers push West each month in search of better land. New forts, such as Pitt, have given the Indians reason to believe the Colonists do not keep their promises.

As odd as it may seem, I see likenesses between the Redman and the Highlander, though I must not dwell on these comparisons if I'm to keep my standing among my English Brothers. Shelby tells me in the same vein that Highland patrols from Fort Pitt have taken to wearing Indian garb and painting their faces many colors so as to increase the odds of treading unmolested through the forests. The Brits are scornful of this and insist on presenting stationary crimson targets for their enemies.

Sweet Friend, I will close this epistle so that the expedition runner can take it (and one written by yer uncle to his wife) in his pouch to Baltimore tomorrow. Let us hope ye'll read it before ye turn seventeen this Hogmanay. Just know I will think of ye that night, and each and every day as yer very own

Tho. Fraser
Lt., 42 Reg. Foot

Lady Maxwell cocked an ear toward the door. She heard footsteps on the stairs outside her chamber. Hurriedly, she read a postscript to the letter before tossing it on the low-burning embers of the fire glowing in the corner.

Jenny, lass—please forgive my melancholic humours. I shall not think them evil if they but express how easily a few drops of rain can make me long for my Flower of Galloway. T.

Following a soft knock, the door opened just as Lady Maxwell turned her back to the fire.

"From my window, I noticed the caddie hand something to Fiona from his pouch," her sister-in-law, Elizabeth Maxwell, said pleasantly. "By chance we havena heard from James or Thomas Fraser?" she inquired, her eyes resting on a small square of parchment curling to cinders on the hearth.

She was eight months pregnant with a child who might not see his father until he was two years old. Elizabeth was anxious for news.

Lady Maxwell flushed slightly, forcing a bright smile to her lips.

"Dinna Fiona tell ye, Beth?" she asked quickly, "or I expect she thought I'd see ye soon at tea. Here," she said, retrieving the other letter from the leaves of the book resting on her desk, "I'm sure ye'll want to read this in privacy. Shall I have Fiona serve ye in yer chamber?"

" 'Twould be most kind of ye, Magdalene," Elizabeth replied carefully, her gaze lingering on the small pile of ashes heaped on the burning coals. "I'll share my news from James at supper tonight, if that would suit. Thank ye."

The two women locked glances briefly before Elizabeth moved slowly toward the door of Magdalene's chamber. Lady Maxwell suspected her sister-in-law had detected her effort to prevent contact between Jane and Thomas, but Magdalene didn't really care what Elizabeth Maxwell thought. Jamie Ferguson had been most attentive to Jane these last weeks, and the gossip in the town was that even the Duke of Gordon would once again be attending Sir Algernon's Hogmanay Ball the night of Jane's birthday. Jane's prospects were infinitely improving!

Soon after Elizabeth's withdrawal, Fiona entered the room and placed a tarnished silver tea tray on the small side table in front of the fire. Lady Maxwell stared thoughtfully into the dying embers smoldering on the hearth. Who could predict what glorious change of fortune 1767 might bring to Hyndford Close?

The Duke of Gordon and his man of business strolled toward a knot of people surrounding the punch bowl in the festive ballroom at Prestonfield House.

"Greetings, everyone!" Charles Gordon cried jovially. "And the best for the New Year to my two golfing partners!" he added, catching sight of Jane Maxwell and Jamie Ferguson.

The guests at Sir Algernon's annual Hogmanay fete were from

the usual circle of acquaintances. Even Simon Fraser and Lady Maxwell ate supper together for the second year running. Charles Gordon noted with some surprise that her beautiful daughter Jane was apparently being escorted this evening by Jamie Ferguson, the homely and sincere Master of Pitfour House—though hadn't someone said Thomas Fraser was in the army? At any rate, it appeared a goodly company and Charles urgently hoped he could interest his patron in forgetting his cares with a little Scottish country dancing.

"I have the honor to present His Grace, Alexander, the Duke of Gordon," Charles said formally, nodding to the duke. Glancing around the circle of people, he made introductions. "Jamie, ye know His Grace, of course . . . Mistress Maxwell?"

"Yes, we met just a year ago," Jane murmured, averting her eyes.

"Birthday felicitations are in order, I believe," Charles added with a courtly bow.

"Why, thank ye," Jane smiled, darting a curious glance in the direction of the duke, who had remained silent.

"And if certain rumors flying around Edinburgh are true, Yer Grace," Charles added for his patron's benefit, "may I introduce ye to the soon-to-be-Master and Mistress Fordyce of Berwickshire. . . ."

Catherine blushed and John Fordyce looked pleased as the Duke of Gordon inclined his head to each one of the group in turn. Despite the gaiety surrounding the assembly, Jane sensed a strange, guarded kind of sadness visible in the young duke's bearing. A muscle in his jaw twitched slightly, as if his teeth were clenched. His hazel eyes were listless. She wondered if he might be feeling ill. Charles Gordon seemed intent on keeping the atmosphere around them buoyant.

"Ye know, I dined out for weeks on my tales of Mistress Jane's phenomenal luck on the links this fall."

"My good *luck*?" Jane replied, falling in good-naturedly with his banter. "I maintain that my pleasing score at Musselburgh Links had more to do with my *swing* than any stroke of good fortune, sir!"

"Aye, I expect that's so . . . though it pains me to admit it," Charles Gordon responded with a broad grin, "but I never saw a lass hit the ball so hard, or for such a distance in my life. When I told His Grace that I suspected ye of witchcraft, he roared with laughter, dinna ye, Yer Grace?" The duke, who presently looked incapable of any mirth whatsoever, merely nodded. "He especially appreciated the way ye sank that last putt," continued Charles gamely, "and beat me by a single point. Tell me the truth, now, lass . . . was it witchcraft?"

"*Witchcraft*?" Jane replied, laughing. "What a curious defense a man can summon when a woman gets the best of him. However, I *do* possess a secret as to why I played so well that day . . . but ye'd burn me at the stake before I'd ever reveal it!"

Charles Gordon responded with a curious look, while Catherine, who remembered how her younger sister had won the match, free of corsets, fluttered her gaily colored fan nervously and quickly attempted to change the subject.

"We're all *delighted*, of course, to welcome the Duke of Gordon, Yer Grace," Catherine interjected quickly.

Once again, the handsome aristocrat nodded slightly, his subdued manner and continuing silence creating a sobering atmosphere, despite the gay music pouring forth from the stringed orchestra on the far side of the ballroom.

"You're very kind," he finally replied, "but Charles . . . I'm afraid I must soon beg to take my leave. I have piles of correspondence to attend to—"

"On *Hogmanay*?" Jane interrupted incredulously.

She wondered why the attractive young duke, so carefully attired in royal blue velvet, had bothered to attend the ball in the first place. She scrutinized his unhappy face and then felt ashamed. Obviously, he didn't feel like celebrating the holiday when the woman he loved lay so recently in her grave.

"Unfortunately, His Grace has been extremely busy with plans to open a meal market in Huntly next month," Charles Gordon said hastily. "I'm sure ye heard he's supporting the project from his own granaries to alleviate some of the suffering."

" 'Tis true, then, Yer Grace," asked Jane, watching the duke closely, "that there've been crop failures again among the tenants up north?"

He nodded as if the weight of the world were on his shoulders.

"Some . . . yes," the duke replied with apparent effort.

"Well, perhaps when the lads who serve His Majesty abroad return to the Highlands this new year, there'll be more hands to plant and harvest," she said hopefully.

"*If* the rumors are true that the westerly forts in the Colonies will be abandoned by the Crown in spring or early summer . . ." The duke's voice drifted off, as if he were too weary to contemplate even this good news.

" 'Tis no longer rumor, m'lord," Jane said, her spirits rising despite the dampening effect the unhappy nobleman's presence was having on the rest of the group. "My Aunt Elizabeth received a letter from her husband in the Black Watch regiment last week. She tells me my uncle, Captain Maxwell, says that now that the program to pacify the Indians has apparently taken effect, the Forty-second has been ordered to pull down Fort Pitt before they leave for home in June, in case the Colonists get any ideas of staging a rebellion."

"Aye," agreed Charles Gordon, grateful that Jane Maxwell had relieved him of some of the burden of keeping a conversation going in view of his patron's dour spirits. "There are voices on both sides of the Atlantic predicting war."

"I canna believe Englishmen would fight Englishmen," Jamie Ferguson commented, shaking his head.

"My guess," Jane speculated thoughtfully, "is that His Majesty is wise to take precautions not to leave ready-made defenses on the frontier for use by his 'ungrateful children,' as he calls them . . . especially, should it eventually come to armed rebellion with the Colonists."

She was enjoying the lively discussion, despite nagging fears concerning Thomas's safety in that savage land. It had been the letter from Uncle James to Elizabeth, actually, that had confirmed this welcome, and—until just recently—censored news that the Black Watch would be sailing from Philadelphia in six months' time. Their tour of duty had been cut ludicrously short.

Thomas would be coming home this new year!

This news was all she could think of, all she could dream about, although she wished she'd heard from Thomas, himself, on *any* subject. But, no matter. The post from America was always unpredictable. Jane glanced at the subdued and morose Duke of Gordon. She only prayed that he, too, would find some measure of happiness in a year's time.

"Since ye seem so pressed with yer estate duties, we wish a good evening to ye, m'lord," Jane said quietly, offering the disconsolate nobleman a graceful means of escape. "And a good New Year to ye."

The duke bestowed on her a look of profound gratitude.

"Thank you . . . you're very kind," Alexander replied bleakly. He bowed slightly and began to take his leave.

"Good night to you all."

And without another word the 4th Duke of Gordon abruptly departed.

"Good heavens!" Catherine exclaimed. "How extraordinary! The poor man couldn't wait to leave!"

Charles Gordon lowered his voice confidentially, and, as the fiddlers struck up a jig, he leaned his head forward into their small group.

"I know I can trust ye not to bandy this about, but, except for his work supplying cheap meal to the crofters, the duke sees no one. He seems not to have shaken the sadness of the year's past events, and only came to Edinburgh because of pressing business and to pay his respects tonight to Sir Algernon and Lady Mary."

" 'Tis sad to see someone suffer so," said Jane with a sigh. "He must have truly loved the lass."

At the far end of the Tapestry Room, the fiddlers began to finger a few strains of the next dance on the program.

" 'Tis 'Montgomery's Rant,' Jane," Jamie Ferguson declared in an attempt to lighten the somber mood that had descended on the group. "May I have the pleasure?" the toothy young man said quickly, bowing courteously to Jane just as Charles Gordon appeared about to ask her to dance.

"Delighted," Jane replied with a look of mild apology to Charles, who merely shrugged good-naturedly.

Lady Maxwell, standing imperiously next to the fireplace at the far end of the ballroom, suspended her tête-à-tête with the paunchy Simon Fraser long enough to nod approvingly at Jane as her daughter and Jamie Ferguson approached the dance floor arm in arm.

Despite the stuffiness of the room and the cloying sweetness of Jamie Ferguson's eau de cologne, Jane felt a shiver slice between her shoulder blades. Fighting an unaccountable sadness that had settled on her since her encounter with the melancholy duke, Jane allowed Jamie to lead her to a place in the long line of dancers strung the length of Prestonfield's ballroom. *In one hour it would be midnight*, she thought, brightening, *1767 . . . the blessed year Thomas would be coming home*.

9

February 1767

Jane's aunt, Elizabeth Maxwell, sank into a chair next to the fireplace in the small guest bedchamber of her sister-in-law's house, her infant asleep in its wooden cradle. She felt exhausted, not only from the preparations for her niece Catherine's recent nuptials, but also from the routine of rising twice each night to feed little Montgomery and keeping a firm hand on her three other boisterous children in the cramped quarters of Hyndford Close.

Elizabeth pulled her shawl more tightly around her shoulders and closed her eyes. Outside the weather had turned bitter, in contrast to the sparkling warmth of Catherine's wedding day earlier in the month. It was only three in the afternoon, and already, sleet scratched against the darkened window pane. She sighed, and allowed her mind to indulge in a recurring daydream, inspired by the news that her husband would soon be sailing back from America.

"Aunt . . . Aunt!"

Elizabeth's eyes flew open. She could hear Jane's shouts and running footsteps from two floors below. The door to her bedchamber burst open and her niece approached her excitedly, heedless of little Montgomery, whose eyes also flew open with a start.

"Jane! Jane, *please*!" Elizabeth hissed, pointing toward the cradle. "Quiet! He's just got off to sleep!"

Jane froze to the spot, her hand covering her lips apologetically.

"Oh, I'm sorry," she whispered loudly, the excitement in her voice translated into a hoarse croak. "But Fiona says there's an officer of the Black Watch downstairs, come lately from America. He says Uncle James has asked him to come by to see ye. He's been shown to the sitting room."

"Go ask Fiona to bring us tea," Elizabeth replied without hesitation. " 'Tis nearly time, as it is. And ye go amuse him while I dress."

As she tidied her blond hair and quickly donned a simple day dress over her shift, she darted a last, quick glance at little Monty, who had settled back into dreamless sleep. As she closed the door gently behind her and proceeded down the chilly corridor to the sitting room, Elizabeth tried to formulate all the questions in her mind about a place that seemed as far away to her as the moon.

"Aunt Elizabeth!" Jane declared with a look of obvious relief when her aunt entered the room. A ruddy-cheeked, stocky gentleman rose awkwardly and crossed over to Elizabeth briskly. The grim set of his mouth and the blue bonnet he was twisting in his broad, bandaged hands told her that he had been an impatient guest for Jane to entertain with polite conversation while waiting for her to appear.

"Ye're Captain James Maxwell's wife, Mistress?" he inquired as formally as if he were an adjutant at a court martial.

"Why yes, I certainly am," Elizabeth replied, attempting to keep the amusement from showing on her face. Jane rolled her eyes to the ceiling in mock despair behind the back of the gruff-mannered officer. "Ye know my husband?" Elizabeth inquired.

"Only met him briefly," the officer answered. "I am Captain Fergus MacEwen, Forty-second Foot. Yer husband was sent as my replacement at Fort Pitt, so we were together just a few days before I left on orders to return to Scotland."

"Well, ye're very kind to take the time to come and tell me something of James," Elizabeth said smoothly, indicating the only comfortable chair in the small room suitable for the rotund officer. "Fiona will be bringing tea shortly, or would ye prefer a whiskey, Captain?"

"Whiskey," MacEwen replied, as if he needed it badly.

He sat down, only to rise again and pace in front of the mantelpiece. Suddenly he turned toward Elizabeth and spoke to her directly, as if Jane weren't in the room.

"Yer husband asked that I call on Simon Fraser, Master of Lovat, first and then proceed to ye—and that I have done."

Jane started at the mention of the Fraser name.

"The dreaded burden has come to me of informing both yer households that Thomas Fraser of Struy was killed in an Indian skirmish in October, less than a month after his arrival at Fort Pitt. Three of our number were slain and two more gravely wounded."

Jane sat transfixed in her chair, staring at Captain Fergus MacEwen as if he were an escaped inmate from a lunatic asylum! The letter they'd received from Uncle James in December had reassured them about the relatively calm state of affairs the troops had encountered en route to Fort Pitt.

"Pray tell us what happened, Captain," Elizabeth said urgently, walking quickly across the room to put a firm hand on Jane's trembling shoulder. All the color had drained from the young girl's face and she seemed hardly to be breathing. As difficult as it would be for the lass to hear the details of Thomas's death, Elizabeth wanted to force her niece to remain where she was and to listen to what, undoubtedly, would be the most accurate account of events occurring many thousands of miles across the sea. Elizabeth had known too many military widows who remained tortured for the rest of their lives because they were told nothing about their husbands' final hours or how they died—merely that their loved ones had been killed in His Majesty's service and were never coming back.

"Ye two are no *relation* to young Fraser?" Captain MacEwen asked, squinting at Jane in the dim afternoon light filtering into the room. "Just friends and neighbors, so to speak?"

"That is correct," Elizabeth intervened quickly, forestalling any attempt by Jane to interrupt. Jane, however, seemed incapable of speech, for she merely stared at the soldier, as if he were mad.

"Well," began MacEwen, who had remained standing, "as ye know, Lieutenant Fraser was a young pup, new to the service, which probably plays a part in what happened, if y'get my meanin'. . . ." His bandaged meaty hands gripped the back of his chair. Elizabeth tightened her hold on Jane's shoulder. "Well, at any rate, young Fraser, along with Captain Maxwell and the other soldiers, arrived at the fort by canoe in early October."

Captain MacEwen seemed more at ease, now that he had launched into the narrative he'd so recently imparted to Simon Fraser.

"Soon after, the Mingos attacked one of the scout's barks as it came up the river, but the lad made it into the fort with only a nick on his arm." MacEwen glanced at both women a moment and then rearranged his bulky form in his chair. "A few days later, yer husband, Mistress Maxwell, was down river for four days at a trading camp and dispatched a letter to ye, he said, telling ye that he and the lads would be sailing home this July. . . ." MacEwen shifted uneasily in his chair. "That was right before the unfortunate incident."

Incident!

Elizabeth felt a rush of anger at MacEwen's incredible insensitivity. Jane's dark eyes had dilated until they seemed black with despair, but still, the lass did not utter a sound.

"There'd been that exchange of fire with the Mingos, so our commander sent me, Lieutenant Fraser, and ten other Highlanders out to try to contact our other scouts. We wanted to see whether this was just a minor brush with the Redskins, or the beginning of troubles, like we had with Pontiac in Sixty-three."

The burly captain licked his dry lips nervously, as if he were getting to the most difficult part of his story. He glanced uneasily at Jane, whose immobile features gave her the appearance of a marble statue standing sentinel at a crypt. Captain MacEwen hesitated and then continued, in spite of the girl's stunned demeanor.

"I had urged the men to adopt the custom of dressing in Indian garb and to fight as we clansmen do, moving between rock and tree to avoid the arrow's shaft, y'see. The Brits in their damn fool red coats are sitting targets, they are, so the men were happy to do a bit of fancy dress. Young Fraser *seemed* the ablest of the lot and I saw that he painted himself up good and proper. In fact, the lads had a fair field day getting ready to go out on patrol," he chuckled, as if enjoying a private joke.

Elizabeth walked over to the sideboard and poured three glasses of whiskey as the heavy-set captain continued his tale. She handed the amber liquid to MacEwen without interrupting his narrative and turned, nodding a silent command for Jane to accept the glass of spirits she held out to her. Obediently, Jane took the glass in her trembling hand, but didn't drink its contents. She merely held it in her lap, unaware that the stub of her right forefinger was no longer masked in the handkerchief she invariably carried in the presence of strangers. The lacy square had fallen to the floor and formed a small, snowy peak at her feet.

"Well," the captain continued, as if to get the worst over quickly, "our patrol was taken by surprise. After a steamin' hot morning, trampin' through thick underbrush and being eaten alive by mosquitoes, I allowed the men to stop by a rivulet for refreshment. With no warnin', out o' the damned bushes—pardon an old campaigner, Mistress—out o' the thicket came this pack o' howling savages war-whoopin' and hollerin' and they set upon us."

Captain MacEwen paused to sip his whiskey and stared balefully out of the sitting room window at the bad weather that had all but obliterated the fading afternoon light. He gazed at the sleet-covered panes as if they were a reminder of the horror that had greeted him on that sultry noonday, the previous October. Jane sat motionless, her drink untouched, her eyes glassy, her gaze unfocused. She breathed in shallow, anguished gasps.

"Both sides were battling at close range," MacEwen continued, his voice animated for the first time since his recitation began. Obviously relishing the memory of combat, his bandaged hands carved semicircles in the air, recreating the scene for his stunned audience. "Our lads picked off at least a dozen of 'em bastards—beggin' yer pardon again, ladies—but war whoops from over the ridge proved our men would soon be far outnumbered. I ordered the lads to retire and all but three headed into the underbrush to try to get back to the fort. Young Fraser and two other men shouted they'd stay behind . . . a kind of diversion, I suppose they thought 'twould be . . . while I lead the rest to safety."

MacEwen eyed both women carefully for any hint of the same scorn that had been implicit in Brigadier General Fraser's reaction when MacEwen had told him this part of the story earlier in the day. As a veteran of the '59 Siege of Quebec, Simon Fraser felt that leaving only three men to act as rear guard had been suicidal. However, the two ladies voiced no censure, but continued to stare at him wordlessly.

"That's the procedure, y'know, ladies. A Captain's duties is to *all* the lads to do his best, so that the majority dinna come to harm."

"We understand perfectly, sir," Elizabeth said quietly.

"Well . . . right," he replied uncertainly. "When the three dinna return, a party was mounted the next morning with every available man for the search. Just before sunset we came upon a sight so monstrous, so foul . . . never in four years in the wilderness have I seen the like o' it. Broadsword or tomahawk—both weapons cut the same." Elizabeth appeared at his side, ready to pour the Captain a second whiskey when he paused for breath. The three of them silently watched the topaz liquid drain into his glass. "The bodies were killed Indian-style, if y'take my meanin'. The lads were so new to our acquaintance, and I'm sorry to say they were scalped and mutilated beyond recognition . . . arms . . . legs . . . 'twas like a grisly puzzle, sortin' it out."

Jane's hand flew to her mouth, her eyes clamped shut. She stood up abruptly from her chair and turned away to face to the window. Elizabeth anticipated her cries, but none came.

"We laid what was left o' the lads side by side on the banks of the Monongahela with all three names on a common marker." MacEwen downed his second whiskey with a quick gulp, wiping his lips with the back of his bandaged hand. "I wonder if 'twas our dressin' as Redskins that made 'em so vengeful . . ." he mused, as if trying with four months' hindsight to fathom the reason for the extreme brutality of the killings. "Captain Maxwell arrived back at the fort some hours after the bodies had been borne to the stockade and buried by the river, but 'twas he who saw to it that a proper stone was made for the grave."

Elizabeth glanced over worriedly at Jane's back. Slowly her niece turned around, her face a mask, revealing no emotion whatsoever. She sat down once again, frozen on the edge of her chair, as if she hadn't heard a word Captain MacEwen had said.

"I know this is one of the most painful duties a fellow officer is called upon to perform," Elizabeth said, offering a cue to their visitor that he could decently bid them farewell. "And the Maxwell household is deeply grateful that ye took the time to inform us of this tragedy so we might better offer comfort to our neighbor, Simon Fraser."

"Well, thank ye, Mistress," Captain MacEwen replied, swiftly setting down his empty glass of whiskey and patting his broad, kilted waist in preparation for a hasty departure. Pointing to the bandages on his hands, he added in explanation, "Almost lost a finger or two in that last bit o' business at Fort Pitt—but I was lucky and the surgeon patched 'em up right and proper. Said I'd be good as new in a couple of months."

Captain Fergus MacEwen took a moment to stare curiously at the dark-haired young woman who hadn't uttered a word since her aunt had joined them. She looked on the verge of hysterics, which made him all the more anxious to take his leave. Reaching for his blue bonnet that he'd dropped on his chair, he wagered that despite the latest skirmish, the rumors that a goodly portion of the Crown Troops would be sent home by summer was probably true. If no one was there to fight off the bloody savages, the white settlers would be too fearful to push west in their quest for land, and thus not violate the Six Nations Treaty. If the treaty were respected, Chief Flat Fish and his followers might not bother anybody, he figured.

He prepared to exit the cold, dreary chamber, with thanks to whatever turn of fate had saved him from being scalped and hatcheted to pieces like those poor lads lying in the muddy soil on the banks of the Monongahela.

"Well . . . good day to ye . . ." Captain MacEwen said to the two women and marched past a maid balancing a tea tray just outside the door. Letting himself out the front entrance, he escaped into the cold winter air of Hyndford Close.

Inside the sitting room, Jane heard Elizabeth direct Fiona to set the tray down on the sideboard. Sitting in stunned silence, she felt as if she were underwater. An overwhelming wave of emotion was pushing at her brain, threatening to crush her with its force. As if peering through a foam-flecked sea, she watched her aunt pour a strong cup of the brew and exchange it for Jane's untouched glass of whiskey still clasped in her hand. *Why would her aunt give her whiskey?* she wondered. *Mama never let them even taste it, since Daddie imbibed far too much and too often.* There was a buzzing in her head. She couldn't think anymore. The teacup in her hand started to rattle as if it were alive.

"Jane?"

Elizabeth stared worriedly at her niece as the cup danced in its saucer, and shudders coursed through the young girl's body. For a long moment, Jane gazed into her aunt's face, seeing in Aunt Elizabeth's melancholy glance the truth that had been pressing on her mind like a vise. Thomas dead? *No!* Jane searched for a different answer in Elizabeth's pitying gaze. Thomas couldn't be gone forever—wiped off the face of the earth! Not strong, steady *Thomas!* But he was. He was dead and buried in foreign soil. That's what that fat captain, anxious to cover up his mistakes, had told them just now. Her beloved Thomas, *cut to pieces,* had been rotting in a mud-filled common grave these past four months, while she had danced and laughed and dreamed of his coming back to her.

Jane's keening cry could be heard echoing throughout Hyndford Close. The rhythmic wails brought Lady Maxwell scurrying into the sitting room just as Elizabeth was easing the girl onto the floor, cradling her in her arms as if she were the infant Montgomery. Shards of Jane's teacup were scattered everywhere. A dark brown pool of tea seeped out in a ragged oval on the floor, staining a corner of Jane's lace handkerchief that lay beside it.

Elizabeth looked up at her sister-in-law who stood paralyzed at the threshold. The blond-haired woman gently rocked her niece, who was by now hysterical. She had to shout to Magdalene above Jane's wild, piercing screams.

" 'Tis Thomas. Thomas Fraser. He's been killed."

10
April 1767

"Jenny, just look at that sky!" exclaimed Catherine to her sister. The pair had been sitting in the window seat for several minutes without exchanging a word. "The rain has stopped and everything looks so clean and fresh! 'Tis *beautiful,* isn't it?"

Jane gazed indifferently at the jagged rooftops of Edinburgh bathed in brilliant hues of pink and peach and remained silent.

"Let's take a walk!" Catherine proposed suddenly. "We still have time before I must go home to dress for the ridotto. 'Twill do us both good."

"Oh, Catherine . . . not now. I dinna really feel like going out and I'm *not* going tonight, no matter what Mama says!"

"But ye're obliged to come," Catherine said, a worried look furrowing her brow.

"I dinna accept the invitation, Mama did! And besides, there'll be so many people at the theater tonight, the Duke of Gordon will hardly notice if I stay home . . . which is exactly what I intend to do!"

Catherine perceived the catch in Jane's voice and the tears gathering in her sister's eyes.

"Ye've been cooped up here for weeks," Catherine protested sympathetically, though she knew that arguing about the matter would only result in an emotional outburst and Jane's shutting herself in her room. Lady Maxwell had all but given up trying to cope with Jane's emotional state and had requested that Catherine drop by Hyndford Close as often as possible to encourage her younger sister to cheer up and get on with the business of finding a suitable husband.

With the perspective gained from living as Mrs. John Fordyce under her own roof at Argyle Square for several months, Catherine could see how manipulative her mother had become, and how unhappy Catherine would have been if Lady Maxwell had opposed her marriage to John and sent him far away from her.

"Come!" said the older girl gently to Jane, who had remained sitting wanly in the window seat. "At least, let's get some air."

Reluctantly, Jane permitted Catherine to drop a cloak around her shoulders and then lead her downstairs, out the door. Hawkers mingled with the many townspeople who were promenading up and down the rain-washed High Street. Catherine and Jane walked along in silence. As they approached Fountain Well, Jane froze at the sight of the ancient landmark, struck by the painful memory of the final pig race. Thomas had stood right where they were at this moment and declared Eglantine the winner. Jane remembered the happy laughter at the sight of all of them slathered with mud. That was surely the last day of her childhood, she thought ruefully. She'd lost a forefinger in the accident with the apple cart that day, and along with it, her good fortune. If only she'd realized she was doomed to lose Thomas in the bargain.

"Jenny, hinny . . .," Catherine said helplessly, watching the tears start to flow down Jane's cheeks. There was simply no way for her to comfort her sister when these waves of grief overtook her. "Ye must try . . ."

Catherine didn't finish her sentence. *Try what?* Catherine wondered. To forget Thomas? To forget her loss? What could anyone say that would help her sister start living her life again?

Suddenly Jane stiffened, staring at an approaching pedestrian on the other side of the street. Simon Fraser, out of uniform and looking somewhat shabby in an ancient greatcoat that probably belonged to his father, the Fox, walked toward them from the opposite direction. Before Catherine could stop her, Jane darted through the traffic and dashed into his path, her cloak streaming out behind her.

"Well . . . can ye imagine! Simon Fraser, Master of Lovat, I see," Jane hissed as Catherine ran up behind her. "Pray forgive me for not paying ye a formal call of condolence . . . but then, I dinna remember yer paying *me* one!"

Simon looked haggard and unkempt. The Maxwell household had had word that he was about to depart with His Majesty's forces for Portugal. He did not reply to Jane, who stood glaring at him, flushed and trembling.

" 'Tisn't it fortunate, *sir*," she emphasized with sarcasm, " 'tisn't it just an amazing twist of *fate* that I was not 'formally' betrothed to Thomas before he went abroad."

"Aye, I suppose it was," the old campaigner said wearily.

"No one expects me to wear widow's weeds or mourn for a dead man whom ye and my mother *never* intended to be part of my future, now do they, Master Simon?" Jane spat back. Simon looked past them both, avoiding Jane's poisonous glare. "But I suppose *ye* realize it was ye and my dear mother who sent Thomas to his death! To be scalped and mutilated beyond recognition . . ."

"Jane—*stop it*!" Catherine implored, tugging on her sister's arm.

"His red hair must have been torn from his head!" Jane shouted, her voice taking on an edge of hysteria. "Afterwards, they dinna even know which body was which!"

Simon Fraser stood stock still on the busy thoroughfare.

"Now, see here, lass—" he began.

"Ye butchered him, sure as if ye'd struck him with yer own claymore!" she shouted, her face contorted with rage. She poked her stubby right forefinger into the middle of Simon's massive chest. She seemed oblivious to everything else around her.

"Ye sent Thomas where he'd be hurt . . . where he could never come back to me . . . I *hate* ye for that! I hate ye, *Simon Fraser*! I will hate ye till I'm in a grave like yer *beloved* godson!"

Jane started to cry uncontrollably, pounding Simon's broad chest with her fists. For a moment, the brigadier stood rooted to the spot where Jane had accosted him. Then he made a grab for Jane's wrists in an effort to fend off her blows. Passers-by stared curiously at the two of them engaged in a furious struggle, noting that the burly gentleman seemed to be taking the worst of it. The tirade issuing from Jane's mouth was shocking to hear, but Catherine assumed it had been building for weeks. She summoned all her strength and grabbed Jane roughly by the arm.

"I said *stop it*, Jane!" Catherine shouted, ignoring the ring of onlookers that had gathered around them. "Master Simon has suffered a loss as well, lass. Ye're behaving abominably!"

Jane clamped her mouth shut, breathing in ragged sobs.

"I'm sorry, sir," Catherine said to Simon, whose color had drained from his face. "I'm so sorry about Thomas . . . ye were always good to the lad since his parents died. Please forgive my sister, if ye can. *Come* now, Jane," she ordered sternly. "We're expected at home."

Catherine caught Jane's hand and half-dragged her down the narrow alley, through the gate, and into the stable yard behind Hyndford Close. Without ceremony she pushed her sister into the stable and slammed the heavy wooden door shut.

"Thomas is *gone*, Jane!" Catherine yelled, holding her sister by her two shoulders so fiercely, her intensity shocked them both. "He was killed in a senseless, stupid, horrible way! I feel terrible, Simon feels terrible—ye feel worst of all—but he's gone! *Gone!* Ye're only hurting yerself to keep blaming . . . *blaming* everyone."

"But they sent him *away* . . ." Jane sobbed, her body sagging against the empty horse stall. "They sent him to die in that horrible way . . . hacked to pieces, from limb to limb—"

"But Thomas *wanted* to be a soldier, Jane," Catherine interrupted, almost shouting. " 'Twas a way to build a life for the two of ye, and perhaps even regain his family lands . . . even the baronetcy! It wasna merely that Simon banished him to America . . . part of Thomas *wanted* to go." Catherine threw her arms around her sister and hugged her close. Tears streamed down both their faces. " 'Tis simply that a very bad thing happened to a very good lad, Jane . . . and whether ye were *married* or not . . . *betrothed* or not—dinna make much difference. Ye'd miss Thomas just as much and yer grief would be as terrible . . . maybe more so . . . so stop blaming everyone else, hinny! Feel yer loss . . . *yer* loss . . . and accept it, and one day life will seem good again. *We're* still here! I love ye."

For a moment, Jane stared at Catherine. Her shoulders started to shake once again and she sobbed quietly for a few minutes while her sister rocked her in her arms. Sniffling, Jane wiped her damp face with the sleeve of her dress.

"I love ye, too, Catherine," Jane whispered, "and I do, truly, appreciate how good ye and John have been to me these last months."

"I know, hinny," Catherine said, stroking Jane's hair soothingly and blinking away her own tears.

"Ye're the only ones who seemed to understand what I've been going through—" Her voice cracked.

"We *do* understand . . . and we are so sorry all this has happened," Catherine replied simply.

The golden light was fading now. Dark shadows had crept into the stable and Catherine suddenly became aware of the lateness of the hour.

"Jane, we must hurry! I'll help ye dress, and then I must get back to Argyle Square to get ready m'self!"

Jane nodded her assent. The two young women ran through the deepening dusk toward the Maxwells' back door.

Upstairs, Jane scrubbed her body with a damp, rough linen cloth, as she often did, despite her mother's dire warnings that it would bring on ague. She splashed her face with cold water in the basin that rested on the bedside table, while Catherine laid out the voluminous petticoats for Jane's new white evening gown.

"I don't know why Mama spent all that money on this," Jane said, shivering as her exposed flesh began to dry. "I could have worn my blue satin to the ridotto just as well."

"Perhaps 'twas her way of saying how sorry she was . . ." Catherine said mildly, lifting the heavy garment over Jane's head.

"Or perhaps it was her way of laying a trap for Charles Gordon or Jamie Ferguson and the like!" Jane retorted, jutting her chin in the air as she settled the nipped-in waistline above her hips.

"Well, whatever it was . . . ye look lovely!"

"I canna hardly *breathe*!" gasped Jane as Catherine struggled to close the back fastenings. "But 'tis pretty, 'tisn't it?" she acknowledged, swaying from side to side to appraise the movement of the skirt.

Jane's smooth shoulders and pale Celtic complexion melded provocatively with the straight lines of the square-cut neckline of the dress, decorated with tiny tucked rows of white bobbin lace.

A knock interrupted their musings over Jane's ensemble.

"This was just delivered, Mistress Jane," Fiona said, handing a small packet to her.

"Hurry . . . open it quickly . . . before I depart," Catherine said excitedly, noting the thick wax stag's head crest that sealed the package. " 'Tis from the Duke of Gordon!"

Jane ripped through the wrappings and opened a long, thin box. Inside lay a delicate white ivory fan. She lifted it out of its nest of thin tissue, carefully opening it to its full extension. It was ornately decorated with silver swans painted on the parchment connecting the ribs. She fingered the incredibly soft white swan feathers that edged its border. A note was wedged between two of the ribs.

A few fine feathers for the Flower of Galloway . . . these come from the Isle of Swans near my home. I look forward to our evening together. I will call for you at eight, if that will suit.
Gordon

"Jane . . ." breathed Catherine in awe, "the duke intends that you be his companion this evening, not just a member of his party. . . ."

"He's downstairs in his *coach*!" Fiona added excitedly. "He says he will wait for yer answer."

Jane eyes widened in shock and she sat down on the bed abruptly, her white gown creating a fan of its own on the coverlet.

"I . . . I canna . . . I—"

Jane fell silent midsentence and simply shook her head. Her breathing became heavy and Catherine feared another outburst of tears. The elder sister looked helplessly toward the housemaid, who returned her worried glance.

"I'll speak to His Grace," Catherine said at length. "Jane, go down to the sitting room and Fiona will fix ye a nice cup of tea or a bit of ale—whatever suits yer fancy. Ye'll need a bit of bracing to steady yer nerves for tonight. I'll just have a word with the duke and explain—well, I'll think of something!"

"I'm not *going*!" Jane cried, sounding as if she were a child. "I'm not going at *all*!"

"Yes, ye *are*!" Catherine replied firmly. "Ye're going with John and me, just as we planned! Down to the sitting room with ye, and wipe yer eyes! 'Twill be all right!"

And without waiting for further protests, Catherine brushed past Fiona, wondering, as she hurried down the several flights of stairs, how in the world one refused a cordial invitation from a duke.

The early evening had grown surprisingly warm for April, and Catherine diffidently approached the handsome black coach emblazoned with its familiar crest. She tapped on the window and immediately the green velvet curtains were drawn back.

"Good evening, Yer Grace," Catherine said awkwardly. "Would it be all right if I spoke to ye in the carriage?"

"But of course," replied Alexander Gordon courteously, the slightest arch of his eyebrow his only sign of surprise at such an unusual request.

Catherine climbed aboard the running step and settled herself opposite his handsome visage. She clasped her hands together nervously in her lap.

"As ye may have . . . heard in the town," she began uncertainly, "my sister has recently suffered the loss of an old friend . . ."

"So, I understand," the Duke of Gordon replied. "My man of business, Charles Gordon, told me of the tragic death of Thomas Fraser at the hands of those savages. Pity. He was rather a hotheaded youth, as I remember, but 'tis a loss, I'm sure, that grieves the entire Maxwell household."

Catherine swallowed and racked her brains for a way to explain Jane's fragile emotional state in a manner that would not be insulting to the duke.

"Tonight will be the first time she's left the house since word of Thomas's death reached us in February, Yer Grace," Catherine began, screwing up her courage. "I think 'twould be best if she passed the evening in the bosom of her family . . . I hope ye understand, 'tis nothing to do with—"

"—With me," Alexander interrupted, his finely chiseled features masking whatever thoughts were in his head. "Actually, I understand the strain Mistress Maxwell must be experiencing only too well. That is why I extended my invitation to her so impulsively this evening. And I concur with your decision, Mrs. Fordyce. However," he continued, "may I be permitted a private word with your sister, since I fear the excitement of tonight's entertainment will preclude an expression of my heartfelt condolences over her loss?"

Catherine was totally nonplussed by his request. He was so correct in his manner, so commanding in his demeanor that she could think of nothing else but acceding to his request and immediately led the way to the small sitting room upstairs.

Jane froze, teacup halfway to her lips, as the two of them entered the chamber. She sat near the fireplace that was black and empty, thanks to the unseasonably warm weather.

"I insisted your kind sister allow me just a word with you before I return to my lodgings to dress for tonight's festivities," the Duke of Gordon announced suavely before Jane could speak. Turning to Catherine, he reached for her hand, brushing his lips across the back of her palm.

Perceiving she had been politely, but firmly dismissed, Catherine glanced quickly at Jane, who appeared as dumbfounded as she was by the Duke of Gordon's courteous but imperious manner, and then retreated in haste.

Alexander paused just inside the door. Jane felt his eyes surveying her white satin gown from hem to shoulders before he crossed the chamber and drew up a chair next to hers. He allowed the silence between them to permeate the room and smiled slightly, drawing the fingers of his slender hands together in a pyramid that supported his chin.

"I'm sorry ye've had such a difficult time," he said finally. "When Charles Gordon told me you'd be coming with your family to the ridotto tonight in my honor, I wanted to tell you privately how sorry I was over your loss. Frankly, I admire your courage.''

Gently, as if trying to soothe a wayward kitten, he reached for her left hand and held it in his own. Jane flushed slightly, curling her right hand into a fist to disguise her amputated finger.

''When I lost someone close to me, I couldn't face even my friends for nearly six months. Perhaps you noticed my unsociability the night I saw you at Prestonfield House last winter?'' he continued, his thumb grazing hers in feathery strokes. ''Alas, 'twas foolish of me. Those close to me only wanted to help.''

His unexpected kindness and heartfelt expression of sympathy took Jane completely off guard. The young aristocrat released her hand from his grasp, but his penetrating gaze forced Jane, almost against her will, to meet his glance. Jane took a deep breath and forced herself to break the spell. She glanced over at the empty fireplace before looking back at the duke's broad, finely etched mouth and clear, intelligent hazel eyes.

''I, too, realize now, Yer Grace, that my friends and family want to help . . . indeed, they have,'' she said softly. ''And I thank ye for yer kindness in paying this call and, not least, for the exquisite fan.''

''I'm pleased it suits you, and trust you'll do me the honor of carrying it this evening,'' the duke replied, his smile broadening. ''Dressed in white, you remind me of the fair inhabitants on the Island of the Swans.''

''That's in the north, 'tisn't it?'' she inquired, deflecting his compliment.

Privately she knew of the vast tracts of land owned by the Gordons in the Highlands, where all manner of wildlife and game flourished, not to speak of the duke's prize-winning cattle and sheep.

''Yes,'' replied the Duke of Gordon, ''on Loch-an-Eilean adjoining my estate at Kinrara, a mere day's ride from Inverness . . . or from Gordon Castle, too, for that matter. A family of swans has been nesting there for years, and when they depart in the late spring, we collect the feathers from the reeds and think of lovely things to do with them!''

The duke continued to gaze at her, his eyes darkening with intensity. Jane blushed for no reason she could think of and looked away.

''I-I thank ye for yer kind invitation to escort me tonight, but . . .'' her voice drifted off.

''I merely thought to spare you the difficulty of coping with the many admirers who haven't seen you these last months," he interjected lightly. "They are bound to want to make your reacquaintance this evening. I thought, perhaps, if they saw you on my arm, they would temper their enthusiasm, until such time as you felt strong enough to reenter society with a happier heart."

A vision of Jamie Ferguson's buck teeth, protruding from his bulbous lips, swam before her eyes. She hadn't answered any of his notes of sympathy, but tonight, he was sure to make another approach, no doubt encouraged by Lady Maxwell.

"Would it be possible for Catherine and John Fordyce to accompany us?" Jane asked softly.

"I've taken the liberty of requesting they be seated next to my box," he replied. "Our mutual friends, Sir Algernon and Lady Mary, will be sharing ours also . . . that is, if you will come with me."

"Ye anticipated I would say yes?" she asked forthrightly.

"I merely hoped I could offer my protection," he replied easily, "and I am most delighted you have accepted."

He rose to make his departure.

"Now I must be off to dress. I pray my rather mundane attire this evening shall not detract from your beauty, Miss Maxwell. Your white satin, with that magnificent chestnut hair, makes you swanlike, indeed. 'Tis nigh impossible to imagine you have ever perched upon a sow!" Before Jane could recover her aplomb, the Duke of Gordon crossed the chamber in a few, swift strides and inclined his head in a gesture of farewell. "I shall return to fetch you one hour hence," he announced, and vanished through the door.

11

As the Duke of Gordon's black carriage pulled up to the play-house on Canongate opposite Shoemaker's Hall, the crowd stepped back a few paces, and two footmen in red and white livery jumped down from their perch. With a theatrical flourish, they threw open the door. Alexander Gordon extended a black satin-clad leg, with its white silk stocking and shining black leather pump distinguished by red kid heels, and alighted gracefully to the cobblestoned pavement.

The onlookers standing near the playhouse entrance exchanged whispered comments about the pleasing cut of his black brocade jacket and smartly embroidered cream-colored waistcoat that set off his lean figure to perfection. The duke's head was crowned with a simply styled, chalk white wig, neatly tied at the nape of his neck with a black satin ribbon. The crowd hardly had time to absorb the unaffected elegance of his appearance before a collective gasp rose from the throng.

"Who *is* that?" they whispered to each other as a vision in white satin emerged from the coach. From their perspective, the mysterious woman's face was obscured by a magnificent mass of white feathers fashioned into an ornate fan.

Inside the playhouse, tallow lamps glowed softly against dark red, silk-covered walls. Jane held on to the duke's arm even more tightly, as he propelled her toward the parted velvet curtains marking the entrance to the auditorium. Everywhere the buzz of the theater crowd seemed to intensify as Jane and Alexander proceeded to their seats.

" 'Tisn't that Jane Maxwell?" a gray-haired matron whispered loudly to the old codger by her side.

"Sink me, will ye look who's with her?" said her companion whose narrowly set eyes and hooked nose gave him the appearance of a ferret. " 'Tis the young Duke of Gordon, I'll be bound!"

"A fine catch for a baronet's brat, wouldna ye say?"

"Aye—if he's not *mad*."

"Or if the lass's not enceinte by that lad—what be his name?"

"Simon Fraser's ward? Oh, he died. In America, I heard. Mistress Jane certainly dinna let any grass grow under her slippers, did she, now?"

Jane quickly turned away. Alexander reached for her gloved hand and gave it a sympathetic squeeze. They continued to make their way past the sea of curious faces, but she was touched by his display of concern for her vulnerability. Perhaps he realized the same cutting remarks that would once have made her laugh, now stung.

Staring across the expanse of the audience hall, Jane was surprised to see that the orchestra pit had been covered with a portable floor abutting the stage. The alteration had created an enormous space where she assumed the public dancing would take place. Above them, the galleries were filled with legions of shop clerks and wigmakers, merchants and caddies—all manner of folk who enjoyed a night at the old playhouse as much as any of the ton. Jane guessed that the more expensive boxes had been patronized by a collection of lawyers and doctors, because the evening had been organized in the duke's honor by Charles Gordon, his kinsman and personal solicitor, and Sir Algernon Dick, his physician, to benefit the city's charity workhouse.

"My dear Gordon!" a voice boomed from behind them.

Alexander and Jane turned around to see Jamie Ferguson striding down the aisle.

"Ah . . . Jamie, man . . . 'tis good to see—"

Alexander stopped midsentence. Ferguson was staring—not at his family friend, the Duke of Gordon, but at Alexander's companion.

"Jane?" the young lawyer asked, dumbfounded.

Ferguson's eyes appraised Jane's figure from the skirt of her white satin gown to the tips of the delicate swan feathers edging the open fan shielding her face. His one-word query revealed his incredulity at seeing her in public. The fact was, he had spent more than two months begging her to respond to his letters and personal entreaties, only to be answered with silence. Now, here she was, standing before him on the arm of a duke, a gent who happened to be one of his oldest friends.

"Hello, Jamie. 'Tis . . . 'tis n-nice to see ye again," Jane faltered.

"I gather you two haven't seen each other recently," Alexander said, one eyebrow arching almost imperceptibly.

"Aye . . . 'tis been a long time . . ." she replied, her glance begging Jamie's forgiveness for the hurt she'd caused him.

"Where are you sitting?" Alexander asked politely, putting a hand on his old friend's shoulder.

"I'm supping with several lads who've taken a box yonder," he replied stiffly. He pointed to one of scores of alcoves that had been transformed into intimate dining areas. "It seems that upstart peacock, Mr. Stanley, thinks he should be playing Romeo tonight in the Shakespeare instead of Mr. Younger," he added with forced cheerfulness. "Stanley's lined up the young barbers over there in his behalf," he complained, indicating a row of boxes filled with boisterous young medical students already plied to the gills with wine punch. "But we advocates are sworn to uphold the honor of Mr. *Younger,* and the management agreed to present *him* as Romeo tonight. G-great sport, eh what?" the young lawyer stuttered, his own cheeks suffused by a quantity of punch already consumed. The theater's side-boxes had been transformed into bars selling wine, ices, cold pheasant, and various other delectables.

"I've heard these theatrical rivalries sometimes become fairly raucous, old man," the duke said mildly.

"Aye, Yer Grace . . . that they do . . . and that's the fun o' it!"

Ferguson was at least making a stab at appearing unruffled about his discovery that Jane was accepting the attentions of the Duke of Gordon. Alexander gestured at the illuminated heads of famous poets fastened over each box.

"What's all this?"

"We wanted to render homage to Yer Grace's writings in a v-visible manner," Jamie said, slurring his words slightly as he made reference to Alex's versifying, for which the duke was duly admired.

"Well, this is all quite splendid, Jamie. My thanks for whatever part you've played in creating such a masterpiece," the duke said with an affectionate pat to his friend's rounded shoulder.

As Jamie retreated unsteadily up the aisle, Jane glanced at Alexander and said quietly, "I suspect ye gathered I have not been of a mind to pretend an interest when there is none?"

"I see that," the duke replied dryly.

"I say what I think," Jane added a shade defensively.

"That's quite evident," he said, casually guiding her toward their seats for the performance. Then, suddenly he stopped Jane's progress down the aisle and looked into her eyes. " 'Tis not a bad thing, you know, Mistress Maxwell," he said, "letting people know what you truly think."

The duke had in mind all the simpering, dissembling, manipulating women of his acquaintance—an assortment that included his own mother. He took her gloved hand, closed his long fingers around it, and led her toward a group of boxes near the edge of the stage where Sir Algernon Dick and his wife, Lady Mary, greeted them both warmly. Once they were settled in their seats, the physician inquired how the Gordon estates were faring.

" 'Tis been a devilish rough winter in the Highlands," Alexander acknowledged, "but instituting our own meal market from the Gordon stores has alleviated some of the suffering from the crop failures of recent years. Let us pray for better weather this season."

Turning in her seat to face the duke, Jane asked, "Do ye plan to clear yer land of tenants and crops to make room for sheep?"

The question caught the two gentlemen off guard.

"I have been forced to run sheep on some of my lands near Kinrara," Alex replied. " 'Tis the only thing that seems profitable these days, what with taxes and the disruption of the economy since the Forty-five."

Jane looked at him with a penetrating stare.

"But how do ye propose to raise crops of wheat or barley or turnips when the weather *does* improve, if ye give all yer land over to sheep and remove the poor tenants?"

"I do not intend to commit all my land to sheep, but 'tis a vexing question, to be sure, Mistress Maxwell," he replied evenly. "And 'tis one I enjoy discussing with people of experience in these matters."

Jane bristled at his inference that she was unsuited, by virtue of being a woman, to such a discussion.

"It dinna take *vast experience*, as ye put it, to determine the want of the people who have no land upon which to grow their crops," she retorted. "If the lands are cleared of crofters—as it's rumored they will be in future years—what will become of them? Yer coffers may be full, but what of the havoc wreaked on the hundreds who depend on yer good will . . . not only for their land, but for their bread?"

"If we land owners are forced by unhappy circumstances out of our control to reclaim land that is ours by right and tradition," he began, "many will find opportunity to seek their own land in the Colonies—"

"The *Colonies*!" she spat. "Ye ask them to leave their land, their very homes and hearth to risk death at sea and God knows *what* barbarity from the savages in that land!"

The flush spreading up Jane's cheeks contrasted sharply with the paleness of the skin revealed by her low-cut gown. Alexander could see that she was trembling.

"Jane, lass," Sir Algernon interjected sharply, "all of America is not as uncivilized as the wilderness in the far west of the Colonies. The jackals in England would like nothing better than to see all Scotland's Highland nobility as homeless as are some of the tenants. Lairds like Alexander Gordon must do everything they can to survive and pay taxes and hold on to the land! Otherwise, Scotland'll have no future at all, dear girl . . . no future at all!"

Jane regarded Sir Algernon with amazement. She could see that her old friend was disturbed that she should judge Alexander Gordon ruthless toward his clansmen and tenants.

"I've not been to the Highlands, Yer Grace," she conceded matter-of-factly, "and perhaps 'twas unseemly of me to pass judgment on matters concerning the Gordon estates, when I know so little of them. I was referring to what I've observed of farming in Galloway, where my father resides."

"Well, I hope one day you will have the opportunity to see that country near Kinrara," Alexander replied pleasantly. "I think you would find it one of the loveliest parts of Scotland. I pray I may be the man to reveal its beauty to you."

Jane flushed once again, this time in embarrassment.

"You were right, Sir Algernon," said Alex, turning in his seat. "So far, 'tis been a fascinating, if not enlightening experience, listening to the opinions of Mistress Maxwell, just as you predicted it would be."

Just then, Charles Gordon and Jane's sister and brother-in-law settled into the box next to theirs with friendly waves and a fluttering of fans. The crowd had grown louder still, clapping and stomping to indicate their impatience. Much to her amazement, Jane recognized some of the same medical students and lawyers she'd danced with sedately at the Hogmanay Balls, now hurling wings of fowl and boiled turnips across the seats at one another in wild abandon.

"We want Stanley . . . we want *Stanley*!" chanted the medical students, clapping their hands for their favorite actor and howling with high-spirited laughter. Jane saw Sir Algernon frown and lean over to speak to Charles.

"Bring on Younger . . . let's have *Younger*!" echoed Jamie Ferguson's crowd, who were stamping their feet to drown out the competition on the other side of the hall.

"How long has this Romeo rivalry existed?" Alexander shouted to Charles.

"All winter long, I'm afraid," Charles shouted back. "Ever since Stanley joined the players and organized his claque. It gets better or worse, depending upon how much wine punch is consumed by the theatergoers."

Charles's last words were lost as the medical students once again roared for the celebrated Mr. Stanley to appear on stage. Alexander leaned closer to Charles and Jane so he could be heard.

"Compared to this, I can see I lead a very sedentary life in the Highlands . . . scribbling verse and separating crofters from their lands!"

He cast a sly glance toward Jane, who pursed her lips to hold back a smile and turned to watch the theater manager, David Beatt, step forward center stage with both hands raised in an effort to restore quiet.

"My lords, ladies, and gentlemen . . ." he shouted. The restless audience settled back a bit, while a few young men continued trading quips and insults. " 'Tis my pleasure to bid ye welcome here tonight. . . ."

The students and their supporters shouted back unsolicited greetings to Beatt, who nodded and again raised his hands beseechingly.

"On behalf of the management of the Canongate Playhouse, I am especially pleased to welcome our guest of honor, His Grace Alexander, the Fourth Duke of Gordon—a man of letters and extraordinary refinement who—"

Drunken cheers rang out from the audience on both sides, led by a flush-faced Jamie Ferguson. Beatt bit his lip apprehensively and glanced down at the duke's stage box.

"In honor of His Grace, and at the *special* request of the most *respected* gentlemen sponsoring this most sublime ridotto for the benefit of the Charity Workhouse, we have arranged for yer special pleasure, a period of dancing to be enjoyed *before* our magnificent program this evening."

"No . . . no!" shouted those few in the forward seats who had heard Beatt's words. "Bring on Stanley . . . we want Romeo!" bellowed the medical students, who were seemingly bent on besting their rivals.

Beatt looked increasingly grim faced.

"In accordance with the wishes of the *sponsors* of this ridotto, the public dancing will commence!"

Without uttering another word, David Beatt turned on his heel and fled backstage.

"Maybe they'll dance themselves sober," grunted Sir Algernon sourly. "The students are a rowdy disgrace. The University provost shall hear about this, ye may be sure!"

"I'm dreadfully sorry about this, Yer Grace—" apologized Charles Gordon, who, along with the doctor, was the principal organizer of the charity event.

"Actually, 'tis quite amusing, Charles," Alexander replied. "I'm enjoying myself enormously," he added, smiling in Jane's direction.

The delicate strains of the traditional opening number could hardly be heard above the din that now grew louder and louder. Dandies draped themselves over the edges of the boxes that girded the audience. Several of them began pouring bumpers of wine on the elaborate coiffures of the patrons below. Despite the deafening tumult, several brave souls attempted to execute the first figures of the minuet.

"Stanley . . . Stanley . . . *Stanley*!" chanted the medical students, oblivious to the couples dancing sedately onstage.

"Younger . . . Younger . . . *Younger*!" shouted the young men reading for the Bar.

Soon the orchestra was entirely drowned out by the sound of wooden chairs crashing against the walls. Splintered pieces rained down on the unsuspecting crowd positioned below the side-boxes. Jane gasped as she saw Jamie Ferguson take a glancing blow to the head from a metal sconce that had been ripped off the wall.

"Yer Grace," shouted Charles, "I've seen these crowds turn nasty. I wonder if we—"

"The *candles*!" Jane called to Alexander and Charles. "They're throwing lighted candles . . . there'll be a *fire*!"

Everyone in his box and on the floor of the theater stared in horror at the chaos raining down from the hordes in the balconies above. Jane suddenly felt sorry for poor Charles Gordon, who sat riveted to his chair. The evening that he'd planned so carefully to reintroduce the Duke of Gordon into Edinburgh society was turning into a fiasco. And how humiliating for the twenty-four-year-old duke to have a ridotto transformed into such bedlam, when she'd heard it had all been specifically designed to put to lie the persistent rumors that Alexander suffered from the notorious Gordon Madness, or even more scurrilous, that he had somehow been responsible for the death of his lover, Bathia Largue.

Jane was spellbound by the tumult surrounding her. Behind the line of dancers scurrying for cover on the stage, a phalanx of men, whom Jane took to be performers, appeared from backstage with flimsy-looking weapons she assumed were theater props. They'd split into two groups—each led by an actor dressed for the part of Romeo—and were battling each other with blows to the head and shoulders.

It seemed to Jane as if a whirlwind had descended on the Canongate Playhouse, complete with thunder and lightning and levitating furniture. Another lighted sconce sailed overhead, landing on stage near the hem of the massive drapes. Through the hole in the curtain bounced Juliet's bed, followed by the shrieking figure of a portly actress, Mrs. Baker, decked out in the diaphanous costume of the ill-fated Capulet heroine.

"*That* is Juliet?" Alexander shouted at Jane. "No wonder they're protesting!" he cried, reaching for her gloved hand. Turning to Charles, he bellowed, "My dear Gordon, I think we should adjourn this revel for the evening. Perhaps you would escort Sir Algernon and Lady Mary out of your box . . . Fordyce will look after his bride . . . come, Mistress Maxwell, we'd best be off."

In a graceful arc, Alexander leapt over the box's low railing. Jane vaulted over the banister, unassisted.

"Follow me," she cried. "I know a way out behind that curtain."

Without waiting for his assent, Jane disappeared behind a curtained doorway as Alexander hurried to keep up with her. An arm, sheathed in white satin, reached back through the drapes and grabbed his sleeve.

"Quickly, Yer Grace . . . *this* way!" Jane panted, unceremoniously tugging him along with her gloved hand. "There's a passage on yer left that lets out behind Watson's Close. We've got to escape this mob!" Reaching the safety of outdoors, Jane and the Duke of Gordon unceremoniously sprinted down a narrow alley. "Have ye seen Catherine or the others?" Jane shouted back over her shoulder.

"I spotted them departing through the other exit," Alexander replied tersely, surveying the angry throng spilling out a side door fifty feet farther up the alley.

The two of them turned away from the mob and bolted down the ill-lit close that veered off sharply from Canongate and the playhouse. A loud crash, followed by a roar from the crowd inside the building, echoed in their wake. Soon the air was filled with high-pitched screams.

"My God!" Alexander exclaimed, picking up speed. "It sounds as if half the roof collapsed!"

"Or the chandelier fell. Come! This way!"

Jane abruptly darted to her left, leading Alexander down another narrow winding passage. He dared not consider what alien, squishy, yielding matter he felt under foot as they fled the ugly scene. It was past the hour of ten when Edinburgh residents were wont to holler "Gardylou," the Scots' equivalent of *Gardez l'eau*—"watch out for the water"—and toss all matter of refuse out their windows into the street. As they slowed to a trot, the stench in the street was so malodorous, Alexander felt himself about to gag.

"You seem to know your way around these back alleys pretty well, Mistress Maxwell," he said between clenched teeth, trying to avoid inhaling an ounce more of the fetid air than necessary. As she led them away from the tumult, he marveled at her deft sense of direction.

"Ye forget, m'lord . . . I grew up on the High Street," she replied, between gasps for breath. Slowing her pace to match his, Jane led Alexander down another narrow passageway to what appeared to be an enclosed square. On one side was a row of townhouses that apparently faced one of the larger wynds. "My friends and I used to creep backstage to watch the performances when we were children," she said, breathing heavily. "I've probably explored every inch of the city."

"I should hope that that redheaded Highlander escorted you when you ventured out like this . . . and I should hope you chose a less treacherous time than the hour of Gardyloo!" he declared between gasps for air.

Panting heavily, Jane halted on the edge of the stone-sided square they'd just entered. Her dark eyes were framed by thick sable lashes. The high planes of her cheekbones were set off by a softly rounded chin. Masses of chestnut hair were swept back from her forehead, piled in a natural style. Alexander found his eyes wandering to the shy little strands that had escaped during their flight and played gently across her ear lobes. From everything he knew of her and had observed for himself, Jane Maxwell was anything but shy. But tonight, in spite of her bravura, he sensed a remoteness about the young woman that bordered on despair.

"Ye remember Thomas well?" she asked unevenly. "Ye only encountered him once or twice, I thought."

"How could I ever forget that famous pig race?" Alex replied, trying to catch his breath. "He must have been a mere twelve or thirteen, and damnably rude, if I remember rightly. I myself, was hardly a man, and acted equally arrogant, I'll wager. And, of course, the two of us almost shared a dance with you the evening of your sixteenth birthday."

Jane vividly recalled Thomas's anger when he discovered her on the dance floor with the duke. She wondered whether Alexander had witnessed her passionate embrace with Thomas in the library, when the duke had returned to retrieve his kid gloves.

Alexander paused to scrape he dared not guess *what* from one of his diamond-buckled brogues on the edge of a granite step. Jane bent over, pushing her wide-hooped skirts flat against her thighs, and rubbed the ankle of her right leg. Alex couldn't help noticing the rounded cleavage exposed by her movements. He marveled at the fullness of her maturing figure and the narrowness of her waist, no larger than a small, porcelain dinner plate.

"Have you hurt yourself?" he asked.

"Just twisted it a bit," she replied, continuing to massage her leg. There was a moment's silence. Then: "I suppose ye know *how* Thomas Fraser died?" she asked with a catch in her voice. Her head remained bowed over her leg.

"I know," he answered quietly. "Charles Gordon told me he was killed in an Indian massacre in America last autumn."

Jane glanced up at him and their eyes met. At that moment, Alexander wondered how much knowledge of her relationship with Thomas he should reveal. When he had queried his solicitor, Charles Gordon, about the lovely lass he'd seen the previous two New Year's eves, he'd discovered it was common knowledge she and Thomas Fraser intended to marry, despite the rumored objections of both Simon Fraser and Lady Maxwell.

"As I said earlier this evening, I was so very sorry to hear the news. I'm told he was a decent chap, if a bit impetuous, and that he was destined to have an excellent career in the military."

There was no point in speaking ill of the dead, Alexander thought, watching Jane carefully. Actually, he thought Lieutenant Fraser had been a hotheaded rogue who, like the rest of his clan, had a penchant for lost causes.

Jane straightened up, allowing the sweeping folds of her white satin gown to fall back into place.

"If Thomas acted rudely toward Yer Grace that evening, 'twas because he was jealous of ye," she replied, tilting her chin defiantly. "Did ye know we were to be wed?"

"That I did, which must make your loss doubly hard," Alex said stiffly.

Jane nodded, holding back tears that had suddenly welled up in her eyes. She reached down and pulled off one of her dainty satin slippers, its raised heel covered with stains.

"These were made for dancing, not mucking about," she said, veering away from the subject of Thomas.

"Why don't we get to a place where you can sit down," he urged. "The Devil knows where my coach has got to! Since you know the neighborhood so well . . . do you have any notion where we *are*?"

Jane gazed up at the towering buildings flanking them on all sides.

"Chessel's Court, I should think . . . ." she said, looking for landmarks that would serve as positive identification. "Aye, that's where we are . . . just a few closes over from St. Mary's Wynd and the Red Lion Inn."

"If it wouldn't destroy your reputation," Alexander said wearily, "I could certainly use a brandy."

"The Red Lion Inn it is, then," she said. "I've been a patron there since I was six . . . or rather a *visitor*," she amended hastily at the sight of Alexander's cocked eyebrow. Jane clasped his arm tightly and, replacing her slipper, tentatively put weight on her right foot. Taking a gingerly step, she asked soberly, "Do ye think everyone in our boxes escaped the theater?"

"They got out, all right," he assured her, and when he saw that she still looked troubled, added, "Don't worry, Jane, my dear." He was aware of using her Christian name for the first time. "My man Charles Gordon said he would lead them to safety and I'll wager you a new pair of satin slippers he has. And what would *I* do with a new pair of satin slippers?" he teased.

Her warm, generous smile in response to his jest radically altered her appearance. Its radiance was like the northern sun unexpectedly emerging from a dull gray sky, shimmering on Lock Alvie or Loch-an-Eilean, where Highland swans spent their winters. They walked in companionable silence across a wide field behind several tall buildings fronting on the High Street. Eventually they turned right into another courtyard that led to St. Mary's Wynd and the welcoming glow of the Red Lion Inn.

The convivial crowd inside whispered behind their tankards as Jane and Alexander entered in their evening finery, looking both elegant and disheveled.

"It might damage yer reputation to be seen in such an unfashionable place" she whispered mischievously. "I think I'll introduce ye as plain Alex Gordon!"

Jane waved at the barman and, still limping, headed for a table at the back of the tavern where ladies were welcome and the high-backed benches afforded a certain amount of privacy. Many of the patrons recognized her, and they greeted her genially, commenting on her curious appearance.

"We've just been in a riot!" she announced to proprietor Peter Ramsay as the patrons hushed to hear more.

"The advocates and the medical students had a row over who should play Romeo at the playhouse tonight. They tore the place to bits . . . or at least we *assume* they did. We left after the chandelier came down.''

"Aye," said Ramsay, shaking his head. "I've just had a word with the constable. The fire was doused, but there was considerable damage to the playhouse. The real miracle is no one got killed.''

"Well, that's a blessing," murmured Alexander, relieved that the entertainment in his name had not created any new widows or orphans.

"Ye should have seen the food fly!" Jane said excitedly. "Poor old Mistress Baker . . . Romeo's 'Juliet' dodged a joint of beef before retreating to the tiring room, I can tell ye that!''

Her eyes sparkled with pleasure as her audience savored the description of the cheeky students in the balcony pouring perfectly good claret down onto their tutors' wigs. Alexander, meanwhile, stood off to one side, watching Jane's animated performance with a look of faint amusement. Finally she turned to him and presented the publican.

"Peter, this is . . . ah . . . Alex Gordon," she said. "We escaped the mob together."

"The truth is, she *saved* me from it," Alexander interjected, enjoying his commoner status.

Ramsay surveyed the young man's smartly cut suit with interest.

"Well, a wee dram for the survivors, and then, Mistress Jane, I think ye should soon be gettin' home. Her ladyship may be worried o'er ye."

Ramsay shot a baleful look in Alexander's direction. It plagued him not to be able to place this Gordon fellow. Nevertheless, he retreated to pour the brandies, thinking to himself how good it was to see Jane once again with a smile on her face. It had tugged at his heart the few times he'd glimpsed her moping in the back garden or lingering in the shed where Thomas used to keep his horse. As Ramsay funneled the amber liquid into snifters, he wondered what was to become of the beautiful Jane Maxwell, now that Thomas was gone. The publican made his way back across the crowded tavern to the rear table where Jane and her mysterious companion were engrossed in conversation and delivered their brandies.

"To survival," Alex said, touching Jane's raised glass. Their eyes met briefly, and Jane sipped a portion of the fiery liquid. "Tell me what it was like, growing up in this teeming metropolis," he went on. "As a youth I only came to Edinburgh occasionally . . . and now visit only when I have business to attend to.''

Jane gave him a surprised look.

"Dinna ye *like* Edinburgh?'' she asked sharply.

Clearly *she* did.

"I don't know it terribly well, as you observed this evening. That's why I'm curious about your childhood here.''

Jane leaned against the back of her bench and toyed with her glass. Her eyes had a dreamy quality about them, as if she were contemplating a painted landscape.

" 'Twas wonderful to grow up in the town. From the time I was six, Catherine and I went anywhere we wished, since Father had decided to spend most of his time in Monreith. Until we were a bit older, Mother had her mind solely on making ends meet, and pretty much let us do as we wished—'' Jane looked at Alexander challengingly. "With two households and six children, there was hardly a farthing to spare—but still, we girls had wonderful fun. Thomas lived three doors away and we went everywhere together. He taught me to climb trees and plant turnips in the kitchen garden . . . he taught me how to ride in Holyrood Park and showed me where to find the sweetest wells in the city. We played golf together at dawn's light at Musselburgh Links. He even taught me how to drink spirits . . . how to hold my liquor!'' she laughed, downing her brandy with a gulp and then signaling for another.

"Did he teach you to dance?'' Alexander asked gently. "I've been told you're quite the best dancer in Edinburgh, and after our brief encounter in the Prestonfield ballroom, I formed the same opinion.''

"No, Thomas and I learned dancing together.'' She smiled, startled by Alex's bold compliment and by the fact that he'd obviously been talking to someone else about her. "Master Davie Strange taught us all the steps at his school in Todrick's Wynd. Thomas practiced with me for hours and hours. I haven't danced since his death . . . I just . . . can't . . .''

Jane's voiced trailed off as Peter Ramsay placed another short snifter in front of them. The innkeeper shot Alexander a quizzical look and walked away.

"I can tell you miss him very much,'' Alexander said quietly.

"I will *always* miss him,'' Jane answered fiercely. "I still canna believe he's gone . . . that he will never come back . . . that I will never see him again.''

Jane looked down at her glass helplessly. Silent tears edged through her lashes.

"I'm sorry . . ." she said in a wan voice. "I keep thinking I'm getting better, but I guess I'm not."

"Yes, you are," Alexander countered, taking her gloved hand in his. "You laughed a little this evening, and you were brave enough to come out with me, a stranger."

"But when I do those things, I feel *terrible*!" she exclaimed suddenly. "Thomas is lying in some muddy grave near a river whose name I canna even pronounce, and my mother says 'Cheer up, lass . . . on to the ball!' "

Alexander gently stroked the soft doeskin of her white glove with his forefinger.

"I know . . . when I lost someone I held dear, I felt guilty too—and angry at the same time," he said quietly.

"Angry?" she asked. A strange look passed across her furrowed brow.

"That *he's* dead and *you're* alive. That he *left*," Alexander said softly.

Tears welled up again in her dark eyes, luminous in the dusky glow of the tallow tapers standing in the wall sconces.

"I *am* angry! I'm angry at my mother! 'Twas she who thought she could make a *better* match for her darling Jane. And I *hate* that Simon Fraser . . ." Jane's bitterness seemed to fade into despair. "Catherine says 'tis wrong of me to keep blaming everyone, but ye know who makes me angriest of all?" she asked, staring at Alexander.

"Who?"

"Thomas," she whispered. "He let it *happen*. I dinna want him to leave. Simon Fraser spirited him away to keep us apart, and but 'twas *Thomas* who gave in to it . . ." Jane added a dash of venom to her pronouncement. "He was trying to please *everybody*—but look what happened!"

The anguish in Jane's voice struck a deep chord in Alexander. Her story had a depressingly familiar ring to it. Bathia had come from solid, respectable people. When Alexander had learned she was carrying his child, he had thought seriously about marrying her. He had loved her, he knew that. No one had ever made him so happy, so capable of dealing with the burdens of his dukedom. But he had shrunk from the conflict their attachment created with his mother and Staats Morris.

"Bathia Largue is a sweet thing, and we shall be forever grateful to her for nursing you back to health," his mother had said, "but surely, Alexander, you can appreciate she's certainly not a suitable match for a *duke*!"

For a while he had fought against their reasoning, their pleas, their threats. But in the end, Jane was right. He had bowed to the pressure to "please" his mother and stepfather. He had been forced to ignore the fact that Bathia had never left his bedside when he himself had been so ill with ague. And she had willingly given him her virginity. She had been hurt terribly when they didn't marry, and eventually, he began to wonder if she would continue to love him at all. Women of his acquaintance often withdrew their affection if they didn't get what they wanted. Bathia, however, had died within days of the birth of their son. He never discovered whether *he* could learn to trust the one woman who had offered such enduring love. By trying to please everyone except Bathia who *deserved* to be pleased above all others, he had lost the one thing he'd ever wanted. And until this night, he had believed there could be no other woman in his life, ever again.

"I'm angry at Thomas for *dying*," Jane said, her voice interrupting his gloomy reverie. "Did ye feel that way when Bathia passed away?"

"So, you know something of my past as well," he responded, smiling sadly at Jane's tear-filled eyes. "Two bruised hearts are here tonight, are they not? Well, yes . . . I suppose I was very angry when Bathia died. But most of all, I was angry at myself for not being strong enough to do what I felt was right." He lifted his hand from Jane's and, with the back of his finger, brushed away the moisture that had spilled down her cheeks. "I don't think I'll make *that* mistake again," he said, lightening his tone.

"But as least ye have a wee bairn to remind ye of her."

Jane said it with such fierce longing that Alexander overcame his surprise that she should know about his Geordie.

"So 'tis all over Edinburgh, is it?"

"Not exactly . . . but people do talk."

"And does such licentious behavior shock you?"

His voice had an edge to it.

"No . . . I'm envious."

Her answer startled him so much he nearly choked on his brandy.

"It doesn't offend you that I have a bastard bairn in the nursery at Gordon Castle?"

"Dinna call yer child that!" she said sharply.

"All right . . . I won't. He's a fine wee thing."

"Handsome as his father?" she said teasingly.

"Aye . . . handsome as the Devil himself," he grinned, patting her hand for emphasis.

His touch was comforting. She liked the way his slightly gaunt visage filled out when he smiled at her.

"What rock-hard fingers you have, lassie," he joked, pinching her gloved hand lightly in wonder. "Whatever have you been doing? Planting turnips all winter?"

Jane's brief smile vanished and a deathly white cast came over her features.

"That's not my finger . . . 'tis a piece of ivory," she whispered. *Why, oh, why, just when she was feeling a bit cheerful, did something like this have to happen?* she wondered bleakly.

"Ivory? What are you talking about, lass?"

Jane put both hands on her lap under the table.

"Remember the day of the pig race on the High Street?"

Alexander nodded, smiling at the memory of a ten-year-old Jane throwing a fit in the mud puddle like an enraged duckling after she'd come up the loser.

"Well, yer fine linen handkerchief probably saved my life," she said, avoiding his eyes. "Right after the race I reached for an apple from a moving cart and, instead, tore off my finger. Thomas ripped yer linen into strips and tied the artery to staunch the blood."

For reasons he didn't clearly understand, Alex wanted to know everything he could about Jane Maxwell.

"May I see?" he asked softly.

"See?" Jane repeated uncertainly. " 'Tis ugly as sin. 'Twas the beginning of all my misfortune."

"Well, we've both survived a lot of muck under our feet tonight, and some bad luck as well . . . why not this?" he replied evenly, holding out his hand. "Please let me see your hurt, Jane."

Slowly, dreading the sight of the now-familiar stub, Jane rested her hands on the tavern table and tugged at the leather fingers of her right glove. As she drew the doeskin gauntlet off her hand, the ivory extension fashioned by a cobbler at Lady Maxwell's direction, clattered to the table. The stubby index finger of her right hand lay exposed against her long slender middle finger.

Alexander picked up her hand and studied it matter-of-factly. As he did so, she was struck by the appearance of his own slender hands with their long, tapering fingers. "One would never suspect . . ." he murmured, turning her hand over, palm up. Her own soft pink flesh contrasted strongly with the hardness of his, probably the product of practicing the sport of archery, for which he had gained some renown. He took her chin in his other hand and forced her to look at him. Slowly he turned over her injured hand once again and bent forward to kiss it. Deliberately, he brushed his lips across its entire surface, briefly caressing the disfigured finger as if it were exquisitely precious. He glanced up and saw she was staring at him in wonder. "There. That's done," he said huskily. "The rest of you, I have no doubt, is perfect as well."

Jane was thrown into confusion by the odd tremors radiating through her body. His lips had felt so soft against her skin. His touch seemed so distinctive, yet so reminiscent of Thomas's caress. Then, Alexander eased himself out of his seat. He walked over to the innkeeper to drop a few coins on the bar, giving her time to insert the ivory finger in her glove and put it back on her hand.

"May I?" he said, extending his arm.

She tested her weight on her strained ankle. It hurt,, but she could walk on it, if she moved slowly. As the two emerged into the April night, Alexander put a hand casually around her waist. Then he fell into step, offering the solid support of his other hand under her elbow.

"I trust, my dear Jane, you know the way home?"

"Aye, Alex Gordon—that I do."

2

1767–1782

The Silver Swanne, who
   had no living note,
When death approacht,
   unlockt her silent throat.
Leaning her breast
   against the reedie shore,
Thus sang her first and last
   and sung no more.
Farewell all joys, O death
   come close mine eyes.
More Geese than Swannes now live,
   more fools than wise.

   Anonymous, seventeenth century

12
May 1767

Arabella O'Brien Delaney tapped her quill on the side of a large red leather-bound ledger, heedless of the ink blotches bleeding into the margins. Her attention had strayed from the jumble of figures and inaccurate calculations committed to the pages of the plantation's accounts book by her brother Beven. Her eyes were focused, instead, on a wooden cart rumbling up the tree-lined avenue, which ended in a circle of gravel outside her window.

The first sunny day in weeks displayed Antrim Hall at its very best. The Maryland plantation's broad front fields were sprinkled with purple and yellow wildflowers, boxed off by white rail fences stretching in every direction. The fences defined the holdings Arabella had worked so hard to preserve since the untimely death of her elderly husband, Hugh Delaney, at the Ogilvy-Delaney Hunt the previous spring. Surely, she thought, a sixty-seven-year-old man should have had the sense to decline her brother Beven's drunken challenge to jump his steed over a five-barred gate. But there you were, she sighed resignedly, snapping shut the heavy ledger. Men were simply an inferior species.

Arabella had been hopelessly distracted from her morning's tasks even before the cart had appeared this warm spring day on the road leading to Antrim Hall. She had sat dreamily at her desk, with the May sunshine bathing her face, her jet black hair pulled back casually and tied at the nape of her neck like a man's periwig. She delighted in the sun's sensuous heat, which penetrated her pores and made her feel like a sleepy kitten. A kind of impatience had been gnawing at her for most of the morning. She was fed up with Beven's inebriated carousing and with trying to make sense of her brother's blatant mismanagement of their jointly held estate. And she was fed up with not ever having any fun.

The slender Arabella sighed once again, returning the quill to its holder. What she really had in mind to do was throw herself into the tall grasses that grew beside the brook beyond the distant ridge, and. . . .

"Spring fever! At the ripe old age of nineteen, I've got myself a *serious* case of spring fever!" She laughed aloud, her cobalt blue eyes carefully charting the slow progress of the vehicle from her vantage point in the morning room. At length, the cart drew up in front of the white pillared porch and graceful front steps of the stately mansion.

"Mehitabel!" Arabella called loudly to her servant, while rising from her desk.

She would have to return to puzzle over Beven's accounts later. The endless months of rain—continuing even into late May—had delayed the wheat planting, and Arabella was concerned that this bit of bad luck, plus Beven's mounting gambling debts, would mean they'd be dangerously short of cash before fall.

"*Mehitabel!*" she repeated crossly. Presently, the black house slave appeared at the door, breathing hard. "Will you please tell Mr. O'Brien that a visitor has arrived. You'll probably have to knock loudly at his door. I think he's still asleep."

The housemaid nodded and retreated from the sun-splattered morning room. Arabella knew full well her brother was asleep. *Unconscious* was probably a more precise description. Here it was midmorning, with a million chores to be attended to, and Beven O'Brien was upstairs, sleeping off his third hangover of the week.

"*Damn him, anyway!*" she said out loud.

She entered the broad hallway and stepped to the narrow window flanking the front door, eyeing the large patches of paint curling away from the pale yellow walls. She peered out at the cart whose wooden sides concealed its contents, although Arabella could make out a round, white shape dipping in and out of sight along the rim of the slats nearest her view. The driver pulled hard on the reins as the vehicle crunched to a halt at the front door. He jumped down from his perch and briefly inspected his mysterious baggage, then swung his thick frame up and over the sides of the cart and leaned down to reach for an object out of her view. He tugged at it, trying to pull it off the floor. A sack of meal, or perhaps a heavy pile of tobacco, she speculated. *Really!* she fumed. *Didn't tradesmen appreciate what a back door was for?*

Suddenly, Arabella gasped when she got a closer look at the

round white sphere she'd spied earlier. It was a human head swathed in bandages! The victim was apparently unconscious, and his buckskinned companion hiked his charge's large body over his own massive shoulders with great difficulty.

"Beven! Mehitabel! Come quickly!" Arabella cried from the bottom of the stairs, rushing back to peer through the thin strip of glass by the side of the front door.

Who in the world were these men? she wondered. *And why were they coming here?* She didn't feel up to playing nursemaid, what with all the problems confronting her regarding the plantation.

"Gadzooks, woman! Couldn't you cope with this yourself?" croaked a voice behind her. "I'm feeling a bit rough this morning. I fear I'm coming down with a touch of influ—"

Arabella whirled around to see her brother Beven stumbling downstairs, barefoot and disheveled. He made an attempt to tuck his linen shirt into his stained and wrinkled breeches, but the simple act of standing on the curving staircase required a herculean effort.

"I could cope with it, brother dear," Arabella retorted sarcastically, "but I don't *care* to! Now see who this is and send them around back."

She turned to look out the window again, just as the older man carried his bandaged burden up the last step onto the mansion's front porch. Arabella's jaw dropped as she stared at the face that was now only inches away from hers through the window. Several small red scars seared the man's upper lip and a longer one sliced across a prominent cheekbone. They were all fresh. It was a very handsome face, she noted with interest, despite the blood-soaked bandages and the ravaged look it bore. She couldn't recall the unfortunate gentleman's name, but she distinctly remembered being introduced to this rugged officer, looking splendid in his Black Watch kilt at Charles Carroll's party in Annapolis exactly a year ago—a celebration held to commemorate the repeal of that odious Stamp Act. If it were the same man who had so caught her eye that night, he would have an arresting mane of claret-colored hair under that bloody bandage.

Before Beven could stagger to the front door, Arabella opened it wide and waited expectantly for the buckskin gentleman to address her.

"Good morning, ma'am . . . name's Shelby. Captain Evan Shelby. This here's Thomas Fraser," the man said by way of explanation for their presence on her front stoop. "He's a lieutenant in the Forty-second Regiment. He said he met you once," he continued, hiking the man's large six-foot-four frame on his bent shoulders. "The lad's not dead yet, but he *will* be if we don't put him right to bed and get a doctor."

Arabella whirled around and started barking orders.

"Beven, I want you to ride over to Dr. Scott's in Annapolis immediately."

Her brother nodded sullenly and retreated to locate his boots. Meanwhile, several of the servants, including Mehitabel, were peeking around the corner of the hallway.

"Mehitabel, go turn down the counterpane in the blue room, next to mine, and be quick about it. Jemma, get me some hot water and some cool—and *fresh* linen! Zeb, help this gentleman carry . . . what's your name again?"

Arabella took a breath and turned to look at the wounded man's rescuer.

"Shelby. Captain Evan Shelby. Mason–Dixon expedition. We . . . ah . . . also met about a year ago . . . at an excellent fox hunt of yours. So sorry about your husband's . . . ah . . . demise," he stammered lamely.

"Yes, I recall our meeting then," fibbed Arabella. There had been hordes of riffraff at the last hunt, and Hugh Delaney's death had offered the excuse she needed to cancel the event this spring, thank heavens! Those spongers had been eating her out of house and home every year.

She gestured toward the curving staircase. Shelby and Zebediah half carried, half dragged the injured man up the long winding stairs and down the carpeted hallway on the second floor.

"In here," Arabella said, pushing the door against the wall of the guest bedchamber with a thud.

Mehitabel adjusted the windows to air out the stale smell permeating the seldom-used chamber while the men eased the unconscious lieutenant's long, lean frame onto the four-poster.

Arabella directed the maid, "Take off his . . . what *are* those?" She was referring to strange objects covering the lieutenant's feet.

"Moccasins . . ." declared Shelby. "They're part of the Indian garb he wore on patrol when his party was ambushed near Fort Pitt last fall," Shelby answered, easing the sweat-soaked shirt off Thomas's body.

Arabella hardly had time to wonder why the poor man had been traveling for months in this condition before she recoiled at the sight of the crimson gashes that streaked the lieutenant's shoulders and chest. On the biceps of his left arm there was an ugly deep cut the circumference of a sovereign.

"Musket shot," Shelby explained, pointing to the circular wound, "and Indian carvings . . . the lad got nicked several times before crawling into the underbrush. He saved himself by rolling into a ditch and covering his body with leaves as his mates were slaughtered. He lay still till the Mingos left. Then he crawled to an abandoned trapper's cabin at Turtle Creek, for safety."

"But that happened *months* ago," Arabella exclaimed, puzzled. "Charley Carroll told me about the skirmish at Fort Pitt . . . let's see . . . it must have been way back in December. Yes, that's it! He told me at his father's Christmas party that several fresh recruits from the fort whom we'd met the previous May had been killed by Indians last autumn."

"Everyone, including me, assumed Fraser, here, had died in early October, along with several other lads," Shelby replied, motioning for Zebediah to help undress Thomas, who was breathing steadily, but lay on the bed with his eyes closed.

"They even had a funeral at the fort. But the soldiers had been hacked up pretty bad and scalped by the braves . . . and since *everybody* was dressed as Injuns . . . well, there was a lot of confusion, I suppose." Shelby and Zebediah began to roll Thomas's leather breeches gently down the unconscious man's muscular thighs. "At any rate, Fraser finally made it to a settlers' compound near Redstone where he collapsed," continued Shelby. "Out like a lantern for days, they told me. Old Enoch Van Dyke's missus nursed him for months, though they hadn't the slightest notion who he was, then."

Arabella modestly busied herself adjusting the drapes in the window next to the bed. Out of the corner of her eye she saw the two men pull the trousers past Thomas's ankles. No scars on his legs, she thought, permitting herself a glimpse of a nest of ruby hair that cushioned a sizable, soft penis at the base of the lieutenant's naked torso. She fumbled for the tie holding back the worn, blue curtain, and waited to hear the sound of the cotton sheet rustling over Thomas's inert body before she turned to face Shelby.

"The poor blighter was in pretty ragged shape all winter," Shelby related. "Cut up like a filet fish, Van Dyke said . . . couldn't even tell you his name. But the old woman poulticed him and pampered him and fed him every herb she had. At any rate, he finally came around . . . and then remembered most everything. He couldn't talk very well, though, for a while. As you can see, he took a blow to the head. Bouncing around in that cart opened the big gash on his crown again," he added, pointing to a spot above Thomas's temple. Arabella wrinkled her nose as she surveyed the dirty linen bandage covering the gash on Thomas's head. "Finally, the lad woke up one day and had his speech back, but he was still weak as a lamb," Shelby continued, while both he and Arabella applied soft cloths soaked in cool water provided by Mehitabel. "Old Sarah Van Dyke wasn't about to let him die, though, what with five eligible daughters in the family. When I arrived on the scene, they had him bundling with the middle girl. Sarina, I believe her name was."

"That must have been quite a tonic for a man in such dreadful condition," Arabella commented dryly, wringing a compress with pronounced vigor.

"Well, I can speak plainly about such things, Mrs. Delaney . . . you being a widow and all. . . ."

"I think it's perfectly appalling," Arabella said, trying to sound outraged. "*Bundling* with a complete stranger? I hope the poor man hasn't contracted a disease . . . or spread one, for that matter!"

Captain Shelby cleared his throat with embarrassment.

"No, ma'am. That type of illness is not his complaint. Believe me, Mrs. Delaney, he only slept *near* the girl. Poor Thomas, here, was in no shape for much recreation, if you get my drift."

Arabella was familiar with the well-known practice of bundling. Impoverished settlers, with their one- or two-room cabins, often put total strangers in bed with female members of the family, given the scarcity of living space on the frontier and the expense of shelter. Arabella knew for a fact that, for want of a wooden board designed to separate a visitor from his sleeping companion, many a dainty miss wound up at the altar with a baby on the way. Still, many a casual drifter found a permanent abode in this fashion, so perhaps bundling performed a necessary social service for the lower orders.

"Well, despite Mrs. Van Dyke's efforts, it looks like a definite relapse to me," Arabella noted sarcastically, indicating the lad's apparent unconsciousness.

Shelby drew a breath and explained.

"Word finally came to me in January at Christiana Bridge where the Mason-Dixon expedition was wintering, that a red-headed white man, dressed in Indian garb, was recuperating at the Van Dykes' at Redstone. I couldn't believe it! I'd visited his commanding officer, Captain Maxwell, in November. He'd told me the sorry tale of how they'd buried the three casualties when Maxwell was down river on other business.'' Shelby rubbed his chin, recalling his conversation with the saddened military man. ''The captain was real struck by it all, because the lad was to marry his favorite niece. Apparently, the Frasers were large landholders in Scotland before some sort of local rebellion there twenty years ago. The lad knows farming and sheep raising, Maxwell told me. The poor sot would have been a 'Sir' something, if his family's fortunes hadn't turned sour.''

''How tragic . . .'' Arabella murmured, as she gently cleansed Thomas's musket wound with her moistened cloth and formed a plan. ''So, what you're telling me is that some Mingo got a decent Christian burial near the walls of Fort Pitt,'' chortled Arabella, gently scraping off a patch of dried blood just below Thomas's hairline. ''But Lieutenant Fraser has such distinctive red hair. Didn't anyone notice that none of the corpses fit his description?''

''Begging your pardon, ma'am,'' Shelby said grimly, ''but those Indians made shepherd's pie out of the bodies. Scalped and chopped 'em up real fine, Captain Maxwell told me. Blood everywhere. That's why I could hardly believe the rumors he was alive before I decided to go to Redstone myself to see if it was true.''

''If he lives through this latest mishap, where will he go? Back to his regiment?'' Arabella inquired, scanning the intriguing form of her new guest beneath the thin sheet.

''A farmer at Frederick told me the Forty-second is already on its way home. They're marching across Pennsylvania and are scheduled to sail from Philadelphia in mid-July. Fraser begged me to get him to his ship on time. He said he wants to get back to his lady. We slogged through the muck and rain for three weeks. I caught a chill myself, I did,'' he said, pounding his barrel chest and coughing loudly to prove it.

''Well, I fear Lieutenant Fraser has caught more than a chill,'' she answered, bending over him and putting her head on his chest. Soft golden hairs tickled her ear as she listened to his breathing and was reassured by the even rhythm of Thomas's heartbeat. His chest sounded raspy, however, and his skin was burning to the touch. She glanced sideways at Shelby as she reached for Thomas's wrist to measure his pulse. It was strong and steady.

Arabella avoided Shelby's eyes. She felt an uncharacteristic blush creep into her cheeks as thoughts of keeping the handsome lieutenant company spun through her mind.

"Don't you think the poor man's too sick to make the trip to Philadelphia any time soon?" she asked solicitously, the rest of her scheme clicking into place.

"God, yes!" Captain Shelby replied. "His lungs were rattlin' the last miles here. You will look after him, won't you, Mrs. Delaney?" Shelby asked earnestly. "I'm a month late catching up with the Mason-Dixon expedition. I'd be most obliged if you'd write Captain James Maxwell, care of the *Victory* in Philadelphia, once you know the outcome. If the lad lives, at least Maxwell can bring the glad tidings to his niece, in the event young Fraser is too ill to risk an ocean voyage, come July." He glanced down at Thomas's unconscious form. "And if he doesn't make it . . . well, they've buried him once already. No need to do it twice."

"Of course, Captain Shelby," Arabella assured him solemnly. "I'll do whatever is necessary. If the Lieutenant lives, he'll have you to thank for bringing him back to civilization. But, you shouldn't waste another minute returning to your Mason-Dixon party. That new boundary line is important to us all. As for your injured friend, here," she said, flashing him her warmest smile, "don't worry. I'll do the best I can."

She cast an appreciative glance at Thomas Fraser. He *had* to know more than Beven about running an eleven thousand acre plantation such as Antrim Hall. And once this good-looking lieutenant recovered his physical powers and was lonely in the night. . . .

The figure in the bed stirred. Much to Shelby and Arabella's surprise, the gray-green eyes of Thomas Fraser flew wide open, and he stared up at her in apparent recognition.

"Jenny?" he rasped, and then closed his eyes, as if the sheer effort of uttering that one word was simply too much for him.

" 'Tis all right, Lieutenant Fraser," Arabella said soothingly, her hand resting lightly on the young man's sinewy shoulder. "That's right . . . just close your eyes and sleep. Everything is going to be just fine."

She quickly bent over and efficiently tucked in the linen bedcovers nearest her. Glancing up at Shelby, she added cheerfully, "You just leave Lieutenant Fraser to me."

Eglantine burst into her sister's bedroom.

"The duke's wearing *plum silk*!" exclaimed Jane's fifteen-year-old sister excitedly. "I just peeked at him sitting in his coach."

"Really, Eglantine," Jane chided her. "There's no need for a fashion report. I'll be seeing His Grace myself in two minutes' time."

"Yer fan, Mistress Jane," Fiona said solemnly, handing her the gift from Alexander.

Jane could only smile at the deference accorded her by her little sister and her maid during the three months the Duke of Gordon had been paying court—if that's how their friendship could be characterized. He had been calling at Hyndford Close quite regularly, when he was in Edinburgh. In fact, the duke's attentions had created a social whirl that was sorely taxing her dressmaker, not to mention the family finances.

"He's so *beautiful*!" sighed Eglantine, sinking down on the bench where Jane had just been sitting, primping her hair in anticipation of the night's round of festivities at Comely Gardens.

"Please, Eglantine. Men aren't beautiful. They're *handsome*," said Jane matter-of-factly.

Her tone masked a sense of bittersweet nostalgia at the memory of her first sight of Thomas resplendent in his Black Watch uniform. Indeed, Thomas *had* been beautiful that day, striding into the Old Ship Hotel wearing his forest green and black kilt and scarlet coat. Now that he was gone, it was too horrible for words to contemplate such wonderful chiseled cheekbones and warm, gray-green eyes suffering disfigurement. *Thomas was dead!* Why couldn't she accept it?

"He's *waiting*!" cried Eglantine impatiently. "Aren't ye excited about dining and dancing at Comely Gardens? And with a *duke*! And a rich one, at that! Maybe he'll ask the question tonight!"

"The question of marriage?" Jane asked mildly, inserting the ivory finger into her glove and pulling the doeskin onto her hand. "Really . . . I wish ye'd believe me when I tell ye Alexander and I are simply good friends. We have . . . uh . . . certain interests in common and feel comfortable in each other's company . . . nothing more."

"Well, why dinna ye try and *make* it more?"

It was her mother's voice. Jane turned abruptly toward the door, startled by the intrusion.

"Ye're an exceedingly beautiful young woman, Jane," said Lady Maxwell as she entered the room briskly, skirts rustling. "Clearly, the Duke of Gordon has taken a fancy to ye, yet ye give him precious little encouragement.'' She signaled to Eglantine and Fiona to leave, and they did so, reluctantly. ''Dinna ye think ye owe it to him to offer him some sign of yer affection?''

''He knows I enjoy his company,'' Jane replied carefully. She was in no mood to argue about her behavior with her mother while the duke awaited her downstairs.

''But how long will he enjoy *yers* if ye exhibit him no more than polite interest?'' her mother demanded.

''If he should tire of me so quickly, then our prospects for spending a lifetime together would not appear propitious, would they, Mama?''

''I'm not as concerned about yer happiness as I am about yer future, missy,'' Lady Maxwell snapped. ''Ye're now nearly eighteen. 'Tis time ye were married. One of the most eligible men in all of Scotland, of Britain for that matter, honors ye by paying court. 'Tis common knowledge he would propose but for a small sign from ye. Yet ye show nothing. I think ye pretend to play the game but only tease—''

''I do not!'' Jane replied angrily. ''The duke and I understand each other, even if ye do not, Mama! He is not as ready as ye may think to bind his heart to any woman.''

''So *that's* it!'' Lady Maxwell said triumphantly. ''If ye believe His Grace thought more of that castle chit than of a moment's pleasure, ye are very naive! And besides, Bathia Largue is dead. The sooner ye rid yourself of all this sentimental nonsense, the better, lass! The duke must marry. The bastard who lies rocking in a cradle in the Gordon Castle nursery may bear his name, but not his title, and the duke *knows* it! He needs a suitable partner, and for some undiscernible reason, he has selected ye as a likely candidate. Ye owe it to me and the entire Maxwell family to play yer part and capture the prize. Either that, or ye shall retire to Monreith to assist yer father with housekeeping chores suitable for a self-declared spinster. Do ye understand, Jane?''

Jane's eyes had narrowed and her body trembled slightly. Lady Maxwell watched her daughter warily. Perhaps she had pushed too hard.

''So yer lofty ambitions would now rule out even Jamie Ferguson or the others ye considered acceptable before the stakes were raised!'' Jane retorted, a flush spreading up her slender throat in stark contrast to her pale white satin evening cloak. ''I suppose if Thomas were alive, the son of a knight and an officer

in His Majesty's Service would no longer be good enough for
Jane Maxwell!''

Lady Maxwell's eyes flashed as angrily as her daughter's. It
sorely tried her patience when the little saucebox succumbed to
these moods.

''I can assure ye, lass, that if it were a contest between the
Duke of Gordon and a lowly lieutenant, ye would find yerself a
duchess, whether ye desired it or not.''

Jane had thrust her chin beyond the satin ruffle of her cape.
Her dark eyes glared venomously. Magdalene decided to be
conciliatory.

''Jane, dear . . . I'm sorry for my hasty words . . .'' she
began, alarmed by the look of undisguised hatred on her daughter's face. '' 'Tis just that yer headstrong actions *vex* me so. I
know how sorely grieved ye've been by Thomas's death. But the
lad is gone, and a most wonderful gentleman begs, I'm told, to
take his place in yer affections.''

''No one can take the place of Thomas!'' Jane spat, glaring
furiously at her mother.

''Well . . . perhaps not . . . but Jane . . . our means are
limited . . . and 'tis so expensive to present ye to society.''

''I dinna ask for all the gowns and gloves and finery!'' Jane
retorted, turning her back on her mother.

Lady Maxwell put her hand lightly on her daughter's cape.

'' 'Tis been such a . . . such a difficult time with all ye
children, since yer father and I cannot seem to—''

''To live happily together—isn't that what ye mean, Mama?''
Jane said, turning around to face Lady Maxwell. ''Yet ye ask me
to encourage a man I hardly know, a man whose life and past are
so different from mine. Ye wish to sell me off to the highest
bidder before even a year's gone by since Thomas's death . . .
less than six months since I learned the news! *I don't even know
this man!*'' she declared vehemently. ''He was raised in the
country . . . in a *castle*! I live in the city in a rented flat. He
writes poetry, I like politics. He's used to having his every wish
obeyed, and I have grown fond of deciding things for myself! I
have to see if these differences will blend like beaten eggs—or
like oil and water. That takes time! Otherwise, Mama, I may end
up spending the rest of my life like ye and Da . . . squabbling
and punishing everyone else for yer mistake . . . and I dinna
think I could bear it!''

Lady Maxwell stared at her daughter, stunned by her harsh

assessment of her parents' married life. Jane swept past her mother before Lady Maxwell could think of a suitable retort.

The Duke of Gordon's black carriage slowly threaded its way out of Edinburgh along the crowded Easter Road toward Jock's Lodge, a village of less than five hundred souls, most of whom were in the employ of one Andrew Gibb, the proprietor of Comely Gardens.

"Comely's but a poor imitation of London's Vauxhall, really, but you may find it amusing," Alexander said, tilting his neatly coiffed head against the coach's padding to gain a better view of Jane, who sat opposite him. "There are acres of grounds and miles of sculptured hedges. You'll like Gibb's faux-marble cherubs, lit by hundreds of Chinese lanterns. And the ham he serves is sliced so thin, you could paper the entire grounds with it."

"Sounds like good business practice to me," Jane laughed. "The thin-sliced ham, I mean."

"Good business or no," replied Alexander, "we'll have to watch out for pickpockets and footpads."

"Nothing to worry about on that score," Jane responded cheerfully, waving her small satin drawstring pouch in front of him. "The Maxwells are in no danger of losing siller they dinna have!"

They both laughed and settled into a companionable silence as the coach wheels crunched along the road. Alexander stared at the night sky through the window.

"It may be vulgar, but I rather enjoy the music at Comely Gardens, and on a night as mild as this . . . with a full moon as well . . . we should enjoy ourselves, don't you think?"

Jane nodded, turning to peer out at the rolling downs, which were flooded with silvery summer moonlight. She could see the outlines of cypress, yew, and tulip trees and felt the warm summer night air waft gently against her cheeks.

" 'Tis lovely, isn't it?" she breathed. "Ye couldna have selected a better evening for such an adventure." She turned to look at Alexander. "And thank ye for inviting Catherine and John yet again. I do so miss her since she moved to Argyle Square."

"I can see that," Alexander replied pleasantly. "And if Eglantine can learn to stop spying on people from behind half-opened doors," he added half in jest, "she'll be included in the next invitation."

A moment passed, and Alexander looked at his companion intently.

"Jane, do you or your mother want for anything . . . anything at all?" he asked earnestly.

Jane studied his face.

"Ye mean money?" she asked wryly, smiling a little at the diplomatic way the duke referred to the precarious Maxwell family finances.

He nodded.

" 'Tis always unpredictable what my father will provide each month, but with Aunt Elizabeth's contribution, at least till Uncle James returns from America this fall, we seem to be managing quite well, thank ye."

"Truly, Jane, you will let me know if I can assist you in any way?" Alexander asked quietly as the coach turned down a lane flanked by a low wall leading to the entrance of Comely Gardens. Jane looked across the coach's luxurious interior, trying to mask her alarm at the drift in the conversation. The duke was offering her money, and if she accepted, it would change their situation entirely.

"That's very kind of ye, Yer Grace, but . . . I must confess I am a bit surprised to think of ye concerning yerself with the subject of the Maxwell household's financial uncertainties."

Without a moment's hesitation, Alexander replied, "It shouldn't surprise you, Jane dear, that I express concern for your family's welfare. The fact is, I intend to make you my wife. Ah, we've arrived!"

Before Jane could recover from her shock at hearing these words, the young duke gracefully exited the coach. Then he extended his hand to assist in her descent. She stared at him with an expression of amazement, heedless of the servants who were approaching to take command of the horses. Alexander said nothing, but simply crooked his arm in Jane's and led her toward the tree-lined esplanade that opened onto the walled gardens.

"Yer Grace!" she exclaimed, stopping their progress through the high arches, festooned with scores of twinkling lanterns.

"Yes?" Alexander answered calmly. "By the way, Jane, could you consider addressing me by my Christian name? 'Your Grace' seems far too formal when one is affianced."

"We are *not* affianced!" Jane replied hotly. "We hardly know each other! Ye've been very kind . . . I don't deny that, but really, Yer Gra—really, Alexander, I have in no way given any indication that—"

"That's true enough," he interrupted. "Until just a moment ago, I had given no indication either . . . but tonight I *choose* to give you a *slight* indication of my affection and esteem."

He led her quickly down a graveled walk, bordered on each side by lofty trees. Without warning, he pulled her into a maze of hedges, which were cut in geometric designs under an espaliered rose tree. Its pink blossoms gave off a faint but sweet perfume. Jane stood there, dumbstruck, as Alexander reached into a small pocket in the lining of his silk coat. He pulled out an object and kept it hidden in his hand.

"I said only that I *intend* to make you my wife. Naturally, it isn't at all clear whether you will have me. But to show you the sincerity of these intentions, I would like you to have these . . . they belonged to my grandmother, Henrietta, the Second Duchess of Gordon."

Alexander held up two exquisite ear fobs in the moonlight. Their faceted sides glittered like the lanterns shining in the distance.

"I was going to wait to present them at some opportune and properly romantic moment, but as I watched your lovely profile in the coach as you gazed out at the moon, I was struck by how perfectly these diamonds would complement your ensemble."

Without waiting for her response, the duke leaned forward and fastened one, then the other clip to her ears.

"Alex—Alexander," she stammered, fingering one of the jewels dangling from her ears with her glove. "I'm touched ye should want me to have these—especially since they belonged to yer grandmother—but . . ." She looked up at him, brows knit pensively. "How can ye be so sure ye want to marry me after such a short introduction? We've led entirely different lives . . . we dinna even know each other properly . . . and we're both . . . we're both—"

Jane left her sentence dangling in the balmy night air. She lowered her eyes and then glanced distractedly into the silvery night. The delicate sounds of a string orchestra playing somewhere on the green expanse of Comely Gardens floated toward them.

"We're both . . . sore of heart?" Alexander questioned softly. "Isn't that what you were trying to say?" he asked, holding her softly rounded chin between his slender fingers.

The gold metal of his ducal ring felt cold against her flesh.

"We must give our hearts a rest," she told him earnestly. "At least *I* must."

Alexander bent forward, gently brushing her lips with his. He lingered there only a moment before pulling his head away.

"How long a trial period would you suggest?" he murmured.

"I canna put a time to it," she replied in a soft, melancholy voice. "I only know that my feelings for Thomas aren't dead. Perhaps they never will be. I like ye too much, Alexander, to—"

"I don't ask you to forget Thomas," Alexander interrupted her shortly, taking her hands in his. "He was a spirited lad, and I acknowledge your love for him. It does you credit that you haven't dismissed his memory with ease, and that you are not easily seduced by the trappings of the House of Gordon, as others of your sex might be."

"But I still love him as if he were *alive*," Jane responded sadly. "What would be left over for ye?"

"Thomas is dead, Jane. The tie has, tragically, been severed by fate."

"I suppose I've accepted the fact he's dead," Jane said, blinking back tears as she looked beyond Alexander's shoulder at the perfect pink blossoms on the rose tree behind him. "It took me months to do that much. But I still feel *attached* somehow . . . connected to him—at least to the memory of him. Until that tie is broken, I'm not fit to be . . . a wife. Especially not the wife of a duke."

"Becoming a duchess is not the point, Jane," answered Alexander, his exasperation showing. "However, what you said before—that you still need time to break the ties you feel—*that*, I will accept and try to understand."

He placed his hands on her shoulders and gradually tightened his grip.

"But the bond you feel with Thomas Fraser *will* be broken, Jane, or your life will be unbearable," Alexander said grimly. "I know. I learned that lesson myself. It took my meeting you to realize how wide the gulf is between the living and the dead. Of course your feelings for Thomas aren't forgotten. Mine for Bathia will never be forgotten either, but we must put those emotions where they belong. They're a precious part of our past, to be remembered . . . but to be just that—a lovely, sad memory. Only one part of the tapestry of a full life."

"I know ye're right," Jane sighed. "But I canna seem to . . ." her voice trailed off. She gazed into his eyes and shook her head sorrowfully. "I know I shouldna live in the past, but I canna seem to go forward in the present. I'm just stuck—like a coach wheel in a rutted road."

He smiled. "I'm just the person to give you a push!"

"I'm stuck too deeply for that, I'm afraid," Jane replied, shaking her head again, this time with resignation. "At least that's the way it seems. So I think I should—"

She began to remove one of the diamond earrings.

"Don't!" Alexander said harshly, staying her hand with his. "Whatever you decide, I want you to have them. Even if you don't wear them."

His words allowed no room for argument, and his demeanor reflected a habit of being obeyed. Presently, the grim line of his mouth softened into a smile, and he laced his long fingers through hers. She wondered if he could feel the ivory extension filling the empty space inside her right glove.

"I'll accept you as you are, for the time being," he said in a bantering tone, pulling her gently against his chest. "However, I can't guarantee I'll always play the gentleman while you try to get your wheels unstuck."

As if to illustrate his words, he slowly skimmed the crested face of his gold signet ring lightly down her cheekbone to her throat, then pressed it to her swelling bosom that thrust out of her gown's low-cut bodice. The cool metal sent chills through her body as Alexander drew her closer to him, the full length of his frame melding with her own.

"Perhaps a little lubrication . . . a little whale oil, or such, would unloosen those wheels a bit," he murmured teasingly, deliberately tilting his pelvis toward hers to offer proof of his rising ardor. His tongue gently flicked around the diamond earrings, and darted briefly inside her ear. Jane tensed, but before long, his insistent, feathery caresses overcame her resistance. "You're a wonder, Mistress Jane," he whispered, returning to the sensitive spot he'd discovered just above her lobes where the earrings dangled.

The flat surface of his signet ring continued to press lightly against the valley between her breasts, causing a peculiar fluttering to ripple through her chest and stomach.

Slowly, languidly, Alexander pulled his body away from hers, resting his hands lightly on her bare shoulders. There was still clear evidence he had interrupted their embrace fully aroused, but he seemed now to take no notice.

"I think we'd better find our supper companions, don't you?" he asked quietly.

Jane thought she perceived a calculating glint flicker in his eye. He made a show of admiring his gift to her by rocking her shoulders gently, causing the earrings to swing softly against her neck.

"Lovely . . . lovely," he said smugly. "My grandmother would pluck them off you from her grave and my mother would snatch them from your ears instantly, if either one of them could see how much more stunning they look on you. You'll understand what I mean this winter when you see their portraits in the gallery at Gordon Castle."

"*Alexander*!" Jane protested in exasperation.

"I know . . . I know! Your wheels are stuck," he laughed. "Well . . . let's just say you'll see what I mean *if* you accompany me to the Highlands . . . someday."

Without further conversation, he led her back up the gravel path toward the center of the gardens where a line of Corinthian columns supported an ornate bandstand, and a string quartet was mechanically playing Handel. There seemed to be a thousand lanterns twinkling along the periphery of the circle of pavilions and its central building, flanked by two domed wings with turrets.

As they entered the pavilion itself, Comely Gardens' owner, Andrew Gibb, greeted the duke with an effusive welcome and directed them to a large, open-air supper box decorated with the same neoclassic motif that Gibb had used throughout his pleasure park.

Jane was soon swept up in a wave of greetings and embraces as Catherine, John Fordyce, and Charles Gordon, among others, said their hellos and bid them join the late night supper. Jane was mildly surprised to see Marietta Buchanan, who seemed even more plump than the last time they met. She was flitting around Jane's erstwhile escort, the toothy Jamie Ferguson.

"We'd begun to worry ye'd never make yer way through that line of carriages," John said, as liveried attendants drew gilded chairs for Jane and Alexander.

"Ye've missed the concert," Marietta said, her envious eyes resting on the jewels dangling from Jane's earlobes. As the pudgy lass began a comparison of the pleasures of smoked salmon versus the delights of potted shrimp, Catherine suddenly gave out a little yelp of pleasure.

"Jane! Those earrings . . . they're beautiful!"

A hush descended on the table. Alexander lifted his glass, gesturing in Jane's direction.

"I remarked the same m'self, Catherine," he said jovially, "when first I saw them sparkling against her throat. Lads, I

propose we drink a toast to the beautiful women in the world—
especially those in our company this evening.''

''Aye . . . Hear! Hear!'' chorused the gentlemen around the
table. ''To the lassies.''

''Hurry now . . . eat your victuals, Mistress Jane,'' Alexander
commanded. ''I desire you to walk with me to the Cascade. We
must see how cleverly this imitation Vauxhall exhibition is
constructed.''

Jane attacked her food and tried to ignore Alex and the
memory of his unorthodox proposal of marriage. She nibbled on
a few bites of ham and sighed. She didn't feel like eating even
the minuscule portions served up by Andrew Gibb. Presently,
she sank back in her gilded chair, unable to taste another
morsel. At first, she thought the gentle brushing against her thigh
was something she imagined. Then she glanced down toward her
lap and saw a flash of gold winking in the candlelight. Alexander's hand, with its distinctive gold crest ring, gently stroked her
leg through the thick folds of her skirt. She found the steady
motion disturbingly pleasant.

''We mustna miss the Cascade,'' she announced, her voice
ringing shrill even in her own ears.

''Right you are, Jane.'' Alexander signaled for the waiters to
attend to her chair. ''Come, everyone . . . the clock strikes
nine.''

The entire party began to stroll among the boxed hedges and
the statues of Diana, Apollo, and the various heroes of Greek
mythology. Eventually reaching an unilluminated section of the
garden, they were soon hemmed in by the milling crowd waiting
for the display to begin. Then, on some silent signal, two
servants magically appeared to light the lanterns surrounding the
construction of a miniature landscape. It depicted a lush country
scene, complete with tiny miller's house, a water mill, trees, and
gardens. A sudden surge of water began cascading over the tops
of model mountains, spilling over a rocky precipice and under
small-scale bridges, and with that, the audience let out a communal gasp of pleasure. The rushing torrent reached the millhouse,
turning the tiny mill wheel around and grinding the authentic
grain contained inside.

''Come,'' Alexander whispered in her ear. ''Gibb has invited
us to see something even more unusual.''

Alexander took her hand and led her around behind the massive display. Andrew Gibb was clearly delighted that such a
prominent member of Scottish society should grace his establish-

ment. He greeted them effusively once again, beckoning Jane and Alexander to follow him behind a curtain at the back of the enormous construction. Wheels and gears creaked and groaned as a revolving turnstile scooped up pailfuls of water and hoisted them up to the top of the contraption, where they were poured down the side of the miniature mountain in a continuous display.

"The basic principle is sheer gravity," Gibb explained. "Gravity . . . and that lad's muscle power."

In the shadows Jane saw a boy she took to be about sixteen methodically turning a crank, his arm muscles bulging from the effort.

"Very ingenious," said the duke, complimenting his host. "I have long enjoyed the study of mechanics. Perhaps this same principle could be applied to a granary in late summer when the rivers run low?"

"Or a sawmill?" Jane suggested, equally captivated by the intricate machinery. "Thomas told me once that logging in the Highlands comes to a complete standstill during the dry months because the timber canna be floated to market," she said eagerly to Alex. "If there were a way of capturing the spring thaw, and then releasing it in this fashion . . . 'twould be a possible solution for yer problems on the River Spey, might it not?"

Jane looked at the duke and Andrew Gibb expectantly. Gibb was nodding as if he found her ideas noteworthy, but Alexander's face had the look of a disapproving tutor, determined to scold a recalcitrant pupil.

"Really, Jane, I hardly think it suitable to venture an opinion on a subject you know virtually nothing about, nor rely on the views of others equally uninformed."

"But *ye* described to me how much more profitable the timber on the estates near Kinrara would be, if only ye could log a greater part of the year!" protested Jane, her eyes on the ingenious model in front of them. "Dinna ye think—"

"I *think* ye should stop prattling on in such a boring fashion, and that we should return to our seats," the duke interrupted sharply, drawing back the curtain and stalking out into the night air.

Jane quickly nodded her thanks to Andrew Gibb and followed the duke outside, hurrying to catch up to him before he joined the throng out front who were still staring in awe at the mechanical display.

"Alex, for pity's sake, what's the matter?" she demanded, her own temper starting to rise.

"As you are my future duchess," he said in low clipped tones, "may I suggest ye not shame the House of Gordon by quoting opinions offered by yer former lover!"

Jane stared at him, dumbfounded. A scarlet flush began spreading up to her cheeks where the diamond earrings glittered, like her flashing eyes.

"Firstly," she hissed, teeth clenched, "as I have already said, ye must cease at once this talk of duchesses. Secondly, yes, indeed, a number of my opinions are founded on conversations with Thomas Fraser. May I remind ye his family's lands lay hard by Gordon territory, m'lord," she continued acidly, "so he had goodly knowledge of such problems of drought and the accompanying hardship. And thirdly, *Yer Grace*, ye are quite mistaken if ye think yer gift of sparkling gems gives ye the right to speak to me abusively, as ye have!" she concluded furiously, unfastening one ear fob with shaking fingers.

"Please, Jane, don't do that," Alexander said with quiet intensity. For the second time that evening, he captured her hand in his before she could completely remove the earring. "You have a right to be angry . . . I'm . . . I'm sorry."

With a gentle touch, he refastened the piece of jewelry to her ear. Then, without warning, he crushed her against him in a fierce embrace that spoke wordlessly of his jealousy even of the dead and his growing desire to possess her affections and her body. He buried his face in her fragrant hair and pressed her unyielding form close to him.

" 'Tis as my *wife*, I long for you," he whispered hoarsely. "Can't you see that, lass? Thomas is dead . . . and I'm—"

He ceased speaking and showered her face and neck with impassioned kisses. Despite her anger, his lips evoked currents of excitement that spread throughout her body. Jane pushed against Alex's plum silk chest, struggling to fend off the onslaught of powerful feelings provoked by such skilled lovemaking. For a few moments, she felt she must be drowning. Then the memory of Thomas and the sheer physical presence of Alexander merged into a passionate blur.

At length, the duke released her and took a step back, his eyes boring into hers with a look of undisguised triumph.

"It seems her nibs might quite like some of the duties attendant on becoming my duchess," he said languidly, pressing his crested ring once more into the valley between her breasts. "I believe we shall both delight in discovering which of those obligations you enjoy most."

13
July 1767

The humid air pressing down on the wheat fields mantled the Tidewater region of Maryland like a hot, damp cloth. As the July heat engulfed Antrim Hall, Thomas Fraser reluctantly agreed with Arabella Delaney that he was not yet sufficiently recovered in time to sail home with his regiment. Lingering headaches continued to plague him, as did a persistent throbbing in his arm where fragments of lead still pierced his flesh.

Arabella had been an attentive nurse and had insisted on leisurely early morning rides to strengthen Thomas's legs. Then, by nine o'clock, the two of them would take refuge under the cool eaves of the old summerhouse, a sort of eight-sided hideaway nestled in the shade of a giant cluster of oaks. Arabella's personal maid, Mehitabel, stocked the little house each morning with hot coffee, fresh biscuits and a delicious variety of cheeses for their enjoyment. After the midday meal and his nap, Thomas would help Arabella sort out the figures scratched into the plantation ledgers. Or they would simply talk.

"Mehitabel has taken a mighty strong liking to you, Thomas," Arabella said suddenly one August morning over coffee in the summerhouse soon after Thomas declared himself finally well enough to begin his journey homeward. "She thinks we'd make a good match, you and I," she continued lightly. "I suspect she has some silly notion of us running Antrim Hall together."

Thomas frowned slightly and set down his coffee cup.

"But dinna she know I'll be leaving for Philadelphia on Friday?" he said, reluctant to bring up the difficult subject of his departure.

Arabella shrugged and remained silent for a moment.

"Like most women, she has her dreams," she said finally, brushing a wisp of coal black hair from her damp forehead. "We are good together, Thomas . . . you do see that, don't you?" she asked, her blue eyes smoky and full of promise. "We could make all this work, you and I," she added softly, her fingers now caressing the linen shirt covering the jagged scar on his upper arm. "If we can just dispense with Beven's interference and put a rein on his gambling with my inheritance, we could turn Antrim Hall into one of the wealthiest plantations in Maryland!"

He had never seen Arabella so unguarded, so willing to reveal herself. Although she had been warmhearted and generous during his long stay, she'd disclosed little of her past, especially the period before her marriage to her late husband, Hugh Delaney. Now, he sensed what she was leading up to, and he wasn't looking forward to hearing it.

"I . . . I'd like to marry you, Lieutenant Fraser," she said abruptly, biting her lower lip. "I find, much to my surprise . . . I am quite partial to you, Thomas." She lowered her eyes to avoid his gaze, and her black lashes cast a crescent shadow on her cheek, moist from the sultry heat.

Thomas parted his lips to speak, and then remained silent. He didn't trust himself to say anything because of his own confused emotions.

" 'Tis not an offer to be sniffed at!" She laughed nervously. "In Scotland, with my holdings, I'd probably be a baroness . . ." Arabella stared at Thomas with her mysterious eyes. "Are you shocked I make myself so plain?"

"No . . ." Thomas replied, "not shocked, really . . . just sad." He took her chin gently in his hand. "Ye're a fine, fair lass, Arabella O'Brien Delaney, and I owe ye my life, but I told ye from the first . . . my heart is claimed by another, and I must hold to that." At the sound of these words, Arabella looked crestfallen. Thomas shifted uncomfortably in his chair. "Arabella, lass," he added, "I truly care for yer future and yer happiness . . . but I canna accept yer generous proposal."

" 'Tis not generous *enough*, I see!" she replied icily.

Arabella stood up from the table abruptly and walked to the summerhouse windows, now shuttered against the heat. She felt Thomas's bewildered eyes on her back, which only intensified her feelings of humiliation. What had begun as a calculated plan to extricate herself from her current predicament with Beven had unexpectedly resulted in her falling in love. Here, she had offered him everything she had, and he had spurned her best offer.

"I'm sorry, Arabella . . . truly sorry," Thomas said quietly. He approached her from behind and put his arms around her waist, kissing her lightly on top of her head, as if she were a little girl. "If another world dinna wait for me across the sea . . ." he said softly, his words trailing off.

Her shoulders began to quiver.

"Sweetheart—" Thomas said helplessly.

"Don't call me that!" she cried, pulling away from him. "I'm not your sweetheart! Your *sweetheart* is in Scotland!"

"Arabella," Thomas said urgently, turning her around and cupping her face in his large hands. A few silent tears spilled from her eyes and rolled down her cheeks. "I should have known we couldna live in the same house so long—and keep from carin' in the end," he added sorrowfully. "I'm sorry, lass. . . ."

"You're just sorry I'm not a baronet's daughter!" she wept. "You're sorry I'm simply the daughter of a drunken Irish rotter and the widow of a fool! Well, I'll tell you something, *Lieutenant* Fraser . . ." she said, an hysterical timbre edging into her voice. "*Your people at home think you're dead*!"

"Arabella . . . please . . . ye're as fine a woman as any man could desire, lass. I *told* ye about Jane Maxwell and our plans for the future. And I've also a duty to my regiment."

Once more, Thomas reached for her comfortingly, but she fought against him, pounding his chest.

"They don't *expect* you!" she cried. "*No one* expects you ever to come home!" She pulled herself free of his embrace and flattened her back against the shuttered casement. "*You're dead to them!*" she shouted. "Don't you understand? *You're dead!* But you're alive to *me!* I washed your naked body, Thomas Fraser. I cleaned your *wounds!* I have given you your *life*, damn you, and *I* need you more than *they* do!"

The silence between them deepened as Thomas stood, staring at her, gripped by a sudden dread. The thin scar on his cheek had blanched white against the natural ruddiness lately restored to his Celtic complexion, and the gash on his arm began to throb painfully.

"What do ye mean, they dinna expect me?" he asked, a dangerous edge creeping into his voice. "Why would they think me dead when I sent Captain Maxwell and Jane letters telling them I had survived?"

A look of fear flickered across Arabella's face. She turned away from him, staring unseeingly through the slits in the wooden shutters.

"Beven was drunk and lost the note to Captain Maxwell on the *Victory*."

"*What!*" growled Thomas. "Why dinna ye tell me of this?"

"I—I just found out," mumbled Arabella, continuing to stare through the shutters.

"Ye're lying!" Thomas shouted, grabbing Arabella by her arm and forcing her to look at him directly. "Ye would have told me or sent another missive."

Arabella stared down at the hem of her riding habit.

"So," he said menacingly, "I've just been waiting to be plucked, have I, all these weeks! I've paid m'way here nicely, havena I? A plantation overseer during the day and someone ye planned to service yer lust at night . . . is that it, lassie?" He pushed her away from him to keep from striking her. "*Slut!*" he spat. "Where's my letter to Jane Maxwell?"

Arabella remained silent, tears streaking her cheeks. Thomas cursed and strode out the door of the summerhouse. He leapt onto the back of the gray stallion tied next to Arabella's mare, and within minutes, had galloped up the hill to the barn where he tossed the reins to a startled stable boy. As he strode toward the house, he could hear the sound of Kerry Girl's hooves pounding on the turf behind him.

Inside Antrim Hall, Thomas turned purposefully into the chamber where Arabella's delicately carved secretary stood next to a fanlight window. He yanked open each desk drawer in rapid succession, riffling through its contents in search of incriminating evidence. Arabella ran into the room, panting.

"What are you doing?" she begged. "Stop it! *Stop it!*" she screamed, as he inspected the contents of each drawer before flinging it across the room.

In a burst of fury, Thomas splintered the wood, forcing the bottom drawer open, and pulled out the heavy account books. One by one, he slammed them on the floor. Beneath the last ledger, Thomas discovered a rosewood letter box with the initials *A O' B D* inlaid in dark mahogany on the top. Inside the box lay a thick missive addressed in his hand to *Jane Maxwell, Hyndford Close, Edinburgh*. It was the same letter he had written in early June, on the day he was first able to sit up in bed.

"Ye dinna send it . . . ye dinna *send* it, *bitch!*" he shouted, his face crimson with rage.

Arabella's voice sounded as faint as the breeze rustling through the massive oaks down by the summerhouse.

"I loved you from the first, but I didn't realize it, you see . . ." she murmured brokenly, as if explaining her conduct to herself. "You were my only hope of saving this place from

Beven's dissipation, but after a while, 'twas more than just the
plantation . . . I wanted you here, with me, Thomas . . . *you*! I
wanted to give you everything I had. . . .''

Arabella faltered, silenced by the murderous look in Thomas's
eye.

"I dinna believe anything ye say . . . anything ye've *ever* said
. . . *Mistress Delaney*!" he raged.

Arabella took a step toward him and raised her hand beseechingly. Thomas stiffened.

"Stay where ye are, or I swear by St. Giles, I'll *kill* ye!" he
said between clenched teeth. He rummaged in one of the drawers
and drew out a pouch of gold coins. "I'm taking the wages due
me as overseer to buy my passage home," he growled. "I'll send
back yer steed when I get to Philadelphia, and I'll post ye
whatever I owe ye from Scotland!"

He stormed up the stairs to the guest bedchamber, still clutching his letter to Jane. Within minutes, Arabella heard Thomas's
booted feet pound past the morning room and out to the front
portico. The door slammed behind him. Soon the crunching
sounds of his hurried strides faded on the gravel path leading
around to the horse stalls at the rear of the mansion. In the
dwindling light of the humid afternoon, a gray stallion bearing
Thomas Fraser streaked past the windows at the side of the house
and thundered down the rows of stately trees leading away from
Antrim Hall.

"Your regiment sailed for Ireland, not Scotland, lad," the
grizzled dock master informed his visitor. The young lieutenant
with the thin scar slashed across his cheek scanned the line of
square-rigged ships tied up along the quay at Philadelphia's
waterfront.

"Seems the Paddies are givin' old King Georgie worse problems than we are!" the dock master chortled. "You're lucky,
lad. In two days time, on August tenth, there's a ship bound for
Cork." He stared curiously at the soldier's woolen kilt, which,
even allowing for the breezes wafting up the backside, looked
deuced hot in the muggy weather. "Shouldn't be too hard for
you to get to Dublin from there."

Thomas Fraser swore softly under his breath.

"Can ye also do me the favor of telling me when the next ship
bound for Leith or London would be leaving?" he inquired. "I
have a letter to post."

"The *Valiant*'s your best bet. She leaves for London on the noontide. You'll have to hire someone to row you out, but you still have time to make it, if you hurry.''

Jane darted past the four central pillars supporting the canopied vaults of St. Giles Cathedral, pausing to catch her breath as she approached a small stone chapel on the far side of the enormous granite edifice. It, in turn, had been built on an earlier Roman church erected on the site. She glanced cursorily at the stone pulpit where Protestant reformer John Knox had railed at his flock some two hundred years earlier, urging all the ornate architectural evidence of Catholicism to be stripped from the church, leaving in its place a stark stone monument to Presbyterianism.

Dwindling shafts of amber sunlight filtered through the cobalt-colored stained glass, casting an azure sheen on the stone paving below. It almost gave the mammoth sanctuary the appearance of being underwater. Jane hurriedly entered the minuscule chapel and stood at the spot where ancient emblems picturing Protestant evangelists were carved in the floor.

"Good afternoon," said a calm voice from the shadows. "I came as soon as the caddie brought your message. I must say, Jane dear, 'tis a rather strange spot for a secret assignation."

Jane squinted in the murky light of the chilly October afternoon, trying to catch sight of the man all Edinburgh expected her to marry in seven days.

"Alexander?" she said uncertainly.

In response to her voice, the figure of the duke emerged from the dark corner of the chapel.

"Aye . . . and what might it be that occasions a rendezvous in such a dank place as this?" he teased, languidly approaching Jane, who stood rigidly near the arched stone entrance to the tiny chamber. "A romantic nook, to be sure, but hardly very comfortable."

Jane remained rooted at the arched entrance, fidgeting with the lace handkerchief she always carried to hide her injured finger. Alexander kissed her gently on the cheek and then allowed his lips to stray casually to her ear.

"Odds fish, but you Presbyterians can be a gloomy lot," he murmured. His breath felt warm against her skin, in contrast to the chill in the small room. "Hard benches, instead of the cushioned pews, as in Anglican churches. I should have liked to see this pile before John Knox ordered its renovation. The good

Reverend would be thundering from that pulpit out there if he knew my unclean thoughts right now.''

Jane pulled away from Alexander's embrace and continued to twist the lace handkerchief in her hands.

''I needed to talk to ye privately and I could think of no other suitable place where we could be alone.''

''How unlike you to be so unimaginative,'' Alexander replied, putting a palm under each of her elbows and drawing her close to him again. ''I could think of one place in particular,'' he added with a raffish grin. '' 'Tis about a mile down the High Street, near the castle walls. My coach is just outside and could whisk us there in a trice,'' he teased, obviously referring to his own elegant lodgings. Without further words, he seized her shoulders and returned his lips to the sensitive spot he'd discovered, over recent weeks, just below her ear. ''I admit I was startled to receive your request for a clandestine meeting,'' he whispered, ''but, now that I'm here, I find such an eager bride much to my liking. . . .''

Jane was aware of Alexander's rising ardor as he pressed her body tightly to his. She struggled to tilt her head back to look at him.

''Please, Alex,'' she pleaded, pushing in vain against his chest. ''I wanted to meet ye here because I have something . . . something very difficult to tell ye.''

The duke did not reply, but held her close to him for a moment before releasing her.

''What is it?'' he asked quietly.

Jane avoided his piercing gaze and crossed the small chamber to the spot where Alexander had been lounging earlier. She turned around and faced him.

''There is no pleasant way to say this,'' she began with effort. She raised her eyes and met his quizzical gaze. ''I canna marry ye next week.''

''No? May I ask why?'' Alexander said evenly.

The welcoming smile had vanished from his lips.

''I was awake all last night trying to sort it out,'' she said, pacing back and forth on her side of the tiny chapel. ''I kept asking myself, what can I say? How can I explain. . . .''

Jane's voice faltered. She watched the duke's lips harden into a straight line. A muscle in his cheek quivered with tension.

''Explain what?'' he asked coolly.

Jane walked toward him and gazed earnestly into his face.

'' 'Tis too soon,'' she said simply. ''There is no other way I can express this feeling that's been twisting my heart. I should never have let ye . . . and Mama . . . and *everyone,* really, persuade me to do something I know will be disastrous for us all.''

Alexander quickly looked away from her and stared, blankly, unseeing, at the stained glass window above their heads. Jane seized his hand, pressing it urgently between hers.

''If we marry now, when those cords binding us to . . . others . . . have not been truly broken, neither of us will be happy,'' she implored. The duke remained silent, and his gaze was fixed on the jewel-like window. ''I've grown to care deeply for ye, Alexander. 'Tis difficult to explain . . .'' she continued apologetically. '' 'Tis just a sense I have that we're proceeding too hastily, considering what we've each endured. We've only really *begun* to know each other, Alex. If we wait a while longer . . . say, another half a year . . . and ye still wish to wed, then we would come together with a free heart, certain of our own happiness as husband and wife.''

''I want you as my wife *now,*'' Alexander said in a low voice. ''It appears to me, Jane, that you are merely suffering from a common case of bridal vapors.'' His tone had become clipped and formal, and Jane felt a chill run down her back as she listened. ''I think you would have to admit that I have been more than patient with you on this subject. Thomas Fraser has been dead for more than a year now. You've had your time of mourning, though you weren't even officially betrothed.'' Alexander gave Jane a sidewise glance and continued to speak, his voice cracking with intensity. ''Six weeks ago you agreed to become my wife. My family and yours are assembling from near and far, not for one, but *two* weddings in a week's time, at your sister's country manse and a repetition of our vows here in Edinburgh. I think 'tis time, Jane, you attended to the feelings of others as well as yourself,'' he added stiffly.

''I *am* thinking of yer feelings,'' Jane interrupted, trying to keep the choking frustration out of her voice. ''I'm thinking of us *both* . . . and of our families. What of the years of unhappiness that lie ahead for everyone if we marry merely to fill a void left by the people we loved and lost? 'Tis no good, Alex, unless we purge the ghosts that still torment us.''

''That's not the way it is for me!'' he retorted fiercely, his fists clenched by his side. ''I've made my peace with Bathia's death. 'Tis *you* who still long for a ghost. Do you suppose I haven't known 'tis *his* arms you think of when we embrace? That 'tis *his* lips you remember when I kiss you?''

Alex stepped a pace closer, boring in on her with his burning eyes. Jane met his glare with her own.

"That is *precisely* the reason I feel we should not be wed next Friday, Alex," Jane flared.

Angrily, he grasped her shoulders, his voice low and slightly menacing, disguising his hurt.

"I warrant you shall soon recognize the difference between your ghost and your husband, lass!"

Savagely he covered her mouth with his, forcing open her lips to accept his tongue, which spoke with silent but frightening intensity. Jane stiffened, wanting to push him away, longing to retreat to the safety of Hyndford Close, wishing fervently she'd written him instead of daring to meet him here to tell him of her doubts. Finally, he released her mouth, only to press his lips to the hollow at the base of her throat. Jane felt the grip on her self-control starting to snap as Alexander probed her lips once again. Her mind had gone blank. Shudders began to pulse through her body in response to his caresses.

"Dinna *do* this!" she cried, shocked at her own unbidden reaction to his passionate embrace.

"I love you, Jane!" he whispered fiercely. "I want you as my wife, though God knows every Gordon from here to John O'Groats has hinted I could aim higher. But *this* is my choice and no one—not even you—is going to prevent this marriage!" Alexander caught hold of Jane's wrist and held it in a viselike grip. She stared at him, shocked at the ravaged look radiating from his hazel eyes. "I don't think we shall wait a week to exorcise this ghost," he said resolutely.

Before she could protest further, he was pulling her down the length of Preston Aisle and out through a side door of the immense cathedral. Jane struggled to break away, crying out as he squeezed her arm even tighter. He propelled the two of them out into the October air.

"Coachman! Over here!" Alexander barked as soon as they emerged.

Instantly, the driver snapped his reins, bringing the black enameled carriage with the stag's head crest to the spot where Jane stood rigidly. With an iron grasp, he thrust her inside the carriage and pulled the curtains closed. The two rode opposite each other without speaking as the coach rolled down the High Street. Jane was frightened by the way Alexander was now staring at her—coolly, as if deciding which of several methods he would employ to brand her as his property.

"A—Alexander . . . please," Jane stammered. "I should be getting home . . ." she added nervously. "They'll be wondering where I am, as it is."

The duke did not reply. An ominous silence grew between them as the coach swayed from side to side, threading its way through the late afternoon traffic in the direction of the town-house he had leased for the season. Finally, Alexander spoke in a voice devoid of emotion.

"We both know that your mother, your sister, and your brother-in-law have preceded you to Berwickshire to prepare Ayton House for the coming nuptials," he said evenly. "So, you see, Jane," he said, leaning forward slightly in the coach, his hand idly stroking her left breast, "when I received your invitation to St. Giles this afternoon, I assumed we had similar ideas in mind, and I made plans accordingly."

Jane shrank back, pressing her body to the tufted leather upholstery. In a swift movement, she bolted to open the carriage door, but Alexander's long arm and slender fingers blocked her escape.

"No," he said matter-of-factly, with something akin to amusement tugging at the corners of his mouth. Jane took a deep breath and tried to steady her nerves. "I am Alexander, Duke of Gordon," he said softly. "From this moment forward, you shall regard me as your husband, with all that that implies. I am the man who will govern your life. It is *my* body that will lie next to yours for years to come. It is *I* who will be the father of your children."

No! she thought wildly. *No one shall govern my life!*

But when his lips seared hers, she felt the sheer force of his will that seemed determined to blot out all rational thought, all memory of Thomas Fraser. Alex's mouth again began to roam her face and neck. His breath was hot on her ear once more, sending an odd tingling coursing through her limbs. The duke suddenly pulled his body from hers, leaving Jane with a peculiar and unexpected sense of loss. He had a stubborn, challenging look in his eye.

"I shall be frank, Mistress Maxwell. I intend to bed you this night," he declared, "and your thoughts shall be of *me*!"

Alexander clasped her hand tightly once more, pulled her from his coach, and quickly led her inside the last building on the High Street, a mansion that flanked the walls of Edinburgh

Castle. Racking her brains for some means of escape, she took little notice of the rich appointments of the downstairs rooms or the imposing family portraits that lined the staircase leading to the top apartments.

Alexander's private suite was large, and luxuriously furnished with rich mahogany paneling. It looked to Jane more like a library than a bedchamber. Leather-bound books decorated an entire wall, except for a small carved wooden fireplace adorned with a polished brass fender.

Jane's eye was immediately drawn to a large bed with enormous down pillows and thick, forest green and brown tartan blankets suitable for a hunting lodge. Dark, moss green velvet curtains hung down around the head of the bed from a half-canopy attached to the ceiling. A large leather trunk with brass corners stood at the foot of the bed, along with a black and tan setter, curled up on the Persian carpet. Next to the sleeping dog, Alexander's riding boots stood in their forms, a promise of outings to come. It was a totally masculine lair, inviting, but at the same time forbidding. Jane shivered, despite the cheerful fire glowing in the grate.

"Affric! Come!" Alexander commanded. The dog opened his soulful brown eyes and gazed at Alex adoringly. His master gestured toward the open door he and Jane had just entered. "Go see Cook. Supper's in the kitchen," he said. "There's a good boy."

Jane's body tensed as she stood poised to spring past Alex and escape down the stairs. But as the dog padded out of the room, Alexander glanced in Jane's direction and swiftly locked the door, pocketing the key. The duke bid her approach a window where a round table displayed a number of silver-covered dishes.

"Come, my dear," he said calmly, removing her cloak from her trembling shoulders. "You must be famished. Here is the meal I ordered for us after I received your summons to the cathedral. Please sit down," he said, pulling out a chair for his disconcerted guest.

Jane could only stare as Alexander set about serving her portions from the assembled platters of roast lamb, potatoes, stewed fruits, and a bowl of buttered crab served with sweet scones. He poured a glass of sparkling wine Jane took to be champagne.

"To the bride . . ." he said, raising his glass in a mock salute. "To us. Now drink it down . . . there's a good girl."

Jane obediently drained her glass, and the two of them began their meal. Alexander kept up a steady stream of pleasantries as he urged her to consume more of everything that lay before them, including the wine, which went down smoothly and gradually infused her tense body with a comforting glow.

"Won't you have some Fochabers gingerbread for a sweet?" he inquired solicitously. " 'Tis a Gordon Castle specialty . . . especially nice with the wine."

" 'Tis quite wonderful," she ventured timidly, feeling suddenly giddy from her third glass of champagne. She took a bite of the gingerbread made from treacle, currants, and ground cloves, speculating what might be in store for her after dessert.

"Good," he said with satisfaction. "I'm glad you like it. Now come here, my dear. Please."

As if sleepwalking, Jane rose from her seat a trifle unsteadily and slowly moved toward Alexander who by this time was comfortably lounging in a high-back leather wing chair. He took her wrist, far more gently than at St. Giles Cathedral, and drew her down to sit in his lap. He resumed his game of playfully nuzzling her neck as he searched for the fastenings of her gown. Jane's first impulse was to struggle against the warm, languorous feeling invading her body. But it was dulled by the effects of the wine and the pleasurable currents coursing downwards from the spot below her ear where Alexander continued to kiss her. She felt the stiffened bodice of her afternoon dress fall away from her flesh, and, after a moment's effort at untying the laces crisscrossing her back, her corset as well.

"There, my love," Alexander said huskily, turning her toward him. "Doesn't that feel better? Now, if you will please rise . . ."

Jane stood before him in an agony of apprehension as he swiftly removed the rest of her clothing. After pausing a long moment to drink in the sight of her nakedness, Alexander quickly gathered her up in his arms and placed her gently on his bed. He drew back the bed linen and the thick woolen blankets and stood towering above her. Then, as he began to divest himself of his own clothing, Alexander hesitated, his hands at the buttons of his breeches.

"Will I be the first, or has the ghost won that contest as well?"

"No," Jane whispered, with a mixture of shyness and sorrow. "Ye are the first."

"Ah," he said softly. "Then perhaps I have a chance."

Jane closed her eyes until she felt the length of his body impose itself next to hers. She waited a moment for him to make his claim on her, but all was silent. After an interlude, she fluttered open her lids to see him smiling at her, a look of unexpected tenderness marking his features.

"The Duchess of Gordon," he said quietly, tracing his slender finger lightly down her cheek, to her throat. "Jane Maxwell, the Duchess of Gordon." He bent over her to brush his lips softly against her forehead as if anointing her in her new role. "That's what you are, my love . . . that's what I want this night to mean. You are *my* duchess. The past is finished. We are the House of Gordon."

Jane rose up on one elbow in order to look him fully in the face, consciously blotting out the vision of Thomas that rose unbidden before her eyes. Slowly, she nodded her assent. The time had come to bury her memories once and for all, she silently lectured herself. She had no doubt, now, this complicated man was in love with her. Perhaps she could one day feel the same blinding commitment she had felt toward—

Jane clamped her eyes shut, willing the very name of Thomas Fraser banished from her mind. When she opened them, she leaned forward, and then, without hesitation, put her arms around Alexander's lean torso. They both sank back against the pillows, his weight settling against her slender frame.

"*Help* me!" she whispered into his ear, nuzzling his lobe as he had hers. "Help me banish all the ghosts, Alex, so we can truly be . . . the House of Gordon. . . ."

Elizabeth Maxwell's spirits were gay, though she longed for her husband to attend her niece Jane's nuptials with her. It still seemed a miracle that the poor lass had finally made peace with the loss of Thomas Fraser, and was about to be married this day . . . and apparently, happily so.

Elizabeth surveyed her trim figure in the looking glass, pleased to see how her waistline had restored itself after Monty's birth, and relieved that James had written her from Dublin to say his Black Watch regiment had arrived safely at its new post. It would only be few short months before he would take his accumulated leave and be home for Hogmany.

An urgent tapping at her door interrupted her pleasant contemplation of her husband's imminent homecoming.

"Excuse me, mum," said Tessa, the Fordyces' upstairs housemaid, in a rather shrill, excited voice, as she approached with a silver tray. "The runner from Edinburgh has just arrived with this from Ireland, and I knew ye'd be anxious to have it, straightaway.''

Elizabeth's heart beat faster as she snatched the parchment addressed to her in James' familiar hand and broke its seal. She had just begun to read its contents, with a stunned expression, when her sister-in-law, Magdalene Maxwell, entered the room.

"Elizabeth, dear, would ye be so kind as to give me yer opinion on the salmon mousse . . . I'm not sure 'tis even edible—'' Lady Maxwell halted midsentence, staring at Elizabeth with a puzzled look. "Elizabeth? Are ye all right? Has anything happened to James?''

Elizabeth cradled the letter in her lap and gazed out the window at the bustling activity taking place on the front lawn of Ayton House in preparation for the wedding.

"Thomas Fraser is alive," she announced in a shocked voice. "He's just arrived in Ireland. Somehow he survived that Indian massacre and made his way from Philadelphia. James must not yet have received my letter about the wedding . . . he writes me that he is allowing Thomas emergency leave to come home to claim Jane's hand.''

"*No!*'' Magdalene nearly shouted, quickly closing the door behind her. "No, no, no!''

Lady Maxwell's royal blue silk skirts crackled ominously as she approached her sister-in-law.

"Ye are *not* to breathe a word of this, Elizabeth!" she commanded menacingly. "I will never forgive ye or speak to ye or James again, if ye do.''

"But the lass has a right to *know* he's alive, Magdalene!'' Elizabeth countered shakily. "She has a right to choose for herself—''

"She's *made* her choice, and ye can see for yerself that since her arrival from Edinburgh, she and the duke have been behaving like genuine lovebirds,'' argued Magdalene forcefully. "And besides, there are four hundred guests milling about outside this window from as far north as the Orkney Islands! We *canna* tell her, Elizabeth! 'Twould be folly of the first order. In an hour's time Jane will be the *Duchess of Gordon!*''

"That's the main thing, 'tisn't it, Magdalene?'' Elizabeth said scornfully. "In an hour's time, *ye'll* be mother-in-law to a *duke!*''

The dancing commenced almost the moment the Presbyterian cleric closed his Bible and the handsome groom, resplendent in a

deep purple velvet coat and embroidered ivory waistcoat, stooped
to kiss the bride. The afternoon of Friday, October 23, 1767, had
turned into a splendid day. Ayton House, scrubbed and refur-
bished for such a momentous occasion, stood bathed in dazzling
autumn sunshine. Two hundred yards from the Fordyces' comfortable pink stone country manse, the soft green hills of
Berwickshire, some forty miles south and east of Edinburgh,
sloped gently down to the River Eye.

A huge tent stood on the lawn to provide shade or shelter as
needed for the guests, and adjacent to it were several great
cauldrons filled with a hundred boiled fowls and mutton hams.
Estate women with pitchforks stirred in leeks, prunes, and Ja-
maica pepper, creating a rich, flavorful version of cock-a-leekie
soup, a dish beloved by all Scots.

As shadows began to lengthen across the green expanse of
lawn, still more wine, whiskey punch, and ale were set out at
each table. While the guests helped themselves, Jane collapsed
into a chair at her place of honor, to watch several of the men,
including the groom, lay crossed sabers on the grass. As the pipe
music droned faster and faster, the men flung themselves into the
"Sword Dance," whirling like dervishes between the sharp blades,
until the dancer who succeeded in avoiding the steel with his feet
emerged victorious. Alexander, placing second, smiled triumphantly at Jane for having made such a good showing in the most
difficult of all Highland dances.

"When do you suppose 'twill be a decent hour to withdraw?"
Alex whispered into Jane's ear, giving her a furtive kiss on her
sensitive ear lobe. "I fear I shall be unfit to perform my duties
as a bridegroom if this frolic continues much longer."

Jane giggled and leaned forward to whisper back.

"No excuses, now, m'lord. I shall claim my bridal rights,
even if ye turn up yer toes at the end of this fine day!"

Reflecting on the sheer gaiety of the occasion, Alexander took
a long, satisfying draught from the wineglass that the liveried
stewards had kept filled to the brim all afternoon. He paused, to
look at his bride who had opened the swan-feathered fan that
he'd given her the night they had first attended the theater
together. With her head tilted against the back of her chair, Jane
fanned her flushed face. Alexander's gaze drifted down her
slender neck to the pale yellow silk wedding gown with its ivory
stripes, small brocaded flowers woven in pink, blue, and green,
and the finest of lace gathered at her elbows. He knew the dress
had been damnably expensive, with its twenty-two yards of silk,

but then again, Jane would wear it on at least one more occasion when they traveled to London in a month to appear before George III and seek his official blessing on their marriage.

The duke was not looking forward to the backstairs intrigue at St. James's Palace, or the filth and bustle of London. His preference was to remove Jane to the Highlands where the two of them could enjoy the simple pleasures of country life.

But for today, at least, Alexander could tolerate the crush and heartily anticipated the moment he would unhook the tiny fastenings of Jane's matching petticoat and stomacher, which filled the front of her wedding gown. He suppressed a chuckle, recalling how they had managed to arrange several illicit rendezvous at his Edinburgh townhouse before she and her brother Hamilton departed together for Berwickshire to prepare for the day's nuptials. Jane had proved a willing pupil in the art of making love, and Alexander longed to be alone with her once more. He had introduced her to the physical side of their relationship with all the skill and care at his command and he had reaped exquisite rewards for his pains. He reckoned that by now, the ghost of Thomas Fraser had finally been put to rest.

"Come, Jane . . . come, Alexander," cried Catherine gaily, entering the bridal tent. " 'Tis the dance of the 'Babbity Bowster' and ye two must lead off!"

Hundreds of couples clapped their hands in anticipation of the "Kissing Reel," traditionally the last dance of the bridal festivities.

"Let's dance beside the dowager duchess and Mr. Morris," Jane said mischievously as they approached the throng hand in hand. "Yer mother and stepfather have hardly acknowledged my existence. Are they really that displeased with yer choice?" she teased. "I should think they'd be grateful ye'd finally married *someone*!"

"Well, at least 'tis finally put an end to the public speculation about my sanity," he replied ruefully. Alexander was thankful when Jane revealed she knew all about the so-called Gordon Madness and that she'd dismissed such rumors out of hand.

Joining the circle of dancers, John Fordyce jovially handed Alexander a bolster cushion—an insider's reference to the name of the dance "Babbity Bowster." As the fiddler struck up the tune "The White Cockade," Alexander circled the group and placed the cushion on the turf in front of his bride, inviting her to kneel with him on it. The crowd cheered, nearly drowning out the music, as Alexander, to the delight of all the spectators, kissed Jane many seconds longer than was seemly. Then, the pair rose, carrying the cushion, and walked around arm in arm, smiling at the many friends and relations who had journeyed from Edinburgh and as far away as the Isle of Barra to attend their wedding.

Jane and Alex continued to circle the hand-holding crowd, nodding warmly as they passed Sir Algernon Dick, now retired from medical practice and looking rather frail and tired. Standing next to him was Elizabeth Maxwell, who appeared unaccountably distressed. Jane smiled warmly at her favorite aunt, guessing she was melancholy at the absence of her husband from such a family event. At least, thought Jane cheerfully, Uncle James was due home soon from what was rumored to be a long-term post in Ireland.

Even pudgy Marietta Buchanan and her bean pole companion, Jamie Ferguson, were among the guests, though there was no sign of Simon Fraser. Jane had adamantly refused her mother's pleas to include his name on the guest list.

She and Alex continued on around the circle, greeting countless other Maxwells of Monreith, Wigtown, and Gatehouse of Fleet, as well as scores of Gordons of Gight, Strathbogie, Huntly, and Aberdeen. At length, Jane threw the bolster down in front of Alex's stepfather, Staats Morris. Momentarily startled, the Dowager's consort scooped up the pillow and chased after Jane, but he was too late to steal a kiss. She had already linked arms with her groom and was running with him gaily toward the front steps of Ayton House. Staats shrugged and began circling the enormous assembly, impulsively tossing the cushion, not before the feet of his wife—a woman ten years his senior—but at the delicately shod satin slippers of a pretty wench from Berwickshire parish. By the time they both had kneeled on the pillow and Staats had kissed the lass firmly on her lips, Jane and Alexander had reached the top of the stone stairs leading to the front door of Ayton House and were engaging in a final passionate embrace before the applauding throng.

Fiona McFarland opened the heavy oaken door to the Maxwell apartments at Hyndford Close, peered outside, and suddenly let out a scream that echoed in both directions down the narrow alley that led off the High Street.

"It canna *be* . . . St. Ninian, have mercy on us all . . . Thomas Fraser, ye be *dead*!" the maid babbled incoherently.

"Nearly, Fiona . . . nearly . . . but not quite," the lieutenant smiled reassuringly. "St. Ninian preserved me and I've returned to Scotland very much alive. Is Mistress Maxwell at home? Dinna announce me . . . I wish to surprise her.''

And surprised she certainly would be to learn his ship landed in Ireland a fortnight ago and that her uncle, Captain Maxwell, had kindly granted Thomas leave to come to Edinburgh. The Forty-second was to be posted over there indefinitely, but it was nice to be on this side of the water again. Thomas wondered at the peculiar look on Fiona's face. The woman kept shaking her head, as if denying his presence at her door this blustery November day.

''Fiona,'' he said gently, ''from yer reaction, I take it Miss Maxwell dinna receive the letter I posted from Philadelphia in early August? I thought it would precede me, as my ship to Cork didn't sail until the tenth.''

''W—we've been in Berwickshire, sir,'' she stuttered, staring at him as if he were a ghost. ''Nobody's been here but me cousin, Meg. Any letters or packets home, they be forwarded to the Fordyces' house in Ayton, as her ladyship directed before she left for the wedding.''

''How splendid! John and Catherine have married!'' he said, trying to disguise his disappointment that Jane was apparently in Berwickshire for her sister's nuptials. ''When are her ladyship and Mistress Maxwell expected to return?''

''I couldna be answering that, as I dinna rightly know, sir,'' Fiona replied, avoiding his gaze.

''Have ye *no* idea, Fiona?'' he pressed, puzzled that the maid persisted in staring at her shoe tops.

''All I can say, sir, is they might be north by Christmas, or mayhap Hogmanay.''

''Hogmanay!'' Thomas repeated, dismayed. ''That's nearly six weeks away. Why should they stay in Berwickshire so long?''

''Och! They winna be in Berwickshire, sir,'' Fiona exclaimed. ''They've gone to London to visit the king! Then they'll make a grand tour of all the family holdings!''

''What? Why . . . ?'' Thomas began.

''I'm sorry, sir, but that's all I ken say,'' Fiona retorted, reaching to close the door. ''Pray, excuse me, sir, but I've me duties to attend to. I'm sorry, sir . . . and welcome home.''

Before Thomas could protest, the heavy door slammed shut, and no amount of pounding persuaded Fiona McFarland to open it.

With a growing sense of unease, Thomas pulled his cloak

more tightly around his shoulders. Rain began to pelt down on the High Street as he headed for Fortune's Tavern, the best source of information available in Edinburgh.

Sure enough, the drinking house was jammed with locals trading gossip and good cheer. No sooner had Thomas entered than a small crowd of friends and half-familiar faces gathered around him, stunned to see the man who had come back from the dead. He soon tired of recounting the amazing tale of how he'd been left for dead by the Mingos following the massacre and of his escape into the dense Pennsylvania underbrush. Pressed by his audience for details, he told them what he'd learned from his rescuer, Captain Shelby—that he had missed his own funeral at Fort Pitt because everyone thought he was one of the poor bastards in his patrol who had been hacked to pieces by the braves.

"Since everybody was dressed as Redskins, and few were left with their scalps," he finished, shrugging, "I suppose there was a lot of confusion."

His short narrative was interrupted by the sound of the ornate tavern doors banging against the walls as a piercingly cold wind swept through the low-ceilinged chamber.

A tall, angular figure burst into the public room, shaking off rivulets of water from his encounter with the storm outside. It was Jamie Ferguson, looking cold and in need of a drink. He looked around and caught sight of Thomas sitting at a small table in front of the fire. Jamie froze. His mouth dropped open and his prominent front teeth protruded beyond the boundary of his receding chin.

"Fraser?" he asked incredulously. " 'Tis that *ye*?"

"Aye, 'tis me, all right, Jamie, lad. Risen from the dead, it seems."

"My God, man . . . 'tis such a shock! There was a long account in the *Edinburgh Courant* of the ambush in . . . where was it now, Mary-land?"

"Pennsylvania," Thomas replied with a short laugh.

Ferguson handed his cloak to a servant and indicated the chair next to Thomas.

"May I join ye?" he said, the expression of shock still imprinted on his pale features.

"Of course," Thomas replied, nodding to his drinking companions, who quickly bid him adieu and melted into the crowd clustered at the bar.

" 'Tis good to be back, despite the weather," Thomas said,

signaling the barmaid to take Jamie's order. "I'm soon off to the Highlands to assist with recruitment. Those savages ye spoke of have thinned our ranks, and we intend to augment the Black Watch by some two hundred men, if we can find them. But, enough of my tales. I've news to catch up on in Edinburgh. Tell me, Jamie . . . why are the Maxwells so long in returning from the Fordyce nuptials?"

"Ye've just arrived?" Ferguson asked, not answering Thomas's query.

"Aye, not more than an hour ago, and I must say, the Maxwells' maid was very mysterious as to Jane's whereabouts. Is it true, she and her mother have been summoned to Court?"

Ferguson glanced up at the buxom barmaid who'd come to take his order.

"Two brandies, and be quick about it!"

Jamie sighed and folded his hands on the table. Thomas settled in his chair and felt a familiar stab of pain that from time to time, invaded his upper arm where the bullet had pierced his flesh so deeply.

"I think it best if I tell ye the news directly," Ferguson said quietly.

"News?" Thomas repeated apprehensively.

"Jane became the Fourth Duchess of Gordon . . . oh, it's been about three or four weeks now."

"The Duchess of . . ." Thomas's words trailed off.

"She thought ye were *dead*, lad," Ferguson said gently. "She grieved for ye as if ye'd been her husband. Wouldna talk to a soul and refused to go out for months."

"Jane . . . the *Duchess of Gordon*?" Thomas echoed his companion's words once more, the shock of their meaning etched painfully on his gaunt features. "But she couldna have heard about the ambush but ten months ago . . ."

"The duke and she met again about six months ago," Jamie continued, anxious to be done with his painful duty. "Alexander pursued her like the fury, from the start." Ferguson was anxious to alleviate some of the lieutenant's distress by a logical explanation of events. "At first, when she finally agreed to accompany him to a ridotto, she seemed merely to enjoy his company. Speculation too, was that because of his rank, he would seek a wife of higher social standing than the daughter of a mere baronet. But soon it became plain that he wouldn't hear of any objections to the match, not even his mother's distress over their different religions."

Ferguson had settled into a recitation of the facts that had helped ease his own painful rejection by Jane.

"They had an Anglican ceremony here in Edinburgh and an enormous fete last month at the Fordyces' country home, presided over by the Presbyterian minister of Ayton parish. After the weddings, they set out for the Court of St. James with both families in tow, to present the bride to the king. She was an astounding success, I hear, and befriended the queen," Jamie continued, awestruck. "Sink me, if the *king*, who loves his wife, didn't offer to stand godfather to their first son! Now Jane and the duke are making a grand tour of all the family estates before returning to Gordon Castle after the holidays."

The pain from Thomas's wound had become excruciating. For a moment, he feared he would humiliate himself by fainting right at the table.

"So ye can see, old man," Ferguson said kindly, "events went forward at a rather rapid pace. I, myself, retired quite quickly from the field, in view of such competition."

Thomas remained silent, rubbing his upper arm in a fruitless attempt to assuage the pain. Ferguson pushed a second brandy toward the young lieutenant and leaned forward sympathetically.

"Look, lad, I think I have some idea what ye're feeling right now. 'Tis a damnable blow to receive so quickly upon yer return. I'm sorry, laddie. . . ."

"*Ye!*" Thomas snarled. "What do *ye* know of this matter?" he shouted, jumping to his feet and toppling his chair with a crash. Jamie stared, speechless, at his enraged companion. "Jane and I were *promised* to each other, ye bastard!" he cried, taking no notice of the startled glances of on-lookers. "The banns were all but official. She was to be my *wife*! What do ye think sustained me through this nightmare?"

An unnatural hush settled over the noisy tavern. Thomas strode to a peg on the wall and angrily retrieved his cloak. He glared at Jamie Ferguson as he furiously rubbed the throbbing pain in his upper arm.

"What would ye know of Jane Maxwell? She thought ye a pleasant enough fool whose teeth occupy most of yer *face*! *Jane Maxwell is mine!* Not the duke's and certainly not *yers*! She's *always* been mine, and I'll make her my wife if I have to drag her out of the Duke o' Gordon's bed to do it!"

He turned on his heel and marched out of Fortune's Tavern, neglecting to shut the door against the howling storm that had descended on Edinburgh his first night home.

14

December 1767

A light December snow dusted the rolling hills that arched down to the River Tweed. Three coaches, their horses pawing and snorting opaque puffs of vapor, pulled away from the Queen's Head Inn, Kelso's finest hostelry. The vehicles lumbered in a line down the town's wide, cobbled square, past the ruins of what was once the largest and finest of the great border abbeys in the territory separating England from Scotland. Jane craned her neck to catch sight of the crumbling twelfth-century Norman tower that stood like a sentinel, guarding the center of the ancient village.

"Warm enough?" asked Alexander, who sat opposite his wife in the swaying coach as it crossed the stone bridge and headed north toward the tiny town of Gordon, their midday destination. Without waiting for her reply, he tucked a thick plaid more snugly around her hips. "We shall pause at the village long enough to let the tenants catch a brief glimpse of their new duchess. Then, I promise you, my dear, we shall speed on to Ayton House in time for the seven-course meal I'm certain your sister Catherine has prepared."

"That sounds like an excellent plan," Jane replied, leaning back contentedly against the coach seat. "Tell me, Alex," she said, looking out the window, "Why are these lands so distant from Gordon Castle and yer northern estates in Strathbogie and Badenoch?"

"Someone has been remiss in teaching you your Scottish history, lass," he smiled. "In the misty past, we Gordons came from Normandy, arriving with William the Conqueror in ten sixty-six. His descendants thought so much of our swordplay and brute strength, they gave us lands in southern Scotland—where we're headed—around the Eden Water, west of Ayton and south of Edinburgh. Of course, three hundred years later, we supported the Scots against the English in the Battle of Bannockburn in thirteen-fourteen, and when Robert the Bruce won, we were handsomely rewarded with *more* spoils, to the far north, where we built Gordon Castle.''

''Ah, so ye Gordons are actually Lowlanders, just like the humble Maxwells!'' Jane teased.

''Exactly!'' he laughed.

While Jane had been listening, she slipped her feet out of her satin shoes. Now, she placed her toes on the flannel-covered brass box on the coach floor that contained a small pile of glowing coals. When her silk-clad foot encountered her husband's stockinged feet, she giggled. With a sly smile, she rubbed her arch against his instep in slow, rhythmic circles.

''Sink me, but ye have chilly extremities, m'lord,'' she said with mock innocence, continuing to stroke his foot with hers.

''One of my extremities is far from cold, dear wife,'' Alexander replied, leaning toward her from the opposite bench. He took her chin in his hand and allowed their noses to touch. ''If you continue your little massage, you may discover that particular part of me burns as feverishly as the coals beneath our feet.''

''I canna think that possible,'' she replied pertly, bringing her other foot to entrap his, ''for my toes are ever so toasty . . . what could be warmer than they?''

''Odds fish, Madam! If you ask such a question, you deserve an answer!'' Alexander replied, bringing his lips hard against hers.

''Alex!'' she protested, but her cry allowed him to plunge his tongue deep within the soft recesses of her mouth.

With one arm he yanked the coach curtains closed against the passing view of the gentle Cheviot Hills, mantled in pre-Christmas snow. With his other arm, he encircled her shoulders and shifted his weight onto the bench where she sat, gasping at the fierceness of his embrace.

This was not the first time the newlyweds had been able to steal a private moment away from the wedding party during their two-month honeymoon tour. From its inception, Alex let it be known he intended to share his black conveyance with no one but his bride. As a result of this edict, Lady Maxwell and Eglantine rode in one coach, and the dowager duchess and her husband, Staats Morris, rode in still another.

''What a lovely way to keep warm . . .'' Alexander murmured, nuzzling Jane's neck. His practiced hand cupped her breast beneath her bodice and she felt a familiar, pleasurable sensation invade her body.

" 'Tisn't it?'' she mumbled, helpless to prevent the surge of desire that he could expertly call forth whenever he chose.

Night after night he brought her to this state of yearning, and she now realized he knew her physical self as well as the coachman over their heads knew which path, or trail or rutted road to steer the horses toward to reach their ultimate destination.

But what did she know, really, of her husband's secret self? He had revealed so little, except for the episode concerning Bathia Largue. He seemed always in control, even during their lovemaking. He never cried out, as she did; never implored her for release from the sweet agony wracking their two bodies in moments like these. Would she ever know his true thoughts and feelings the way she had known Thomas's? Quickly, she shied away from such dangerous speculation.

She recognized, of course, that she greatly pleased her husband in bed—probably far beyond his original expectations—but there were times when she sorely wished she had the power to make him feel as helpless as she did when the tide of physical longing engulfed her.

"What is your pleasure this fine day, m'lady?" he whispered huskily, pulling her into his lap.

"My pleasure today . . . is to give *ye* pleasure," she said boldly, studying his face for his reaction. She almost laughed out loud when his countenance remained impassive, but a pronounced swelling expanded beneath her thighs.

"Then you shall," he murmured, his arms encircling her shoulders under her cloak as he lowered his head to kiss the summit of her breasts through her traveling costume.

His right hand fumbled for the buttons on her tight-fitted jacket. She shivered involuntarily when his cool hands slipped within her bodice and his fingers grazed her sensitive nipple. Soon the steady strokes of his thumb both warmed and stiffened the pink tips of her breasts.

"You please me when you let me do this," he whispered, trailing kisses down her neck, seeking to nuzzle the small mole nestled in the hollow of her throat.

Unbidden, the thought of Thomas suddenly cut through the haze of pounding pleasure.

Oh, why does Alex have to kiss me there? she thought desperately.

As her husband relentlessly pushed his body against hers, she felt her mind suddenly divided. She ached with every fiber to keep pace with Alex's urgings, but part of her broke away from his sheer physical domination, longing for the knowledge of what these powerful intimacies would have been like with the man she couldn't forget. Would she have felt bullied as well as desired? Would the physical act of love with Thomas have been so intense—almost antagonistic?

This is Alex! she cried to herself in silent anguish. *These are his arms, his body! Ye know nothing else, nor ever shall!*

Frantically pulling away from the lips pressing against her throat, she placed her hands along the gaunt planes of his jaw and drew his face toward hers, kissing him fully on the mouth. She was oblivious to the inhospitable confines of the carriage, which swayed along the rutted road leading toward the village of Gordon. In Edinburgh, on their first night together, Alex had ordered her to blot all thoughts of Thomas out of her mind—out of her life. He had been right, and now, as some primal instinct drove her on, she met his almost brutal kisses with quick, sharp bites to his lips. A voice echoed deep within her, urging her to commit her soul as well as her body to the flesh-and-blood man clinging to her so violently. If she did not, whatever chance they had for happiness would be lost. Hurtling herself against Alex's chest even more fiercely, Jane felt overwhelmed by a searing desperation.

"Alex! Alex!" she cried brokenly, raking her fingernails against his velvet-clad shoulders. "Please . . . oh, please!" she sobbed incoherently. She couldn't put the reason for her lament into words. Tears streamed down her cheeks. Despairingly, she leaned her perspiring forehead against the cool nap of his coat. Alex ceased kissing her and held her firmly for a moment. "Dinna stop," she begged, sobs wracking her body. "Ye mustna stop! But don't *toy* with me . . . just want me. *Want* me! Please, Alex! *Please!*"

"I do, my love . . . shhh . . . don't be frightened."

"But I *am*," she moaned. "I'm so frightened . . . ye winna let me feel as if I'm giving something to *ye*. It seems as if ye merely tell me what I may *have* . . . and what I may *not!* Do ye understand?" she pleaded, her cheeks wet from tears of frustration. "I want ye to *need* me as well as want me . . . 'tis so difficult to explain . . ."

"Sweeting . . ." Alex murmured, stroking her hair. "You've been trying so hard, haven't you? Trying so hard. . . ."

Jane tensed. What disturbed her most of all was that this man seemed able to read her mind regarding her own fears, but didn't seem to understand that the only way to allay those fears was to disclose to her some of his own feelings and needs. Heaving a sigh, she slumped in his arms. She supposed that dukes were not in the habit of showing their vulnerabilities, especially not to women.

Sensing she had calmed down, Alexander pressed his lips gently against her ear.

"You are winning the battle over your ghost," he whispered against the damp strands of hair clinging to her temple.

"*Ye* have a battle to win as well, m'lord," Jane declared softly, the truth of that statement settling over her with soothing effect. She tilted her head back to meet his gaze. "I know something which may surprise ye, Alex," she said quietly. "Ye keep a part of yerself hidden from everyone . . . even from me . . . *even* when we're as close as two naked bodies can be." She reached up to nibble gently on his ear. She heard his quick intake of breath, but he remained silent. "I intend to know that secret part of ye one day, Alexander Gordon . . . the part of ye that wants looking after, though ye trust no soul on this earth with yer fate."

Alex still did not reply, but, with a sudden look of hot determination, he slid one palm beneath her voluminous skirts, tracing his fingers along the length of her silk-clad leg. Jane stiffened and closed her eyes. The memory of the hard, narrow cot aboard the *Providence* lying at anchor in Leith Harbor flashed across her mind, and, helpless to surpress it, she saw Thomas repeating that same gesture as a kind of torturous echo.

"Alex . . ." she protested weakly, as his fingers invaded her most private realm.

"Let me pleasure you like this, darling," he urged, lightly kneading the flesh between her thighs. "This lovely part of you, I think, is what needs looking after. . . ."

The coach rocked them to and fro like a sensuous cradle, heightening Jane's arousal as Alex stroked her. He seemed bent on prolonging her physical delight, challenging her to cry out for relief from the cascade of pleasure assaulting her senses. Gradually, he began to set a different pace—swift and deeply penetrating. At length, exhausted, Jane could not control the voluptuous shudders overtaking her body as she arched against him. She heard herself whispering Alexander's name over and over in a kind of litany.

A few minutes passed in silence. Jane was puzzled by her feeling of deep, physical contentment, when part of her longed for their lovemaking to be gentler—less a contest of wills. *Would the day ever come,* she wondered, *when she and Alexander could blend their passion together with a desire to disclose their deepest feelings and give of themselves fully—without reservation?* Her silent query was met by the sounds of distant cheers from the assortment of yeomen and goodwives lining the streets of the tiny border town of Gordon, named for her husband's family eight centuries ago.

A discreet knock on the bedchamber door was followed by the sound of the door opening and the rattle of cups on a tray.

"Just put it on the table over there," Alex directed the maid from behind the closed curtains of their four-poster. Jane listened sleepily to the sound of the woman who scurried to do the duke's bidding. "I'll see to the fire," he said, pushing the peach-colored velvet hangings to one side. "Are Mr. and Mrs. Fordyce up and about yet?"

"Yes, Yer Grace. Mr. Fordyce asks if eleven would be a suitable hour for yer ride, sir?" the maid inquired, averting her eyes as Alex pulled back the other bed curtain, revealing Jane leaning contentedly against plump linen pillows.

"That will be fine," he replied, dismissing the maid with a nod. Jane watched with amusement as he padded over to the fireplace, poking at the dormant coals until the brazier glowed invitingly. "Jane, will you be riding with us this morning?" he asked, heading toward the bed in his bare feet.

"No-o-o," she groaned, sinking languidly into the feathery softness beneath her head. "I have scores of letters to attend to. All those people were so hospitable to us in London, and I shall stay right here to write them. Ye and John and Catherine may freeze if ye choose . . . I shall be cozy and warm, awaiting yer return."

"What a lovely thought." He grinned, slipping back under the bed linen and enfolding her in his arms. "Perhaps I shall change my mind about our ride. . . ."

"*Alex!*" she giggled as his head ducked under the covers and his lips trailed kisses toward her breasts.

A preemptory knock interrupted them. Alexander hastily emerged from beneath the coverlet. Jane's sister and brother-in-law entered the room, their arms laden with wrapped packages and letters, part of the bridal booty that continued to accumulate at Ayton House during the ducal honeymoon tour.

"Forgive us for intruding . . . Tessa told us ye were awake and having breakfast. Look!" Catherine said excitedly, indicat-

ing one of the packages. "This one came only two days ago, by
special equerry. It's from Their Majesties! Things were in such a
tumult last night when ye arrived, I completely forgot. And look
at all these others! Ye'll need an extra carriage to transport all
yer wedding gifts to Gordon Castle. The post alone will take ye
weeks to sort through."

"Put the letters on the bed here, and the packages over
there," Jane directed. "At least half the letters are addressed to
ye, Alex," Jane said with a laugh. "I shall be more than happy
to allow ye to dispense with those as ye wish!"

" 'Tisn't that why I married you, wench?" he teased, kissing
her on the nose before getting out of bed once again. "To take
care of such things?"

"Aye, and to minister to yer other needs as well, I suppose,"
she retorted saucily. "I fear I am too fatigued today to see to
such matters!"

"Jane!" Catherine exclaimed, blushing, but her husband John
and Alex laughed heartily. The men withdrew to Alex's dressing
room as Catherine poured a cup of coffee for herself and her
sister and sat on the bed. "All seems quite well with ye," she
said tentatively, a flush beginning to spread up her neck once
again.

Jane smiled.

"Aye . . . Alex and I have no problems in *this* department,"
she said, lightly patting the bed's pale peach damask coverlet.
"We still have much to learn about each other, and I wish Alex
weren't so closemouthed about problems that bother him . . .
but all in all, everyone's advice, including yours, urging me to
marry the man against my inclinations, has proved quite sensible. And how about ye?"

"I'm breeding," Catherine said in a soft, low voice. "At least
I think I am . . . but dinna tell Mama till I'm sure!"

"Of *course* . . . but that's wonderful!" Jane exclaimed, bouncing up and down on the bed excitedly and scattering the piles of
letters in all directions. "Darling, Catherine's enceinte!" Jane
called, summoning Alex and John from the next room. "Isn't
that *wonderful*?"

"Congratulations, my good man!" Alexander exclaimed, thumping Fordyce on the back. "This is capital news! Jane, get
dressed, lass! This calls for a wee dram or two, wouldna ye
say?" he added, adopting their Scottish brogue for a moment in
jest. "Let us drink to your health in the drawing room in five
minutes! And we can open the packet from Their Majesties."

All of them cheered his proposal and scattered to comply with the duke's suggestion. Alexander hurried downstairs with the wedding gift from the king and queen while Catherine's maid, Tessa, returned to brush Jane's hair. Hurriedly she piled it atop her head and secured it with pins.

"Now where are my blue slippers!" Jane exclaimed aloud, yanking open the tall armoire that towered against the wall. "Will ye be so kind as to look in the trunk over there?" she directed the maid, "and I'll look under the bed." Jane got down on her hands and knees, next to the four-poster, in a most unladylike fashion and lifted the valance. Peering under the mattress, she cried in triumph, "Ah . . . I've found one!" as she pushed aside several letters that had fallen to the floor in the earlier excitement. "And here's the other!" she said, pulling both the lost slipper and another stray letter toward her.

As she bent down once more to slip her foot into the dainty shoe, something caught her eye. A watermarked letter beside her satin-clad toe read:

> *Jane Maxwell*
> *Hyndford Close*
> *Edinburgh, Scotland.*

Jane immediately recognized the hand. She began to tremble as she slowly retrieved the missive.

"Ye may go now," she said faintly to the maid, as she sank onto the bed, staring at the yellowed epistle in her shaking fingers.

Her breathing had become labored, and blood seemed to be pounding in her temples. The post frank said *Philadelphia*. The date at the top, when she finally broke the seal, read: *Antrim Hall . . . Maryland . . . 1 August 1767 . . . My dearest Jenny. . . .*

Thomas's familiar handwriting swam before her eyes.

This canna be happening! her mind screamed. *This letter was written five months ago . . . months after Thomas died!*

Her mind trembled so violently, she could hardly hold on to the vellum on which a postscript was written.

. . . by the time you read this, I should be in Ireland . . . the fantastical tale of my survival proves I was saved to come back to ye, Jenny, my love . . . I shall be by yer side in November, at the latest . . . my love for ye was the

single thing that saw me through the darkest days . . . I
love ye with my life, sweet lass, and return with only one
thought in my heart: to make ye my bride . . . and to
remain with ye till the grave . . .

Carefully, Jane folded the pages and reached for her cloak. It
was an hour or more before they found her shivering and sobbing
on the stone bench in the church cemetery that sloped down to
the River Eye. The sluggish waters were nearly frozen over in
the December chill. Alexander collected the pages of Thomas's
letter, scattered like dead leaves at Jane's feet, while John Fordyce
directed two footmen to carry the half-delirious young woman
back to the house. They placed her on a makeshift litter and
slowly, the melancholy cortege wound its way across the snow
past a row of headstones marked Martin, Cameron, and Graham.
Jane struggled frantically, crying out that she must wait for
Thomas Fraser beside the church, where he would come soon to
marry her.

Once inside the house, Alexander gently lowered Jane's prostrate form on the peach-colored counterpane that graced the
four-poster and then immediately walked out of their bedchamber. The entire household spoke in whispers when the duke's
black carriage and another, hastily outfitted for the dowager
duchess and Staats Morris, were brought around a few hours
later to the front of the pink stone country house. Catherine,
silent tears streaming down her cheeks, rose from her vigil
beside Jane's bed to watch through the casement window as the
two vehicles began the long journey north to Gordon Castle. She
turned to bury her head in the hollow of her husband's shoulder,
weeping quietly, while Jane's mother stared, dumbstruck, at the
carriages disappearing over the snow-clad hill at the end of the
drive.

"Dear God!" was Lady Maxwell's stricken cry, as she turned
to stare at her daughter, slumbering fitfully in a laudanum-
induced stupor. "What's to become of the lass? What's to
become of us *all*?"

Katherine, the Dowager Duchess of Gordon, laid her hands
along the sides of the silver teapot that rested on a small table in
the drafty drawing room. The pot was distinctly cool. She gazed
out the window, and a look of irritation creased her powdered
brow.

Her son Alexander's behavior during the past month and a half had been trying beyond words. How many days could a man disappear with his longbow and shoot deer for sport? The larder at Huntly Lodge was overflowing with carcasses! It was time the Duke of Gordon ceased his interminable stalking and made some decisions.

Katherine resettled her shawl on her plump shoulders and sighed.

"Stir up that bloody fire, will you, Moira?" she said crossly. "You've let it dwindle down to a pathetic wee thing!"

"Yes, Yer Grace," the maid replied, chastised. She reached for a brass poker and gave the logs a good thwack.

"I must really see to having new hangings made for this room," the dowager duchess said, more to herself than to the maid. "The wind positively whistles through this chamber. I had no idea this property was so ill-kempt when I accepted the duke's offer of it as a dower house!" She glanced once again through the window and started in her chair. In the distance she noted several shaggy ponies emerging from a stand of trees on the right and three figures plodding beside them through the light snowfall. "God's wounds! He's shot another two stag!" the dowager duchess groaned.

Moira walked to the window and looked out.

"I do believe he's got a royal, mum!"

"That makes sense," her employer replied grimly. "Now he's got a matched pair. We skinned his twin yesterday. Now, please add some scalding water to this," she said, indicating the tepid teapot. " 'Tis undrinkable."

Katherine waited impatiently for Alexander and her husband to divest themselves of their outer garments and come in to tea. She noted the firm set of her son's mouth and the slope of his shoulders. The perpetual air of melancholy surrounding the man was really too boring to endure. To her the choice was simple: either cast the chit aside, or make the best of it. *After all,* she thought, *'twould certainly not enhance the Gordons' standing at Court if rumors of this unholy mess filtered down to St. James's.*

"Alex, darling . . . here's a nice cup of tea," she said to her son solicitously.

Alexander walked directly toward the hearth, ignoring his mother's offer, and held his hands up to the fire. Staats sank into a chair and waited for his wife to pour him some hot refreshment.

"I see you're aware how chilly this room remains," his mother noted pointedly. "Our teeth've been chattering since the day Staats and I vacated Gordon Castle and took possession

of Huntly Lodge. We *must* order new draperies, immediately!
'Twill make the place far more livable. And perhaps, while
we're about it, we should do this for all the main rooms.'' Alex
turned around and looked at her steadily, but did not reply.
''Well . . .'' she said uneasily, sensing the tension permeating
the room. ''I see you've stalked more deer today,'' she added
lamely. ''Cook says she's quite besieged with meat, not to
mention antlers.''

''Aye,'' Alex said shortly.

Katherine glanced quickly at her husband, who stirred restlessly in his chair. She absently poured two cups of tea and
handed them to the men.

''Really, Alex, how much longer do you intend to carry on
like this?'' she asked petulantly. ''We have venison coming out
of our ears, and Staats and I have been nearly frozen to death in
this threadbare place for weeks! I distinctly remember telling you
last year that Huntly Lodge simply will not do as a dower house
unless some major repairs and refinements are made. You will
simply have to authorize me to—''

''You are not authorized to do *anything*, Mother!'' Alex snarled,
suddenly breaking his silence. ''You are not authorized to spend
any more of my money, or give me advice, or tell me to make
the best of it, or any other damn thing!''

Katherine stared at her son, stunned by his insulting tone.
Staats merely looked down at his shoes.

''You and Staats will not have to concern yourself with my
moods any longer, mother dear,'' Alex added icily, ''for I depart
for Gordon Castle at dawn. Alone.''

''To do exactly *what*, if I may be so bold to ask?'' Katherine
responded acidly. ''Live like a hermit? Sulk like a child? I
warned you that little nobody would cause you grief, and now
look at you. You went ahead, ignoring the advice of your father
and me.''

''Staats Morris is not my father!'' Alex growled, ''so leave
him out of it!''

''Perhaps I should withdraw, Your Grace,'' Staats interjected
hastily, rising as if to leave.

''Stay right where you are!'' Katherine commanded.

Her husband sank back into his chair like a wilting flower.

''You thought the lass was taken with *you* and *not* your title,
didn't you?'' Katherine said sarcastically. She rose from her
chair and stalked over to her son's side. ''And now that she's
gone all weepy and mad over this lost lover of hers who's risen

from the grave, you have to face facts. Your precious bride whom you thought so besotted with you was far cleverer than you gave her credit for. When that baronet's brat thought her lieutenant dead, she played the harlot in order to ensnare you and to make sure she would be Duchess of Gordon one way or the other!''

Katherine glared at her son triumphantly. Alex's features had become completely expressionless, but the color brought to his cheeks by the frigid wind blowing through the deer forest had drained from his face.

''Don't think I don't know what goes on under every Gordon roof, dear boy,'' she continued venomously. ''I heard of your little rendezvous with that strumpet in Edinburgh before your wedding day. Well, Mistress Jane played you for a fool, and now you're stuck with her. The sooner you stop behaving like a pitiful victim, the better—or you'll disgrace us all. 'Tis Bathia Largue, all over again, isn't it, Staats?'' she said to her husband, not waiting for him to reply, ''only, unfortunately, this time you didn't listen to *us*, Alex. And now you'll have to pay the piper, laddie.''

''I will leave you now,'' Alexander said, his face still a perfect mask, except for an almost imperceptible twitch in his jaw. ''You'll find there are no funds for you to do anything but remain here quietly at Huntly Lodge for the rest of the winter.'' Both Katherine and Staats Morris appeared horrified at the prospect, but Alex took no notice. ''Your allowance will continue, as before, but I will instruct all the shops in the village to extend you no more credit, and the same policy will be in effect with my agents in Aberdeen and Edinburgh, so don't even consider going there. Within these chilly walls, mother dear, you can continue to be as nasty as you please. Like so many of your sex, you come to it naturally.''

True to his promise, by dawn's light the 4th Duke of Gordon had departed on horseback for Gordon Castle. He arrived at his family seat, just in time for the feast of St. Valentine on February 14, which he observed alone, except for the silent companionship of his butler.

15
March 1768

Even at midday, Fochabers, a little village near the mouth of the River Spey, beholden to generations of Gordons for its very existence, was deserted. The sodden mists of early March clung to the lime and larch trees dotting the muddy square, and everything looked bleak and cold.

As the coach pitched and rolled over the last miles of rutted road that led to her destination, Jane strained to catch her first glimpse of Gordon Castle. The massive stone entrance gates filled the carriage window for an instant, giving way to a view of a natural park area, devoid of formal planting, but dotted with leafless trees and an occasional hare scurrying across the icy fields. After several minutes of traversing this desolate landscape, the coach reached a curve in the drive. Jane's heart sank. Ahead of her stood a gaunt gray manse with a six-storied tower and a cluster of inelegant outbuildings. It looked more like a prison than a castle built for a duke's pleasure, and, as far as her future was concerned, Jane supposed that was exactly what it was.

Staring moodily out the window as the vehicle drew nearer the forbidding structure, she saw the heavy front door open and a woman step out just beyond its threshold. Jane felt restless and uncomfortable, having been cooped up in the coach for more than a fortnight. During her long journey she had felt either too ill or too weak to do anything more than put on the same soiled traveling costume and push pins back into her unruly coiffure. The closer she drew to Fochabers, the more heartsick and depressed she became. As the tower of Gordon Castle loomed menacingly ahead, she wished she had followed everyone's advice and waited for some word from Alexander before traveling north.

The carriage pulled up before the open front door. Its oak expanse framed a thin woman dressed in dark blue with an apron and a cluster of keys hanging from her waist. The authority in the rawboned housekeeper's grim demeanor bespoke her position on the estate.

A thin, spare man who introduced himself as William Marshall, the duke's butler, appeared at the carriage door. He was followed by the steward, who ran forward to hold the horses steady as a footman opened the door of the coach.

The housekeeper with the chiseled face wore a cambric cap that ballooned out over her sharp features like a swollen sheep's stomach. As Jane set her foot for the first time on the castle grounds, the servant stepped forward and sank into a perfunctory curtsy.

"I be Mrs. Christie, Yer Grace," she said in an accent so strange, Jane could hardly comprehend her. "Seein' ye're fashed and sickly lookin', I'll have Ellie draw a bath for ye in yer chambers upstairs."

Too tired to rebuke the woman for her rude observations, Jane wordlessly followed her into the dim stone entrance that funneled into an even gloomier foyer. She was too exhausted to inquire why Alexander hadn't met her, despite her having sent a messenger from the little farmhouse she had stayed at on the duke's other estate at Kinrara, a half-day's journey from Gordon Castle. Mrs. Christie paused on the first landing of the broad staircase and made an announcement, faintly tinged with scorn.

"His Grace received the post yesterday tellin' ye'd be comin'. He asked me to beg yer leave, but he has business in Aberdeen concerning renovations he's planned for the castle. Mayhap, he'll not return for a fortnight or more, he told me."

Numbly, Jane accepted the information that Alex had fled on receiving word of her imminent arrival. For the next several days, the bone-deep fatigue that had invaded her body during the preceding two months took complete possession of her. She could rouse herself only for brief periods to sip a little broth brought to her chamber by the forbidding Mrs. Christie or one of her minions. Then she would fall immediately into a restless slumber that occasionally lasted eight to ten hours at a stretch.

At length, one morning, nine days following her arrival at Gordon Castle, Jane awoke, feeling rested for the first time in more than two months and determined to explore her surroundings. As she peered down the long, dim hallway that stretched from her bedchamber door, she had no idea in which wing of the castle she had been housed. She surmised that the damp chill pervading her chamber was likely the temperature throughout the place. She gathered a woolen plaid around her shoulders and ventured down the passageway.

As she slowly paced down the corridor, flanked by somber family portraits of long-dead members of Clan Gordon, she noted that some doors were ajar along the hall. She peeked in one or two to discover bedchambers and dressing rooms, mostly unused, their furniture draped to protect it from dust. In a hallway veering to the left off the main landing, Jane discovered what must have been the nursery where Alex spent his childhood. Jane remembered his telling her that his mother, the Dowager Duchess Katherine, had produced six children in ten years of marriage to the 3rd Duke. Hence, the six miniature brass beds lining one wall. From an adjoining room, which Jane assumed had once accommodated a nanny, she could hear the soft strains of Scottish lullaby being sung by a disembodied voice.

> *Sleep ye wee bairn . . . Yer Da's comin' home.*
> *Ye've no leave to cry, for yer Da's comin' home. . . .*

Jane advanced stealthily into the room. A young girl in an indigo blue skirt and striped apron sat in a chair near a small fireplace. A child who looked to be about eighteen months old perched in her lap. The nursemaid herself didn't appear to be more than eleven or twelve.

"Dinna be startled," Jane said softly, "but please tell me, who is this child?" The young girl bolted out of her chair and the baby began to howl with fright. "I'm sorry," Jane said hastily, rushing over to take the child in her arms and comfort it.

"Ye shouldna do that, ma'am," the nursemaid protested as Jane rocked the baby gently, crooning to soothe its fears. " 'Tis me neck if Ma sees ye in here!"

"And who might yer mother be?" Jane asked, cradling the curly headed babe in her arms.

"Mrs. Christie. . . ."

"Ah . . . Mrs. Christie . . ." Jane replied, noting the girl's angular features which mirrored the bony countenance of the housekeeper. She glanced down at the round-faced bundle in her arms. "Is this the duke's son?"

"Aye, he is." The young girl nodded, wide-eyed that such a question should be asked so casually by the duke's new bride. "My ma warned me to be scarce, so the sight o' him might not offend ye," she said, looking as if she should retrieve the baby from Jane's arms.

"What a pretty wee thing ye are," Jane crooned, smiling at the little boy who had stopped crying but was looking at her quizzically. "He's called George, I believe?"

"Aye, but we call him Geordie."

"Hello, Geordie," Jane said, tickling him lightly under his plump little ribs. "Yer a fine, fair lad, aren't ye now? Handsome as yer da, just as he said."

Jane smiled at the neatly kempt nursemaid who stood open-mouthedly, watching the duke's new bride cuddle his bastard.

"And what might yer name be?" Jane asked kindly.

"N-Nancy, Yer Grace. Nancy Christie."

"Well, Nancy, ye're just a few years younger than my sister Eglantine, and ye seem a very responsible young miss, if I can make that comparison with that madcap lass."

"Why, thank ye, Yer Grace," Nancy replied, pleased by the compliment. "My ma has two bairns more and seems unlikely to stop havin' 'em, so I've had lots of practice lookin' after the wee ones. I feel a bit sorry for this little lad, dinna ye?" she asked seriously, her young brow knit in a pensive frown. "No mama to coddle 'im, and the duke, such a grand man. I been tellin' Geordie I prayed ye'd be kind to 'im, and here ye are, holdin' 'im in yer arms!"

"How sweet ye are, Nancy," Jane said, touched by the young girl's concern for the little lad. "I shall come and visit him every day, would ye like that? And I shall tell yer mother there's no need to keep him hidden away. The duke has determined the lad shall have the protection of the House of Gordon, and I am happy to comply. I shall see ye both tomorrow . . . yes?"

"That 'twould be lovely, Yer Grace. I'll have him scrubbed and in his best tucker for ye!"

"Fine . . . tea in the nursery then, tomorrow." Jane smiled, her spirits lifting.

She quietly let herself out of the nursery, venturing down another mysterious corridor. Soon, she found herself at the top of a dark, narrow stairway. She walked down several flights till she reckoned she must be in a section of the castle that was below the ground. A stone passageway led to a room packed with furniture in various stages of construction. In an adjoining room, scores of clocks hung on the walls or spilled their innards across a worktable. Jane examined what appeared to be a chronometer of some sort. A paper with minute mathematical calculations stood next to an inkwell and quill pen.

"Does science interest ye, Yer Grace?"

Jane let out a startled cry and whirled around to face William Marshall, who stood in the doorway, clothed in his butler's livery. Jane hadn't laid eyes on him since the day she'd arrived at the castle, and she was shaken by his sudden appearance in such strange surroundings. His manner was cool, as if he had some secret knowledge that led him to disapprove of her presence within his domain.

"I know nothing of science, Mr. Marshall, but I was interested to see more of my new *home*," she replied with deliberate emphasis.

"These are the duke's workshops," Marshall said, easing his compact frame into the room. He absently fingered a dismantled telescope that was apparently in the process of being cleaned. "His Grace and I have shared a mutual interest in things mechanical ever since we were lads."

"Is that so?" Jane responded politely.

"When I entered the service of the dowager duchess at around the age of twelve as a novice house steward, his Grace and I were near in age. I was honored to be allowed to spend many idle hours as his youthful companion. The duke and I studied astronomy together as well as mechanics. As no doubt ye've seen, he is also a skilled woodworker—a hobby I also enjoy, thanks to the duke's indulgence."

"Do ye write poetry as well?" Jane asked in a slightly mocking tone, referring to the duke's pastime with which she was most familiar. "Or perhaps ye're a champion archer, like His Grace?"

"No, m'lady," Marshall answered, looking at her steadily. Jane felt as if he were measuring her as he would an adversary. "But as for music, His Grace writes the words and I write the tunes. The duke does me the honor of asking me to play my violin for festivities here at Gordon Castle."

"'Twould appear, Mr. Marshall, that ye and my lord Gordon have much in common," Jane commented dryly, wondering at such intimacy between a butler and a duke. Her conversation with the smug servant had given her a chilling glimpse of the isolated childhood Alex must have experienced, growing up in this mausoleum. "Now, if ye'll excuse me, I'm feeling a bit tired from my little excursion." Jane turned to leave the strange basement chamber. At the threshold, she turned back to face

William Marshall. ''I should like to hear ye play yer fiddle of an evening, Mr. Marshall. 'Tis been ages since I've heard a sprightly air.''

''As ye wish, Yer Grace,'' Marshall replied without enthusiasm.

''Around eight, shall we say?'' she persisted, pleased to make him do her bidding. ''Is there a music room in this tomb?''

''Aye, on the ground floor. Ellie can tell ye where to find it.''

''Thank ye, Marshall.'' Jane smiled brightly, despite her sudden sense of fatigue. ''Till eight, then.''

Another fortnight passed and still Jane had received no word or written message from Alexander. Two or three times she requested Mr. Marshall play for her after a solitary dinner in the ornate dining hall. A brace of stags with massive antlers stared down at the unlikely pair in the music room, while the talented fiddler rather morosely played his own compositions. Some days she wondered if she shouldn't pack her trunk and retire to Ayton House permanently.

Though slowly recovering from the shock of receiving Thomas's letter, Jane continued to suffer from the fatigue that would come over her suddenly, forcing her to take to her bed for long hours of heavy slumber.

It was probably just as well that she kept to her chambers most of the time, for she sensed the growing disquiet within the household, due to the duke's extended absence and her presence in the castle. ''What bridegroom ignored his new bride to this extent?'' whispered the servants among themselves. At night she dreamed repeatedly of trying to reach St. Giles Cathedral, only to see Thomas departing through the side door without noticing her, and Alexander shaking his fist at her from John Knox's pulpit. Only with Alex's bastard son, little Geordie, could she relax, relishing their times together in the nursery and the games they played.

Another week passed before her spirits took a turn for the better, when an unusually warm first week of April ushered in the daffodils. Patches of green turf were now peeking through the slush surrounding the gloomy castle walls.

''Several letters for ye in today's post, m'lady,'' Mrs. Christie greeted her as Jane returned with muddy boots from her short walk. ''Will ye be takin' yer morning tea in yer room, as usual, Yer Grace?''

''Is there a fire in the small drawing room?'' Jane asked impulsively.

"Always, ma'am," Mrs. Christie said with a shade of hauteur.

"Then bring the tea in there," Jane replied shortly. She was growing weary of the increasing disrespect she felt her uncertain position had thrust her in.

Drawing a large leather chair near the cheerful fire, Jane eagerly flipped through the small stack of correspondence handed her by the housekeeper. Perhaps there would finally be some word from Alex. There were several letters from strangers wishing her well on the occasion of her arrival in their native Highlands. She noted her mother's familiar hand on a thick packet she correctly predicted were pages of recriminations over what had transpired at Ayton House. By the time Jane had read a half page, Lady Maxwell's words had drained her of the fragile feeling of cheer she had been nuturing during her sun-filled morning walk. She set the sheets aside, unfinished, and saw there was another letter, this one from her sister Catherine.

Eagerly she turned over Catherine's correspondence, and was about to open it when she noticed that beneath it lay a smaller, thin missive.

Thomas! she gasped under her breath.

Heart lurching, hands trembling, she studied the bold letters on the parchment.

Jane was stunned to discover he was writing from Beauly, near his home village of Struy, less than a day's ride from Gordon Castle. Aunt Elizabeth had written that Uncle James would be in Ireland with the Black Watch until further notice and that she and all her children would be joining him soon in Dublin. Why, then, was Thomas in the Highlands? The letter was addressed to her using her new title, positive evidence that he had discovered she was married. Slowly, fighting the dizziness that filled her head, she broke the seal.

> *2 April 1768*
> *Balblair House, Beauly*

> *My congratulations to*
> *Her Grace, the Duchess of Gordon.*
>   *Before my departure for permanent assignment in Ireland next month, may I present my compliments to ye and Alexander, 4th Duke of Gordon.*
>   *Tho. Fraser*
>   *Lt. 42nd Reg. Foot*

Jane stared at the message, shocked by its brevity and lack of emotion. Slowly, she crumpled it into her hand and angrily threw it into the fire. She yanked several times on the bellpull next to her chair and began to pace up and down before the ornately carved stone fireplace emblazoned with the crest of the House of Gordon, the ancient family shield flanked by two rearing stags. Within minutes, Mrs. Christie scurried into the room with Ellie following along behind, bearing a tea tray.

"Tea was detained, ma'am, because a messenger just arrived from His Grace in Aberdeen," Mrs. Christie said hastily, unsettled by the flashing brown eyes of her mistress. "He asked me to inform ye he will return to Gordon Castle in a week's time."

Jane suspended her pacing and stared into the fire where she had tossed Thomas's cryptic letter.

"How convenient," Jane replied, at length. "I shall have just returned from Kinrara by then. Since the weather has turned so fine, I wish to see the swans at Loch-an-Eilean and Loch Alvie before they depart their nesting sites for the year. The duke has told me so much about them and the loveliness of his lands in Badenoch this time of year, I've decided a little change of scene will do me good. Please order my carriage for tomorrow at dawn and send word to the factor at Badenoch to prepare that little shieling on the River Spey at Kinrara, where I lodged on my journey north. I shall require a small bateau at my disposal at Loch-an-Eilean, as well. See to the arrangements, will you please, Mrs. Christie?"

"But Mr. Marshall has joined the duke in Aberdeen, Yer Grace. 'Tis he who always makes such arrangements . . ." she said, faltering.

"In that case, Mrs. Christie, the burden shall fall on yer own capable shoulders. I should like to borrow yer Nancy and little Geordie for company. See to their packing as well, if ye please."

"Oh, Yer Grace," Mrs. Christie protested, "I couldna do *that!* Mr. Marshall is the one who carries out the duke's orders, and with both of 'em away in Aberdeen, I—"

"*Mrs. Christie!*" Jane interrupted with as much imperiousness in her voice as she could muster. "May I remind ye that I am the *Duchess* of Gordon, and in the duke's absence, ye will do *exactly* as I direct." Jane quickly took a sip of scalding tea and looked Mrs. Christie in the eye. "Oh . . . and I will have several letters to well-wishers I wish to post immediately. Send the duke's runner to me in half an hour. Now good day to ye, and leave me to enjoy my tea!"

*   *   *

The sure-footed Highland pony picked its way along a series of rocky precipices in the Monadhliath Mountains and down along the windswept ridge which melded into Kinveachy Forest. Thomas Fraser emerged from the dark woods and caught his first glimpse of the River Spey. Shafts of pale April sunlight sliced through the morning fog, which blanketed the glens branching out from the valley floor. After riding all night, the lieutenant had finally reached the district of Badenoch, most of it owned by the Duke of Gordon, and the rest by the chieftain of Clan Grant. He made his way to the solitary inn west of Loch Alvie to seek more specific directions to a place called Loch-an-Eilean.

"Aye, sir, there are swans at Loch Alvie," said the grizzled proprietor of the Lynvuilg Inn. He cast a skeptical gaze at Thomas's regimental kilt. Thomas sensed the old hotelier thought bird watching an inappropriate pastime for a member of His Majesty's forces.

Thomas tossed a few coins on the table, which more than covered his tankard of ale.

"Since my recruiting mission took me through this district, I thought it worth half a day to see the birds," Thomas lied, casually sipping his brew. "My godfather, Master of Lovat, told me these Swan Isles are a fine, fair sight in spring."

"That they are," agreed the innkeeper, the tone of his voice warming noticeably at the mention of one of the few heroes to survive the fiasco with Bonnie Prince Charlie. "In fact, some say that the word 'Alvie' means Isle of Swans. But if it be sheer poetry yer after, Loch-an-Eilean's the spot. Now *there's* an isle for ye, and with swans too! 'Tis a bit out of yer way and has fewer birds, but a glimpse of the old, abandoned castle's well worth the trek."

Thomas fingered the note from Jane he carried in a pocket of his red flannel coat. Her answer to his short missive congratulating her and the duke on their marriage had merely said:

> *Search for the swans at the lair*
> *of the Wolf of Badenoch . . . Friday.*

His breath nearly caught in his throat as he asked, "Is that the ancient stronghold of the famous brigand?"

"The Wolf of Badenoch?" queried the innkeeper, squinting curiously at Thomas. "Aye, the very spot where that devil himself would retreat after doin' his evil across the countryside. Some say ghosts still walk the parapets. . . .''

Within a day of receiving Jane's cryptic instructions to meet her at the abandoned castle, Thomas had set out for the district of Badenoch, pausing only for a few hours' rest. He had been uncertain as to the exact location of his rendezvous, and now that Friday morning had finally dawned, he was filled with conflicting emotions as to its outcome.

"I suppose ye've heard the tales of the notorious Wolf who lived here in this very glen four hundred years past?'' the innkeeper asked, warming to a subject on which he felt himself to be an expert.

"Only a bit o' lore my godfather has mentioned over the years,'' Thomas replied, encouraging the garrulous old man.

The innkeeper described to Thomas a lake less than a mile in length, surrounded by pines and studded by a small, abandoned castle that nearly covered the little island on which it sat.

"The Wolf, who was the third son of the first Stuart King, badly needed such a refuge in the year thirteen hundred and ninety,'' the innkeeper lectured, leaning his bulk against the wooden post supporting the low tavern roof. "Every Christian in the Highlands had been hoping to kill the ruthless laird to avenge his putting Elgin Cathedral, north o' here, to the torch. He was engaged in a mighty struggle, ye see, with his rival, the Bishop of Moray, who held sway over the land.'' The innkeeper chuckled. "The Wolf pretty near burnt everything in his path. He was redheaded, like ye are, but a wild, fiery orange color, they say, and he was mad as a hatter. The Bishop excommunicated him and the Wolf just *laughed*!'' The innkeeper slapped his knee to emphasize his apparent admiration for such derring-do.

"To this day,'' he went on, shaking his head, "the old women around here swear there's spirits and sprites at Loch-an-Eilean. Not the Wolf of Badenoch, of course—he's fryin' in Hell—but all the innocents he killed, whose heads he put on pikes around the castle walls. Nasty lad, that one,'' continued the innkeeper, savoring his tale. "Nowadays, the place's as peaceful as a crypt. Few relish meetin' a ghostie, if ye take my meanin'. But the birds pay no mind. Swans mate for life, ye know . . . the same pairs come back to Loch Alvie and Loch-an-Eilean every fall. If one of 'em dies, 'tis many moons before the other takes a new mate . . . and some never do. Not like us frail mortals, eh laddie!'' his informant whooped, slapping an untidy barmaid on her rump as she passed by.

Thomas's genial storyteller tugged on the wench's skirts, signaling her to pour them each another ale. As soon as Thomas had finished his second tankard, he set out from the inn, anxious to be on his way. He threaded his way among the tall stands of birch, larch, and Caledonian pines lining the path toward the River Spey. The towering trees flung deep shadows across the trail. The woods grew dense near the river, cloaked in the damp fog, which still boiled along the ground. After fording the stream at a crossing, he made his way in the direction pointed out by the innkeeper. He glanced above the treetops. A thinning mist flung a gauze veil across the azure sky arching over his head. The unpredictable mist continued to hover close to the ground, obscuring the landscape, except for a few ghostly trees flanking the trail on either side of him.

Within a half hour, the haze began to thin out once again as the sun, rising higher overhead, burned through the moist air. Emerging from the thicket of pines, Thomas halted his pony and stared in wonder at Loch-en-Eilean. There before him lay a body of water in the shape of a perfect oval sapphire. A small green island on which stood a miniature, vine-covered fortress, studded its center like a precious emerald jewel. Sun poured down on the center of the loch, leaving the gravel beaches at its edge shrouded in billowing mist. It appeared as if a virgin lake had just bubbled up from Creation. Thomas had the uncanny feeling that if he blinked his eyes, the magical sight might suddenly vanish.

Two bateaux were tied to a stake at a spot where the water was narrowest between the shore and the deserted castle. Thomas dismounted and led his pony back into the forest, securing it out of sight. As he emerged from the shadows, he hesitated, spellbound by the sight before him. Two large white swans, their necks arching proudly, swam in a stately procession from behind a thicket of reeds encircling the castle walls. Behind the male swan glided five gray cygnets, newly hatched. Bringing up the rear, the mother trailed her mate and their brood at a discreet distance. The male suddenly cocked his head in Thomas's direction and trumpeted a warning *Ko-hoh . . . ko-hoh* as the regal birds circled away from the edge of the shore, ruffling their feathers in alarm.

The innkeeper had described to Thomas how this mother and father swan would soon teach their young the art of flying in preparation for their annual summer pilgrimage north. But each fall, this same pair would return to Loch-an-Eilean to build its nest and raise its young in graceful harmony with nature and the sumptuous beauty that surrounded the lake.

Thomas skulled his boat around the sheer stone walls of the castle's base, keeping a safe distance from the wary family of swans. The mother and father were paddling like sentries a few yards from the castle's small granite pier. All was silent, except for the lapping of the water against the stones. Thomas pulled himself onto the boat landing and vaulted a low wall that formed the ancient entrance to the crumbling stronghold. A small courtyard led into a roofless chamber, which Thomas guessed had once been the great hall. Ahead of him, a spiral stone staircase led to the tower.

Cautiously, Thomas ascended the dank passageway. The walls felt slightly spongy to his touch from the lichen feasting on the weeping stones. Recalling the innkeeper's tales of the barbarous Wolf of Badenoch, he wondered what bloodcurdling screams had echoed up this passage in eons past.

Thomas felt smothered by the deathly silence in the stairwell to the tower. All he could hear was the slapping sound of his boots against the time-worn granite steps. The mists he had seen earlier, clinging to the trees at the water's edge, had blown to the far end of the loch, and brilliant spring sunshine blinded him momentarily as he emerged from the arched doorway into the light.

An osprey nest sat twenty feet above him on the only remaining section of the castle tower that hadn't succumbed to the ravages of four hundred Scottish winters. Gazing back at the shore, his breath caught at the sight of a small, gray palfrey just disappearing into the forest near the remaining boat. He had only a second's glimpse of the rider seated sidesaddle on the little mare, but he knew instantly that the cloaked figure was Jane.

Leaning against the stone side of the tower, Thomas watched as she emerged from the forest where she had apparently tethered her horse next to his. Her face was hidden by the hood of her cloak as she untied the bateau and quickly pushed off across the glassy surface of the loch.

The flap of swans' wings beating against the water and the caw of birds jolted him out of his temporary paralysis. He hurtled down the winding stone staircase, round and round the central support, until he was dizzy. When he arrived at the floor of the great hall, he paused, transfixed, staring through the open doorway that led to the boat landing.

Suddenly, Jane was running toward him. Her tartan hood flew

back and settled on her cloaked shoulders, revealing her dark chestnut hair and the face he had dreamt about for two long years. She didn't throw herself in his arms, as he expected, but clasped his hands, while tears streamed down her cheeks.

She gazed at his face wordlessly and he could feel her absorb the changes their separation had wrought: the tiny scars marring his upper lip and the longer one that slashed across his left cheekbone. She lifted her fingertips, tracing the slightly raised surfaces that gave silent evidence of the ordeal he'd endured since last they'd met.

Jane raised her hands to her own face and wept, turning away from him to lean against a stone wall for support.

"Jenny . . . Jenny, I . . ."

The sobs wracking Jane's body emanated from the same raw grief filling his own chest. He watched her, unable to offer comfort, because he had no hidden source from which to provide it.

"I canna think how to begin. . . ." She choked out the words, turning away from him once more. Thomas continued to stare at her, heedless of the tears moistening his own cheeks. Her voice was muffled. " 'Tis no one's evil doing . . . yet look what hell we've all been through!" she wept. "My dreams of ye never stopped, Thomas . . . even after—"

"After yer marriage to the duke," Thomas finished her sentence for her, his voice cracking despite a herculean effort to control his emotions.

"Aye," Jane acknowledged, turning toward him, her eyes revealing her pain.

Thomas abruptly walked over to a section in the wall of the great hall whose windows overlooked the loch. He slammed his fist against the stones, bruising the edge of his hand.

"For all ye knew, I was hardly in the ground *half a year,* Jenny, before ye forsook our promises!"

"But Captain MacEwan said he *saw* the blow that felled ye . . . he *buried* yer dismembered body, he told us . . . ye'd been scalped and pulled apart limb from limb! How could I *not* think ye dead!"

"I understand that part of the puzzle," Thomas replied in a low voice, whirling to face her with pent-up anger, "but ye married yer duke a mite fast for a lass who swore she'd love another man the rest of her life!"

"I'll *always* love you, Thomas Fraser . . . *that will be my curse!*" she cried, her face contorted with misery. "But every-

one badgered me to accept the duke . . . pushed me into a
position I couldna escape . . . and . . .'' Jane hesitated, searching for words as if she, herself, needed an explanation of how
she'd arrived at this terrible crossroad. "Alexander is a good
man. He understood how wild with grief I was over the loss of
ye. He'd suffered a similar loss, and, at first, he merely offered
friendship.''

Jane approached Thomas and put a gloved hand on his arm.
Before he jerked his hand away, he observed that the soft leather
was exquisitely tooled with Gordon's stag's head crest on its
edge. He winced to see it was similar to the Fraser Crest—
which was also a proud stag, though etched in profile.

"Later, when Alexander did everything he could to make me
love him, I reached out to him as a drowning swimmer lunges
for a tether!'' Jane said, her eyes pleading for forgiveness. "It
had become impossible to live in a world bereft of your kindness
or affection. . . .''

"Aye,'' Thomas replied, his eyes narrowing grimly, "I imagine m'lord heartily enjoyed bestowing such *affection* on ye these
past months.'' He felt his gorge rise at the thought of the young
duke and Jane together . . . together in bed.

Jane almost seemed to wince at his bitter sarcasm.

"And *ye*?'' he asked, scanning her tear-streaked face. "Have
ye found such affection much to yer liking? Perhaps His Grace,
with his wealth and power and the pleasant luxuries that accompany a duchess's state, have persuaded ye that yer love for me
was . . . but a childish fancy?''

"Stop it, Thomas!'' Jane responded, stiffening in sudden
anger. "This nightmare dinna concern the question of who con-
trols my affections more firmly!'' she cried. "Ye and Alex are
not two stags butting heads over a fawn! No one—*ever*—will
replace what ye are to me! But I cannot *stand* ye to cast what has
happened to all of us in this jealous, canting fashion!''

Thomas felt ashamed. He was aware for the first time how
much Jane had changed—and how much she had suffered. She
was as beautiful as he remembered, but there was a darkness in
her eyes that was new.

"Ah, Jenny, love . . . forgive me . . . 'tis just . . . if only
ye'd *believed* in the miracle that brought me back . . . if only
ye'd waited, even a year before ye'd given me up for lost,'' he
blurted, reaching for her.

Jane spun away, out of his grasp, and then turned, fists
clenched at her side.

"That's true enough," she said bitterly, "and for that lack of
faith, I can only blame myself. But ye, too, played yer part in
this disaster," she said, her eyes flashing. "If only ye'd never
left before marrying me!" she exclaimed furiously. "I begged ye
to elope to Gretna Green, but ye played lackey to Simon, letting
him whisk ye to the coach straight from the ball. 'Twas *ambition*
that seduced ye, Thomas, not yer Jenny of Monreith. Ye thought
ye could have me *and* yer lieutenancy *and*, someday, yer lands and
title back, dinna ye? But it dinna come to pass. Ye dinna *fight* for
me, Thomas Fraser . . . yer *ambition* called the tune . . . yer
ambition and that bastard, Simon Fraser!"

Jane whirled on her heel and darted blindly for the spiral
staircase, running as fast as she could. Thomas raced to catch up
with her, taking the twisting steps two at a time.

"Jenny . . . Jenny . . . wait . . . please wait!" he shouted,
filled with a sense of dread he had never experienced before. He
half expected her to be poised on the parapet, high over the loch,
but, instead, he found her leaning, defeated, against the stone
tower's curved wall, her head tilted back, her eyes closed, as she
gasped for breath.

"I'm here, Jenny," he said softly. "I dinna ever want to leave
ye again. Please, love, look at me . . . I've a plan ye should
know . . . a plan that can mean a new life for us both."

Wearily, Jane opened her eyes and looked at him sadly. She
didn't speak.

"All during my ride from Beauly, I thought about what
possible remedies there might be for this . . . this nightmare,
as ye call it . . ." he began. "And . . . there *is* a way we can be
together." He walked toward her, but hesitated to touch her.
Her eyes seemed almost glazed, as if her body were there with
him on the tower, but her mind was floating far off like a swan
on the wing. "Jenny, lass," he begged earnestly, "we can go to
America. I've money put by, plus a small cache my godfather
has given me over the years. I can resign my Commission and
we can go to Maryland or Pennsylvania, where my travels took
me. Annapolis is a fine, fair city, much like many here in
Scotland . . . but a wee bit warmer," he said, smiling before he
realized she wouldn't understand his little joke about Maryland's
steaming summers. He tried to stir her from her peculiar lethargy. "Ye say ye love me . . . that ye'll always love me . . .
well . . . here's yer chance to change the fates which deceived
us so cruelly! Come with me to America!" he pleaded.

Without waiting for her reply, he strode to her side and folded her in his arms. Her body trembled for a few moments as she buried her cheek against his shoulder. It was difficult to embrace her fully because of the bulky folds of her cloak. Jane continued to rest her head against him, before finally pulling away.

"I love ye, Thomas. I never stopped loving ye, nor will I— ever," she said quietly. Her eyes, having lost their glazed look, stared at him from their sable depths. "But I canna go with ye," she said, barely above a whisper. She parted her cloak to reveal a belly swelling firmly against the fabric of her muslin dress. Soon its waistline would be too tight for her and she would have to have larger clothes made for her rapidly expanding figure. " 'Tis the duke's heir . . . four months along. I expect 'twill be born in September, just before we mark one year of marriage," she said with finality.

Thomas stared at her rounded abdomen, and a wave of bitterness engulfed him.

"That should be *my* bairn growin' inside o' ye!" he cried in anguish, grabbing her shoulders roughly. "*Mine's* the seed that should be planted in yer womb! That bastard duke has stolen every blessed thing . . ."

With a strangled cry, he crushed her lips to his, seeking to infuse her with the same hopelessness and rage that he feared would accompany him from this day forward. He realized he was probably hurting her, but he clasped Jane in a crushing embrace. The Gordons had now robbed him of everything! Thanks to the faithlessness of families like the Gordons toward the Bonnie Prince in 1745, the Frasers had lost it all: their homes, their lands, their patrimony. And now Thomas Fraser had lost Jane to the 4th Duke of Gordon.

Jane whimpered softly beneath his torturous embrace, but she didn't fight against him. Suddenly both were weeping, clinging to each other, giving vent to the months of anxiety and longing they had endured since the day, two years earlier, they had parted in the golden twilight aboard the *Providence*.

The swans, forty feet beneath the castle tower of the Wolf of Badenoch, rustled uneasily in the reedy grass. Then, with lightning grace, the birds pushed off, swimming in agitated circles around their five offspring, who poked their tiny heads below the surface of the water, imitating their parents in their search for food.

Jane and Thomas appeared at the arched stone entrance to the keep, their faces ashen and still moist with the tears they had shed together. The swans cocked their heads and waited, watch-

ing warily as Thomas tied his boat to the stern of Jane's. He
handed her into the first bateau and climbed in, opposite her,
reaching for the oars. As the two craft came around the far end
of the island, the largest swan followed at a safe distance behind
the boats, shadowed by the rest of his family.

By now, the spring sunshine was fast losing ground to the
mists, which had been held in abeyance for a few hours. The
cooler air had simply overpowered the lukewarm rays of the sun
with a new blanket of fog. The swans glided back and forth in
the smoky waters off shore, staking out the perimeter of their
island territory. Wordlessly, Thomas offered his hand to Jane to
assist her out of the skiff, securing the boats to their moorings on
the gravelly beach.

"They're safe in their island home," Jane said, gazing at the
picturesque grouping of swans and their young. "If only we
could have been *them,* in this remote place . . . away from . . .
everything." Gently, Jane placed her gloved hand on Thomas's
arm. "Let them be *us,*" she said softly, watching the larger
swan usher his family back toward the castle walls. "Let our
minds fly back to them whenever we feel sad or lonely . . .
whenever we feel that longing for each other that will never go
away. . . ."

Thomas remained silent.

With a stifled sob, Jane threw her arms around him, holding
him close. His arms remained at his side and she knew he was
aware of the unfamiliar hardness of her rounded belly pressing
against him. Tenderly, she pulled his head toward hers, tasting
the saltiness of their mingled tears.

"We're like the swans, Thomas," she said softly. " 'Tis for a
lifetime I've chosen to love ye—and ye, me."

Their eyes locked, and, finally, Thomas unclenched his fists
and wrapped his arms around her hooded figure. They stood
together silently for some moments and then walked quietly into
the woods where their two horses were grazing peacefully, oblivious to the cold mists swooping down from the crags above.

Gently, Thomas placed Jane sidesaddle on her palfrey and led
the sweet-tempered mare toward the path Jane had taken from
the old farmhouse at Kinrara. The hood of her cloak nearly hid
her face from his sight until she turned toward him in her saddle
and nodded a brief, melancholy farewell. With a tap of her boot,
she urged her pony forward.

Slowly he watched her form melt like an apparition into the
cloud of moisture curling along a stand of pines that edged the

loch. When he looked back across the water, Loch-an-Eilean and the swans had disappeared from view behind a billowing gray blanket of fog.

Jane was shivering with cold by the time her pony reached the whitewashed crofter's cottage nestled in a hollow near the River Spey on the estate at Kinrara. As she entered the simple abode, the Gordon nursemaid, Nancy Christie, gave her a concerned look and pulled back the bed linen on the straw-filled pallet that rested in a dim corner of the chamber. The one-room cottage was plain and functional, but a welcoming fire glowed in the grate. Jane stood forlornly in the middle of the humble dwelling. Suddenly, she sneezed—once, twice, three times—and then put her hand to her throat, which felt painful and raw.

"Ye've caught a chill, Yer Grace," said Nancy anxiously, hanging Jane's tartan cloak on a peg next to the door. "Let's get ye out of those clothes and into bed while I just put some barley broth on to heat."

"Sick?" piped a small voice from the shadows.

"Aye, Geordie," Nancy replied tersely. "The duchess is feeling poorly, so ye must be extra good, lad, and not disturb her ladyship."

The little boy stared at Jane solemnly and, once Nancy had tucked her into bed, he sat cross-legged on the floor, stroking her hot and feverish hand, which lay on the homespun counterpane. For several days Jane permitted herself the luxury of feeling miserable, preferring to concentrate on her physical discomforts instead of allowing herself to dwell on the fact that she would probably never see Thomas Fraser again.

Never see Thomas again.

Her congestion traveled to her chest and she grew wan and listless. Sleeping nearly around the clock, Jane found herself drifting into a semiconscious state in which she could hide from the finality of Thomas's departure for Ireland.

She survived for several days in this condition, until one morning, when she was already noticeably overdue at Gordon castle, she heard the jingling of harnesses outside the small window of Kinrara cottage. Male voices mingled in the chill spring air with little Geordie's high-pitched shouts of welcome.

"She's had a bout of ague, Yer Grace," she heard Nancy say as footsteps resounded on the wooden floor near her bed. "But she's much improved, m'lord . . ." the maid added nervously. "We thought to travel to Fochabers the day after tomorrow."

"What the devil were you doing here in the *first* place?" Alex's voice asked gruffly. "Never mind. Will you please leave me to attend Her Grace," he added shortly.

Jane heard Nancy and Geordie depart and then the sound of a chair being dragged toward her sickbed. Silence. Jane listened to her own uneven breathing.

"Jane . . . Jane? Are you awake?"

"Yes," she replied weakly, keeping her eyes closed.

"Would you please tell me why you are here, living like a peasant in a one-room crofter's cottage?"

Jane sighed and opened her eyes. Alex still had his traveling cloak draped around his shoulders and he was in the process of removing his gloves. His features were as she remembered them during their long separation: patrician and impassive. She hadn't a clue what was passing through his mind. His manner was cool, and utterly controlled, and he spoke to her in the tone one would use to address a child or a disobedient servant.

Jane sat up in bed and immediately regretted the abrupt movement. Alex's face became a gray blank for a moment until her dizzy spell passed.

"I came here for several reasons, Yer Grace," she said finally, "not the least of which was that I couldna stand Gordon Castle one more second! I waited weeks for ye to come, or write, or give me some signal, and ye did *nothing*!"

"There doesn't seem much we *can* do, does there?" Alex said unemotionally. "You love Thomas Fraser, but, unfortunately, you are married to me."

Jane looked at him, feeling her anger rise with each clipped, careful sentence he uttered.

"That's right!" she retorted. "I am married to you: Alexander, Fourth Duke of Gordon. And that's why I came to Kinrara. To tell Thomas Fraser that I couldn't run away from this marriage. That I wouldna go to America with him."

Alex's eyes revealed that he was far from the unruffled inquisitor he had, at first, appeared.

"You've *seen* him? Here?" he growled, his eyes darting around the dimly lit cottage.

"No, not *here*," she said quietly. "No one saw us. Thomas has rejoined his regiment in Ireland. 'Tis finished, Alex."

Alex remained silent, an unfathomable look flickering in his eyes.

"You've been ill," he said at length.

"Aye," she said, tilting her chin defensively. "But I'm better now."

"Are you able to travel?"

"In a day or so, I expect."

"Do you wish to return to Gordon Castle with me?" he asked evenly.

"As *what*, I wish to know?"

"That can't be decided yet."

Jane stared at him in disbelief.

"What in God's name do ye *mean* by that?"

"Mrs. Christie told me you weren't well at Gordon Castle either."

"That's true," Jane answered cautiously, her lips drawing together in a grim line. "I felt miserable for days."

"Mrs. Christie says your courses never appeared during your stay in Fochabers—"

"She said *what*!" Jane choked.

Her mind flashed on an image of the old crone sorting through her cambric underclothes and petticoats.

"She tells me you may be with child," Alex declared.

"I am."

"Is it mine?" he asked coolly.

Jane stared at him, stunned into silence by the outrageous insult his words represented. Alex's eyes were hooded, and a mirthless smile traced his lips.

"My dear Jane, since 'tis possible that you saw Fraser after my departure while you were still at your sister's in Ayton, this child could be—"

Before Jane even realized what she was doing, she leaned over the bed and raked her nails with all her might across Alex's cheeks.

"Ye *bastard*! Ye worthless *sot*!" she screamed. "The devil take ye and all yer damned, brainsick Gordons with ye!" She threw the bedcovers off her body and plastered her nightdress against her abdomen, revealing the firm, round bulge that testified to her advancing pregnancy. "Look at this! *Look at this,* ye swine! This is *yer* bairn . . . this is what *ye* made with that instrument between yer legs, thanks to all those nights when ye played me like a harp, holding yerself aloof . . . posing as my lord and master. This is *yer* baby, God help it!" Alex stared at her wordlessly. Jane rolled to her side, turning her back to him. "In actual fact, my lord Gordon," she said, spitting out her words over her shoulder, "I dinna care whether ye believe me or not. Just leave."

"Jane, I—"

"Just *leave*!" she shouted, pounding her fist furiously against the wall.

Alex bent down to retrieve his cloak from the floor where it had fallen during Jane's attack.

"Will you come back to Gordon Castle?" he asked soberly.

"What choice do I have?" she replied bitterly, refusing to look at him. "I'm four months gone—with not a farthing of my own."

There was a momentary silence. Then Alex walked out of the cottage, leaving Jane shivering in her nightdress despite the warmth of the crackling fire. Wearily, she tugged at the bed linen that lay piled around her knees and pulled it over her rounded abdomen. She lay on her back like a corpse, her hands folded on her chest, anticipating the sound of the coachman's cry and the crack of a whip. When, at length, she heard them, she heaved a sigh and closed her eyes. Alex had begun his journey north, along a route she would have to follow only too soon.

16

September 1768

Jane's bedchamber was suffocatingly hot, but she seemed hardly able to catch her breath long enough between her labor pains to beg the midwife to open a window. In any case, the woman probably would think her daft for asking, since Scottish custom was to keep the birthing room airtight to ward off any evil humors that might take possession of the newborn.

If only this fetal prisoner could escape her body soon, Jane thought, gasping, with sweat pouring down her cheeks. She clutched at the headboard of the massive four-poster and bore down hard, as she'd been instructed. The pain was relentless as it reached crescendo after crescendo. It would subside for a few moments and then overwhelm her again with tremendous force. During the brief respites, Jane's mind wandered to a memory of the sound of Aunt Elizabeth's low moans floating down the hall at Hyndford Close. She remembered Thomas describing how the sheep he tended would bleat and pant between contractions. It comforted her, somehow, to know that the ordeal her body was enduring was as normal as the rising of the sun or the migration of the birds. The youthful Thomas had told her all about the mystery of what would happen to her one day . . . Thomas . . . if *only* Thomas were by her side. . . .

Jane's eyes widened in fear. Had she said anything aloud? Had Thomas's name escaped her lips? Where was Dr. Ogilvy? Where was Alex? Did he care if she lived or died? Would she die? Would the baby?

Suddenly she was more frightened than she had ever been in her life. She knew Bathia Largue had died like this. Would anyone look after her bairn the way she had nurtured Geordie this past year? Silent tears slid down her cheeks. Another wave of pain swept over her. It caught her up with the force of a storm at sea and hurled her down into blackness where she could hear far-off voices whispering like the lapping of the ocean on the shores of Monreith.

"Soon, 'twill be over . . . very soon," said a deep voice penetrating the fog of pain. She felt a cool cloth wipe her brow and then circle her face gently. "You're doing fine, darling . . . all's well, my love," the voice told her urgently. She heard someone whisper, " 'Tis so *hard*! I dinna think 'twould be so hard"—and realized, much to her amazement, that the second voice was her own.

After a few moments, she ceased hearing the deeper voice. A door had closed on the other side of the bedchamber. Once again, she was alone with her agony. Suddenly, Jane felt an urge to push the baby out with all her might. The midwife was barking orders, and there were rustling sounds in the room. She strained in the darkness of her struggle to free the child inside her body, until, miraculously, the pain vanished and she heard the loud, insistent cries of a newborn baby, far off, as if from high on a heather-clad moor.

A cart pulled by a stout-hearted Highland pony stopped a hundred yards from the still roofless new addition to Gordon Castle. Stones stood in neat piles nearby, waiting to be added to the exterior walls of the half-finished pavilion.

"Careful, now!" shouted Alexander to the crew of gardeners attempting to lift an eight-foot lime sapling out of the cart. "We can't have you killing the Duchess Tree before it's even planted. Easy, now!"

Jane watched as estate workmen shoveled mounds of rich

moist soil into the hole her husband had ordered dug. The silver lime tree was merely the most recent of many tokens of affection he had lavished on her since her tiny, perfect daughter—who, in truth, was the picture of Alex—made her appearance in the fall.

Charlotte had been baptized on a day selected by her father: October 23, 1768, the date that marked her parents' first wedding anniversary. Alex had presented Jane with a diamond necklace, one that matched the earrings he had given her on that memorable night at Comely Gardens, when they were still friends and not yet affianced.

As Jane watched her husband grab a shovel, she wondered if the planting of the tree somehow symbolized a new beginning for their marriage—a new beginning of which Alex was reluctant to speak. Not once had he mentioned how much the baby looked like him, nor had he revealed his own desolation following the arrival of Thomas's letter at Ayton House during their honeymoon. Without warning, the duke had simply reassumed the role of husband following her recovery from childbirth.

Jane felt a flush rise to her cheeks when she thought of the cool and rather deliberate way Alex aroused her, once they again shared a marriage bed. Without alluding to their complicated past, she had willingly succumbed to his lovemaking. To do otherwise would have risked upsetting everything once more, and she didn't think she would survive more turmoil. Yet she longed to tell him of her grief that he, along with Thomas, had been so terribly wounded by all the turns that fate had taken. She wanted him to know how much she wished to make peace with the past—a past she now realized could never include Thomas Fraser of Struy.

But, just like her husband, Jane couldn't bring herself to put her feelings into words. Something in Alex's manner and in her own heart prevented it. Her body responded almost instinctively to her husband's skilled touch, but in moments of private, searing honesty, Jane knew that she, too, kept in check the flood gates of her emotions.

Stifling a sigh, she glanced over at little Geordie, who was hopping up and down excitedly as the men patted down the dirt around the new tree with the backs of their shovels. She didn't give a fig if the servants or their neighbors thought it peculiar that the duke's illegitimate son was treated as an equal in the nursery. He was sweet with Charlotte and dear to Jane herself, and that's all that mattered, as far as she was concerned.

"Jane, darling," Alex said, startling her from her wandering thoughts. "Would you come over here, please."

The gardening crew leaned on their shovels as Alex handed her his, gesturing that she add a final topping of dirt at the base of the new sapling. When she obliged, Alex exclaimed, "Bravo, dearheart . . . you've just christened the Duchess Tree! May she grow and flourish!"

"Which branch of the Duchess Tree is for *me*?" demanded little Geordie, speaking his first complete sentence, much to everyone's surprise and amusement.

Alex reached past his son's head and grasped a thin reed bursting with delicate buds.

"This is you, my lad . . . and this little twig is baby Charlotte." While the bystanders applauded, Alex leaned over to whisper to Jane, his breath warm and sensuous against her ear. "Now, what say you, my dear lady? Shall we retire to our chamber to do some planting of another kind? Who knows," he added softly, "perhaps such bucolic pleasures will soon graft an heir-apparent on this lovely sapling?"

Jane enjoyed less than a year's respite between Charlotte's birth and her next pregnancy. In 1770, her second child, Alex's heir, was born. From her bed on a bitterly cold morning in early February, Jane could hear the bells in the Bellie Church Tower in Fochabers, tolling the joyous news for a solid hour. Much to his father's delight, the newly arrived Marquess of Huntly cried in unison for nearly that long.

Later in the day, when Alex appeared in Jane's bedchamber, she greeted him with undisguised pride.

"Now, there's the matter of a Christian name for this heir to the House of Gordon," Jane said, sipping from a steaming cup of caudle, a fortifying liquid made of eggs, milk, and brandy. Leaning against a mound of pillows, she watched Nancy Christie tuck the baby into its cradle after its first feeding.

"A name . . . ah yes," Alex murmured, staring down at the tiny bundle, sleeping peacefully at last. "Well, we named our daughter after Queen Charlotte. I'd like to call my heir George, in honor of the king."

Jane's heart thudded painfully. It was hard to imagine a child of hers named after the sovereign whose coronation proclamations she and Thomas had ripped to shreds when they were young.

"Winna that be a mite confusing," she replied hastily, "with yer firstborn named George as well?"

"Well, I've had cousins named Alexander," the duke answered thoughtfully, "and we always managed to sort it out. The principal factor in all this is the impression you made at court. The king was so taken with you the day you were first presented, you must recall how he volunteered to stand as godfather to our first son. 'Twould be an affront if we didn't ask him now, and, naturally, if we *do* ask him, we must name the bairn for him."

"I see . . ." Jane said quietly.

Thus, six weeks later, after the requisite exchange of correspondence with the palace, the 8th Marquess of Huntly and the future 5th Duke of Gordon was given the Christian name of George, after King George III. Jane tried not to think about what Thomas Fraser would say, if ever he should hear of it.

It wasn't long, however, before Jane no longer cared whether outsiders considered it strange that the Duke of Gordon had two sons called George, and one, a bastard at that. She was too preoccupied with her own cares and with an emerging cycle of pregnancy and delivery that occurred every other year. In 1771, Jane's father died from an outsized liver that no longer functioned. Alex had seen to it that Baronet, Sir William Maxwell of Monreith was buried in high style, much to the relief of all concerned, and that lodgings of her own were purchased for Lady Maxwell, to keep her in Edinburgh. Jane's second daughter, Lady Madelina, was born the following year, and two years after that, on the exact anniversary of little Huntly's birth, another daughter, Lady Susan, made her appearance on February second.

"Think of how convenient 'twill be to have their birthday fetes on the same day," Alex teased her, bringing to her bedside the now familiar caudle. In addition to the milk, egg, and brandy, Nancy Christie now added a few spoonfuls of oatmeal, sugar, nutmeg, and a little lemon juice to make it more palatable in hopes of bolstering Jane's depleted strength.

Jane smiled at Alex weakly, and obediently sipped the concoction. She focused on the necessity of hiring additional help for Nancy, now that five of the six little brass beds in the nursery were occupied.

By August, Jane had established a routine regarding the children and longed for a change of scene.

"Alex?" she said, one evening, sinking exhaustedly into a

chair in the library. "Do ye think it possible for us to visit Edinburgh so that I may see Eglantine? I dinna think all's well with her."

Alex looked up from some papers he had been perusing at his desk.

"Problems with Wallace?" he asked.

He had always been amused by Jane's flighty sister, dating from the time he caught the wench spying on him from behind her front door in Hyndford Close when he first began courting Jane. Something had bothered him about the chap Eglantine had married two years ago, the eccentric Sir Thomas Wallace of Craigie.

Jane glanced down at the letter from Eglantine she held in her hand.

"Thomas Wallace may be no baronet at all."

Alex stared at her in disbelief.

"Surely, you jest?"

Jane sighed and shook her head.

"It seems he inherited the estate of his grandfather through his mother and simply styled himself a 'Sir'—a title he apparently is *not* authorized to claim!" Jane pointed to Eglantine's latest missive. "Now Eglantine has discovered there's no money, a mountain of debts, and that they must sell Craigie House and all the land."

"The deuce, you say!" Alex declared. He glanced at Jane's drawn face, which mirrored both worry about her sister's unorthodox situation and fatigue from months of late-night vigils, for she had insisted on breast-feeding all four of her children during their infancy, rather than summon in a wetnurse.

"What would you say if we took Eglantine to London with us for a few months? Get her away from that rogue for a time?" Alex asked casually.

Jane stared at her husband, wide-eyed, an excited flush brightening her tired features.

"London!" she cried, clapping her hands. "What a wonderful idea! And with Eglantine! Oh, Alex, ye're dear to think of such a thing! Could we really?"

She jumped up from her chair and threw her arms impulsively around her husband. She kissed him firmly on the cheek. Then, just as quickly, she bit her lip and furrowed her brow.

"But, what about the children? I canna leave little Susan . . . she's still at the breast. . . ."

"We'll take the two youngest ones with us and leave Charlotte

and the two Georges in William Marshall's care. 'Twill be just
for six weeks. You deserve a rest from those little savages!''

Jane looked at Alex ambivalently. She had never warmed to
the butler, despite Alex's obvious regard for him. However, a
tutor could be engaged, and she realized a change of scenery
would be restorative, especially if it involved an indulgence in
the glittering life of sophisticated London. Sure enough, within a
few weeks, the Duke and Duchess of Gordon, along with Eglantine Maxwell Wallace, took up residence for the winter and
spring in a leased house on St. James's Square. Jane and her
sister were immediately caught up in a glamorous round of
parties, balls, and routs, while Alex dutifully attended the House
of Lords.

One day in early May, 1775, as the Gordon coach rolled
through Hyde Park on its customary afternoon outing, Eglantine
nodded to a passing carriage filled with admiring dandies proceeding at a fast clip.

''My dear husband may not be a genuine Scottish baronet,''
Jane's sister said gaily, ''but that's no reason to cease being
called Lady Wallace here in London, do ye think?''

Jane laughed, happy to see her younger sister appear so cheerful, considering the series of harrowing discoveries she'd made
about her ne'er-do-well husband. Dating from Eglantine's re-
moval to London, Sir Thomas had reportedly been frequenting
all the brothels between Edinburgh and Dumfries, and was currently recovering from a severe bout of the clap.

''What are ye going to do about this . . . this predicament?''
Jane asked Eglantine gently.

''Oh,'' replied her sister airily. ''I expect I shall eventually
divorce the sot.''

''*Divorce*?'' Jane said, shocked at the suggestion. ''Ye know
as well as I do, practically no woman alive is granted a divorce,
and rarely is a *man,* unless he's Henry the Eighth!''

''I've had yer solicitor, Charles Gordon, do some checking. I
might win if I charge fraud,'' said Eglantine, matter-of-factly.

''Ah . . . I see,'' Jane said thoughtfully. ''Very clever. Are ye
sure ye should be introduced to the king next week as Lady
Wallace?'' she wondered aloud.

''Absolutely!'' her sister replied tartly. ''Dinna our dear Mama
always say we must keep up appearances!''

Indeed, eight days later, ''Lady'' Wallace was presented by
the Duke and Duchess of Gordon to King George III in the grand
reception hall of St. James's Palace. Jane noted that the monarch

had gained a substantial amount of weight since last they'd met and now resembled nothing so much as a large, bewigged pear. Nevertheless, he was resplendent in ivory silk breeches and a dark blue velvet coat emblazoned with gold braid and the Order of the Garter affixed to his breast.

After the introductions were made, the king turned to Alex and questioned him about his reaction to the growing unrest in the American Colonies.

"Do you not consider them ungrateful children?" the king asked morosely. His double chin trembled as it nestled in the white linen stock encircling his neck. "Parliament merely asks them to pay a minimum of the expenses incurred defending their borders, and they call such taxes 'The Intolerable Acts!' "

" 'Twas regrettable, that business at Lexington and Concord in April," Alex replied delicately.

"Those self-styled 'Minutemen' were given plenty of warning to lay down their arms," continued the king.

"Americans are all savages, Yer Majesty," Jane interjected with a tone of disgust. "Our Redcoats will teach them a lesson in loyalty that's sorely needed."

"Do you expect the violence to continue, Your Majesty?" Alex asked quietly.

King George sighed and readjusted his bulky form on his gilded chair. "Let us hope not. But if it comes," he went on, eyeing Alex shrewdly. "I trust I shall be able to count on you Scots to raise regiments, if we need them?"

"Of course," Jane and Alex replied in unison.

"That is gratifying," replied the king. "And what of my godson, young George?" he inquired, suddenly shifting away from the troubling topic of his rebellious American subjects. The king cast an appreciative glance at Jane's elaborate court gown of ivory silk, shot through with gold threads. "Is the lad here in London with you?"

"No, Yer Majesty," Jane answered, giving the thirty-six-year-old sovereign a mischievous smile. "I doubt our Capital is fortified enough for such an assault. Our littlest bairns are with us, though."

"Ah, yes . . . I had heard you'd added another babe to your brood . . . a girl, I think I heard it was. How many is it now?"

Jane hesitated for a brief second, unsure whether to number Bathia's son among the count. She decided to include him.

"We've five children in the nursery, Yer Majesty," she smiled. " 'Tis a paltry number, when compared with yer nine."

"Quite right," the king answered, obviously pleased by her apparent admiration for his ability to father such a gaggle of royal heirs. "Our dearest queen devotes herself to me and her adopted country. For this, I consider her a jewel more precious than any in my crown." Jane found herself warming to George III's simple, homey virtues, despite the prejudices she had adopted as a youth. There was something almost touching about a king who seemed fond of his wife. " 'Tis a pity our queen is so lately delivered from childbed," he continued. "I shall tell her I have seen you pay us Court."

"If ye would be so kind as to send her my warmest good wishes for her continued recovery," Jane murmured, taking his cue that their audience was at an end.

Once the three visitors were safely inside their coach, Eglantine emitted an unladylike giggle.

"If His Majesty ever had a word with Constable Munro, Jane, they'd lock ye in the Tower!"

"Pray, who is Constable Munro?" Alex asked, puzzled.

" 'Tis simple," teased Eglantine. "Munro was the man who suspected yer dear wife was the perpetrator in a shocking wave of vandalism which occurred along the High Street many years ago."

The duke cocked an eyebrow in the direction of his magnificently attired spouse.

"What did you do, my dear? Steal fish from a hawker's basket?"

Jane smiled uneasily, but remained silent.

"Oh much worse than that!" Eglantine chortled, unmindful of the dangerous emotional waters she was treading. "On Coronation Day in 1760, she and Thomas Fraser crept down the High Street and tore down every single billboard proclaiming George III King of Britain! And here we are in 1775, and everyone in London is saying that the Duchess of Gordon is practically the king's favorite female! Next to Queen Charlotte, of course! Can ye imagine?" she laughed uproariously.

Jane could hardly keep from flinching at the sound of Thomas's name. Neither she nor Alex had mentioned him in six years. Her sister's innocent indiscretion had bared an old wound. Jane glanced at her husband. His face showed no discernible emotion, yet she could guess precisely what he was thinking: 'twas always bad luck to speak of the Devil.

*   *   *

Jane glanced out of the sitting room window at Gordon Castle, startled by the sudden shrieking sounds that wafted up to her from the direction of the tall tower. Looking out, she could see the Duchess Tree, which had grown steadily to a height of some thirty-five feet. As the child's alarm grew more shrill, Jane dashed down the corridor to the library.

"Alex . . . Alex! Come quickly. The two Geordies are playing in the scaffolding and they canna get down!" she exclaimed.

Without waiting for the duke's reply, she dashed out the side door onto the terrace and ran across the manicured lawn toward the tower. Arriving breathlessly at the scene, Jane shifted her worried gaze from her daredevil five-year-old son to his equally boisterous nine-year-old half-brother perched atop the scaffolding cradling the old castle tower during the ongoing repairs and additions. Jane kept a concerned eye on the littler George who by this time had lost his courage and was whimpering with fright. The older George was perched on the wooden plank above him, looking out at the surrounding estate with studied nonchalance.

On the ground, Alexander hurried across the lawn with his architect, John Baxter, along with the duke's ever-present butler-confidant, William Marshall. The trio had been discussing the planting of still more trees and shrubs to decorate the evolving parkland. The carefully designed landscape would eventually provide a fitting setting for the princely mansion, which was now all but completed. The castle's two new Georgian pavilions surrounded the stark original fourteenth-century tower, and it was the construction scaffolding that had tempted the two little Georges to wager which of them could climb higher.

"Dinna either of ye scamps move a muscle, do ye hear me!" Jane shouted up through the gold and red October foliage of a larch tree that stood nearby. "Stay right where ye are, ye wee devils!"

The Gordon's seven-year-old daughter, Charlotte, stood next to the tower, twisting the strands of her dark curls. She smirked up at her nemeses.

"Now you'll catch it, you naughty boys," Charlotte crowed. "Mother warned you."

Jane ruefully noted the little girl's clipped accent, reflecting the influence of the English tutor the duke had engaged for the lass's education. In fact, none of Jane's children had a hint of the Scottish burr that still clung to her own speech inflections, despite her frequent exposure to the court of St. James and the grandest social circles in London.

"Shush, Charlotte," Jane said sharply, as little Madelina, aged three, began to wail, fearing she, too, might soon receive a measure of her papa's wrath. The baby, Susan, lay on a soft tartan rug under a tree, sleeping soundly through the uproar caused by the rowdy antics of the two Georges. Nancy Christie, the nursemaid who was now of marriageable age, wrung her hands distractedly.

"Och! Those Geordies . . ." stammered the eighteen-year-old to the assembled adults. "I was playing a game with the lassies, ma'am, and minding my sister Jean as well," she said, referring to the pretty, five-year-old daughter of their housekeeper, Mrs. Christie. The child had pale hair and none of the sharpness of features that marred her mother and sister's looks. She was about the same age as the Duchess's George, as everyone referred to the mischievous Marquess of Huntly. "The Duke's George scampered up there when I wasna looking!" Nancy lamented, pointing to the scaffolding embracing the old castle tower. "And sure, if yer Duchess's George weren't right behind 'im!"

Jane smiled to herself over the name the family and staff had adopted for the duke's two sons. Jane supposed it was the talk of the Highlands that the two half-brothers looked so much alike and were being brought up together, as if their parentage were the same. The Duke's George, however, could be a holy terror, as he had certainly proved this very afternoon.

Jane watched Alexander sternly lecture his two sons perched overhead. Her eyes drifted to the brilliant hues of the seasonal foliage. Suddenly, a memory flashed before her of the sheaves of Thomas's letter from America, tumbling among the russet leaves, which had dotted the graveyard by the banks of the River Eye near Ayton House. Despite all that had happened between Alex and her, despite her seven-year struggle to disavow the deep bond she felt for another man, nothing seemed to lessen the void she continued to feel over her loss of Thomas . . . a loss that struck her at times she least expected it.

Sternly, Jane forced herself to mentally recite a familiar litany of happy times, times when she and Alex had been able to share a sense of satisfaction over their life together. Both took great joy in the children's small accomplishments and she hastily reminded herself of the many times Alex had honored her by soliciting her opinions and incorporating many of them in his day-to-day decisions over his northern empire. He had supported her plans to encourage weaving and other cottage industries among the poor, and he often credited her publicly for the fact that a new way of life was slowly emerging for women tenants in the region who spun wool and knitted stockings with materials supplied by the estate. The products were then sold and the monies split with the wives of the crofters.

Forcing her thoughts back to the problem at hand, Jane watched with relief as Alex coaxed the elder George down to a plank within striking distance of his rescuers. Her husband reached up effortlessly and lifted his elder son to the ground. However, George Gordon, the Marquess of Huntly, resolutely refused to budge an inch farther.

"Well, Mr. Baxter . . . you're the architect," Alex said jovially. "Any notions of how we get this last wee lad down from the tower?"

"Excuse me, Yer Grace," said William Marshall, "but perhaps a tether thrown up to the boy that he could tie around his waist . . . then we could lower him slowly, pulley fashion."

"That scaffolding's far too unstable!" snapped Jane, her distaste for the butler barely disguised. "Nancy, lift Susan off that tartan rug. We can all hold it for this kelpie to fall into."

"What a capital idea, Yer Grace!" said Baxter, the architect, admiringly. Marshall looked subdued at her suggestion and remained silent.

Nancy Christie shooed her little sister Jean to one side and scooped up the sleeping toddler, Susan. Jane snatched the blanket from the freshly clipped grass and handed the corners of it to the three men. The adults gathered in a circle, creating a wool basket out of the tartan blanket. With a sigh, little Huntly closed his eyes and pushed off, tumbling harmlessly into the blanket held tautly on all sides by the adults. The lad bounced a few times on the stretched wool tartan, squealing with delight by the time he came to rest.

"Again! Papa . . . please . . . may I jump again?"

Everyone, including Jane, burst out laughing as Alex scooped up his son, bringing his face close to the boy's tear-smudged countenance, which was now wreathed in smiles.

"No, you may not, you little savage! And both you and your brother had better not let me see you up there—*ever*!"

Alex's lecture was suddenly interrupted by the sound of horse's hooves pounding along the gracefully curving entrance drive to Gordon Castle. Coming toward them at a dead run was Jane's brother, Hamilton Maxwell, who urged his mount off the path in the direction of the tower. Grass divots flew from the turf in his wake as he reined his horse to an abrupt stop.

"Ye'll not be riding my Dougal Dan again, if ye abuse him so, brother mine," Jane said indignantly, pointing to the necklace of sweat on her favorite horse.

Hamilton was in the army now and appeared totally preoccupied with military life. This attitude quite annoyed their mother, Lady Maxwell, who felt her middle son should be seriously looking for a wife. But Ham liked riflery, wine and wenching, in that order, and thus far, had shown no signs of settling down.

" 'Tis official!" Hamilton panted, ignoring Jane's caustic comment and throwing himself out of the saddle. "Master Simon has today received a warrant from the king to raise the Seventy-first Fraser Highlanders to fight the American rebels!" he continued excitedly. "They've ordered two Highland battalions, Alex . . . that's more than twenty-three hundred men who must be recruited up here by next April! The ships will sail from Greenock by the first of May to join General Howe in Boston. His Majesty's government has finally decided to send the kind of lads who can put an end to the bumptious nonsense going on over there!"

Two Fraser battalions! Jane thought excitedly. Surely Thomas would want to transfer from the Black Watch in Ireland to his godfather's own regiment. Such shifts were accomplished all the time. After all, he'd been with the forty-second nearly ten years now. Hamilton's news could mean Thomas would be returning to Scotland—at least for a while. *Perhaps they would meet . . .*

Twisting the corner of the tartan fabric she still grasped in her hand, Jane soundly chastised herself for her disloyalty and turned her thoughts to her old enemy, Simon Fraser, Master of Lovat.

Grudgingly, she had to admire that canny laird. He had played the English bootlick for thirty years since the disastrous affair with Bonnie Prince Charlie, and, finally, it had won him the prize. His years as a respectable lawyer and soldier, during which he had maneuvered to recover his father's estates in Beauly from the Crown, had achieved their purpose. The man she blamed most for Thomas's departure to America had finally gotten his Highland lands back from the king—at a price tag of twenty thousand pounds, paid in 1774 to the Treasury. The old goat would now achieve the further honor of having a regiment created in the name of Clan Fraser, and receiving a promotion to the rank of General in the bargain.

Over the years, she had made efforts to shrug off her long-buried resentment toward her neighbor—once in Edinburgh, now in the Highlands. Yet, whenever Jane had encountered Queen Charlotte during the fashionable winter seasons she and Alexander spent in London, she always managed to convey something mildly disparaging about the almighty Simon Fraser. He might be able to supply the highest quality cannon fodder for Britain's overseas adventures, but, thanks to her influence through the queen, Jane doubted the king would ever truly trust the son of the Fox. Much to Jane's satisfaction, George III had declined Simon's bid to have his title of Baron restored. She *was a duchess,* she thought with grim pleasure, *and Simon, still a commoner!*

Jane felt her husband's piercing stare even before she turned toward him. Alex was studying her features as if he were trying to read her thoughts.

I should be praying to St. Ninian that Thomas stays with his old comrades in Ireland and leaves me in peace! Jane lectured herself sternly, secreting away the longing that the news had instantly aroused in her.

But the thought of seeing him again could not be so easily extinguished. Try as she might, in these last years there had not been a day she didn't think of Thomas, wonder of his whereabouts, worry for his safety. She had forced herself to accept the fact that she could never be Thomas's wife, but she knew, with the awful certainty of the damned, that she could never completely give her heart to Alex. The price of Thomas's survival was the terrible burden that all three of them carried wherever they went.

"Master Simon has *personally* asked me to form a company within the regiment," Hamilton continued excitedly, "and he asked me to convey to ye his hopes that Yer Graces will sponsor my attempts at recruitment on Gordon lands. My reward will be a captaincy," he said proudly.

"Why, of course, Hamilton," Alex said quietly, continuing to stare at Jane with a look she found exceedingly unsettling. "Jane and I will do everything we can to assist your success in this venture with the Frasers, won't we, my dear?"

"I wouldna go much out of my way to help Simon Fraser, I can tell ye that!" Jane retorted, before she could check herself. "But since 'tis to be yer own company, Ham, I-I'll do whatever Alex deems fitting." Jane turned abruptly to face the children who were staring at their Uncle Hamilton in awe. "Now, 'tis time for all this foolishness to end!"

"That's right," Alex agreed. "Back to the nursery with the lot of you. Ham, will you join me for a dram of whiskey in the library? I'd like to hear more of this recruiting venture."

Alex and the men headed for the castle entrance, leaving Jane with whining children tugging at her skirts. She would have preferred nothing more than to follow the men into the library to hear every word of what Hamilton had learned about the new British offensive to subdue the rebellious Colonies. She had always found it extremely irksome that women were excluded from such discussions as a matter of course.

"All right, children," Jane shouted above the din of the youngsters' chirping voices. "Nancy is going to take ye in for yer tea. I want the boys cleaned up and ye, girls, minding yer manners when the cake is passed out. I will see ye in the nursery in three-quarters of an hour and I expect ye to behave like proper lads and lassies."

She ruffled the hair of both Georges, despite her best resolve to be stern with them. The two troublemakers looked at her adoringly, grateful she had miraculously spared them from their father's wrath.

"Yes, Mama," her George said dutifully.

"We'll be extra good all day, Yer Grace," echoed the Duke's George, and, like ducklings, they followed Nancy Christie and her pretty little sister Jean, along the path to the house.

Jane walked across the green and leaned against the bark of the Duchess Tree, attempting to sort out the jumble of feelings inside her. If Thomas transferred to the Fraser Highlanders, she was bound to see him before the regiment sailed for America, if only at a distance on a parade field. She wondered if Thomas would find her much changed after seven years? Despite four full-term pregnancies, her figure, at age twenty-five, was as trim as ever.

Jane reflected on the startling news Hamilton had brought to her cloistered world at Gordon Castle: Scottish troops were being mobilized for duty in America; there was an excellent chance that Thomas Fraser would be returning to the Highlands, if only briefly, from his long exile in Ireland; and Alex had all but endorsed the idea of her helping Hamilton recruit for the 71st Fraser Highlanders within the vast stretches of Gordon land. *Where, oh where, would such a journey take her?* she wondered.

17

November 1775

The fist pounding on the brothel door might as well have been pummeling Thomas Fraser's skull. The continuous thuds reverberated loudly across the bedchamber, penetrating his fog-shrouded brain like the noise of cannon fire.

"Holy Mother," mumbled a voice emanating from the feminine figure whose ample thighs draped heavily across his own. "G'way! The loo-tenen's not here, are ye?"

The harlot's voice was slurred and laced with the scent of the ample whiskey she had shared with him the previous night. Thomas turned over in the rumpled bed. A bottle of spirits wasn't the only thing he and the wench had shared. His groin was sore, not to mention certain other parts of his anatomy. He glanced over at his bed partner's touseled locks. Her name was Katie, he remembered. Yes, Katie Connelly. He had chosen her instead of his usual companion, Brigid, who understandably had glared at him venomously as he retreated upstairs, his palm pressing against Katie's broad bottom. Mistress Connelly's enormous, pendulous breasts and bovine figure were unique in his experience. What's more, her blue-black hair and blue eyes brought to mind that damnable vixen, Arabella O'Brien Delaney. When he'd spotted those ebony tresses earlier in the evening, Thomas had had a sudden fancy to plough the strumpet within an inch of her life. Katie Connelly had proved more than a match for him, however, cheerfully writhing beneath him most of the night on a lumpy horsehair mattress in Madame Geraghty's finest boudoir.

"Fraser! Fraser, lad? Are ye in there?"

Dumbfounded, Thomas recognized the voice. James Maxwell had somehow tracked him to the most disreputable whorehouse in all of Dublin, the retreat where Thomas assuaged his moments of loneliness and despair.

"Is Lieutenant Thomas Fraser *in* there?" Captain Maxwell bellowed. "Because if he is, I am going to wait exactly one more minute for him, and then, the Devil take him and his damnable Commission in the Fraser Highlanders!''

''Ho, there, James!'' Thomas answered Jane's uncle. Over the years, the older man had become a fast friend and mentor.

Suppressing a groan, he swung his long legs over Katie's soft hips and slid off the bed. The room seemed to wobble around him. He was naked and the room was icy cold. Shivering, he wrapped his wrinkled kilt around his waist and cracked open the door a few inches.

''Ah . . . greetings, James,'' he said sheepishly. ''I fear I've overslept.''

''That's right,'' his longtime comrade said, tight-lipped. ''And ye've also missed parade. Again.''

''I dinna think these Irish potatoes are much impressed by our fancy drills, James, old boy. Really, I—''

''God's wounds, Fraser! Ye look like ye've been in a coal mine for a month. Pull yerself together, lad! Ye'll need yer strength for yer journey across the Irish Sea.''

''What . . . ?'' Thomas faltered, staring at the thick parchment Maxwell thrust into his hands.

''Yer Commission, I expect,'' James said shortly.

Thomas was aware that Jane's uncle soundly disapproved of the hedonistic lifestyle he'd succumbed to in this wretched outpost these past seven years, but the older man made no further comment. He merely gestured toward the missive Thomas held in his hand.

'' 'Tis affixed with yer godfather's seal. A few of the other lads received theirs today as well. There's a ship bound for Greenock tomorrow.''

Thomas broke the wax crest, stared at his orders for a long moment, and closed his eyes.

''I'll see her, ye know,'' he said, his voice cracking. ''Simon's asked yer nephew Hamilton to raise a company.''

''And ye'll say, 'Good morning, Yer Grace' when ye do,'' James Maxwell said gruffly. ''Dash it, man! Yer life's going by and ye're living it like a dirty dog!''

''I know,'' Thomas replied quietly.

''This is a chance to change all that,'' his friend urged. ''Ye'll get out of this hovel and see some action!''

''I had enough action at Fort Pitt to last a lifetime,'' Thomas said, looking over his shoulder to observe whether the prostitute was awake. Katie had flopped on her back and was snoring like a trooper.

"Now ye'll be a Fraser Highlander, lad," James Maxwell said kindly. "Ye'll be with yer own kin."

"Aye," Thomas said thoughtfully. "And I'll be going home to Scotland—at least for a while."

The potbellied sergeant by the name of Dougal Fraser hiked his heavy drum against his well-worn red and moss green kilt. He began to beat out a solemn cadence as the Gordon party approached the hulking ruins of Elgin Cathedral. The ragged stones of the ancient church etched themselves bleakly against a clear winter's sky. The group, which included a piper and a corporal carrying a banner with the Fraser coat of arms, was headed for the market square to try its luck recruiting one more time. Hamilton Maxwell's company of 71st Fraser Highlanders was still shy at least a dozen men.

Their journey this crisp December day took them to several villages and hamlets on the main route leading to Inverness. It seemed to Jane that the mere sight of the distinctive Fraser tartan slung about the sergeant's broad hips had put Alex into a foul temper. Neither Hamilton, nor Alex's brother Lord George, a local MP anxious to be seen engaging in such patriotic activities, nor even young Charlotte, could draw the duke out of his dark humor. The rest of them grew gloomy, too, as they had failed to enroll a single recruit, despite their morning's efforts. Jane decided once more to try to rouse her husband from this glum state as the party entered the outskirts of the market town of Elgin, which flanked both sides of the River Lossie.

"Alex . . . look! The cathedral," she exclaimed, pointing to the enormous, roofless structure put to the torch in the fourteenth century by the infamous Wolf of Badenoch.

The place was imposing, even in its desolation. She tried to push away thoughts of that other ruin associated with the demented Wolf—the miniature castle at Loch-an-Eilean guarded by wild swans where she'd last seen Thomas nearly eight years before. Though neither she nor Alex had mentioned the subject all morning, both were trying to adjust to the shock of the casual announcement made by Hamilton over breakfast earlier in the day, that Thomas Fraser was transferring from the Black Watch to his godfather's regiment.

Shifting her weight on her pony, Jane addressed her husband sharply. "Alex!" she repeated as the huge religious edifice loomed ahead, "We're nearly there! Look at the *cathedral*!"

"We'll all be buried there one day," Alex replied grimly,

nodding at the crumbling gable of the cathedral's south transept. "St. Mary's Aisle has long been reserved for the Gordons."

"For pity's sake!" Jane retorted in exasperation. "If ye persist with this gloomy attitude, we'll not get one lad to sign the rolls. Come, now, m'lord . . . aren't we supposed to be the 'Gay Gordons?' Well, then, let's have a little gaiety! Sergeant, beat the drum faster . . . *faster*, I say!"

Alex merely stared ahead as the soldier hastened to respond to Jane's command. He flailed his stick against the taut, stretched hide of the drum, picking up the pace.

"Aye, that's the spirit, Jane!" enthused Hamilton, grateful his sister was attempting to lighten the leaden atmosphere.

"Mama, will the men in Elgin be pleased to join His Majesty's army?" piped Charlotte, sitting primly on the small Highland pony Alex had recently given her for her seventh birthday.

"We shall see when we get there, pet." She smiled fondly at her daughter who sat sidesaddle on her small mount, trying her best to appear ladylike. "That's why we brought ye with us, moppet, to charm the lads into enlisting!"

"A knock on the head's the most likely persuader," Lord George, the duke's brother, commented sourly, compressing his prissy lips into a thin line. "That, and a few well-placed threats against the heathen."

Gradually, Jane had learned that, as far as her eccentric brother-in-law was concerned, anyone who wasn't a member of the Protestant Association, of which he was a rabid supporter, was a heathen, regardless of religious affiliation. Jane wagered that Lord George's primary motivation for helping them recruit was to force Alex into an obligation to pay off his latest round of drinking and gambling debts.

Her cynical reflections were interrupted by the sight of window sashes flying up in the rows of houses flanking the cobbled streets of the quaint town. Elgin lay ten miles west of Gordon Castle and the appearance of a duke was cause for celebration. Before long, their party halted in the open square in front of the local tavern, known as the Star Inn. The duke nodded morosely to the sergeant, who gave the drum several thunderous claps. Then the corpulent recruiter ceased his banging and spoke to the assembled throng in stentorian tones.

"Drinks for ye, lads! Drinks, and a chance to serve in one of His Majesty's finest regiments. And ye'll be paid in the bargain!"

As the sergeant continued to harangue the apathetic crowd, Jane sat quietly on her pony. Slowly, the better part of the throng began to melt away. Hamilton dismounted and waded into a knot of young men who were gazing skeptically at the recruiting sergeant.

"Now ye might ask . . . what're Maxwells and Gordons doing, recruiting for a company of *Frasers*?" Hamilton interrupted loudly, slowing the departure of a knot of likely looking recruits. Quickly, he launched into his well-practiced speech designed to lure potential enlistees into the ranks. "Well, lads, 'tis a chance for us to put porridge in yer bellies, give ye a fine kilt to wear proudly after the dark years of the Diskilting, and offer ye a chance to serve with yer brother Highlanders! Come now, lads, have ye a drink!"

Hamilton thumped the back of the boy nearest him and proffered his own tankard of ale. Bystanders on the circle's periphery self-consciously began to edge away, despite Hamilton's stirring words and the spirits being passed out in increasing quantity.

Alex slouched in his saddle, remaining aloof from the effort. Taking note of the rapidly thinning crowd, Jane shouted impulsively, "Ye, there . . . Piper! Play us a bonnie tune in honor of His Majesty's new regiment. My daughter and I will dance with any man who enlists this day in the Seventy-first Fraser Highlanders, the finest fighting force Scotland has ever produced!"

Stirred from his lethargy by Jane's unexpected announcement, Alex stared at her incredulously. The piper struck up "Hielan Laddie," and Jane, without waiting for assistance, sprang down from her horse and lifted Charlotte from her saddle. The little girl was thrilled to be the center of attention, along with her beautiful mother. She fell in behind Jane, who skipped in and out of the crowd in time to the music. A roar of approval rose from the throng, attracting the attention of bystanders who had drifted off to survey the open stalls of the Elgin marketplace.

As Jane and her little daughter commenced a merry jig, a strapping young man of six feet joined them in performing the dance's high, hopping steps. Soon, a second young man, and then another took advantage of the rare opportunity to dance with a duchess. The five of them commenced whirling and turning to the wild skirl of the pipes.

" 'Tis worth the risk of facing rebel cannon to step lively with ye, m'lady," gasped her gallant partner as the music came to its boisterous conclusion.

"Then ye'll accept the King's Shilling?" Jane panted, attempting to catch her breath. She smiled up at the lad as provocatively as she dared without compromising her dignity as a duchess.

"Aye, m'lady," he replied with a rakish grin and turned to shake Hamilton's hand, taking the coin to seal the bargain. "And here's me pledge!"

"Here's mine too, Yer Grace," shouted his companion, not to be outdone.

"And mine, Duchess!" chimed in the third, accepting the King's Shilling.

"Huzzah!" Jane exclaimed to the multitude, which echoed her shout with cheers and whistles. "What's yer name, laddie?" she asked of the strapping six-footer.

"T-Thornton, m'lady," he stammered, suddenly tongue-tied. "C-Christopher Thornton."

"Three cheers for Corporal Christopher Thornton and the brave Fraser Highlanders!" she shouted happily, and the crowd roared with delight.

Buoyed by the success of her impromptu ploy, Jane turned toward Alex and held out her hand.

"Come, m'lord . . . will ye not dance for such a noble endeavor?" she asked, expecting him to take her cue enthusiastically. Surely a dancing duke would bring in many more recruits than her own modest efforts had produced.

Without responding, Alex swung off his horse and strode into the circle of bystanders. The crowd began applauding their local laird and his daring duchess, and the piper squeezed his instrument, summoning up another rousing tune.

"Why, certainly, Your Grace," Alex said brusquely, bowing perfunctorily as he began the dance. "Since you've found the Seventy-first Fraser Highlanders *such* a worthy cause, how could I refuse?"

The piper wailed the tune and Alex began the hornpipe "Jack on the Green," a strenuous jig that simulated the fertilizing spirit of spring. Alex's calf muscles bulged as his feet cut in and out in the complicated, suggestive steps. The dance pantomimed the planting of seeds and the plucking of fruits of such labor. The duke's eyes bore into Jane's as he whirled faster and faster, his kilt spraying out in a circle, revealing his sinewy thighs. When, at last, the pipes skirled to a climax, the cheers from the crowd were genuine and rousing. Staring straight ahead, Alex strode over to Jane in the midst of the tumult and bent low to whisper in her ear.

"Are you pleased your husband plays lickspittal to Fraser's

kin?'' he hissed, unmindful of several more men who'd stepped up to accept the King's Shilling. ''You are perfectly welcome to put yourself on exhibition if you wish, dancing like a strumpet on the green, but I'll thank you to leave me out of such patent pandering to Fraser and his ilk!''

Ignoring Jane's look of astonishment, he stalked inside the Star Inn without another word.

The sound of shouts and hoofbeats and creaking harnesses outside her coach roused Jane from an exhausted slumber. A week of touring had brought her and the recruiting party, at last, to within six miles of Inverness where, mercifully, their carriage had met them. Their toil had been more than repaid, however, thanks primarily to Jane's inspiration to offer to dance with any lad willing to enlist in the 71st Fraser Highlanders. At Hamilton's urging, she continued to perform her favorite Highland dances, and her brother continued to sign on his full complement of men. And the more Jane danced, the less the duke participated in the recruitment effort. Nevertheless, eighty-nine lads had followed them to their present destination—Culloden House—on the banks of the River Nairn where all the new companies making up the 71st Fraser Highland regiment were gathered in the chilly December dusk.

''I doubt John Forbes has a footman to spare, by the looks of things,'' Jane heard Alex grumble as she pulled herself upright and peered outside the carriage window at the mass of confusion reigning in front of the large Georgian structure she knew to be Culloden House.

A small tent city had been erected on the frozen ground, which comprised a portion of the forty acres of parkland surrounding the mansion. The dark red brick of the imposing house was trimmed with white sandstone. Its high roof and balustraded facade had a slightly raw look, since it had been built only three years previously, in 1772. The stately manse had replaced an ancient, fortified castle that, nearly thirty years earlier, had housed Clan Fraser and Prince Charles on the eve of the disastrous Battle of Culloden Moor fought on the soggy heath a mile away. Today, Jane couldn't help but note the irony that the hundreds of newly enlisted soldiers bivouacked outside their coach wore the Fraser colors now, as King's Men. Political necessity had certainly made strange bedfellows, Jane thought to herself as she stared across the frozen expanse of the huge estate.

Some of the soldiers were tending their horses, others were

cooking their supper over small open fires, and still others were
bundled up inside their tents catching the last solid hours of sleep
before commencing the training of hundreds of green recruits. In a
few months time, they would all march to Glasgow where they
would meet the other battalions of the 71st Fraser Highlanders
and, in May, sail from Greenock, at the mouth of the River
Clyde, for America.

Jane gathered her cloak tightly about her shoulders to ward off
the chill winds blowing toward them from the Moray Firth. She
clasped her daughter Charlotte's hand as the welcome warmth of
Culloden House's front entry greeted the weary travelers.

"Yer Grace! How delighted we are ye've arrived before dusk!"
boomed their host, John Forbes, advancing to greet them in the
entryway. "M'lady, a light supper has been laid and a fire is
already crackling in yer chambers upstairs," he said kindly,
perceiving the fatigue written on the tired faces of his guests.
"Ye should have time for a sound nap before the evening's
festivities begin!"

"How very kind," Jane said, rallying from her exhaustion to
convey her appreciation for her host's hospitality in the face of
such frantic activity.

"We're a wee bit cramped, as ye can see," apologized John
Forbes, nodding toward a group of officers ascending a sweeping
staircase in the hall, "but I hope ye find the guest quarters
satisfactory."

"I'm sure we'll be more than comfortable," Alex said, taking
Jane's elbow.

"Oh, my lady Duchess . . . an old friend was asking after ye
this afternoon," Forbes said, halting their progress toward the
staircase. "A Captain Thomas Fraser of Struy. Tells me the two
of ye were neighbors in Edinburgh and used to race pigs down
the High Street when ye were wee bairns!" Duncan Forbes
slapped his thigh and gave a hearty laugh. "I'd heard that tale
before, but 'twas like a breath of spring air to have the truth o' it
confirmed!" he teased. "Are ye sure ye're not a Highlander,
born and bred?"

" 'Tis true . . ." she replied faintly. "The part about racing
pigs. . . ."

Jane felt as if an invisible hand had clutched her shoulder and
instinctively, she reached for the bannister to prevent herself
from pitching forward down the stairs.

"If you see Captain Fraser before we do," Alex intervened
smoothly, "I beg you to congratulate him for us on his promo-

tion and please convey our pleasure at the prospect of this unexpected reunion. Now if you will excuse us. . . .''

In a daze, Jane allowed herself to be led upstairs and down a darkened corridor to their rooms. A maid assigned to Charlotte took the little girl to the nursery at the end of the hall. Jane soon found herself alone with her husband in the ornate bedroom, festooned with bloodred brocade curtains and matching silk-upholstered furniture. She felt Alex's eyes boring into her back as she sank to the small stool facing the mirrored mahogany dressing table.

''Fatigued, my dear?'' he asked in a soft voice whose edges curled in unpleasant sarcasm.

''I'm utterly exhausted,'' Jane breathed, shutting her eyes against the world that seemed to be closing in on her.

''A bath and a nap should restore your spirits,'' he replied. ''That, and the anticipated pleasure of seeing old friends.''

Slowly Jane opened her eyes and gazed up at Alex's reflection in the looking glass.

''I fear the journey has made me feel unwell,'' she said, her eyes sliding away from his face. ''I dinna think I'm up to coping with those hordes tonight, Alex. I shall have a tray and go to bed.''

''I doubt that mere fatigue has put you in this unhappy state, my dear Jane,'' Alex answered, his face darkening dangerously. ''Could it be you are feeling rather giddy at the prospect of seeing *Captain* Fraser after all these years?''

He had emphasized Thomas's promotion in a voice laced with bitter mockery. Alex's next words overrode her feeble protests.

''Any fool can see you are shaken by the effect of our host's announcement, so let's not perpetuate your little masquerade. No, my dear wife, 'tis *I* who shall take ill this night, and you must represent the Gordons in my place!''

''Alex, dinna *do* this!'' Jane pleaded in a low voice. ''Dinna put more trouble than need be in our path! Try to understand . . .'tis true . . . 'tis . . . *unsettling* . . . to have Thomas appear in our lives so suddenly, after all this time, but ye are my true husband, and I yer wife. We have four children . . . five, counting Geordie, and I do count the lad! We've been happy! We mustna let anything destroy what we've built!''

'' 'Tis not *I* who destroy what we have!'' Alex replied, his voice rising angrily, ''but your *love* for him! Don't think I can't read your thoughts at times, Jane, when the expression on your face tells all! Don't bother to deny it! You dream, while we make love, of *him* lying at your side! You wonder what our babes would have looked like, had *he* been their sire. You—''

''*Stop it*, Alex!'' Jane cried, jumping up from the dressing table seat and whirling around to face him.

Her skin was flushed, and her voice shook slightly. She was shocked by Alex's uncanny perception regarding the feelings and thoughts she had tried hard to suppress for so long. Stunned by the murderous look he gave her, she quickly turned her head to avoid his gaze and walked toward the bedroom window. The heavy damask curtains were drawn shut against the icy winds whistling outside.

''We should never have raised a company for Hamilton . . .'' she despaired, holding back tears. ''We should never have *come* here!''

''You think by merely avoiding Thomas Fraser, you can play the loyal, dutiful wife?'' Alex snarled, following her. From behind he grabbed both her shoulders with his hands and dug his fingers into her flesh.

''Alex, please . . . stop!'' she said weakly, wincing at the pressure his hands were exerting against her arms. ''I could see ye've been upset all week long, and there's no need! Ye know how much I care for ye . . . this jealousy of yers is . . . well . . .'tis unhealthy . . . *I am yer wife!*'' she cried.

''Well, let's see how convincing you are in that role, knowing he's here, at Culloden House, mayhap in this very *wing*!'' he hissed into her ear.

''Alex, please—'' Jane stammered, twisting out of his grasp. When she turned to face him, she was frightened by the unnatural glitter in his eyes.

Ignoring her pleas, he crushed his lips against hers, bruising her mouth roughly with his own. It was not an act of passion, it was an act of rage. Jane's body stiffened with alarm. Releasing her briefly from his embrace, Alex led her swiftly to the canopied bed, richly appointed in red brocade. She stood, paralyzed, while he held on to a newel post of the four-poster for support and yanked off his boots.

''Undress yourself, lass,'' he commanded harshly, peeling off his coat and waistcoat and tossing them across the room.

''I will *not*!'' Jane replied defiantly, staring at him as he continued to divest himself of his clothing.

''But, Jane, my dear,'' he said, his voice low and slightly menacing, ''I only wish to gauge the degree of affection you truly hold for me, your husband. 'Tis a matter of trust, you see. I don't know for certain if I trust you. I wish you to *demonstrate* the affection for me you claim is in your heart.''

Alex shed his breeches, kicking them into a heap on the floor. His white linen shirt could not conceal evidence of the heat coursing through his body. He took several paces toward Jane and smiled grimly.

''No words of love? No heartfelt preliminaries?'' He took her chin between his tense fingers and stared stonily into her eyes. Jane willed herself not to flinch from his gaze. At length, he shrugged. ''Suit yourself. Since I know in your heart that you long to behave like Fraser's slut, you shall be treated like one!''

Before she could protest, he roughly forced her face down on the bed and savagely pushed up the hem of her traveling gown with both hands. With one violent motion, he ripped off her undergarments, leaving them in shreds.

Jane reeled from the shock of Alex's sudden assault, appalled that their years of passionate lovemaking could degenerate in the space of an instant into this repugnant act. His kisses sought not to arouse her, but to wound, his lips bruising the back of her neck, his teeth sharp, as he angrily nipped the flesh of her shoulder through the material of her bodice. Her fingers clutched at the bedcovers as she tried to escape from under him, but Alex's sheer strength and weight made that impossible.

At length, she stopped struggling and lay silently beneath him, a numbness supplanting her feelings of outrage. He entered her quickly and without concern for her comfort, pounding the message of his furious jealousy to the very core of her being. Soon the pain of his relentless battering receded and Jane was barely aware of his final release. The heat radiating from his body was stifling and the glistening sweat on his torso soaked the back of her gown.

Except for the sound of Alex's jagged breathing, the silence permeating the room was palpable. His weight was oppressive, but Jane forced herself to remain still. A cold core of rage, centered in her chest, began to spread throughout her body and even seemed to fill the room. Floating in Jane's memory, the drowned corpse of her old Edinburgh friend Matilda Sinclair rose before her. The woman stared at her with lifeless eyes, another victim of another husband's fury.

Alex withdrew from Jane and stood beside to the bed. She rolled over onto her side and gazed at her husband's profile, recalling the scene, etched permanently in her mind's eye, of Jock Sinclair, clad in his tanner's apron, lying along the bank of

North Loch, dead from an apoplectic seizure exactly ten years ago.

Sighing deeply, Alex sat next to her on the bed and idly stroked her arm.

"Jane, I—I'm—"

He ran a slender finger along the line of her clenched jaw. Jane flinched slightly and reached down to smooth her skirt along the length of her bruised legs. Wordlessly, she turned away from him onto her left side, curling her legs against her stomach to gather warmth from her own body. After a few minutes, she felt Alex rise from the bed. A gentle breeze caressed her body as he drew up the blood-red counterpane to cover her.

A curtain of fog seemed to drift over her, blanking out all thought of what had just occurred and bringing with it, a blessed unconsciousness.

When she awoke two hours later, Alex was not in the room. Two maids carrying a heavy brass tub slung between them deposited their burden with a thud in front of the chamber's roaring fire.

Jane raised her throbbing head from the pillow as one of the maids poured scalding water from the first of several steaming kettles the two lasses had hauled up from the kitchen.

"His Grace asked me to tell ye, m'lady, that an urgent matter of estate business forced him to return immediately to Gordon Castle," said the maid with a mass of carrot red ringlets capping her head. The other young maid turned to hoist a second kettle of water over the tub while her companion stirred in a mixture of highland herbs, including elderflower, comfrey, coltsfoot, dried heather, and thyme, which gave the water a pungent fragrance Jane could smell from across the room. "The duke asks that ye follow him to Fochabers in a few days' time," Jane's informant continued, knitting her orange brows together in concentration in order to recite the duke's words exactly as he'd told them before his abrupt departure. "He begs ye to stand for him as chief representative of Clan Gordon at the troop's reception tonight."

"Thank ye," Jane said wearily. "And now, please leave me for an hour. I can manage on my own."

Hundreds of candles glowed in the grand salon of Culloden House. The mellow light transformed its pale lemon-colored walls, enlivened with ornately carved molding, to the shade of golden amber. The sounds of a string quartet playing pieces by the fashionable German George Frideric Handel washed over the room now filled to capacity with the scarlet-coated officers in formal attire. Their swords and epaulets glittered among the taffeta and silk gowns worn by the small number of women in attendance.

Jane held her brother Hamilton's arm tightly to steady herself as the pair descended the broad staircase and entered the ballroom. Despite her long, soothing bath, Jane felt stiff and sore with each step. If the two maids had seen several small bruises on their mistress's body as they assisted Jane into her sea green taffeta dress, the young women had kept these observations to themselves. The burning coal of anger and humiliation embedded in Jane's breast flared momentarily at the memory of Alex's behavior toward her. Husband or not, he had assaulted her . . . raped her, was a more accurate description, she thought wretchedly. No doubt, there were many soldiers in this very room who had similarly attacked women who'd crossed their paths in the lands they had conquered. With an overriding sense of despair, Jane wondered how she would ever survive the long reception ahead.

Looking around the room, she knew instinctively that somewhere among the blur of red jackets stood Thomas—tall, broad-shouldered, his garnet mane making him stand out from the crowd. Would his features still be as sharply defined, given the years since last they'd met? She wondered how time had changed him.

A chill passed through her body, despite the hot room and the heady odors generated by the assembly of humanity pressed together in the stuffy chamber. Judging from the pungent smell assaulting her nostrils, many of the King's Cavaliers had foregone the luxury of bathing for some time. Perhaps Thomas, too, was less fastidious in his person, having lived so long among the heathen Irish. Did he, too, now assume the male prerogative of taking a woman sexually, whether she desired it or not? As Hamilton led her across the large chamber, Jane attempted to blot out the image of Alex and the blood-red bedchamber upstairs.

Perhaps Thomas had decided, after all, to avoid a meeting altogether. *'Twould be for the best,* Jane thought glumly. Better to live with the dream of a kind and loving man than to discover Thomas had become like Alex, a man for whom love, jealousy, and vengeance seemed one and the same.

Jane's head began to ache fiercely once again. She longed for a breath of fresh air and wished fervently she were miles from this crush of bodies and ripe odors.

"Have ye seen to the arrangements, Ham, so I may leave at dawn for Kinrara?" she said in a low voice while smiling and nodding greetings to a few familiar passing faces.

"I canna think why ye must rush off in such a hurry!" he replied, his exasperation apparent in his voice.

The unexpected change of plans caused by the duke's abrupt departure, and now Jane's unaccountable desire to depart for the most remote corner of the Gordon estates was a damned inconvenience.

"Why do ye insist on such an out-of-the-way route back to Gordon Castle? Kinrara's but a poor farmhouse, and here, there'll be several more days of festivities before the officers get down to the business of whipping the recruits into shape," he complained.

"I wish to be far from the sound of drums beating their tattoos and troops drilling beneath my window," Jane replied, trying to keep her tone light, as Hamilton held a gilt chair for her. Sitting down was no mean feat in a gown with yards of sea green flowered silk taffeta swirling over wide panniers that extended on either side of her tight, corseted waistline.

"Had yer fill of Army life so soon, Jenny mine?" Hamilton teased, his good humor returning at the sight of the punch bowl a few yards away. "Ye certainly seemed to enjoy yerself, dancing with those brawny lads in the village squares."

"Aye, that I did, but now I long for peace and quiet, and *that* brought to mind Kinrara. A few day's rest is what I want, so I expect all to be in readiness tomorrow at sunup," she commanded, attempting to sound every inch a duchess.

What she didn't tell her brother was her determination not to see Alex again until she had time to consider whether she wanted to see him at all.

"Duchess! How lovely ye look!"

Jane's meandering thoughts were interrupted by their host, John Forbes, who bowed before Jane's chair, kissing her gloved hand.

"M'lady," he said with an appreciative glance at her full bosom swelling above the low-cut neckline of the gown's bodice, "I'm so sorry the duke was called away but, if ye will do me the honor of taking my arm, we shall form the reception line straightaway."

"That is most agreeable," Jane replied, grateful for the chance to escape the ballroom's oppressive heat as quickly as possible.

John Forbes led the Duchess of Gordon to the far end of the room, indicating to Hamilton and several other officers enroute to join in their wake. Before she was quite prepared for it, she was face to face with her old nemesis, Simon Fraser, Master of Lovat. *General* Fraser, Jane corrected herself ironically.

She could hardly believe that at her last encounter with the stocky campaign veteran, she had flailed against his chest in the middle of Edinburgh's High Street, screaming curses at him. He'd actually looked gaunt and haggard then, but all that had changed with the miraculous reappearance of his godson from beyond the grave and the return of the Fraser lands by the Crown. She gazed at Simon's well-fed countenance and took measure of the son of the Fox. She had to admit to herself that at age forty-nine, decked out this night like a peacock in full Highland regalia, he looked healthy and prosperous. And why not? The escalating conflict in the Colonies had been good for the Scottish landed gentry. Troops needed warm clothing spun from the wool of Scottish sheep to shield against New England winters. Fighting men required all sorts of provisions that Simon Fraser and the Duke of Gordon and others were only too happy to supply—for a price.

"Good evening, Yer Grace," Simon said stiffly, regarding her warily.

"Master Simon," Jane answered curtly, inclining her head only slightly in greeting. "I canna believe the rumors I hear that ye aren't accompanying yer troops to fight for the king in America. Can such slander be true?" she asked, wide-eyed, knowing full well it was.

"His Majesty has assured me that the homage I pay in supplying such fierce, fightin' men as these be sacrifice enough," Simon replied testily. "My estates require my full attention, if they're to contribute to the needs o' the Crown in fightin' this war."

"Surely, 'tis not yet considered a *war*?" Jane parried. " 'Tis only a serious disagreement."

"Well, whatever the Parliamentarians wish to call it, 'twill soon be an all-out battle, and no one can say the Frasers havena answered the king's call!" he replied grimly. He scrutinized her closely, and a goading look crinkled the corners of his eyes. " 'Tis the talk of the Highlands how even the Duchess of Gordon rallied to our standard."

"My loyalties, sir, lay first and foremost with my own family and my wish to serve my brother's cause," she said, bristling. Abruptly, Jane turned from Simon as if she had dismissed him, which she had.

Forbes signaled for the string quartet to cease playing, and a sudden silence fell over the throng. The host of Culloden House stepped forward as a piper entered the room, the wails of his instrument echoing throughout the hall. As the last notes drifted off, Forbes officially welcomed his guests. A long scarlet line of officers began to wind its way past the fireplace. The soldiers chatted briefly with their commanders and filed past Jane with more than a curious glance. As rumor had it, she raised troops in a most unorthodox manner.

Jane drew a sharp intake of breath when, out of the corner of her eye, she caught a glimpse of a garnet-maned head a foot taller than the other officers in the procession. Soon she saw Thomas Fraser making his way down the reception line. Her back straightened slightly and she prepared the warm but impersonal smile she had graced so many others with in the preceding minutes. In an instant, Thomas was towering over her, the sweep of his tartan sash all but shielding her face from view. He extended his hand. Jane found she could only stare wordlessly into the depths of his eyes, their unusual gray-green color reminding her of the waters of the River Spey on a day of sun and shadow.

Thomas's hand served to steady her and prevented her from swaying dangerously on the heels of her satin slippers.

"Good evening, C-Captain," she stammered, painfully aware that Simon Fraser was standing not four feet from them.

"Duchess—" Thomas replied formally, bowing respectfully, though his eyes conveyed a far different message.

" 'Tis good to see ye, Thomas," she said sincerely, not caring any longer who overheard them, as long as she could keep hold of his hand.

"Aye . . . and ye too, Jenny," he replied softly, gently extricating his fingers from hers and preparing to move down the line.

"Would ye be so kind as to ask the footman for a glass of that punch . . ." she blurted, inventing an excuse to prevent his leaving her side. For the first time in her life, she felt she was about to faint. "I'm feeling the need of refreshment . . . 'tis so warm in here. Perhaps he could bring it over to that chair by the window?"

"I shall deliver it myself, m'lady," Thomas replied, his eyes flitting across her face as if reacquainting himself with her features. Then, without another word, he moved on down the receiving line.

It seemed an eternity to Jane before the last subaltern paid his respects. She quickly grabbed the arm of the startled young soldier and commanded him to escort her across the floor where Thomas was waiting beside a chair, holding two cut-crystal punch cups in his hands. Hamilton and Simon, engrossed in conversation, hardly noticed her departure.

"Thank ye, lad," Jane said to the young soldier she'd commandeered, the tone of her voice a clear dismissal.

"Yer refreshment, m'lady," Thomas said wryly, offering her the glass as the bemused subaltern melted into the crowd.

"Dinna do that," Jane said sharply.

"Offer ye some punch?" Thomas asked mildly.

"No," Jane replied. "Dinna call me m'lady."

"Ah, but ye are, and a duchess to boot."

"I'm not of a mind to spar with ye, Thomas," Jane said wearily. "What's done is done. Canna we at least be the friends we always were? I'd like to know how ye truly are . . . what ye do as a soldier . . . what yer life was like in Ireland. Are the Irish as savage as the Indians in America?"

Thomas tilted back his head and laughed loudly. Jane noticed that the scars on his face had faded considerably since the last time she'd seen him and, rather than detracting from the twenty-eight-year-old's good looks, gave his features character. Assisting her to sit down, he pulled up another gilt chair and clinked her glass with his.

"Here's to friendship and the woman whose friendship I have never forgotten," he said lightly, but his eyes sought out hers, intently questioning.

"Nor have I forgotten yer friendship," she answered simply, resting her punch cup in her gloved hand and staring at its crystal rim.

"Are ye all right, Jenny?" Thomas asked suddenly, his voice filled with concern. "Ye look . . . sad."

"I *am* sad, Thomas," she answered, surprised at the sensation of tears brimming her eyes as she glanced up at him. She was too emotionally exhausted—and he was too perceptive—for dissembling.

Thomas remained silent for a few moments, and then asked her quietly, "Why dinna the Duke of Gordon grace us with his company this evening? Is he ill?"

"Ill?" Jane repeated thoughtfully. "Yes, in a fashion. I fear he is sick with jealousy at the thought that ye and I should meet again. He returned to Gordon Castle—on urgent estate business, I was told—but that 'twasna the reason."

"And *ye*?" Thomas prompted softly. "Is the duke's jealousy, after eight years of marriage, what's making ye sad? I would have thought just the opposite. Hasna he just demonstrated his feelings for ye are still strong?"

" 'Tis not a *game* we're playing here, Thomas, to see who cares for whom the most, or keeps the upper hand!" Jane replied heatedly. " 'Tis people's *lives*! I said I was sad . . . and I am. For the three of us . . . and now there are the children—"

Jane looked away to stem the tide of anguish that suddenly swept over her. She could never abandon her children, and that's what she would have to do if she separated from Alex and went to live with Catherine and John Fordyce in Berwickshire. She would have to leave them in her husband's custody. Scottish law clearly favored men in all domestic matters—especially men as powerful as the Duke of Gordon. As far as the law was concerned, she and the children were mere possessions. Suddenly, Jane recalled her husband's overwhelming strength as he pressed his weight against her rebellious body on the bed upstairs. He had defiled the trust implicit in their intimacy by demonstrating to her he could take her against her will, whenever and however he wished. Alexander Gordon held all the cards. Perhaps it *was* all a game, this contract of marriage. A game she could never win.

"Yer first born is well?" Thomas asked quietly, observing the emotions that had played across her face.

Charlotte, she thought, disconsolately. The babe she carried when she'd last met Thomas at Loch-an-Eilean.

"Aye, she's well," Jane answered, swallowing hard. "She's just turned seven years. She's here at Culloden House, upstairs in the nursery. Lord Huntly and the babies remained at Gordon Castle."

"Ah, yes, John Forbes told me ye'd had several bairns, including an heir," he continued gently, "and that yer the best of mothers to them all."

Jane turned and smiled weakly.

"That's dear of him to say," she answered, turning to stare out the window, which overlooked the rows and rows of tents scattered among the stark trees and hedges of the estate's parkland. She thought of the cozy hours in the nursery where she had taken it on herself to read to her children and drill the older ones in their sums. "Aye, I love my children very much," she said finally, gazing at Thomas once again. "Susan's the wee one . . .

and there's Madelina, who's three, and little George—Lord Huntly—he'll be six in February.''

"Twenty-five years old and the beautiful mother of such a braw brood . . . Then *why* are ye sad, my Jenny of Monreith?" Thomas asked, his voice vibrating with intensity.

"Because I wish they were *yours*!" Jenny whispered in anguish, a feeling of recklessness taking possession of her. "I'm sad because I canna stop cursing the fate that condemned the three of us to be miserable all our lives, with nothing solid to hold on to, and always feeling . . . feeling something's *missing*! Alex knows he can never have *all* my love; ye know ye never can possess *any* of it . . . and I . . . *I* feel as if I'm being carved in two *every day of my life*!" Jane felt the tears starting to brim over her eyelids. She stood up hastily. "I must leave this room or I'm going to faint or be sick!"

"Jenny!" Thomas said, rising quickly, "I *must* see you again!"

"That's not possible," she replied agitatedly, searching the milling crowd for a glimpse of Hamilton to escort her out of the reception. "I leave at dawn for Kinrara."

Their eyes met, and for an instant, each knew that the other held in mind the same memory of standing side by side atop the tower of the small, crumbling castle, set like a jewel in the center of Loch-an-Eilean.

"Kinrara?" Thomas repeated softly.

Jane nodded.

"I'll *be* there the day after tomorrow," he whispered fiercely, taking her arm. "I swear it!"

"No, Thomas . . . ye mustna come to Kinrara—" she began.

"I'm granted three days' leave before the regiment starts training in earnest," he interrupted, his eyes boring into hers. "I shall spend them at Loch-an-Eilean, whether ye come to the castle or not! And now," he said more calmly, "May I offer ye my arm? I'm sure ye must wish to retire to prepare for yer journey."

Jane was virtually unable to reply. In a trancelike state, she allowed Thomas to return her to Hamilton's side, and, within minutes, her brother had escorted her out of the stiflingly hot room to the broad staircase that led to the blessed solitude of her chambers.

18

Late the following afternoon, the Gordon party arrived in the heart of the Spey Valley. Jane marveled at the spate of unseasonably mild weather that greeted them as they passed the pile of stones marking the entrance of the estate. The small entourage of carriage and ponies arrived at a cluster of whitewashed shielings, capped with thatched roofs, which stood in a clearing. Rust-colored roe deer foraged among the dried grasses for a winter's meal. The small animals froze at the sound of the coach, and then bounded in a jagged pattern out of sight.

The farmhouse, which was merely the largest of several cottages, sat in the hollow that flanked a bend in the River Spey. It was just as Jane remembered it from her brief sojourn almost eight years earlier. The whitewashed stone building with its shaggy roof nestled into the ground, and a curl of smoke drifting up from the chimney told them they were expected.

Jane inhaled the pungent scent of pine in the air and let out a contented sigh. Its delicious smell told her she could only be in one place: Kinrara.

Angus Grant, the estate's sharp-eyed factor, had reacted swiftly to the message that had preceded Jane's arrival by only eight hours. Despite such short notice, the dwarfish Highlander had seen to it that the interior of the small, one-room structure had been aired and swept. Jane noted with pleasure that a pattern of worn Turkish carpets forming richly colored rectangles covered the plain pine floor. The straw bedding stuffed between lengths of stiff linen in the corner had been freshened, and there were oatcakes and bannocks resting in fragrant profusion on a wooden table near the cooking hearth. Tallow candles placed strategically around the room illuminated the cozy space, casting a warm, inviting glow as Jane stepped from the dwindling daylight across the threshold.

The stone walls and simple furniture were in stark contrast to the elegant rooms at Culloden House, and the appointments compared poorly to the magnificence of Gordon Castle. Yet, Jane felt at home. Utterly at home. She smiled broadly as she turned around, her roving eye drinking in the smallest detail of the humble cottage.

" 'Tis lovely, Angus," Jane breathed happily. "Thank ye for making us feel so welcome."

For the first time since she had stared into Alex's thunderous reflection in the mirror in the ornate bedchamber of Culloden House, the knot of tension in her breast began to ease.

"I've taken the liberty of readying the old bothy down the lane for Lady Charlotte and yer maid, Nancy," the estate factor said, pointing through the small window toward the neat white bungalow a hundred yards away. "Yer footmen are welcome at my cottage, and the driver will be snug in the wee stable to the back, looking after the ponies."

"Ye've fit us into this magical place like fingers in a glove, Angus." Jane smiled at the gnome of a man, stooped from his years of hard labor, which had ultimately won him the prized position of estate factor. "I plan to closet myself right here for a few days and do nothing but rest. Our journeys these last weeks have been exhausting."

"Aye," said Angus Grant with the natural ease of a native Highlander, one who respected his laird and lady, but was never subservient toward them. "Ye deserve a respite, Duchess, after all the recruiting ye did for the regiment."

"Mama, are we to have that other little cottage all to ourselves?" squealed Charlotte, hopping up and down at the window that overlooked her assigned residence. " 'Tis like a doll's house, only Nancy and I'll have it for our very own!"

"That's right, pet," Jane smiled, pleased that her eldest child didn't complain of a lack of luxury or common comforts. She seemed to sense the magic of Kinrara just as Jane had that first time she'd traveled here.

"Mama . . . look! Mrs. Grant has come with our supper!" Charlotte said excitedly, gesturing through the window at a plump woman, her arms pulled taut to her sides as she toted two enormous woven baskets of food.

"A thousand Highland welcomes, m'lady!" beamed Flora Grant, setting down her burdens on the stone hearth so she could bob a curtsy. "Unusual fair weather we be havin' for this time of year, but no complaints, no complaints! 'Tis fit for a duchess, so we are blessed that ye're here!"

Nancy Christie retrieved one of the baskets under Flora's direction, after being assured by her mistress that she could cope perfectly well without a lady's maid in such a simple setting.

The young lass and a very animated Charlotte headed off to explore their own accommodations.

"Sleep well, poppet," Jane called after them gaily through the front door, her spirits soaring as she caught sight of her first swan, winging back to its nest on Loch-an-Eilean. "Breakfast will be waiting for ye both when ye awake."

"Thank ye, m'lady," Nancy called, whirling around to make one final curtsy.

"I've brought roasted grouse and oatcake and some cheese and tea, and a wee dram of whiskey, m'lady," said Flora Grant, unloading the contents of her second basket onto the deep-set windowsill including a jug of Kinrara's own brew. "'Tis simple enough fare, but wholesome for ye."

"Aye, Flora," Jane thanked her, "'tis the simple life I long for—and the food to go with it. Thank ye for yer kindness . . . and ye too, Angus," she said, turning to Flora's husband, who stood at least a head shorter than his wife. "I know our unexpected arrival made much work for ye both, but 'tis wonderful to see Kinrara again."

"Och! Dinna fash yerself," Angus replied, reddening at her compliments. He gestured abruptly with his woolen cap at his wife of forty years, and the two of them vanished down the pony track that led to their own shieling a mile away.

The fire crackled in its grate as Jane walked slowly around the room, luxuriating in the solitude permeating the cottage. She unbuttoned the confining jacket of her heavy woolen traveling costume. Tossing the garment over one of the few chairs in the single room, she breathed deeply, savoring the peace and tranquillity that surrounded her. Finally, she reflected, she would have time to *think*. Finally, there'd be time to sift through the jumble of emotions that had tormented her in the last few days. She tried to push from her mind Thomas's vow to see her once more. So many events could intervene to prevent his coming to Kinrara. The sensible side of her nature told her she had problems enough, and she prayed he would never appear.

Jane measured out the tea and poured several cupfuls of scalding water into a small stoneware pot from the cauldron that Flora had provided on the hearth. She delighted in serving herself and reveled in the first privacy—devoid of both family and servants—that she had enjoyed in years, perhaps in her entire life, she reflected.

Jane sipped her tea and stared into the fire. Its warmth and darting flames compelled her to do nothing but gaze into its incandescent embers for well over half an hour. When she had finished her tea and had nibbled on an oatcake and a slice of the grouse, she undressed leisurely in front of the fire. After some initial difficulties escaping from her stays without Nancy's help, she slipped into her soft cambric nightdress and dragged the linen mattress across the floor, plumping up its straw a safe distance from the glowing grate.

Wrapping herself in one of the many thick woolen plaids left by the Grants, Jane felt the tension continue to drain from her body. The patches of sky visible through the two small windows grew dark, and a moon the size of a dinner platter rose over the soft hills that encircled the shieling.

Jane snuggled down in her makeshift bed. She would wrestle with the dilemma of Alex tomorrow, she thought sleepily. Tonight, all she wanted was what surrounded her at this moment: the peace of her second home, Kinrara.

She awoke several hours later with a start, her heart racing. As she lifted her head off the mattress, the metallic sound of the door latch snapping open pierced the silence. A tall figure stood framed by the threshold, moonlight pouring over his shoulder. From her line of vision lying on her linen pallet on the floor, it looked like a giant, come to stalk the earth.

"Jenny . . . Jenny, 'tis me . . . Thomas . . . dinna be frightened . . ." a voice said softly.

Jane could see by the way Thomas glanced anxiously around the room that the brightness of the moon bathing the Spey Valley made it impossible for him to see clearly inside the darkened cottage.

"I'm here, Thomas," she answered softly, "in front of the hearth."

Thomas turned toward the sound of her voice and quietly closed the door behind him, cutting off the path of moonlight that had led from the threshold to where Jane lay before the fire. With three quick strides he was kneeling in front of her, pulling her to her knees and enfolding her in his arms. He began to kiss her hair, her forehead, her cheeks, drawing away from her briefly to cup her face between his two enormous hands. He stared at her as if she were an apparition about to dissolve before his eyes. Then he threw his arms around her once more, clasping her to him and burying his hand in the chestnut hair tumbling down around her shoulders.

"Ye said ye'd be at Loch-an-Eilean," she whispered. "I spent all day telling myself I wouldn't come to ye . . . that I mustna come to ye, or I'd be lost. . . .''

"I was yer shadow all the way from Culloden House,'' he said into her hair. He raised his head and the two looked into each other's eyes. "I watched the factor and his wife take leave of ye and gave thanks to St. Ninian when yer daughter skipped down the lane with yer maid. I was going to go to Loch-an-Eilean and wait there, but I couldna, Jenny. I've waited for ye so long—I couldna wait any longer.''

He had withdrawn his hands from her and only their knees were touching. Then, slowly, he raised his hand and ran his fingers lightly down the side of one cheek, gently skimming past her neck, until he grazed the roundness of her breast beneath her thin nightdress. She felt her flesh stiffen. Suddenly, the ugly memory of Alex's assault clashed with her instinctive response to Thomas's tender caress. She shrank back, feeling her heart thudding painfully.

"Jenny . . . ?'' Thomas asked, immediately sensing the shift in the emotional currents flowing between them. "What is it, love?''

Her eyes searched his. She was touched beyond words by his look of concern. She felt the love they'd shared as children well up within her, blending with an undercurrent of passion she'd kept in check for years.

"Oh . . . my dear, sweet love,'' she said softly, reaching up to run her fingers through his hair where the soft night winds of Kinrara had ruffled it. "There's to be no more waiting this night, Thomas . . . no more longing for what we canna have. . . .''

And, with a woman's full knowledge of the consequences of her actions, Jane drew him to her, pressing her body along his, tilting her pelvis to revel in the fullness of desire she had aroused in him. She fumbled for the brass buttons on his scarlet uniform. Unmindful of her ministrations, he bent his head forward, smothering off her lips, her eyes, her throat with kisses. Frantically, she peeled off his jacket and set to work on the line of buttons on his waistcoat. Thomas quickly dispensed with his other clothing. All her mind would admit to was a burning compulsion to feel his skin against hers, to cover his chest with kisses of her own.

The taper in the candlestick she had set on the stone hearth before drifting off to sleep gave a hiss, sputtered, and then gutted out, leaving only the tangerine glow of the low-burning fire to illuminate their litany of love.

Thomas's naked body cast a giant's shadow on the whitewashed wall of the cottage as he tugged gently on the silk bow that closed the neckline of her nightdress. Jane's eyes drifted back from the silhouette on the wall to Thomas himself. His fingers trembled slightly as he sought to release the fastenings on the front of her bodice. His knuckles pressed lightly against the fabric covering her breasts. Jane felt as if a warm, golden liquid were being poured through her veins.

She reached out to grasp his forearm in order to steady herself. Her gaze traveled down to his chest, which was sprinkled with auburn hair. Her fingers traced a line along the thick, knotted scar slicing into his left biceps. She leaned forward slightly and brushed her lips against it. Her hand strayed lower, encountering the ridges of hardened muscle on his abdomen. His waist tapered to slim hips, and her eyes drifted inexorably down toward his powerful thighs and the object of her consuming desire.

Thomas's restless fingers had reached the last of the night-dress's fastenings and he playfully captured her wandering hand with his own.

"Ah . . . minx . . . ye'll not be teasing me quite so much or ye'll miss the bounty I've been savin' for ye." He gathered her other hand and, for a moment, gazed at her missing right forefinger, injured when they were both mere children. She felt a sharp intake of breath as he placed the stub on the jagged scar disfiguring his arm. "Our hurts are as one, now, Jenny," he said, his bantering mood evaporating suddenly as he looked at her gravely. "Let our love heal these wounds."

Slowly and with deliberation, he drew her nightdress over her head, tossing it aside. He sank back on his heels, his eyes devouring the sight of her naked form, which cast soft shadows opposite his silhouette painted on the far wall, bathed in amber firelight.

"Oh, God, Jenny . . . when I thought I was dying in that Pennsylvania wood, 'twas the thought of ye that kept me alive. But when I came back and found ye lost to me . . . I *wanted* to die! I cursed ye for being my safe beacon home, only to lose ye again at Loch-an-Eilean."

"And do ye curse me now, Thomas, for having been with Alex first?" she asked, her voice raw with the heartache they'd all suffered during those terrible months following her wedding to the duke. "Can ye take me tonight and not punish me for it tomorrow?"

"There's been far too much punishment to wish for any more," he said soberly. He kissed each eyelid in turn. "Ye were right, ye know,'' he whispered, ''about what ye said to me on Swan Isle. There's naught to blame . . . 'tis been hellish for us all, but 'twas no one's fault.'' He reached for her hand and pressed his lips against her palm. ''Ye were just a lass when I left ye . . . now yer a woman. A knowing, loving woman. I suppose I must thank Alex for some of that.''

Jane sighed inwardly. Until so recently, what Thomas said had been true. Alex had taught her to welcome the physical side of love and had made her aware of what it was to be a woman. The rage he'd expressed upon the silk-strewn bed at Culloden House had been a perversion of everything her husband had shown her lovemaking could be.

Gazing on Thomas's beautiful form kneeling on the straw-filled pallet, his skin golden in the firelight, she felt oddly humbled by the enduring love this roan-haired man had always held for her. She knew that she could put the memory of Alex's angry actions at Culloden House to rest. No matter how harsh the blows of fate had been, Thomas would never punish her for the hurt he had endured. To do that would be to harm himself. She could never fear Thomas, and that knowledge was a healing balm for her soul.

Suddenly, she felt an overwhelming physical need for him that went beyond anything she had ever known.

''Thomas . . . please love me! Love me now!''

Slowly, as though he'd thought about this moment all his life, Thomas bent down and seized her lips with his, searing them with a deep, prolonged kiss. His tongue stroked hers, exploring the velvet lining just beyond her lips. Before she could pull him to her on the pallet, he lowered his head to her breasts, brushing one with light feathery kisses, and teasing the other with his thumb, as if to extract her very essence.

Jane was frantic to feel his weight on her, but the pleasurable sensations called forth by his lips and fingers on her breasts suspended her own desires and melded them with his. She buried her hands in his hair, threading her fingers through its garnet strands, and pulling his head even closer.

As if reading her mind, Thomas shifted one hand that was cupping her breast and encircled it around her waist, lowering her gently onto her back. Jane stretched her arms up over her head and stared at him boldly as he surveyed her form. His eyes drifted down to the nest between her thighs. Gently, he separated her legs and knelt between them. Bending over her, he brushed his tongue lightly along a line running from between her breasts to just below her waist. He hesitated for an agonizing instant at her navel, and then darted the tip of his tongue deeply into its recess.

Jane moaned softly and thrust her hands into his hair once again, pressing him close to her in a vain attempt to fuse their flesh.

"Jenny . . . yer so beautiful . . . I—"

His words were lost as he moved his head lower . . . lower, nibbling and licking her flesh until she thought she would go mad. His palms slid down to stroke her inner thighs. Unbidden, Jane parted her legs wider, and boldly thrust her pelvis forward to meet his lips, which sought the soft hidden spot she longed for him to kiss. His hands slipped beneath her bottom, raising her up to meet the relentless pressure of his lips . . . calling her to him in a way she'd never known. There was no shame, no shadow, only the reality of the pleasure coursing through her. She was on the brink of an abyss. One more second of pleasure and she'd drown in the voluptuousness that was fast overtaking her.

"Please . . . *please*, Thomas . . . I want you—I want us . . . *please!*" she implored, tugging fiercely to raise his head.

In one fluid movement, he slid up the length of her body, hovering over her briefly, his shadow filling the opposite wall. In an instant he had entered her and Jane reveled in the feel of his flesh inside her, in the weight of him. Her arms wound tightly around his back.

"No matter what happens, we'll have this moment always, Thomas," she whispered brokenly, staring into his eyes, their lashes nearly touching. "The others in our lives who came before . . . we must bless them . . ."

"I do . . . I do bless them," Thomas replied huskily. "But now, 'tis just us, darling girl . . . and what a wonder it all is." He smiled, kissing the lid of each eye in turn while moving his body gently against hers.

In response, Jane began to tease his pelvis with her own, pushing forward slightly before retreating a distance in a movement calculated to send shudders through Thomas's long, lean frame.

"Two can play such wicked games, saucebox . . ." Thomas said gruffly, staring down at her with a rakish gleam in his eye. Slowly, at first, he began to shunt his hips back and forth in an easy, steady rhythm.

"Yes . . . oh, dear God . . . *yes!*" Jane heard herself cry.

Thomas buried his lips in the hollow at the base of her neck, calling to her as they hurtled, unafraid, toward a longed-for oblivion. As if the winds off the moors were sighing in the trees, Jane heard Thomas whispering his love for her over and over in a kind of sacred chant until they both cried out for the pleasure and joy of the song they sang together.

The embers on the hearth crumbled to bare flickerings. No shadows danced on the walls, and a peaceful silence enveloped Kinrara cottage.

Thomas lay on his side, with Jane tucked, spoon fashion, into the contours of his body. He had wrapped them both in the thick, bark brown plaid, careful that no December drafts should chill them. Through the small windows facing the river, the first light of dawn painted a brush stroke of amethyst across the morning sky.

The distant call of a swan to its mate nesting in the reeds surrounding the crumbling castle on Loch-an-Eilean wafted faintly through the stand of Caledonian pines that marched up the glen beside the Spey.

"Koh-hoh . . . koh-hoh . . ."

Thomas winced slightly at the mournful sound and tightened his embrace around Jane, who slept in his arms like a contented child.

A log from the freshly stoked fire fell from the grate with a thud. The sound roused Jane from the depths of the most peaceful slumber she could ever remember. With her eyes still closed, she stretched her arms above her head and felt the heat from the crackling hearth warm her hands. Her shoulders felt chilled, however, outside the plaid blanket, and she realized, with a start, she wasn't wearing her nightdress.

Jane's eyes flew open. For a confused instant, she wondered where she was. She noted the rumpled bedcovers next to her and spotted her cambric nightdress folded neatly on a nearby chair. Thomas! It wasn't a dream. She and Thomas had—

Even before her eyes searched the room, she knew with heart-thumping certainty that he had departed, having stoked the fire and having left her neatly folded nightdress as a teasing symbol of the passion they had shared the night before.

Shafts of morning sun slanted across the cottage floor, illuminating segments of the blue and gold Turkish carpets on which her pallet lay. By this time, she mused, Thomas would be rowing over to the derelict castle on Loch-an-Eilean, where, in their final, whispered words of love just before dawn, they had agreed to meet this day. She snuggled back under the warm covers, her mind full of sensuous reveries after so many years of longing and regret.

They had slept for several hours before Jane had been awakened by gentle but unrelenting kisses on her shoulders and along her spine. Thomas had buried his face in her hair near the nape of her neck. His lips nuzzled the back of her earlobes while he reached around to encase both her breasts in his hands. Jane blushed, remembering how he had made love to her without turning her around to face him, just as the purple light of dawn inched across the pine forests in the valley. Soon afterward, they had fallen asleep again, still linked by their love, driven by a thirst for closeness that had been whetted, not slaked, by their joyful intimacy.

The sun rose steadily above the mountains flanking the valley. At length, the thought of Thomas lying alone at the abandoned castle nearby prompted her to rise from the warm cocoon of her makeshift bed and put on a simple blue gown. She laid out a cup for tea and sliced the bread with the knife left by Mrs. Grant. She drank the scalding liquid and consumed a bit of oatcake while searching her belongings for her writing case to pen a short note that she had gone for a long walk.

She threw a warm, thick tartan cloak around her shoulders, tucked the jug of Kinrara-brewed whiskey and several bannocks in a small sack, and struck out toward the river, searching for a shallow spot where she could ford the Spey. From her last trip to Loch-an-Eilean, she knew it was not more than a mile or so along the old logging path.

The unseasonably mild weather had held, and though the air was crisp, the sky overhead was a clear pale blue. Jane's first glimpse of the Wolf of Badenoch's crumbling castle, with its ragged sandstone towers standing sentinel over the lake's smooth surface, prompted her to quicken her pace. Her heart raced at the thought that behind its forbidding walls was Thomas, waiting for her. She laughed giddily. He was probably exhausted and miserably cold, but with her whiskey and her love, she would see to his comfort, she thought with a smile.

As she reached the edge of Loch-an-Eilean, Jane commandeered one of several loggers' bateaux that the factor always left moored on the loch until the onset of the first winter storm. She rowed across the narrow channel of water and around the steep, thick walls of the miniature fortress.

Two swans swam in agitated circles several yards from the stone dock where an arched entryway led into the castle's court. Jane wondered if they were the same pair that had greeted her in early spring, almost eight years before. There were no cygnets trailing along behind and Jane surmised this year's young were yet to be hatched. The nest was probably hidden in the reeds somewhere near the docks, since the large male emitted a series of throaty honks as she approached.

Reassured by the sight of a second small boat tied to an iron ring embedded in the castle's stone dock, Jane darted through the weed-strewn forecourt. Softly, she called out Thomas's name. He was not in the great hall or in a room Jane took to be the ancient kitchen, judging from the gigantic black cauldron tipped over on its side next to the hearth. She mounted the winding staircase that led to the rooms above the main floor. The stone stairs, as far as she could remember, led up to the tower.

She climbed the stairs with growing trepidation and peered into the first room to which she came. Suddenly, a bat flapped its wings and made a hasty retreat out the small window facing her. Startled, Jane caught her breath.

"Thomas . . . Thomas, where are you!" she cried uneasily.

"Here, Jenny, love . . . here I am," a voice wafted toward her, "a poor excuse of a man, though I be, with sleep in my eyes. . . ."

Trembling with relief, Jane dashed up three more steps to a small landing and peered into a tiny chamber constructed entirely of stone. Two slits in the thick walls afforded a modicum of light, which played across the barrel-vaulted ceiling. There was no furniture in the room, only a small fireplace containing a cheerful blaze. Jane stepped across the threshold and saw that Thomas was lying on a bed of pine boughs, wrapped in a length of tobacco brown Fraser tartan. He ran his fingers through his touseled hair and grinned.

"Ho there! I was quite exhausted from a recent encounter with a wicked wench up the lane . . . a lass from Kinrara. Perhaps ye know her? Och! What a charmer! I quite lost my head over the chit, and have been sleeping it off since dawn's light."

"Aye . . . I know just the one ye speak of, lad," Jane smiled saucily, lowering her bundles of food to the floor and approaching his makeshift bed. "She's a handful, to be sure! Are ye certain yer man enough for her, Captain?"

"There's but one way to find out, now 'tisn't there?" he replied, lifting the blanket in which he'd wrapped himself. "Come, darling girl. . . .'' He beckoned her with a grin. ''Take pity on my frozen bones and lie here beside me.''

Jane sank to her knees, and parted her cloak so she could wrap her arms around him.

''Last night . . . 'twas like a dream,'' she whispered between kisses. ''And when I woke and ye were gone. . . .''

''I wanted to stay and greet the morning sun with ye, but I feared. . . .''

''I know. . . .'' She shushed him, unwilling at this moment of reunion to consider what the events of the previous night could mean. She settled herself alongside him and nuzzled her lips against his throat. ''I *am* wicked,'' she whispered, inhaling the pungent freshness of the pine boughs he'd gathered for a bed. ''All my feeble brain can contemplate is being near ye . . . touching ye—and ye touching me.''

Thomas grasped her face between his hands and gazed somberly into her eyes.

''I canna bear for ye to come to harm because of our lovemaking, Jenny. I couldna get to sleep at first, for the thought of it.''

Jane's heart filled with a boundless love for Thomas. She laid her palm along his cheek and kissed him tenderly.

''Listen well to what I tell ye, Thomas Fraser of Struy. 'Twould be my heart's joy if we created life together. 'Tis what I long for, more than I can say.''

''But Jenny—'' he began, as she silenced him with another kiss.

''I've been thinking, too, my love,'' she continued, ''as I walked through the forest to Loch-an-Eilean. Ye leave for America in four months' time, and who knows where this journey will end for ye? If I canna have ye in my life, I'll have yer seed . . . I'll have yer bairn. 'Twill be a precious thing between us in this life or the next.''

''But, the duke . . . 'twould be of terrible consequence for ye''

''There's no way to predict the future, Thomas,'' she said cryptically. For a fleeting instant, she struggled to erase the image of the last time she and Alex had been together. *I may already be with child*, she thought soberly, staring into Thomas's gray-green eyes. His brows drew together with concern. ''Ye mustna worry . . . or spoil the time we have together.''

''But Jenny, if ye'll forgive me for saying it—ye're a proven breeder, pet. Ye'll be left to face the scandal on yer own.''

'' 'Twill be no scandal, Thomas, I can promise ye that!'' she said heatedly. "I've given His Grace an heir and daughters to boot. I've raised Bathia Largue's child as if he were my own!" Thomas looked at her quizzically. "Alex was in love with the woman who took care of him during an illness, before we ever met. She had his child, but died when the laddie was a bairn." Jane shrugged. "The Duke's George is a sweet lad . . . Alex canna find fault with me or with the way I've conducted myself these last eight years." She gazed through the narrow window of their stone chamber. "Believe me, Thomas, there are many marriages at Court that have produced bairns born on the wrong side of the blanket! As long as there's an heir to continue the line, there's no great fuss, if matters are handled discreetly."

She wondered momentarily whether Alex would be so sanguine about the thought of her bearing Thomas's child.

"I dinna want any child of mine condemned to be a bastard!" Thomas answered hotly.

"Darling!" Jane exclaimed soothingly, holding him tightly and laying her cheek on his chest. "Ye must trust me. Any child of ours would forever be shielded from harm in my care."

"I want ye to know this, Miss Maxwell of Monteith," he replied, raising her chin with his fingers so he could gaze into her eyes. "Since I've proven I'm a cat with nine lives, I fully intend to survive this coming skirmish against those ragtag Revolutionaries. I shall come back to Scotland to claim ye and the babe, and *then* what will ye do?"

" 'Tis all speculation," Jane said, shaking her head ruefully. "For me, 'tis enough for the moment that I'm in yer arms, though I must say, I pray ye'll call on me at Kinrara cottage tonight, where the accommodations are more salubrious."

Thomas kissed her nose and settled back against the pile of pine boughs he had bunched together for a pillow.

"Ye're not pleased with my castle, m'lady?" he replied in mock indignation. "I've gone to great trouble to furnish it with the finest Caledonian pine and keep it toasty-warm—not to mention ensuring plenty of fresh air!" He gestured toward the open slits in the walls that served as windows, and laughed.

" 'Tis not the *only* way to maintain comfort," she replied slyly, shifting her weight on top of him and straddling his thighs.

"Aye . . . that'll do quite nicely, strumpet!" he retorted, deliberately tweaking her nipples through the fabric of her bodice, prompting them to stand at attention.

"Will this do as well?" she asked huskily, unbuttoning the

few closings of her gown's bodice and pulling it over her head.

"Excellently," he breathed, his eyes devouring the fullness of her figure. He reached to cradle each of her breasts, and pulled himself up on his elbows to suck gently on her pink nipples.

Jane was as aware as Thomas when it came to the presence of the mound of hard flesh straining against the woolen blanket covering his lap. Goosebumps began to dimple her skin.

"Lass, I shall take pity on ye and invite ye into my warm lair," he whispered with a mischievous twinkle in his eye, "but only if ye shed yer knickers!"

"I'm not wearing any, ye randy rogue!" she retorted, divesting herself of skirt and petticoat. She slipped under the tartan coverlet, using her own cloak to add to its warmth. Slowly and deliberately, she began to kiss the smooth skin of Thomas's shoulders, lingering on the jagged impression made by the deep scar on his arm. Her lips trailed down to the small aureoles nestled amid the claret-colored hair on his chest. She licked each lightly in turn, gratified at the sound of his sharp intake of breath.

Her only desire was to please him, to pleasure him as he had pleasured her. She began to move her mouth lightly across his abdomen, teasing the sensitive flesh around his navel. Delicately, she darted her tongue inside it with butterfly kisses.

Thomas plunged his hands into her hair, scattering the few pins securing her coiffure.

"May I kiss ye here?" Jane whispered, trailing her fingers lightly along the crease between his thigh and torso. His answer was to gently guide her head toward the spot. "And here?" she asked, suddenly shy, touching him intimately.

Thomas merely gazed at her with a sensuous smile.

Jane found herself eager to bear bold witness to her passion. She kissed and stroked him, licked and nuzzled his body everywhere, tormenting him sweetly and wantonly, until he cried for release.

"Aye, Thomas . . . I want that too . . . I want to give ye the joy and love ye deserve . . . that ye've always deserved."

Straddling his thighs, she retraced her trail of kisses back up his chest, placing one of his palms on each of her breasts. Creating a kind of tent with the blanket and cloak draped around her shoulders, she positioned herself above him.

"May I have ye inside me, my darling?" she whispered, her voice trembling with emotion.

Thomas looked up at her with a kind of awe. Never had he experienced a woman so demure and demanding all at once. Smiling gently, she allowed her body to envelop his. They both moaned softly.

"Ye're exquisite. . . ." he breathed, opening his eyes wider.

"I've always thought ye quite the most beautiful of men," she replied simply, settling her weight comfortably against his abdomen. Then she grinned. "Ye've driven me to such wicked debauchery!"

"Do ye have any idea what power ye have over me?" he replied hoarsely, lifting his hips for emphasis. "I want ye to know that, Jenny . . . that 'tis the same for me as 'tis for ye."

"I know, love," she replied, unexpected tears catching in her throat.

Falling silent, she stretched herself along the length of him and gently began to rock, to and fro. Meeting the languorous pace she'd set, Thomas glided his hands down her back and cupped her derriere, sending cascades of pleasure coursing through her limbs. She could feel the muscles of his thighs gathering strength as he lifted her higher and higher. Suddenly, the rhythm had changed and she was no longer the rider and he the steed. A sense of abandonment enveloped her and she felt an urgent desire to fling herself over the precipice. The next instant she was on her back with Thomas's weight full on her.

"Yes?" he cried, raising his head to gaze at her with blazing eyes.

"Yes!" She repeated the question, which was its own answer, because the wonder of it was that they were *one* . . . their pleasure was the same. Their cries of joy and tears mingled in the crystalline December air, their world enclosed by three-foot-thick stone walls, their love protected by the Wolf's lair and the lake below, guarded by wild swans. Whatever came after this moment, they both knew with a certainty born of pain, they were bonded for all time.

19

December 31, 1775

The sound of a festive tune played on William Marshall's fiddle wafted under the crack of Jane's bedchamber door, borne along by the December drafts that perpetually chilled the inhabitants of Gordon Castle. A soft knock at her door announced Nancy Christie, who entered the room to help with her mistress's dress and attend to her coiffure.

"The children are nearly daft with excitement, ma'am, waitin' to gift ye with the trinkets they've made for yer birthday," Nancy said cheerfully, pulling the laces of Jane's stays tight. Jane winced. Her breasts, so tender to the touch lately, were pushed up to a fashionable but nonetheless uncomfortable height.

Nancy scooped up the voluminous rose silk gown and lifted it over Jane's head. Its panniers weighed heavily against her pinched waist, and yards of the material making up the overskirt settled around her hips in deep folds like soft spokes on a wheel. The music downstairs blared momentarily as the door opened again, and Alexander stood framed at the threshold of his wife's bedchamber.

" 'Tis the perfect shade with your hair and coloring, my dear," he said, advancing into the room. "Our friends await you downstairs. Hamilton has arrived with several fellow officers, and the children are in an absolute lather to present you with your birthday gifts. They have commanded me to escort you to the drawing room immediately." His eyes absorbed the sight of Jane's decolletage spilling over the top of the evening gown. "I must say, 'tis an assignment I undertake with some relish," he continued. "You look magnificent, Jane."

At that, he turned to Nancy, who was putting the finishing touches on Jane's coiffeur. He relieved her of Jane's silver-plated hairbrush, and nodded a signal of dismissal.

"There are just a few wee strands here," he said to Jane in a low, intimate voice. With light, feathery strokes, he caressed her hair forward with the soft bristles of the hairbrush and then bent down and grazed his lips along the same path just below her hairline. Jane stiffened at his touch, but remained silent. "Ham has asked permission for several companies of the Seventy-first to assemble here in February, once their training is completed," he commented casually, continuing to nuzzle her neck with soft kisses. "From the castle, they'll march south to their ships."

Jane's eyes widened at this startling bit of intelligence. Would Thomas's company be among these men? Would she be forced once again to encounter him in the confines of a crowded room or perhaps to bid him a final farewell from across a parade field? Especially considering the nightmare at Culloden House, she knew it would be dangerous for all concerned to place Alexander and Thomas anywhere near each other, let alone under the same roof.

Ignoring Alex's attempt to smooth things over between them, Jane rose abruptly from the padded satin stool stationed in front of her looking glass and walked toward a dresser containing her jewelry.

During the ten days following her return from Kinrara, Alexander—much to her relief—had been sleeping on the day-bed in his dressing room after late evenings alone in his study or in the company of the ubiquitous musical butler, Mr. Marshall. Not once had Alex broached the subject of his brutal treatment of her at Culloden House, nor had she mentioned her sojourn to Kinrara. A profound sense of bereavement had enveloped Jane after Thomas's departure to regimental headquarters at Inverness. It numbed what would otherwise have been a feeling of tremendous guilt for the betrayal of her marriage vows. Her deep bond with Thomas only complicated the anger she had harbored toward Alexander as a result of her husband's act of cruelty. She found herself utterly unable even to respond appropriately in casual conversation since the debacle of their violent evening together.

Now, on the eve of her twenty-sixth birthday, Alex leaned one palm on her dressing table and silently watched Jane rummage through yet another velvet box until, at length, she retrieved a pair of tourmaline earrings and a matching necklace. She tried unsuccessfully to fasten the necklace, but her truncated forefinger made snapping the platinum clasp difficult. She glanced up at Alex, her chin jutting slightly in the air as she anticipated reproval.

"Here, let me help with that," he said quietly, startling her with an unexpectedly gentle tone. He flicked the catch closed and once again kissed the nape of her neck. "You look so lovely tonight," he said, his eyes searching her face. "Every year, it seems, you grow more beautiful." He drew her close to him and savored her appearance. "You have that look, again, Jane," he said huskily. "The voluptuous appearance of a woman with the spark of new life growing inside her. 'Tis a look that can heat a man's blood beyond endurance."

His hazel eyes bore into hers, and with one swift motion, he pressed his hand and gold signet ring between her cleavage, the signal they'd shared during their eight-year marriage of his desire to make love.

" 'Twill never be like Culloden House again, Jane," he whispered, leaning forward to kiss her lips. "I swear it! Let's start the year anew, for the bairn's sake."

"No!" she spat, "dinna be daft! I am *not* with child!" She fiercely clasped his wrist with her hand and flung his arm away from her breasts in a violent movement. "No, no, *no!*" she shouted, her voice rising to an hysterical pitch.

She rushed out of the room without seeing the stricken look etched across her husband's features, and ran down the stone staircase into the drawing room filled with family and friends.

A shaft of pale afternoon sun struggled to pierce the leaden skies arching over the grounds of Gordon Castle. A small band of pipers and rows of kilted soldiers fanned out in a sea of scarlet coats, marching smartly in step before their senior officers. The pipers' regimental tune, "Morair Sim," dubbed "Lord Lovat's Welcome," was played in honor of their commander, General Simon Fraser.

Jane shivered beneath her cloak and looked down at her four children, plus the Duke's George. They seemed unmindful of the frigid February air sweeping over the impromptu parade grounds, and gazed with rapt attention at the members of their Uncle Hamilton's company passing in review.

In spite of the celebratory atmosphere, Jane was feeling queasy. The steady beat of the regimental drummers and the skirl of the pipes aggravated her headache, and the greasy mutton stew she'd had at the noon-day meal rested uneasily in her stomach. She longed for the privacy of her bedchamber, especially since Captain Thomas Fraser was among those officers quartered in Fochabers in anticipation of the 71st's final departure at dawn tomorrow. Jane grew faint at the thought of the calamity enveloping her. She found herself swaying. The heel of her slipper sank into the soggy ground.

Alex had been right. She was pregnant again. Of that there could be no doubt. Her courses had stopped following that fateful week in early December, when both her husband and Thomas had taken her to bed within a few days of each other. Since then, she and Alex had slept apart, but the simple truth was, the baby growing inside her could be either man's. Jane thought back to the ecstasy of those precious days with Thomas at Kinrara and Loch-an-Eilean. How sure she had been back then that only Thomas's seed could have created life in her. She had been positive that Alex's degrading assault at Culloden House could only have come to naught. But now . . . now that the reality of her condition had engulfed her, she couldn't bear to contemplate that the child was anyone but Thomas's!

For the first time in five pregnancies, attacks of violent nausea plagued her during every waking hour. Seven months of cruel uncertainty stretched ahead, before she would be in a position to guess who was the father of this child.

Jane clenched her skirts between white knuckles as Thomas's company of eighty-nine men approached the reviewing stand. The last few weeks had been sheer torment. She'd caught only fleeting glimpses of her lover as he sipped brandy with his fellow officers, or barked orders at the raw recruits under his charge while they drilled in formation under her bedroom window. The greatest shock of all was that Alex had been astoundingly civil to Thomas. He had proffered him the best cognac and treated him with the same easy graciousness he extended to all the officers.

Whose baby am I carrying? cried Jane silently, as a brisk wind snapped the edges of her cloak.

The Fraser company halted directly in front of her. Thomas himself stood at attention not fifty yards from where she was stationed, feeling miserable and chilled to the bone. Her throat constricted at the sight of his beloved profile and tears misted her eyes. She turned toward Simon Fraser, Master of Lovat, seated imperiously astride his black stallion, wearing his scarlet uniform with its general's epaulets. He complacently surveyed the ranks of his soldiers—all clad in his family tartan.

"Clansmen, kinsmen, brothers all," Simon shouted in a booming voice. "Ye will go forth from this day to reclaim in America the glory denied ye in Scotland for so long by circumstances best left forgotten. However, *never* forget," he said fiercely, "that ye wear the colors of Clan Fraser and carry the glorious history of a thousand years of Highlanders in yer veins."

Simon surveyed the field of men who gazed up at him with

rapt attention. To Jane's consternation, Thomas, too, was among those who stared at their leader with awe as he addressed the throng gathered in his name under his family's coat of arms.

"Remember, ye are *MacShimi*'s men—the sons of Simon—not merely bonded to me by blood or fealty, but bonded to all Frasers who came before."

Jane suddenly felt the bile rise within her. Stayed by the thought of disgracing herself in front of everyone, she mumbled something to Alexander about feeling ill and took refuge behind the stout trunk of the Duchess Tree. Then, with as much dignity as she could muster, Jane escaped through the side door of the west wing and disappeared inside the castle without a word.

Three hours later, the door of her bedchamber opened quietly, and she lifted her head weakly from the pillow. She held a cold cloth pressed against her closed eyelids.

"Feeling any better, my dear?" inquired Alex's voice.

"A little," she replied, although the truth was she felt wretched.

She felt Alex's weight press against the mattress of their large four-poster as he sat beside her.

"You're having quite a time with this one, aren't you, poor dear?"

Jane didn't answer, hoping Alex would think her too weak to reply.

"Dr. Ogilvy advises me that within another month or so, your indisposition should abate."

"Dr. Ogilvy has *had* a baby? He knows these things?" Jane replied sarcastically, breaking her temporary vow of silence.

She removed the compress from her eyes and stared moodily at Alex. Perhaps the misery of this pregnancy was a form of punishment meted out by the Highland Fairies for the hours of bliss she'd spent with Thomas. *One always seems to pay a price for joy,* she thought desolately reminded of dour Presbyterian dictums drummed into her as a child. 'She Is A Joy Who Doth Obey,' her tattered sampler had once prophesied. It was certainly evident, she concluded morosely, that obedience was not in her character.

"Dr. Ogilvy's delivered many a bairn," Alexander replied pleasantly, interrupting the stillness that had grown between them, "so I suppose he does know something about these things."

"Did he deliver yer George for Bathia Largue?," Jane inquired with a nasty edge to her voice. "He was so drunk last time, he nearly dropped Susan."

"You may engage anyone you wish, Jane," Alex answered

evenly, his features remaining as composed as his tone. "The most important thing is that you have someone looking after you who gives you confidence."

"I suppose Ogilvy's as good as the next man in this godforsaken place," Jane responded sullenly.

She knew she sounded like a spoiled child but she was beyond recovering her usual good humor.

Alex abruptly changed the subject.

"I've brought you some hot tea and a little dry bannock," he said, pouring from the teapot he'd set down on a tray. "If you sip some of this, perhaps you'll feel well enough to attend tonight's farewell dinner for the officers."

"No!" wailed Jane.

Much to her surprise, Alex leaned toward her and put his arms around her and drew her gently to his chest, whispering to her soothingly.

"There, there, my dear . . . you don't have to come downstairs if you aren't up to it. 'Tis just that so many of our friends have been distressed to hear you're feeling so poorly. Captain Fraser asked specifically to convey his regards."

Jane felt her body go rigid within the circle of Alex's arms.

"He spoke to ye?" she inquired cautiously, stunned that the two men might have exchanged more than civilities.

"Why, yes," Alex answered calmly. "Since both he and Hamilton are to serve in the same Fraser regiment, I thought it was time the Frasers and the Gordons put their enmities behind us."

"And what was his response . . . ?" Jane asked incredulously.

"Well," Alex said evenly, "this afternoon over brandy, he shook the hand I extended to him."

"I see . . ." Jane faltered, wondering how the meeting would have unfolded if Thomas knew she might be carrying the duke's child, or if Alex suspected the new baby was fathered by the very man whose hand he'd grasped in an offer of truce.

"I acted the jealous fool at Culloden House, Jane," Alex said quietly, "and I beg you to forgive me. You must let me prove to you, 'twill never happen again."

Jane stared at her husband, uncertain whether she had heard him correctly.

"The only good to come from that shameful night is the new babe," he said, his voice cracking with emotion. "For that I bless heaven—even as you rightly curse it. I will do everything I can to see you safely through your ordeal. I swear, by the honor of the House of Gordon, to return the trust and support you've offered to me as my faithful wife these last eight years.''

" 'Tis not certain I'm breeding,'' she whispered.

"Of course you are,'' Alex replied calmly. "Mrs. Christie tells me your courses ceased at least two months ago.''

Jane felt the last bit of energy drain from her body. Once again, apparently, Alex had instructed his housekeeper to spy on her for him. The wretched woman had probably interrogated the maids about the most intimate details of their household duties: the cleansing of a duchess's bloody rags after her monthly flux. It was an outrage!

"I'm so very happy about our new babe,'' Alex said, remaining oblivious to her fury. "As I told Captain Fraser, I'm wagering 'twill be another boy.''

He rose from the bed and gently rearranged the counterpane, tucking it neatly under the mattress. Jane closed her eyes as he tiptoed from her chamber. Moaning softly, she rolled over, and prayed fervently for sleep.

Standing in front of the enormous fireplace at the end of the hall, William Marshall sawed away at his fiddle. He was accompanied by the Fraser Highlander's pipe major who stood six feet five inches tall and made his music by blowing lustily into the chanter, a thin reed pipe with holes on which the melody was played. The tartan-covered bag lodged under his arm also sprouted three larger pipes, or drones, which produced the low, moaning bass notes.

The Duchess of Gordon slipped quietly into her seat at the head of the long dining table. Simon Fraser, as protocol required, was seated to Jane's right. As she took her place beside the general, he rose and bowed stiffly, while the footman held her chair. She took great pleasure in ignoring his reflexive courtesy, and turned to smile stiffly at her brother seated on her left.

Her heart thumped loudly in her chest as she glanced down the table, searching for Thomas's face. He was placed halfway down the row of guests, and he met her gaze immediately. She felt her cheeks flush with color, despite her determination to maintain her composure. There was no way for them to talk, which precluded her revealing to him her plan.

Fine claret and bowls of savory barley broth began the five-course banquet—all of which had been arranged, not by Jane, but in conferences between Mrs. Christie and the butler, Mr.

Marshall. The odious duo continued their subtle power struggle with Jane for control of affairs backstairs that, in truth, influenced much of what went on at Gordon Castle.

The officers attacked the repast with gusto, but the very smell of joints of beef, steaming potatoes, and turnips wafting toward Jane disquieted her stomach once again. She glanced down at her lavender silk gown, whose heavy folds and styling cleverly disguised the slight thickening of her waistline. Her svelte appearance, however, had been achieved at the price of considerable discomfort, and Jane longed to escape the stuffy room.

After numerous toasts offered around the table in praise of various accomplishments of several officers, the Duke of Gordon tapped his bone-handled knife against his crystal goblet, and rose, glass in hand.

"I think we would be remiss," he began, "if we failed to toast the person who, in no small way, is responsible for the fine complement of men under the command of my esteemed brother-in-law, Captain Hamilton Maxwell. I am referring, of course, to my dear wife, whose efforts in the field of recruitment have earned her much-deserved fame. So, gentlemen, I ask you to rise and join me in a toast to my beloved wife, Jane, the Duchess of Gordon!"

Cries of "Hear! Hear!" and "To the Duchess!" burst forth from the host of kilted soldiers who'd risen to their feet to pay her homage.

Jane nodded bleakly and acknowledged the compliment. Then, once the toasts were finished, she glanced at Thomas, who looked back at her steadily. He proceeded to whisper something to the major seated next to him and then withdrew, unnoticed, during the hubbub of conversation that bubbled throughout the room as Alexander bade his guests join him in a brandy.

Trying to maintain her poise, Jane led the small group of women who had accompanied their officer-husbands to Gordon Castle out of the dining hall to the smaller sitting room. As soon as coffee was poured, she quickly excused herself, pleading a headache that, unfortunately, was all too genuine.

Bursts of masculine laughter echoed in the foyer between the great hall and the parlor where the covey of ladies daintily sipped a thick Turkish brew from steaming cups. Jane mounted the stairs slowly, wondering how she would locate Thomas among the labyrinth of bedchambers assigned to visiting officers. She sincerely doubted Alexander's claim that he had conquered his jealousy of Thomas. Following her intuition, she quickly headed down the corridor toward the new wing, in the opposite direction from her own suite of rooms.

The farther she strayed from the castle's public rooms, the colder the evening air became. Without her cloak, she shivered in the icy dankness that permeated the stone walls in the new pavilion. The last door along the corridor was cracked open six inches, allowing a view of Thomas's broad back as he threw several pieces of clothing into a leather trunk at the end of his bed.

He reached for a pair of doeskin breeches folded on a chair, but his hand froze as he spied Jane standing in the doorway with her teeth chattering.

"Ye shouldna come here," he said gruffly, grabbing the breeches and slamming them roughly into the trunk.

"Thomas!" Jane replied heatedly. "The last time I saw ye, 'twas when ye were lying naked in a pile of Caledonian pine boughs. Now, all ye can say in greeting is, 'Ye shouldna *come* here?'"

"'Twas nearly three months ago, Jane," he replied, avoiding her gaze. "Much has changed between us since then."

"And what is *that*, may I ask," she retorted angrily as he crossed to the dresser to retrieve several articles.

He rested his fists on the dresser top, his head sunk below his shoulders:

"Ye're breeding, for one thing. Yer husband hinted as much to everyone within ear shot. 'A Christmas bairn,' I think he said."

Jane stood stock still at the door.

"The babe might be yers, ye know," she said in a low, raw voice. "Alex and I've not been to bed together since before I was at Kinrara."

"And *before* then?" he shot back. "'Twas clear ye dinna come to *me* a virgin bride!"

Jane clutched her waist, almost as if she had been struck by a blow.

"Ye *promised* ye'd not punish me for having been with Alex first!" she cried, angry tears welling up in her eyes. "I am his wife!" she said despairingly. "I am his *property*! I pray this will be *yer* baby, but all *ye* can do is pose and prance like some stag who's lost his doe!"

For several moments, the two of them glared at each other across the small chamber. Jane's cheeks were glistening with silent tears.

As Thomas stared back at her, he seemed almost to wince. At length, he shook his head.

"Ah, Jenny, love," he said, his own eyes shot with pain. "Ye know what I'm meaning. 'Tis a fine mess our lives have become. Ye canna know what 'tis been to see ye here at Gordon Castle . . . as ye *really are*—a *Duchess* in a fine house, with a gaggle of bairns clustered by yer skirts, and a husband who adores ye and can give ye everything this life can surely offer—"

"Adores me," she laughed bitterly. "He has a strange way of showing it."

Thomas looked at her oddly, but resumed packing his belongings into his campaign chest.

"He *does*, ye know," he replied, a tight smile on his lips. "Who would recognize that better than I?" Jane didn't respond, but stared at him silently as Thomas continued. "He even had the grace to *apologize* for his rudeness to me all these years. He said his father's . . . frailty . . . during the Rebellion in Forty-five had, in effect, caused much unwarranted discord and suffering among many Highland neighbors—"

"And ye believed him?" she demanded angrily. "Ye believed he was sincere?" Jane began to pace up and down the small chamber. "Rouse yerself, laddie," she said scornfully. " 'Tis time ye understood the truth about yer rival. Though Alex and I have never spoken of it, my noble husband knows I still love ye, Thomas. His fine words to ye over brandy are merely designed to persuade ye to give him back his property. 'Tis as simple as that!" She halted her restless pacing and stared up at him. "He *knew* he could play on yer sensibilities as a man of honor, as an *aristocrat* yourself, title or no, to abide by the *Gentlemen*'s Code," she added caustically. "Oh, I'm sure he used his fine phrases of how wrongheaded all the Gordons were who came before him, but, believe me, he was playing ye for a kindhearted fool!"

"I assume him to be at least a man of honor," Thomas replied stiffly.

"Thomas," she said wearily, "ye make a fatal mistake if ye think the Fourth Duke of Gordon is like yerself. He may act the gentleman, but he is merely a gentleman thoroughly accustomed to having things *his* way! And his *honor* is employed in keeping a tight rein on his *possessions*!"

Jane walked to the bedchamber window and stared down at the neat rows of tents where the crack troops were camped a hundred yards from the castle walls. Thomas remained silent, stationed behind her. At length, she turned to face him, fighting to suppress a wail of anguish.

"So that's it, then . . ." she forced herself to say calmly.

"What would ye have me *do*?" Thomas exploded, pounding his fist on top of the mahogany dresser.

"Take me with you!" she cried, grabbing hold of his arm. "Run away with me to London or to France. *Be* with me, no matter what the cost, because ye say ye love me and canna imagine life without me by yer side! 'Tis how I feel about *you*! 'Tis what I came here to tell ye!"

Jane stared at him, feeling bitter tears begin to spill down her cheeks once more. Thomas stared back, his face haggard. From the far end of the hallway, the sound of raucous laughter and off-key singing floated through the door. Apparently, several of the younger officers were making their way back to their rooms so they could continue drinking themselves insensible till their departure at dawn.

"I canna run away with ye," Thomas said, his voice rasping. "I love ye with my life, Jenny, but ye're with child—"

"And ye dinna want me, unless yer certain 'tis *yers*, is that it?" she flared.

"No, 'tis *not* the way of it," he shot back, a look of anguish etched on his face. "But I canna take ye from yer home and children at a time like this . . . and I canna abandon the men in my charge." His fists relaxed by his sides and he shook his head in a melancholy way. "Jenny, darling," he said gently, taking her hands in his and raising them to his lips. "If either of us is to have any happiness in this life at all . . . we must give all this up. . . ."

Jane stared at him, cut to the quick.

" 'Tis the only choice we have." A look of searing pain passed across his features as he gazed into her eyes. "Truly, pet," he said, releasing her hands, "I've thought of nothing else these past months . . . and seeing ye and Alex side-by-side with the bairns. . . ." He turned away from her, his shoulders slumped in defeat. "We must give it up . . ." he repeated, his voice cracking with emotion. " 'Tis what I must do. 'Tis what I *shall* do."

Give it up!

He'd said it like a litany he was attempting to commit to memory.

"Then *do so*!" she cried. "But *I—I* canna just *stop* loving ye—though, as God is my witness, I wish I *could*!"

Jane spun blindly around on her heel and made a headlong dash for the door. By the time she arrived back at her room in the original wing of the castle, she was doubled over and retching, holding her pale lavender skirts to her lips.

Two hours later, Alex returned from the festivities downstairs and found his wife splayed on the floor near their bed, huddled over the chamber pot, losing the last of the elegant meal they'd served to the departing officers of the 71st Fraser Highlanders.

"My poor darling," he said. To Jane, his sympathetic words sounded hollow. Obviously, he hadn't the slightest idea of what it felt like to long for death.

Jane's eyes followed Alex listlessly as he reached for a linen towel and dipped it in cool water from the pitcher on a small table near the velvet-curtained window. He wiped the sour taste from her lips and patted dry the beads of clammy perspiration from her forehead, lifting her gently to the bed. Then he stripped her of her gown and undergarments. His hands lingered a moment on the soft mound of her belly. She closed her eyes to blot out the gesture from her sight. Soon she heard him removing his own clothing. She waited apprehensively as she felt his body slipping next to hers between the linen bed clothes.

A heavy cloak of misery settled over Jane as Alex gently gathered her in his arms. The room was filled with silence. His body relaxed against hers and he sighed. Slowly he stroked her hair and whispered, "Sleep . . . just sleep, my dear. By morning, he'll be gone and all will be well."

The wheels of the small trap skimmed over the golden leaves lying in dusty profusion along the gated entrance to the castle grounds. The Duke of Gordon himself waited by the heavy oaken door as Nancy Christie emerged from the carriage looking distraught.

"Where's Dr. Ogilvy?" demanded Alex to Jane's maid.

"I found him in his room at the Gordon Arms," Nancy explained nervously. "The publican said he'd made quite a night o' it, sir. I found a pitcher of heather ale next to his bed drained to the dregs, and nothing I could do seemed to rouse 'im!"

"Blast the bastard!" the duke swore swiftly. "I'll have him horsewhipped!"

"How goes Her Grace?" Nancy asked timidly as the two of them hurried up the wide oak staircase toward Jane's bedchamber.

"Poorly," the duke answered cryptically. "The duchess appears to be in great distress, but the midwife claims there's no sign of the bairn.''

What he neglected to add was that the morning's sequence of events had seemed hauntingly familiar to Alex: Bathia Largue had endured an excruciatingly difficult delivery like this. And then she died.

Slowly Alex opened the door to Jane's bedchamber. His wife, pale and perspiring, gripped the bed's mahogany newel post and uttered a low, guttural moan that rose to an agonized shriek. Drucilla Perkins, a plump matron of about fifty-five, stepped forward to speak to the duke.

"She's been laboring since cock's crow," whispered the midwife, "with still nary a bit o' progress to show for it. The pains are farther apart now than they were when I was first called. 'Tis a puzzle, it is . . . not like the duchess's other bairns a'tall." She shook her head and sighed. "The bairn's head is down . . . and that's a good sign," she added hopefully, "but I suspect the wee thing is facing the wrong direction, banging the back of its head against the duchess's spine. That's why the labor is so slow and the pain so intense."

Alex clasped Jane's clammy hand in his own and gently kissed her forehead. She stiffened at his touch. In the past nine months an emotional desert had existed between them, but now all he could think of was that Jane might die.

"Where's Dr. Ogilvy?" Jane gasped between pains. When Alex didn't answer immediately, Jane smiled grimly. "The drunken sot!"

The fingers of her free hand began to pluck at the coverlet shielding the enormous bulge that was her unborn child. Her body suddenly grew rigid and she began to whimper.

"Sir, perhaps 'twould be better—" the midwife began tentatively.

"Leave us *alone!*" the duke growled. "Fetch your mistress some cool water, and be quick about it!"

As Perkins and Nancy Christie retreated quickly from the room, Jane's moans crescendoed into primordial wails of an animal suffering excruciating pain.

"Hold on to me, dearheart," he whispered fiercely into her ear as her fingers dug into his arm. "Try to breathe . . . that's it . . . *breathe!*"

Jane's ragged sobs slowly evened out as the wave of pain receded.

"My b-back . . . my back is on fire!" Jane gasped when she could finally speak.

"Can you roll on your side?" Alex asked. "Let's try. . . ." With great effort, Jane shifted her body to the left while Alex pulled away the bed linen. "How does that feel?" he inquired, rhythmically kneading the small of her back.

"Oh, God . . . 'tis good . . . oh . . ." Her hoarse whisper faded and he felt the muscles beneath his fingers release some of their tension. He sat on the bed in silence for five or ten minutes, continuing to massage the area on either side of her spine.

"Alex?"

He was startled to hear her call his name.

"Yes, Jane?"

"There's no more pain."

"I'm glad."

"But 'tis not natural. Something's happened. Where's Perkins?"

"Here I be, ma'am," said the midwife, entering the room. "I've brought ye some nice cool water."

"The duchess feels no more pain," Alex said abruptly.

"Aye?" frowned the old matron. "I think Her Grace should try to stand up . . . or at least sit . . . the weight of the bairn itself might encourage her labors. . . ."

"Do you think you could do that, Jane?" Alex said. "Do you think you could sit on the edge of the bed if we helped you?"

"And walk a wee bit, if ye can," the midwife said emphatically. "If that bairn's head is pressing on your ladyship's back bone, we must get it to push past it on its own."

With supreme effort, Jane raised herself on her elbows while Alex and Perkins flanked her. Together they helped her to sit up, and, when her dizziness had passed, they each took her by an arm and raised her to her feet.

"Shall we try to walk?" Alex said, masking his own concern with a smile. "Where would you like to go, m'lady?"

"Anywhere, if 'twill finish this. . . ."

Slowly they walked down the long, gloomy corridor, back and forth, for more than an hour. Occasionally, Jane would be gripped by a mild contraction of her uterine muscles. She leaned against the corridor walls till it passed.

"Are ye tired, Yer Grace?" the midwife asked anxiously.

"Yes . . . but let's keep walking . . . I want to—"

Suddenly, Jane doubled over with a gasp.

"Oh, my God!" she hissed between clenched teeth. "Now *that* feels like the pain I remember!"

"We should get her back to her room!" Alex said to the

midwife, unable to conceal his concern. He held on tightly to Jane's arm as his wife sagged against the wall, shuddering.

"I'd like to sit in that big chair," Jane said tiredly, when they'd returned to her bedchamber. "Just for a while, at least. It feels so much better than when I'm on my back in bed."

Alex looked questioningly at the midwife. Despite the fact that this was their fifth child, in the past he had felt decorum dictated he remain in his study, awaiting word that Jane's ordeal was over. This time, however, he felt that he, too, was becoming the parent of a new baby. He found he quite liked the prospect, though he felt like an untutored schoolboy as far as the practical side of childbirth was concerned.

"When yer ladyship feels ye must push—begging yer pardon, sir—" Perkins glanced at the duke with some embarrassment, "then ye should return to yer bed."

Jane winced as another contraction swept through her body. This time, though, she held tight to Alex's hand. Her face glistened with perspiration as her labor intensified. Suddenly her cry startled them both.

"Oh my God, Alex! 'Tis coming! Oh, God!"

The duke and the midwife quickly lifted her onto the bed, propping up her back with every pillow in the room.

"If Yer Grace would hold her shoulders," Perkins ordered briskly, casting Jane's nightdress unceremoniously above her knees. "When I nod to ye, tell her ladyship to push."

There was only a moment of silence before the midwife dipped her head emphatically.

"Push, darling!" Alex said, his arms around Jane. "That's a good lass . . . *push!*"

As Jane bore down with all her might, a kaleidoscope of images flashed through Alex's brain. He remembered the little girl riding so jauntily aboard the pig down Edinburgh's High Street. He thought of how exquisite Jane had looked as a seventeen-year-old in her white satin gown the night she had saved him from the riotous mob at the Canongate Playhouse. A vision of her smiling happily at him as they danced down the line of guests at their wedding melded with the memory of her frozen countenance when he had abandoned her in the guest bedchamber at Culloden House. And now, the result of that passion and pain was about to be born. If anything should happen to Jane or the babe now, because of his unforgivable behavior nine months ago. . . . The midwife furiously bobbed her head up and down.

"Push . . . push *hard*, darling!" Alex urged his wife, an icy fear gripping him as he felt Jane's body become as rigid as his ceremonial steel sword.

Jane's cries rent his heart, but he exhorted her to bear down each time Perkins shook her head in their direction.

"Please, Jane . . . try, darling. . . . I love you, darling. . . . I'm here . . . *please try*!" he murmured incoherently.

Jane emitted one, bloodcurdling scream and appeared to faint.

" 'Tis come, Yer Grace," the midwife announced triumphantly. "And a fine Scottish bairn she is, with her copper tresses!"

" 'Tis a lass, Jane," Alex said excitedly as the midwife held the squirming, bawling baby up for his inspection. "And she's kicking her arms and legs in all directions!"

The infant's tiny nose was flattened somewhat from the difficult journey she had taken into the world, and her auburn hair, still damp from birth fluids, glistened orangey gold in the afternoon sun that streamed through the window. Jane's eyes fluttered open at the sound of his voice.

"Another girl," she sighed exhaustedly. "Are ye pleased, though, Alex?"

"Of course," he replied, attempting to steady his voice as he continued to stare at the baby's arresting pumpkin-colored locks. He forced himself to shift his gaze to his wife's chestnut hair, a shade darker than his own, which lay tangled on the pillow. As shafts of autumn sun singed her curls, he wondered if his wife's hair didn't seem of a more reddish cast than ever he had noticed.

The midwife had tied off the cord and cut it. She swaddled the child in clean linen with lightning speed.

"What shall we call her?" Jane asked sleepily.

Alex didn't answer because his mind was utterly blank.

"She's all right, isna she?" Jane asked suddenly, her eyes widening with concern when Alex did not speak.

"She's as perfect as a *peach*," chimed in the midwife with a pride of authorship that was especially sweet, since Dr. Ogilvy had so thoroughly discredited himself at the crucial moment.

"We could . . . call her . . . Louisa . . . after my uncle Lewis," the duke said finally, surprised at the name that had involuntarily come to him.

"The uncle who fought against the Crown for Bonnie Prince Charlie?" Jane asked cautiously.

"Aye," Alex replied wearily, an overwhelming sense of fatigue invading his body. "The only Gordon in my family who fought beside Simon the Fox, at Culloden Moor."

He gazed down at the tiny bundle cooing softly in Perkins' arms. Louisa's hair had partially dried, and in the shadows of the curtained bed, it appeared to be only slightly more auburn than her mother's brunette mane. He must have been imagining. . . .

"I think you should rest now," he said, rising from the bed as Perkins lay the newborn in his wife's arms.

The soaring happiness that had filled his heart at the moment of the baby's birth had drained away, leaving only the dregs of doubt and mistrust that once again ate at him like a canker.

"A-Alex . . ." Jane said softly, staring at the russet top of her new daughter's head.

"Yes," he replied dully, preventing himself from musing about the brief period the previous December when Jane and Thomas Fraser were together at Culloden House. Surely, he, Alex, had left her that night in no condition to seek another man's bed. He'd learned through his brother-in-law, Hamilton, that she had left the next day for Kinrara and then, home. Alex closed his eyes to shut out the memory of that first blinding vision of Louisa's reddish hair. He breathed deeply. Louisa was his. The baby *had* to be his! He felt Jane's hand touching his sleeve. Opening his eyes, he flinched for the first time in his life at the sight of his wife's missing forefinger.

"I think I would have died without ye, Alex . . . truly, I do."

"I think not," he answered stiffly, turning to leave the room. "Just as I've always said, you're a proven breeder, Jane. Now, I suggest you get some sleep."

20

September 1777

Thomas Fraser observed the dense fog enveloping the Old Kennett Meeting House with a profound sense of foreboding.

It was nine o'clock on this sultry September morning, and already, sweat was pouring down his back. The peculiar vapor obscured a long line of British infantry who, together with a company of Hessian mercenaries, were advancing along the Baltimore-Philadelphia road toward Chadd's Ford in pursuit of

General Washington's army. Thomas squinted through the haze. His scouts had sworn the Continentals were posted on the heights across the Brandywine, but he couldn't even see the rebel troops.

"Do ye think General Howe did right to split us into two forces like this, Captain Fraser, sir?" Corporal Christopher Thornton whispered nervously, nodding in the direction of General Knyphausen who rode at the head of the long column of soldiers disappearing into the mist.

Thomas was annoyed by the persistent questions posed by this young recruit who, he'd lately learned, hailed from the cathedral town of Elgin and had accepted the King's Shilling from the Duchess of Gordon herself.

Can I never escape from the shadow of that blasted clan? Thomas thought morosely.

"Look, Thornton," Thomas replied to the eighteen-year-old recruit, " 'Tis a sound plan for our battalion and the Hessians to engage the main American force while the others encircle them from behind."

General Howe and Lord Cornwallis had first listened carefully as Thomas and the other intelligence officers reported the latest information collected from a network of agents and royalist sympathizers who'd crawled out of the woodwork in Pennsylvania as soon as His Majesty's troops landed on August 25. Thomas glanced back at the column of kilted soldiers of the 71st Fraser Highlanders. Their ranks were thinned by the capture of a whole company, including Jane's brother, Hamilton Maxwell, aboard the *Ann* just as the ship approached Boston Harbor in June of 1776. Thomas wondered if Jane even knew yet that her brother and his fellow soldiers had wound up in prison as soon as they touched American soil, and without having fired a single shot.

He shifted his musket onto his left shoulder and tried not to speculate further about *anything* having to do with Jane Maxwell, even the fate of her brother. Despite his resolve, he found his mind drifting back to the night they'd parted in his room at Gordon Castle. What if she had actually been carrying his child? What if—

Give it up! he silently lectured himself. *'Tis finished. Finally finished.*

Thomas eyed the pack horses tramping past Welch's Tavern. The region they were marching through presently was shaded by hickory trees and Penn oaks. The rolling green hills and rich bottomlands of Chester County, Pennsylvania, supplied much of the grain that fed Washington's Army, as well as most of the iron, the furnaces, and the forges that produced the muskets and cannonballs fired at the British troops. Thomas and the rest of the 71st Fraser Highlanders were aching for a chance to repay the rebels, who had managed to recover from their ignominious rout at a place called Brooklyn Heights in New York and had subsequently outflanked and outsmarted Cornwallis during the latter part of 1776 in campaigns all over New Jersey.

Thomas pulled his collar away from his sweat-damp neck and was suddenly reminded of those stiflingly humid days he'd spent not so very far from here, just over the border in Maryland. His hand involuntarily traced the scar slicing across his cheek. It had been ten years since he'd lived at Antrim Hall, recuperating from wounds he'd received in the Indian ambush. If it hadn't been for Arabella O'Brien Delaney's hiding his letters to Jane and no doubt to Captain James Maxwell as well, he might be married to Jane this very day. Thanks to Arabella's perfidy, he was marching along a fog-choked road in Pennsylvania, facing death from an American musket fired by a soldier he might never see.

If I live to see another dawn, he thought grimly, *I will pay my respects to that raven-haired vixen.*

Events had moved swiftly following the sound defeat of Washington's troops at Brandywine. After the battle, the British General Howe established his headquarters six miles north of Philadelphia with nine thousand men, and then, on September 26, he had marched into the capital, unopposed. The Revolutionary leaders had barely enough time to flee to nearby Lancaster, Pennsylvania, with their personal belongings and their quill pens.

"Are ye *sure* the lad said Antrim Hall? Antrim Hall outside of Annapolis?" Thomas quizzed the agent who'd arrived in camp following its hasty construction.

"Right. That's what he said," the peddler insisted. "He told me the mistress of Antrim Hall has married one of Washington's aides. A Colonel Boyd, he said. Much older than her, but they tied the knot about a year ago."

"And ye're *positive* the colonel paid his wife a visit just after Brandywine?"

"Yes, sir. That's what the other agent said. He heard Colonel Boyd speak of his wife at the inn in Annapolis on his return to Lancaster."

"I see . . ." Thomas said absently, turning this fortuitous bit of information over in his mind. Perhaps he could both settle an old score and glean some much-needed intelligence as to Washington's next moves at the same time. He opened his pouch of gold coins. "Until next trip, then." He smiled grimly, extending payment to the itinerant traveler.

Within twenty-four hours, Lord Cornwallis had agreed with Thomas that he and a party of nine men should travel to the Maryland Tidewater region, ostensibly to "liberate" foodstuffs and supplies for their newly established headquarters in Germantown, just outside Philadelphia. However, Thomas's real mission would be to persuade the new Mrs. Boyd, by whatever means were at Thomas's disposal, to reveal what her husband had undoubtedly told her about General Washington's future battle plans.

The ancient oaks arched in a tunnel along the entrance to Antrim Hall. Their branches cast a spiderweb of shadows in the moonlight, which shone overhead with dazzling silver brilliance.

"The cook house and the stores lie in two low brick buildings in the back, behind the main house," Thomas whispered to the soldier next to him. "Ye'll gather as much as ye can. Thornton, report to my lord Cornwallis that I will return to Germantown by Friday, but that I think my interview with Mistress Boyd may quickly yield some valuable information regarding General Washington's plans to recapture Philadelphia."

"Aye, Captain," responded Corporal Christopher Thornton with a sly smile.

The pink-cheeked recruit, who had an appreciative eye for the ladies, was obviously titillated to learn that an old acquaintance of Captain Fraser's had married an aide to General Washington. Whether the lady in question would be forthcoming about what she knew, or would require some amusing form of persuasion, was a mystery to spark Corporal Thornton's imagination.

"All right, lads," Thomas said gruffly, "just get the stores and then be on yer way. I doubt there are many men left on the plantation, so, no nonsense with the servant women . . . d'ye take my meaning?"

"Aye . . ." the nine men mumbled in unison, looking disappointed at the order. As far as they were concerned, intelligence officers had all the luck.

With Thomas in the lead, the small band of men rode down the shaded driveway until they were within view of the porticoed, white-shuttered brick mansion standing on the gentle rise. Thomas couldn't help but recall the towering rage he had been in when last he'd thundered past this mighty avenue of oaks on his

way to catch his ship in Philadelphia. Now, as he gazed down along the shaded drive, the house looked as picturesque as a wedding cake, iced with moonlight.

Stealthily, the party dismounted and tied their horses to the branches of the last oak flanking the road. Thomas passed along the rose garden by the side of the house, and around to the back porch. Then he waved his men toward the two squat buildings that stood a hundred yards from the Greek revival manse.

With the tip of his dagger, Thomas jimmied open the flimsy lock and let himself into the back pantry. The sounds of dogs barking in the kennels down by the summerhouse made him feel uneasy as he crept up the back stairs. He quickly reached the passageway that ran past his former sickroom. Shafts of moonlight spilled through the fanlight window at the end of the hall onto the worn carpet and peeling wallpaper. Apparently, Arabella's nuptials with Washington's aide-de-camp had not brought with it vast wealth. Or perhaps the general shabbiness of the place indicated that the British blockade had effectively prevented luxury goods from reaching the hands of Americans who could pay for them.

The door to Arabella's brother's bedchamber stood open a few inches. Its bareness assured Thomas that Beven O'Brien had apparently sobered up long enough to volunteer for the Maryland militia. He paused at Arabella's door, listening intently. He could hear nothing. Carefully, he lifted the latch, but, despite his efforts to open the door noiselessly, it creaked loudly on its rusty hinges.

"Mehitabel? What is it?" Arabella's husky voice cried out. "Don't tell me that mare's come up with the colic *again*?"

"Why no, *Mrs.* Boyd," Thomas said into the darkness. " 'Tis merely His Majesty's troops, come to pay a call."

There was enough moonlight flooding the room for him to see Arabella sit bolt upright in her high, four-poster bed.

"Not *again*!" she moaned. "Who goes there?" she said boldly, though Thomas detected a slight tremor in her voice. "How dare you enter my boudoir!"

The silvery light pouring through the window glinted off the barrel of an unwieldy pistol Arabella had snatched from beneath her pillow and held in her shaking hand.

" 'Tisn't it just what ye always *wanted* of me, Mrs. Boyd?" Thomas said sardonically, advancing toward the bed.

"Who *are* you?" Arabella demanded, shrinking to the far side of the bed. "Get out at once or I'll pull the trigger!"

"Now, is that any way to treat a former guest?" he said softly, resting his boot on the mahogany bed frame and leaning an elbow on his knee. "Perhaps I should reintroduce myself. Former Lieutenant—now Captain—Thomas Fraser of Struy, Scotland, mum, come to pay my humble respects."

"Thomas Fra—? What are *you* doing here?" Arabella shrieked, plainly shocked by his sudden reappearance. She relaxed her hunched shoulders, and the bedlinen slipped to her waist, revealing ample breasts outlined beneath her cambric nightdress.

"I'm here to renew an old acquaintance," Thomas said pleasantly, "and to request a favor."

"Thomas, stop talking in riddles," Arabella said nervously, lowering the pistol onto the pillow by her side. "I certainly never thought to see *you* again, after what happened."

Her sheepish words trailed off and she stared at him uncertainly. Embarrassed, she fumbled for a flint to light the candle standing in a pewter holder beside her bed.

As she reached toward the bedside table, Thomas grabbed her hand and held it in a viselike grip. Her face was illuminated by a shaft of moonlight and a flicker of fear flared in the blue depths of her eyes. After a long moment, he released her arm, taking the flint from her fingers and the gun from its perch on her pillow. He tucked the pistol into his belt.

Arabella shifted uncomfortably under Thomas's steady gaze as he ignited the candle. Her former guest sat down casually on the mattress. His eyes wandered leisurely over her form clad in the filmy nightdress while she stared up at him from a mountain of linen-covered pillows cushioning her back. The silence hung heavily between them.

"Just as comely as ever," he commented, as if to himself. "Marriage to the Colonel seems to agree with ye, even if it hasna brought ye the prosperity ye'd desired."

In the ten years since he had stormed out of Antrim Hall, Arabella had aged in the way of women blessed with high cheekbones and trim figures: her face had held its striking contours, and her body had become only slightly fuller, hinting at a voluptuousness she might achieve in her early thirties. Her jet black hair was as glossy as ever, pulled back from her face and secured by a length of white satin ribbon, salvaged from better days. Although tiny lines fanned out from the corner of her distinctive eyes, their arresting gaze was still framed by long dark eyelashes that cast shadows on her cheeks in the mellow candlelight.

"Antrim Hall was *finally* starting to show a profit when this blasted war broke out," she complained. Her voice was full of bravado, but her eyes watched him warily. "Mr. Boyd sold his own farm and the money was put to good use—under *my* management, I must say—after my dear brother Beven ran off with his Annapolis cronies to play soldier. But then Boyd, that old goat, *volunteered*! General Washington had to go and make him a Colonel, which cost us a pretty farthing, I can tell you! Now, there's no one but the oldest slaves left to pick the crops, and no way to get them to market safely, thanks to *you* lot." She lifted her chin and flashed him an angry look. "You English are running all over the countryside, raiding our storehouses, killing whomever you please. . . . No farmer's safe from the Limeys *or* the Colonials! 'Tis disgusting!"

"I'm *not* English!" Thomas interrupted stiffly.

"English . . . Scottish . . . Continentals . . . what's the difference?" she demanded petulantly. "You men merely *take* what pleases you and cloak your actions in fine sentiment and flowery words about liberty and sovereignty. I find the entire situation absurd!"

"Did ye express yer opinions to yer dear husband, the Colonel, during his visit here last week?" Thomas asked calmly, nodding in the direction of a small porcelain miniature standing beside the candlestick.

It portrayed a slightly balding, heavyset man of middle years whose nose was too large for his face. Studying it, Thomas found himself discomfited by Arabella's cynical assessment of the reasons why some thirty thousand men had fought and died in places such as Brandywine, Pennsylvania. Less than two weeks previously, on a dark September night, Thomas, personally, had supervised a military detail that had buried some five hundred bodies in Colonial soil. Those good men had gone to their graves without regard to their red or blue uniforms, soldiers from both armies forever entombed beneath the bloodstained battlefield near Chadd's Ford.

"I told Colonel Boyd *exactly* how I felt about being left here, virtually unprotected, only a stone's throw from the Baltimore-Philadelphia road!" Arabella said, bristling. Then she looked at Thomas sharply. "How, pray tell, did *you* know my husband came to Antrim Hall five days ago?" she demanded.

" 'Tis part of my job to keep track of the movements of our enemy's spies."

"*Spies*?" Arabella sniffed. "Colonel Boyd, a *spy*? Don't talk nonsense!"

"How well do ye know yer dear husband, Mrs. Boyd?" Thomas asked with mock politeness.

"Stop calling me Mrs. Boyd," Arabella said irritably. "Then I shall have to call you Lieutenant . . . or Captain or whatever you said you were now," she retorted with matching sarcasm.

"A mere Captain," he replied, inclining his head with a derisive smile. "A Colonel's Commission is beyond my means, I'm afraid."

"Ah . . . so the baronet's daughter is a bit stingy with the purse strings, is she?" Arabella said with a flash of malice. When Thomas remained silent, she continued with a brittle smile. "Actually, the Colonel and I hadn't conversed much when we decided upon . . . rather . . . ah . . . hasty nuptials. War had just been declared when I discovered I was . . . how shall I put it delicately? I was, as they say, *breeding*."

She shot him a challenging look, veiled by something in her eyes he couldn't quite discern.

"Ah . . . so ye are a mother now, as well . . ." he said.

"No, I lost the baby," she replied shortly. "The entire exercise snared me a reluctant husband. Of course, he's more than delighted to be called the Laird of Antrim Hall and strut around behind General Washington, dealing in tittle-tattle, just as you do! Meanwhile, I've been trying to keep this place afloat—and I was doing just *that*—that is, until the damned *British* headed south!" She glanced over at a small, round table near the window on which rested a square cut-glass decanter and several glasses.

"Would you like a whiskey?" she said abruptly. "I'm thirsty."

Without waiting for his reply, she slid out of her four-poster and quickly donned a dressing gown that lay on one of two chairs positioned next to her private liquor supply.

"Ye dinna approve of the war, I take it?" Thomas asked. The kernel of a plan began to unfold in his mind as he watched her pour out the amber-colored spirits.

"I *dinna*, as you say, approve of anything that makes my job harder!" she retorted, handing him a glass and indicating he should be seated in one of the two chairs facing each other across the Chippendale table. "I think your fat English king should mind his own business, and I think those hotheads in Philadelphia should mind theirs!"

"Ye *are* a cynic," he said thoughtfully, sipping his drink. "And a very beautiful one, at that."

He stared boldly at the top of her nightdress where a button had become dislodged, revealing a patch of her lovely rounded bosom. Feeling his eyes on her, Arabella set down her glass on the table with a clunk.

"I think you should leave now," she said in a flustered voice. "I'm sure by now your men have stolen every last rasher of bacon and every bushel of grain I have, so you might as well go."

"I will see that they leave us enough for breakfast, my dear Arabella," he said softly, relishing the prospect of capturing such prey. "And enough for supper, and dinner and breakfast again."

"W-what are you talking about?" she stammered, glancing nervously out the window, which faced the rose garden below.

"Ye see before ye a man as weary of war as yerself," he said quietly, his eyes boring into hers. "I merely long for a brief respite, enjoying the civilized company of an old friend."

"*Friend*!" she countered sharply. "You don't regard *me* as a friend. I was bold enough to ask you to marry me, once, and to share Antrim Hall, but that wasn't good enough for you!" She waited for Thomas to respond. Goaded by his continuing silence, Arabella lowered her eyes and added in a low voice, "You'll always hate me because I didn't send your letter to your precious Jane Maxwell! Do you still hold her in such high regard after ten years of close proximity?"

Thomas felt his gorge rise, but he fought to keep his temper.

"We never married," he replied evenly, draining the rest of his whiskey in one gulp.

"Ah . . ." Arabella said with a note of rancor. "The great love of your life didn't have the grace to wait for you?"

"That's right," he said shortly, setting his glass next to the near-empty decanter. "She dinna. That's why I'm back in service to His Royal Majesty . . . and why I'm mighty sick of the entire business." He reached across the table to grasp her hand and lifted it quickly to his lips before she could withdraw it. "So soft . . ." he murmured against the back of her fingers. He was surprised, despite his calculated gesture, to feel himself genuinely aroused by her proximity and the faint scent of jasmine rising to his nostrils. It had been more than a year since he had lain with anyone but whores. What's more, the plan that was slowly evolving in his mind had increasing appeal: dish out to

Arabella a sample of what she'd served up to him a decade
earlier and, in the process, perhaps gain some important intelligence as to when General Washington would move on Philadelphia. "My dear Arabella," he said, ignoring her puzzled frown
as he released her hand, "I've disturbed yer sleep long enough. I
must excuse myself. I want to be sure that my men do not strip
yer stores of more than they need to spur them on their journey
back to Germantown."

Her startled look told him his strategic retreat was precisely
the correct maneuver to bend her to his will.

"And . . . you?" she inquired uncertainly, like a wallflower
whose favors remain unclaimed at a ball.

"I shall avail myself of the bed in my old sickroom, if I
may," he said lightly, "and look forward to joining ye on the
morrow for some of that bacon. I havna had a bite of anything
decent to eat in a month. And I relish the thought of a hot bath
and a day's holiday." He picked up the candlestick and held it
above his head until Arabella slid back into bed. Then he blew it
out. "Good night, Arabella," he said into the semidarkness.

"G-good night, Thomas," she replied hesitantly.

He was nearly to the door when she spoke again.

"Thomas?"

"What?"

" 'Twas very bad of me not to post your letters as I promised.
You left so quickly that day . . . I couldn't tell you how ashamed
I was to have done such a thing. . . ."

Thomas stared at the shaft of moonlight pouring through her
bedchamber's window.

" 'Twas a long time ago," he managed to say, perplexed by
an onslaught of contrary emotions.

"I pray such childish actions played no role in your not
marrying—"

"Dinna speak of it!" he interrupted harshly. " 'Tis in the
past!"

"Thomas . . ." she said softly. "I'm truly, truly sorry for
what I did."

Her abject apology sounded so unlike the tough little piece of
baggage he'd always taken her for. Such meek words from the
strong-willed plantation owner made him wonder. What was she
up to? And who was about to set a trap for whom?

Two horses, one gray and one black, walked together across
the little creek that flowed toward Antrim Hall.

"Are you hungry?" Arabella asked, glancing at Thomas through thick black lashes.

"Aye, that I am . . . and hot. 'Tis so strange to feel the sun so warm in autumn. A nice bit o' shade would be in order too, dinna ye think?"

Arabella O'Brien Delaney Boyd looked fetching indeed aboard the finely bred hunter whose silky flanks matched the color of her own dark tresses, tucked neatly under her riding hat.

"Follow me," she said, urging her horse into a faster walk and gesturing toward the summit of a gentle, moss-covered incline. "I've arranged the perfect spot for our picnic." The horses entered a grove of oaks on the north side of the hill. "There!" Arabella said, pointing to a small white structure flanked by two magnificent oaks. "Do you remember drinking coffee and eating Mehitabel's cream biscuits in the old summerhouse? I told her to air it out."

" 'Tis not exactly a place for a *picnic*," Thomas noted dryly, jumping to the ground. He was wearing a pair of Beven's old riding boots and breeches and a shirt borrowed from the drawers of the mahogany highboy in the guest room he'd occupied the previous night.

Arabella did not reply, but tied the horses to a post while Thomas eased a saddlebag with their refreshments off the back of his mount. As he entered through the low-slung door of the miniature house, he ducked just in time to avoid hitting his head. It just was as he remembered it: an octagonally shaped room studded with eight shuttered windows and rough-hewn furniture painted pure white. There was a daybed with calico cushions positioned against one wall and two chairs and a round white table, set for two. An enormous peach-colored rose floated in a glass bowl between the place settings. Two crystal glasses stood on the side table, and next to them sat a bottle of wine, uncorked. The stage was set—but for what play?

"Would you mind pouring?" Arabella said to Thomas as she dished out plump cold chicken breasts drizzled with herbs next to a rice dish dotted with raisins and pine nuts. "Apparently, your men did leave us some stores," she said with a wry smile as she sliced two thick pieces of freshly baked bread and topped them with slabs of green-veined cheese from a stone crock. "May I raise my glass in a toast of thanks?" she added, taking the goblet he offered her and grazing his fingers with hers.

"And here's to yer kindness to a man in need of a comfortable

bed and a long, soapy bath,'' he replied, bowing slightly, trying
to ignore the sensations prompted by her subtle touch.

''Have you any other needs I could assist you with before you
leave us, Captain?'' Arabella asked calmly, sipping her wine and
looking directly into his eyes above the rim of her glass. Her
own blue eyes had taken on a smoky quality in the dim, cool
atmosphere of the summerhouse's shuttered interior.

Thomas stared back. There was no mistaking her meaning. He
watched her carefully cut into her chicken breast.

''''Yes . . . actually, there is,'' he said quietly.

Arabella lay down her knife and fork.

''And pray, what might that be?'' she asked, chewing slowly
and looking at him steadily.

''Ye say ye dinna care who wins this skirmish—am I right?''

Arabella cocked an eyebrow and then picked up her eating
utensils.

'' 'Tis all a bloody nuisance, if that's what you mean,'' she
replied shortly, attacking her meal with her silver knife. ''Another year of raids like we've been having, with no markets to
sell our crops, and Antrim Hall will be finished.''

''What if I told ye I could pay ye a hundred guineas right now
for something ye already have in yer possession?''

''You're *not* taking my crystal for your headquarters, if that's
what you're thinking!'' she retorted hotly. ''The silver's long
gone, except for these few pieces you're dining with, and my
goblets are the only things that make this place feel civilized!''

''I dinna want yer goblets, my dear Arabella,'' he chuckled.
''I want information.''

''Information? For a hundred guineas?'' she asked incredulously.

''Right,'' he said simply. ''Information.''

''What *kind* of information?'' she asked, tilting her head to
one side and eyeing him suspiciously.

''Well . . . for instance . . . how long did yer husband remain
with ye at Antrim Hall on his last visit?''

''That's none of your business!'' she retorted, ''and how
could *that* be worth a hundred guineas?''

''Well, 'tis *not*,'' Thomas laughed, taking a long draught of
wine and pouring her another glass. ''But if he should have told
ye what General Washington might be planning in the near
future . . . well . . . *that* would be worth siller, I can promise
ye.''

Arabella stared at him, her eyes widening slightly.

"Why, you *are* a spy!" she said, her voice tinged in wonder, "and you're asking *me* to spy!"

"I'm not a spy . . . exactly," he laughed loudly. "But ye're right about one thing . . . I *am* asking ye to keep yer eyes and ears open—and His Majesty's government is prepared to pay for it."

"What are you, then, if you're not a spy?" she demanded.

"I'm an intelligence officer," he replied evenly. "I receive and disseminate information that our agents bring to me."

"And you're asking me to tell you what my husband told me?" she said. "You're asking me to be one of your agents."

"In a manner of speaking." He smiled, topping off her wine glass.

"And whom, may I ask, are *you* going to tell whatever it is I tell *you*?"

"My Lord Cornwallis," he answered without preamble.

"My point exactly!" she said triumphantly. "*That's* spying!"

"No," he replied patiently. "I dinna masquerade as anything I'm not. I am simply a captain in His Majesty's forces, authorized to pay for some information that is very valuable to my Lord Cornwallis and perfectly worthless to ye, besieged as ye are by both camps, here at Antrim Hall." He glanced around the summerhouse, which was sorely in need of fresh whitewash. "And I would imagine a hundred guineas would be most welcome to ye."

"You're right," she said, much to his surprise. "I haven't two farthings to rub together at present and no hope of borrowing any to pay for seed next spring." She sipped her wine thoughtfully. "As I have indicated, I harbor few passionate sentiments toward Colonel Harrison Boyd—who barely speaks to me, now that there's no baby—and I have no feelings whatsoever for either General Washington or your Lord Cornwallis. . . . In fact," she said challengingly, "there's not a man I've ever met whom I could depend upon in a pinch, and that's a fact." She took a large sip of wine and cheerfully looked at him across the table. "What do you want to know?" she said.

"Did yer colonel say anything about a surprise attack to retake Philadelphia?"

Arabella stared thoughtfully at the remains of her breast of chicken.

"Well, as I mentioned, he was not exactly pleased to have ended his long years of happy bachelorhood for a lady who then miscarried his son and heir," Arabella related bitterly, "but

among the few subjects he deigned to speak of was that he swore
they'd run your lot out of Pennsylvania in the near future. He didn't
mention a date. Just something about turning Cornwallis's old
tricks against him . . . something of the sort.''

"So," Thomas murmured, "perhaps he plans to try flanking
us outside Philadelphia as we did him at Brandywine.''

"Flanking?" Arabella asked, puzzled.

"That's a maneuver where the army is divided into columns,
attacking from all sides, rather than as one body.''

"Well," Arabella noted thoughtfully, "if Washington is going
to try to retake Philadelphia, wouldn't he do it before the
weather changes? Otherwise, they'll not have time to establish
winter quarters in Valley Forge, if they fail—and my dear Colonel will have no need for his dress uniform after all—''

"Did Colonel Boyd say that?" Thomas interrupted.

"Yes," Arabella replied slowly, searching her memory for
shreds of conversation she'd completely dismissed during the
brief time her portly husband had been home. "The Colonel said
that he'd be sending a runner from Philadelphia for his dress
uniform by mid-October . . . if he'd be needing it at all.''

" 'Tis the thirtieth of September, today," Thomas mused
aloud. "That must mean General Washington plans to advance
within the week!''

"Perhaps," Arabella shrugged. "Surely, you're not going to
pay me a hundred guineas for *that*?" she added, a note of
disappointment creeping into her voice. "I may have got it all
wrong, you know.''

"We shall see, soon enough," Thomas said, pulling a small
pouch of gold coins out of his jacket. " 'Tis King Geordie's
siller," he laughed. "What do I care?''

Arabella opened the pouch and peeped inside, catching her
breath.

"This will get us through the winter and allow me to purchase
everything I need for the spring planting . . . and more!" she
exulted, her eyes sparkling. She tucked the coin purse in the
pocket of her riding habit.

"If ye hear of anything more ye think might be of use, I can
probably get ye further payment," Thomas said casually. "That
way, I could return to Antrim Hall from time to time. I find it a
good deal more pleasant than I'd remembered.''

Without replying to his suggestive tone, Arabella downed the
contents of her third glass of wine with surprising dispatch.

Thomas leaned over the table, taking her hand and lacing his fingers through hers.

"Ye apologized to me last night. And I'd like ye to know, I truly appreciate that."

"Well, I meant it," Arabella mumbled, staring down at their joined hands. "I was a fool then . . . a mere child."

"And if I'm not mistaken," he continued, watching her face intently and stroking her palm with his thumb, "there's a slight chance that ye *still* would find me a man to catch yer fancy, if ye were free to do so?"

"I told you that ten years ago, Thomas, when we were *both* free," she retorted, her low voice cracking with its distinctive huskiness.

"Since we have reached an understanding concerning the past," he said slowly, "perhaps we could arrive at another, with regard to the present."

"And the *future*?" Arabella said snappishly, pulling her hand away from his grasp. "What about *that*?"

He rose from his chair and stood behind her, his hands resting lightly on her shoulders.

"I understand—and *ye* understand that—what we're feeling for each other right now is separate from yer obligations toward the colonel," he murmured into her ear. "But for now, since we *have* that understanding . . . and since we both feel a certain *attraction* as friends who will soon part. . . ." She rose like a sleepwalker and turned to face him. Her lips were inches away from his. A tantalizing hint of jasmine wafted about his nostrils. "Ye're a lovely woman," he whispered softly. "I had a difficult time getting to sleep last night as I lay in my bed, imagining ye in yers. I stole into yer chamber before sunup today—just to watch ye sleep. The bed linen was twisted at yer feet, as the day dawned warm . . . very warm—just as it is now."

Arabella closed the short distance between their bodies, pressing herself against him, her cheek against his chest. She wrapped her arms around his back and tilted her face toward his, waiting to be kissed. He quickly obliged, feeling her lips part invitingly. Her arms tightened around him and she seemed to meld right to his frame. At first, he consciously commanded himself to kiss her deeply in a deliberate attempt to arouse her, but, within seconds, his thoughts had flown to the far corners of the eight-sided summerhouse. Instead, he experienced the pure sensation of inhaling Arabella's fragrant skin, threading his hands through her silken hair, caressing the soft, yielding curves of her body, which pressed against his.

"Thomas . . ." she began, when, finally, they pulled away from each other breathlessly.

He was surprised and slightly chagrinned by the clear evidence of desire she had aroused in him.

"Arabella, I—"

"Sh . . . 'tis all right," she crooned, once again wrapping her arms around him and kneading her fingers along his spine. "I'm a married woman, remember?" she said, releasing a throaty laugh. "Goodness knows, I'm no blushing virgin, about to be deflowered."

From the swelling in his breeches and the rush of sensation pulsating through the rest of his body, Thomas recognized, to his amazement, that he was fast losing all sense of control over the situation.

Arabella led him by the hand to the daybed pushed against one of the walls of the summerhouse. Smiling mischievously, she seated him on the quilted coverlet and sank to her knees on the floor in front of him. With tantalizing slowness, she peeled her riding jacket and blouse off her shoulders, while continuing to gaze directly into his eyes.

Thomas realized that he had been holding his breath at the sight of her white shoulders. She wore no corset and her breasts were clearly visible beneath the thin cambric shift clinging to her torso. She reached behind her waist and swiftly removed her skirt and petticoats, letting them fall in a sea of cotton around her knees. Carefully, she removed the strap from one side of her shift, then from the other. She reached for his hand.

"Will you help me, Thomas?" she asked quietly, placing his hand on one breast and hooking his fingers on the neckline of the flimsy bodice. Slowly, he eased the fabric down to her waistline, where she pushed it to her knees. The sheer undergarment joined her riding habit in a frothy pile. "Do I please you, Thomas?" she asked with a diffidence that took him off guard. She rose to her feet, her arms resting quietly at her sides. She stood naked before him, totally without shame. She seemed proud, in fact, of what she was offering him. "Am I what you imagined when you came into my room this morning?" she questioned him again. She paused, reaching toward him to stroke the hair on his temples with her fingertips. "Despite your feelings for . . . for others," she added softly, "You've thought of me too, haven't you? Even the first time you were at Antrim Hall."

His eyes traced an imaginary line from the hollow of her neck, down between her breasts, to her dimpled navel.

"Aye, I've thought of ye . . ." he said. With some lust, but not kindly, he added to himself.

Could he ever forget the burning fury that had coursed through his veins on that wild ride from Antrim Hall to Philadelphia, where a ship waited at anchor to take him across the ocean and back to Jane—or so he had thought? Had Arabella truly asked for forgiveness? Or was this . . . display . . . simply part of some trick?

Arabella interrupted his silent musings by placing one of her hands behind his neck, pulling him toward her, and offering her right breast to him to be kissed. A low, almost purring sound erupted from her throat as his lips touched her. She urged him to explore her other breast, its nipple as erect as the one that had grown firm under his caress. He moved his hands to her naked back and marveled at the softness of her flesh. He could feel an urgency flowing from her in the way she kissed his hair and licked his earlobe, just as he sensed her own physical need rising hot within him. She was hungry for him to touch her, and made no pretense of her desire to envelop him with the warmth of her body.

"Ah . . . yes!" she breathed, as he began tracing kisses from her breast, up along her neck, to just below her ear. "There . . . and *there*!" she moaned, guiding his hand with hers to the soft velvet place between her thighs.

She was a woman who understood men, understood *him*, he thought, drawing on that tiny portion of his mind still functioning rationally. She seemed to revel in showing him what pleased her, what transformed her into the passionate, demanding woman she had become. She merely wanted him to fill her need, just as she was willing to fill his, he thought, as his bones seemed to liquify. She was twice married, initiated into the mysteries of human passion. He was violating no code. No doubt this rendezvous in the summerhouse was just as much a part of her plan as it was his.

Arabella's lips, her voluptuous breasts, her long legs, firm from years of riding along the creeks and bottomlands, all combined to offer him a startling revelation: that his inability to separate himself from the warm, soft body clinging to him had nothing to do with that secret place in which he hid away his abiding love for Jane. The woman who kissed him fiercely this sultry afternoon, so far from Scotland and home . . . this woman was a vessel aching to be filled . . . just for the moment . . . just for today. She was *here* . . . in his life *now*. For today, at least, she could make him forget. . . .

"This may be madness, Arabella . . ." he groaned, making one last effort to break the spell of her bewitchment. "I dinna fancy leaving a bastard Fraser to add to yer cares."

Arabella stared at him with a look of such undisguised tenderness, he was flooded with guilt.

"There's no danger," she said softly, her hand seeking the fastenings of his trousers. "I've just finished my flux . . . there'll be no baby. But you were sweet to think of—"

He stilled her lips with another kiss and quickly shed his clothes. Settling her beside him on the bed, he watched the corners of her mouth turn up provocatively as her hand closed around the object of her desire.

"Does this please you?" she asked, smiling saucily at the expression spreading across his face.

Thomas leaned against the large cushions at his back and closed his eyes, allowing pure sensation to sweep over him. He felt as if he were about to sail effortlessly over a tall barrier, like a sixteen-hand hunter at a five-barred gate. With a pleasurable moan, he flung his arms around her, pressing her body beneath his own. She cried out softly when he entered her, and quickly matched the cadence of his thrusting hips.

"Aye, lass, ye please me, wench," he whispered hoarsely, angered somehow that she should have the power to give him such pleasure—when she had caused him such terrible pain. "Now, 'tis my turn to please *myself*."

Bearing down on her with his pelvis and longer legs, he held on tightly to each of her wrists, pressing them against the pillow that supported her head.

"I find this pleasing—do *ye*?" he demanded, shunting his torso sharply against her. "And this . . . and *this*?" he cried, ignoring her low whimpers.

He kissed her with a fervor that could not quite erase thoughts of Jane that now flashed, unwanted, through his brain. He cursed the vision, and roughly grasped Arabella's white shoulders, silently cursing her as well for the role she had played in the traumatic events of a decade earlier.

"Am I goin' about this rightly, *Mrs.* Boyd?" he demanded, fighting a wave of desolation welling up within him.

Settle an old score . . . part of him raged.

Arabella ceased meeting his thrusts. He felt her stiffen beneath him just as he found his release. Tears escaped from beneath her dark lashes, and spilled down her flushed cheeks. When, at length, his breathing returned to normal, he raised himself on his elbows, absently smoothing a few wayward strands of her hair from her perspiring forehead. Bitter shame flooded through him as her shoulders began to shake. The sounds of her quiet crying filled the room. Thomas closed his eyes and heaved a sigh.

"I ask ye to forgive me for the unforgivable, Arabella," he said abjectly. " 'Tis punishing, I've been to ye, and I'm truly sorry," he added, noting ruefully, "What a way to accept yer apology. . . ."

Thomas withdrew from her gently and sank onto his side, reaching to comfort her. He was surprised when she allowed herself to be held, although tears still streamed down her face. Suddenly, she sat up abruptly, pounding her fists against the bed with a fury that shocked them both.

"Filthy wretch!" Her curse slid into a sob. "A pox on it *all*!"

"Arabella, lass . . . I'm sorry . . . I—"

"That *not* why I'm crying!" she wept.

Propelled by some inner turmoil he didn't understand, she jumped up from the bed and reached for her petticoat among the heap of clothing on the floor, clumsily wrapping it around her body.

"Then why *are* you crying?" he said, reaching out to stay her hand.

"Because I-I can n-never have what I *want*!" she hiccupped. "I fell in love with you ten years ago, and I told you so," she said brokenly. "But you'll *never* forgive me for what I did . . . and maybe you shouldn't! You needn't put on a show—*now*—when you don't care about me at all . . . when all you're trying to do is hurt me for my having hurt you!" Fresh tears cascaded down her cheeks. She turned away from him and leaned against the wall, her face covered in her hands. "Nobody cares how *I* feel . . . nobody *ever has* cared! But I thought, at *least* you weren't like every other man I've taken to my bed. But I was wrong," she cried, turning to face him, her eyes suddenly flashing. "You're just like the rest. You *pretend* to have a thought for my feelings when it suits you, but all you *really* care about is—is—*servicing yourselves*! You . . . Colonel Boyd . . . Hugh Delaney . . . even my own *father*!"

Arabella stopped stock-still. She was breathing heavily, and her eyes dilated unnaturally.

"What are ye saying, lass?" Thomas asked, taken aback by

what he thought he had heard. "Are ye telling me that yer father and *you* . . . ?"

"*Nothing!*" she screamed, her hands clenched at her sides.

Thomas stared at the frozen mask her features had become. Gently, he reached for her hand.

" 'Tis *not* nothing, Arabella," he said quietly. "What are ye saying? That yer own father bedded ye. . . ."

His question hung between them like a corpse on a gibbet.

Her face remained immobile, but her eyes stared away from him with a haunted look. She pulled away from his grasp and walked toward a window half-shuttered against the suffocating afternoon sun. Dark, shameful images loomed before her glassy eyes as she tried to shut from her brain the long-hidden memories of the year preceding her father's death. She leaned her forehead against the wooden casement and felt sick to her stomach. She wondered whether she would ever escape the nausea that swept over her whenever she remembered the events of that terrible night.

Helpless to prevent the vision that rose before her eyes, she once again saw Seamus O'Brien stumbling down the hall, drunk from a month of dreadful binges, which had followed her mother's funeral.

"We had to bury my mother quickly, because of the heat," Arabella murmured, as if to herself. "For days, Father just sat on the porch, hour after hour, drinking homemade gin. One night, he started slamming doors and shouting at the servants, so I ran to my room to hide."

"How old were ye?" asked Thomas softly, watching her gaze listlessly out the shuttered window of the summerhouse.

"Fourteen," she replied, biting her lip. "In the middle of the night he came scratching and pounding at my door, begging me to open it. 'Bella, I need you' he said, and he was crying. He kept pleading for my mother, sobbing that she always turned away from him . . . and then he started asking me why *I* didn't love him. It frightened me that he seemed to confuse my mother with me, and he kept pounding and pounding on my door!"

She began to weep.

"You let him in, dinna ye?" Thomas said sympathetically. "You let him in because ye felt such pity for the man."

Arabella turned to face Thomas, tears bathing her cheeks.

"My father's hands were shaking so much, he dropped the candlestick he'd been holding. His breath reeked of gin when he kissed me and it made me feel sick." She swallowed hard. "His hands . . . his *hands*, Thomas . . . they were so *strong*. And then he pushed me onto my bed and—'' Arabella's beautiful features crumpled into a child's face, and her lips quivered with unchecked sobs. ''I screamed, which roused the household, but Father stopped Mehitabel at the door, saying I'd just had a nightmare.''

''Did he do it again?'' Thomas asked, disgust for the long-dead Seamus O'Brien tinging his voice.

''In the ten months it took him to drink himself to death, he never came near my bedchamber again, and everyone here behaved as if nothing had happened. But Mehitabel knows. . . .''

''Ye were frightened until the day ye put him in the ground, weren't ye, hinny?'' Thomas probed gently.

He spoke to her from the short distance separating them. She shook her head affirmatively, but was unable to speak. In the past, she had tried to assuage the pain of that terrible night of betrayal by using men—before they could use her. She'd actually seduced the Irish stableboy . . . and then there'd been a series of Beven's cronies—young and old—each behaving like more of a bastard than the one before. What had prompted her hasty marriage to Colonel Boyd last year had, strangely enough, forced old Hugh Delaney to marry her as well: in 1763, she'd become pregnant at age sixteen, and had lost that child, too, in her third month.

Arabella gazed dejectedly at the lean, handsome man whose russet hair made her think of precious rubies. She wondered, now, if he, like all the others, had somehow sensed her guilt, her shame, all along? All the men who wished to bed her had claimed they *cared* about her—just like her father—but the cads had treated her like a whore, and the kind ones never stayed. They always moved on, or married the good, unsullied girls— and God knows, she was far from that.

Thomas started to speak.

''Don't *say* anything!'' she cried. ''Just don't say a *thing*!''

He drew her unyielding body toward him, enfolding her in his arms, which were still deeply scarred from wounds she had tended so carefully a decade earlier.

''I winna say another word,'' he whispered, gently kissing her forehead, ''except to tell ye 'twas cruel of me to show ye anger that's owing partly to others.''

Some of the tension in her body eased, but her voice remained harsh.

"You'll always be angry with me for what I did," Arabella said, wiping her eyes with the back of her hand.

"Perhaps I will," he agreed, taking her chin between his fingers and tilting her head until she was forced to look at him. "But my ill fortune is also due to fate—and other forces—and not merely to ye and yer willful ways, my dear Arabella. . . ." He kissed her again softly on the lips. "And I would suspect that 'tis much the same for what happened between ye and yer da. 'Tis time for both of us to try to put such sadness behind us." Gently, he led her back to the daybed and pulled her down along the length of his body, lightly brushing his lips against each eyelid in turn. "Poor us," he murmured into her ear, inhaling the scent of her moist and fragrant skin. "We've had quite a time of it, havna we, pet?"

He continued to stroke her hair, until slowly she relaxed against him.

"No one should ever hurt a child as ye've been hurt," he whispered. "Whatever happened between ye and yer da so long ago . . . 'twas not in the least *yer* doing, dearheart."

She closed her eyes and shuddered slightly, and then began to breathe evenly. Her features assumed a look of composure that rendered her more beautiful than he had ever seen her, for all her flashing eyes and fiery temper. In a twinkling, she fell fast asleep.

Thomas carefully eased himself off the bed and gingerly draped Arabella's dimity petticoat over her slumbering form. When he returned to his room in the mansion, he quickly donned his uniform. He descended the broad staircase and strode across the parquet foyer into the morning room. He sat down at Arabella's desk, glancing briefly at the drawers where he had once discovered the unposted letter to Jane. Hastily, he reached for his hostess's quill pen.

> *To the Mistress of Antrim Hall:*
> *I know ye've never met a man ye could "depend on in a pinch," but, should fate and fortune allow . . . 'Tis my hope we shall meet again.*
> *T. F.*

21

May 1780

Within three days of Thomas's return to Germantown, General Howe and Lord Cornwallis repulsed the anticipated four-pronged attack boldly mounted by Washington to regain Philadelphia for the Patriots. Then, within three weeks, Cornwallis and his men were on the march again, embarking on a two-and-a-half year odyssey that was to take them from the Jersey palisades to the swamps of Savannah.

By the spring of 1780, Thomas found himself far from Antrim Hall, among the conquerors of Charleston, South Carolina, sharing quarters with his fellow officers at Number 10 Atlantic Street. His flatmates included Hamilton Maxwell, who had been traded late in 1778—along with Colonel Archibald Campbell— for the rebel colonel, Ethan Allen. Ham had caught up with the 71st in time to take part in the siege of the southern port city.

The house where Jane's brother and Thomas were billeted was a handsome red brick edifice overlooking the convergence of the Ashley and Cooper rivers. One night, shortly after the British occupied the beautiful city of Charleston, Thomas stood in the fading twilight, relishing the absence of the cannon's roar and the sound of crackling muskets. Leaning against the frame of the French doors that opened on to the piazza outside his elegantly furnished room, he quietly drank in the musky scent of the night-blooming jasmine floating on the soft May air. Its languorous perfume recalled a jumble of memories of his last visit to Antrim Hall: an octagonally shaped summerhouse, cool in the sweltering heat; Arabella lying alone in a four-poster, a pistol beneath her pillow.

Savoring erotic thoughts of that voluptuous creature, he wondered, idly, how soon the rebels would surrender. If they did, and if he could manage it somehow, he fully intended to pay at least one more call on the mistress of Antrim Hall . . . that is, if the good Colonel were not at home.

Thomas yawned and stretched, cheerfully anticipating the comfort of the soft feather bed awaiting him. Considering the fact that Arabella O'Brien Delaney Boyd had ruined his life, he acknowledged to himself with some surprise that he *liked* the wench! She could never call forth from him the love or blinding emotion that the mere memory of Jane Maxwell would forever evoke. But Jenny was irrevocably lost to him, he firmly reminded himself, and his glimpse of Arabella's vulnerability under that tough exterior had touched him somehow.

"Thomas, my man," Hamilton Maxwell called genially from the far end of the veranda, interrupting his thoughts. "Come see this. A letter from home's finally caught up with me."

From time to time, Thomas and Ham had shared a brandy on the wide piazza after dinner while they awaited for official word that the 71st was to leave Charleston. Thus far, Thomas had studiously avoided all but the most perfunctory mentions of his fellow captain's sister—all part of his current campaign to attempt to dissolve, once and for all, the bonds linking Jenny to him. Bonds that could only continue to bring them both unhappiness and pain.

Hamilton held in his hand a letter with a distinctive stag's head crest stamped in crimson wax.

"It arrived with a packet for Lord Cornwallis this morning," he said genially.

Hamilton Maxwell had never been one for subtleties. In fact, Thomas doubted whether the blustery captain even suspected that he and Jane had ever been anything more than childhood sweethearts.

"Jane writes that the Dowager Duchess of Gordon breathed her last just before Christmas," Ham noted cheerfully, pointing to the date *1779* at the top of Jane's lengthy missive. "That must have reduced Alex's estate expenses considerably!" he added wryly. "No wonder my sister and the duke can afford to take a fashionable house in St. James's Square again for the season in London." He scanned a few pages of the letter and smiled broadly. "Here . . . here's the part I wanted ye to hear. Jane says, 'With the wee one just three, now'—she means little Louisa . . . this was written last September—" Ham interjected helpfully, " 'I find myself with more time to pursue those interests which ye, dear brother, most likely would consider unfeminine in the extreme. Eglantine and I have taken to donning men's attire several days a week, and stealthily invading the gallery in Parliament to hear debates on subjects most intriguing. The Duchess of Devonshire is ever so put out when I can converse with that rising young barrister, William Pitt (and others who enjoy the king's confidence) in an informed and lively manner that her ladyship simply cannot fathom. She prides herself on her intelligence and finds it all most distressing!' "

Hamilton rested the letter in his lap and laughed uproariously.

"Can ye imagine *that*, Thomas?" he said, wiping the mirth from his eyes. "A mother of five, and she's dressing up like a lad to hear the debates! Sounds like some of the antics the two of *ye* used to get up to, eh, laddie?"

"A mother of five? Jenny had another child?" Thomas inquired carefully, hoping his voice sounded steady. *The child had lived! Who was its sire?* he thought, his heart thumping in his chest.

"Aye, as I said, a little lass, named Louisa . . . born in early September, back in seventy-six when I was languishing in that Boston prison." Hamilton smiled. "*Ye* should be especially pleased . . . they named the bairn after Alex's uncle Lewis, the only Gordon to fight with Prince Charlie in the Forty-five!"

"Aye . . . ?" Thomas replied faintly. "Is the child as comely as her mother?" he added lamely, for he realized as soon as the words were out of his mouth that Ham had never seen his niece, born after the regiment sailed for America—exactly nine months following the idyll Thomas had spent with Jane on the Island of Swans.

"See for yerself," Hamilton said jovially, pulling a small round object from the pocket of his scarlet officer's coat. "This came wrapped inside Jane's missive."

Thomas's eyes widened. In the palm of Hamilton Maxwell's hand was a painted miniature of a child with rich, russet curls and high cheekbones who reminded Thomas of no one in the world so much as himself.

The day was hot for early June, and the London alleys and wynds reeked of rubbish and rotting refuse even more than they usually did. A handsome carriage rolled through Leicester Fields and drew up in front of the impressive residence of Sir Joshua Reynolds, who had been duly knighted in 1768 as the founder of the Royal Academy of Art. First to emerge from the coach was a sea-green parasol that shielded the elegant passenger from the sun's unrelenting rays.

"Good afternoon, Your Grace," a young woman said politely as she opened the door to her visitor. She inclined her head respectfully toward the Duchess of Gordon who had arrived for the first sitting for her portrait precisely at the agreed-on hour of two. "I'm pleased to see you've not been inconvenienced crossing the city, what with the troubles brewing at St. George's Fields today. Imagine that riffraff—"

Sir Joshua's young niece and housekeeper, Offy Palmer, froze, midsentence, and clapped her palm over her mouth.

"B-begging your pardon, mum," stammered the portraitist's niece, blushing crimson. "I meant no—"

"Dinna trouble yerself to apologize to *me* for the insane actions of my husband's brother . . . that blithering demagogue!" Jane replied crossly, stepping over the threshold of Number 47 Leicester Square. She shut the parasol with an irritated snap. "I canna think that two chimney sweeps would turn up for Lord George Gordon, that impudent pup—let alone forty thousand Londoners!"

They both referred to the platoons of pious Protestants who had responded to the call of Alex's eccentric sibling to assemble outside Parliament and publicly demand the repeal of the Catholic Relief Act. It was totally preposterous, Jane thought crossly. Couldn't Lord George, that idiot M.P., *see* that the deuced war in the Colonies demanded that the government relax the rules against Catholics? That way, the army could attract more Irish recruits to fill the depleted ranks. Lord George's wild ravings against the "Popish Devils" had surely raised the specter of Gordon Madness in earnest, this time.

"Then, you haven't heard the news, mum?" Miss Palmer said timidly.

Jane handed the young woman her parasol.

"Pray, what news, Miss Palmer?" she asked warily.

"The mob has already crossed Westminster Bridge. Some say there's sixty thousand or more, all wearing the blue cockade and chanting 'No Popery!' 'Tis far more than just Lord George's Protestant Association, mum. They've got flags and banners and Scottish bagpipes skirling, and they say they're going to storm the very doors of Parliament!"

"Ye canna be *serious*," Jane scoffed with a toss of her head.

" 'Tis what Sir Joshua's groom told me when he returned from delivering a portrait of the Duchess of Devonshire—"

"Georgiana Cavendish has commissioned *another* work by Sir Joshua?" Jane demanded incredulously.

A handsome, full-length canvas of the celebrated and charming duchess had been completed in 1776, depicting one specific detail for which the Duchess of Devonshire was famous—a set of plumes worn in her hair, some a foot and a half tall! So associated were these feathers with Georgiana and the great ladies of the Whig party—which often locked horns with the king—that Queen Charlotte forbade the wearing of plumes at court. One might wear a model of a British Man-of-War or even a genuine candelabrum attached to one's gargantuan wig, but not plumes.

"Oh, no, mum," Miss Palmer hastened to explain. "The Duchess of D is not sitting for Uncle again. We've merely changed the frame and cleaned the likeness for Her Grace."

"Ah . . . I see," Jane murmured, relieved to hear her own future portrait would not compete with a new work depicting her current rival. After having admired Reynolds's likeness of the angelic-looking Duchess of Devonshire, Jane had decided on the spot to have Sir Joshua's assistant render a miniature of little Louisa to send to Hamilton, who had never seen his niece. She had wondered for months if he ever received it . . . or had ever showed it to Thomas.

Jane slowly removed her gloves, her thoughts drawn to her youngest daughter. Louisa was now three years old and so like her true father in looks and nature, Jane's heart almost jumped each time she beheld her redheaded child. It was because of Louisa, and Alex's subtle rejection of the lass, that Jane had pleaded with her husband to lease the house on St. James's Square once again. When Louisa was but a year old, Jane had left Alex to his clock making, archery, and estate business for a few months, and fled with the children and the nursemaid, Nancy Christie, for London to fill the void left by Alex's studied indifference toward her. Thereafter, for at least half of each year, Jane exchanged the gloom and silences of Gordon Castle and its dour laird for the city's hectic social scene.

Tucking her gloves into her reticule, Jane acknowledged to herself ruefully that she was now counted among London's fashionable inner circle at court. She had even become an intimate of Queen Charlotte. For reasons that seemed rather silly to Jane, people had begun to speak of her and the beautiful Duchess of Devonshire in the same breath. They had been dubbed "The Two Duchesses," as if they were in some kind of competition. Jane and Georgiana—who held violent Whig sympathies, in contrast to Jane's more moderate political outlook—argued about everything and anything: from the day's gossip to the latest battle fought in the Colonies.

The Colonies. . . .

Thomas's words of farewell spoken in his room at Gordon

Castle when he was packing to leave for America had haunted her for four years.

Give it up. . . .

Sternly, Jane forced her thoughts back to the matter at hand as she followed Offy Palmer toward a sweeping staircase at the far end of the foyer.

"Did my groom deliver my gown and court robes?" Jane asked Reynolds's niece brusquely as they reached the landing and headed down a dim passageway.

"To be sure, m'lady," Offy replied quickly. "I hung it in the studio dressing room myself."

Fighting an onslaught of unwelcome memories, Jane followed Miss Palmer up a second flight of the stairs toward what she assumed to be the location of the artist's studio, acknowledging bleakly to herself that nothing she did really seemed to numb the pain of Thomas's departure.

Give it up. . . .

Blessed St. Ninian, how she'd tried to forget Thomas Fraser! She'd been a loyal wife to Alex, though her husband had shared her bed infrequently after Louisa was born, and showed fatherly interest only in their ten-year-old son, Huntly. To his eldest daughter, Charlotte, and to Madelina and Susan, he extended passing pleasantries, if he took note of them at all. Louisa, with her bright curls and lovely oval face, had essentially been ignored by the duke since birth.

Jane followed along as Offy Palmer led her down another long passageway on the second floor. There was good reason for her husband to shun her last-born child, she thought glumly. However, if Alex had any suspicions that Louisa was not his, he adamantly refused to confront her with them whenever she took her courage in hand and attempted to broach the subject. He had once again erected an impenetrable fortress around himself, as he had after Thomas Fraser's miraculous return from the dead, so soon after Alex's marriage to Jane. To outsiders, their lives appeared perfectly normal. But Jane knew the truth. The Duke of Gordon treated all the females in his household, including her, with a cool detachment that brooked no intrusion.

Sir Joshua Reynolds's niece opened a door that led into a large unfurnished room. Jane was conscious, suddenly, of the pungent odor of oil paints and bitumen. She gave closer inspection to rows of celebrated faces adorning the spacious gallery.

"Ah, that's Dr. Samuel Johnson, is it not?" Jane inquired of a marvelously rendered figure. "And next to it, Gibbon, the historian?"

"Yes, mum," answered Offy proudly.

"Now here's a difficult subject," Jane said wryly, nodding toward a rather large canvas of the Prince of Wales.

King George III's son, a young man of eighteen, was quite handsome, but Jane considered him rather dissolute in character. The lad was constantly wrangling with his father over his allowance and his unfortunate habit of wooing unsuitable women into his bed. Jane heard the murmur of people chatting in the next room, punctuated by explosive bursts of merriment.

"Sir Joshua is receiving at this hour?" Jane asked archly.

"Just a small group of friends, due to leave shortly," Offy Palmer explained nervously. "There's Fanny Burney, the novelist, whom I'm sure you know—I adored *Evelina*, didn't you, Your Grace?" the young woman exclaimed. She was plainly enthralled with the rather charming account of an amiable young girl's entrance into society. "And Angelica Kauffmann, who, I believe, painted *you* the same year my uncle did that charming half-canvas of you in fancy dress . . . wasn't that in seventy-four? Dr. Johnson was due for tea," Offy prattled on, "but I heard not a soul can cross the city because there are masses of people parading in the streets."

Jane attempted to shrug off a sense of foreboding concerning her brother-in-law's latest antics as they entered Sir Joshua Reynolds's celebrated painting room. It was an odd-angled chamber, some twenty by sixteen feet in size, with windows positioned nine feet off the ground. The sunshine pooled in bright patches on the floor, highlighting the spackles of time-worn paint from portraits long completed. In the center of the room, as if sitting on a stage, stood a large wooden easel, and on it, an imposing frame of blank canvas. Nearby was Sir Joshua's five-drawer box of oils overflowing with small pots of color.

"Why, Duchess!" Sir Joshua said, quickly rising from a small table flanked by two women Jane recognized as the Misses Kauffmann and Burney. "We quite forgot the time. Will you take tea?"

"No, thank ye, Sir Joshua," Jane replied, noting that Reynolds's guests were in the process of bidding adieu.

"Shall we both change, Your Grace?" Reynolds said genially, pointing to a small attiring room off his studio. Jane could see her court gown hanging in readiness. "A maid will assist you. I must find my smock."

''That will suit admirably,'' Jane answered in a loud voice, remembering the gossip that Sir Joshua's hearing was failing him at an alarming rate, though he was only fifty-six. Sure enough, this bit of intelligence was confirmed by the curved ear trumpet lying next to a teacup on the table.

The heavy velvet folds and tight bodice of Jane's formal gown were stiflingly hot. As she assumed various postures for Reynolds's scrutiny, she began to doubt the wisdom of commencing a series of sittings in such a warm season. Beads of perspiration bubbled above her lip as she and the artist discussed the effect both hoped to achieve with the painting—and its price: one hundred and fifty pounds.

The artist's assistant, Mr. Toms, who'd created the lovely miniature of little Louisa, stood to one side, watching the painter intently as Reynolds sketched several quick drawings on paper to give Jane an idea of his vision for the work. At length, he chose to have her stand slightly in profile. He set to work outlining a preliminary drawing on a small canvas, which would eventually serve as a guide to the life-size canvas leaning against the easel.

Jane surreptitiously studied the celebrated artist. He was not a handsome man, but had a pleasant, broad, clean-shaven countenance that might be taken for that of an apothecary, or perhaps a linen merchant. His hands were large and capable—beautiful, actually, despite a darkish caste to them from years of handling oils. Sir Joshua noticed her staring at him and smiled.

''You were studying me rather like I must study you, Your Grace,'' he said. Glancing at her injured finger, he added gently, ''Rather than wear the ducal coronet, Duchess, I'd prefer you hold it in your right hand.''

''Excellent,'' Jane answered calmly, convinced more than ever of the man's talent and tact. Her amputated forefinger was now completely disguised.

Suddenly Reynolds's niece Offy Palmer burst through the door and began whispering to Mr. Toms in an agitated fashion.

''What *is* it, Offy?'' Reynolds asked, irritably. ''Speak up! You know I can't hear anything when you talk like that! What do you mean, disturbing us like this?''

''I'm so sorry, Uncle,'' Offy apologized, wringing her hands and glancing distractedly in Jane's direction. She ran to the tea table and handed Reynolds his ear trumpet. ''Ralph Kirkley has just returned, sir, and says the mob's headed for Leicester Square!'' she shouted into the horn.

''That valet's afraid of his own shadow, Offy, you know

that," Sir Joshua scoffed, waving his curved hearing aid in the air. "Now, be gone with you! The duchess is, no doubt, melting in her finery, and I want to finish this preliminary sketch as quickly as I can."

"But Uncle!" Offy protested. "It was Sir George Savile who *introduced* the Catholic Relief Act. Kirkley says he heard some of the rabble swear they'd burn his house to the *ground*!"

"Sir George lives across the square, does he not?" Jane asked.

Offy and Mr. Toms nodded emphatically.

"Yes, but I doubt—" began Sir Joshua.

A low rumble that sounded like a barrel being rolled across a wooden floor drifted into the room through the studio's clerestory windows. Jane glanced at the wide-eyed Offy and Toms and quickly stepped down from the low riser and velvet backdrop where she'd been posing.

"Sir Joshua," she said loudly, "I think it wise if we conclude this first appointment and ye instruct yer servants to make fast the doors and windows of yer house."

"My dear Duchess, I don't think that will be necess—"

A wave of shouting that even the nearly deaf Reynolds could hear interrupted the painter, midsentence. Offy and Mr. Toms exchanged frightened looks, as Jane hurried to don the simply styled dress she'd worn earlier. By the time she emerged from the dressing room, a rhythmic chanting could clearly be heard in the square outside.

"No Popery! No Popery!"

"Down with Savile!"

"May the Devil take the Pope!"

The shouts seemed to come from every direction. She made her way back through the house and down the stairs. Reynolds and his household were gathered in the front foyer, staring out the window in amazement at Leicester Square. The tree-lined area was packed from one end to the other with the ill-clad, obviously inebriated rabble, numbering in the thousands.

"They was *everywhere*, Sir Joshua!" exclaimed a man Jane took to be the servant Ralph Kirkley. "One group came over Blackfriars Bridge and another, London Bridge; but the main mob marched over Westminster and choked near every entrance to Commons 'n Lords. 'Twas frightening, Sir . . . I ken tell ye that!"

"Tell him how they accosted the carriages," Offy said excitedly. "The Archbishop *himself* was catcalled and howled at and

spattered with mud. How he ever escaped inside Parliament must
be the Lord's own knowledge. Sir George Savile's coach was
demolished, I heard . . . had its wheels wrenched *right off*!''

"I saw it with me own eyes," Kirkley confirmed. "The
House has adjourned, so the mob's spreading through the town,
up to no good."

"Have ye heard what role Lord George Gordon played in the
melee?'' Jane asked evenly, though dreading to hear the answer.

"A footman in Commons told me that the Reverend Thomas
Bowen, the chaplain of the House of Commons, asked Lord
George to disperse the mob, but when he went outside to speak,
he only told them the king would instruct the Ministers to repeal
the Bill, as they wanted," Kirkley related.

"Oh, God . . ." Jane groaned aloud. *A pox on that demented
brother-in-law of hers!* she thought.

"Now, I'm told," the servant continued, "they're torching
Catholic chapels all over the city and attacking the embassies of
Catholic countries. Lord Mansfield's house is burnt to cinders!''

The sound of shattering glass from across the square riveted
their attention.

"Oh, no!'' cried Offy, " 'tis Sir George's house. Look!''

All the windows in Savile's fashionable residence across the
way were broken, one by one, by rocks thrown by the throng
clogging the square. The iron railings surrounding the house
were yanked from their moorings, as if they were mere matchsticks.

"I think we should leave this house at once, Sir Joshua," Jane
said decisively. "We could go out the back alley to St. Martin's
Lane and down Pall Mall to my house in St. James's Square.''

Sir Joshua stared silently out the front window. "My friend,
Edmund Burke, also lives in St. James's Square," he mused
aloud. "Perhaps 'twould be a prudent precaution.''

"But what of the *work*!'' declared his assistant, Mr. Toms.

"We shall cram as many canvases into the coach as we can,''
Jane said. "Come, let's not tarry, Sir Joshua," she added urgently, recalling the violence of the mob that she and Alex had
barely escaped at Edinburgh's Canongate Playhouse. "That rabble will soon tire of merely breaking windows.''

The chanting of the hordes in the square grew deafening as
Reynolds, his servants, and the Duchess of Gordon each made
several trips from the gallery out the back door to the mews
where Sir Joshua's carriage was being harnessed to a team of
grays. Portraits of every size and description were hurriedly
carried out of the house and stuffed into the cab or tied down on

top of the vehicle. Jane had heard of Reynolds's famous ''chariot,'' as he called it, but she was not prepared for such an enormous, richly carved and gilded coach, adorned with painted panels representing the four seasons. The showy equipage was good for business, no doubt, but Jane worried they would be set on the minute the crowd spotted such ostentatious livery.

Ralph Kirkley and the other servants climbed on top of the huge carriage, each holding onto a painting of the size appropriate to his or her stature. Inside the coach, scores of portraits were stacked high on the seat against one wall and on the floor beneath their feet, leaving barely enough room for Sir Joshua, Offy, and Jane to squeeze in on the opposite bench. The coachman fiercely cracked his whip and the magnificent conveyance, pulled by a perfectly matched pair of geldings, sailed down the back alley and into St. Martin's Lane.

The coach curtains were discreetly drawn closed, but Jane peeked out the window at the stragglers from the main mob, who brandished scythes and sticks and pelted the carriage from time to time with small stones. Smoke had started to drift into the cloudless sky and Jane could smell the fire she assumed was burning at poor Sir George Savile's abode.

As the carriage turned the corner into Pall Mall, Jane was horrified to see an ocean of dirty faces, sporting the Protestant blue cockade, clogging the thoroughfare and preventing their progress. Soon, the sea of bodies surrounded the coach. She felt it rocking back and forth, almost as if the throng would soon lift it overhead and toss it like so much cotton, into the crowd.

The sound of a whip's crack rent the air and, in an instant, Jane could hear men and women howling in pain. The cracks and the screams went on for some time and then, slowly, the coach continued along the street. A chorus of obscenities shouted by the throng followed them as Sir Joshua's carriage ploughed through the teeming masses. At one point, the coach seemed about to topple as its wheels rolled over something formidable. Probably someone's body, Jane thought, shuddering.

Oddly, St. James's Square itself was quiet when the horses, their sides heaving and their eyes darting wildly, pulled in front of the sedate residence marked Number 6.

''I thank ye for yer protection, Sir Joshua,'' Jane said, alighting from the coach. ''I'm only sorry a relative of my husband's should have anything to do with such abominations as we've seen this day.''

Reynolds let the ear trumpet he was holding fall to his side.

"You're a quick-thinking, coolheaded woman, Your Grace," he replied kindly, "and I especially appreciated your concern for my paintings. I trust I'll see you in a fortnight for our next sitting? Your court gown will look magnificent, I promise you. A capital choice of garment, I must say!"

Jane summoned a wan smile to her lips and nodded farewell to her fellow escapees, who looked as pale and shaken by what they had just experienced as she felt. Tiredly, she turned and slowly walked up to her front door, wondering what the ultimate damage of this day's events would be for the House of Gordon.

Alex arrived at the leased house in St. James's Square ten days later. As soon as he received Jane's frantic summons, he had hurriedly departed from Glasgow where he had been living since Christmas, preparing to review a home guard of Fencibles he had raised at the king's request. Around the time France had formed an alliance with the American Revolutionaries, the Duke of Gordon had responded to His Majesty's bid to recruit the regiment. At that point, the government was worried that the French might dare to actually invade England, even as far north as Scotland.

Exhausted from his breakneck journey to London, Alex listened silently in the library as Jane gave her account of the shocking affair involving his brother, who'd been arrested and clapped in the Tower of London.

Even some of Alex's close friends had been among those attacked and manhandled by the mob. Lord Germain had had ale thrown in his face, and the Bishop of Lincoln's throat had been squeezed so ruthlessly by a ruffian, the poor man had spouted blood from the corners of his mouth.

Something had to be done about Lord George, and done *quickly,* or the future prospects of every member of their immediate family would be ruined.

"Well, I suppose we shall have to cope with it on the morrow," he said wearily. "I'll just finish my brandy and look over a few things on my desk. Good night, Jane."

Rebuffed, she watched him take up his quill pen and jot down a few notes. She had been dismissed and, cut to the quick, she retreated upstairs. Within the hour, she heard him pass her door and retire to a bedchamber down the hall, as had been his custom since the birth of Louisa. Trying to take her mind off the myriad of troubles besetting her, Jane reached for a copy of Fanny

Burney's *Evelina*, hoping a second reading would provide an effective diversion.

The spires of the Tower of London stood out starkly against the leaden skies. The hot weather of the previous week had reversed itself. The heavens were about to unleash the downpour that had been threatening all day. Soon, a light rain began spattering fitfully against the handsome black carriage, its door emblazoned with a gold, stag's head crest. The carriage passed the barrel-shaped Lion Tower and drew to a halt next to another coach that had also paused in front of the gated entrance to the prison.

Jane studied her husband's profile, his composed features giving no hint of the turmoil he must be feeling. Following the riots that had ripped through London for five days, Alex's brother had become this bastion's most celebrated inhabitant, and it didn't bode well for any of them. Glumly, Jane sank back against the padded upholstery lining the carriage, waiting for the footman to open the door. No charges had yet been lodged against Lord George, but when they were, no doubt it would be for High Treason.

Jane saw the wiry figure of the barrister, Thomas Erskine, descend from his carriage. She had engaged his services before Alex had arrived back in London, and since her husband hadn't challenged her choice, she assumed he considered it a wise one. The famous defense lawyer took shelter from the rain under a gray stone archway, standing with his cloak held tightly beneath his chin.

Thanks to the change in the weather, and the harsh military response ordered by the king during the worst of the disturbances, the city at last was quiet, but the scars of the tumult—now dubbed by the press and the people, alike, as the Gordon Riots—were everywhere to be seen.

Alex and Jane merely nodded to Erskine, with whom they'd conferred at their house in St. James's Square earlier in the day. The three walked silently through the Byward Tower gate. They were escorted through another gate by a yeoman warden, resplendent in scarlet livery and white neck ruff.

Jane grimly attempted to assess the overall damage wrought, in part, by the man they were about to visit. Nearly five hundred people had been killed or injured in the melee. Several beautiful Catholic chapels had been gutted by fire, their sacred altars and wooden pews tossed out on the cobbled streets. Many of those

same thoroughfares still had deep potholes created when the
rabble dug up the paving stones and tossed them at those unfor-
tunates not wearing the Protestant blue cockade.

Jane sighed as they were led through the Tower's inner courtyard. She paused to stare at a large wooden block. Its top edge
was partially hollowed out, allowing a head to rest there comfortably, if its owner were kneeling. The yeoman followed her
gaze, which rested on an outsized executioner's axe suspended
nearby from a wall of Portland stone.

"Last time that little charmer was used was in Forty-seven,"
the yeoman offered cheerfully. "Lopped off the 'ead of the
Fox—Simon Fraser, Lord Lovat, one of Charlie's lads. Did a
fine, proper job o' it, I can tell ye that! We just hang 'em, these
days," he added sadly.

What a pity they didn't lop off his son's *head, while they were
at it,* Jane thought to herself, staring straight ahead and following
the men up a gloomy, winding stone staircase in the forbidding
Waterloo Barracks. Simon Fraser, Master of Lovat, was now an
M.P. for Inverness, as well as a Commissioned General in the
71st Fraser Highlanders. Nevertheless, he continued to sit out the
American War and she'd heard he was currently in London to
attend the House of Commons. *He was probably among those
calling for George Gordon to be hung by the neck until dead,*
she thought glumly.

The ducal couple and their lawyer, Thomas Erskine, stood
quietly in the drafty stone corridor as the yeoman pulled a large
key from his pocket. He inserted it into a square iron lock on a
massive wooden door with bars crisscrossing a window in its
center. From inside they could hear low moans and sobs, punctuated occasionally by a high-pitched wail.

"Oh, God . . . Oh, my God!" the voice cried.

"His lordship's been doin' poorly, Yer Grace, oi'm sorry to
report," the yeoman commented. "Seems he claims he never
intended to incite a riot. But he sure did a good'n, wouldn't ye
say? We've hung twenty-one of the buggers so far. We builds
the gallows right at the spots where they committed their mischief!"

Jane peered through the bars on the door as the yeoman
struggled with the ancient lock. Lord George, pale and emaciated, paced up and down his gloomy cell, agitatedly running
both hands through his thinning hair. He turned and stared as
they entered the chamber, and then sank his head into his hands
and turned away.

"I believe you know Mr. Erskine, George," Alex said quietly.

"He is going to try to help you, but you must do *exactly* as he says."

"Look . . . *look!*" the younger man whined, pointing out a small window set into the thick stone wall of his cell. "Oh, God! Is *that* to be my fate?"

Jane stood on tiptoe and gazed out at two men in rags, hanging by their broken necks from a scaffold erected outside the prison walls. Their faces were of a bluish hue, and their bodies twisted slowly in the freshening wind that heralded the approaching storm.

"Hanging's certainly a possibility, unless you follow my instructions to the letter," Erskine replied mildly, sitting down gingerly on one of two narrow cots pushed against the granite walls. "To begin with, sir," Erskine said briskly, "I'll need some information about precisely what you said when you addressed the throng at St. George's Fields on Friday, June the second. . . ."

An hour later, Jane and Alex were back in their carriage for the return trip to St. James's Square.

"Erskine may just *do* it!" Jane said excitedly, believing for the first time that the situation wasn't absolutely hopeless.

"Do what?" Alex asked, pulling the coach curtain back an inch to stare moodily out the window at the steady downpour.

"Succeed in getting yer dotty brother acquitted, that's what! He'll manage it as long as no other hard evidence suddenly appears which proves that Lord George *intended* to commit the felonies which were enacted by the mob. 'Tis a perfectly *brilliant* defense!"

"I hope it works," Alex replied glumly.

"And what about the rest of us?" she persisted. "What are we to do while this case drags on, as 'tis bound to?"

Alex shrugged. "We go on as before."

"We canna go on as before," Jane countered. "No one will speak to us . . . no one will have us in their homes . . . yer friends will snub ye in the House of Lords and at yer club . . . and worse."

"There's not much we can do about such things, Jane," Alex replied with his usual remoteness.

"Oh, yes there is!" Jane said suddenly. "We can apologize!"

"Apologize? For what?" he said testily. "I was in Glasgow during the riots, drilling His Majesty's Fencibles, and you were . . . well, I have no idea *where* you were, but let's merely hope you were committing no transgression worthy of capital punishment!''

Stung by his veiled accusation, Jane remained silent for a moment and then spoke in a voice that vibrated with intensity.

"I know there are many things between us, Alex, about which we have remained silent," she said, forcing him to look at her. "They have festered and eaten away at our marriage. But this business concerning Lord George threatens the very House of Gordon! I dinna want that, and ye dinna want that for either us or our children—especially young Huntly. I think 'twould make a great difference in the public's opinion of us if we went to each and every person of importance who was damaged by the disturbances, either in their person or property, and told them how sorry we are for this misfortune. We can pay calls together or separately, but I think it should be done.''

The sound of the horses' hooves and the patter of the heavy rain on the carriage roof grew louder in the silence that hung between them. Alex pursed his lips a moment, lost in thought. Then he looked at her and smiled wryly.

"You're a clever lass, Jane Maxwell. Bold and clever. You recruited lads for Hamilton's regiment when the Highlands had been bled dry and the scheme you've suggested to save our sorry reputations just might work. Are you willing to risk being re-buffed by every aristocratic family in London?''

"That I am, Yer Grace," she replied, looking at him steadily.

"And despite our . . . estrangement . . . these past years, you are willing to stand by my side?''

"Aye," she said slowly. "For the past four years I've wanted to do just that, m'lord.''

Alex continued to return her measured glance for what seemed like an eternity before he spoke again.

"No need to address me so formally, my sweet," he said finally, bending forward to take her face gently between his hands. "I am, after all, your husband," he murmured with studied irony. "You *do* still acknowledge that, don't you, Jane?''

She nodded, remaining silent and staring across the carriage at the enigmatic man to whom she'd been married almost thirteen years.

His hands brought her face inches from his and he kissed her lightly at first, and then with a hunger stoked by denial. Like a man possessed, his lips sought her eyelids, her cheek, the hollow of her throat. She allowed the effects of his urgent lovemaking to wash over her. *Give it up*, she told herself for the thousandth time, praying that the magic of his hands and lips would banish all thoughts of Thomas Fraser from her brain. Alex's touch was achingly familiar, and yet she almost felt as if she were watching from afar as her husband passionately kissed someone else. Then, mercifully, a quickening took hold deep inside her. An arousal of sensation so long held in check finally supplanted the jumble of half-thoughts whirring inside her head, and she surrendered to the warm waves of pleasure Alex had always been able to call forth from her.

The coach halted in front of Number 6, St. James's Square. In the pelting downpour, footmen scrambled to assist the Duke and Duchess of Gordon as they made a dash for the front door. As soon as the pair had handed their cloaks to the phalanx of waiting servants, the ducal couple marched past their startled English housekeeper, without so much as a nod in greeting. Hand in hand, they mounted the stairs with an urgency that appeared highly unseemly, considering the fact that it was high noon and Their Graces' brother had been clapped into the Tower of London for the most heinous crimes. The door to the duchess's bedchamber at the top of the stairs slammed shut.

Well! sniffed the housekeeper, retreating to the kitchen for a bracing cup of tea. What could one expect from Scots? They were probably *all* wild fanatics like Lord George Gordon!

For two days following their visit to the Tower, the Duke and Duchess of Gordon rarely left their bedchamber overlooking St. James's Square. They were like a pair of travelers who had been stranded in a desert, prepared to breathe their last, only to stumble on a crystal pool of water that beckoned them to drink their fill.

"Really, Alex," Jane chided her husband one morning, smiling slyly. They were still lying abed, although the hour was late. "I shall never be able to face that disapproving English housekeeper if we dinna stop this . . . this unseemly display!" She gently ran her fingers through the dark hair peppering his chest.

"Let the housekeeper be hanged!" Alex retorted, pulling her to him and nuzzling her neck with his lips.

"But we have work to do," she insisted, ignoring his invitation to yet another bout of love. She sat upright in bed and crossed her legs under the bed linen. "Whom should we call upon first?"

Reluctantly, Alex rolled onto his side, propping his head up with the palm of his hand. Together, they planned their strategy, while in another part of her mind, Jane calculated how soon it would be before she would be pregnant again.

However, to her relief, Jane's monthly flux began soon afterward. She wondered, as she and Alex made their appointed rounds in London of friends and acquaintances harmed by the mob, whether her childbearing years were perhaps at an end. She speculated that after such a long period of celibacy, perhaps her body had ceased to be a haven for the miracle of new life. With the crush of responsibilities and the strain of attempting to make amends for Lord George's transgressions, Jane pushed the notion of having another baby to the far recesses of her mind.

At first, their peers were slow to respond to the Gordons' direct expressions of sorrow. Lord George still languished in the Tower of London during the summer, but he had been moved to more commodious chambers in another section of the prison. This was due in great part to Thomas Erskine's entreaties and the general respect most members of the House of Lords held for the duke himself. Several times each week, Lord George had taken to hosting dinner parties in his new prison cell—even after he had officially been charged with High Treason. He had the accounts for such frivolities sent directly to Alex for payment.

Among the scores of victims Alex and Jane called on from June through October, many had reacted quite favorably. The majority were stunned, in fact, to be singled out for the honor of being visited personally by a duke and his lady.

Sir George Savile, the originator of the Catholic Relief Act, whose house in Leicester Square had been gutted, remained cool to any apologies. However, Lord Mansfield, whose residence on Bloomsbury Street, including his famous library, had been destroyed, received them cordially. Jane was overjoyed, because Mansfield was sure to sit on the case when Lord George was brought to trial. After this particular visit, Alex and Jane noticed the atmosphere around them warmed perceptibly.

It was mid-November, however, before Jane mustered sufficient courage to venture an appearance in Court.

"Don't worry, my dear," Alex reassured her as they mounted the steps to St. James's Palace. "You've been a favorite of Queen Charlotte from the first." He squeezed her arm to bolster her resolve. "You were clever enough to realize at the outset that the king has very great respect for his wife's opinions—God help him!"

The duke and duchess were ushered into a large reception room filled with peers, merchants, and hangers-on, all milling about. Servants dressed in all manner and color of livery wove in and out of the assembly, delivering messages to clusters of people scattered around the room. Life-size portraits of male members of the Royal Family on horseback adorned the high walls of the ornate chamber, and the riders seemed to survey the bustling scene below.

Jane glanced about the room uneasily. She and Alex waited in one corner of the chamber until such time as they would be summoned to greet the king, by whose angry order Alex's brother had been clapped into the Tower. Ladies whispered behind their fluttering fans and gentlemen exchanged knowing glances. *'Twould be great sport,* Jane concluded morosely, *if the assembled throng observed Alex and her being utterly snubbed or, worse yet, actually removed from the king's chamber.*

Jane groaned inwardly when she spotted the Duchess of Devonshire having a tête-à-tête with the bombastic Whig Parliamentarian, Charles Fox. The politician known as the Eyebrow whispered to Georgiana behind an upraised palm, his bushy black eyebrows knitting together above his sly, brown eyes. His portly frame sported an elaborately embroidered pearl gray coat and matching waistcoat, set off at the throat by a linen stock folded and twisted in an intricate fashion. This dandy had allied himself with the Devonshires and the Prince of Wales in hopes, no doubt, that such friendship would one day make him chief minister when young George ascended the throne. Jane had no doubt that hanging a member of Clan Gordon, a family so identified with King and Court, would please this wily politician no end.

William Pitt the Younger approached the Duke and Duchess of Gordon to pay his respects. Turning her back on Fox and the Duchess of Devonshire, Jane smiled warmly at the attractive young man. At age twenty, the amiable Mr. Pitt had recently stood for one of the Parliamentary seats from the University of Cambridge and had lost, but had been offered another seat by a powerful magnate who controlled nine northern boroughs. Jane and Alex chatted with Pitt for a few moments, which took Jane's mind off their impending interview with the king.

"Is it true, sir," she asked, "that ye're totally opposed to the war in America?"

"I support a rapprochement with our Colonial cousins," he answered lightly, eyeing her low-cut court gown with a certain restrained, but obvious, appreciation.

"But we hear the war goes so well for us now," she countered.

"Cornwallis has nearly secured the south and Clinton plans to mop up the last resistance in the Mid-Atlantic and the north. . . ."

"I see you read the accounts of this conflict with as much attention as I do. But I wouldn't count those chickens yet, my dear Duchess," he said seriously.

"Perhaps not," she replied thoughtfully, wondering, despite her best resolve, how Thomas would be affected if the war didn't end as quickly as so many military men were predicting these days.

A letter from Hamilton had caught up with them in London. He wrote, in passing, that Thomas Fraser had been involved in a series of daring forays behind enemy lines to gather information from Loyalists, an effort that undoubtedly had helped the war. The captain had apparently made several mysterious excursions up to Maryland and back to retrieve vital intelligence from a disaffected wife of one of General Washington's aides-de-camp. Angry with herself for her lack of self-discipline, Jane had found herself wondering if his travels ever took him in the direction of Antrim Hall and its seductive plantation owner. Thomas had told her during their three-day idyll at Loch-an-Eilean that a vixen named Arabella Delaney had been responsible for the late arrival of the fateful letter that had so changed her life. Jane forced another smile to her lips as she addressed Mr. Pitt.

"Well," she said, "either way the conflict in America resolves itself, I shall look forward to reports of yer maiden speech next session."

"I'm honored, madam," he said, bowing gallantly.

During this exchange, Jane sensed the presence of someone else standing behind her.

"I trust yer maiden speech winna be defeatist twaddle, my good man!" growled Simon Fraser, who suddenly had appeared in their midst. "Or I shall have to beg for time to answer yeⁱ"

Jane paled visibly. *Why was Thomas's godfather always materializing in her life at the worst moments?* she thought angrily. Simon, for all his bulk, looked unwell, and was apparently as ill-humored as ever. The veteran campaigner, whose skin had a sallow cast to it, nodded curtly to acknowledge her presence.

"Word is, come spring, they'll head for Delaware and Virginia, and that should finish it," Simon allowed, glaring at William Pitt as if that concluded any discussion about the war in America.

Mercifully, the king's majordomo gave them a sign, and soon Alex and she were standing before the king and queen.

"The Duke and Duchess of Gordon, Your Majesties," intoned the majordomo.

Conversations were suspended, fans ceased fluttering, and all eyes were drawn to the drama unfolding.

"Duke . . . Duchess . . ." King George III murmured noncommittally.

Jane sank into a low curtsy and Alex bowed deeply.

"You do us great honor by receiving us today, Your Majesty," Alex said carefully.

The king merely nodded and Queen Charlotte looked on silently, offering Jane the merest nod. However, her eyes seemed friendly, and Jane took a deep breath.

"We are not only honored to be in yer presence," Jane said quietly, trying her best to control her Scottish burr, "but profoundly grateful to be allowed to express our sorrow at the disruptions in the city last June. 'Twas only due to the decisive actions taken by Yer Majesty," she added, looking directly at the king, "that a far worse fate dinna engulf the town."

A hush entombed the entire room. Queen Charlotte, increasingly plump following the birth of the thirteenth child she had borne the king, extended her hands to Alex and Jane. She spoke in French with a heavy Teutonic accent.

"Je suis très content de vous voir encore," she said, smiling. *"Ma chère duchesse, peut-être vous viendrez chez Buckingham bientôt, non?"*

"Ah, oui, Madame," Jane replied in her halting French. *"Vous êtes très gentille."*

" 'Tis pleasant, indeed, to have you among us once again," King George commented with considerably more warmth then he had expressed a few moments before. "We must compare notes on our Reynolds portraits when yours is completed, my dear Duchess," he added with a twinkle.

"Thank ye, Yer Majesty," Jane murmured, curtsying deeply once again. "I should like very much to do that."

She and Alex backed away from the two sovereigns in formal fashion. Jane could hardly contain her delight. The room resumed its buzz of conversation, and several people who had pointedly ignored the duke and duchess since the Gordon riots came forward to pay their respects. Nevertheless, Alex and Jane departed as quickly as was seemly. During the carriage ride home, they examined the scene in the palace drawing room from every angle.

"Odds fish! I vow the Duchess of D was actually gnashing her teeth at our triumph!" Jane crowed as their carriage rolled down the broad expanse of Pall Mall. "No doubt she'll be driven to make double wagers at faro tonight to assuage her fury, the saucy wretch!"

"Bless me, but the Eyebrow looked none too pleased either," Alex chuckled. "Did you catch his grimaces as we were leaving?"

Later, that crisp November night, Alex dismissed Jane's maid and undressed her himself, taking a slow, sensual delight in removing the layers of her court gown and unlacing the stays of her stiff corset. At length, he peeled the thin cambric shift from her body. Sinking to his knees, he bade her kneel beside him as he covered her face and form with passionate kisses. Then, they made love on a fur rug in front of the fire with an abandon new to them both, though at the moment of Alex's release, Jane fought against the vision of another night of love in front of another fire, in a simple stone cottage at Kinrara.

Give it up . . . her heart cried into the night.

22

February 1781

Jane pulled her shawl more tightly around her shoulders, attempting to ward off the frigid February drafts that no architect at Gordon Castle seemed able to remedy. She peered out the front sitting room window at the wide expanse of parkland, mantled in a snowy crust, which had fallen the previous day and frozen overnight.

The winter weather in the Highlands had been appalling during the weeks following New Year's Eve when she and Alex had rung in 1781 with a quiet celebration at Gordon Castle in honor of her thirty-first birthday. Both of them had been glad to quit London to escape the uproar caused by Lord George's impending trial. Then word arrived on Twelfth Night that Alex's brother finally had to face his Royal accusers. By mid-January, Alex had returned to London to endure the indignity of watching his younger brother tried for treason. The trial finally had begun in London's Court of King's Bench the next Monday, the sixth of February. Jane despised having to endure the uncertainty regarding its outcome, especially from such a distance.

Jane glanced down at her waistline beneath her light woolen gown. Once again, her belly had that provocative curve of a woman four months gone. Any hint of nausea had faded from memory. She felt fine . . . wonderful, in fact, with energy to spare for her boisterous brood.

Jane cupped her hands lovingly around her abdomen.

"Ye'll see the light of this world in July, my little one," she whispered aloud. She had said nothing to Alex when her courses stopped before Christmas, afraid to believe that the interruption of this bodily function meant she was breeding. When the second month came and went, she feared she might miscarry, after nearly five years of no childbearing.

This bairn is our chance to start again, Jane thought, *a chance to make up for the sadness and the hurt we have caused one another.*

As she gazed at the castle's frozen parkland for a sign that Alex was finally returning from London, Jane vowed she would never again jeopardize the fragile happiness that was blossoming between them. As soon as Alex arrived, she would tell him the joyous news that he was to be a father again. Regardless of the outcome of Lord George's trial, she would have her own tidings to share, which would either increase his joy or salve his wounds.

An hour later, she was startled by the sound of jingling harnesses and the thud of the heavy front door slamming downstairs.

"Jane! Jane!" Alex was shouting. "Wonderful news!"

In an instant, she ran into the foyer and was in his arms. She pressed her warm cheek against his frigid one.

"George was *acquitted*!" he shouted, dancing her around in a circle with uncharacteristic abandon. "Erskine was positively *brilliant* and Lord Mansfield's instructions to the jury, scrupulously fair. It took them less than *half an hour* to find him not guilty of *intending* to incite the riot!"

"Oh, Alex," she cried, unconcerned that the entire castle staff might see her throw her arms around his neck, "I'm so *pleased*!"

William Marshall and the hawk-faced housekeeper, Mrs. Christie, appeared in the front hall simultaneously. Mrs. Christie's daughter Jean stood shyly in the shadow of the stairs, dressed in her new housemaid's uniform. The pretty girl unabashedly stared at her employers with her enormous gray eyes.

"May I offer my heartiest congratulations, sir," Marshall said, pumping the duke's arm vigorously.

"And I, Yer Grace," Mrs. Christie said, bobbing. "The staff'll be so happy to hear the news . . . eh, Jeannie, lass?"

"Aye, Mama," the young girl agreed, clapping her dainty hands, which would soon grow red and raw from scrubbing stone stairs. The comely lass continued to gaze admiringly at Alex, who, Jane noted pleasurably, looked dashingly handsome in his black traveling cloak.

"Why dinna ye tell the staff the duke has returned, then?" Jane interjected quickly, casting an annoyed glance in the direction of the housekeeper's daughter, who continued to ogle Alex like the moonstruck maid she undoubtedly was. "Tonight his lordship and I will dine by the fire in my bedchamber, Mrs. Christie. And instruct yer daughter *Nancy* to bring up hot water for the duke's bath immediately," she added pointedly. She turned to face Alex and said, proprietarily, "Come, my good sir."

Alex suppressed a smile.

"Happy to oblige, my dear," he said, following her up the curving staircase and giving her derriere a caress when Marshall and the Christies were out of view.

The copper bathtub had been long removed and their dinner plates whisked downstairs when Jane sat playfully in Alex's lap. He held a brandy in his free hand and draped his other arm loosely around her waist. They both stared silently into the fireplace, mesmerized by the glow of the chunky logs crackling cheerfully on the grate.

Carefully, Alex set down his snifter on the small table next to his chair. He kissed her long and lingeringly. One hand grazed her breast beneath her thin wool bodice, while his other massaged her spine.

Jane sighed contentedly.

"That feels so wonderful . . ." she breathed.

"Does it?" Alex chuckled. "Don't get too relaxed and sleepy. . . ."

"Why not?" she teased, her eyes drooping lazily, her body sinking into his.

"You know why," he said, nuzzling her neck, his voice low and intimate.

She felt him becoming rigid against her thigh. With a knowing smile, she rubbed her leg against his.

"Aye, I know why . . ." she whispered, pressing her lips softly against his ear. "But I'm *very* sleepy. . . ."

In a swift movement, he pushed her firmly to her feet and stood up himself. Scooping her into his arms, he carried her to the massive canopied bed, its forest green velvet hangings reminiscent of the furnishings in Edinburgh when he'd bedded her for the first time the week before their wedding.

"Wake up, you little baggage!" He laughed, unceremoniously laying her on the bed.

She watched while he slowly and deliberately removed all his clothing.

"What a fine specimen ye are, even if ye *are* a ripe old thirty-seven!" she said, boldly surveying him from shoulder to toes, her eyes lingering on the proof of his obvious desire.

"I'm just about to hit my stride, wench," he mocked, sitting naked beside her, unfastening the hooks that marched down the front of her bodice.

She got up off the bed and let the dress and her petticoats fall to the floor. Alex unlaced her stays, flinging them across the room into a chair. Keeping her back to him, she slowly removed the rest of her undergarments and turned to face him.

"God, you're so beautiful, Jane . . ." he murmured, staring at her full breasts.

In a swift movement, he was on his knees, his arms around her waist, scattering kisses all over her torso, finally taking one breast gently between his lips and sucking the swollen nipple in a manner that caused her legs to buckle under her. An amazing liquid fire flowed through all her limbs. Frantically, she offered him her other breast because it, too, ached for his caress. He did her bidding—for a while. Soon, his lips trailed down to her waist, his tongue darting like a small dagger into her navel.

He sank back on his heels and with feathery strokes, strafed his fingers along the inside of each thigh in turn.

"Alex . . . Alex . . ." Jane moaned, feeling as if she would dissolve into a molten mass if he didn't stop coaxing the essence from between her legs. Yet, she could not bear it if he halted his exquisite ministrations. He raised his head and she held him tightly to her, his stubbled cheek pressed against her breasts.

"Yes, Jane," he whispered hoarsely. "Tell me . . . *tell* me what you'd have me do. . . ."

He was goading her into complete wantonness . . . to confess

her most secret physical longings. It was their old contest of
wills, his familiar demand to extract from her complete capitula-
tion. A throbbing warmth blotted out everything but the sheer
presence of him tracing the contours of her body with his lips. If
it satisfied something in him to hear her say she longed to be
pleasured like this, so be it! She ached for him to continue his
odyssey, and it didn't seem to matter if part of his satisfaction
came from hearing her say the words.

"Yes, Alex," she cried out, pushing his head lower. "Please,
love me there . . . oh God . . . *please* . . . yes!"

She started to tremble and was forced to regain her balance by
digging her fingers into Alex's shoulders. A cry ripped from her
throat and her entire body quivered uncontrollably. Heat centered
deep inside her spread in luminous waves from her abdomen.
Her breasts and scalp tingled; a hot flush fanned down her legs.
Even her toes curled. Suddenly, she was sobbing—whether with
sadness or joy, she couldn't discern in her trembling state. As
her cries subsided, Alex, still kneeling before her, placed his
cheek against her belly and held her gently. The only sounds in
the room were the crackling of the fire and the ticking of the
ornate clock on the mantel.

When she began to breathe evenly again, he carefully placed
her on the silk coverlet and stretched out next to her. He held her
close to him with infinite gentleness. Finally, his hand came to
rest on her abdomen.

"Alex?" she whispered.

"What, Jane?"

"Ye know, dinna ye?"

"I knew when I first caught sight of you as I walked in the
door."

"Ye *did*?"

"Yes, my sweet. You had that look."

Jane remained silent, thinking back to the time Alex had
known instinctively she was pregnant with Louisa. But, of course,
everything had changed after the baby was born. Now, his
loving glances scanned her face and body and the faint protru-
sion of her belly. Suddenly, Jane had an overpowering urge to
make a clean slate of it all. She longed to blurt out to Alex that
she knew *he* had concluded from the first that he was not
Louisa's father. That there must be total honesty between them
for them to build anew upon the strong foundation of their last
months together. He leaned forward to kiss her with infinite
tenderness, and she felt herself drowning in the unexpected

sweetness of his gaze. Phrases formed in her brain, but, some-how, the words wouldn't rise to her lips. They had so many secrets between them, she thought helplessly. So many doors they had kept closed. And now, to prevent dealing a blow to Alex she knew he might not be able to sustain, she would for-ever keep the secret of Louisa's parentage from Thomas as well.

A wave of abject loneliness engulfed her, and Jane turned her head away from Alex's tender embrace to stare into the inky darkness outside their bedchamber window. Her bond with Thomas had been forged in youth and preserved in adulthood because they'd always told each other the truth. Now, this *unspoken* truth about Louisa separated her from both Alex and Thomas, creating a chasm between each man and herself, a separation that left her feeling totally bereft and frighteningly alone.

"Are ye happy about it, Alex?" she asked finally, turning her head on the pillow to stare once more into his eyes. "The new bairn, I mean?"

"Very much, my love." He kissed her gently on the tip of her nose, then pulled up a soft tartan blanket from the foot of the bed to cover their nakedness. "I'm very, very happy."

She reached under the bed clothes and boldly lay claim to him, willing herself, by this wanton act of deliberately arousing him, to bind herself to him once and for all time.

Please, dear God . . . she prayed, *let Thomas stay in America when this dreadful conflict ceases . . . let us all, finally, find some peace. . . .*

"If 'tis a boy, we'll name him Alexander," she whispered fiercely as she tantalized him with strong, sensuous strokes of her hand.

Alex gazed at his wife who hovered above him, a dark-haired temptress who would fulfill any man's wildest fantasies. He searched for words to thank her for the gift of this baby growing inside her and to bless her for the extraordinary loyalty she had exhibited toward him throughout this year's dreadful challenge to the House of Gordon. Her wide, expressive eyes searched his face, seeking some answer from him, some sign that he accepted the precious nature of the gifts she had bestowed on him at such emotional sacrifice to herself. He felt his eyes welling with tears. He couldn't allow himself to speak.

Instead, he responded to the steady rhythm of Jane's erotic touch with a low, involuntary moan. Slowly, he gave himself up to the overwhelming sensations rippling through his groin. De-spite the voluptuous chaos gathering within him, he commanded his arms to remain at his sides, granting Jane, as he had no women before her, absolute power over him.

"Tell me what ye'd have me do, Alex," he heard her say gently, mocking his earlier demands of her. "Tell me, husband!" she demanded.

The hypnotic rhythmns of her hand soon began to swallow up the night.

"Love me," he whispered. "Please love me, my dearest wife."

Captain Thomas Fraser squatted in the mud collecting at the bottom of the small fortification dubbed Redoubt Number 9. He pressed his back against the slanted dirt wall that had been hastily constructed by Lord Cornwallis's earthworks experts. It was honeycombed with rivulets carved by the steady downpour that had been falling for more than an hour.

The rain-filled clouds overhead deepened to black in the growing dusk. In another hour, the sky would look like a pot of ink, with no moon rising. Thomas's bowels grumbled uneasily. Provisions had been scarce, and the putrid meat and wormy biscuits handed out to the men in recent days had done their mischief. Many of Cornwallis's troops had sickened with dysentery or the bloody flux, and Thomas feared he might be the next victim. He wondered how the devil the events of the last year and a half could have led so quickly from his luxurious feather bed in Charleston to this hellhole in Virginia called Yorktown.

The actual siege of Yorktown had begun the ninth of October at around three in the afternoon, and the sound and fury had not let up for five days. Thomas watched a cannonball plummet to the ground, just short of the small fort. It spun furiously as it burrowed down into the sandy earth and then exploded, splintering many of the logs masking the front of the redoubt and scattering the protective wooden pickets in every direction.

York River ran fast and cold at his back, emptying into Chesapeake Bay where a forest of ships' masts in the twilight told him that the worst had happened: the French admiral, de Grasse, evading the British fleet sent to block him, had arrived from the West Indies in aid of the Americans.

Corporal Christopher Thornton stood beside Captain Fraser, shivering in his ragged trousers that, like Thomas's own tattered uniform, had been issued for use in the soggy trenches in lieu of the regimental kilt. The young soldier followed his comrade's gaze and shook his head disgustedly.

"Canna believe that bastard, Admiral Graves," Thornton growled under his breath. "Left us like sittin' ducks, he has!"

The opposing navies had engaged in battle midwater between Cape Charles and Cape Henry at the entrance of the Chesapeake on the fifth of September. Their skirmish lasted less than three hours. Within the week, the British Admiral Graves had unaccountably sailed for New York, leaving the waters to de Grasse. Staring glumly through the rain, Thomas acknowledged to himself the British were outnumbered two to one.

"General Cornwallis has done the best that's to be expected," Thornton continued, more to himself than to his superior. "Fortifying Yorktown and Gloucester, opposite us, was the only thing to do . . . but puttin' us Highlanders in this wee fort, here . . . I dinna know, Lieutenant . . . I'm gettin' an awful feeling, sir . . . that—"

"Enough!" Thomas interrupted his subaltern, though his own thoughts had been running along parallel lines as he watched the evening gloom envelop the gutted landscape.

The Fraser Highlanders were holed up with the Welsh Fusiliers and some German Hessians in a small five-sided fort adjacent to another smaller redoubt a few yards from the York River itself—outposts along the first line of defense against the American allies. Half the time, Thomas couldn't even understand a word uttered by either group of his compatriots.

Nothing had gone right in this latest campaign, Thomas thought morosely, shaking the water from the top of his bonnet. Idly, he noticed a tall officer in a heavy woolen cloak duck into the redoubt from the trench that ran in an undulating line toward Yorktown. The firing had halted momentarily, and an eerie quiet descended over the soggy, pockmarked fields. Thomas watched the visiting captain hand orders to Major Campbell. Suddenly, he realized that the messenger was Hamilton Maxwell. Thomas hailed him and sloshed through the mud to his side.

"Thomas, man!" Hamilton greeted him heartily, though his face was drawn. "Good to see ye, laddie."

It always gave Thomas pause whenever he saw his old acquaintance whose features so reminded him of Jane. Hamilton looked as if he'd had as little sleep at Headquarters as Thomas had had in the earthen labyrinth that had been his home for a week.

"Been keepin' good and wet, I see," Hamilton joked grimly.

"And ye, Ham?" Thomas replied, extending his hand toward Captain Maxwell, whose cloak was soaked through with the rain. ''Where've ye been? Haven't seen ye since before the march to this godforsaken swamp.''

A random cannonball burst overhead in the direction of the besieged town itself. Ham laughed sympathetically and shook his head.

''Cornwallis sent me north with dispatches for General Clinton in New York,'' he explained.

''And?'' Thomas asked pointedly.

Hamilton shrugged.

''Dinna know . . .'' he said softly, not wanting to be overheard. ''Clinton sent back word that he would send a relief expedition by sea from New York no later than October fifth, but no one knows if, in fact, the troops are on their way.''

''Well, they'd better get here soon,'' Thomas said in a low voice, indicating the sorry state of the men holed up in the star-shaped fort.

Hamilton nodded agreement and turned as if to go. Smiling crookedly, he looked back at Thomas.

''Ah . . . I have some domestic news, man! A letter from my brother William caught up with me in New York. Sink me, if Jane and Alex havena produced yet another lassie! That makes six children in all, plus the Duke's Geordie . . . can ye fancy that? The Duke of Gordon got a breeder in m'sister Jenny, all right!''

Thomas hunched his shoulders, as if warding off the blow of Ham's latest news from home.

''Christened Georgina, in honor of the king, on the eighteenth of July, just past,'' Ham chuckled, calling over his shoulder as he ducked into the trench that would lead him back toward Yorktown under the cover of night. ''A son named George and a daughter named Georgina. Trust m'dear sister Jane to cozy up to the Crown after that deuced Gordon Riot business, eh what? Well . . . so long, laddie! I'll buy ye a brandy when this is over. . . .''

Thomas took a deep breath and stared into the starless sky. In vain, he struggled to banish painful images of the lass who once stood by his side and ripped down coronation posters. Now she played the toady to George III by naming another brat after him! Thomas tried not to imagine Jenny and Alex together—and the product of that coupling—their new bairn. The little garnethaired girl named Louisa would have just had her fifth birthday in September, he thought wistfully, pushing all other memories aside.

Oh, God, Jenny. . . .

A familiar and piercing sense of loss took possession of him, though he fought it as he had fought the rebel Americans for five years. Jane had changed in many ways, it seemed, and *he* had somehow become a man with no home, no family, no proof he had ever existed on this earth, but for that flame-haired child named Lady Louisa Gordon. For years, now, he had told himself that Jane was lost to him forever, but Louisa. . . .

His knuckles whitened around his musket as another ball burst fifty feet to his right, the explosion briefly illuminating the onyx sky. A man screamed in agony.

Jenny! Jenny . . . Thomas cried silently, echoing the sobs of the wounded soldier who lay writhing in the mud in a trench he couldn't see. And he knew then, no mater how he tried to deny it, that if the next ball should strike him, Jane Maxwell and a child he'd never seen would be the last vision to rise before his eyes.

Once again, an uncanny silence descended along the earthen fortifications. A discomforting premonition of disaster settled over Thomas, along with the acrid smoke that drifted into the redoubt. General Washington's entire force numbered some sixteen thousand men to their seven thousand or so. The enemy was dispersed in an encircling series of trenches matching their own, which the rebels had dug within a thousand feet of the British forces during the previous few days.

Six single shots rang out. Then silence again. A German Hessian several yards from Thomas suddenly cried into the blackness, *"Wer da?"*

Thomas flung himself on his stomach against the earthworks. Squinting down his musket barrel, he waited for an answer to his comrade's question, "Who goes there?"

The response came soon enough. Bursts of fire erupted everywhere. Screams of pain and cries of fury in three languages spilled out into the darkness, which was punctuated with renewed flashes of cannon fire and musket shot.

A figure materialized on the wall above him and the Hessian shot at it point blank, shattering the knees of the invader. The soldier fell back on the sharp pointed pickets stationed below the miniature fort. His agonized screams could be heard over the steady sound of musket fire. A wave of French and American Continentals took the place of the hideously wounded soldier. Suddenly, Thomas found himself engaged in hand-to-hand combat within the extreme confines of the redoubt. Arms and elbows dug into his back as the British and German mercenaries tried to

fend off the onslaught of enemy soldiers cascading over the walls
of the fortification.

In the haze of smoke, he saw Thornton take a vicious bayonet
thrust to the chest. The lad crumpled into the mud, and the
soldier in the tattered blue Continental uniform who'd struck him
down turned quickly to face Thomas. Oddly, few shots were
being fired within the fort. The struggle was far more deadly—
man-to-man. Amid the groans of men fighting for their lives, a
new downpour was unleashed from the heavens. Flashing blades
and bloodcurdling screams rent the air, along with lightning
crackling across the night sky.

"Nein! Nein! Nein!" screamed Thomas's Hessian neighbor
suddenly. The German soldier threw down his musket and raised
his hands in surrender. Soon, other Hessians in Thomas's immediate vicinity followed suit, though he and the Continental remained locked in a deadly struggle. Thomas could hear the
clatter of arms being pitched to the ground all around him as he
and several other Fraser Highlanders continued to battle the
onslaught of French and American troops overrunning the redoubt.

"Vive le Roi!" shouted a French soldier, the breast of his blue
jacket smeared with blood and mud.

"Vive le Roi!" roared back his comrades, some still holding
their enemies at bayonet point or by the scruff of their collars.

The French soldiers' triumphant cries were echoed by those of
the Americans, including the man who had killed Corporal Thornton and was currently battling with Thomas. Rain and sweat
mingled on their faces as they grappled with each other in a
lethal duel. The Continental suddenly caught the tip of his
bayonet on the underside of Thomas's musket barrel and flung it
across the rain-swept redoubt. The two adversaries riveted their
eyes on each other momentarily. Then, quickly, Thomas ducked
to avoid having his head severed from his shoulders. Recovering
his balance, he tackled the American soldier around the waist
and the two of them pitched forward into the mud, fighting
furiously. Scores of bodies hemmed them in, making it difficult
to inflict major bodily harm. Thomas's breathing had grown
ragged, and he knew he had little strength left. Somehow, the
Continental pulled himself upright and suddenly straddled Thomas's hips, pinning him in the muck. His enemy pressed the tip of
his bayonet to Thomas's throat at the same moment Thomas
brought up a small dirk that had been strapped to his waist and
thrust it against the menacing steel blade.

"Stand back! Stand back!" a voice cried in the distance.

Out of the corner of his eye, Thomas saw Major Campbell slam his weapon into a pile of muskets in the center of the fort.

"Throw down your arms, man!" Thomas's adversary muttered fiercely under his breath. "There's no reason to die in a mud hole like this! We've bested ya, son. . . ."

Major Campbell shouted at the British soldiers who were still fighting on all sides of the redoubt.

"Stand back, lads! Surrender yer arms! *Stand back!*"

Numb with cold and humiliation, Thomas acknowledged his compassionate adversary's brief nod of the head and allowed his dirk to slip into the mud. He had no doubt but that similar surrenders were taking place at that moment over the entire battlefield at Yorktown. Slowly, the blue-coated American rose to his feet.

The rain beat down in full force on victors and vanquished alike. The soldier who had chosen not to kill Thomas extended his hand, pulling Fraser roughly to his feet and shoving him into the milling crowd of defeated British Redcoats. Falling into line with his compatriots, Thomas realized grimly that Cornwallis had been beaten, not so much by the Americans and their allies, but by that damned Clinton in New York, whose promised reinforcements hadn't arrived in time, and by that idiot, Admiral Graves, who'd sailed blithely out of the Chesapeake Bay before a shot had been fired at Yorktown.

Shivering uncontrollably because of the damp, Thomas gazed at the crumpled form of Corporal Thornton whose eyes stared fixedly at nothing and whose chest was caked with blood. Thomas's own eyes swept over the other bodies twisted into odd shapes and frozen in macabre attitudes, as if a mad sculptor had created this terrible scene. He suddenly thought of his father, Sir Thomas Fraser of Struy, who undoubtedly had surveyed an even more horrifying sight after the debacle at Culloden Moor more than thirty years earlier. In a very real sense, thought Thomas bitterly, that terrible day had led to *this* pit of carnage and death, where stout Scots lads such as Corporal Thornton sacrificed their lives in exchange for Britain's mismanaged dreams of Empire.

Thomas clenched his fists to his sides as a wall of rage rose up inside him. The unwelcomed Union of Parliaments in 1707 and the failure of the Rebellion of '45 had obliterated the last of Scotland's claims to sovereignty. During Thomas's lifetime, he realized, as Thornton's life blood drained from his wounds into a pool of murky rainwater, an entire country and culture had been destroyed as surely as the wily George Washington's troops had hacked to death the men of the Scottish regiments such as his young comrade who lay dead in the mud.

Swallowing hard, Thomas inventoried the few remaining members of the battalion he'd served with since 1776. Once again, he had survived. But for *what*? What was left to him? There had to be some *reason* for all this, he thought wildly, staring at the dead and dying bodies scattered everywhere. His chest began to heave and the tears on his cheeks blended with the rain bathing his face. He closed his eyes, fighting for control over his emotions. Minutes passed while wounded men prayed aloud for death. When he opened his eyes, the edges of his vision began to turn gray and he felt his knees buckle. The soiled blue arm of Thornton's killer grabbed his own red sleeve to prevent him from pitching forward. The Continental soldier lifted Thomas by his armpits. He dragged him across the redoubt and leaned the captain's crumpled form against the fort's slanted dirt wall.

Just as he was losing consciousness, Thomas suddenly saw in his mind's eye Hamilton Maxwell handing him a likeness of a pink-cheeked child with copper hair, painted on an oval miniature. The tiny portrait fit perfectly in the palm of his hand.

A boy of about seventeen, clad in ragged breeches and a dirty white shirt, walked barefoot through the brown grass, beating a drum methodically and shouting announcements. He passed groups of men in tattered uniforms stretched out on the ground. The British prisoners of war lazed in the crisp November sunshine, awaiting dispersal to various parts of the Colonies. The victors had neither the money nor the manpower to set up prison camps for the vanquished, so most would serve out this war as indentured servants wherever they were needed most. The Yorktown campaign had been decisive, to be sure, but until Parliament and King George III signed an official peace treaty, General Washington had made it clear: no one was going home.

"Captain Thomas Fraser!" the lad called out between drum beats. "Message for Captain Thomas Fraser of the Seventy-first!"

Startled to hear his name called out, Thomas rose weakly to his feet and made himself known. He cast a puzzled glance toward Hamilton Maxwell who had been idly whittling a stick.

Standing upright, Thomas felt dizzy and slightly nauseated. His uniform hung loosely on his shoulders. The dysentery he'd feared would strike during the battle had plagued him for nearly a month now.

The boy in the ragged clothing handed him a small piece of parchment. As he read it, Thomas felt a smile threatening to spread across his lips, despite his miserable condition.

Captain Fraser:

You have been assigned to accompany the Widow Boyd and the body of her late husband, a Colonel with His Excellency, General Washington, to Antrim Hall, near Annapolis, where you will remain as a prisoner until Peace is declared and your regiment, officially disbanded. Report immediately upon receipt of this summons to the Somerwell House, Yorktown.

Major Lilburn Williams
Third Regiment, Maryland

"What is it?" Hamilton queried.

"A rather unusual summons," Thomas answered, handing the note over to Hamilton to read.

" 'Tis not so unusual," Hamilton replied, studying its contents. Then he glanced sharply at Thomas. "Someone ye know?" Hamilton pressed.

"Ah, yes," Thomas laughed. "The Widow Boyd."

"Who the deuced is 'the Widow Boyd?' "

"The plantation owner I told ye about once . . . Arabella O'Brien Delaney Boyd, who saved my life after the Mingos made mincemeat of me when I was in the Black Watch."

"The wench that Corporal Thornton and ye visited in Maryland after Brandywine, ye mean?" Hamilton said, a smirk lighting up his face. "He said ye took a bit o' French leave that time, eh, Thomas m'lad! And what about those missions ye made north from Charleston! Why, ye old dog, ye—"

"Shh!" Thomas growled, adding under his breath, " 'Twouldna do for the Yanks to know I'd met the Widow Boyd *before*, now would it?"

"Och! No, lad, that it wouldna," Hamilton agreed quickly. "Especially since she wasna a widow at the time ye paid her those calls," he whispered. "I figured intelligence wasna the *only* thing ye were gathering from the beauteous Mistress Boyd!" he added with a lecherous wink.

Hamilton stood up and shook Thomas's hand heartily.

"Well, laddie, the best of luck to ye, ye fortunate rogue! God knows where the rest of us will be sent till this bloody thing is over.''

Thomas walked slowly, like an old man, behind the drummer boy while the lad completed his rounds delivering messages. Soon, Fraser and the urchin were trudging along a dusty road into Yorktown itself. The journey from camp was less than two miles, but Thomas thought he would collapse from exhaustion. Arms and legs of dead soldiers poked up through the sandy alluvial soil lining their hastily dug graves. The human limbs, stiffened now, created a macabre picket fence along their route. At length, the boy pointed to a small brick house with square-paned windows and a neat white door. Miraculously, it had somehow survived the siege, though the road that passed in front of it was pocked with gaping holes made by cannonballs and other explosives.

Thomas painfully approached the short flight of stone stairs fronting the small brick structure. Without warning, the door flew back on its hinges and Arabella O'Brien Delaney Boyd appeared, looking fetching, indeed, in widow's weeds made of bombazine as black as her thick, shining hair.

She registered her shock at his appearance only by a slight widening of her eyes, but their blue depths seemed to darken as she surveyed his emaciated form and sallow complexion.

''You are Captain Fraser, I presume?'' she asked formally.

A man Thomas took to be Major Lilburn Williams, Third Maryland Regiment, appeared at her shoulder.

''You want *this* man to escort you home, Arabella?'' he asked, staring at Thomas incredulously.

''Well, Lilburn, I haven't seen the Captain since Sixty-seven,'' she snapped. The lie seemed to convince Major Williams, who continued to look with disdain at Thomas's disheveled state. ''How was I to know you starved your prisoners of war?'' she demanded.

''I must hasten to correct you, madam,'' Major Williams said stiffly. ''The enemy is in this condition due to the failure of their *own* provisioners, not ours!'' His glance swept over Thomas from his cracked and splitting boots to his matted, dirty hair. '' 'Tis a wonder you remembered his name all these years, let alone, his rank and regiment.''

''Before the war, Captain Fraser became a close and treasured friend of my brother Beven, isn't that right, Captain?'' Arabella prompted, her eyes warning him to pick up her cue.

''Aye,'' Thomas answered, doing his best to hide the smile

that threatened to curl his lips, despite the gnawing pain in his belly. "Tell me, Mistress Boyd, I pray Beven has not met the same fate as yer dear, departed husband."

"Beven is missing in action," Arabella said solemnly.

"Missing in *inaction* is more like it, my dear," Major Williams said nastily.

Thomas could see that the soldier was familiar with Beven's undisciplined habits. Perhaps, too, the Major's ill-humor indicated his own lack of success in rekindling what was apparently once a close association with Lieutenant O'Brien's fair sister.

"Beven disappeared into a tavern in Philadelphia a year ago and was never seen or heard from since!" Williams added maliciously.

Thomas swayed slightly on his feet, feeling increasingly lightheaded as he stood in the road.

"Pray, Captain, do come in and sit down," Arabella said, tripping down the stairs to take his arm. "The good Major has offered to share his quarters. Lean on me a bit. Lilburn—quick! Take Captain Fraser's other arm, man! Can't you see he's about to swoon?"

The next thing Thomas remembered was the feel of a cold cloth patting his forehead and the pressure of someone sitting next to him on a small settee where he had been placed while unconscious. The parlor was quite dark but, as his eyes began to focus in the gloom, he could see several candles burning at the foot of a large rectangular box, which rested on a trestle table in the middle of the chamber. For a moment, he thought perhaps he had died, and was attending his own wake, but then he realized it was Colonel Boyd's wooden coffin.

"Better?" Arabella asked, with a smile.

"I think so," Thomas answered uncertainly, "though the accommodations ye've offered me aren't exactly the most cheerful. . . ."

Arabella's throaty laugh sounded soothingly familiar. She continued to daub his face with the cool cloth and lowered her voice to a whisper.

"Thank God they nailed the coffin shut three weeks ago and the weather turned crisp," she confided. "Otherwise, I fear our journey to Antrim Hall would be most unpleasant."

He laughed weakly. "Ye vixen. How'd ye manage to have me 'assigned' to ye, if I may ask?"

"A favor returned," she answered lightly. "Since I hadn't seen or heard from you for months, I came as soon as word reached us that the battle had been won . . . or lost, depending upon one's point of view. Imagine my shock to discover enroute that I'd become a grieving widow . . . 'Twas fortunate my stopover in Philadelphia allowed for a quick trip to the dressmakers!'' she laughed, smoothing her widow's weeds.

Thomas chuckled in spite of the increasing turmoil churning in his gut.

"Ah, Arabella . . ." he sighed. " 'Tis good to see ye again, dearheart.''

"And 'tis good to see you too, Thomas, though you look about as dreadful as you did the day you arrived at Antrim Hall in the back of that cart with your head bandaged in dirty rags.''

"I feel *worse*," he groaned, concerned that the pain suddenly gripping his bowels again would cause him to disgrace himself on the parlor settee. "Oh, God, Arabella . . .'' he gasped.

"Up we go, my friend," Arabella commanded, helping him rise.

Quickly, she led him out the back of the little brick house and opened the door to the privy, pushing him playfully inside and slamming it shut. He leaned against the wall as an excruciating cramp seized his abdomen. A low moan escaped his lips as he attempted to unbutton his breeches in the dim light.

The door suddenly opened and he stared at Arabella miserably.

"Let me help you with that," she said quietly.

"Jesu, Arabella . . . no . . ." he mumbled, a look of misery etching his haggard features.

"Yes, let me . . ." she repeated. "There is nothing about you, dear Thomas, that disgusts me, so you may as well allow me to lend a hand.'' Swiftly, she rendered him assistance and shut the door once again.

By the time he reappeared in the brick house, she had brewed a pot of tea and handed him a cup, along with a warm cream biscuit. A large tin bathtub three-quarters full of steaming water stood in the middle of the floor in front of the kitchen fireplace.

"I'm afraid you must remove your clothes once again," she said firmly.

"What about Major Williams?" Thomas whispered. "I'm not sure he swallowed yer tale about my being Beven's best friend.''

"The Major has departed for Philadelphia, bequeathing me his assigned billet till my nerves are steady enough to travel back to Antrim Hall,'' she assured him with a sly smile. "Now off with those rags and throw them out the back door.''

Feeling suddenly sheepish, despite their previous intimacies, romantic and otherwise, Thomas stripped off his filth-encrusted uniform and gratefully sank his emaciated body into the metal tub, his knees tucked under his chin. Arabella rolled up the sleeves of her mourning dress, grabbed a bar of tallow soap, and knelt next to the bath.

"How does this feel?" she asked, scrubbing his back in brisk circles.

"Mmmm . . ." he sighed, as months of dirt and grime peeled away from his skin.

Arabella washed every inch of his body as impersonally as a medical orderly, and shampooed his hair for good measure.

"Out," she ordered, holding a blanket for him to wrap himself in.

"Arabella?" he said, allowing her to wrap the cloth around his shoulders. He stood before her draped like an Indian squaw.

"What?" she replied, reaching up to comb her fingers through his wet, tousled hair. The moisture had dimmed its hue to the color of cinnabar.

"Ye seem forever destined to be my guardian angel, lass."

Arabella smiled contentedly. Then, she stood on tiptoe, cupped his face in her hands, and kissed him on the lips.

"Let's just get you well, Captain," she said softly, leading him to a chair positioned next to a wooden table where a bowl of barley broth awaited him.

As he began to spoon the soup slowly into his mouth, he paused.

"Remember Corporal Thornton?" he said suddenly.

"Aye, and so do half the serving women on the plantation," she smiled.

"He died the day our redoubt was taken."

Arabella looked at Thomas sharply, noting how he gazed out the window with a faraway look in his eye.

"I'm sorry. He was a lively lad. I liked him," she said gently.

"Aye," Thomas replied, his glance fixed on the road outside. "All those journeys he made with me to Antrim Hall and the other rendezvous spots . . he was never afraid. Yet, that last day, he seemed to know he was going to die."

"So did Harrison Boyd," she said somberly. "He'd written his brother a letter about it just before he was killed. I found it in his trunk."

Arabella stooped and retrieved the bar of soap that lay on the floor, next to the tin wash tub. She kept her back to him for some moments.

"Ye're a bit sad for the loss of him, aren't ye?" Thomas said with some amazement, watching her intently.

"He was a hard man, and he merely married me to get an heir, which, of course, he didn't succeed in doing," she said, turning to face him. "But he put his money into the plantation, and without those funds, plus what I got from you for my part in this little drama, I would have lost the place long ago." She leaned over Thomas's chair and kissed him lightly on his drying hair. "Now, eat your soup, please," she said in a bantering tone. "We must build your stamina for the journey home. I seem to bury a lot of men at Antrim Hall," she added, her voice low and husky, "and I certainly do not intend for you to become one of them."

Jane tucked Hamilton's latest letter, written from the New World outpost of Yorktown, Virginia, in her reticule and strode into the cheerful nursery. The wing had been fashioned out of two former bedchambers at the top of the townhouse on St. James's Square. She bent over Georgina's cradle and pressed her lips gently against the baby's soft, fragrant cheek. Even at seven months, the little lass had clearly begun to take after the Maxwell side of the family, with her dark hair and eyes and lusty lungs.

"I shall return in time for tea," she instructed Nancy Christie, whom she had brought down to London from Gordon Castle to supervise the nursery, now that there was a baby in residence once again. "Please tell the other children we shall continue with *Don Quixote* at four and I will have several questions to ask them on the subject of Honor."

Nancy nodded and bobbed a curtsy, watching her mistress sweep out of the room in her stunning suit of burgundy wool, piped around the collar and cuffs with black silk braid. It was the full-skirted ensemble she often wore when paying her most important calls on people of note in London.

As the coach pulled up to a small, three-storied house half a block from Number 10 Downing Street, Jane stared at the letter she held in her gloved hand. It contained news she was duty-bound to deliver to the ailing Simon Fraser, but oh, how she longed to forget much of its contents.

Heaving a sigh, she allowed her footman to assist her out of her carriage and up the icy walkway leading to Simon's newly leased London residence. The chilly February wind pulled at the dark red skirt whipping her ankles. She lifted the heavy door knocker and held her breath. The butler led her into a small, sparsely furnished drawing room.

"I'll just go summon Mrs. Fraser, Yer Grace," he said solicitously.

"*Mrs.* Fraser?" Jane repeated incredulously. How had she failed to hear such astounding news?

"Oh, yes, mum," the butler said politely. "The General and Miss Bristo were married recently, just before the master became seriously ill."

Simon Fraser, married! Jane thought, stunned. *He* must *be ill . . . either that, or Miss Bristo was!*

Within a few minutes, an extraordinarily tall woman of middle age appeared at the door, her hands clenched together nervously.

"Ye dinna know me, Mrs. Fraser," Jane said, eyeing the rather ungainly woman's approach, "but I am Jane, Duchess of Gordon, and I have news for yer husband that I think might raise his spirits in his time of trial."

She had heard Thomas's godfather was suffering from a weakening of the heart and had not long to live. He had never seemed to *have* a heart, she thought with some bitterness. Perhaps it was only justice that such an organ should cause him pain and suffering as he approached old age.

The new Mrs. Fraser looked at Jane uncertainly.

"F-forgive my appearance, Your Grace," she stammered. "I have been waiting two days for my husband's solicitor to complete certain matters regarding his will. Simon's half-brother, Archibald, is due here from Scotland with certain papers for him to sign so all will be in readiness when—"

The bony-faced woman's eyes began to mist and she fell silent. Jane looked at her uncomprehendingly. That Simon Fraser could rouse such feeling in a woman was incomprehensible to her.

"Well," Jane said hastily, preparing to depart as quickly as possible. "Perhaps ye could just tell yer husband that my brother Hamilton writes that the General's godson, Thomas Fraser of Struy, has survived the late lamented defeat at Yorktown last year." She pulled Ham's letter out of her reticule as evidence of the truth of her words. "He has been taken prisoner, of course, but Hamilton says Thomas is . . . in . . . ah . . . completely safe hands. If ye can provide pen and paper, I'll write where letters can be sent 'til the Peace is signed and the Seventy-first is released to sail home."

"Oh, Simon will be so relieved!" the woman exclaimed, tears

spilling down her lined cheeks. "Pray, Duchess, would you be so good as to tell him the news yourself? I know 'twould mean so much for him to see the letter himself."

Jane sighed and searched the kind face of Simon's new bride. Perhaps the old goat had softened, she mused. And after all, he was desperately ill.

"All right," she agreed reluctantly. "If ye're sure. . . ."

"Oh, yes, please!" Mrs. Fraser said excitedly. " 'Twould be best if ye only stayed a short time, but I think 'twould truly make these last hours so much easier if he knew the lad lives!"

As Jane followed Simon's wife up a narrow staircase, she felt the same, familiar jumble of emotions well up inside that she had felt when she'd opened Hamilton's letter the previous day. First, sheer, unfettered joy at learning Thomas had survived. Then, a wave of anger and despair to be told by Hamilton that Thomas was a "happy captive at Antrim Hall, enjoying being kept prisoner on this spacious plantation by a pulchritudinous widow-jailor by the name of Arabella O'Brien Delaney Boyd"—the very woman, Jane remembered instantly, who had wreaked havoc in their lives with her deceit. How could such a coincidence occur, unless Thomas and she had come to some unusual accommodation? The man who had fathered Louisa had never written or sent one message to Scotland since he had set sail for America in 1776, knowing full well Jane might be carrying his child. Yet he would live under the same roof as that strumpet, Arabella Boyd! Worse, he had apparently followed his own advice without a qualm.

Give it up. . . .

Thomas's last words to her would remain with her all her life. Even so, Jane knew that, regardless of how hard she tried to forget him completely or how deeply she cared for Alex and the welfare of her family, there would always be Louisa to remind her of the man she had loved so passionately . . . and there would always be some essential piece of her past missing from her heart.

Simon Fraser's wife slowly opened a door at the top of the stairs and admitted them both into a chamber made gloomy by heavy curtains pulled tight against the glowering February skies outside. A shrunken figure lay deathly pale against the smooth linen pillow propped under his head. Simon Fraser, Master of Lovat, son of a Baron, General of the heroic 71st Fraser Highlanders, survivor of Culloden Moor and the dungeon below Edinburgh Castle, legendary commander in the wars against the French in

Canada, family despot, noted barrister and M.P. for Inverness—
this shriveled remnant of a man stared at Jane with hollow eyes,
his massive jowls drooping below his chin, his neck scrawny and
wrinkled.

"Why is *she* here?" he rasped, his eyes darting with some of
his old fire in the direction of his nurse-wife.

"She has wonderful news, Simon!" his spouse replied with
forced cheerfulness. "But I'll let the duchess tell you herself."

Jane approached the bed warily. She looked down at Simon
quietly for a moment, noting his shallow breathing and the
parchment quality of the hand that lay trembling on the bed
linen.

"Yer godson, Thomas Fraser, survived the Battle of Yorktown,"
Jane said simply. "He is alive and well, living as a prisoner of
war on a plantation in Maryland." She held up Hamilton's letter.
"I've just received this from my brother, Captain Maxwell.
Thomas is *alive*."

Simon closed his eyes. His breathing became more labored.
When he resumed staring at Jane, she saw with amazement that
tears had begun to slide down his cheeks.

"Thank you so much, Duchess," Mrs. Fraser said in a choked
whisper. "At least he knows a part of his line will continue,
thanks to his half-brother, Archie, and now, this news. He took
the surrender at Yorktown very hard."

Jane looked at the man who had schemed with her mother so
long ago to keep Thomas and her apart, and felt only sadness.
He was dying—and childless. His driving ambition to restore his
lands and titles had consumed his life to such a degree that he'd
had no time in his youth for women such as the former Miss
Bristo. His machinations, in the end, had even kept Thomas
from producing a male heir. Simon Fraser had many acres to
pass on, and no son to pass them on *to*. At least Archie and
Thomas were still alive to serve as some sort of substitutes,
though the dynastic dominance of the Frasers known in the days
of Simon the Fox might never again be felt in the Highlands.
The way of life General Simon Fraser had fought so ferociously
to preserve was dying with him.

"Duchess . . ." he whispered hoarsely.

Jane bent her ear close to the old man's lips. She laid her right
hand lightly on his shoulder.

"What is it, General?" she asked softly.

"Thank ye for bringing me such news."

"Y-ye're welcome . . . 'tis blessed news for us all . . ." she said, tears stinging her own eyes.

It had taken Simon a great deal of effort to produce his last words and he appeared to be having difficulty catching his breath. Suddenly, he seemed to choke. His wife ran to the other side of the bed, clutching at his hand agitatedly.

"Oh, no! Simon!" she cried, glancing across at Jane distractedly.

The general gave a strangled cry and then appeared to sigh. A strange rattling sound gurgled in the back of his throat. Suddenly, he shuddered, and then his body became completely still. Simon's face settled into a mask that looked like a marble bust of a Roman senator. His mouth lay slightly open, as if he were about to address the multitudes.

His wife began to sob quietly as Jane reached down and closed each of his eyes with her gloved, ivory forefinger.

The great Highland warrior had died in his own bed.

3

1783–1789

*Her Grace, whose flambeaux flash against
the morning sky
And guild our chamber ceilings as they
pass by . . .*

                                    Robert Burns

23

June 1783

The hills dotting Maryland's rich bottomland rose gently from the banks of Antrim Creek. The moist earth was carved in neat furrows, and shoots of wheat were just beginning to peep above the ground. If all went well, thought Thomas, surveying the scene astride his dappled gray, the 1783 crop of wheat would be safely on its way to Jenkin's Mill by autumn. Eighteen months of sensible management and an unofficial peace in the Colonies had made all the difference to the plus and minus columns of Arabella's ledger books.

Thomas and Arabella saluted jauntily to the men weeding the northwest section of Antrim's arable land, pressed their heels against their horses' flanks, and cantered toward the stream.

"Race you to the creek," Arabella said, her eyes sparkling and her lips pursed in what Thomas recognized was a familiar, provocative pout.

Thomas spurred his mount without giving her a gentlemanly head start, hoping to heaven he could best such a superb horse-woman. Their horses tore into the dense woods at a flat-out gallop. The oaks flying by them stretched up the hill on the left toward the small octagonally shaped summerhouse. The couple arrived at Antrim Creek in a dead heat and nearly overran the small, free-running stream that cut across the plantation. Both their mounts were well lathered, thanks to the warm June sunshine and their breakneck pace.

They had halted in a secluded glen where the creek flowed gently along a stretch of soft, mossy bank. Arabella jumped down from her mare and flung herself on her back, panting heavily, her arms stretched out like a cross on a field of apple green velvet. Gasping for breath, Thomas slid off his horse and flopped down beside her.

"God, lassie!" he exploded. "No Scottish fox could ever keep ahead of the likes of ye!"

Arabella laughed her throaty laugh and heaved a happy sigh.

"Do you realize, Thomas, that if we manage to harvest what we've just planted, we're going to be *rich*!"

"I think 'rich' is overstating the facts just a wee mite," Thomas chuckled, chewing on a long blade of grass. "Ye could call Antrim Hall prosperous, mayhap . . . if we have a good crop again this year. But rich? No, lass, 'twould be stretching the truth too far."

"But we've made the switch to wheat, when others strive for more tobacco, which only depletes the soil. This year, don't you think, there's bound to be a decent profit? What do you plan to do with your share?" she asked suddenly.

Her manner was bantering, but the strangely diffident look in her eye told Thomas she was asking more than a friendly question.

"I dinna know," he answered lightly, rolling onto his knees and stripping off his jacket. "Depends on how long I remain yer 'prisoner of war.' "

"Ah . . . I see," she said, closing her eyes against a shaft of sunshine slicing through the leafy bower overhead. "I've heard nothing from Washington's people, so . . . I guess you'll just have to stay."

"Canna be forever, dearheart," he said gently. " 'Tis only a matter of time before the peace treaty's signed."

"So, you're *serious* about returning to Scotland when the peace is official, are you, Thomas?" she said, opening her eyes.

Moodily, she flicked her horse's reins along the soft grass beside the bank, avoiding his glance. In all the time he'd shared her home at Antrim Hall, she had made no reference to the future. Arabella was not a woman to be turned down twice when she asked a man to marry her. But her latest question led them into uncomfortable terrain.

"To a man, the Fraser Highlanders took an oath in Seventy-five that we'd disband at Perth when all this was over, and not before," he replied evenly, dunking his head into the stream and trying to cool off. "And to that promise I must be true. And besides, Arabella, as a woman of property, ye must surely understand that I must see to certain affairs, now that my godfather has died."

A confusion of emotions invaded his chest whenever he thought of the short letter he'd received last May from Archibald Fraser. Simon's half-brother had written to tell him of Simon Fraser's death in February 1782, from some sort of disease affecting the heart. Thomas felt a strange combination of anger and grief when he recalled the man who had saved him from starvation as a child in the Highlands, who had scraped together the shillings to buy him his first army Commission, and who had so ruthlessly intervened against his desire to make Jane Maxwell his bride. There were so many unanswered questions regarding Thomas's inheritance. Archibald had neglected to relate how—or even whether—Simon had provided for him in his will. Thomas *had* to return to the Highlands to see Struy House and Beauly again. And Louisa. And Jane . . . ?

He pulled himself up short and splashed his face again with icy water. His gray hunter, its sides still heaving, sucked noisily from the steady flow that ran beside him. Suddenly, Thomas felt a pair of reins brushing lightly between his shoulder blades. Still scooping water with his cupped hands, he twitched, as something tickled his neck.

"You've soaked clean through your linen, Thomas," Arabella said quietly, substituting her long, tapered fingers for her bridle. He shivered slightly with pleasure as she sketched seductive circles on his back. "I'm hot, too," she complained.

Thomas brushed his face with his sleeve to clear the water out of his eyes. When he opened them, the snug jacket of Arabella's riding habit was lying on the moss and she was unbuttoning the last closure of her cotton bodice. Her corset stopped short of her breasts, which strained against her shift's sheer material. Involuntarily, Thomas felt his breath catch in his throat.

Sinking to her knees beside him, Arabella calmly dipped both hands into the stream and splashed water over her chest. Soon the shift was plastered to her bosom, her erect nipples clearly outlined through the cloth. They stared at each other in silence.

"Would ye be of a mind to kindly remove yer remaining garments?" he inquired with mock politeness, knowing full well such commands excited her. "And I assure ye . . . I shall do the same in good time, dearheart."

As Arabella shed the rest of her attire, Thomas gazed boldly at the full curves of her exquisite form. As she resumed kneeling in the grass, her smoldering dark blue eyes had their usual effect on him. He felt a stirring between his legs and the familiar pounding in his chest. With lightning grace, she reached out and drew a line with her forefinger from the hollow of his throat, down alongside the fastenings of his damp shirt, never hesitating until she gently caressed the bulge clearly visible beneath his riding breeches.

"Why, Captain Fraser," she drawled with a wink, "I do

believe your temperature's rising.'' The two of them knelt before one another, motionless except for Arabella's hand slowly stroking his groin. "What a pity you're not wearing your kilt, Thomas,'' she added mischievously, narrowing her eyes to his waist and below. '' 'Twould make things so much simpler.''

Her hands strayed to his thigh and back again, continuing its agonizing, circular motion. Arabella's practiced fingers firmly strafed his crotch. Unaccountably, he found himself comparing her bold strokes with the sweetness of Jane's shy touch that afternoon so many years ago when they had lain below deck on his hard bunk aboard the *Providence*. As Arabella continued expertly kneading the swelling between his legs, an even sharper image of Jane sprang into Thomas's memory—that of her kneeling in the moonlight in Kinrara cottage, crying out for him to make love to her.

He cursed inwardly and seized Arabella by the shoulders, smothering those pouting lips with his own mouth.

Will I never be free of this longing? a silent voice asked as he commanded the vision of Jane to disappear.

Tremors coursed through his body, tremors reminiscent of erotic dreams, vaguely recalled. He drowned himself in Arabella's cobalt eyes, willing their glowing intensity to pull him toward her and surrendering gratefully to the magnetism inexorably drawing their two bodies closer.

As soon as he had shed his clothes, Arabella pulled him down on the sweet-smelling grass beside the creek. He smothered her form with his, and found her damp breasts cool against his perspiring chest. Her lips opened like a flower in the sun as soon as he pressed them once more to his own. The soft scent of jasmine filled his nostrils, while unseen insects droned in tune with the stream gurgling over the amber-colored rocks.

Memories of other languid hours of lovemaking in this emerald wood drifted through his mind. Their particular magic had them in its grip, he thought with some relief. Arabella's low, husky murmurs and the parting of her thighs signaled more strongly than words how much she wanted him inside her. Moving quickly, he entered her, a strange jubilation taking hold of him that he should have the power to bring her to such a state of rampant desire.

"Please, Thomas . . . oh, *please* . . .'' he heard her cry.

He felt himself consumed by the heat of her incandescent passion. For his part, he knew it wasn't love. At least, he had accepted the truth that Arabella would never have the hold on his soul he had granted to Jane. But her friendship and generosity this last year and a half, her frank appreciation for the sexual compatibility they shared, and yes, the love he knew she bore him were powerful aphrodisiacs, and their sorcery cast a kind of bewitchment on him. This time, too, all thoughts were finally banished from his mind, allowing pure, physical sensation to invade every fiber of his body.

At last, there was only the sound of the clear spring runoff rushing over the stones in the creek that coursed past them. His own vital force flowed from him in an affirmation of life, challenging the shadows of death that had for so long been stalking him.

Thomas and Arabella walked hand in hand toward the stable yard to the left of the house, with their horses plodding along behind them, secured by their reins.

"What do you suppose you'll find when you return to the Highlands?" Arabella asked quietly.

"Poverty," he replied, "but I hope, not starvation."

"I meant, what do *you* think you'll find," she said. "Do you think Simon has made you a bequest?"

" 'Tis hard to fathom," Thomas answered, handing the reins of Arabella's mare and his stallion to a black stable boy. "If he knew he was dying, he might have left me some money . . . that is, providing he hadna spent it all buying his own lands back from the Crown. But if death came suddenly, 'tis anybody's guess what I'll find."

"If the worst comes to pass, Thomas," Arabella said carefully, as they approached the path to the rose garden, "you'll always be welcome at Antrim Hall."

He stopped and turned to face her.

"Arabella," he said, taking her chin gently between his fingers. "I canna be making any predictions about the future . . . but one thing I *do* know . . . ye're a dear, dear lass to me, and ye've seen me through two of the worst times in my life. I love ye for that and I'll ne'er forget ye."

She looked at him strangely and then gazed off in the direction of a rose bed, riotous with pink and white blooms.

"You plan to live in Scotland, then," she said finally.

"I dinna know the answer to that," he replied slowly. "There's always the chance I might return to live among ye rebels."

"As you've said, there's no predicting the future," she repeated obliquely.

Thomas took her hand and kissed it.

"One thing ye must promise me," he said soberly. "If ye discover after I'm gone that we've made a baby . . . *swear* ye'll tell me."

"Yes," Arabella replied softly. "I will. Though I think if that were still a possibility, 'twould have happened ere now. But yes, Thomas, I promise."

Before he could reply, she walked on ahead. Then, abruptly, she turned to face him.

"Whatever happens, you can always come back," she said suddenly. "You're the best friend I've ever had and I'd never shut you out of my life."

He strode to her side and folded her in his arms, kissing her fully on the mouth.

"Arabella . . ." he murmured into her hair, still fragrant with the faint smell of jasmine. "I wish I was clear in my mind what our future together could be, but I have to go back."

"I know," Arabella replied, sounding desolate. "There's the question of the will . . . and Louisa . . . and . . . "

She didn't finish her sentence. There had been no secrets between them during the year and a half they'd spent together, but the subject of Jane Maxwell was one they had both scrupulously avoided during the last few months, along with the topic of future commitments. Arabella was not going to replay the hand that had failed so disastrously before.

"Ye're aware, are ye not, dearheart," he said, kissing her lightly on the tip of her nose, "that when ye save another's life, yer bound to them forever? Ye saved mine *twice*. Ye'll not get rid of me so easily."

"I'm glad for that," she said simply, "but you know, Thomas . . . sometime soon you're going to have to choose between the present and the past—or you'll lose both."

He gave her a startled glance.

"And that's all I have to say on this subject."

She gathered her riding habit's voluminous skirts and proceeded up the garden path toward the house. Both she and Thomas were unaware of two figures who had been standing on the veranda of Antrim Hall, taking in the tender pantomime enacted between Thomas and Arabella in the rose garden.

Hamilton Maxwell took the porch stairs three at a time and strode in the direction of the colorful plantings. Beven O'Brien remained in the wooden rocking chair, sipping a tall drink.

"Thomas, my man!" Hamilton hailed, waving his arm overhead.

"Who is that?" Arabella demanded, shading her eyes in order to see the rangy figure approaching them at a lope.

"Why, 'tis Hamilton Maxwell! From my regiment," he said, his surprise reflected in his voice. He walked quickly ahead of her with an outstretched hand extended toward the unexpected visitor. "And I believe the gentleman lounging on the veranda is yer brother, looking a bit worse for wear," he called over his shoulder. He pumped Hamilton's hand, asking incredulously, "Ham . . . what are *you* doing here?"

"I'm here in an official capacity, laddie mine," Ham said heartily, with an appreciative glance at Arabella, who had caught up with the two men. "Believe it or not, I've been ordered to visit all the so-called prisoners of war officers in this area. The Peace Treaty is on its way to Parliament, and *ye*, my friend, are a free man . . . that is, as far as yer prisoner status is concerned." He laughed, pleased with his little joke. "What's left of the Seventy-first sails from Philadelphia in September," he continued. "Forgive my blurting out my news before I have made the acquaintance of yer lovely jailer," he added, with a bow to her.

"And *your* hostess, as well, Captain Maxwell," Arabella said smoothly, extending her hand. "I hope you will make Antrim Hall your home for as long as you like," she amended.

"Yer kind brother, Squire O'Brien, offered the same when we met so fortuitously in a tavern in Annapolis and he learned of my destination. I accept with pleasure, madam."

Her mind was beset with questions. Why had Beven suddenly returned after nearly two years of silence? What did Jane Maxwell's brother know of the outcome of Simon Fraser's will? She decided to concern herself with one problem at a time and turned to smile warmly at Hamilton. The more she could learn about the woman whose hold on Thomas had endured all these years, the better she could devise a strategy to induce her lover to surrender his past.

"I would imagine Hamilton has many more men he must notify concerning the journey home," Thomas said stiffly.

Arabella glanced at him, surprised. Thomas's open, friendly countenance suddenly looked pinched, as if he had an excruciating headache. Clearly, he wasn't pleased with the notion that Jane's brother would remain at Antrim Hall for an extended period.

"Actually," Hamilton said, oblivious to the undercurrents swirling around him, "I saved ye for last, laddie. I thought 'twould be capital to spend time with an old comrade in this beautiful region before going home. Ye're kind, indeed, madam, to extend such gracious hospitality."

"Please call me Arabella, Captain." She smiled, wondering, as always, what kind of condition Beven was in. "Shall we go in? I'm sure you'd like to spend a moment speaking with Thomas alone and would appreciate some rest and refreshment."

"Yer serving woman was kind enough to offer both while Beven and I awaited yer return," Hamilton said cordially, offering his arm to Arabella. "But I do have quite a bit of news from home. . . ."

"Then by all means, Captain, you and Thomas please retire to the library, and Mehitabel will bring you another cool drink. I'll just greet my brother and go see to your comfort."

"I have a packet, Thomas, from Archibald Fraser," Hamilton said, patting his chest pocket as they entered the paneled library. Ham sank into a leather chair, grateful to be free of that sot on the veranda who seemed to keep himself perpetually inebriated. "This missive has been chasing ye . . . oh . . . for at least three months now."

Thomas moved to place the letter on a desk that stood against the wall, but Hamilton urged him to open it while he examined the contents of the bookshelves around the room.

"Well, well . . ." Thomas breathed.

"Good news?" Hamilton asked hopefully.

"Apparently, Simon Fraser was in the process of purchasing back Struy House as my legacy when he died," Thomas said, indicating the pages of fine script he held in his hand.

"Good show!" Hamilton said enthusiastically.

"Not quite," Thomas replied soberly. "The transactions were not completed before he died. According to Archie, 'tis all in a terrible muddle, and that's why he made no mention of the will in his brief letter telling me of Simon's death. I may inherit the entire estate my father once owned, I may inherit just the house, or I may have only a few hectares of land left to me. 'Tis up to the lawyers, it seems."

"Bad luck!" Hamilton sympathized, but then he brightened, glancing around the well-stocked library shelves. "I'm sure 'twill all come right in the end, old boy. Ye seem to land on yer feet, no matter what blows are dealt ye by fate." He winked slyly and sat down. "I imagine life as the laird of Antrim Hall would prove a tidy patrimony, eh what? Any chance ye'll not be sailing home with the regiment? It could take *years* to sort out that tangle at Struy, if the courts are involved. Ye dinna want to miss out on a sure bet with the Widow Boyd, now do ye, laddie?"

"I took that oath to disband at Perth after the war, same as ye, remember?" Thomas said lightly. "And what news of home? Is everyone well?"

"Aye . . . who do ye want to know of first?"

Thomas shrugged and smiled, but his eyes seemed watchful and cautious.

"My sister Jane is very well and specifically said in her last letter that she'd welcome a visit the minute ye return to Edinburgh."

"She knows where I am?"

"Oh, aye!" Hamilton said smiling. "After the surrender, I wrote immediately to let them know we were all right. The post is still so unreliable, I thought it prudent to tell of yer good fortune to have been made prisoner at Antrim Hall, should any missive ye might write go astray," he added.

"A-and Eglantine and Catherine?" Thomas asked quickly, wondering if Jane had rightly concluded that he had spent the last year and a half with the woman whose rash actions had dealt Jane and him such a blow sixteen years earlier. "And what of the others? Is Lady Maxwell in good health?" he inquired unsteadily.

"Mother enjoys being mama to a duchess, to be sure, though Jane, I fear, does her best to avoid her company whenever she can. Catherine continues to be a happy matron at Ayton House. And the scandal about Eglantine marrying that phony baronet and divorcing him is nearly forgotten. Now, she's busy scribbling *theatrical pieces*, can ye fancy? Jane says one may be performed at Covent Garden, though I canna truly believe that, can ye?" Thomas remained silent, almost brooding. "Since ye seem to have found yerself such a hospitable situation with Mistress Boyd," Hamilton continued cheerfully, "I wonder if ye winna yerself think of settling down soon, Thomas?"

"Of course not! Why should I?" he snapped. Then, he smiled bleakly at Hamilton, as if apologizing. "Arabella has been a . . . friend. A true friend. But I have much that awaits me in Scotland and I must hasten home."

Hamilton Maxwell had always accepted the youthful relationship between Thomas Fraser and his sister at its face value. They

had been childhood sweethearts, of course, but when Thomas
had been reported killed outside of Fort Pitt in 1766 and Jane had
married the Duke of Gordon, he chalked up her earlier romance
with Fraser to mere puppy love. Hamilton had been posted
abroad when the ducal Gordons returned from their grand honeymoon trip to discover Thomas was still alive. Indeed, Ham had
utterly dismissed Thomas from his thoughts until Fraser returned
from eight years' service in Ireland to join the 71st Fraser
Highlanders.

Hamilton's eyes narrowed as he studied Thomas's gloomy
countenance. It struck him as odd that his comrade and boyhood
acquaintance—who had obviously spent these eighteen months
of the war in such comfortable circumstances—should be so
testy at the mention of the possibility of marrying the winsome
Arabella.

A startling notion was beginning to invade his thoughts. Hamilton surveyed Thomas's gaunt features. The man seemed tense
and extremely edgy. Could it be the flame still burned? Was it
possible that even after all these years and Jane's passel of six
children, the man still felt an attachment for his sister?

"Ye wouldna still be harboring fond feelings for Jane, would
ye now?" he asked bluntly.

"I will always feel deep affection toward yer family who was
so kind to me when I was a lad," he said, avoiding Hamilton's
piercing stare. "But as for Jenny—the fates decreed 'twas not to
be."

Thomas busied himself folding the letter Hamilton had delivered and said no more. Captain Maxwell suddenly recalled the
miniature portrait of little Louisa. He remembered Thomas's
look of utter astonishment when he had showed it to him in
Charleston. Hamilton had been surprised himself to see all those
red curls. . . .

Poor blighter, Ham thought silently, staring with new eyes at
Thomas's burgundy-colored mane. The man's hair looked slightly
damp, as if he'd been swimming within the hour, but its distinctive roan color caused Jane's brother to pause. He did some
quick mental arithmetic concerning Louisa's birthday. Nine months
before that child was born, they'd all been at Culloden House—
Alex, Jane, Thomas, and himself. But hadn't Jane insisted she
depart for Kinrara when Alex left Inverness so suddenly? His
mind drifted back to that frenzied time before the regiment sailed
for the Colonies. Had there been a quarrel that had rashly pushed
Jane into Thomas's arms—and into bed? Hamilton dredged his

memory. He vaguely recalled Alex leaving abruptly for Gordon Castle the night of the officers' reception . . . and hadn't Fraser requested leave about that time to go to Beauly that same week? 'Twas merely a day's ride from Beauly to Kinrara. *So it* was *possible!*

At that moment, Arabella entered the library, carrying a silver tray of refreshments. Hamilton watched the striking young woman set down her burden, imagining to himself how shocked his circle of family and friends would be if they knew Jane's fourth daughter might not have been fathered by the duke. Another scandal to add to the Gordon Riots and Eglantine's divorce would be disastrous for everyone concerned, including himself, Ham thought. In the reign of Their Most Prudish Majesties, King George III and Queen Charlotte, army promotions during peace-time went to people with powerful connections who kept their noses clean, along with those of their relatives. In the interests of family propriety, it would not do for Thomas to think Jane still cared for him, though her latest letter—on reflection—more than hinted that she still did. Reaching a decision, Hamilton Maxwell rose to assist his hostess.

"Ah, Mrs. Boyd . . . Arabella," he said gallantly, "do let me help ye with that. I was just telling Thomas some domestic intelligence about my sister Jane."

"Really, Captain?" Arabella said, with a peculiar glance in Thomas's direction. "All is well with the duchess, I hope," she added, handing him a glass.

"Capital," he said, taking a long draught of his drink to give himself time to think clearly. "Thomas may have told ye, the Duke and Duchess of Gordon have children hanging from the chandeliers. I must say," he said with a confidential wink at his hostess, "I'm not one for these marriages promoted by ambitious matrons, but Gordon's a first-rate chap, and, over the years, Jenny and he have become absolutely devoted to one another— especially of late. So *rare* in these kinds of situations, dinna ye think?" he said heartily. "If ye need proof of that, just count the bairns!" he laughed uproariously, slapping his thigh. "Little Georgina makes six . . . and she's barely two. My guess is, at the rate they're going, they'll keep having 'em till the *babes* have babes, eh Thomas?"

Thomas nodded polite agreement and stood up abruptly. Ignoring the light refreshment Arabella had brought on the silver tray, he stalked over to a side table and poured himself a tumblerful of brandy, then downed a third of it in one gulp. He

quickly finished the rest of it, not even attempting to feign
interest in the banter being exchanged between Hamilton and the
mistress of Antrim Hall.

"Pray, forgive me," Thomas interrupted suddenly, pouring
himself another stiff drink, "but I must answer Archibald's letter
immediately and send it to Annapolis with a runner before
sundown. I shall see ye both when we sup."

And without waiting for their answer, Thomas withdrew from
the library, leaving Hamilton and Arabella to share a long moment of embarrassed silence.

24

April 1784

Hamilton Maxwell climbed wearily down from his hired London livery, paid the driver, and directed the footman to deposit
his heavy campaign trunk around the back of the house at the
servants' entrance.

Even from the roadway, he could hear crystal glasses tinkling
softly in the mild evening air, providing a lively counterpoint to
the convivial conversation drifting through the open windows of
the elegant Pall Mall townhouse. The gray stone residence was
situated in London's most fashionable neighborhood, hard by the
apartments of the Duke of York and the Prince of Wales.

Bursts of laughter exploded from the crowded sitting room of
his sister's newly rented abode. Feeling travel-worn and out of
sorts, Hamilton lifted the heavy door knocker and pounded it
against its matching brass plate. The last thing Captain Maxwell
was in the mood for was talking politics or coping with hordes of
people he didn't know. After eight years away from home, he
wondered if he'd even recognize his own kin!

Idly, he gazed to his left through the square-paned window
while waiting for someone to open the door. He easily identified
the Duke of Gordon standing in a corner of the well-appointed
drawing room. Hamilton's forty-one-year-old brother-in-law stood
silent among a group of well-dressed, talkative men lounging on
the far side of the chamber. His companions were no doubt

debating the hotly contested upcoming Parliamentary elections, but Alex looked a trifle bored.

Jane, in contrast to her taciturn husband, was conversing animatedly with a good-looking, intense young man in his mid-twenties. His elegant linen cravat and well-cut, bottle green coat bespoke a gentleman of power and influence, despite his youth. *Could that be William Pitt, the upstart son of the elder William Pitt, Lord Chatham?* Hamilton wondered.

Ham had to admit that his sister still looked ravishing at age thirty-four in a spring frock the color of French lavender. He marveled that with her tiny waist and full, high bosom, she could be the mother of so many children. From the look of her circle of friends, she was also a powerful behind-the-scenes player in London's contentious political arena.

Hamilton stared through Jane's drawing room window in momentary confusion at the figures of four young people clustered together on the far side of a table laden with refreshments. Captain Maxwell realized, with a start, that this quartet must be his own nieces and nephews—and wondered which one was Alex's legitimate heir, Lord Huntly, just graduated from Eton and about to enter Cambridge.

Hamilton's gaze swept the rest of the assembled guests. He speculated apprehensively about his other niece—the flame-haired Louisa. Neither she nor his niece Susan, who must be nearly ten now, nor little Georgina, still a toddler, were to be seen among the glittering assemblage. Just as well to keep Louisa in the background, he thought. If a bastard's to be flaunted in the Pall Mall drawing room, he thought crossly, better for all concerned it should be the Duke of Gordon's, rather than his sister's.

Hamilton's eyes were drawn to the figure of a female of about thirty, aimlessly plucking the strings of a harp positioned near the window.

Locking glances with the woman suddenly, Hamilton flinched as his sister, Eglantine, emitted an unladylike shriek, nearly toppling the harp onto its side. Despite his fatigue, a smile creased his features as he watched her run out the door of the salon, leaving a line of surprised guests in her wake. She dashed across the parquet foyer, almost knocking over the Gordons' sedate butler, Mr. Marshall, whose imperious expression reflected his displeasure at her lack of decorum when he opened the front door.

"Ham!" Eglantine cried unrestrainedly, stepping in front of the servant to throw her arms around her brother's neck. "Ye're back!"

"Sink me, if it isna' my long lost brother!" Jane cried delightedly, coming up behind her sister to kiss him soundly on the cheek as he received Eglantine's effusive affections.

A general hubbub ensued, and, as Hamilton had feared, Jane linked her arm through his and drew him into the salon to be introduced to the guests crowding around them.

"Uncle Ham! Uncle Ham!" his nieces cried excitedly, flinging themselves around his neck while the boys commenced pumping both his hands simultaneously.

Jane shushed her youngsters good-naturedly and pulled him into the center of the room where the young man in the green coat was standing, a pleasantly expectant look on his youthful face.

"Mr. Pitt," Jane said formally, though with a broad smile illuminating her fine features, "May I present my brother, Captain Hamilton Maxwell, Seventy-first Fraser Highlanders and late of the unfortunate conflict in America."

William Pitt, at twenty-five, was England's youngest-ever First Lord of the Treasury, Chancellor of the Exchequer, and, as of December 19, 1783, Prime Minister. For all intents and purposes, the slim, attractive young bachelor ran the entire country. Pitt nodded cordially and shook Hamilton's hand, apparently pleased to make the acquaintance of a man whose sister had so ably functioned as his hostess these last crucial weeks of the 1784 campaign.

"Delighted that a brother of such a sensible patriot as the Duchess of Gordon has returned safely home, Captain," Pitt said. "Welcome back, my good man. I am pleased no more British blood is to be spilt in such senseless folly."

Before Hamilton could reply that he would have welcomed another chance to have at those American upstarts, Jane introduced him to the rest of the company who all seemed, in one way or another, to be key figures in Pitt's current election effort. The hope was to whip the Foxites soundly and return to Parliament with a healthy majority those candidates loyal to King and Constitution.

"With the loss of the Colonies, political life in London has been in a rather fluid state," Jane murmured confidentially. She led Hamilton, with Elgantine draped on his other arm, across the room toward the refreshment table and the infamous Gordon punch. "Last December, the king asked Mr. Pitt to form a government, and he's been leader of the minority only three months now." Jane pulled gently on his arm and whispered into his ear. "Minister Pitt requested King George dissolve Parliament and call for new elections just this month. This little soiree is to assure him of the support of a few . . . uh . . . uncertain votes." She turned toward her sister with a satisfied smile, adding in a normal voice, "Mr. Pitt's sure to return with an overwhelming majority, dinna ye think, Eglantine? 'Tis the perfect time to turn out that impudent Charles Fox and all his hangers-on!"

"Including the Duchess of Devonshire?" Eglantine replied teasingly. "Jane and the Duchess of D are quite the rivals these days, Hamilton. Mr. Pitt even credits our dear sister as his most effective 'whipper-in.' She delivers the votes of wavering members by virtue of the potent punch served in her sitting room— *and* promises of wealth and honors to come!"

"Eglantine!" Jane reproved heatedly, glancing around her to see if any of her guests overheard her sister's wry comments.

" 'Tis absolutely true, Ham," Eglantine laughed. "Mr. Pitt says he's counting on Jane's support to win him this coming election!"

"Women have not become so forward in my absence," Hamilton said sourly, "that they, too, now stand for Parliament?"

"Not yet," shot back Jane tartly, "but we *do* wield some power in the salons, I believe."

"Well, ye seem to have become uncommonly fond of politics. 'Tis not a normal female pursuit—or have those popular sensibilities changed as well?"

"She's the talk of the town, to be sure," Eglantine agreed admiringly.

"Ye've not enough to do as the wife of a duke and the mother of all those bairns?" he asked disagreeably.

"Alex has his own pursuits," she said enigmatically. "Ah, here he is now," she added, as the Duke of Gordon approached to welcome his brother-in-law home from the war. "I bid ye greet the conquering hero, Alex," she added with adequate sarcasm to pay back her older brother for his criticism.

The duke shook hands and motioned for the liveried servant to offer Hamilton a crystal cup of punch from a heavy silver tray. Hamilton's flagging spirits revived considerably as he sipped the brandy-laced concoction, inhaling its heady, spicy aroma.

"The other children are perishing to see ye," Jane said by way of steering the conversation into safer waters. "They've been all agog since we heard ye'd be home in time for little Georgina's third birthday in July."

"What's the grand total of my Gordon nephews and nieces these days?" Hamilton replied, smiling at the two Georges, who looked remarkably alike, and at Charlotte and Madelina. "Five girls and the Marquess of Huntly . . . plus the Duke's George? To think I've been away so long, I've never seen Georgina. . . ."

"Or Louisa," Eglantine prompted.

Jane darted a glance at Alex, whose friendly countenance was suddenly transformed into a stone mask. The air seemed charged and oppressive, as if a summer storm were about to break.

"Louisa's not so little," Alex said stiffly. "She'll be eight years old this September."

"Wait till ye see those copper tresses, Ham!" Elgantine enthused, unmindful of the current of tension crackling between Alex and her elder sister. "They flow all the way to the lass's waist like a rippling red flag!"

"Both Louisa and Georgina are extremely comely, if I do say so myself," Jane interposed quickly, "though I fear the first thing they'll ask ye, Ham, is if ye brought them some frippery from the Indians, or some such nonsense."

"Tell me, Ham," Alex said with slow deliberation, the angry edge to his voice barely concealed, "what news have you of Jane's old friend, Thomas Fraser? Has *he* returned the conquering hero since his imprisonment?"

Hamilton surreptitiously studied Alex's clenched jaw and Jane's tight-lipped countenance. His sister's high color had paled somewhat, and he noticed her twisting the handkerchief she constantly clutched in her hand to disguise her injured finger. His suspicions were finally confirmed. He knew, without question now, the role Thomas Fraser had played in the Gordon family drama over the years. Well, many an aristocratic family had a similar tale to tell, if the truth were known. But the truth could be damaging now, not only to Jane and Alex, but to anyone with ambitions, such as he held, for advancement in a peacetime army. Thomas Fraser stirring up this volatile mix by intruding in all their lives again, could be dangerous. Hamilton wondered what he could do to keep a tight lid on this treacherous brew.

He allowed himself a lecherous smile in response to the reference by Alex to Captain Fraser.

"I would have to say, Alex m'lad, that our old neighbor Thomas has found himself the perfect solution to his impecunious dilemma in one Arabella O'Brien Delaney Boyd—a buxom, beautiful, *bountiful* lady who not only became his keeper after the war, but apparently shares her Maryland plantation with him, *and* her . . . ah . . . profits as well.''

There! he thought to himself, *that should do something to stifle any plans Jane might have to renew her relationship with her lover.*

Alex's tight features relaxed somewhat, and a mocking smile lit his face. Jane's eyes widened slightly. She remained uncharacteristically silent.

''He's found an American bride, you say?'' the duke inquired softly.

''As of my last visit to Antrim Hall. They hadna tied the knot yet, but I surely expect they will.''

''Then Thomas is not coming home?'' Eglantine asked, darting a glance at Jane, who stared straight ahead.

Hamilton hesitated. He considered lying about the fact that Thomas had landed with him at Plymouth less than a day earlier, and departed on the next coach north for Inverness. But, on quick consideration, Hamilton thought better of out-and-out subterfuge.

''Before Thomas marries, he must officially muster out of the Seventy-first with the rest of us at Perth next month. And, of course, there's the matter of that legal tangle concerning his godfather's will, as, no doubt, ye've heard. He's gone straight to Struy. Simon Fraser was in the midst—''

''We *know!*'' Jane interrupted shortly, cutting him off midsentence. ''Simon's servants were left unprovided for in the will. His Edinburgh townhouse is becoming derelict, and *all* affairs were left in disarray, including his attempt to buy Struy.''

''Typical of that self-centered wretch!'' Eglantine commented acidly. ''The Master of Lovat waited till 'twas too late to get his affairs in order,'' she continued. ''I suppose he was too busy purchasing favors from the War Ministry in the attempt to recover his title. Well, at least the scheming old goat never managed *that!*'' She laughed with a hint of malice. ''In the end, his black heart failed him, it seems!''

''The man couldna help dying,'' Hamilton protested, coming to the late Simon's defense.

Jane remained silent on the subject of visiting her old enemy on his deathbed, but faced Hamilton squarely, her chin raised.

''So ye say Thomas may be in Scotland only a short time, and then back to a new life in America.'' She turned to Alex, adding with a strange kind of determination, ''We all certainly wish him well, dinna we, Alex?''

"But of course," Alex replied grimly. "The man's had many a disappointment. Perhaps his luck is changing if he seeks his fortune with the beauteous Widow Boyd."

Alex and Hamilton fell into small talk about her brother's voyage home. It was obvious to Jane that Alex was disturbed to learn that Thomas was back in Scotland. She attempted to still the pounding in her chest as she watched the two men converse. Well, *she* was just as unsettled as *he* was to hear the news. The problem was, her own distress concerning Thomas's return emanated from the same source as Alex's—and therein lay the perpetual difficulty between them. Despite their reconciliation four years earlier, Alex had never ceased to fear Thomas's potent hold on her affections . . . and with good reason, she was forced to admit to herself. Jane could see that the mere *mention* of Thomas Fraser instantly disrupted the delicate balance they had maintained with reasonable success following the Gordon Riots.

The same tenuousness was true regarding Alex's relationship with Louisa. As the child's auburn curls had deepened over the years, taking on a rich, ruby hue so like Thomas's distinctive mane, the duke had grown pensive and withdrawn whenever the youngster was in his presence. This happened seldom, of late, because of a mutual, but unarticulated pact between Jane and Alex that Louisa be kept in the background.

Yet, despite Jane's best efforts and the bone-deep sweetness of Louisa, Alex had become moodier and more unapproachable, the older Louisa became. Alex resented, too, the time Jane had devoted to William Pitt's important Parliamentary effort. However, the election campaign had become a convenient and absorbing antidote to the lonely days and hours Alex habitually spent away from her.

The strikingly similar images of Thomas and his daughter Louisa suddenly crowded Jane's mind like shafts of sunlight pouring through a tiny prison window. Would Thomas want to see his daughter, if he realized Louisa was his? Jane felt her resolve to sever all ties with even the memory of Thomas Fraser begin to weaken. The steady hum of chattering guests faded into the distance, and Jane was conscious only of Alex's familiar, penetrating stare. Once again, she felt he could see through her soul.

"Alex," she said, trying to keep the tone of resignation from her voice. "I see that our guests are leaving. Hamilton, do let us show ye to yer chamber. In the morning ye'll hear the breakfast gong at nine, but come down whenever ye like. Eglantine, the lassies, and I will be off early to help with canvassing votes in Westminster tomorrow, but Alex will keep ye company."

"Egad!" Hamilton exclaimed with a horrified look on his face, as dark as the duke's somber features. "Ye mean women of fashion now take to the hustings? With their *children*? Alex, man? Ye canna be seriously considering letting yer wife *do* such a thing!"

Alex's eyes had a dangerous glint to them but he merely shrugged.

" 'Tis long been Jane's pleasure to mingle with the rabble, hasna it, my dear?" he said acidly. "Louisa, too, comes by it naturally, I suppose." Jane flinched at the insult. "To date, Jane has avoided press censure," the duke continued caustically, "but not so, I fear, her rival, the Duchess of Devonshire, who was lampooned in this morning's paper, riding a bushy, four-legged fox—backwards. Did you see it, my dear?"

"Or course . . . but never fear, Alex darling," Jane replied, her eyes narrowing slightly as she tilted her head toward him in a gesture of mock obeisance. "I will, of course, have the protection of my good Gordon name, as that other duchess does not. As everyone well knows, Georgiana Cavendish shares her husband with her best friend, Lady Foster." She nodded toward the handsome young William Pitt whose relationship with Jane had been the subject of some inevitable, but only mildly malicious gossip lately. "I have absolutely no intention of falling into a similar . . . *pit*."

Alex surveyed with blazing eyes the distinguished young gentleman's well-cut coat and shiny black boots. Pitt had been waylaid by a garrulous old man in dreadfully dated attire, but the young minister inclined his head to listen graciously. Alex lowered his voice to a growl.

"I'm not convinced your admirer, the audacious young minister, will benefit from such feminine interference as you plan at the polls tomorrow," he said cuttingly. "To many men, including your own brother, such forwardness and meddling on your part could actually do harm to your cause. We've had one Gordon too many stirring the masses to riot." His brother Lord George, after miraculously gaining acquittal, had converted to Judaism and fled to the Continent.

"As ye may remember," Jane retorted archly, glancing testily toward Hamilton, "my 'forwardness' and 'meddling' produced excellent results at Court, despite the crazed activities of yer unfortunate brother. As for 'mixing with the rabble,' as ye call it,'' she added between clenched teeth, ''the shop-worn second sons of the aristocracy dinna seem to win many votes these days *without* a lady's smile to encourage the electorate. I'll wager, such feminine *forwardness* on my part will be *most* welcome this election!''

Before Alex could reply, she extended her hands graciously to the approaching William Pitt, who was oblivious to the sparks of dissension flying between his hosts.

''Ah, my dear Mr. Pitt . . . are ye departing? I'm glad to see ye'll be rested for the morrow,'' Jane said brightly.

''Duchess . . .'' he murmured as his lips brushed lingeringly against her hand. ''Till tomorrow, then. . . .''

The Duchess of Gordon linked arms with the attractive, dark-haired minister, and left Hamilton and the Duke to follow them into the foyer. Alex's anger was palpable, growing in intensity as Jane continued to bid goodnight to her departing guests who were filing out of the Pall Mall residence into the April evening air.

As the last visitor murmured thanks to his hosts at the front door, the Duke of Gordon whirled abruptly on his heel and departed for his study. The door was slammed shut. Jane stared at it for an instant, then wearily led Hamilton upstairs and, without further discussion, directed him toward his chamber.

Hesitating only a moment, she continued on along the hallway to the children's rooms.

''Goodnight, darlings,'' she said from the doorway.

''Good night, Mama,'' came a chorus of voices from the collection of beds positioned around the large room.

'' 'Twas a lovely party, Mama,'' Charlotte volunteered.

''Wasn't Mr. Pitt handsome in his green coat?'' sighed Susan, who, along with her younger sister, Louisa, had peeked down at the arriving guests from between the newel posts on the staircase landing.

Two-year-old Georgina whimpered in her cot in the small room adjacent.

Jane smiled. ''Shh . . . ye'll wake the bairn.''

''Mama, you look so pretty,'' Louisa whispered sleepily, also awakened by the chatter.

''Thank ye, dearest,'' Jane said, trying to keep the sadness out of her smile.

What a sweet, loving child she was, Jane thought, bending over the bed to kiss Louisa gently on the forehead. So much like her father in temperament, as well as looks. She smoothed the tangle of dark red hair away from her daughter's cheek.

"Charlotte said Uncle Ham came back."

"Aye . . . he asked after ye, sweetheart."

"He did?" Louisa asked happily.

The little girl reacted to kindness like a flower soaking up sunshine. She bloomed in the warmth of the slightest attention. If only Alex would show her the same genuine affection, Jane sighed. She snuffed out the candle near the door and bid them all goodnight. "Now, all of you, off to sleep. We have an exciting day tomorrow, helping Mr. Pitt's men garner the votes."

In the library, Alex filled a tumbler with brandy far more potent than even the remnants of the famous Gordon punch, which languished in scores of crystal glasses abandoned in the sitting room. He tossed his head back and drank the amber liquid to the dregs. Resting his boot on the brass fender that guarded the hearth and its low-burning fire, he glanced above the mantelpiece to the Reynolds portrait of Jane in her burgundy velvet coronation gown. The painting's vibrant colors mocked the bleakness invading his soul. After some minutes, he averted his eyes from the remarkable likeness of his wife and stared at the coals crumbling into molten powder on the iron grate.

Suddenly, the duke pounded his clenched fist sharply against the mantelpiece. Then, he cradled his forehead in the palm of his hand.

Thomas Fraser has come back . . . again!

He listened distractedly to the sounds of the staff clearing up the debris in the next room. His thoughts drifted to the lass with the russet curls who lay asleep upstairs with her sisters. *Her half-sisters*, Alex reminded himself bitterly. A part of him adored the child he had delivered into the world, literally with his own hands. But riddling his conscience was the overwhelming desire to banish Louisa from his life. Sometimes it was all he could do to keep from visiting on this sweet, innocent child the barely controlled fury he felt toward her father. And now her damnable sire had come back to Britain!

Alex stared moodily into the fire. At length, the house on Pall Mall settled into silence, and everyone but the Duke of Gordon drifted off to sleep.

Thousands of bystanders packed themselves tightly around the platforms hastily raised in honor of the candidates stumping the hustings near Covent Garden in the shadow of the parish church.

Jane peered through her carriage window at a blue banner proclaiming 'Fox and Liberty' that hung on one side of the square. She was pleased to note that the other party was well represented with another banner that proclaimed 'Pitt and Constitution'. She pointed it out proudly to Eglantine, Charlotte, Susan, Madelina, and Louisa, all of whom she had brought with her to enjoy the spectacle.

The banners said it all: this election of 1784 could be distilled to a question of balancing the rights of a few great and powerful governing families in Parliament, embodied in the candidacy of Charles Fox, against the age-old rights of the Crown *in consultation* with Parliament, a philosophy embraced by William Pitt, the Younger, and his famous father, the late Lord Chatham—not to mention King George III.

Even children Louisa's age knew that the House of Lords was made up of the first-born sons of aristocratic families—such as the fabulously wealthy Duke of Devonshire. The House of Commons was reserved mostly for those *other* sons of the ruling classes unlucky enough to have made their appearance in the world *after* their elder siblings. These men had to stand for election, all right, but bribes and inducements and tradition nearly guaranteed certain powerful families their accustomed places as supposedly "elected" officials of Great Britain.

But this election year was different, Jane mused, as the carriage rolled to a stop in the teeming street. Many of the members of the prospering middle class whom she could see from her coach window were mightily sick of aristocrats—whatever their birth order—lining their pockets with money from the Treasury. The hardworking milliners and mantua makers and wigmakers and apothecaries whose shops lined the city streets of Westminster admired their straitlaced king and queen, and had become deeply distressed by rumors of licentiousness among Fox and his circle, including the flamboyant Duchess of Devonshire and the disaffected Prince of Wales.

The twenty-two-year-old heir to the throne had long been estranged from his father. Thanks to his gambling binges, his mistresses, and his highly expensive tastes, he was gravely in need of capital with which to pay his enormous debts. Therefore the Prince, too, supported Fox's vision of an aristocratic monopoly with supremacy over his father, King George III—in return for the promise of more money deposited in his personal account.

Young Pitt, on the other hand, was untainted by the sort of financial and sexual excess associated with the Prince, Charles

Fox, Georgiana Cavendish, and their set. He called for reform of this stranglehold enjoyed by a few of the country's most powerful families. In ringing tones, he backed the constitutionally ordained *balance* between King and Parliament—or at least, he *said* that he did in brilliant speeches made to the benches.

Jane wrinkled her nose in disdain as she spied the olive-skinned, heavy-set figure of Charles Fox himself, holding forth from a platform near the front of the church. It was the Duchess of Devonshire who had been the first to call Fox the Eyebrow. Her nickname was certainly apt, Jane thought, noting how the man's brows knit in a single line of thick black hair across the broad expanse of his forehead. In stentorian tones, Fox accused King George III of obstructing Parliament's ability to act in the country's best interest.

"What absolute *twaddle*!" Jane exclaimed to her companions in the carriage. "That man grows worse each day of this contest! A *true* aristocrat supports King *and* Country—not just the interests of a narrow minority, bent solely on feathering its own nest! Where's Mr. Pitt? He should answer the scoundrel forthwith!"

"I'm sure he or somebody else will," Eglantine soothed, craning her neck to survey the burgeoning crowds clustered near the speaking platform.

Jane's lips set in a determined line as she cast a professional eye toward the crowd, which was listening inattentively to the caustic comments tossed off by Charles Fox. Votes would actually be cast today and throughout the month in the open air, first by a show of hands, and then every male householder would commit his choice to paper. Westminster was one of the few boroughs where Fox could not depend on patronage and intimidation alone to retain his seat.

Supporters of Fox and Pitt were yelling slogans at each other as another grand carriage, pulled by six horses bedecked with blue ribbons, careened around the corner. As soon as it halted in the square, an army of grand ladies spilled out into the grimy streets that peeled off from Covent Garden, London's great market for fresh produce.

" 'Tis the Duchess of Devonshire, to be sure!" Charlotte cried, pointing at the magnificently dressed woman.

"Why are they all wearing buff and blue, Mama?" Louisa asked curiously, as several other women descended from Georgiana Cavendish's grand equipage. "Are they in the army?"

"No, dearheart." She smiled fondly at her seven-year-old

daughter. "Those are the colors associated with Charles Fox and his party."

Pitt had felt the handling of the American War by previous ministers fraught with folly, but he remained a loyal supporter of the King. Fox and the Whigs showed their disrespect to the Crown by adopting the colors associated with the uniforms worn by the rebellious George Washington and his troops.

The Duchess of Devonshire was cheered by the crowd as she waved a friendly greeting to the throng. Jane was forced to admit that her rival was, indeed, exquisite: her face was a perfect oval; her alabaster skin, sparkling blue eyes, and even her teeth were arresting. Her glorious reddish blond hair was capped fetchingly by an enormous blue ruched bonnet. The duchess—reputed to have wagered and lost thousands of pounds recently in a single all-night game of faro—marched gaily up to the establishment of a registered voter and pounded on the door.

"I'll be bound if that's not her sister, Lady Duncannon, with her," Eglantine added in awe.

"*And* the Duchess of Portland," Jane murmured, staring at yet another fabulously adorned woman of fashion. She was also dressed in buff and blue. She shook hands with the enthusiastic throng crowding near her, who were delighted to have a brace of real, live duchesses in their midst.

"Ye dinna suppose the Prince himself will appear today in behalf of Fox?" Eglantine said worriedly.

" 'Tis a cool reception he'd get, to be sure, and he knows it, I'll warrant," Jane replied.

"Aye . . ." Eglantine mused thoughtfully. " 'Tis a pity he and the king are at such loggerheads. After all, they are father and son."

Through her open carriage window, Jane resumed surveying the progress of Georgiana Cavendish, who daintily trod up several steps of another shop and rapped sharply on a sagging front door.

"This kiss will seal your vote, kind sir!" Georgiana cried gaily, curtsying prettily to the burgher who, under normal circumstances, would be constrained to use the trade entrance at the fabulous Devonshire House in Picadilly.

"All right, lasses!" Jane announced with determination to the others in her carriage. "We have work to do. Out with ye and march directly into that food shop there!"

Jane emerged from her carriage and purposefully stood on its running step a moment, to give the crowd time to admire her white and gold gown and to recognize the fact that yet another duchess graced the neighborhood.

The Duchess of Devonshire glared at her when she spied Jane's entourage wading into the crowd and greeting the local constituents.

"Ho, worthy sir!" Jane hailed a chimney sweep passing by with several filthy brooms balanced against his stooped shoulders. "How fortunate that Westminster grants votes to all honest working men. I ask for yer vote for Mr. Hood, the candidate supporting William Pitt. Will ye give it?" she asked, boldly offering her gloved hand, and placing it in the sweep's paw, which was sprinkled with soot.

"A-aye, m'lady . . ." he stammered, nearly overcome by the shock of shaking hands with such a dazzling vision.

Cheers resounded as Jane and her party moved quickly to a shop where vegetables were displayed on low stalls outside the store. Out of the corner of her eye, she saw the Duchess of Devonshire pause on the opposite side of the street, clearly annoyed that Jane had dared to challenge her so directly in the pursuit of votes for Mr. Pitt.

"Good day to ye, sir," Jane called warmly to the vegetable vendor. "Have ye any fresh broccoli today?"

"Broccoli?" repeated the astonished shopkeeper, alternately eyeing Jane's and Georgiana's magnificent finery.

"Yes, broccoli," Jane repeated calmly to the merchant. "Have ye any today?"

"Why, yes, mum, I have some very fine broccoli," the wizened greengrocer said timidly. "If ye'd be so kind as to inspect it to yer satisfaction."

" 'Tis lovely, sir," Jane said, hardly glancing at the wilted vegetables. "Would five guineas be sufficient?"

Before the astonished shopkeeper could respond to such an outrageously high sum for a pound of tired produce, Jane had moved on to the tailor shop next door and was canvassing the wide-eyed owner who stood outside with a pincushion clamped on his arm.

"Be sure to give Mr. Pitt's man yer vote, winna ye, kind sir?" she called back quickly to the greengrocer before extending her hand to her next prey with a friendly "How d'ye do!" for Mr. Snickworth, Tailor and Mender, Ltd.

Across the street, the Duchess of Devonshire glanced at Jane sharply and squared her shoulders. She proceeded to march to the bake shop directly opposite the tailor's establishment. Within minutes, the beautiful Georgiana emerged bearing a basketful of sugar buns, which were quickly passed out to the worshipful crowd. As the throng eagerly accepted her offering, she cast a look of triumph in Jane's direction.

"I'll wager she paid a pretty pence for those!" Jane grumbled, and directed her own feminine army to head for the soap maker's shop on the corner.

From morning till the sun set along the back streets and alleyways of Westminster, the dazzling ladies of fashion personally petitioned the electorate, using every wile and trick they could conjure to procure votes for Fox, or the candidates who supported the popular William Pitt. Jane was pleased when, impulsively kissing a blacksmith on the cheek for the promise of his vote, she soon heard from the Cockney elector in the next arcade that her rival had immediately begun to mimic Jane's singular vote-getting technique by bussing a butcher.

"Lord, mum, 'twas a fine sight to see a grand lady come right up and smack us hardworking mortals with her cherry lips," the laborer chortled.

"And if I kiss ye, as well, which one will get yer vote? Fox, or Pitt's man, Mr. Hood?" she inquired mischievously.

"Why, the man what's supported by the last great lady to give an old sot like me such a lift in me old age," he answered slyly, lifting his cheek toward her for the expected peck.

Jane planted a chaste kiss on the old codger's weathered skin and grandly continued on her rounds of the Covent Garden neighborhood. Jane was more determined than ever to help defeat—or at least diminish the vote count—of the odious Fox in his own ward.

Moonlight was reflecting off the rooftops of the city by the time Jane's carriage returned to Pall Mall. Inside the coach, Madelina and Susan leaned against the plush upholstery, quietly reviewing the day's exciting events. It was long after the normal supper hour and Louisa had fallen asleep in the corner. Her dark red locks spread like fingers of fire across her sister Charlotte's shoulder. Charlotte herself was barely awake.

"We're home, darlings," Jane said, gently shaking them.

"Zooks! I'm exhausted," sighed Eglantine.

"Before we left this morning, I ordered a light meal to be sent up to yer rooms in three-quarters of an hour," Jane said, as they trudged up to the short flight of stone stairs to the front landing. "Ye'll all have lovely baths, then off to sleep!"

Marshall, the butler, opened the door, his face impassive, as always.

"His Grace waited dinner an hour for ye, m'lady," he said stiffly, "then departed to eat at his club."

"I distinctly left instructions with Mrs. Christie this morning that ye should inform the duke we would return by eight o'clock, so that he and I might sup together," she replied with annoyance. "Dinna ye say as much to the duke, Marshall?"

"Those instructions never reached me, yer ladyship," Marshall said with an innocence that made Jane immediately suspicious. During her almost seventeen years of marriage to Alex, his butler and his housekeeper had persisted in their absurd rivalry for Alex's time and attention. Such petty acts of sabotage as witholding her messages to her husband were commonplace.

"Well, then, thank ye, Marshall," she said evenly. "I trust our baths are ready. Or did Mrs. Christie not pass on those instructions, either?"

"Aye, of course, Yer Grace," Marshall replied, with a hint of the disdain the commonfolk and many aristocrats held toward those who practiced the self-indulgent, and probably dangerous, habit of bathing more than once every six weeks.

"That will be all," Jane retorted shortly, sweeping past him toward the stairs.

"Really," Eglantine agreed under her breath as Jane and her daughters reached the second-story landing. "That pair are the height of insolence!"

"That they are," Jane agreed with resignation. "Pay them no mind. But, blessings to all of ye," she added fondly, "and thank ye for lending yer support."

"Ye were truly a marvel today, sister mine," Eglantine said, brushing her lips against her Jane's cheek.

" 'Twas exciting to be part of it all, wasna it?" Jane smiled tiredly. "Sleep well."

Eglantine waited while her nieces trooped down the hallway to their rooms.

"Will ye wait up for Alex?" Eglantine said in as diplomatic a voice as she could muster.

"I imagine . . . for a while," Jane replied evasively.

"The other night," Eglantine ventured, "Alex seemed . . . perturbed, I think, to hear of Thomas's return. Is that why he's been in such a black mood lately, do ye suppose?"

"Aye," Jane said shortly. "But there seems to be no help for it. Goodnight, Eglantine,'' she added quickly, anxious to be done with the subject. "And, again, thank ye."

"What are sisters for?" Eglantine responded wryly, accepting her dismissal.

Within an hour, Jane had scrubbed the soot and grime of the streets of London from her skin and donned her cambric night-dress. As her two housemaids retreated, lugging the heavy copper bathtub between them, she pulled an upholstered chair near the fire and idly stabbed at her potted meat, bread, and cheese. This evening had ended like so many others of late. Once again she was eating alone, exhausted from her day's labors. Alex was off at his club. His *fortress*, was more like it, Jane thought gloomily.

Eating pensively, Jane marveled at the customs of London society in which a husband and wife, living in the same house, could go literally days without seeing more than a glimpse of each other. Yet, no outsider would consider anything amiss. With a sigh, Jane wondered if the reason she saw so little of Alex lately was because of her consuming involvement in politics—or whether she was so consumed by politics because she saw so little of her husband.

She stared into the fire, reflecting on the heady excitement of the campaign. She adored the challenge and thrill of being part of something more stimulating than sitting-room small talk. To think she had actually garnered votes for the premier minister of all of England! 'Twould be so much more enjoyable, she mused, if Alex shared her love of London and her passion for politics. Instead, she suspected that he saw the walls of Gordon Castle as a means of shutting them both away from that stimulating world.

Jane nibbled on a pungent slice of Stilton, its sea-green veins running through the ivory-colored cheese like babbling burns into the River Spey. She suddenly thought of Thomas, back in Scotland, wandering along the streams that flowed past his home village Struy. Jane felt a familiar restlessness invading her body. It was hard to believe he had now returned to Britain after eight years abroad! Perhaps his current legal tangle would bring him to the London Courts of Chancery . . . perhaps. . . .

"*No!*" she scolded herself aloud, jumping up from her chair suddenly and scattering the half-eaten cheese in all directions. As she was gathering up the spongy crumbs, there was a soft knock at her door.

"Alone?" Eglantine said, poking her head into the chamber.

"What on earth are ye doing?" she added, noting Jane was on her hands and knees.

"I spilled the deuced cheese!" Jane replied testily. "Yes, I'm alone."

"I dinna hear any carriage," Eglantine said, pulling another chair closer to the crackling fire. "Do ye fancy some company?"

Jane shrugged and then smiled, in spite of her moodiness. Eglantine pulled her wrap close to her body and tucked her feet under her as she sat down.

"Jenny . . ." she began cautiously. "Plain and simple . . . I've been sitting in my bedchamber, worrying about ye, lass. Worried that Thomas's coming back to Scotland has—"

"Made Alex irrationally jealous?" Jane interrupted shortly.

"Aye, it has," she confirmed grimly. "But, in case ye hadna noticed, Alex sees a rival in William Pitt as well. The only thing that would make my Duke of Gordon happy would be to insure his duchess never spoke to another man and was pliant, obedient, and breeding more bairns."

"Aren't ye being a wee bit harsh?" Eglantine said gently. "Forgive me for saying it, Jenny, but half of ye has always been wedded to the *fantasy* of Thomas Fraser. Alex is too intelligent a man not to sense this. His jealousy and black moods, I'll wager, mask a profound hurt."

" 'Tis not a matter of hurt . . ." Jane countered defensively. " 'Tis his notion of possession."

"Take care to hear what I'm saying," Eglantine urged, leaning forward in her chair. "Thomas's coming back from the dead was perhaps a bigger shock to Alex than to ye, who'd always held him safe in yer heart. I think Alex feels the love he bears ye is not *enough* in yer eyes . . . and when he sees how infatuated young Pitt is with ye, perhaps it brings to mind the ghost of his old rival. Now that Thomas has actually returned to Scotland, Alex saw for himself how affected ye were by the news. We all saw it, even Hamilton. Alex may be possessive, Jenny, but he loves you in the same, blind way he loved Bathia Largue. Believe me, there are many lasses who would gladly take yer place."

"But that kind of love leaves no room to breathe . . . to have one's own interests or plot one's own course in life."

"Ye're right . . . Alex is a difficult, demanding man," Eglantine agreed. "But ye married him, ye had six bairns by him, and now . . ." Her voice trailed off as she was puzzled to see a stricken look pass over Jane's features at her mention of the children. Rather than questioning her, Eglantine took Jane's right hand and held it gently. "Ye lost part of yer forefinger, but ye still have yer hand. Ye lost Thomas to an accident of fate, but ye still have the rest of yer *life* . . . and Alex is a part of that life! Dinna risk the happiness that's right in front of ye, Jane," Eglantine said simply. "Mayhap I see this more clearly than ye do. Compare Alex to that sod *I* married!"

Jane heaved a sigh and smiled wanly.

"It canna be easy for Alex, I'll admit that," Jane said dejectedly, thinking of a crucial factor that Eglantine didn't know: Louisa's true parentage. "What a muddle 'tis all become . . ." she sighed.

Both women were startled by the sound of the front door slamming and footsteps taking the stairs, two at a time. There was a sharp knock at the door before it flew open and crashed against the chamber wall. Suddenly, Alex filled the doorframe, holding a newspaper wadded into his hand.

"You've not seen this, I suppose!" he growled, ignoring Eglantine's presence in his wife's bedchamber and stomping across the Persian carpet. He threw the paper into Jane's lap.

Jane's heart thudded in her chest while she studied a pointed, but rather amusing cartoon depicting two gorgeously dressed duchesses offering pecks on the cheeks to a butcher, a baker, and a candlestick maker. The caption read, "Consorting with the Ton."

After a moment, Jane threw her head back and laughed, rather pleased that the part women had played in the current election had garnered such attention, for a change. Even Eglantine was repressing a smile.

"Alex, 'tis perfectly harmless," Jane chuckled.

" 'Tis certainly less offensive than the one with Her Grace *mounted* on a fox—backwards, no less!" Eglantine allowed cheerfully. She appraised Alex's glowering countenance. "But, pray, excuse me, ye two. I'm utterly fashed by today's excursion. I bid ye both goodnight." She squeezed Jane's hand and impulsively kissed her brother-in-law's flushed cheek.

Alex paced in front of Jane's four-poster until Eglantine had shut the door and her footsteps receded down the passageway.

"Strumpet!" he snapped at Jane, his hands clenched by his sides.

"Oh, do stop being so silly!" she retorted angrily.

The sound of the clock on the mantel chiming eleven bells pierced the highly charged atmosphere.

"I am not a strumpet, or a whore, or a wanton," Jane said finally, rising from her chair. "I have not slept with William Pitt . . . or even the butcher, the baker, or the candlestick maker. Now, please come sit down, Alex. I need to say many things to ye."

"Aye, perhaps you've not slept with that young pup," he said, looking at her speculatively. His eyes narrowed slightly as he gazed at her, the firelight silhouetting the outlines of her body beneath the sheerness of her cambric bed gown. "But ye're not entirely blameless, are ye, my dear? There's the matter of a certain *Captain*, 'tisn't there?" he continued bitterly. "Our darling little redhead speaks to that point pretty well, doesn't she, Jane?"

Jane remained silent for a moment, and then walked quietly toward him and embraced him without responding to his bitter words. His arms remained rigidly against his sides. Jane continued to hold him gently. Then she stood on tiptoe and kissed his neck.

"Alex . . . let's not argue, or use Louisa to hurt each other," she said softly. "Please . . . please stay with me tonight," she whispered, unbuttoning the fastenings of her nightdress. The thin material fell away from her throat.

A dark swath of Alex's disheveled hair cast a shadow across his forehead. He stared at her uncertainly. She speculated that her husband had drunk a fair quantity of brandy, but he wasn't in his cups. Or at least, she didn't think he was. Her calm reaction to his insult and her frank invitation had completely unsettled him. She flashed him a warm smile, and then reached for his hand. Silently, she led him toward their four-poster, which he had slept in only rarely, of late. He stared at her and then pulled at his knotted neck linen.

"I'll bed you, wench," he growled, "but I won't make love to you."

"Ye'll make love to me, or nothing else!" Jane cried sharply, her dark eyes glittering angrily. Alex hesitated. His hands now merely fingered his cravat tied neatly around his throat. "Ye'll not be crushing my bones like ye did at Culloden House!" she exclaimed. "Ye *swore* ye'd never do that again!" She caught his sleeve and stared up at him with a look that was pleading and demanding at once. " 'Tis time we *stopped* wishing for what isna to be ours! I *loved* Thomas, but I—"

"You *still* love him and always will!" Alex interrupted fiercely, his voice betraying an anguish he rarely revealed.

"I canna help that, Alex," Jane blurted, "but, as God is my witness, I love ye too! I care terribly what happens to ye, and I adore the children—yer George, my George, the lassies. . . . We've built a *life*! I want us to be *happy* together—"

"But don't you see, Jane? I *can't* be happy if you love another man," Alex protested wearily. " 'Tis as simple as that. Every time I see Louisa, I'm reminded of that love you still bear Thomas Fraser."

"And what about the elder George?" she countered quickly. "What if each time I laid my eyes upon Bathia's son these last seventeen years, I raved and drove myself into a fury, as ye've done?"

"Bathia's been *dead* for nearly twenty years now!" he shot back defensively, sitting on the bed with his back to her.

"And can ye honestly say ye dinna still love her . . . love the sweet memories . . . love the goodness of her . . . love her son?" Jane inquired softly. "The fondness ye bear her never diminished the love ye offered me all these years."

"Bathia's dead," he repeated hoarsely. "Thomas is alive."

"He's been *absent* from our lives for a decade, Alex!" Jane said urgently.

"He's *in* this country now," he countered. "He has only to appear and you'll—"

His shoulders sagged in defeat.

"I'm yer wife, Alex. If ye'd treat me as if that pleased ye, ye'd have less to fear on that score," Jane replied heatedly. Her chin jutted forward in the air. "And, besides, Thomas winna be here for long, it seems." Alex didn't reply. "To me, he might as well be dead, Alex," she said softly. "He has done what I'm trying to do. He's moved on in his life."

"But you and I are like two strangers, these days," Alex said, turning his head to glance at her briefly. " 'Tis *more* than just Thomas—I can see that now. 'Tis the old story of the City Mouse and the Country Mouse." His sad, sardonic smile made her wonder if the two of them could ever find a common path. "All this hubbub concerning the elections," he added. " 'Tis one pack of jackals pitted against another, as far as I can see. I can't think why you want to be a part of it."

"Dinna ye see a *difference* between Pitt and Fox!" Jane demanded incredulously. "Between our king and his dissolute son? Can ye imagine what 'twould be like for the nation if that impudent puppy wore the crown or his retinue had the entire nation under their thumbs?"

"Actually, I don't see much difference between Whig and Tory," Alex said shortly. "And, besides, it appears to me that you merely enjoy being in the center of things, like that bankrupt harlot, Georgiana Cavendish, with whom your name is now linked. At the club tonight I was told that, as a last resort to support her failing credit, she has opened a faro table at Devonshire House!"

"Her unhealthy passion for gambling has nothing to do with me, nor is it the reason I take such an interest in politics," Jane retorted. "I enjoy the conversation and wit of men like Pitt. I find affairs of state stimulating. Ye have yer club," she argued, trying to make him understand. "Ye canna imagine, I assure ye, how deadly dull is the tittle-tattle with which most women occupy themselves."

He didn't reply. She stared at him in frustration and he gazed back at her, apparently unmoved by her words.

A thought suddenly struck her. Perhaps if she showed Alex that she honestly was trying to see their dilemma from *his* perspective, he would do more to see it from hers.

"Once the election is over," Jane ventured, "we'll have all summer to spend together at Gordon Castle." She sat beside him on the bed. "Pitt will win a majority, I'm sure, even if Fox survives the count in his home territory of Westminster. And we could stay north through the Fall Shoot. . . ."

She fought the twinge of regret she felt momentarily, as she recalled the exhilarating success of her soiree the previous evening and her bold actions earlier at Covent Garden. But these were just the kinds of events that always seemed to come between Alex and her. She reflected on the evening's conversation with Eglantine.

Ye married him and had six children by the man. . . .

Well, not quite, Jane thought ruefully. But they had shared much history these tumultuous years. She reached toward Alex and lightly touched the nape of his neck with her scarred hand.

"My job is finished here," she said, swallowing hard. "I'd like us to be together—*really* together."

"Am I correct in assuming you're unwilling to stay on during the winter in Fochabers?" he said, his lips pursed in a tight line. "After the life you've made for yourself in London, I suppose you'd be miserable rattling around in Gordon Castle."

Alex was right, Jane thought morosely. A bleak, Highland winter with the likes of Marshall and the dour Mrs. Christie for company, and she'd go mad. Besides, she couldn't shut up a sixteen-year-old like Charlotte, just when she should be going to parties and assemblies, to meet a man she could love—and marry. Jane wrinkled her forehead pensively. She stood up from the bed and walked over to the fire, poking the embers with a brass pike.

"What if the City Lass and the Country Lad struck a compromise, Alex?" she coaxed, setting the andiron in its metal holder with a decisive thrust. "What if we took a house for the winter season in Edinburgh? After this London whirl, 'twill seem like a small village to us both!"

"I doubt that—"

"God's wounds, Alex!" she exploded. "I canna be the *only* one to compromise!" she cried. "If I'm willing to give up London . . . please . . . at least let's try life in Edinburgh this winter!"

Alex swiveled his body on the edge of the bed to scan her face. His gaze swept the length of her thinly clad form standing in front of the fire. Warily, he rose from the bed and walked toward her. She stared back at him, wondering, in that instant, what path her life would be taking from now on. An excruciating sense of relief enveloped her as Alex's arms tightened around her back.

After a few moments, her shoulders began to tremble. She was astonished to find herself crying.

"Jane . . . shhh . . . 'tis all right, dearheart," he soothed. "Edinburgh's a lovely idea, darling . . . shh. . . ."

"Please, Alex!" she whispered brokenly against his chest, "let us make peace with one another." Tears glazed her luminous brown eyes as she drew away from him to look questioningly into his face. " 'Tis a debt owed each of us that's long past due."

"Peace . . ." he murmured, as he took her in his arms.

25

January 1786

Intermittent snow flurries scratched at the windows of the townhouse on George Square as the temperature outside continued to plummet. Snow-laden clouds scudded across a full moon whose radiance cast an eerie glow over Edinburgh's rooftops. A piercing wind blew up from the port of Leith, promising the city even more frigid weather in the coming days.

Jane exited from her bedchamber and briskly headed down the hallway of their rented townhouse, tying the ribbons of her scarlet woolen cloak under her chin as she walked. The garment's cowl-like hood settled on her shoulders with comforting warmth, thanks to fabric, which had been double-milled to make it more weatherproof. A door opened into the passageway, and her five daughters rushed toward her excitedly.

"Ohh . . . Mama," cried Charlotte, who took note of every thread of clothing her fashionable mother wore. "Your cloak is magnificent!"

" 'Twas a lovely gift from yer da," Jane said with a smile, allowing herself to be pulled into her older girls' suite of rooms situated across from the nursery. "Yer brother Lord Huntly placed the order on his way back to Cambridge last fall. Now then," she said with mock sternness. "Have ye all been studying yer French? Monsieur Varney will be drilling ye on yer verbs this Monday, and I want ye all to do splendidly."

"Aye, Mama," nine-year-old Louisa said sincerely. "*Je t'aime, Mama!*"

Madelina, thirteen, and Susan, almost twelve, giggled and poked their younger sister in the ribs.

"*Nous aimerons Papa!*"

"Where *is* Papa?" demanded four-year-old Georgina. "I want to see Papa!"

"He's with little Alexander, I expect," Jane said soothingly. Her youngest daughter had not taken kindly to the male rival who had made his appearance at seven pounds in the nursery the previous November.

"He's *always* with baby Alex," Georgina pouted. "He likes him better than us."

"Why, nonsense!" Jane said, taken aback by the child's brutal frankness.

"He does, Mama," said Louisa quietly. " 'Tis the truth."

"Now, I winna have ye say such things!" Jane admonished sharply. "Of course yer Papa loves ye . . . 'tis just that he's so delighted with a second son. Now, let's not hear another word of such trumpery!" She turned toward her eldest child. "Charlotte, I think this blustery night calls for hot chocolate and some cake, dinna ye? Have Nancy tell Cook ye can all have yer own little fete while Papa and I are at our party. Would ye like that?"

"Yes . . . oh, yes!" came the chorus, except for Louisa, who remained silent and stepped closer to Jane.

"I must just look in on the bairn," Jane said, trying to appear more cheerful than she felt. "Good night, my darlings," she added, squeezing Louisa's hand lovingly, to show her she was not really angry for her daughter's honest words. The lass had grown four inches in a single year and was going to be tall, like the father she had never met. Forcing a smile to her lips, Jane blew them all a kiss. "I'll tell ye all about the dancing on the morrow."

Approaching the nursery door, Jane paused to listen to the sounds of a baby's gurgle, overridden by a deep male voice speaking in childish, singsong tones.

"There, there, laddie . . . 'tis time for wee ones to be asleep . . . there, there. . . ."

Nancy Christie, who had grown into a scrawny but kindly version of her mother, the formidable housekeeper, smiled knowingly at Jane as she entered the chamber, as if to say, *Have ye ever seen the likes o' it? The Duke's besotted with this babe!*

"Alex, we'll be late," Jane whispered loudly. Her husband cut an elegant figure in a new, grape-colored coat studded with large onyx buttons. Nevertheless, he was holding a tiny bundle swaddled in a thin woolen blanket against his broad shoulder. "If ye put Alexander in his cradle, he'll go right off to sleep . . . I'm sure he will. If we tarry much longer, there winna be an oyster left!"

"He seemed a bit fussy after you fed him," Alex replied, as if he hadn't heard a word she'd said. Gently, he patted the tiny back of the two-month-old. "I wonder—"

A loud belch interrupted his words. The adults, including Nancy, the nursemaid, laughed at the infant's indiscretion.

"There's yer answer," Jane smiled. "Now put him down, and let's be off! 'Tis my first evening out since the babe was born, and I intend eating at least three dozen of Lucky Middlemass's *best*, before I'm through!"

Within ten minutes, the Duke of Gordon's gold-crested black carriage was bumping along Nicholson Road in the direction of Edinburgh's most popular oyster cellar. Oyster parties were held in a variety of Edinburgh taverns that specialized in serving raw oysters from the Firth of Forth, and hearty porter or ale with which to wash them down. Jane had missed many such convivial gatherings this past winter, due to her recent lying-in.

There had been times during the past two years when Jane had longed to be in London once again, but she loved the special flavor of Edinburgh social life at watering holes such as the oyster houses, where ladies took part in the revelry without restraint. She was especially fond of the custom afterward of clearing out the tables at these unique taverns for some spirited country dancing.

The coach began to rock alarmingly as the two of them continued up Nicholson Road. Jane held on even more tightly to the leather strap as the carriage swayed and dipped among gigantic potholes. The thoroughfare was in a sorry state, due to the construction in progress on the new South Bridge, which crossed the High Street. In the last year, Jane had been struck by the significant changes in the old town that had taken place since her girlhood in Edinburgh. North Loch, the scene of poor Matilda Sinclair's drowning, had been completely drained, and a park laid out where the old tannery had once stood. North Bridge, along the lake's former banks, led off the High Street to the New Town, where speculators had been building row after row of townhouses according to the designs of Robert Adam. Even their own house, on George Square, south of the Royal Mile, was in one of the new residential areas that had been developed outside the old city walls.

"I dinna know whether to think of tonight's party at Lucky's as a celebration or a wake," Jane mused aloud, staring at the snow swirling outside the coach. " 'Tis hard to believe, after all these years, that they'll soon be tearing down Lucky Middlemass's Tavern to build South Bridge. 'Tis a shame, really."

"Never fear, Jane, darling, there are lots of oyster houses still in the town," Alex teased her. "I shall be sure you never want for them. They always seem to work such potent magic upon your affections. . . ." He leaned toward her, brushing his lips on the sensitive skin below her ear lobe.

" 'Tis the porter *you* drink with them, ye impertinent wretch!" she retorted with feigned indignation. "It makes ye feel ye're a randy lad of eighteen again."

Alex slipped his hands inside her scarlet hood and cupped his wife's face. He kissed her slowly, inserting his tongue between her lips in a not-so-subtle attempt to arouse her ardor.

"We're not doing too badly for middle-aged lovers, are we, Jane?" he whispered. One hand had drifted down to her engorged breasts, which strained against the bodice of her claret-colored velvet gown. She was nursing little Alexander, and felt that if Alex didn't curtail his actions, his mere touch would summon milk to her bosom in a moment. As it was, a familiar throbbing sensation coursed through her.

"Imagine . . . a baby at our age," she murmured mockingly. Despite her better judgment, she welcomed the pulsing stimulation suddenly resonating through her highly sensitive nipples.

"I'm sure people thought 'twas most unseemly," Alex mumbled, nibbling at her ear.

"It *was* unseemly," she laughed, pushing him away from her half-heartedly.

"That's what made it all so wonderful," Alex said, suddenly serious. He stared at her with an intensity that made her unaccountably ill-at-ease. "I want another bairn . . . as many as we can have! You've never looked more beautiful, Jane."

"Nor so exhausted," she chided lightly. "I havna done a thing for two months but sleep, nurse, and tend to little Alexander."

"But isn't that why you're such a capital mum?" he said with a wary smile.

Jane glanced at him briefly, and then stared out the coach window. The snow was falling more heavily now as the carriage drew to a halt in front of Lucky Middlemass's Tavern. The veil of white all but obscured the brilliant full moon overhead.

"Alex," she said gently, taking his hand. "I love the babe very much, and I'm very glad we had him, but I'm thirty-seven . . . 'twas a difficult birth. . . ." Her chin rose in a small sign of defiance. "I have borne *seven* children, Alex . . . and I love them *all*. But there is more to my life than the world of the nursery. . . ."

"I thought you were pleased, as I was . . ." he said slowly, averting his eyes.

"I am," she said quietly. "But the doctor says there's likely to be no more bairns . . . ye know that."

" 'Tis not impossible—" he began.

" 'Tis *unlikely*, though," she overrode him. "And, to tell ye the truth, I'm not sorry about it." She took his right hand in hers and forced him to look at her. " 'Tis useless to think we'll be happy together only if I am occupied solely with the children. We must share more than that, as the years go on. I have a *mind*, as *ye* have, and I need the diversions of books and music and good conversation, just as *ye* do."

The carriage door was snapped open by a footman dressed in the Gordons' red and white livery, but Alex didn't stir from his seat. He stared moodily past the velvet curtains at the snow swirling at the window.

"Come now, m'lord," Jane said with as much cheer as she could muster. "Let us repair to our friends—and our oysters."

The footman assisted Jane down from the coach. The snow stung her cheeks and she drew her cloak tightly to her. Still subdued, Alex stared straight ahead as he took her arm and they proceeded down the steps to the smoke-filled oyster cellar. A familiar figure, slightly more stooped than in years past, approached them jovially, his arms outstretched.

"Ah . . . Alex . . . and Jane!" he exclaimed. "How delightful, my dear, to have ye amongst our company once again."

"Charles Gordon!" Jane exclaimed to Alex's lawyer and man of business in Edinburgh. "How could we forego a party given in our honor by the very man whose good offices introduced me to His Grace? I trust no unruly students of the medical or legal professions have been invited tonight?" she teased, recalling that tumultuous evening, nearly twenty years earlier, when Charles had given a ridotto in Alex's honor that had ended in a riot of bun-slinging at the Canongate Playhouse.

"No, my guest list is confined to old reprobates, like myself—too full of lumbago these days to cause a riot. But," he laughed mischievously, "ye two are quite the pair! How is the newest Master Gordon?" he inquired.

"The spitting image of his namesake, and just as demanding," Jane replied, looking pointedly at Alex. "That's why I insisted on calling him Alexander."

"Good evening, Charles," Alex said quietly. His tone contrasted markedly with the cheerful timbre of Jane's voice. " 'Tis good to see you again. I spy the Earl of Glencairn over there . . . if you'll both excuse me a moment. . . ."

Jane stared thoughtfully at Alex's retreating back until a host of friends crowded around her, celebrating her appearance after so long an absence. She chatted briefly with Ian Dalrymple, an Ayrshire man who hailed from a village not far from her birthplace of Monreith. Their lively discussion about Freemasonry and the clever rhymes of a local poet he knew there named Robert Burns was soon augmented by the presence of William Creech, the eminent publisher who had, in his youth, been tutor to the Earl of Glencairn. Soon, Glencairn's relative, the Earl of Buchan joined their circle, followed by his brother, Harry Erskine, a relative of the man who had so ably defended Lord George after the Gordon Riots. It was a lively, stimulating crowd, and Jane found herself quickly pushing to the back of her mind Alex's sudden attack of ill-humor.

The low-ceilinged room was suitably cozy for the cellar that it was, illuminated only by tallow candles on the walls, which cast their glow on huge dishes piled high with plump, raw oysters. The mountainous plates of seafood and jugs of porter sat on coarse round tables.

"Dinna ye miss the gay life in London, Yer Grace?" Charles inquired, a trickle of broth running down his chin.

"Only when I dinna have such marvelous evenings as this to look forward to," Jane answered sincerely, sliding a succulent oyster into her mouth. " 'Tis a lovely gathering, Charles. Thank ye so much for arranging it."

"My pleasure, m'lady . . . my pleasure," he chuckled, visibly pleased by her compliment. He quickly returned one of his own. "From what I hear, ye're certainly missed in London after Pitt's great triumph in the elections. The M.P. from Penicuik told me yer admirer, Mr. Pitt, asks after ye whenever he sees the man. He wants to know if ye'll ever grace a salon there again. Says he's been forced to press his sister into service as his hostess in yer stead, but now she's engaged to marry and will leave him soon. He wants ye to hurry back."

"How kind . . ." Jane murmured, aware that Alex, who'd taken his seat on Charles's left, was within earshot of them. "But perhaps Mr. Pitt will marry soon?" she suggested pointedly.

"Not if he canna find the likes of ye to wed," Charles replied. Jane knew full well he meant only to compliment her once again, but, as a result of Charles's words, Alex's features had composed themselves into a kind of impassive sculpture.

A jolly-looking, rotund fiddler, his violin in one hand and a bow in the other, entered the room with a theatrical flourish.

Immediately, the guests—who'd had more than their fill of oysters—jumped up to help the staff remove the tables and chairs to the sidelines to prepare for dancing.

"I've secured Neil Gow for this evening's entertainment," Charles Gordon said, a note of pride creeping into his voice.

Gow was fast gaining a reputation as one of the premier fiddlers and composers of Scotland. In fact, he rarely entertained in oyster cellars any more, preferring the more lucrative engagements at private parties in the newly built homes across town when he visited Edinburgh from his little village of Inver.

"How absolutely wonderful!" Jane exclaimed. "Alex! Ye've so admired Neil Gow's work. How lovely we're to dance to him tonight. Charles . . . this is really too kind of ye!"

"Nonsense!" their old friend said, embarrassed, but more pleased than ever. " 'Tis so good to see ye both again, and in such good spirits!"

Spirits indeed! Jane glanced over at the unfathomable mask enveloping Alex's features. *He's only happy when I am a prisoner of hearth and home,* she thought irritably. *Any man who seems a friend of mine is suddenly a rival in his mind. 'Tis ridiculous!*

Jane was forced to acknowledge that in recent weeks, Alex's mood had grown more anxious and wary as she had recovered her strength and returned to a normal life. The more he tried to fence her in with remarks about having more babies, the more she longed for evenings such as this—with good friends, good food, and good conversation.

Why does it all worry him so? she asked herself for the hundredth time.

She didn't devote any more thoughts to such unanswerable questions. By this time, Neil Gow had struck up "Captain MacIntosh" on his fiddle, and the entire company set to dancing. Soon, patrons from the tavern on the street level filtered downstairs to observe the fun, attracted by the sprightly music and the opportunity to see some of Edinburgh's leading social lights cavorting gaily around the chamber. Jane felt exhilarated dancing to the jigs and reels that followed one after the other. Everyone but her husband was vying to be her partner.

Alex lounged against the far wall, speaking to no one. He only danced if a friend of long-standing, such as the nimble Dowager Countess of Glencairn, dragged him onto the floor. Jane noticed that he would thank his partner politely when the music ended, but then did not seek out another. Rather, he would return to the darkest corner he could find and survey the scene with hooded, brooding eyes.

At length, there was a pause for Neil Gow to rest and refresh himself with a tankard of porter. The fiddler went out the low-linteled door, which led up the stairs to Cowgate, for a breath of air.

"I think we should be going, Jane," Alex said in a low voice as he appeared suddenly by her side. "The bairn will wish to be fed and—"

"I saw to that before we left," Jane whispered back, trying to keep the irritation out of her voice. "I expelled some milk into a brass-nippled cup. Nancy will already have fed the lad. Please, Alex . . . let us stay. Be my partner for "The Nymph." 'Tis been so long since we've danced together."

"I can see you've plenty of partners," he replied curtly. "I find the smoke in this place insufferable. As you wish . . . I shall ask Charles Gordon to see you home."

Before Jane could protest, he strode away from her and stopped to confer briefly with his man of business. Charles shot a startled look in Jane's direction and nodded. Then, without a backward glance, the Duke of Gordon lifted his cloak off the peg next to Jane's crimson one, and flung open the cellar door. Her husband had taken a few steps, when he froze, as if the mighty winds off the Firth of Forth had turned him into a glacier.

An enormous, broad-shouldered figure stooped low to cross the doorframe, his head and body covered by a mantle of snow. With a sweeping, fluid gesture, the stranger divested himself of his cloak, and shook his head like a border collie emerging from a stream.

Jane gasped aloud. The man's white hair turned the color of port wine as the snow quickly evaporated in the warm air permeating the stuffy room. The newcomer headed immediately toward the table offering rum punch near the spot where Alex had abandoned Jane. He nearly bumped into the Duke of Gordon, who stood rooted to the floor.

The two men stared silently at each other for what seemed to Jane to be an eternity. She approached the pair, terrified at what might happen next. Fortunately, the lively chatter and general hubbub in the cellar muffled their exchange.

"Why Captain Fraser," Alex said at last, "I made a wager with myself 'twould only be a matter of time before you tipped up. I'd heard rumors you and your Edinburgh counselors still wrangle in the courts over Simon Fraser's will."

"Yer Grace," Thomas greeted him stiffly, his eyes sweeping the room.

"Aye, she's here," Alex growled, "behind you."

Thomas whirled around. As Jane and Thomas saw each other, amazement, joy, and dismay flashed across their features in rapid succession.

"Believe me," Thomas said in a low voice, turning back to address Alex, "I had no idea ye'd be here."

"Oh, I believe you," Alex said caustically, glancing beyond Thomas's broad shoulders to stare at his wife's stricken countenance. "Jane, are you coming home now, or would you prefer to spend some time catching up with your old acquaintance? No doubt, you have some rather important news to impart to the Captain, here."

Jane could only stare at the two men in shock. Alex hesitated a moment, waiting for her to speak, and then abruptly turned toward the door Thomas Fraser had just entered. He stalked up the stairs and into the street, his figure soon disappearing into the opaque veil of snow whirling around his waiting carriage.

The frolicking strains of "The Nymph" quickly set the Middlemass crowd to dancing once again. The publisher, William Creech, suddenly appeared by Jane's side.

"Yer Grace," he said, staring curiously at the tall stranger standing next to the Duchess of Gordon. "I do believe we're promised for this one."

In a daze, Jane allowed the portly gentleman to lead her onto the floor. She executed the dance's complicated steps like a wooden marionette. As soon as the dance concluded, Thomas came across the smoke-filled chamber.

This is a dream, she thought wildly, watching him walk toward her. *This is not actually happening!*

But it *was* happening. Few people present in the room would remember a garnet-haired lad from the Highlands who was given up as dead some twenty years before.

Charles Gordon remembered, though. A look of surprise and concern etched the features of the Gordon family solicitor as he observed Thomas Fraser striding across the room. He saw the veteran of the ill-fated American War nod rather grimly at William Creech before taking the hand of the Duchess of Gordon as if it were his, alone, to possess.

"Yer Grace," Charles heard Fraser say formally to the guest of honor. " 'Tis so good to see ye after this long while."

Thomas's woolen breeches looked worn, and the cuffs of his

dark green coat had been turned and restitched in an attempt to disguise how threadbare they'd become. Nevertheless, the man's enormous height and proud bearing gave him the appearance of the aristocrat he should have been, and made him quite the equal of the beautiful woman whom he addressed.

"May I have the honor of the next dance?" he continued in a strong, clear voice. " 'Tis "The Nightcap Reel," if memory serves. I will be the luckiest of men, if I have the pleasure of the evening's last tune."

Charles saw that Jane did not exchange a word with her new dancing partner, but allowed Thomas to lead her to the bottom of the set, where the low-burning candles cast murky shadows on the wooden floor planks.

As the crowd serpentined around the room, Charles soon lost sight of the singularly handsome couple. At the conclusion of the dance, many of the guests seemed reluctant to call a halt to such an enjoyable evening. They continued to chat with friends who lingered near the smoking hearth, sipping the dregs of the rum punch, long after Neil Gow had packed his fiddle in its case and departed up the steep stairway to the street. With a feeling of foreboding, the host of the eminently successful oyster party noticed that the scarlet hooded cloak was missing from its peg, and the woman he had promised to escort home was no longer in the room.

"Where are ye taking me!" Jane shouted into the snow swirling around Thomas's shoulders. He pulled her by her gloved hand along Cowgate and darted up a narrow alley she guessed to be Middle Close. "I must go home!"

Thomas spun around and caught her in his arms, his flowing black cape enveloping her own red one.

"No!" he shouted at her, snowflakes clinging to his eyebrows, his breath visible in the frigid night air. He stared down at her face which was framed within its scarlet hood, and, like a man with a desperate thirst, crushed his lips to hers.

His skin was cool and dusted with flecks of snow, but his passionate kiss infused her with an incandescent warmth that left her breathless. Finally, Jane and Thomas pulled their lips apart.

"Oh, God, Jenny," he whispered hoarsely. " 'Tis like a *dream*, my seein' ye so. . . ."

Without waiting for her reply, he kissed her again, slowly and without his previous anxiety that she might disappear into the snowy night.

"Come," he murmured into her hair, clutching her hand in his.

They covered the short distance to the High Street and ducked through a wooden gate set into a thick stone wall. The neglected patch of land backing up to the late Simon Fraser's abandoned townhouse was strewn with broken carriage wheels. In one corner stood an animal pen long since devoid of chickens. They entered the five-story tenement through the back door, the bottom hinges of which pulled away from the wall.

"Mind the loose steps," Thomas warned as he led her up four rickety flights to a small gambrel-roofed room at the top of the house. He quickly struck a flint and lit a small candle resting on a table next to a narrow bed. Patches of damp and mold dotted the walls. Jane shivered, despite her cloak. Thomas poured each of them a brandy from a dented silver flask, which he then tucked away in a saddlebag flung over the single chair standing in the corner of the bleak chamber. He set the glasses next to the candlestick.

" 'Tis dreadfully cold in here," he apologized, his eyes searching her face. "Keep yer cape around yer shoulders and drink this," he urged, seating her gently on the bed and handing her a glass with a small crack on its lip.

He removed his own black cloak and wrapped it around her legs for extra warmth. Silence hung heavily in the frigid air.

Ten years! Her mind whirled. It had been *ten years* since she'd last laid eyes on Thomas Fraser of Struy! And suddenly, there he was, amidst the smoke and din at Lucky Middlemass's oyster cellar. The next thing she knew, they were dancing "The Nightcap Reel," and then he was pulling her down the road in a snowstorm like some mad Highlander, without so much as a by-your-leave or explanation after a decade of utter silence! Anger flooded through every pore of her body as she jumped to her feet, flinging Thomas's cloak to the floor.

"What in the world do ye think ye're doing, dragging me here?" she said in a low, smoldering voice. "Not a word . . . not one letter . . . not a message have I received in *ten years*, Thomas Fraser! And ye think a few kisses will mend it all!" She was shouting now and trembling from head to foot. "We're past kisses, and soulful glances, and looks of regret! *Ten years!*" she shouted and headed for the door.

Thomas's long arm caught her elbow and yanked her back. He was staring at her strangely, as if working out a puzzle in his

head. His eyes glinted with a flash of anger that seemed equal to
her own.

"I'll tell ye why I've been remiss, *Duchess*!" he said acidly.
"Ye've been a mite busy yerself these ten years. Let's see . . .
after our Louisa was born, ye had another child. *Georgina*, 'tisna
that her name?"

Jane stared at Thomas, speechless to realize that he had apparently deduced long ago that her fifth-born child was fathered by
him.

"Louisa's sister must be nearly five years old by now," he
continued, jaw clenched. "Spawned by yer duke about the time
the Seventy-first Fraser Highlanders were routed at the Battle of
Cowpens in the autumn of Eighty." His eyes dilated slightly and
his voice lowered to a growl. "And now, yet a *new* bairn has
made his appearance, I'm told," he jeered. "The Duke of
Gordon's bed hasna' been so *cold* these ten years, has it, hinny?"
His words were laced with sarcasm. "And ye're quite the heart-
breaker in London town, Ham told me. 'Tis hard to fathom that
Jenny of Monreith, who tore down placards on the day fat
Geordie was crowned, is now the darling of the Court. 'Tis true,
though, 'tisna it? Even Mr. Pitt is still a bachelor like me—
pining away for what he canna have. Quite the little tease, aren't
ye, *Duchess*!"

The pair glared at each other for a long moment. Jane's gloved
hand stung like nettles as she slapped Thomas across the face as
hard as she could. Her breathing was ragged, and she tried
desperately to swallow her rage at the cruelty of his words. She
bit her lip, staring at the red streaks she'd slashed across his
cheek. The angry marks paralleled the scar cut by Mingo Indians
when Thomas was nineteen years old. The white line slicing
across the plane of his gaunt cheekbones swam before her eyes.
Her shoulders started to tremble and uncontrollable sobs wracked
her body. She covered her face with her hands and sank to her
knees. Her cloak, like a pool of blood, fanned out around her.

"Oh, God, Jenny, forgive me . . ." Thomas exclaimed, resting his hand on her heaving shoulder. " 'Tis just that I swore to
m'self I'd never see ye again . . . never try to find ye . . . and
then, there ye were . . . so beautiful in yer velvet finery. There
ye were, *right before my eyes,* dancing and smiling, and looking
every inch the grand duchess ye've become. 'Twas as if everything we'd suffered dinna count a farthing to ye. . . ."

The hood of Jane's cloak completely shielded her face from
his view. Slowly, she looked up at him.

"And what of *yer* betrayal of the dream . . . for that's all it's become," she said in a voice so low he had to strain to hear her. "Hamilton told us of the Widow Boyd and yer plans to solve yer troubles with Simon's will by marrying her. He described to us how *heartily* ye enjoyed serving yer time after the war in a comfortable prison called Antrim Hall."

"There's been nothing comfortable about the last twenty years of wantin' ye for my wife," Thomas replied dully, sinking to his knees beside her. "When I found myself alive in Charleston and caught up with Hamilton, he showed me the miniature ye'd sent of Louisa, and I knew she was mine. . . ."

"Aye," Jane murmured, averting her eyes from his solemn gaze. "And never a word from ye, even when ye left knowing I might be carrying yer child."

"Ham spoke of how *happy* ye were with Alex in eighty-one . . . that a difficult marriage had turned into a rapturous idyll . . . that yet *another* bairn was on the way. I was like a man who'd lost his mind. I saw I would never be able to claim my child. I couldna face the thought that ye'd gone back to Alex's bed without a qualm. Even so, when I returned, I determined I would see ye, once this legal nightmare with Simon's will was sorted out. Then some gossip in Inverness informed me that ye'd had *another* babe and named him Alexander after the duke ye were so devoted to. Well, everything Hamilton had said seemed to be—"

"Is there *no* way to explain to ye the war *I've* fought these years?" she interrupted fiercely. "When last we met at Gordon Castle, ye begged me to . . . to . . . *give it up*, ye said. Oh, how I tried!" she cried, her eyes glittering. "But half of me has battled to make something of my marriage to Alex, and the other half fights to hold onto a fairyland where I live with *ye*! Whichever side eventually wins, 'tis my *body* that holds *me* prisoner! Whether I like it or not, each time I've joined my body with a man's—*whether I wish to or not—I* . . . not *ye*, not *Alex* . . . *I* have borne the burden of that union! I have *seven children* I'm responsible for! How many do ye have?"

Jane glared at Thomas whose russet hair was now brushed with silver at the temples. It was Thomas's turn to avert his eyes.

"I expect ye've bedded plenty of wenches since we lay upon the pine boughs at Loch-an-Eilean," she added caustically, "and gone off yer merry way with nary a thought—"

"Actually, that's not been the case, as ye may remember from our parting that day," he said, his voice cracking slightly. "I dread the thought of any child of mine living in this harsh world without my protection.''

Jane paused and looked down at her hands clasped in her lap. She was ashamed.

"Of course. Ye're right. Forgive me,'' she replied quietly. The bittersweet memory of their time at Loch-an-Eilean returned to her with a poignant rush. "Ye're not at all like most men, Thomas. Who knows that better than I? But, it seemed as heartless to me as my actions must have seemed to ye when Hamilton told me ye'd found the perfect solution to yer financial and personal troubles . . . *the Widow Boyd*! The very jade who caused us so much grief! I was told that as soon as the problems of Struy were settled, 'twas back to America and the lovely Arabella. . . .''

"I'm not allowed to try to make a life for m'self . . . to try to give up the dream, as ye have?'' he asked defensively.

"With the very lass who'd *betrayed* us by not sending yer letter to me in time?'' Jane flashed back, pounding her fist against her thigh. " 'Tis not so much that ye're trying to make a new life for yerself that upset me so—but that ye've chosen Arabella O'Brien Delaney Boyd! 'Twas *that* I couldna bear!''

Jane glanced down at her right hand, encased in its doeskin glove. The soft leather covered the ivory digit, skillfully concealing her missing finger.

"So,'' she finished simply, "I did the best I could these ten years past. I tried to make peace with everything that had happened to me. But, somehow, I've never quite been able to do it.''

Thomas sighed and took her hand in his, gently rubbing his thumb against her glove.

"Nor have I,'' he acknowledged sadly. "Till this business with Simon's will is finished, I have no real life in Scotland. Struy is a ruin. The Highland countryside is desolate. Thousands of men have enlisted in the army over the years, and the rest just wandered away.'' He shook his head dejectedly. "Ye were right, Jane, when ye told me as a lass . . . an entire way of life in the Highlands is at an end. We Scots are merely lackeys to our English overlords.''

"And so ye'd go to America, too?'' Jane asked quietly. "Ye'd actually marry the woman who kept us apart. . . .''

"What Arabella did so many years ago was wrong, terribly wrong,'' Thomas replied heavily. "And she'd look ye in the eye today and tell ye that straightaway, if ye two ever came face-to-face. But she, too, was doing the best she could, twenty years ago.''

"So there *is* a life waiting for ye in America?" Jane asked in a small voice.

"If I want it," he answered steadily. "Just as yer life is here—or in America. With me—or without me. Whatever ye want it to be. If ye really wish to be with me, ye may."

" 'Tis not that *simple*!" Jane cried out. "There's more to it than just the two of us. There's Alex, who's driven mad by the mere *thought* of ye! There are *five girls* to marry off suitably, and Lord Huntly to settle, not to mention finding a position for the Duke's George, and now there's Alexander. Good God, Thomas! I am a thirty-seven-year-old woman and I've still a bairn at the breast!"

She paused, pulling herself to her feet, and began to pace the small chamber under its gambrel roof. Thomas moved quietly to sit on the edge of the narrow bed, watching her walk to and fro.

"I almost died when yer Louisa was born," she said shortly. "Alex saved my life. And the same with wee Alexander. He's my last. The midwife told me so. Are ye as ready as ye think never to have another child in yer life?"

"We have Louisa . . ." he interrupted.

"Are ye satisfied *never* to have a son?"

"We have Louisa . . ." he repeated.

Jane suspended her agitated pacing and smiled sadly, her sable eyes growing soft as she scanned his figure sitting on the bed.

"Aye . . ." she said quietly. "She's so like ye, Thomas, it stops my heart sometimes."

"Is Alex good to her?"

Jane's eyes darted away from his briefly.

"He's not cruel to the lass . . . 'tis just, he knows she's yers. 'Tis natural it should be hard for him."

Thomas stood up abruptly and took her in his arms.

"Come to the Highlands with me," he whispered hoarsely. "The three of us can live a good, simple life. I've enough sterling to last until the case is heard. Struy will be ours. Just today, the advocate said it winna be too much longer now. . . . Come with me!"

Before she could protest, Thomas's lips traced a path of fire down her neck to where her cloak's ribbons still hung, loosely tied. The cape fell to the floor, but Jane didn't sense the cold. Rather, she pressed her body the length of his, seeking the warmth radiating from his chest and legs.

With trembling fingers, Thomas sought the fastenings of her bodice. As the cloth parted, he slipped his hands beneath her velvet gown. His thumbs grazed the pink tips of her breasts. Jane experienced a tremendous tingling sensation. He bent forward and took first one nipple gently between his lips, then the other.

"Dear God, ye're so beautiful . . ." he murmured, tugging on her sensitive areola like a man deprived of all sustenance.

Her bosom suddenly became hard, filled with a flush of milk. Droplets sprayed his lips like the tiny snowflakes brushing against the chamber's window.

"Thomas . . . no," she cried weakly, shaken to the core by the forbidden sensuousness of what was happening between them. "I canna be with ye this way . . . 'tis for the bairn. I must go to my baby. . . ."

Jane tried to push Thomas from her, her maternal instincts battling in a deadly clash with her instincts as a woman who longed for this man to fuse his body to hers.

Thomas clung to her a moment and then released her. A look of utter despair passed between them. Slowly, Jane straightened her gown and reached for her scarlet cloak.

"I dinna know the answer to any of this," she whispered brokenly. "I only know I love ye with my life and I find it impossible to imagine life without ye."

"I leave for Struy at dawn. I'll stay in the Highlands at least until I know what land's to be restored to me," he replied dully. "Dinna come to me there unless ye want me *in* yer life— forever."

Jane's eyes searched his face as if she were storing the memory of his features to give her strength to face the future. Then, before Thomas could stop her, she fled out the door, her footsteps padding lightly on the stairs. He stared down five stories from his small window at the lane below.

The night sky was clearing as stars pierced through wisps of clouds drifting on the horizon. Below, the narrow path was illuminated by a full moon shining down on Castle Hill, which was thickly blanketed with new-fallen snow. Soon, a tiny figure clad in cardinal red emerged from the back of the Lovat town-house. Jane's cloak contrasted with the whiteness mantling the ground like a drop of his own lifeblood. She rounded the corner of Middle Close and disappeared into the dark alley that funneled south of the city in the direction of George Square, half a mile away. Thomas rested his flushed forehead against the icy windowpane. The ivory world outside seemed blank and void, drained forever of all laughter and life.

Another pair of sleepless eyes stared down from a third-floor bedchamber. The hour was late, past two, according to the French marble clock on the shelf. For several minutes, Alex had listened to the small, fretful cries of his infant son in the nursery down the hall. The heavy snowfall had ceased, and outside, absolute stillness settled over George Square.

The Duke of Gordon was startled by the sight of a cloaked figure who dashed into the square and ran along the wrought iron fence guarding a small park. The tiny oasis, verdant in summer, sported a few leafless trees whose stark branches were weighted down with snow and silhouetted by crystalline moonlight that illuminated the scene. He heard the front doorlatch click shut and, soon, the sound of Jane's steps passing by their bedchamber and fading into the distance. The door to the nursery was ajar.

Jane sat in a corner of the room awash in moonlight. Little Alexander sucked greedily at her breast. She was crying quietly. Alex observed her silently for a few moments from the threshold and then pushed the door open wider.

"You saw him," he said tonelessly.

"Aye," she said, looking up at him with no attempt to mask the misery etched on her tearstained face.

Her scarlet cloak hung loosely around her shoulders, shielding his son from the drafty room. Only the baby's tiny feet were visible.

"And ye went with him?" Alex continued.

"Aye," she confirmed, defeat resonating in her voice.

"And ye've lain with him?"

"No. But what matter? 'Tis all the same to ye."

Alex watched his wife transfer their son's pouting lips to her other breast. It was hard and round and bursting with milk. He could not disguise the wave of desolation that invaded his body. Jane was correct. Whether she made love with Thomas Fraser this night or not, she still loved the man. She always would. It was all the same.

Wordlessly, Alex retreated to the library downstairs. Still clothed in his grape velvet coat, he stretched out on the leather chaise. Cold shafts of moonlight dissolved into gray fingers of dawn before he finally closed his eyes.

26

December 1786

The year 1786 seemed to Jane to be one long, desolate winter with no renewal of spring, or lovely autumnal season of reflection. She had known from the instant she had put the baby Alexander to her breast that she couldn't abandon her children and flee to Thomas's side. Having made this painful decision, she and Alex attempted to resume their lives as if Thomas Fraser had not suddenly materialized out of a January snowstorm. But, with each passing month, there was still no restoration of warmth or closeness between them.

Alex spent much of that summer shut up in Gordon Castle, looking after the estate, grooming his menacing falcons, and crossing the progeny of his famous setter, Affric, with other dogs to develop the distinctive black and tan coat to which he was quite partial. There had been four "Affrics" during the nineteen years of their marriage, and Jane sometimes thought Alex's dogs were the only living things in which her husband had complete trust. In idle moments, the duke would pen rhymes in the dour company of his fiddler-butler, William Marshall, while Mrs. Christie and her young daughter Jean kept house for him. He entertained few visitors.

Meanwhile, Jane and the children, with Nancy Christie to look after them, repaired in June to the old cottages at Kinrara. They lived like woodsmen in the simple thatched abode and surrounding outbuildings of the estate in Badenoch, scandalizing the district by swimming nude on fine days in the River Spey.

The runner from Gordon Castle arrived once a week with a satchel full of missives for Kinrara's pint-size estate factor, Angus Grant. Sometimes these consisted of terse scribbled messages for the children, but Alex communicated nothing in writing to Jane. His silence spoke eloquently of the abyss that once again had opened between them.

As the August heather burst forth on the moors in all its purple majesty, Jane busied herself accompanying Angus to the logging operations, which were winding down for the year near Loch-an-Eilean.

"We should be matchin' last year's production, Yer Grace," Angus speculated one morning, as they watched a cluster of stout pine trunks bumping along the river into the sluice that led to one of the mills. "With the Frenchies so restive, I'll wager the shipyards will be wantin' our wood for the Navy vessels, wouldna ye think?"

"I hope there winna be war with France, but ye're right, Angus," she said, squinting into the sun. " 'Twas a good year for lumbering."

It was a lovely summer. From time to time Jane would row over alone to the Island of the Swans, as she'd come to call the small dab of land in the middle of the loch with its tiny, abandoned castle. She took comfort in the sight of its inhabitants: two stately birds and their cygnets swimming in a solemn parade. The swans still made both Loch Alvie and nearby Lochan-Eilean their home. At the sight of them, Jane's mind would drift back to those precious few days she had spent in the tower room at the top of the twisting stone stairs. But each time she returned to Kinrara Cottage and saw her children gathered in front of the hearth, or fishing on the river for salmon, or rushing to greet her with a bouquet of wildflowers or an armful of heather, she knew she could never leave them. Then, she would spend the next days trying to convince herself that, by this time, Thomas must have given up hope she would come to him. Presumably, he had wound up his legal affairs and had sailed for Baltimore and a new life at Antrim Hall.

By November, the ducal Gordons and their brood, with the exception of Lord Huntly, who returned to Cambridge for the fall term, were installed once again in the Edinburgh house on George Square. By the time Jane and her daughters and small son arrived, Alex was established in a chamber at the far end of the hall. She ordered her trunk unpacked in their former bedchamber and attempted to take an interest in the winter social season, which was in full swing.

Over breakfast one morning in mid-December, Jane set down her cup of tea and addressed her estranged husband directly.

"I've invited a young Ayrshire poet to read his work aloud tonight."

Alex looked at her from the far end of the dining table. Remaining silent, he merely arched an eyebrow.

"Lord Glencairn and Lord Monboddo are singing the lad's

praises," Jane continued briskly, "and *The Lounger* calls him a 'heaven-taught ploughman.' 'Tis hoped William Creech will bring out an Edinburgh edition of the bard's Kilmarnock poems, if he can generate enough subscribers."

Jane assumed such an evening's entertainment would intrigue Alex. After all, he himself was an accomplished poet.

"So . . . you plan a bit of campaigning for this rhyming farmer from Ayr, do you?" Alex replied in a snide tone, folding his linen beside his plate as if preparing to depart. "Have you met the man—or read his poems?"

"I've read a few, yes," Jane replied carefully, "and I quite like them, but we've yet to be introduced. Glencairn asked me if we'd host the soiree. 'Twould give the man the support he needs among the *literati* to persuade Creech to publish him in Edinburgh."

"Ah . . . so you consider yourself one of the *literati* these days?" Alex replied mockingly.

"No, of course not!" she snapped, her patience wearing thin. "But I thought the evening would be something that might interest ye, Alex," she continued, trying to keep her temper in check. "Ye've a love of poetry yerself and write beautifully . . . winna ye come to listen to Robert Burns?"

"Perhaps," he replied noncommittally.

"Oh, do stop this nonsense!" Jane exclaimed exasperatedly. "Come—or dinna come. Suit yerself!"

She abruptly pushed her chair from the table and stalked out of the dining hall, vowing a silent oath to make no more such foolish overtures toward her husband.

That evening, Jane was pleased to discover that the duke's butler, William Marshall, turned out to greet with more grace than usual the parade of distinguished guests that trooped into the drawing room in George Square. *And well he should,* she thought crossly. The assembly consisted of the leading literary lights of Edinburgh.

"Good evening, Dr. Blacklock," Jane said warmly. She extended her hand to the good reverend who had been the first in Edinburgh to rave about the poems written by the unknown farmer from the Lowland county of Ayrshire.

Nearly blind, Dr. Blacklock was a distinguished poet himself, despite his handicap.

"So kind of ye to include a sightless old bard like me, Yer

Grace," he replied genially. He drew his face close to hers, squinting his eyes to catch a hazy view of his hostess.

" 'Tis because of ye, sir, that we all gather here tonight,' she answered. "Please partake of our punch. Marshall, here, will see to yer comfort."

The original, crudely printed Kilmarnock edition of Burns's work had been sent to Dr. Blacklock by a country parson. After it had been read to him by his curate, the reverend had immediately shared it with Professor Dugald Stewart, who was entering Jane's drawing room behind the portly historian Fraser Tytler.

The Earl and Dowager Countess of Glencairn swept through the door, followed by Lord Monteith, and the painter Alexander Nasmyth. Next to arrive was Henry Mackenzie, whose word was law on literary matters in the city, as proven by the enthusiastic response to his review of Burns in *The Lounger* the previous week. The gray-haired gentleman-poet Lord Monboddo literally had William Creech's arm in a vise grip as he propelled the reluctant publisher toward Jane.

"So delighted ye could join us tonight, Mr. Creech," Jane said graciously.

"Well," said the crusty bookseller, "I came to see whether that redheaded giant who stole the last dance from me at the oyster celler would be in attendance tonight."

Jane fought to maintain her composure.

"Why no," she replied, thankful that Alex had not yet made an appearance. "Thomas Fraser was a childhood friend I hadna set eyes on in more than ten years. I hear he's emigrated to America."

Jane eyed the ill-tempered publisher. She had a sudden urge to use all her charm on this skeptical man on behalf of the young poet she had never met.

"I've read some of the work of our guest of honor tonight," she said, abruptly changing the subject. " 'Tis quite noteworthy, though I'm certainly no judge, I assure you. However, I'm pleased to tell ye I will subscribe to at least twenty copies of Burns's poetry, should ye decide to bring forth an Edinburgh edition. The one I read from was slipshod and badly presented . . . a poor effort by a small publisher in Ayr, I believe."

"I'll take sixteen copies!" chimed in the Countess of Glencairn, not to be outdone.

"Will the duke be joining us?" Creech asked pointedly, as if the literary fancies of women were of no particular import. "He's a fine master of rhymes, and since I have an inkling all of yě here tonight will try to persuade me to wager good siller on this young bard, I'd like to have His Grace's opinion of the work."

"I would be most happy to comply," a voice behind Jane interjected sharply. Alex had suddenly appeared in the drawing room and greeted Creech cordially. "I'm just as curious—and skeptical—about our guest of honor, my good fellow."

To Jane's annoyance, Alex proceeded to lead Creech to a far corner. She assumed the two of them would trade quips about the foolishness of taking such an untutored writer seriously.

Jane returned her attention to the entrance to the drawing room. Framed by the door's graceful molding stood a well-proportioned young man of about twenty-seven or eight. The new arrival stared at his hostess with dark eyes that glowed with peculiar intensity as he surveyed the room. His luminous gaze paused momentarily on her lemon-colored bodice trimmed with white lace stitched around the scooped neckline, and lingered a second too long for delicacy. Jane sensed an almost animal-like magnetism about the man she immediately surmised was Robert Burns. He exuded a vibrant force that seemed to be alerting her that here was an artist who, despite his humble origins, and despite the fact he was possibly ten years her junior, might feel himself entitled to lure her into any compromising situation of his choosing.

She felt a prickling on her skin as she stared at Burn's strong, even features and unpowdered, dark brown hair pulled back simply in periwig fashion. Her face felt unaccountably flushed as he approached her, his eyes locking glances with hers, and refusing to look away.

His buckskin breeches stretched tautly over his muscular thighs, which were developed to outsized proportions, presumably by years of pushing a plow on his farm near Mauchline in the south. His blue coat, studded with brass buttons, was obviously new, as was his yellow-striped waistcoat and the snowy linen and ruffles that gathered at his massive throat. His unmistakable maleness was not diminished by such recently purchased finery suitable for an aristocratic drawing room in Edinburgh. Despite the cut of his coat, nothing could mask an essential earthiness in the man.

Burns strode to Jane's side and inclined his head in greeting. With unexpected grace, he reached for her hand and kissed it. Much to her horror and chagrin, Jane found herself conjuring up an image of this beautiful specimen of manhood lying naked in a hay barn.

"My Lowland countrywoman . . ." he murmured over her hand, his breath blowing sensuously through the sheer cambric handkerchief she held tightly, as always, to hide her injured finger.

Startled by his forwardness, she assumed he was referring to the fact that Ayrshire lay hard by the county of Galloway and her father's rundown estates in Monreith. Alex, having witnessed the unusual and intense manner in which the poet had greeted his wife, smiled sardonically.

"Jane, my dear, please introduce me to our guest of honor," he said.

"W-why certainly," Jane stammered, furious with herself for her obvious lack of composure.

"Good evening, Yer Grace," Burns said cheerfully to his host, as if undressing the duchess with his eyes was a perfectly acceptable way of paying a compliment to her duke. " 'Tis extremely kind of ye both to welcome such a poor poet as m'self to this grand town."

"No doubt, it is," Alex replied dryly, making his own survey of the man's slightly rustic, but commanding presence.

"Please take some refreshment, Mr. Burns," Jane interposed quickly, regaining her sense of self-control. "Marshall!" she called sharply to the butler, "See to Mr. Burns."

Before long, the entire company settled themselves in the chairs Jane had ordered placed in the drawing room, so as to create a small, cozy theater. Burns stood in the center of the flowered carpet and appeared remarkably unselfconscious in such august company. He withdrew several sheafs of what Jane took to be his handwritten poems. In a deep, resonating voice, interspersed with the rich inflections of his native Ayrshire dialect, he began to read from a work titled "Winter Night."

Jane sank into a wing-backed chair and rested her feet on a small, needlepoint footstool. She allowed the poet's rolling cadences to sweep over her.

> *. . . Blow, blow, ye winds with heavier gust!*
> *And freeze thou bitter, biting frost!*
> *Descend, ye chilly, smothering snows*
> *Not all your rage, as now united, shows*
> *More unkindness, unrelenting,*
> *Vengeful, malice unrepenting*
> *Than heaven-illumen'd*
> *Man on Brother man bestows!*

The poet seemed to be suspended in a half-conscious state. He was no longer even looking at his written poem, but reciting from memory, his eyes slightly closed, his face like chiseled marble. The brilliance of his words, their melody, their power moved Jane deeply. Her eyes grew moist, though she was at a loss to know whether it was due to the poem itself, the riveting manner in which Burns recited it, or the unshed tears of loss she'd been holding back so many months.

When Burns finished "Winter Night" there was awestruck silence. Then the room burst into applause.

"Splendid!" roared old Lord Monboddo. "Simply splendid!" he repeated, amid a chorus of general praise.

Burns's ruddy faced glowed with pleasure. He thanked everyone with a simple grace and seemed genuinely surprised when several members of his audience begged to hear more of his work.

As he began the first lines of a poem he called "My Highland Lassie," Burns's words flowed easily, and he stared intently in Jane's direction. Alex's immobile features gave no hint of his judgment of the work. Although the poetic lines were clearly about Burns's own lost love, Jane had the uncanny sense that the poet was staring at her so intently because, somehow, he knew that this particular poem characterized the woman she had been at eighteen. Perhaps, he instinctively recognized she had suffered great loss. In any event, the words he recited in his deep clear voice spoke to her of a woman's love for the wild Scottish countryside and the visceral pull exerted by the woods and lochs and braes of the Highlands. The biblical phrase, *and he knew her*, with all its emotional and sexual connotations, floated through her head as she listened to him recite. She was mesmerized by his compelling manner and button black eyes, which were fastened unflinchingly on hers.

When he had completed his recitation, the chamber suddenly erupted with applause and praise for the ploughman poet. Startled from her former state of suspended animation, Jane quickly glanced around the room at the excited assembly and noticed that Alex had slipped out of the room at some point during the poet's remarkable performance.

Robert Burns accepted another glass of Gordon punch from an uncharacteristically jovial William Marshall. He nodded his thanks for the butler's compliments and walked directly toward Jane, who was still seated in her wing-backed chair. He smiled down at her, his dark eyes kindling with frank admiration.

"Well, madam?" he said, his tone both challenging and diffident.

"That Highland lass . . . must have touched ye greatly," Jane said quietly.

"Aye, that she did," he replied, his voice a peculiar blend of tenderness and sensuality.

"And ye took great pleasure in . . . ah . . . knowing her," she added, unsettled by the man's silent but unrelenting appraisal of her face and figure.

"I sometimes feel that way about beautiful lassies, aye," he said, a mischievous smile playing across his well-defined lips.

The cheek of the peasant, she thought, suddenly annoyed at his presumption. She told herself that she felt an odd attraction to him only because he was a talented, handsome devil, and because Alex and she had been sleeping apart these many months. She interrupted her thoughts midstream and abruptly stood up.

"Ye've met the Dowager Countess of Glencairn?" Jane declared with forced politeness, nodding her head toward the least beautiful example of womanhood in nearly all of Edinburgh. "She's quite an admirer of yers," she added with deliberate condescension.

"But are *ye?*" Robert Burns asked boldly, his gaze lingering once again on her bodice.

"An admirer of yer rhymes?" she asked, feigning an innocent interest in his writing. "I am no judge of things literary, of course, but I quite like what I've heard. Do ye write cheerful ones as well?"

"Aye, Duchess . . ." he murmured. "Mayhap ye'll permit me to present them to ye sometime soon. I'd very much like that . . ." he added, his meaning unmistakable.

Before she could summon a tart dismissal to her lips, the parsimonious publisher, William Creech, approached them. After a few moments, he nodded curtly to his hostess and led Burns away to confer in a corner.

"I doubt much these poems of yers will sell, mind ye," he began, "but I might be willing to print an edition, if we could come to an equitable arrangement."

Within a month, Robert Burns and his poetry were the rage of Edinburgh. The party given at the home of the Duke and Duchess of Gordon had launched the farmer from Ayrshire into a whirlwind of social activity and acclaim. With his lightning wit and brilliant, if sometimes impertinent conversation, he wooed the city like a brazen lover. When he wasn't basking in the praise of duchesses and countesses, he was singing drunken songs (whose lyrics he was more than likely to have scribbled down hastily with a borrowed quill) in half the taverns along the High Street.

As the new year wore on, Jane found herself increasingly enjoying Burns's company. Despite the man's impudence, she was dazzled by his talent and found it amusing to introduce the poet to the cream of Edinburgh society. At the Caledonian Hunt Ball in mid-January, one hundred people signed up on the spot for Creech's forthcoming edition of Burns's poems. Soon after, Jane and Burns attended the Theatre Royale's production of *The School for Scandal* and laughed themselves silly, even though the frippery was from the pen of Richard Sheridan, a rascally confidante of Charles Fox and Jane's rival, the Duchess of Devonshire.

Every men's club in the town wanted Burns to join their circle. The Kilwinning Masonic Lodge made him one of their own, and on April 21, the Edinburgh edition of three thousand copies of Burns's *Poems Chiefly in the Scottish Dialect* was published by Creech. The book sold so briskly that the canny bookseller bought the copyright for a hundred guineas, promising Burns four hundred pounds on the sales and subscriptions of the book itself.

As the crocuses and dwarf iris opened their colorful petals in the little park outside the Gordon's Edinburgh townhouse on George Square, Jane found herself looking forward more and more to Burns's visits. The homage he extended to her was flattering, especially at a time when her husband paid her little attention. She thought it was truly remarkable the way his newly published book of poems so captured the spirit of her homeland, and she reassured herself that the younger man's writing was the basis for her admiration.

"I've yet to see much o' any sterling, I pledge ye," Burns commented with a grin one afternoon during one of his frequent— and usually unsolicited—visits to George Square.

The poet lounged comfortably in the solid wing-backed chair in Jane's drawing room, nursing a whiskey with his customary relish. He had taken to calling regularly on his "Patroness" as he described her to his friends, and today, as usual, his stocky, five-foot nine-inch frame seemed bursting with vigor. Meanwhile, Alex had made it obvious he had little liking for the young man, although he grudgingly acknowledged the upstart had a certain talent for rhymes. But the duke rarely made an appearance at these intimate gatherings.

"Well, ye may have little siller," Jane smiled at her handsome visitor, "but ye have plenty of fame, if all these notices in the papers are any measure. What plans have ye for yer future? More writing, I hope, Rabbie."

Burns flashed her a dazzling smile for using his Christian name, a request she had, until now, declined to honor. Jane, at this point, was happy to oblige. During the months of the poet's meteoric rise in the fashionable circles of the city, she had convinced herself that serving as his patroness was a harmless means of filling the void created in her life by Alex's deliberate avoidance of her on all but the most formal occasions.

All in all, Jane mused, refilling Burns's glass to the brim with amber-colored spirits, she'd thoroughly enjoyed herself in the company of this talented rogue.

As for Burns himself, he'd made no attempt to hide his admiration for her—or her person. But then again, Jane realized Robert Burns was a lover of women. All women. She had heard the whispered stories about his numerous love affairs and the astounding number of bastards he had fathered. But what was most endearing about him to Jane was that he was perfectly frank about his rustic indelicacies and his checkered past.

"I am better pleased to make one more bairn in this world than to make war and be the death of twenty," he'd told her during one of their frequent tête-à-têtes.

It was amusing and stimulating to be in his company, and today was no less an example of that than usual.

"Ye know, Yer Grace, I *refuse* to be castrated by Calvinism!" Burns suddenly exclaimed. "Yet half of what I wish to write would be declared bawdy and debauched, and that thought sometimes stays my hand."

"Does it now?" Jane teased. "From what I hear of those rowdy meeting of the Crochallan Fencibles at Dawney Douglas's Tavern, bawdiness and debauchery are the order of the day."

Burns cocked a lecherous eyebrow and then laughed heartily.

" 'Tis the influence of Edinburgh upon me, m'lady," he chortled. "Have ye ever seen such a fine, fair, uninhibited city as this? Houses abuilding, bucks strutting the High Street, blackguards skulking . . . whores leering . . . 'tis the fault of Edinburgh herself that I should have sunk into such dissipation as I have!"

"No doubt," Jane said dryly. "But yer work. Will ye write more?" she insisted.

"I have much in me to write, if only I could say what's in m'heart, Duchess," he said, suddenly serious, his black eyes boring into hers with riveting intensity.

"Ah . . . then we can all look forward to more poems soon, I hope," Jane replied evenly, rising from her chair to break the spell his eyes had cast on her.

She crossed to the drawing room windows and gazed into the small park in George Square, surrounded by a neat wrought iron fence. Yellow daffodils poked their bonnets through the greenery, reminding her of the abundance of spring flowers that must be blooming along the verdant River Spey, which ran through the estate at Kinrara. And on the Island of the Swans, she thought to herself, purple clematis must be clinging to the pale sandstone castle walls. . . .

"If only I could write the song I've heard in my head since the day I first met ye in this very room," said Rabbie, standing behind her, abruptly ending her reveries. The poet's plea rang with the rich inflections of Jane's youth. " 'Twould be a rhyme of such passion and truth, the Kirk would stone me for it."

Suddenly, Jane felt two enormously strong hands clutch her shoulders. Startled, she turned around. Her lips parted with surprise an instant before Robert Burns kissed her with explosive desire. His muscular arms enfolded her in a bear's grip so tight she could hardly breathe.

"Rabbie!" she protested.

His kisses grew more passionate, as if by his sheer strength he would master her resistance. Her immediate response was to feel laughter bubbling to her throat. However, his increasing ardor manifesting itself against her thigh signaled that his declarations of affection were taking a serious turn.

"Beauty," he mumbled, kissing her with mounting passion.

The rigid mound swelling in Burns's breeches filled Jane with alarm. His lips seared the tops of her breasts, calling forth gooseflesh all over her body as he whispered a string of endearments against her skin.

In a corner of her brain she exasperatedly chastised this impudent rake, awestruck by the outrageous cheek of a man who was a decade younger than she. However, her body, so long denied the comfort or pleasure of a man, was responding instinctively to his deliberate and feverish attempt to arouse her. Despite Jane's best efforts to repel him, Burns's large, farmer's hand insinuated itself within her bodice and his calloused thumb expertly caressed her hardening nipple.

"Ye must *stop* this!" Jane panted, tugging with all her might against Burns's hand, which now firmly cupped her breast.

"Oh, m'lady . . ." Burns groaned, still intent on the conquest of her bodice.

In some dim recess of her mind, Jane thought she heard the sound of masculine voices in the front foyer filtering through the closed door of the drawing room.

"Stop!" she choked, wrenching herself away from the poet's forceful grip, and tearing a lace ruffle on her velvet gown in the process.

A few moments later, the door to the drawing room opened and Jane found herself face-to-face with her husband and the butler, William Marshall. The quartet stared at each other blankly for a second before Alex shifted his gaze to the figure of Robert Burns. The poet was wearing his only presentable attire: form-fitting buckskin breeches and a blue coat studded with brass buttons. His sunburnt ploughman's face seemed a ruddier hue than customary, and his breathing was somewhat labored.

Alex's startled glance encompassed the telltale swatch of dainty lace dangling from the neckline of Jane's dove gray bodice. A thunderous look spread across his face. The Duke of Gordon abruptly turned on his heel and stalked out of the drawing room, nearly running down his astounded butler in the process.

"I'm so sorry ye must leave before the duke takes tea," Jane managed to say to her guest, waving a distracted arm in William Marshall's direction. "Do show Mr. Burns out, please, Marshall," she added in a strangled voice. "I must excuse myself and look in on the children. Good day."

Jane had reached the top landing by the time Robert Burns found himself standing on the cobblestone streets of George Square. She pounded on Alex's door, but he refused to answer.

"Please, Alex!" she whispered hoarsely, "Let me in! I must talk to ye!"

He didn't reply, but she heard the sound of a heavy object being dragged across the floor. Drawers opened and slammed shut. She waited outside his door for several minutes, but Alex still did not emerge from his self-imposed exile. At length, her duties in the nursery and the need to keep up appearances in front of the staff forced her to retreat to her own bedchamber. Less than an hour later she heard the sound of a carriage and hoofbeats on the street in front of the townhouse.

Peering down from her window, Jane watched William Marshall assist the housekeeper, Mrs. Christie, in taking a seat next to the carriage driver, while a footman loaded Alex's trunk on the roof. Alex himself emerged through the front door, his traveling cape slung over his shoulders, its high collar obscuring his face. There was a moment's conference between Marshall and the duke before the butler assisted his employer inside the carriage.

Jane tore herself away from her vantage point at the window and took the stairs two at a time, hurtling through the front door and onto the street.

"Wait . . . wait, driver!" she shouted up at the horseman.

Ignoring the disapproving glances of Mrs. Christie from atop the carriage, and the disdain imprinted on William Marshall's thin lips, Jane wrenched open the coach door and leapt inside.

"There is no point, Jane—" Alex began icily.

"This is absolutely ridiculous!" Jane interrupted him angrily, slamming shut the carriage door.

Her plan to approach her husband calmly and sensibly went out the carriage window.

"At least draw the curtains, if you insist on this display!" he said between clenched teeth.

Jane yanked the velvet blinds shut and faced Alex across the upholstered coach.

"I am not *infatuated* with Robert Burns," she whispered hoarsely into the gloom. "I was tempted to seek some comfort from him, I'll admit, because ye've been so cold and horrible this entire year. But the minute that rustic kissed me, I knew I was not at *all* infatuated—and that's the God's truth, Alex!"

Alex stared at her for a moment, considering her outburst, and then shook his head.

"And Thomas Fraser? Can you say the same of him?" he said coldly.

"I can say in all truth I am not infatuated with Thomas Fraser," she said wearily. " 'Tis not been our problem, nor ever has been." She looked at him intently, continuing, "When will ye see, Alex, that Thomas and I had a dream that couldna come true . . . through nobody's fault! Now I'm trying to learn to live without that dream. To care for and honor and enjoy the people closest to me . . . and the person closest to me is *ye!*" she said hotly. "When will ye begin to *trust* that I truly care for ye and cease punishing me for what canna be helped?"

"Please get out of the carriage," Alex replied darkly. "Please leave me be."

Jane stared at him, stunned that he did not respond in the slightest to her heartfelt words.

"If ye canna *possess* every fiber of my body and every corner of my soul, then ye winna *trust* me, or have me in yer life—is that it?" she shouted in frustration.

Alex maintained his icy silence. Jane waited quietly for a long moment, hoping for any response. There was none. Despondently, she pushed against the leather-lined carriage door and stepped into the cool spring sunshine.

William Marshall's smug countenance indicated that he had heard every word of their conversation. Without a glance in Jane's direction, he nodded to the driver, who snapped the reins smartly. The horses trotted around the miniature park, past the yellow daffodils nodding a silent farewell. Jane watched the carriage turn the corner and head down Nicholson Road toward the coach station located at the White Horse Inn.

Jane waited nearly a month for some word from Alex. She hoped that during the time he spent alone in drafty Gordon Castle, without the company of the children or even the presence of his butler-confidant, he would reflect, as she had, that the two of them had much to conserve. But no word came. Not even a message to the girls or little Alexander was included in the fat missives sent to William Marshall and then forwarded to Charles Gordon for his attention.

When the first week of May came and went, and still there was no communication from Fochabers, Jane quietly ordered Nancy Christie and the other maids to prepare to depart for Gordon Castle, uninivited. For her trip north, Jane was forced to divide her large household into two coaches. Overriding Marshall's protests, she determined that she, Charlotte, Madelina, and Susan would set out immediately in the first coach, followed by the butler, Nancy Christie, and the younger children on the next run north to Inverness scheduled for two days later. She hired local livery for the last leg to Fochabers, with instructions for a second hack to take the Marshall group to Gordon Castle as soon as they arrived.

Jane's carriage rolled past the stone gates after midnight on a chilly clear evening in mid-May. She directed the coachman to proceed to the stables where he could sleep for the night before making the return journey to Inverness in the morning.

The latest of the Affrics gave a low yelp of pleasure when Jane and her party quietly let themselves into the chilly foyer. The great-grandson of Alex's original setter wagged a greeting with his thick black tail and then curled up on the Turkish carpet in front of the low-burning fire.

"Poor Affric," said Charlotte, shivering in her cloak. "I wonder why Papa made him sleep here, instead of in his bedchamber?"

" 'Tis bitter cold," Susan agreed, her teeth starting to chatter. "May we bring him up with us, Mama?" she pleaded.

"If ye wish," Jane whispered, anxious that their arrival should not rouse the household. "Yer beds aren't likely to be made up, darling, since the plan was to surprise yer papa." She said it nervously and herded the sleepy young women up the massive oak staircase in the newer wing.

"We'll be fine, Mama," Madelina said, kissing her cheek.

"Good night, Mama," Charlotte said, her eyes searching her mother's anxiously. "Our love to Papa."

"Of course, sweetling. Ye'll all see him in the morning. There's the good lassies."

"Come, Affric," Charlotte commanded.

The dog happily trooped behind the girls to their rooms while Jane headed down the corridor in the opposite direction toward the old wing.

She noticed the light of a candle approaching her from one of the first bedrooms along the lengthy hallway. Mrs. Christie suddenly appeared in the gloom, blocking Jane's passage. The housekeeper's stringy hair streamed down her bony shoulders cloaked in a threadbare nightdress. The sharp-faced woman stared dumbly at Jane. Her openmouthed surprise was quickly replaced by a look of cunning that spread across her craggy features.

"Ye wasn't expected," the housekeeper said abruptly.

"Obviously not," Jane snapped. "Now, step aside!"

The scrawny harridan returned to her room in a huff, slammed the door and turned the key in the lock.

A feeling of unease stole over Jane as she continued down the silent corridor. From the door of her old bedchamber, the massive four-poster loomed menacingly against the wall, its forest green bed curtains drawn shut like a velvet tomb. Jane rested her carpetbag on the floor and shrugged off her cloak. Fatigue numbed her body, and she quickly slipped out of her traveling suit and stays and stumbled toward the bed, clothed only in a light shift.

"Who goes there!" whispered a muffled voice from behind the bed curtains.

" 'Tis I . . . Jane," she replied softly, startled by the suddenness of Alex's words. "I know we've arrived at an ungodly hour, but I was so longing to see ye, Alex, that I—"

She parted the heavy drapery and stared into the blackness.

"Don't come in here!" Alex replied sharply.

"Oh, Alex . . . please! Dinna let's argue about—" Jane began, groping for the edge of the bed. Her hand encountered soft flesh and she heard a woman's gasp.

"I told you, *don't*!" Alex repeated hoarsely. "You must leave at once. *Leave here at once, do you hear me*!" he shouted.

Dumbfounded by the vehemence of his tone, she stumbled back a few steps. Her breath came in ragged gulps. A knot of anguish rose in her breast and she fumbled for the flint that Alex invariably kept on the side table.

"Who *is* that?" she screamed at him. "Who in God's name *is* that!"

The candle's wick flared, illuminating the interior of the room. Alex, oblivious to the fact that he was stark naked, leapt out from the far side of the bed and wrested the candlestick out of her hand. Before its light sputtered out, Jane glimpsed a form huddled beneath bed sheets which bore a large, monogrammed *G* flanked by an embroidered *A* and a *J*.

"Dear God, not *her*!" Jane gasped, her arms rigid at her sides.

Just before the room plunged back into darkness, she had clearly caught sight of the wide-eyed, winsome housemaid Jean Christie, Nancy's younger, much prettier sister.

Jane half-ran, half-stumbled down the hallway, stifling her sobs with the back of her hand. Her mind reeled at the memory of little Jean Christie, a plump, pleasing five-year-old sitting on the tartan blanket with Jane's small daughters Susan and Madelina. It was the day, more than a decade ago, when the two Geordies found themselves marooned on the scaffolding that had encased the new wing of the castle during its construction.

Alex had taken to bed a seventeen-year-old chit, twenty years younger than his wife! Jane glanced back wildly at Alex, who, still barechested, had hurriedly donned a pair of riding breeches and was pursuing her down the passageway.

"*She's younger than Charlotte*!" she screamed, hurtling herself inside his dressing room.

"I *told* you not to come in!" Alex shouted at her as he slammed the door behind them.

A cry like that of a wounded animal tore at Jane's throat. She sank to the floor, pressing her face into the folds of Alex's silk dressing gown, which was draped over a chair. A hand rested lightly on her shoulder.

"Jane, I—" Alex began.

"Oh, please, go away," Jane moaned. "Go away. I canna bear the sight of ye."

A pale, peach dawn stole over the parkland of Gordon Castle. Charlotte, Madelina, and Susan tiptoed downstairs and stood silently in front of the forbidding entrance to the massive house, waiting for their mother to join them. Jane appeared at the door, staring straight ahead. Her eyes were sunken hollows. Wordlessly, the quartet wedged themselves back into the hired livery whose uncomprehending driver sat ready to depart, whip in hand. Jane sagged against the worn upholstery of the conveyance as the carriage wheels twisted in the graveled driveway and the coach lurched forward.

London . . . London . . . London was the only thought that registered in Jane's brain as the coach rocked to and fro and the wheels crunched past the stone gates.

The future . . . I must make some sort of life for myself . . . for the children . . . I must . . . I must . . . I must . . .

Unable to think anymore, Jane sank into the oblivion of exhausted sleep while her daughters looked at each other with frightened eyes.

27

May 1787

Dawn was just breaking through the tall pines and Thomas could smell wood smoke from one of the few crofters' cottages still inhabited along the glen. His eyes skimmed over the bracken-covered rocks and underbrush that flanked the deserted narrow lane. If matters continued as they had these last years, he thought grimly, the population of the entire valley of Struy would soon emigrate to the New World, including himself.

Thomas grazed his leather whip across the flanks of his cadaverous cart horse and cursed under his breath. The pathetically thin steed strained between the wooden shafts encasing its emaciated form and plodded stoically down the path at a snail's pace. Soon the cart rolled past the one-room stone thatched cottage Thomas had called home for more than a year, and headed toward the Inverness Road.

He glanced back at the four skimpy bags of wool bound together in the cart and wondered why he bothered. What more would it take to convince him Jane wasn't coming? Why didn't he simply put the remainder of his money into ship's passage to Baltimore? The last winter in the Highlands had been so bitter, he'd lost a third of his small flock. Between buying new lambs and paying the solicitor he'd hired to clear his title to Struy House and the rest of his father's former estate, he'd be lucky if he had a farthing left at the end of this day to buy himself a tankard of ale at the Church Street Inn!

The broad-shouldered Highlander gazed through the morning mist at the shrouded outlines of his family's former homestead perched at the top of a rise. The acreage surrounding it lay fallow, devoid of braying sheep and shaggy cattle. The land and deserted manse looked as desolate as his mood this chilly May morning. The case to settle the intent of Simon's will continued to drag on, winding its way through this Commission, and that Chancery Court, and yet another hearing. Thomas's solicitor, who prepared the case, and the barrister, who represented him in court, were forever promising the end was in sight, and that the Struy estate would soon be his again, all the while asking for further funds to pursue the matter. Thomas had no choice but to wait—and to pay.

The wooden cart creaked over Struy Bridge as Thomas hiked his moth-eaten kilt more comfortably around his hips and trudged on along the pitted road, which ran parallel to the River Beauly.

He rubbed the beard he'd grown during the long, dark winter. The russet growth on his face collided at his ears with his dark red hair. But what concern was it of his if he looked like some deranged Viking and would no longer be admitted to civilized drawing rooms in Edinburgh and London—or even Inverness, for that matter? He'd just as soon his old friends and acquaintances remained ignorant of the ill-fortune besetting him these days. *'Twas lucky Sir Thomas was not alive to see the condition of his son and heir,* he thought gloomily.

It was well past noon when Thomas yanked on the cart horse's bridle in the market square. After months of solitude, subsisting on the miserably few acres left to him, his senses were assaulted by the sights, smells, and sounds of this bustling market town. He wedged his cart into one of the few spaces available and began to call out his wares at a price he hoped would garner some interested buyers.

"Merino, is it?" asked a gnarled old man Thomas nearly took to be a dwarf. "Good quality, ye say?"

"Aye . . . 'tis from merino sheep," Thomas replied, looking down at his questioner. The top of the canny bargainer's grizzled head barely came up to his own belt buckle. "As for the quality, I'd have to call it only fair. We've had a bleak, bitter time of it this year."

"I know, lad . . . I know," the old man sympathized, "and I appreciate yer being honest wi'me. Let's see what ye've got there."

Thomas pulled on the ropes and opened his four meager bags of wool for the old man's inspection.

"I'll buy the whole lot from ye, for the price I've paid everyone else," he said slowly. "Yers is no better and certainly no worse than what's been sold to me by the braggarts I've met here today."

In a twinkling, the two men agreed on the price and Thomas felt the comforting weight of several heavy coins in the leather pouch he wore around his neck.

"I've finished here as well, lad," his patron said. "Ye look like a wild savage and ye may frighten the lassies in the town, but will ye join me in an ale to seal the bargain? M'name's Angus Grant, estate factor at Kinrara down in Spey Valley. We'll be spinnin' yarn and makin' hose from what I've bought from ye and the others. Our good duchess, ye may know, has encouraged such industry on Gordon lands to keep the tenants from emigrating."

Thomas stood rooted to the spot next to his cart as if struck dumb. *Angus Grant!* This was the wisp of a man Jane had told him about years ago who ran the Kinrara Estate with such vigor and care. It suddenly galled him to think his winter's labors would enhance the coffers of the Duke of Gordon. But perhaps, he quickly rationalized to himself, a little of the profit the duke made from spinning Fraser wool would buy something for the daughter Thomas had never seen . . . something Louisa would hold dear: a doll, or a ribbon for her hair.

"Well, laddie? What do ye say?" Angus asked impatiently, interrupting Thomas's reverie. "Ye'll be my guest, if that's what's bothering ye. . . ."

"No! Of course not," Thomas countered quickly. "The name's Thomas Fraser and the Church Street Inn it is!"

The tavern section of the inn was crowded with refugees from market day, so Angus suggested they take their tankards into the quieter chamber where guests lodging at the inn were made welcome. The two men chatted amiably, although Thomas was careful not to indicate he knew much about the Spey Valley or Kinrara. Before long, a spare, dour, middle-aged man shepherded two young lasses of about eleven and seven years old, respectively, through the room. They were followed by a young servant girl with a thin, pinched face.

"Well, sink me, if 'tisn't William Marshall, without his fiddle!" hailed Angus Grant with a surprised look on his face. He rose and quickly crossed the small space separating him from the somber quartet making its way toward the door and awaiting the coach outside.

Thomas watched with curiosity as the old man slipped off his woolen cap and made a courtly bow to the two young misses in the other man's charge.

"Good day to ye, m'ladies," Angus said with a look of genuine affection. "And where might ye be off to in such a fine coach?"

"M-Mama came to Gordon Castle ahead of us, and now she's *gone!*" the littler lass wailed. "We just arrived at Fochabers and now we have to *leave* . . . 'tis not fair wee Alex can be with Papa and we can't stay too!"

"That will be *enough*, missy!" William Marshall said gruffly. "The duke has seen to yer affairs as he deems fit. Now, out with ye! Nancy, see that the footman puts all the baggage aboard. Hurry, now. Otherwise, the coach'll leave without ye!"

Thomas stared at the two well-dressed lasses who sadly made their way toward the coach where several other passengers were waiting to take their seats.

The duke has seen to yer affairs. . . .

These, then, were two of Jane's children! His mind was racing. The older one . . . which was she? Thomas's thoughts whirled at a dizzing pace, as he recalled the few tendrils of soft, burgundy-colored hair that had escaped from the lass's silk bonnet. If she was ten or eleven years old, as she looked to be, that meant that she would have been born around 1776. He closed his eyes to brace himself from the cascade of memories careening within his brain.

Kinrara. The tiny castle at Loch-an-Eilean. Three days of the most exquisite lovemaking he had ever known.

Jane . . . dear God, Jane . . . this is our daughter!

He breathed deeply to calm his racing pulse. He stared through the entrance of the inn at the child he knew to be his own Louisa. It must be she! The lass who stood not twenty paces from him was his own flesh and blood . . . his own daughter . . . the proof of the love he had tried to erase from his life.

Oh God, Jane! Louisa. . . .

"There's been a terrible row at Gordon Castle," William Marshall was confiding to Angus Grant with a certain degree of relish. "Her Grace has found to her distress that what's good for the goose 'tis not so good for the gander!"

"Be plain, man!" Angus snorted. "Ye're not speaking ill of the mistress, are ye?"

"No more than the rest of Edinburgh, where her *patronage* of that ploughman poet, with his swaggering ways, was the talk of the town!" Marshall replied acidly.

"The duke has taken offense?" Angus asked warily.

"Aye . . . and His Grace has taken a *mistress* as well," Marshall retorted with a leer. "Jean Christie's her name. The younger sister of the serving wench standing out there with the lassies . . . but a farsight more comely, if ye take my meaning. Her Grace had the misfortune to come upon them in . . . ah . . . well, the duchess arrived unexpectedly at Fochabers in the dead of night a few days ago. I, m'self, knew nothing of the tempest until I arrived with their ladyships in the second coach two days later."

"What's to happen?" Angus asked worriedly, with a glance toward the melancholy children standing outside the inn's entrance. In his distress, he had ignored the presence of Thomas, who sat not ten feet from him.

"Oh . . . 'twill all blow by, I expect," Marshall said with a shrug. "The lasses will stay with the duchess in London, but the duke has kept both lads with him, in case Her Grace has any notions of running off with what's his name . . . that Rabbie Burns fellow. Have ye heard of 'im? He's all the rage in Edinburgh these days."

Unnoticed by Kinrara's estate factor, Thomas leapt to his feet.

His blood raced and he had to restrain himself from beating the backbiting Marshall to a bloody pulp. He stalked past the two men, shouldering his way through the knot of passengers gathered outside near the stagecoach.

So, Thomas thought as he strode into the fading sunlight, the Duke of Gordon was obviously jealous—but not of *him* this time. Thomas didn't wonder that Jane attracted many admirers. He tried to subdue the nagging doubts swirling in his head. Had she shunned his own most recent overtures, only to succumb to a writer of rhymes? And what of her marriage? The duke had apparently taken a mistress, and the House of Gordon was openly divided.

In the secret place Thomas held Jane most dear, he was confident she hadn't fallen for the charms of this Robert Burns, whoever he might be. Her pride in herself and her abiding loyalty to those she loved would never allow her to forsake her family in such tawdry fashion.

He sighed. Jane's husband would wreak much grief in his married life if he didn't understand *that* much about his wife. Instinctively, Thomas's heart ached for the pain Jane must be feeling at the discovery that the man she'd sacrificed so much for had shunned her for a serving wench.

The damnable blighter dinna deserve her! Thomas fumed as a wave of anger rushed over him.

His eyes rested on an apricot silk bonnet a few feet away from where he stood.

"May I?" he asked softly of Louisa, who was clutching a heavy carpetbag. "May I give this to the footman, m'lady?"

The youngster stared up at him in wonder and silently released her hold on the baggage.

"Who are you?" demanded the girl's younger sister imperiously.

Thomas was suddenly aware of how disheveled he must look to the children.

"Ye see before ye a-a friend of Angus Grant, the factor at Kinrara," Thomas answered quickly with a smile. "I've been living on the moors this past winter, so ye must forgive my appearance. 'Tis my first trip to Inverness in many a month."

"You have funny red hair, sir!" the younger sister said speculatively, surveying his unkempt locks. " 'Tis much worse than yours, Louisa!"

Louisa shot Thomas a mortified look and flushed crimson.

He smiled down softly at his daughter. "We flame-haired ones must hold our heads proudly. 'Tis a reminder to everyone else what fire and spirit we have *inside* ourselves with which to face the difficulties life presents us, eh, wee one?"

Louisa bestowed on him a grateful smile, one that warmed him as no other had in his entire life. The lass had Jane's dark brown eyes set off with flecks of green to make them sparkle when she was happy. If Thomas were shorn of his scraggly beard, the shape of his face with its high cheekbones and straight nose would match Louisa's own.

"Am I right that yer name is Lady Louisa?" Thomas confirmed, wanting to be certain.

"Yes, sir," Louisa replied, looking up at Thomas with timid curiosity.

"And ye, m'lady?" he asked of her younger sister. "What's yer name?"

"Georgina!" the child answered promptly. "*Lady* Georgina."

"Heigh-ho!" shouted the coach driver. "Is everybody aboard?"

In an instant, Thomas scooped up Georgina by her waist and deposited the dainty lass inside the crowded coach beside the maid named Nancy Christie. He bowed solemnly to Louisa and offered her his hand as if she were a full-grown woman.

"Adieu, m'lady," he said quietly, brushing his lips against the lass's soft, sweet-smelling flesh. "A safe journey to ye," he added, assisting her up the step. "God speed ye to yer mother."

"Thank you, sir," she said without the trace of a Scottish accent.

A Fraser speaking the King's English, thanks to tutors hired by the Duke of Gordon! Thomas's mind was reeling from the day's discoveries! He raised his arm to bid farewell as the cumbersome vehicle began to move away from the inn. Louisa's face reflected puzzlement as she looked through the coach window at the man she had no way of knowing was her father. Then, finally, the team of horses strained against the loaded carriage and trundled down Church Street, accompanied by the creak of turning axles. William Marshall and Angus Grant came up behind Thomas in time to see the coach turn the corner, as it headed for the Edinburgh Road.

"Good riddance," breathed the Gordons' butler.

"How so?" said Angus Grant angrily.

"Oh, not *them*," Marshall corrected himself quickly. "But I winna miss taking orders from their mother, I ken tell ye that!"

"She's a fine, fair lady, and a grand duchess, and I winna hear ye talking such rot in front of strangers!" the estate factor exploded, glowering up at William Marshall.

''The whole district knows what happened!'' Marshall retorted defensively. ''Everybody's heard about the duchess and Rabbie Burns. I've not been spreading secrets, if that's what ye're implying.''

''Come, Fraser,'' the old man bellowed even more loudly and turned his back on the stooped-shouldered William Marshall. ''I feel the need o' something stronger than ale to wash away the taste o' all o' this. *Whiskey*, my lad! That's what we need! I'll buy ye a whiskey to help us forget such scum!''

Thomas and his new acquaintance left William Marshall, speechless with surprise and indignation, at the entrance of the Church Street Inn. The butler's eyes narrowed as he stared at Thomas's retreating figure. His gaze focused speculatively on the shaggy russet hair tied loosely at the nape of the neck of the man whose face he now recognized from Captain Fraser's days at Gordon Castle prior to his and Hamilton Maxwell's departure for America. Very interesting, he thought, rubbing his bony chin. The man who'd risen from the grave and caused his master such grief still dwelled in the Highlands.

Inside the tavern, old Angus patted Thomas on the elbow.

''Ye must come down to Kinrara one day, laddie,'' he said, hailing the tavern wench and ordering two whiskeys. ''Have ye heard about the Wolf o' Badenoch? Yer flamin' mane puts me in mind o' 'im. He dwelt at Loch-an-Eilean many years ago. Kinrara's a piece o' heaven 'twould make the Lord himself forget such scoundrels like that man Marshall! Ye must come down to see it sometime, m'lad. M'wife, Flora, would be ever so pleased to make ye welcome.''

Two exhausted children watched Nancy Christie wearily ring the brass bell outside the leased apartments of the Marquess of Buckingham's mansion in London's Pall Mall. It was Jane herself who answered the door. She stared at her wide-eyed daughter Louisa, who stood uncertainly next to five-year-old Georgina on the front stoop.

''And little Alexander?'' Jane queried anxiously after hugging both daughters fiercely. She attempted to keep the quaver out of her voice. ''Where is he, sweetlings?''

''Mr. Marshall told us that Papa says that Alexander is to remain at Gordon Castle. Papa said for Nancy to bring Georgina and me to you here.''

But Alexander's only eighteen months old! her heart cried out. *He's a wee bairn, yet!*

''Did ye see Papa in yer time at Gordon Castle?'' she asked, swallowing hard.

Jane hardly trusted herself to speak without weeping. She had spent two weeks in complete retirement in London in an attempt to recover from the shock of what had happened at Gordon Castle and to gird herself for the lonely months and years to come.

''No, Mama. Papa never even visited the nursery,'' Louisa said in a near whisper, averting her eyes. ''But Mr. Marshall asked me to give you this packet. 'Tis a bank draft and some sterling, he said, for our m-m-maintenance.'' Louisa's rich burgundy hair fanned out in a halo that reached her slim shoulders. She looked up at Jane with eyes that were filled with pain and bit her lip bravely. ''What is 'maintenance,' Mama?'' she asked, tears starting to spill down her cheeks.

A wall of misery rose up and nearly suffocated Jane as she gazed down at the unhappy faces of her two youngest daughters. Charlotte, Madelina, and Susan were huddled together, silent and equally morose, on the settee in the sitting room across the foyer.

''Maintenance, pet, is what yer Papa shares with us from the Gordon Estates so we can pay tradesmen and live together in this house,'' she replied carefully, fighting a wave of cold rage that had begun to clutch at her.

It was a rage born of the knowledge that she and the children were, under British law, merely chattel of the Duke of Gordon, to be dispensed with in whatever manner the lord of the manor should choose, like his sheep and horses and retainers. And despite her contributions to the Gordon Estates by her sensible counsel on such matters as the wool, the weaving, and logging industries, which had greatly enhanced Alex's coffers over the years, Jane was, in essence, penniless and powerless in her current situation, totally dependent on whatever goodwill—or lack of it—Alex chose to extend. Jane had learned this lesson all too well during her own childhood.

The boys against the girls, her heart mourned.

Alex had apparently decided to keep the two Georges and little Alexander with him as hostages and to abandon her and the girls to whatever life he ultimately condescended to provide for them. Her rage deepened as she recalled the years of genteel poverty her mother and her sisters had endured in Hyndford Close in frighteningly similar circumstances.

He's just like my father! she thought suddenly, anguished by the memory of the heartless behavior of Baronet Maxwell, so many years ago.

Bitter thoughts, long buried—thoughts she had held back during the agonizing fortnight she had spent since arriving in London—now rushed to her consciousness, making her dizzy with anger and regret. *How in God's name had things come to such an impasse?* she wondered, sick at heart. She held the short, formal note accompanying the packet in her unsteady hand.

I will arrive in London at the end of the month, soon to depart for the Continent with Lord Huntly. Enclosed is a draft for funds sufficient for your keep until then.
Gordon.

Gordon! she thought, with another explosion of anger bubbling to her lips. Alex signed his last name *only* when addressing missives to servants and hirelings! She clamped her eyes shut, fighting the jumble of emotions churning inside her. Nancy Christie hung in the background, twisting a corner of her traveling cloak.

"Nancy, see to the lassies' suppers, will ye, please?" Jane mumbled to the gaunt servant who, herself, was still reeling from the events of the past few weeks.

Jane quickly retrieved her own cloak and hurried down the short flight of stairs, which led to Pall Mall, anxious to escape into the chill air so her children wouldn't see the tears that finally overwhelmed her.

Alex arrived in London in early June and prepared to depart for the Continent with seventeen-year-old Lord Huntly in tow. Jane communicated almost nothing to her husband during the few days he remained in town, except to pass along what Prime Minister William Pitt had told her of the rumors of unrest in Paris. Apparently, crowds of angry French citizens were chanting in the streets for bread.

"Nonsense!" Alex replied curtly when Jane found him at his desk in the library one morning. He didn't even look up from his papers.

Jane stood in front of the fireplace, the full-length Reynolds portrait at her back. The silence between them grew oppressive.

"Alex?" Jane said at length. "Couldna we talk about. . . ."

She couldn't bring herself to finish her sentence as memories of the buxom Jean Christie lying on her side in their canopied bed came back with a rush.

"Talk about what?" Alex said, looking up from his papers warily.

"About the *disaster* our life together has become!" she challenged.

"Before our marriage? After our marriage? Before Thomas Fraser rose from the dead? After you saw him last? *Where do we start, Jane!*" he replied, his voice rising ominously.

"How about commencing from the moment I found that harlot in our bed, 'neath our monogrammed linen!" Jane spat back.

Alex studied her with narrowed eyes, unable to mask a flint of triumph.

"So . . . your pride is hurt, is it?"

"My *pride*?" she replied, outraged. "Is that all ye think is at stake here? My *pride*!" Jane paced in front of her portrait, attempting to gain control of her turbulent emotions. "I found a *child* in my bed, Alex!" she exploded. "I had come to Gordon Castle to tell ye . . . *beg* ye to allow me to be yer wife again . . . to plead with ye on behalf of Huntly and the girls, and ye betrayed me with a *child*!"

"So, you've found betrayal as bitter as I have!" he retorted.

Jane stared at him helplessly, unable to sort out in words the vast differences she felt existed between the events leading to Louisa's birth, and Alex's bedding of a seventeen-year-old serving wench as a means of seeking retribution for long-held hurts.

"Do ye care for Jean Christie?" Jane whispered at length, tears welling up in her chest.

Alex stared at her stonily.

"That, my dear duchess, is none of your affair," he replied cuttingly, revealing a satisfied smile.

"Well then," she said bitterly, barely able to control her voice, "I can see there's nothing left to discuss. I pray ye will protect our son from getting a disease in whatever brothels ye lead him to. For I have no doubt that is the purpose of these father-son Grand Tours upon the Continent!"

Fearful she would disgrace herself by bursting into tears, the Duchess of Gordon stormed out of the chamber before the duke could summon a reply.

28

September 1787

By autumn, Alex had returned with Lord Huntly from abroad and headed directly for Scotland. Jane, meanwhile, had again plunged into London's dizzying social whirl. She sought out anything and everything to try to ease the gnawing pain of Alex's public rejection and the humiliation she felt whenever she allowed herself to think of Jean Christie and her husband fornicating in the bed in which Jane had borne her children.

She invited her sister Eglantine to spend the winter with her, and together they went from morning until far into the night, attending routs and balls, hazarding at faro and piquet, and keeping up with the Parliamentary debates on the growing menace of revolution in France.

In the midst of the hectic social life into which Jane had thrust herself, and unnoticed by the rest of the family, Lady Madelina attracted the eye of one Sir Robert Sinclair, a baronet. Not long after he began paying court, Sir Robert appeared one autumn afternoon to ask for the young woman's hand.

"She's barely fifteen," Jane said to him bluntly as her daughter's suitor gazed at her anxiously across a desk in Alex's deserted library piled high with unpaid bills. "I would like ye to be unofficially engaged for one year to be sure ye know each other's hearts. Is that agreeable?"

Actually, she knew she required Alex's approval for any formal betrothal, but Sinclair needn't know that. He seemed a nice enough chap, not taken to drink, and provided with an ample inheritance for Madelina's sensible tastes. What's more, since their return from Gordon Castle, the lass seemed smitten. Sir Robert smiled broadly, a look of relief etched on his plain features.

"That is *most* agreeable, Your Grace. You're very kind," he added.

How simple all this was for the lad, she thought enviously. He and Madelina had fallen in love. He'd asked for her hand. He'd been accepted, and they would be married in a year. A pang of jealousy twisted Jane's heart. How different life had been for her and Thomas. . . .

Her thoughts quickly turned to Charlotte who would need to forge an acceptable alliance quickly, now that her younger sister was spoken for. Then, a moment later, Jane paused, feeling a sense of shame at her increasingly unromantic view of marriage. She was becoming a regular matchmaker, just like her mother, whom she arranged to visit as seldom as possible. What had become of the lass who flew like the wind to the shores of Loch-an-Eilean? she wondered sadly.

She forced such fruitless thoughts from her mind and turned her attentions to matters at hand. Thankfully, marrying off Maddy to Sinclair would mean one less lass to worry about and fewer bills to pay. Bidding the young man adieu, she was left feeling faintly ashamed of the new cynicism she could feel creeping into her bones.

Oh well, Jane thought, watching Robert Sinclair close the library door after himself, *'twas done.*

December came and went with little but perfunctory communications between Alex and Jane, although he did give his written consent to Madelina's nuptials, scheduled for the following October. Jane celebrated her thirty-eighth birthday and the dawn of 1788 on her own at a quiet Hogmanay party she hosted in her Pall Mall residence. Though her figure was trim and her dark hair as luxuriant as ever, giving her the appearance of not being a day over thirty, she felt the weight of her years and the burden of her sorrows throughout the dark, bitter-cold days of January.

Late in the month, her neighbor next door, the Duke of Cumberland, brother of King George III, invited her to a small supper. He had recently rented the adjacent apartments on Pall-Mall, and was hosting his nephews, the Prince of Wales and the Prince's brother, the Duke of York. Jane supposed she was to be included as a means of livening up the festivities without creating scandal.

However, as the time approached to depart for the engagement, Jane found herself sitting in her room, half-dressed, a kind of numbing depression deadening her body. For the first time in her life, she didn't feel like going anywhere or doing anything.

Around seven, she sent a short note to her host, the Duke of Cumberland, pleading a severe headache, and took to her four-poster bed with a copy of James Boswell's *Journal of a Tour to the Hebrides* for cold comfort.

"Is there anything else I can get ye, Yer Grace?" inquired Nancy Christie, a look of concern etched on her hawklike features.

Despite Jane's abiding hatred for the woman's mother and younger sister, her affection for the young maid turned house-keeper hadn't wavered, and it had been returned in full measure over the years.

"No, thank ye, Nancy," Jane replied wearily. "I'll read by the candle here till I fall asleep." She hesitated a moment, and then added, "I know these last months have been trying for ye as well, lass. I do so much appreciate yer loyalty."

Nancy Christie sighed.

" 'Tis shame I feel for the Christie name, Yer Grace," she murmured. "And I thank ye for yer confidence."

Jane smiled at her wanly.

"That will be all, Nancy."

Jane had turned only a few pages of the book before she felt herself nodding off.

Ghostly images of empty corridors and the eerie sound of footsteps filled her frightening dreams. Her unconscious mind wandered down, down, down into the bowels of Gordon Castle, through room after room of half-constructed furniture and broken clocks, until she reached a dungeon that was dank and cold.

Thomas lay on a pallet of filthy straw shackled to the wall by iron cuffs branded with a stag's head crest and the letter *G*. His Fraser Highlander kilt was ripped to shreds and blood trickled from a wound slashed across his prominent cheekbone. She tried to scream, horrified at the sight of him. She was sure he had been tortured, but no sound would issue from her throat. The blood on Thomas's face began to spurt up like a hideous foun-tain, until the bleak, stone cell was filled to overflowing. His blood was hot to the touch, a deeper crimson than any she had ever seen. She could hear someone faintly pounding on the trap door that had closed over her head, blocking her escape from the dungeon. She tried to scream again, terrified that she would drown in her lover's blood. Finally, a piercing wail tore from her chest, awakening her. She was drenched in a bath of sweat.

The first thing she was conscious of was that her bedchamber was filled with smoke and heat. Flames from her bedside candle, which had fallen out of its brass holder, were licking at the velvet hangings on the four-poster, and the wall behind her was alive with fire.

"Duchess! Duchess!" she heard voices shouting.

It took her several moments to realize someone was pounding downstairs on the front door.

Sheer instinct for survival prompted Jane to roll out of bed and drop to the floor. Her lungs were choking with smoke, but she crawled on her hands and knees to the door of her bedchamber, burning her hand on the brass doorknob as she yanked it open.

"Fire! Fire!" she screamed, as she pounded on the doors of her daughters' rooms. "Quickly! Quickly! Come, darlings! We must escape!"

The sounds of heavy footsteps thundered toward her.

"Dear heavens, Your Grace, are you all right?" demanded a gruff voice whose owner was shrouded in the thick smoke now pouring from Jane's bedchamber door.

"Yes . . . I'm fine," she replied shakily. "Just help me rouse the lassies!"

"Frederick, thank God we stayed at Uncle's for that last glass of claret," shouted a second familiar voice.

Jane stared through the gloom at the gentleman whose elegant, elaborate linen and starched high collar could only belong to the Prince of Wales himself. He might be a wastrel and a scamp when it came to his bed partners, but Jane had never been so glad to see the young man in her life!

"Dear lady, let me assist you," he said gallantly, grasping her by the arm as Madelina, Charlotte, and Susan appeared in the hallway. All three gave little gasps of shock as they recognized their future sovereign and his brother, the Duke of York. Smoke was billowing out of the open door to Jane's bedchamber and the sound of crackling flames grew more intense.

"Georgina and Louisa!" Jane gasped hoarsely, pointing at another room farther down the corridor. "We must find them!"

At that moment, Jane's two youngest daughters padded into the smoke-filled passageway looking dazed and bewildered. Jane flung her arms around their thin shoulders, crying with relief.

"Come, come, Mama . . . 'tis all right . . . we're all fine, Mama darling," Charlotte soothed, urging her Mother and the rest of the small crowd to hurry downstairs.

"I've roused all your servants, Your Grace," chimed the Duke of York as they poured into the foyer. "They should be seeing to the coach and horses in the mews."

"And I've raised the alarm," puffed the gout-ridden Duke of Cumberland, reaching their side as they stood shivering in the street. "The army and the Palace fire brigade will be here in a tick!"

The duke was as good as his word. The fire was promptly put out with the worst damage confined to Jane's bedchamber and adjoining dressing room.

"Come, m'ladies," said the Prince of Wales heartily, "shall we adjourn this soiree to Uncle's for a shot of whiskey? I'm glad you decided to come to our little party after all, Duchess," he added with a rakish twinkle in his eye. "I was *desolait* when I learned you'd taken to your bed and would not be joining us."

Jane smiled weakly as the bedraggled party quickly trooped next door into the welcome shelter of the Duke of Cumberland's apartments.

Sipping a brandy in the comfort of the Duke of Cumberland's sitting room, which nearly matched her own smoke-damaged chamber next door, Jane surveyed her daughters thoughtfully.

"While the workers are at their labors repairing our chambers, I think we should return to Gordon Castle."

The five girls looked at each other uneasily. They would never forget their mother's wounded cries echoing throughout Gordon Castle the night she discovered that harlot, Jean Christie, in their father's bed.

"Yer Papa narrowly escaped losing all of us in this near tragedy," Jane said quietly. " 'Tis time the breach is healed."

Her daughters gazed at her, wide-eyed.

"Can I rely on yer help?" Jane asked simply.

The Gordon lasses solemnly nodded their assent.

Within the week, Jane had hired a stagecoach for her sole use. On the appointed day, her exclusively female household happily crammed themselves inside the conveyance and settled back to endure the long, demanding two-week journey north to the snow-covered Highlands.

Jane dreaded the last few miles of the journey from the village of Fochabers to the gates of Gordon Castle. They'd already fought their way through snowdrifts and endured the howling February winds along the Moray Firth, which rolled against the rocky shores near Inverness. But now, as the coach lumbered past the gates that stood sentry at the entrance of the castle grounds, Jane gave an involuntary shudder. She recalled all too clearly that previous nocturnal arrival less than a year before. Could she face the scene she imagined lay ahead of her? Her daughters were also subdued. They ceased chattering for the first time during the long day's trip.

"We've discussed the situation, Mama," Charlotte suddenly

blurted in the silence of the darkened coach. "And we want to be with you when you see Papa."

Jane was touched at her daughters' concern, but she shook her head.

"I know, dearhearts, that ye want this . . . meeting . . . to go well," she said quietly, "but whatever happens, 'tis between yer father and me. Ye're not to blame for any of what's gone on before, and 'tis not yer problem to shoulder, even now."

"But Papa consorts with that *serving wench*!" Charlotte said disdainfully. "The whole district knows about it!"

"Charlotte!" Jane said sternly with a glance at the younger children. "There are many things ye dinna understand," she continued in a gentler tone, "nor should ye be expected to. 'Tis up to your father and me to see if we can find a way to make peace." She kissed Charlotte lightly on the cheek. "But thank ye for yer concern, hinny. I'm hopeful we can sort it out," she said with far more bravado than she actually felt.

As planned, they drew up in front of the heavy oak door to the castle just after midnight. Quickly, the six of them made their way stealthily into the mansion and crept quietly to their rooms. Shivers stole up Jane's spine as she tread softly down the same corridor of the old wing of Gordon Castle that she had passed through so confidently the night she had come on Alex and Jean Christie in her marriage bed.

Surprise is my weapon, she thought, steeling herself. No doubt there would be a terrible scene when she threw Jean Christie out of the bedchamber the strumpet had been sharing with her husband. Her breath caught at the sound of the creaking chamber door when she opened it. Then she tiptoed into the room. The flint was in its customary place on the small table beside the enormous four-poster. The bed was shrouded by its heavy velvet bed curtains drawn shut against the chill of the night. It seemed to Jane as if she had simply been thrust back to the terrible midnight hour almost one year ago when she had entered this room—unannounced.

The flint sparked, then flared as she lit the bedside candle. Her slim shadow danced on the wall behind her. Carefully she parted the drapery and then felt her heart turn over in her breast as the candlelight illuminated the square area of the enormous bed. Alex lay alone, his head cradled against a mountain of feather pillows.

He moved restlessly, but didn't awake. He had kicked off the bed linen during the night. A tartan blanket lay tangled about his knees. Jane stared at his long, lean form, so familiar and yet so foreign after these many months. He wore no nightcap and his unpowdered hair looked dark as onyx, pulled back in a simple style. His face, expressionless in sleep, was handsome still, but Jane detected, even in the dim light, several lines furrowing his cheeks and faint cobwebs fanning out from the corners of his eyes. With an eerie sense of premonition, she glimpsed what this forty-four-year-old man would look like at sixty—even eighty, if they both lived that long. Her intuition told her that if his attitude toward life continued as dour and unforgiving as fresh lines on his face indicated, his aquiline nose would soon dominate his face, while his cheeks and eye sockets would sink into a death's head as old age approached.

Jane shivered again and closed her eyes. When she opened them, Alex had shifted his weight slightly and appeared once again to be the man she had known so intimately for over twenty years. She chastised herself for her flight of fancy, created, no doubt, by the dark shadows cloaking the room. Alex lay naked across the big bed, now looking handsome and virile as ever, his upper body still trim and muscular, thanks to his continuing passion for the sport of archery. Her eyes traveled down past a nest of dark chest hairs to his slim waist and compact hips. As she stood next to the bed, bathed in the candle's murky light, her eyes were riveted on the soft, vulnerable shaft of his manhood nestled in a dark thicket between his legs. Her celibacy throughout this long year had been oppressive and unnatural to her, and she longed to be rid of it.

She was totally unprepared, however, for the rush of warmth that infused her cheeks. His unguarded nakedness produced in her a physical longing for the touch of his caresses that took her breath away. Whatever their problems had been over the years, the sight reminded Jane that Alex had been a consummate lover.

She quickly shed her garments with trembling fingers and stood next to the bed, like a bride on her wedding night, unsure of what to do next. If he rejected her at this moment, it would be more than she could bear. Tears pricked her eyes. She felt she couldn't fight him any longer. She couldn't battle Alex's unwillingness to accept her as she was: a complicated, independent woman who would always love Thomas Fraser in some dim recess of her soul, but who loved him also and wanted to forge a life together—for as long as they both should live—just as they'd promised in their marriage vows. Tears rolled down her cheeks and she buried her face in her hands, wondering desperately why she had ever come to this desolate house.

"Jean?" she heard Alex say sleepily. "Jeannie, are you all right, lass?"

His words reverberated like a knife thrust into her heart. Unable to choke back the sound, a sob erupted from her throat.

"No! 'Tis *not* yer bonnie Jean . . ." she cried out, " 'tis *I*, Jane Maxwell . . . *yer wife!*"

She turned blindly to gather up her clothing and flee the wretched chamber when Alex leapt from bed and caught her arm.

"Jane!" he breathed, a look of complete astonishment on his face. "Please . . . don't go. . . . I never—"

"Expected me here," she finished his sentence for him. "Obviously not!"

Despite her firm resolve, she began to weep unconsolably, sinking into a small chair positioned next to the beside table. For several minutes, her sobs rent the silence in the room. She felt Alex's hands on her shoulders and realized with some surprise he was kneeling next to her chair.

"A-as soon as I stop crying, I'll l-leave ye," Jane stuttered tearfully, trying to regain some semblance of control. The thought of his calling out Jean Christie's name into the chill darkness of the chamber was more than she could stand.

"Jane . . . Jane . . . poor poppet . . ." he soothed, cradling her against his naked chest. "You've come all this way in the bitter weather we've been having? Poor, poor poppet."

He spoke to her as if she were a child, which was exactly how she felt: small and helpless. He stroked her hair and shoulders, his hands warm against her cold flesh, and, after a few minutes her breathing became less ragged and she realized that instinctively, she had been cleaving to him, clinging to the comfort offered by his calming touch.

He kissed each eyelid and brushed the back of his slender fingers against her cheek. Jane pulled away from his chest and stared up at him, attempting to blink away the tears welling from her eyes.

"You look beautiful," he said suddenly.

"I'm th-thirty-eight," she hiccuped. "Ye forgot my birthday."

"No, I didn't," he said, kissing her lightly on the ear.

"W-why isn't Jean Christie here?" she sniffed.

"We've not been sleeping together these last months," he replied evenly.

Jane's breath caught in her throat. Alex's whispered words blew softly against her earlobe and Jane found her mind slipping back to that night, an age ago, when he had wooed her sensuously among the climbing roses in Comely Gardens. It was the same balmy June evening that he had presented her with his grandmother's diamond earrings. Now, these twenty-one years later, he was adeptly kissing her sensitive earlobes with increasing fervor.

Alex methodically stroked the nape of her neck while, with his other hand, he cupped her breast. His thumb played a rondelay against her nipple and it grew stiff as a thorn—whether from the chill in the room or his expert touch, Jane would not hazard a guess.

"I've missed you, you know," he murmured into her ear, easing his tongue into its shell.

She felt his erection press against her thigh and suddenly the many questions that had tormented her slipped away like so much sand trickling through an hourglass.

His hand drifted lower, pressing hard against her abdomen, and lower still, kneading her upper thighs.

" 'Tis difficult to believe you've borne seven children," he whispered, his lips trailing down her neck. "You're flat as a young lass. . . ."

Jane's head fell against the back of the chair. A tiny gasp escaped her lips as Alex bent his head lower to kiss her breasts. She moaned and threaded her hands through his dark hair, pressing his head closer, closer, seeking she knew not what in her delirium of being touched once again.

"You came here to join me in my bed, did you not?" he demanded huskily, yanking his head away from her body, leaving her feeling suspended on a precipice, dizzy with desire.

A torrent of words ran through her head . . . words that would explain how she had come to be sitting naked on a straight-backed chair in the dead of night within arm's length of the bed her unclothed husband had recently shared with his mistress. His mistress. Jean Christie. The serving girl more than half his age, whose name he had whispered into the darkness, only moments ago. Incoherent thoughts collided in her brain and faded into the chilly night, unuttered. Jane merely continued to stare into Alex's hypnotic dark eyes, trembling at the physical sensations cascading through her body.

"Say it!" he demanded roughly. "Say what you want me to do, Jane!"

"I . . . I . . ."

No words would come.

"*Say it*!"

He was almost shouting. It was their old dueling match once again.

"Yes! I *want* ye!" she sobbed brokenly. "I want ye and I want my family back. I was so frightened by the fire in London . . . we could have all been kill—"

His lips crushed hers, silencing her plea. He scooped her up off the chair and strode toward the four-poster. In a trice, they were on the bed, and in a remote part of her brain, Jane wondered how recently Jean Christie had vacated these embroidered sheets.

Alex's body blanketed hers until she could no longer feel where her form ended and his began. He covered her with rough, furious kisses, though Jane could sense he was containing whatever anger he still felt toward her, lest it might spill over as it had that day in the burgundy silk bedchamber at Culloden House. What she had to say about the current chaos of their lives would have to wait until morning. The sensations he was coaxing from her body blotted out everything but the demand that she must have him inside her at all costs.

He knelt on the mattress, prodding open her thighs. In a swift, surprising move, he lifted her legs and draped them over his broad shoulders, pulling her close to him. She stared up at him wordlessly, her eyes dilating in anticipation of what he was about to do. He utterly dominated their lovemaking, demonstrating to her in some primal way the physical mastery of his sex.

"Raise your hips," he ordered softly. As she obeyed his command, he slipped a feather pillow beneath her.

Slowly, with a kind of torturing deliberation, he sheathed himself within her by degrees.

"Jesu . . ." he groaned, acknowledging for the first time the pleasure she was affording him.

" 'Tis like that, Alex," Jane whispered defiantly, "because no man has touched me since ye left my bed for *hers*!"

Alex stared down at her, and his expression suddenly darkened.

"You swear that, upon our children's lives?"

"Yes, goddamn ye!" she cried. "Will this never *end*? 'Tis *ye* who've been the faithless one!"

His face drew into a grimace as he watched tears once again moisten her cheeks. He closed his eyes as if the sight of her weeping was unspeakably painful.

"I know, dearheart," he whispered, as if he were a small, lost boy. "Please . . . please forgive me, Jane."

He remained on his knees, a supplicant before her. His body didn't move, but Jane was suddenly aware that he had begun to pleasure her. His face, too, was impassive, while his strong, deliberate contractions inside her produced a delicious cramping within her pelvis. The strange, silent throbbing of his rigid flesh fused with hers was deeply sensual. It was as if he wanted to take her to a secret place where their sins would be washed away, making them whole again.

"Let me—" he began in a strangled voice. "Let me show you with my body how much I . . ."

His words trailed off and she was astonished to see tears in his eyes as he stared down at her. He looked like a man condemned to die at dawn.

The pulsing sensations inside her grew even stronger as Alex began slowly to shunt his hips back and forth against her. He reached down and swirled the palm of his hand against her breasts, caressing each one in turn. The tension within Jane grew unbearable. She began to move against Alex with hard, fervent strokes. She felt totally unlike herself, as a desire to, once and for all, break down Alex's wall of self-protection took control of her. She felt herself engaged in a battle with some unseen devil and she was determined to exorcise it. Now, or never.

A subtle shift had taken place between them. Alex still knelt above her, motionless, as she moved furiously against him like a woman possessed.

"I am yer *wife*!" she stormed, rhythmically throwing her body against his. "I am yer *duchess*! Tell me, Alex . . . say that *nothing* shall come between us ever again! *Tell me that*!" she demanded with a sob.

He stared down at her, a stricken look invading his eyes. He remained silent as she continued to assault him with the most intimate part of her body.

"Canna ye say it?" she cried out. "Dinna ye love me anymore? 'Tis that the way of it?"

And still he remained silent and motionless, hovering above her, his head framed by the velvet canopy arching over them. She felt him swelling even larger within her, threatening to burst. Before she comprehended what was happening, Alex cried out as if struck in the back by one of his own arrows. With a single motion, he lay her legs flat against the bed clothes, pinioning them beneath his, his entire body stretched the length of hers.

"I love you," he cried brokenly. "I've always loved you, Jane, but now—"

His words ceased and he commenced communicating that love with the sinews of his body. He rested his upper torso on his elbows and thrust against her with powerful motions—alternating quick and slow strokes with exquisite timing. His heat inside her expanded and she felt his crisis rapidly approaching.

"I can't wait, darling," he cried forlornly. "I want you so much. . . ."

A terrible sadness for him filled her heart. She flung her arms around his back and pulled him down to her.

" 'Tis all right," she soothed, "I'm here, Alex. Come, darling. Let me have yer love. . . ."

A warm explosion bathed her, more sweet in its way than all the wild nights of passion they had shared over the years. She felt a gentle tugging within herself and found her own calm release washing over the two of them. Alex's breathing remained ragged. At length, she realized that the man in her arms who had caused her so much pain was crying quietly—wrenching, soft sobs that shuddered through his body.

"Sh . . . sh . . ." she whispered, pressing her lips against his brow slick with sweat. " 'Tis all right. We'll sort it all out on the morrow, Alex. Sleep, now, darling . . . sh . . ."

Alex's breath seemed to catch, and then his shoulders trembled as another wave of emotion overtook him. Jane remained silent, holding his touseled head next to her breast and rocking him gently in her arms. Sheer physical and emotional exhaustion soon overwhelmed her, and, within minutes, she fell into a dreamless sleep.

Jane woke with a start, calculating that it must be around five. She raised her head off the pillow, roused by a high-pitched sound that cut through the chill, dark morning. She lay there, spoon fashion, in Alex's arms, listening intently. One of his long, slender hands cradled her stomach and the other possessively cupped her right breast.

There! She heard the same sound once again! Could it be the mewing of a kitten, or a rusty hinge on an open window down the hall? She slid across the bed without waking Alex and quickly slipped from the high four-poster onto the floor. The Turkish carpet felt cold and clammy under her bare feet. Rummaging as quietly as she could in Alex's armoire to find something to clothe her nakedness, she froze and listened again. The mewing had grown louder and more fretful. She donned Alex's silk dressing gown and opened the chamber door.

A strange dread clutched at her as she sped down the passageway that was illuminated only by the dim light filtering through the window at the end of the long hallway. She paused at the open door of the old nursery, catching a glimpse of the empty brass beds Alex and his children had slept in during their youth. She wondered vaguely why little Alexander was not asleep in his normal place. She prayed that her youngest son had not been banished to a bedchamber where no one could hear his cries if he woke at night. It pained Jane to remember how Alex had refused to allow the child to stay with her in London during the duke's recent trip to France with Lord Huntly, leaving the wee lad in the care of Mrs. Christie and the austere William Marshall in this draft-plagued castle.

Jane pushed the door to the nursery open wider and stared like a sleepwalker at the small fire glowing in the grate. Sitting in the chair in which she, herself, had nursed her own children was Jean Christie, her blond hair untidily fanned about her shoulders. A tiny, mewling babe suckled at the girl's pendulous breasts. She wore one of Jane's own dressing gowns. Jane's favorite woolen plaid hung loosely around her shoulders to ward off the chill. The network of blue veins etched on each bosom reminded Jane in some macabre way of the spidery lines she had seen for the first time around Alex's eyes when he lay sleeping.

"What are ye doing . . ." Jane's voice trailed off. Her heart was pounding.

The servant girl stared at Jane, slack-jawed.

"M-master'll be angry at ye if ye harm—" she said defiantly as Jane advanced toward the rocking chair.

"Ye *viper*!" Jane heard herself screaming at the lass she had housed under her roof for eighteen years. "Ye *bloodsucker*! Get out! *Get out*!"

" 'Tis *ye* who's not wanted here!" the voluptuous young woman said truculently. "M'lord sleeps with *me* now . . . this is our bairn. He gives me fine clothes to wear, like I was his duchess, sure and proper!" she concluded triumphantly.

Jane sagged against the wall nearest the fireplace. The life she had envisioned, just before dropping off to sleep in Alex's arms, dissolved around her. Jean Christie stared at her insolently, although her look turned to alarm as she saw the thunderous

expression taking possession of her adversary. The babe in Jean
Christie's arms pulled away from her teat with a startled jerk and
began to wail in the high-pitched, ragged squawls of a newborn.

"Get out! Get out!" Jane continued to shout, her voice rising
in a near hysterical crescendo. "Get *out of my house, ye filthy
wretch*!"

She heard footsteps pounding down the hallway. Behind her,
Alex stormed into the room and grabbed her by the shoulders,
shaking her roughly.

"Stop it, Jane!" he cried loudly. Anguish and horror, guilt
and anger swept across his features. "Stop it, I say! The lass's
just risen from childbed! The bairn is two days *old*!"

"*I dinna care*!" Jane wailed, whirling to face her husband.
"Jesu! Do ye have no decency a'tall? Ye bed me like I was yer
strumpet with this harlot down the hall!"

"Jane . . . please," Alex interrupted her in a gentler tone of
voice. "I know 'tis a shock—"

Jane pointed a shaking finger at the bawling infant.

"I raised one of yer bastards for twenty years and the devil
take me, I winna raise another!"

"And I raised one of *yours*!" he shouted back at her.

Jane stared at her husband, speechless with rage. How could
she sort out the glaring differences in the conception of these two
children at a time like this? How could she remind him of his
brutal treatment of her at Culloden House and the love and kindness and *history* she had shared with Thomas Fraser since she
was a child? Bedding Jean Christie was merely an act of revenge.

Ignoring Alex, she ran across the room where she towered
over Jean who sat cringing in her rocking chair. "Get out, ye
trollop! Ye doxy! *Get out of my sight*!"

Alex and Jean's newborn wailed all the louder.

"That's *enough*, Jane!" Alex growled, striding to her side.

"Be still, ye son-of-a-whore!" she shrieked at him, totally
losing control of herself. She slapped Jean Christie soundly
across the face and grabbed the tartan shawl from around her
shoulders, slashing the girl's head with it like a leather whip.
"*Dinna ye dare to wear my clothes or sleep in my bed! Get out
of my house, ye thieving slut! Get out or I'll kill ye!*"

Alex looked as if he would strike Jane, but, instead, he
grabbed his wife's arm and yanked her screaming toward the
door. He half-dragged, half-carried her down the hall that led to
their bedchamber. Charlotte and Louisa suddenly appeared at the
end of the passageway.

"Mama! What is it?" cried the elder girl, huddled in her nightdress on the landing, her arms around her trembling sister.

"Go to your rooms!" their father shouted menacingly. "Be gone with you, damn it!"

Alex hauled Jane through the doorway and slammed shut the bedchamber door and locked it. Jane broke away from his grasp and threw herself on the rumpled bed linen of their four-poster. A kaleidoscope of feelings stormed through her brain until she thought she would go mad. She could hear her own heaving sobs as if it were someone else crying in this frigid prison of a room. A cold resolve was forming in the pit of her stomach, independent of the raw emotions raging inside her. Finally, her sobs were spent and she felt totally empty, devoid of all emotion, including grief for what was irretrievably lost.

"I know full well I've dealt you a terrible blow—" Alex began tentatively. He had drawn the chair Jane had sat on last night closer to the bed and addressed her back.

"Ye even gave her my clothes to wear . . ." Jane moaned, fresh tears cascading down her cheeks.

"What—" Alex said.

"Ye gave her my dressing gown . . ."

"I didn't give her anything," he said wearily. "I never even noticed what the chit wears . . ."

"No," Jane replied bitterly. "I expect ye dinna." She took a corner of the monogrammed bed linen and wiped her eyes. "Ye should have told me about the child last night," Jane added dully over her shoulder. "Ye should have told me before we—"

"I know," he answered, his voice raw. "But I couldn't. I wouldn't. I wanted you so. . . ."

"Ye merely wanted what ye thought ye couldna have," she replied tiredly, rolling over on the bed to stare at him with dead eyes. "I've been yers for the asking for years now . . . but instead, ye've smothered me with silence and mistrust. And now, 'tis too late."

"Why, Jane?" he asked earnestly. "Why can't we sort this out, as you said last night?"

"Because we canna!" she snapped. "Because neither of us can change enough to make it work. Because there's a newborn bairn brought forth in my marriage bed!"

"She wasn't born in here," Alex said in a low voice, looking at the floor.

"But she was *conceived* in here," Jane retorted angrily. "Probably the night I found ye two together!" Jane sat up in bed pulling Alex's dressing gown tightly to her breasts. She stared at him with the same coldness she felt encrusting the core of her being. "After all this time, dinna ye understand *anything* at all about me, Alex?" She asked, her voice quivering. "No matter how much I loved Thomas or longed for the touch of an understanding man, I would *never* have betrayed you like this . . . in the house we'd lived in together! With one of our *servants*! As soon as Thomas left for Struy, I saw 'twould never be possible for me to be with him. Yet, when I chose to be with ye, ye were quick to think the worst of me with Rabbie Burns. When I came to ye and found Jean Christie in my bed . . . I *still* thought to m'self, 'twas only some aberration typical of a man of middle years. I thought ye'd see that we had too much we'd built together . . . too much that bound us. But now, ye've cut those ties . . . just like ye've cut out the feelings of love I held for ye."

"Jane, *please*, I—" Alex interrupted.

"I know . . . I know . . ." Jane silenced him, "yer tears last night . . . for a moment, ye let a tiny chink in the wall ye've built around yerself since ye were a boy come tumbling down, but 'tis not in yer nature to lay yerself bare to me—or anyone else. 'Tis not in yer bones to trust in my good will. And if I canna have *that* in my life, I'd rather live alone."

"What are ye saying?" he asked, his voice laced with misery.

"I am saying that I will yield to ye the duties I owe ye as yer duchess. I will support yer estate and honor ye in public. But for giving ye that, ye will grant me an *independent* life and the *means* to live it!"

She took a deep breath, for she knew that if he didn't agree to her next request, there was no hope whatsoever she and Alex could heal their breach.

"As long as that *bloodsucker* and her bastard lives under this roof, I'll not remain in Gordon Castle."

"I will not abandon my child," Alex said stubbornly.

"Then I shall leave today."

"But why?" he cried. "You tolerated Bathia's son. You're quite fond of him, in fact. And what about Louisa. . . ."

"Ye're too stupid for words," she snapped, feeling hot tears filling her eyes once again. "Ye know perfectly well what led to the siring of Louisa. And Bathia's George came from a woman ye *loved* long before ye knew me. He wasn't my *punishment*, as this babe is!"

" 'Tis only an *innocent child*!" Alex pleaded.

"The child is innocent, sure enough, but *ye* are not," Jane replied. "Louisa was innocent too, and look how ye've treated her all her life! No, Alex . . . most likely ye have some genuine feelings for the mother, now that she's had yer child, but ye took her to bed for *spite*, to *hurt* me, and for that, I canna forgive ye."

"But the child lives and I will not forsake her," Alex said, gazing at her warily.

"So 'tis a lass . . . what've ye named her?"

"Katherine. . . ."

For a moment, Jane was confused. Why would he name his bastard for her sister?

"In my mother's memory," he added, as if reading her thoughts. " 'Twas Jean's wish."

"Suits the saucebox, I'm sure," Jane replied bitterly, the hurt she thought she had subdued doubling over on itself. "The Christies and the Marshalls have always licked boots in this house!" A silence ensued. At length, Jane broke it. "I will not stay under the same roof with Jean Christie," she announced dully.

"And I will not turn out this newborn babe—my own flesh and blood—and his mother to a thatched cottage in the woods, as I did with Bathia!" he retorted defensively.

"Then, we are at an impasse."

Alex and she locked glances for many minutes, staring at each other across the wide expanse of their four-postered bed. Finally, Alex broke the stillness, rising from his chair and striding toward the door.

"I've loved you mightily, Jane Maxwell," he said, his features devoid of emotion. "But, I've discovered to my sorrow—you're too damn much *trouble*."

At a loss to reply to such a final pronouncement, she watched him in stunned silence while he carefully unlocked the door to their bedchamber and retreated down the hall.

All that was left to them later in the day was to discuss the terms of their formal separation.

Alex poured a whiskey for each of them in the paneled library. Outside the door, Jane could hear the sounds of servants carrying boxes and trunks down the staircase and out to the enormous coach she had hired in London.

"I will pay four thousand pounds a year to maintain you and the lasses at the apartments in Pall Mall."

"May I take Alexander with me?" she asked in a tight voice. "You can, of course, be with him whenever you wish."

"Do you wish to keep to what you said earlier? Continue in your public role as Duchess of Gordon?"

"Yes," she said abruptly.

"Then Alexander may travel with you," he said, "and I will come to London as my duties at the House of Lords require. Is that still a satisfactory arrangement or should I stay at my club?"

"That will be fine," she answered in a clipped tone, aching for their division of the spoils to be over and done with.

"Which?" he pressed.

"Whatever ye wish," she said, glancing away.

Alex leaned toward her, the guarded look in his eyes softening slightly.

"Perhaps, in time, you'll return to Gordon Castle—"

"Only," Jane said icily, "if *she* and the babe are no longer under this roof."

"My children will always call Gordon Castle their home," he replied quietly.

"Then I'll be an ugly, old woman when I next see these walls again," she retorted, rising from the leather wing-backed chair in which she'd been sitting.

She stared at her husband, and the lump in her throat threatened to cut off her breath. She swallowed and fingered the corner of his mahogany desk with the stub of her forefinger.

"I'd like to build a small country house at Kinrara. I'd like to live there in the summer, and grant it as separate property to my daughters," she said quietly.

Alex looked as if he was about to refuse her, and then bit his lip. After a moment he replied.

"Very well. I'll draw the deeds. Twenty thousand pounds will be put in a separate account for you in London."

"I'll need twenty-five. I wish to raise my own sheep."

Alex sighed and half-smiled sardonically.

"Can we *never* agree? Twenty-five thousand pounds, then."

"And some decent acreage."

"Done."

"Thank ye," she said evenly.

Alex took a sip of whiskey, averting his eyes.

"One thing more," she said, her voice nearly breaking.

"Yes?" he answered with a hint of annoyance.

"I'd like to be buried there."

"Kinrara?" he asked in a puzzled voice. "Not at Elgin Cathedral?"

"Kinrara," she confirmed.

"And may I ask why? Members of the House of Gordon have lain in St. Mary's Aisle since the mists of time—"

"Ye might have a *second* duchess," she retorted bleakly.

"Jane!"

"Ye might. And I must know *now* that my bones will rest where they'll be at peace. *Promise me I'll lie at Kinrara!*"

"You're being ridiculously morbid! Your temper will put *me* in my grave long before *you* succumb, I assure you. . . ."

"*Promise me,* Alex . . . or this arrangement is void!" she cried, her voice rising dangerously.

"All right . . . all right!" he agreed quickly, forestalling the outburst he sensed was gathering. They both were holding themselves behind a thin line of pent-up emotion.

"Well, then," she said finally. "I'll bid ye farewell . . . till London . . ." she added, the reality of what they had just accomplished permeating her final words to him.

"Till London . . . And Madelina's wedding."

She gazed up at him, her eyes mirroring the pain of their mutual loss.

"Take care of yerself, Alex. I'll wait in the coach while ye bid adieu to the children."

Summoning a small, sad smile to her lips, she stiffened her back and walked out of his study.

The duke's five daughters stood in the foyer with downcast eyes while two-year-old Alexander sucked his thumb and pulled on Nancy Christie's skirts.

"I wish you all a safe journey," he said formally.

The girls merely nodded their heads and continued to stare at their shoe tops.

"I shall look forward to meeting Sir Robert Sinclair, Maddy," he said to Madelina, who ducked her head to hide the tears coursing down her cheeks. "We'll have a fine wedding soon, won't we?"

Madelina merely nodded as if it were the most miserable idea in the world. Alex sighed. Suddenly, from a door beneath the stairway, Jean Christie appeared. She was adorned in another of Jane's gowns, this one, a soft sheer lawn with little flowers embroidered everywhere.

"Nancy!" she said imperiously to her sister, though her rough country accent was at odds with her high-flown manner. "I would like hot water to be brought up for my bath. And hurry, will ye? The baby's due to awake in a tick.''

Alex's daughters stared at the comely young wench, their mouths gaping in shock. The duke frowned slightly, and then spoke in a tone that brooked no further discussion.

"Nancy, would you please take Alexander to his mother?"

"Yes, Yer Grace," Nancy said, looking greatly relieved. In a trice, she whisked the little boy out the castle's front door.

"Please attend to your daughter," he said gruffly to Jean Christie. Charlotte and her sisters gazed in stunned silence as their father's paramour slowly mounted the stairs and shot them a triumphant glance from the landing before she disappeared. "Please . . . all of you, look at me," Alex said quietly. "Your mother and I have had a serious misunderstanding . . . but my hope is that one day, we'll sort it through—"

"You consider having a baby with that slut a mere *misunderstanding*?" Charlotte said incredulously.

Alex's shoulders slumped.

"Yes . . . there's a new baby," he said in a low voice. "Like your half-brother, George."

"But George was born *before* you married Mama," Madelina said, sniffling. "That's quite a different matter, it seems to— "

"How *dare* you presume to judge your elders!" Alex exploded, glaring at all of them. His glance rested on Louisa, who stared up at him with tears glistening in her eyes. "You know only pieces of this sad puzzle—"

"But, Papa . . ." the flame-haired girl cried out miserably, "how could you hurt Mama so?"

Louisa put her face in her hands to hid her quiet sobs.

"Come, lassies," Charlotte cut in imperiously. "Let us leave our father to his *serving wench*! I far prefer the company of Mama, don't you?"

And with that, Alex's five daughters, their backs straight as ramrods, marched out of his house. The crunch of the carriage wheels rolling along the gravel drive faded in the distance, and soon, another sound drifting down the staircase attracted his attention. It was the ragged, high-pitched cry of the newest inhabitant of the Gordon Castle nursery. Alex cocked his head and listened intently for a moment, his face engraved with the misery of his last twenty-four hours. Then, he walked slowly into his library and shut the door.

29

April 1788

The coach began its melancholy journey southward from Fochabers, passing through the Spey Valley enroute to Edinburgh. From the moment she and Alex parted, Jane found it impossible to hide her sorrow, so she simply succumbed to her despair. She ordered Nancy Christie to continue on to the George Square townhouse with the children, while she remained alone for a month nursing her wounds in the tiny cottage at Kinrara by the banks of the Spey.

Clearly, Angus and Flora Grant had been shocked by the events described to them by Nancy, but they tended to Jane's needs like a pair of kindly, indulgent grandparents, refraining from asking any probing questions, and seeing to her every whim.

By the end of April, the daffodils and crocuses were pushing through the damp soil in the fields. On an afternoon outing with her estate factor, Jane disclosed her plans to build a country house on a small rise overlooking a bend in the river.

" 'Tis it to be a grand place?" Angus asked, his brow furrowing pensively.

"Oh, heavens no!" Jane assured him. "Just six or seven bedchambers . . . just enough for the lasses and m'self."

"I see," Angus said. "And what's this about a sheep farm?"

"The new house is to have eleven thousand acres attached to it," she replied evenly. "I'd like to run enough sheep to help support it."

"Sounds like ye're planning to retire permanently from London, m'lady," Angus noted. "That's a fair piece of land to be lookin' after all on yer own."

"Well . . ." she said uncertainly. "Winna *ye* be helping us to see to the place?"

"M'lady," Angus said as gently as he could, "I'm an old man and have more than I can manage already. His Grace keeps me busy counting *his* sheep and seeing to the industries ye yerself have founded here in Badenoch. Eleven thousand acres with sheep on 'em and a real house is a handful.''

"What about training a lad from the district to be estate factor?" Jane inquired hopefully.

"Let me think on it," Angus said, scratching his woolen cap thoughtfully. He paused. "Ye need a man with experience, Yer Grace." His face suddenly brightened. "Ye know, I've met someone recently who might be perfect for the job! His family had a large estate in Struy before the Forty-five. 'Tis tied up in the courts just now. He's been struggling on a few pitiful acres, barely subsisting. Dinna have enough capital to see him through the lean winters up there. But he knows sheep, I ken tell ye that! I'll wager he's just the sort of person to take on such a job.''

"R-really?" Jane said shakily, stunned by the unbelievable coincidence that, of all the people in the Highlands, Thomas Fraser might be Angus's choice for the job of Kinrara's estate factor. "Pray tell me," she asked, "how'd ye make this lad's acquaintance?"

"Oh, he sold me some wool on market day in Inverness last year. But he's no mere youth, Yer Grace . . . he's a man of about forty. Looked like a wildman, when first we met. He had this huge thatch of flamin' hair, ye see. Came to visit Flora and me, he did, and thank the goodness he'd trimmed himself up quite a bit, or he would have frightened Flora for sure. I'd been bragging that day in Inverness about our little piece o' heaven here and invited him to come see it for himself—and he did . . . oh, nearly a year ago.''

"And did he like Kinrara?" she asked, swallowing hard.

"That he did," Angus beamed proudly. "Even rowed out to see that fusty old castle on Loch-an-Eilean after I recited the tale of the Wolf o' Badenoch. I *told* him that nobody's been over there for a century or two, but nothing would do, but that he had to row over and see it himself. I think he'd make a fine estate factor for ye, m'lady—if he'd take the job. Shall I make inquiries? I'm to see him at the Inverness Wool Market in a month's time.''

"Well . . ." Jane hesitated, her heart pounding. "Let me think on it. First I must see to designing the house. Then we'll worry about the sheep.''

From then on, she said no more about the subject of estate factor. Angus had revealed that Thomas still lived at Struy. Jane knew that if she even *laid eyes* on him, she could never again summon the strength to leave him. Remembering the look of sorrow etched on the faces of her children as their carriage departed for the south without her. Jane knew what she had to do. Within the week, she departed Kinrara, still sick at heart, for her native city, Edinburgh.

Jane and Eglantine sat quietly talking in front of the fire while a steady spring downpour glazed the windows of the Gordons' Edinburgh townhouse on George Square. Charlotte was supervising the other children's lessons upstairs, allowing her mother and her aunt some much-needed privacy.

"So, ye'll live in London?" Eglantine asked.

"Aye . . . though four thousand pounds a year is hardly a fortune with seven children in such an expensive place. But I think remaining there will be best for the lasses' prospects."

"Is there no way this breach can be healed, Jenny?" Eglantine asked somberly.

" 'Tis come too far for that, I'm afraid," Jane answered wearily. "Alex wants his wife and his mistress, too."

"Are ye sure that's what he wants?" her sister asked gently.

"To be fair, 'tis the babe he winna give up, not that serving wench, I suspect," Jane acknowledged. "But a bairn so young needs its mama, and I canna live in the same house with that viper Jean Christie and her mother!"

"Perhaps, when the child is a bit older, ye'll be able to see yer way clear . . ."

Eglantine's words drifted off as she saw the painful expression invading Jane's eyes.

"I understand Alex's wanting the babe to be acknowledged as his, and provided for . . . but I just canna face being constantly reminded of what he did to hurt and humiliate me."

"Perhaps he also feels hurt and humiliated," Eglantine said softly.

"Perhaps he does . . ." Jane sighed. "But, whatever my sins, I never deliberately set out to do him injury, as he did to me."

The two women were suddenly aware of a commotion in the foyer outside the downstairs sitting room. The parlor doors swung open violently, and there, framed by the threshold, stood Lady Magdalene Maxwell. Her steel-gray hair was partially covered by a puce silk bonnet shaped like a balloon, and it framed her deeply lined face in a less than flattering fashion. The Maxwell matriarch had not even surrendered her cloak to the startled maid who stood wringing her hands behind her. Lady

Maxwell leaned on a silver-handled cane and stared disapprovingly down her nose at her two daughters.

"I have yet to receive a message, a summons, any dispatch whatsoever to indicate that ye've returned to Edinburgh!" Lady Maxwell exclaimed. "Nor was I privy to the shocking news that tittle-tattles are whispering all about the town! How dare ye, Jane, disgrace us all with this *separation* from yer duke? I command ye to stop this nonsense at once! Think of yer children! Think of poor Eglantine, here, who hasna a farthing, but what she is provided so generously by yer husband, the duke!"

Lady Maxwell put her hand on her heart and took a breath, leaning dramatically against the doorjamb.

"What's amiss between Alex and me is none of yer concern, Mother," Jane replied sharply.

"It costs a pretty penny, I assure ye, to run my house on Leith Walk, what with the doubling of prices of everything these days! How could ye think so little of others and do something as ridiculous and selfish as offending the duke!"

"Oh, do be quiet!" Jane fumed, rising from her chair. "Ye know nothing of the situation, so just leave off with yer eternal meddling."

Eglantine, who had listened to her mother's tirade with increasing annoyance and exasperation, also rose from her chair.

"Jane's right, Mama!" she cried. "Stay out of this, I beg ye! Ye know naught of the problems, but ye're forever dishing out advice till it makes us want to *scream*! For yer information, the duke has taken a mistress and has had a brat by her. Jane has a right to be upset."

"So, after twenty years of marriage, he puffs himself up by snaring some local partridge? Is that any reason to pull a house down?" Lady Maxwell demanded.

"So, ye're suggesting that I just accept whatever my lord and master serves up, is that it, Mama dear? Swallow it all, just as long as *ye* get *yer* allowance! Well, I have something to say to ye that ye should have heard long ere now! *I do not live my life to satisfy ye*, Magdalene Maxwell! If only . . . if *only* I had had the courage to act on that twenty years ago!" Jane stalked toward her mother who shrank back into the foyer in alarm. "Get out! *Get out of my house*!" she shouted, her fists clenched at her side to keep from striking her mother. "And dinna come back unless ye're *invited*!"

*   *   *

The quarrel with Lady Maxwell was just one of several factors prompting Jane to close up the George Square house and remove to London soon afterward. Fortunately, the residence at Number 6, St. James's Square was available and Jane decided to lease it again, rather than return to the apartments on Pall Mall where the memories of the fire were all too fresh in her mind.

In the following six months in London, she once again threw herself into a whirlwind of activities, including showing off her eldest unmarried daughters to Society. Her exhausting social life required an expensive and elaborate wardrobe, and Jane sighed at the thought of the pile of unpaid bills on the desk downstairs in the library.

And I used to criticize the debts of the Duchess of D, she thought ruefully, gazing at her own reflection in the looking glass.

"What do ye think, Monsieur D'Amour?" she inquired of the Belgian hairdresser now in her employ. "Too much?"

She was debating whether to add another jewel to her elaborate coiffure. The round-faced artiste cocked his head to one side and gazed at Jane, deep in thought. He scratched his broad forehead, wrinkled his Gallic nose, and continued to stare at his patron's profile critically as she handed him the amythest bauble.

"Ah . . . but, Your Graze . . . if zee Duchess of Devonshire can put—how you say—zee carrots and zee turnips in her coiffure for zee decoration, surely zee queen will not object to one more *objet, n'est-ce pas?*"

"Ah, but she might," Jane mused. "The sovereign is displeased with the outlandish hairstyles espoused by the likes of the Duchess of D this season."

"Ooh, but madam . . . eets so good for zee biz-a-ness for such as I! Can you not persuade zee queen otherwise?" he pleaded with a twinkle in his eye. Jane found Matthew D'Amour too amusing to take offense at his familiarity.

"I'm afraid that is not the purpose of this audience, though I'm sure I dinna know why Her Majesty has summoned me to Kew Gardens today," Jane replied. "And remember, Monsieur D'Amour, that 'twas *I* who said it: one day our dear Duchess of D will go too far."

As D'Amour put the finishing touches on his masterful creation, Jane wondered idly if Alex wouldn't think the same of her. No doubt he would consider her hiring her own personal hairdresser a frivolous expense, but as far as Jane was concerned, it had become an absolute necessity. Neither she nor her maids could even attempt the elaborate styles that were all the rage now in London.

The Duke of Gordon was due to arrive at St. James's Square from Gordon Castle any day, his presence required by the convocation of the House of Lords. Jane was definitely *not* looking forward to seeing him, nor to discussing the financial straits in which she currently found herself. With five daughters to clothe, and her own gowns to purchase, she had come close to spending her four thousand pound annuity on the family wardrobe alone. She presently found herself in the uncomfortable position of having to ask her estranged husband for more money.

"Have you no hint, madam, why zee queen wishes to see you zis day?" Monsieur D'Amour murmured, interrupting her reverie.

"None whatsoever," Jane confided. "Mr. Pitt's summons merely said 'tis to be a private audience . . . just the three of us, thank heavens! I needn't dress as if for a court appearance—but do ye think this gown is—"

"*C'est parfait!*" he interrupted. "Elegant, but not too . . . how you say . . . formal."

Jane admitted to herself she was pleased to be invited to visit the queen. It apparently signaled that, thus far, no one seemed to think it strange that the Duchess of Gordon had taken up residence without the duke. *That was London for you,* Jane thought, sighing.

"Absolutely *no* feathers, Monsieur," Jane said decisively, pointing to a silver plume D'Amour had inserted among her curls. "The queen despises them."

"You are correct, Madame Duchess. *Exactement!*"

Jane thanked Monsieur D'Amour for his labors and he withdrew. She glanced at the clock ticking on the marble mantel and smoothed the folds of her skirt. She retrieved her cloak from the armoire and laid it on the bed. William Pitt would be arriving momentarily to escort her to this mysterious tête-à-tête with the queen. The youthful Prime Minister had been extremely cryptic in his note asking her to accompany him to Kew Gardens. In fact, Jane had been most surprised at receiving an invitation to visit the queen, quite apart from her fears about the scandal of her separation from Alex. She had heard rumors that the king had been somewhat indisposed, of late.

She heard a soft tap at her door.

"The Prime Minister is here, madam," her upstairs maid reported.

"Thank ye, Mavis. I shall join him straightway," Jane replied, lifting her gray satin cloak from the bed.

Jane gave a final glance into the looking glass at her pewter-colored gown trimmed with yards of silver lace. Once again, she smoothed the folds in her skirt, thankful that the prevailing fashion allowed a softer silhouette, with far fewer hoops and stays to pinch her flesh.

Within minutes, Pitt had whisked her into his carriage and they were heading at a fast trot toward Kew Gardens and their afternoon rendezvous with Queen Charlotte.

"Why so mysterious?" Jane teased her companion. "Ye've hardly said a word to me."

"Oh . . . what?" Pitt responded with a start. "Forgive me, Duchess . . . 'twas just that . . . well, ye'll discover the need for secrecy soon enough, I'm afraid."

"Canna ye give me the merest *hint* of what this is all about?"

Pitt shook his head.

"No," he said in a low voice, with a glance toward the driver and footmen accompanying them. "I truly cannot."

Jane grew even more baffled when they pulled up to Kew Gardens and were quickly led past several equerries, pages, and ladies-in-waiting who appeared exceedingly careworn and preoccupied. Immediately, Jane and Pitt were admitted into a small suite of apartments facing the gardens themselves.

A door opened and a woman in her mid-thirties entered the small gallery where they had been left standing alone for several minutes.

"Ah, Miss Burney," Pitt said graciously. "How pleased I am 'tis you who greet us. Have you met the Duchess of Gordon? Your Grace, this is Fanny Burney, the Queen's Keeper of the Robes."

"I doubt the Duchess recalls that we met briefly at the studio of Sir Joshua Reynolds, years ago," Fanny replied graciously. "You were about to have your first sitting for your portrait in your coronation robes, Your Grace. I remember that it was a beastly hot day in June and I thought you extraordinarily brave to do it."

"No wonder ye're such an excellent novelist!" Jane smiled cordially at her. "What a memory ye have! Of course, I remember ye. How could I forget? 'Twas the day the infamous Gordon Riots began," she said matter-of-factly. "I'm so delighted to see ye again."

"How fares Her Majesty?" Pitt interposed quickly.

Fanny Burney's cheerful face fell.

'' 'Tis all quite disturbing,'' she said, lowering her voice. ''I just met His Majesty in the passage leading from the queen's room and he was all agitation, all emotion. He walks like a gouty man and talks without ceasing. For some reason, he is obsessed upon the subject of the composer, Handel, though little of what he says about him makes sense. His poor voice is so hoarse, 'tis painful to hear him. The queen, as you can imagine, is greatly disquieted by it all.'' Her voice sank to a whisper. ''At dinner last night, he broke forth into positive delirium. The queen was so upset, she fell into violent hysterics. The princesses were all in misery. Even the Prince of Wales burst into tears.''

''Really?'' Pitt responded with obvious disbelief. ''I would have thought just the opposite.''

Fanny looked carefully around her to be sure the three of them were quite alone.

''The queen would agree with you that the prince's conduct in the presence of the Court is all for effect,'' she continued to whisper. ''She believes he has been heartless, assuming to himself certain powers here at the palace and elsewhere that have not yet been *legally* granted him—and doing so without any consideration or regard for his mother's feelings.''

''Rumor has it that the king's mind is utterly gone,'' the Prime Minister said bluntly. ''What say you, Miss Burney?''

She looked from Pitt's face to Jane's, as if appraising their trustworthiness.

''These seizures began after he'd gotten chilled last month. The doctors tell us his urine is full of blood. In truth, though I've been here every day, I don't know *what* to say. This is why Her Majesty has summoned you both. We all run some risk, you realize, if the king does not recover his wits.''

''There is always danger for those in service to a king who falls ill,'' Pitt said quietly. ''Will you take us to Her Majesty now?''

''She awaits you in the drawing room.''

''Where is the king?'' Jane asked apprehensively.

''In the apartments next door. The rooms above us are locked so he won't wonder at any footsteps overhead. It sets off endless upset and concern in him, for some reason.''

Jane exchanged glances with William Pitt, wondering silently why the queen should want to see *her* at such a critical time of crisis. When at last they were ushered into the royal apartments,

Jane had difficulty covering her surprise at the condition in which Queen Charlotte received them. She was clad only in a silk banyan, which looked as though it might have been the king's own dressing gown, and her face, ghastly pale, was devoid of makeup. Indeed, her haggard countenance made her look as though she had aged ten years since last Jane had been in her presence.

Nevertheless, Pitt's formal greeting to his sovereign was no different than if they had been in the throne room at St. James's Palace. He bowed low and kissed her hand. Jane curtsied and tried to smile pleasantly.

"Please sit down," the queen said tiredly, indicating two chairs near the chaise on which she reclined. "Thanks to you both for coming. I will speak English, yes?" sighed the former Princess of Mecklenburg-Strelitz, whose native tongue was German.

" 'Twould be most kind of ye," Jane said, much relieved.

"You've heard?" the queen inquired directly, her eyes misting over.

"We've heard the king has not been well and that the doctors are most puzzled," Pitt said carefully.

"S-sometimes he does not know me . . . *not know me!*" the queen exclaimed, stifling a sob. "He talks incessantly until he has no voice left to him. . . . Oh, blessed God, what are we to do?"

"The doctors have no plan . . . no course of treatment they think would help?" Jane asked.

"*Doctors!*" Queen Charlotte spat. "The fools know nothing. They have no explanation for the blood in his urine, yet they bleed him 'til he's deathly pale and close to expiring! They have bound him in a strait-waistcoat without my assent! Now they apply *leeches* to his head. If he wasn't yet mad, their treatment will make him so!"

"And what says the Prince of Wales?" Pitt inquired gingerly.

Jane observed how the queen's nostrils twitched indignantly.

"My son says *little* to my face, but tells everyone else his father has *cracked* . . ." her voice broke.

Jane could readily imagine how the monarch's wayward son must be now relishing the heady position of power his father's illness had placed within his grasp.

"Pray, tell me, Mr. Pitt . . . have Fox and his followers pressed any claims in Parliament to establish a Regent?" Queen Charlotte asked in a low voice.

" 'Tis only a matter of time, Your Majesty. If conditions remain the same with the king—"

"We must *stop* this naked grab for power!" the queen said angrily. "His Majesty had a short-lived malady much like this when first we married. He recovered then and he will recover now! We cannot let the Prince usurp the throne. 'Twould break His Majesty's heart to know such mischief was plotted by his own son while he was ill. I fear he'd quit the throne! And with events in France. . . ."

Jane and Pitt knew she referred to the reports of growing civil unrest across the Channel. There were even rumors that a certain group of English aristocrats might be following suit by plotting to bring revolution to England.

"You must help me!" Queen Charlotte implored. "We must not allow the king to think we've abandoned him!"

"What thoughts have you, Your Majesty, upon this matter?" Pitt asked carefully. "What would you have us do?"

Queen Charlotte looked at Jane closely.

"We must let *them* know many rally to our cause!" she exclaimed, referring to her eldest son, the Prince of Wales, and his brother Frederick, the Duke of York, who was known to support the idea of the Prince becoming Regent. "I have been told, Duchess, that you did much to support Mr. Pitt in the elections in Eighty-four and have much influence in the City. . . ."

"Ye're very kind to have taken such notice of the small part I played . . ." Jane demurred.

"Perhaps you could help Mr. Pitt now as you did then . . . marshaling support . . . fighting those who say the king's malady is incurable. I abhor meddling in politics. 'Tis almost a sin for me to do this, I feel. But I must do *something*!" she cried. Lowering her voice, she added bitterly, "At times, I think the game is won neither in the Privy Council nor the Chambers of Parliament, but in the bedchambers and drawing rooms of London."

"I believe ye're right," responded Jane, impressed by the hapless queen's grasp of current realities.

"We must have Loyalists on *our* side, battling that coven of degenerates—Fox and Sheridan and the Duchess of Devonshire. Mr. Pitt, if a Regency is declared, you must seek to *restrict* my son's powers severely. 'Tis unseemly to do otherwise until we know the outcome of the king's unhappy state."

"Yes, of course, Your Majesty," Pitt replied.

"I will be happy to do what little I can to assist the prime minister," Jane added quickly. "Have ye heard of Dr. John Willis?" she asked with sudden inspiration. "He is quite well known for treating . . . uh . . . mental maladies."

"No," the queen replied, at once interested. "Tell me about him."

"W-well," Jane began hesitantly, wondering why she put herself forward in such a dangerous game. "He's well known in Lincoln for his knowledge concerning this kind of . . . problem. I gather he is a kind man who makes reforms in exercise and such and shuns the use of leeches and restraints. He believes if the mind is allowed complete rest, it will often recover on its own accord."

"You know him to be skilled in this regard?" Pitt said, gazing at her intently.

"Aye. Dr. Willis was consulted over the situation concerning Lord George's conduct while he was . . . uh . . . awaiting trial in the Tower," Jane began "The duke's brother apparently impressed the judges sufficiently that he was sane when he stated to them he never intended to do mischief. . . . 'Tis only a trifling suggestion, Yer Majesty—since ye've said ye're displeased with the physicians—"

"I am," the queen interrupted. "I thank you for this intelligence."

As their audience with the queen drew to a close, Jane concluded that the situation couldn't be more desperate. If the king proved irretrievably mad, there would be a grim fate awaiting those who opposed the prince and the Eyebrow—men who were hungry for power and saw, now, their chance to grab it.

"Pray for me, Duchess," Queen Charlotte said. "And stand fast by Mr. Pitt."

"I will, Yer Majesty," she murmured, executing a deep curtsy.

Fanny Burney magically reappeared to lead them back to their coach. As they exited the queen's chambers, Pitt exchanged glances with Jane at the strange noises emanating from behind one of the palace doors.

" 'Tis *him!*" Fanny Burney whispered with alarm.

At that moment, the door flew open and a chambermaid hurried past them carrying two tin bowls half-filled with blood. Then a pale figure appeared in the doorway whose fearsome appearance caused Jane to swallow hard. The king was wigless, and several ugly red patches scarred his forehead where the leeches had been attached to his skin. He was strapped into a peculiar coat whose sleeves crisscrossed his stomach and were tied at his waist in the back. His eyes widened at the sight of the three of them, and his mouth opened, but his speech consisted of a few pathetic hoarse croaks that were indecipherable. Quickly, an enormous liveried servant grabbed the monarch roughly by the shoulders and hauled him back into the chamber, slamming the door shut.

" 'Tis frightful, absolutely frightful!" mumbled Pitt as he and Jane hurried down the passageway and out into their carriage.

The day's events left Jane shaken and filled with dread. For days afterward, she remained haunted by the experience of having heard incoherent gibberish spouted in her presence by one of the mightiest sovereigns in the world.

Throughout December 1788, a number of wild scenes were played out in the House of Commons involving the matter that in polite circles was referred to as the Regency Question.

"That damned Eyebrow today claimed the evidence shows the king is *incurable!*" Prime Minister William Pitt fumed one evening at a strategy dinner held at Jane's St. James residence. "The evidence is so far inconclusive, but the prince and that rakish brother of his, the Duke of York, openly side with the opposition in trying to wrest His Majesty's power! 'Tis absolutely *disgraceful!*"

Jane, on the other hand, couldn't deny she had a soft place in her heart for the prince, who had so bravely saved her in the fire. Accordingly, she tried to soothe the prime minister's feelings.

"Dundas will be here soon," she countered in a reassuring voice. "I'm told he's bringing a company of M.P.s who vow to assist ye in implementing yer delaying tactics, my dear Pitt."

She ordered the servants to lay out the food and wine on a sideboard so they could continue their conference without interruption, though such generous provisions were placing a great strain on Jane's household budget.

" 'Tis not merely a contest for power within England," Pitt confided later to the assembly seated in a ragged circle in Jane's sitting room. He and Jane hoped the delicious food and strong spirits would help convince these men to remain steadfast behind the king. "There is a major political upheaval building in France—we all know that. 'Tis not the time for England to be in the throes of uncertain succession to the throne. There are larger dangers here, if only those scoundrels would see them. There are traitors among the great families in England who would like nothing better than to abolish the monarchy to garner more spoils for *themselves*, don't you see?'' he added darkly.

However, both Jane and Pitt could see that there was little they could do to prevent the cronies of the profligate Prince of Wales from grabbing power if the king didn't recover soon.

After several such nocturnal discussions, Pitt remained perplexed and upset. One evening, he slouched in a chair in Jane's drawing room, long after the other strategists had departed for the night. Pitt's partisans had only narrowly avoided a vote in Parliament on the Regency Question that very afternoon.

''William,'' Jane said quietly, pouring Pitt what she hoped would be his last whiskey for the evening. ''What's troubling ye now?''

''Have these damned scoundrels no decency at all?'' he exploded. ''Now they stoop to assassinate the queen's character! Her own son has started a rumor that *I* am having a dalliance with Her Majesty now that the monarch is lying prostrate and raving!''

Jane's eyes widened. If the prince was the source of these libelous rumors, he really was an unprincipled lout!

''Say nothing,'' Jane advised firmly. ''Dinna even respond to such twaddle.''

''But—''

''The people are loyal to His Majesty, William,'' she interrupted. ''Even in the synagogues they pray for his recovery. The Prince's estrangement and dissolute ways are well known. I say: hold fast.''

Pitt looked at her admiringly. A wistful smile formed on his lips.

''You're an amazing woman, Duchess,'' William Pitt murmured quietly.

''And a tired one at that, I'm afraid.'' She smiled back at him in her most motherly fashion. ''Come now . . . off with ye. Ye must have yer wits about ye for the coming grand debate, even if the king has, for the moment, lost his.''

Pitt heaved himself out of the chair and accepted his coat from the Gordon footman.

''Are there *any* signs of improvement since Dr. Willis was summoned?'' she inquired as they waited in her foyer for the prime minister's carriage to be brought around from the mews.

''The doctor seems to be having a positive effect on his royal patient,'' Pitt replied, brightening. ''A few days ago, the king had his first good night since this episode began. There was none of his usual nocturnal ranting and pacing . . . but . . . well, no one knows whether he's truly improving.''

The footman opened her front door, but the carriage standing in front of her house was not the prime minister's. It belonged to the Duke of Gordon.

''Ah . . . good evening, Minister,'' Alex said icily, glancing with narrowing eyes from Pitt to his wife as he stepped from the coach. ''Rather late for paying social calls, isn't it?''

England's premier politician flushed slightly, and merely inclined his head as a second carriage appeared around the corner.

''I hope you've had a pleasant journey to London, Your Grace,'' Pitt said with clipped politeness. ''A good evening to you both,'' he added, nodding briefly to Jane before he strode away.

''Hello, Alex,'' Jane said uneasily, feeling defensive for no good reason.

''Good evening, my dear,'' the duke replied coolly. He handed his traveling cape to the liveried servant and directed his trunks to be brought up to his bedchamber. ''You must fill me in on the coming debate. Obviously, you are privy to all the details on matters requiring our vote this session. You seem to be on the most *intimate* terms with our young minister. . . .''

''Oh, *please*, Alex!'' Jane replied crossly as she mounted the stairs.

Alex's taunting voice halted her progress.

''I heard some interesting gossip at the tavern where I supped at the edge of the city tonight, my dear,'' he said mockingly. '' 'Tis said that Pitt dandles a Saxon queen on one knee and a Scottish duchess on the other these days. . . .''

Jane stiffened and turned to stare down at him from the dimly lit landing.

''A pox on ye, Alex Gordon!'' she hissed. ''Ye will *stop* making these vile insinuations! Ye will *stop* treating me thus! Let us get one item straight between us, m'lord,'' she continued, her eyes narrowing. ''I am *nothing* to ye, and ye are *nothing* to me any longer. If ye're not civil to me in *private* as well as in public, I will broadcast it about that the blight of Gordon Madness has struck again: that there is good reason to conclude the Duke of Gordon is a *pederast*! And in London, I assure ye, Yer Grace, the populace will believe *anything*!''

30
February 1789

For all Jane saw of Alex during the next weeks, he could have still been living at Gordon Castle, or deep in the forests of the estates in Badenoch. When the duke wasn't attending Parliament, he generally repaired to that other impregnable fortress: his club. Meanwhile, Pitt continued to employ his delaying tactics, hatched in Jane's drawing room in St. James's Square, in a desperate attempt to save George III his crown.

By the dawn of the New Year, 1789, the king's condition began to improve markedly for no reason other than Dr. Willis's attempts to countermand many of the regular court physicians' repellent prescriptions.

"I've received the most extraordinary news from Fanny Burney," Pitt said in a low voice as soon as he arrived at Jane's for a small dinner in early February. "She's just had a rather startling encounter with His Majesty in Kew Gardens, where he spoke interminably—but nonetheless *sensibly*—of his favorite composer, Handel."

"Hold fast, Minister!" Jane said smilingly as they joined the other guests in the dining room. "Hold fast!"

Then, by the middle of February, Burney reported to Pitt who repeated to Jane that the king was "infinitely better."

In spite of such signs of improvement, the question of the Regency continued to rage in Parliament until March, during which time Pitt had forced debate on every issue related to the crisis he could think of, causing delay after delay—much to the delight of the Tories supporting him.

"I'm about at my wit's end," the prime minister confided to Jane one afternoon when she had called for him in her coach and insisted he drive with her through Hyde Park to escape the constant din and wrangling within the halls of Parliament. "It has become eminently clear on both sides of the chamber that my points of order are simply delaying tactics," he admitted glumly. " 'Tis a matter of days or hours before the question will be called for a vote."

Jane could think of no encouragement to offer Pitt other than her company, so she returned with him to Parliament and repaired to a chamber set aside for ladies, promising to wait for the minister at the end of the day's session. Within minutes of having been served a glass of ale, Jane was startled to see Pitt rush into the female sanctuary, his face beaming.

" 'Tis a miracle!" he exulted, pulling her to her feet. "A messenger has just arrived with a report that this morning His Majesty walked arm in arm with Queen Charlotte in Richmond Gardens! The tenor of his conversation was as wise as an owl's!"

"Sink me . . . canna it be true?" Jane asked incredulously.

"Not only that," Pitt chortled, "but the entire chamber has just learned that the king has been *told* of the proposals to strip him of his powers!"

"God's wounds . . . *'tis* a miracle!" Jane replied excitedly, thinking she would like to see the chagrin on the faces of such turncoats as Sheridan, Fox, and the Duchess of Devonshire—not to mention the Prince of Wales himself! "*Now* we shall see the rats scurrying to reboard the Ship of State!"

"The *miracle* is, the urine no longer runs bloody, and his mind is clear again," Pitt added excitedly.

"We won! We won!" she exclaimed, impulsively skipping in a circle around the prime minister. "The news of his recovery will spread like wildfire!" she predicted happily. "All the fence-straddlers wouldna *dare* try to slip the Regency Bill through now! We *won*!"

On the following day, the vote on the Regency Bill was quietly put off. By March first, prayers of Thanksgiving were read in all the churches and cathedrals in England. As promised, the king went to Parliament on the eleventh to prove he was as fit as the Court party had claimed. Three days later, he was seen riding on horseback at Windsor, and the crowds there paid him enthusiastic homage.

Jane and Alex and their elder children were among the first to receive their invitation to the service of Public Thanksgiving at St. Paul's. It was to be the ducal Gordons' first public appearance together in months, and Jane was on edge.

That morning, she merely nodded when he offered her his hand to assist her into their coach. Fortunately, the children kept the conversation lively on their way to the church.

Lord Huntly had come to London, by special permission, from Cambridge to attend the festivities. Their son had become something of a connoisseur of horseflesh.

"Gadzooks, Papa!" Huntly exclaimed as they alighted in front of the cathedral. "Can you fancy *that*!" He pointed toward the king's coach, drawn by eight cream-colored horses, pulling up in majestic splendor next to the steps of the cathedral. Trumpets and kettledrums heralded the sovereign's arrival. Emerging from his magnificent chariot, the king was in his full dress Windsor uniform.

"Oh, Mama . . ." breathed Susan, her eyes widening at the appearance of Queen Charlotte and the entire Royal Family. The Royals were each attired in purple silk, edged with gold fringe.

"Look . . . *look*!" squealed Louisa excitedly. "The entire family's come to pay homage to the king!"

The Prince of Wales and his brother, the Duke of York, were among the trail of family members following in the wake of the king and queen.

"The royal scamp appears suitably chastened," Alex murmured in Jane's ear as the prince dutifully walked several paces behind his victorious parents.

The wild cacophony of pealing church bells brought back to Jane a childhood vision of herself at age ten, helping Thomas pull down George III's coronation placards while the bells of St. Giles rang incessantly and the old battery on Edinburgh's Castle Hill belched fire. 'Twas hard to believe, she thought ruefully, that today she was credited among the cognoscenti for having helped preserve the king's throne during this fateful time which parlimentarians were privately calling The Madness Crisis.

"There's Mr. Pitt!" Charlotte exclaimed.

The throng roared its approval as the prime minister emerged from his coach in front of St. Paul's. Shortly afterward, the Whig leader, Charles Fox, stepped out of his carriage to a chorus of boos from the bystanders.

"So much for the Eyebrow," Jane said dryly.

"Let's just pray the king is truly cured and this cursed affliction will ne'er come back," Alex replied under his breath.

A series of gala Thanksgiving Balls soon followed in the wake of the king's recovery, but as the country celebrated, the Gordons were in the throes of preparing for the wedding of Madelina, whose marriage to Robert Sinclair had been postponed when the king had fallen ill the previous autumn.

Jane hesitated outside the library door, her hand on the brass knob. Whether she liked it or not, she was forced by her penury to take up the matter of money with her husband.

"I've come to ask ye about the deeds to Kinrara," she asked, approaching his desk. "Have they been drawn up?"

"Yes, good wife, they have," he answered carefully. "They're right here for your inspection."

Jane took the sheaf of papers he proferred her and began to riffle through them. She couldn't help allowing a small smile of triumph to creep across her features. She was about to raise the subject of her household allowance when Alex caught her wrist in a forceful grip.

"Not a farthing more than we agreed upon, do you understand?" he growled. "Not for Kinrara, and not for here!"

"Of course," Jane replied with icy control. "I realize full well ye must save yer pennies to pay for the passel of *bastards* ye'll be fathering by that bloodsucking wench of yers!"

She yanked her arm out of his grip and fled the chamber, clutching the papers to her breast.

Lady Madelina Gordon was duly married to Sir Robert Sinclair in a small ceremony on the second of April. Jane and Alex hardly spoke, which, accordingly, cast a pall over the event.

In early May, the Duke and Duchess of Gordon and their children made a command appearance at a lavish dinner given in honor of the king's recovery by Sir Simpson Gideon, a wealthy M.P. This time, Jane severely doubted she could go through with another evening pretending to be the dutiful, affectionate duchess she had once been.

Fortunately, in view of Alex's refusal to increase her allowance, Jane could wear her Windsor court dress of blue, scarlet and white. Like the other ladies, she had a bandeau around her head imprinted with the words God Save the King. Still, it was against her better judgment that she consented to go.

As the gala evening progressed, Jane took satisfaction in being asked to dance by nearly every gallant in the room. Even the king himself, acknowledging publicly all she had done for his cause, led her to the floor for a lively strathspey.

"You dance with uncommon agility," the portly sovereign complimented her, slightly out of breath from his exertions.

"Why, thank ye, Yer Majesty," she beamed. " 'Tis a dance from one of the loveliest regions in the kingdom."

"The Spey Valley?" he inquired vaguely. "That's in Scotland, isn't it?"

"Aye . . . Scotland," she repeated, nonplussed that he should not know that.

"I've never been there," he added. "There was that unpleasantness of the Rebellion of Forty-five, you know. . . ."

"Well, that's mostly forgotten, sir," Jane said, whereupon she immediately felt she'd committed a heinous betrayal of everything Thomas had stood for in her life. " 'Tis time those wounds were healed completely," she amended.

"You are right, as usual!" her sovereign agreed, leading her with great politeness to Alex's table where, Jane was pleased to note, Colonel Charles Lennox, heir to the Dukedom of Richmond, was conversing avidly with her daughter Charlotte. "You must tell me more of Scotland sometime, Your Grace," declared King George before repairing once more to his waiting queen. "Perhaps we will someday pay a visit to that part of our realm."

"We would be honored mightily, should ye chose to come to Gordon Castle," Jane murmured and sank into her chair.

Louisa, her pink cheeks glowing with the excitement of attending such a glittering affair, sat down next to Alex.

"Papa . . . didn't Mama look magnificent, dancing with the king!"

Alex briefly appraised his wife's flushed condition and nodded shortly.

"P-Papa . . ." Louisa ventured timidly, "I know I'm only twelve, but I would so like to dance with you. . . Huntly refuses to be my partner, though I begged and begged . . . would you dance with me . . . just a short one?" she finished with a rush.

Jane held her breath and watched Alex gaze at Louisa somberly. He looked as if he were about to assent, when his glance rested briefly on the lass's deep rich garnet curls.

"You're far too young to be gallivanting like a strumpet before the king. No. Absolutely not. What in the world gave you such an impudent notion?"

Jane's throat ached at the sight of Louisa's stricken face. She could see the girl's eyes filling with tears.

"Huntly!" she said sharply to her son, who was leaning against a nearby wall discussing the merits of several horses soon to be offered at auction. "The 'Gay Gordons' is on the program tonight. When ye hear them strike up the tune, ye will dance with yer sister Louisa, is that clear?"

Lord Huntly appeared startled by the angry tone he detected in his mother's voice. He glanced at his younger sister and noted the look of misery creasing her pretty features. His father was staring impassively at the dancers gliding across the floor.

"Oh, all right, poppet," Huntly said kindly. "I didn't realize

dancing with your brother was of such consequence.'' He made
a teasing bow. ''Your servant, madam,'' he added, kissing his
young sister's hand.

As if nothing were amiss, Alex poured some wine into an
empty goblet and offered it to Jane. Startled, she took it from his
hand, aware when his slender fingers deliberately brushed against
hers.

''No minuets with Mr. Pitt?'' he asked with an ironic glint in
his eye.

''He dinna dance,'' she retorted, ''and besides, he's ten years
my junior. We're merely friends. Of course,'' she added for
good measure, '' 'twould be impossible for ye to understand,
with yer notions of women as merely playthings or *property*.''

''That's right,'' Alex agreed evenly, as if his exchange with
Louisa had never taken place. ''Would this piece of baggage I
own care to dance? I too am a 'Gay Gordon,' remember? Tis
only fitting the Duke and Duchess of Gordon should lead the set,
don't you think? And besides, 'tis an old favorite of ours, isn't
it?''

''*No*!'' she snapped. ''I wouldna like to dance with ye!''

''But you *do* remember how much we both like this one, don't
you, my dear?''

Jane refused to answer. Her eyes darted about the room,
hoping someone—anyone—would come and rescue her from
Alex's miserable company.

Alex stood up abruptly and clasped her hand. Jane glared at
him, but allowed herself to be led to the floor to avoid an
embarrassing scene. As they began the familiar steps of the
dance, Jane, in order to avoid returning Alex's piercing gaze,
surreptitiously observed Lord Huntly and Louisa. The girl's
countenance had brightened considerably as she threw herself
into the steps of the lively dance. Couples formed an enormous
circle around the room. They paced four steps forward, and four
steps back, with the lady circling gaily under the gentleman's
arm. Then, the last measures of each chorus were spent in
skipping cadence, as the entire company whirled madly around
the room.

As Jane twirled in Alex's arms, refusing to look him full in
the face, she caught sight of Charlotte and young Charles Lennox.
The Third Duke of Richmond's heir was the great-great-grandson
of Charles II and his mistress Louise de Keroualle. The slim,
handsome young man had just the qualifications to satisfy Jane's
growing ambitions for her children.

"I don't like him," Alex whispered in her ear, as their bodies passed close to one another. "He can be an ill-humored lout. Known for mutilating prey when he hunts, rather than making a clean kill. I'd steer her clear of him."

"Oh, do be quiet!" she whispered back, a fixed smile on her lips. "He's merely high-spirited, and I winna have ye interfering—"

"I . . . interfering with a matchmaking Mama?" he snorted, twirling her under his arm. "Heaven forbid. Nonetheless, I wouldn't encourage it, Jane," he continued sotto voce.

"I dinna need to," she whispered back tartly. "They seem to be doing splendidly on their own!" They bowed to each other with mock graciousness as the music drew to a close.

The Duke and Duchess of Gordon, both panting furiously from their exertions, reclaimed their seats. They glanced at Charlotte and her suitor, who were staring into each other's eyes.

Jane suddenly felt a hand on her knee and jumped. The hand belonged to Alex.

"I'd like to go home now," he murmured. "To protect the virtue of my daughter and destroy that claimed by my wife."

"As the king and queen have withdrawn, I am happy to comply with yer first request, but I pray ye, sir, put the second far from yer mind." She was still seething from Alex's casual dismissal of Louisa. The air in the stuffy ballroom suddenly seemed insufferable. She stood abruptly, urging her brood to make their farewells, and, in a trice, they were all heading home for St. James's Square.

"Colonel Lennox has asked to call, Mama," Charlotte confided excitedly when Jane came to her bedchamber to bid goodnight. The other lasses were already fast asleep from sheer exhaustion and excitement.

"How wonderful!" Jane replied with a warm smile. "When?"

"Tomorrow," Charlotte said shyly.

Jane's spirits rose. An alliance with the Dukedom of Richmond would relieve her nagging anxiety about Charlotte's future, but what of Alex's objections? Were they merely grounded in spite?

"Well," Jane replied carefully. "We've just had one wedding. Perhaps we shall have another before long—but only if he'll agree to settle twenty-five thousand pounds on ye as yer very own!"

Shades of her mother, Jane thought grimly. But what choices did she have? She still had three other daughters whose futures she must attend to, and Alex seemed steadfast in his refusal to grant her a larger allowance.

Charlotte threw her arms around her mother and hugged her.

"Do ye find him kind?" Jane asked quietly, taking her daughters hands in hers. "Do ye find Charles Lennox a man ye can talk to like a friend?"

Charlotte looked puzzled.

"Not like Madelina or you, Mama," she replied, her brows knit. "But, when he squeezes my hand, shivers run up my spine," she added shyly.

"Um . . ." Jane replied. "It takes more than shivers to make a life together, dearheart," she said lightly. She thought of the piles of bills awaiting her attention on her desk downstairs. "But, I'm glad he makes ye happy, pet."

Charlotte slipped into bed and pulled the bed linen to her shoulders. She stared up at her mother with a serious frown puckering her brow.

" 'Tis time I married, Mama, especially now that Madelina's a wife. 'Tis by far the best proposal I'm likely to get, that is, if I do get one . . . and with Papa so tight with the purse strings. . . ."

"That's none of yer concern!" Jane said more sharply than she intended. Charlotte averted her eyes and stared at the bed linen. "Ye're a lovely lass, and ye can have yer pick!" she continued, but, as Charlotte and she locked glances, they both knew the truth of the young girl's observations.

Jane found Alex leaning on the mantel, sipping a whiskey, as she opened the door to her suite of rooms.

"Lennox wishes to pay suit?" Alex asked abruptly.

"Aye," Jane answered warily. "Pray, why are ye in my bedchamber? I believe earlier I made my preference clear to ye."

"I came to tell you I've heard the lad's had some sort of skirmish with the Duke of York. There's talk of a duel."

"That impudent royal puppy! All credit to Lennox, then," Jane exclaimed.

Alex arched an eyebrow, but remained silent on the subject of Charlotte's new suitor. Then he stared for a moment into the amber liquid in his glass.

"I also came to claim my sacred conjugal rights . . ." he said over his glass with a wolfish grin.

"Ye canna be serious!"

"I am your husband, I will remind you." He smiled mockingly. "Wasn't it *you* who said that we could continue to appear to be man and wife?"

"In *public,* and certainly not after . . . after. . . ."

"After what?" he asked, apparently puzzled.

"Not after the meanness ye constantly display to poor Louisa . . . nor the way ye are forever goading me about Pitt and Burns!"

"Jane. Why don't you ever realize I do that as a kind of tribute to your charms?" he asked lightly, ignoring her first accusation, because they both knew his behavior troubled him more than he was willing to admit.

" 'Tis no tribute to be accused of cuckolding ye."

"Ah, but you did, in fact, cuckold me," he replied shortly.

"And ye, me . . . and continue to do so—so we're even."

"What a good place to begin a new chapter," he said huskily, reaching suddenly for her hand and kissing the inside of her palm.

"Or a new battle," she replied, pulling her hand away from his. " 'Tis no good, Alex. We've tried and tried. . . ."

"Let's try one more time," he coaxed, grasping her chin between his fingers and pulling her close to him. "I watched you tonight, Duchess. You were radiant . . . the center of attention." His lips probed hers in a sensuous kiss. "I wanted to take you right then and there—right on the floor—in the middle of all those mincing dancers."

"Alex!"

Roughly, he folded her into his arms. She could feel his intense arousal through his satin breeches.

"You knew you excited me tonight, didn't you, wench?" he whispered. "And you are perfectly aware you're exciting me right now, *aren't* you?" he added, seductively pressing his groin against her skirts.

She had to admit that his kisses still had the power to arouse her, just as her appearance at the ball obviously had excited him. After all, she thought bitterly to herself, he had been without the charms of Jean Christie for some weeks now.

As Alex skillfully caressed her breasts through her gown's thin fabric, Jane felt an odd detachment steal over her, a wariness invade her soul, a kind of protective shield envelop her. She experienced the old, familiar heat seeping into her body, making her moist and receptive, but somehow she stood apart, as if watching two people, expert in the art of lovemaking, go through the motions of making love.

Alex didn't seem to sense anything amiss. He nuzzled her neck and began to remove the pins fastening her coiffure.

"Still so beautiful," he murmured, inhaling the scent of lavender she always wore. "I love the smell of you . . . the way you taste." He licked with a serpent's tongue the flesh stretched across her collarbone. He pulled his body away from her to stare into her eyes. "I want to smell you, Jane Maxwell . . . taste every crevice. Right now."

Unprotestingly, she allowed him to strip her of her clothing, carry her to the bed, and deposit her on the feather mattress.

While he quickly shed his own clothes, he continued his seduction verbally, evoking erotic images describing the manner in which he intended to give her pleasure this night. She felt herself sucked into a vortex of artful caresses, lavish praise and whispered promises.

When she attempted to reach out to him, to return his voluptuous embrace, he merely brushed her hands aside. He was the sculptor. She was the clay. He was the master . . . she, the pampered slave. At length, she gave herself up to his total control of their lovemaking, luxuriating in it—and yet she felt despair.

Surprisingly, when she could fight him no longer, her climax was intense. For Alex had known her most intimate secrets and called on that knowledge to bear witness to his own prowess in pleasing her, in pleasing any woman, she supposed. Theirs was still a battle of wits, she thought sadly as she lay by his side, her breathing slowly returning to normal. His head rested on her breast. Absently, she brushed a lock of his dark hair, burnished, now, with a faint dusting of silver. The battle between them still raged—and, no doubt, it always would.

"Come back to Fochabers," his voice said huskily into the darkness.

Her heart thudded in her chest. Perhaps his making love to her this night had not been merely in lieu of having his mistress beside him. He reached toward the bed side table, found the flint and struck it. The candle's light cast a mellow wash upon the pale silk walls. Alex turned back to her and took her by the wrist, kissing her pulse point.

"Be my own true wife again," he said in a low voice. "We've almost twenty-two stormy years to our credit. We'll ride this out." When she didn't respond, he smiled crookedly and shook his head. "As you've come to discover, dearheart, running two households is simply unmanageable, and with Kinrara, we'd have three! By any measure, you'll need to draw upon my bank drafts to marry off your daughters in style. You'd best remarry me first.''

The perpetual turmoil of her life with Alex bubbled like a cauldron.

Come back to Fochabers.

It had been difficult to live in London, a woman alone, prey to every lecher and ne'er-do-well who considered a woman unprotected by her husband to be fair game. It had been taxing to count every farthing and still come up short, no matter how hard she tried to economize. It was damned unnerving to make decisions about the children's futures without being able to consult Alex. And his treatment of Louisa, though perhaps understandable, was beneath her contempt. She was tired of being the one to shoulder all the responsibility—and yet, hadn't she done that even when she was *with* Alex? In order to glean a modicum of comfort during their years together, she'd assumed the entire emotional burden of their life together as man and wife. Because of her enduring love for another man, she had always assumed that everything missing between Alex and herself was *her* responsibility.

Jane stared at the canopy over her head and wondered what life with Alex would have been like if Thomas had actually died in the Indian massacre? Wouldn't Alex have *still* been jealous of Robert Burns? Wouldn't he have harbored suspicions of her friendship with William Pitt? Would he ever, under any circumstances, have encouraged her interest in politics and state affairs? And what of his long periods of emotional withdrawal when she made her own desires known? Would he ever have found her involvement in social and political life appropriately feminine or "suitable?"

Jane bit her lip, lost in thought, unaware that Alex was staring at her, looking perplexed.

The Duke of Gordon is who he is, she concluded ruefully. Little would have changed that—and little could. It was simply out of her control.

Accept him as he is, and stay . . . or accept him as he is, and leave, a small voice whispered.

Jane suddenly recalled the memory of Louisa's tear-filled eyes earlier in the evening. She glanced toward the darkness engulfing the corners of the chamber. She found herself taking a mental inventory of the ways in which she had assumed responsibility all her life for things that were not hers to influence. All she could master, she realized, was *herself*. All she could do was ask for what she wanted in life. Whether she *got* what she wanted depended on what kind of company she kept.

Come back to Fochabers.

Alex's slender fingers gently touched the damp valley between her breasts.

"Well?" he asked softly. "Will ye no come back ag'in?" he whispered in a teasing Scottish brogue.

"I-I would consider becoming yer wife again in deed, as well as name, if ye'll do two things for me, Alex," she replied quietly.

"And they are. . . ?" he inquired warily.

"Be kinder to Louisa . . . 'tis not her fault her presence pains ye so."

"And your other request?" he asked, without acceding to her first.

"Send Jean Christie and the child away."

Alex suspended his gentle caresses. Silence filled the bed-chamber.

"I can understand your not wanting to have Jean Christie in our lives, because I feel the same way about Louisa, sometimes. As I am sure you can understand, I will not abandon a child of mine."

"I do not ask ye to abandon yer child," Jane said carefully. "I want ye to provide amply for them both, but I'm asking ye to send Jean Christie and the child away."

"Dear God!" Alex exploded. "Why do you always have to make everything so damn difficult? 'Tis not the Gordon way! We do not hide our children behind a cloak of shame and hypocrisy!"

"No," Jane snapped, pulling the bed linen under her arms and sitting straight up in bed. "Ye brag about them! Ye flaunt them. They puff ye up!"

"What the *Devil* are you talking like this for?" he cried, losing his temper. "You raised my George . . . and I, your Louisa. Damn it, Jane! We've been over this before—"

"I *will not* raise someone else's child ye've brought into this world as *punishment* for something I dinna do!" she shouted back at him, pounding the mattress in frustration. "I dinna cuckold ye with Robert Burns! I've been no light o' love to Pitt! And I will no longer allow you to punish Louisa and me for what I *did* do for love at a time when ye were bullying and berating me at every turn! The *bloody* muddle of our marriage is not only *my* doing—but ye've never been willing to claim *yer* part in this wretched mess!''

Alex averted his eyes and remained silent. Jane leaned toward him, touching his arm with her hand. Her voice was low and almost gentle.

''I am so weary, Alex, of trying to fathom what's gone amiss when ye're angry or upset or simply moody. I've finished with wondering if ye'll ever change yer unpredictable ways—or wishing ye'd be kind to me or gentle with me and Louisa. I'm through with wondering if ye'll ever trust me and do something that is in *my* interest only—*just once!*''

When he refused to respond, Jane leapt from the bed and threw on her dressing gown to cover her nakedness.

''Ye never comprehended that about me, did ye, Alex? Ye were so like my parents in that regard. Ye never took note that I respond *pathetically* well to a little kindness, a little understanding. Ye said when last we parted that I was '*too much trouble*' . . . and how *much* trouble I must have seemed to ye.''

''Jane, I didn't mean that to sound—''

Jane waved at him distractedly and began to pace the room.

''I've thought about those words for months . . . and I've decided . . . 'tis *true*. I *was* trouble, as ye said, because I was part of the problem too. Somehow I got the notion as a bairn that everything bad that happened was *my fault*. That if I'd been a better lass, my parents would have made a better life together. 'Twas Father's *drinking* and Mother's overriding ambition that caused their rift, not the doings of wee lasses like Catherine and Eglantine and me!''

Alex remained silent. His lips had formed a thin line and his eyes looked at her dully.

''No need to go all glassy-eyed!'' she exclaimed. ''I'm telling ye why I've been so much trouble to ye! From the very first, 'twas up to me to heed what I knew to be true: that you and I shouldna marry till we'd both given our hearts a chance to mend!''

Jane stopped pacing and faced Alex squarely, bare feet planted on the Turkish carpet, hands on hips. She gazed steadily at his face, which had grown ashen. His eyes had now assumed a haunted look. He looked tired and suddenly far older than his forty-six years.

''And then there's *ye*, yerself, Alexander Gordon,'' Jane continued. ''Sometimes I'd say to m'self these twenty-two years; 'if only I could be a more compliant, more obedient *wife*, ye'd not have shunned me when Thomas's letter arrived on our honeymoon. If only I had done even more than I have to enhance yer estate, or make yer tenants respect me more, maybe *then* I could count on yer love.' But *our* problem, O husband mine . . . our problem from the moment we met is that ye've never trusted or respected a single woman in yer whole *life*—starting with yer mother, who used yer title and yer estate for her own ends until she went to her grave. If *only* ye could have seen I wasna *like* her . . . that yer daughters—and certainly sweet-tempered Louisa— aren't like her! But, of course, ye never could . . . and there is nothing, absolutely *nothing* that's happened here tonight that leads me to believe ye ever would!''

Jane strode to the door exclaiming, ''If—if—*if*! I'm sick to death of *if's*!'' She turned around, her hand on the knob.

''The only 'ifs' in *my* future, my dear laddie, are going to be: *if I like it—I will do it*!''

And with that, she flung open the door, indicating with her outstretched hand that he should walk through it. ''No. I will not come to Fochabers and have no future *of my own*. I will not come to Fochabers and have my daughters and myself treated like so much chattel!'' Alex stared at her, all color drained from his cheeks.

''Alex . . .'' Jane said, lowering her voice. ''We still have much to share. We have the children . . . the good we've accomplished in the Highlands . . . but not *this*!'' she finished, gesturing to the crumpled bed linens. ''Not anymore.''

''Am I to believe my lady duchess no longer appreciates such carnal pleasures?'' Alex asked sarcastically, his eyes darkening ominously. ''The 'Flower of Galloway' isn't yet a shriveled up old hag! Look at you!'' he exclaimed, staring boldly at Jane's cleavage, which showed above the dressing gown she had hastily draped around her naked form. ''On the contrary, my guess is my good wife gets her satisfaction elsewhere these days . . . a stableboy, a politician, perhaps . . . even old Angus. . . .''

Jane gasped and spun away from him.

''Get out of my sight!'' she choked. ''Yer damned jealousy and distrust of everything in yer rotten world will be the *death* of ye, and of me!'' She yanked open the bedroom door wider and turned to face her husband, her eyes filled with fury. ''Be gone, ye punishing Devil! Be *gone*!''

''I'll be gone,'' he growled, ''but if I ever have evidence ye're taking yer pleasure elsewhere, I swear by God, I'll ruin you!''

''And what of that Bloodsucker of Gordon Castle?'' Jane

demanded, shaking with a rage that made her nearly faint. "Ye accuse me of doing what ye do yerself with that fornicating slut!"

"That, my dear, is the joy of being a *duke* and not a duchess," he said malevolently, crossing her threshold into the hall. "I do as I please. Good night, my sweet."

4

1789–1797

Thou beauteous star whose silvery light
Enchanting came upon my youthful sight.
Ah, what a blaze was hid by virgin rays
Whilst I, in woods retired, have past my days
Now silver'd o'er by Times eventful hand,
I greet thy evening beam in Scotia's stand.

Poem To The Duchess of Gordon
by the Earl of Buchan

31

September 1789

Jane's estrangement from the duke was now all but official. Alex remained silent when, after a courtship of several months, twenty-one-year-old Charlotte and Colonel Charles Lennox, heir to the Dukedom of Richmond, were betrothed.

Soon after the ceremony, Jane packed her trunks once again and headed for the glorious autumn foliage blanketing the Spey Valley, to begin planning the construction of Kinrara House. With Charlotte and Madelina now the mistresses of their own manor houses, Jane brought with her her third daughter, fifteen-year-old Susan, and the two younger girls—Louisa, whose thirteenth birthday fell three days after Charlotte's wedding, and eight-year-old Georgina. Even Alexander, who would be four in November, was included in the party. Petted and spoiled by his three sisters, he chased after butterflies with a net in the bottom of the garden and was taught how to fish the Spey by old Angus Grant.

During those moments when the estate factor wasn't overseeing the logging and spinning and cottage knitting operations, or instructing little Alexander on the fine points of scooping up a brown trout or salmon sculling in a nearby pool, he met with Jane, and together they paced out the foundations for the new country house.

"Do ye like these renderings, Angus?" Jane asked earnestly, pointing to several drawings of the proposed dwelling, which showed two tall, rounded half-towers studded with large, paned glass windows facing the river. "Do ye think the design is suitable?"

"Aye, m'lady," Angus said thoughtfully, studying the graceful lines of the roof. The bantam-sized retainer was perched on his haunches in the shade of a tree, studying the duchess's drawings, looking for all the world like a forest gnome sitting under a toadstool. "I like it. 'Tis a style that seems to harmonize with the natural beauty surroundin' it."

"I was so hoping ye'd say that." Jane smiled, pleased with his verdict. "Let's see . . . 'tis nearly October . . . if we wish to start raising the timbers by spring, we'd best be seeing to the brick making."

"Inverness is the best place for that, Yer Grace," Angus replied. "There's a factory there that was founded when Culloden House was built."

Jane flinched at the mention of the place where Alex had treated her so brutally. However, since Kinrara House was to be made of brick and plastered over in an eggshell color, the sooner she put in her order for materials, the sooner the house would be standing on this very knoll.

She looked out over the fragrant birch and Caledonian pines covering the surrounding hills and breathed in the slightly musky smell of dying leaves and wilting heather.

"Will ye be traveling to Inverness to see to the bricks yerself, Yer Grace?" Angus inquired.

"Aye . . . I'll place the order when I go north to join the duke in November," she replied, referring to her obligatory appearance at the annual Inverness Gathering early the following month.

"Have ye thought about that man I apprised ye of a while back as a possible factor . . . Thomas Fraser of Struy? I havna run into him in a long while and dinna know if he's still raising sheep, but I think 'tis worth considering, m'lady."

It shocked Jane to hear the name spoken aloud so casually.

Thomas. . . .

Her mind raced back to the last time she'd seen him that night in the room at the top of the stairs of Simon Fraser's tumbledown townhouse in Edinburgh. *Come to the Highlands with me,* he had begged her, before she'd fled into the snowy night. *We can live a good, simple life.*

How ironic that this was the same sort of existence she was seeking at Kinrara. Angus had said Thomas was barely subsisting on the few acres left to him as the courts endlessly debated the complications surrounding Simon's will.

Dinna come to me unless ye want me in yer life, he had told her that night.

Jane looked down on the sparkling River Spey dancing over the amber rocks. The water's mossy banks were studded with heather and lush ferns. Across the glen and behind the hill lay Loch-an-Eilean, crowned by its jewellike castle. Kinrara was her touchstone, her confirmation that there was, indeed, love in the world. She would build a beautiful house and devote herself to the simpler life Thomas alluded to that night. If only she could *share* this life with Thomas. If only—

An involuntary gasp escaped her lips. She had vowed there were to be no more "if onlys" in her life!

Yes! Oh, yes, Thomas, her heart cried out. *I very much want to be with ye in the Highlands!*

Jane took a deep breath and looked over Angus's stooped figure and stared blankly at the river. She had lived her life at the behest of others long enough! Why should she continue to punish herself? She wanted Thomas with her any way it might be possible . . . and she would do whatever she had to do to have him. *Propriety be damned!* she thought fiercely. If Alex could flaunt Jean Christie in the corridors and drawing rooms of Gordon Castle and along the High Street in Fochabers, *she and Thomas* could find a way to be together in the remote outpost called Kinrara. If they were discreet. . . .

Her heart ached at the thought of his scratching out a living these last years in one of the most desolate districts of Scotland. Thomas had waited for her such a very long time. . . .

Angus Grant looked up and was gazing at Jane with a puzzled frown. She had not responded to his inquiry about seeking an estate factor.

"I will send to Struy for the chap myself after the Inverness Gathering," Jane said, recovering the train of their conversation. "How shall I find this Thomas Fraser?" she asked casually, trying to keep her voice steady.

"Och! 'Tis simple as can be," Angus chuckled. "He told me once he's the only crofter left south of Erchless Castle on the Cannich-Struy Road. 'Tis a half-day's ride from Inverness to Beauly, and half that to Struy."

The Duke of Gordon departed for Gordon Castle the day following the annual autumn festivities in Inverness. There had been the market fair, the Highland Games, and the Harvest Ball, all of which Jane and Alex attended side by side. Jane awoke at the Church Street Inn exhausted from the strain of so much pretending.

Pulling herself upright in bed, she stared out of the window of a low-ceilinged room at the crisp November day, and felt apprehensive. She was forced to acknowledge to herself that her determination to have Thomas live with her at Kinrara was fraught with peril. What if Alex found out? What if he—

. . . *living life at the behest of others* . . .

The phrase whirled around and around in her brain. Suddenly, she kicked off the bed linen and hurriedly got out of bed. Prudently disguising herself as she prepared to seek out Thomas, she donned a pair of Lord Huntly's breeches, which she'd found stuffed in a chest at Kinrara. She secured her hair on top of her head and clamped a tattered black tricornered hat over her tresses. Looking like a disreputable footman, she requested a horse from the local livery in the name of the Duchess of Gordon.

"And who's to be saying 'tis all right for ye to have this pony, laddie?" the sharp-eyed stableman asked, cocking his head sideways and staring at her.

"I've a note from my mistress," Jane said in the deepest voice she could muster. "I shall be back before evening."

The stableman glanced briefly at the scrap of parchment Jane had penned herself and handed it back. Jane realized instantly the man could not read.

"All right, laddie. This nag ought to do ye. See that ye feed and water her, now . . . and no running her too hard, ye hear me—or the good duchess'll have yer hide!"

"Oh no, sir," Jane replied obediently, anxious to be on her way. "Ye can count on me to be kind to 'er."

The road toward Struy led over the stone bridge from the center of Inverness and along the rutted lane that flanked the Beauly Firth. Dawn's light was just bathing the bay the color of slate. Jane soon passed the point of land where the water funneled into the blue River Ness, home of a monster said to dwell in the depths of the loch several miles downstream. A cold, brisk wind blew off the bay, giving a hint of the winter storms, which would soon be thundering out of the Arctic north, blanketing northern Scotland in snow and ice.

Jane spurred her Highland pony to a trot. The forests on both sides of the steep-sided glen grew more dense, casting deep shadows across the road. The air was damp and silvery, with an alpine tang to it. Only the sound of the wind reached her ears, a sighing, lonely whisper that seemed to convey a secret message she couldn't discern. She sensed she had entered a magical kingdom, ruled by some ancient chieftain unanswerable to any king.

Her pony plodded on, deep into the valley bisected by the ribbon of the River Beauly, which wound its way toward the remote lochs and braes seen only by stags and hawks. Jane felt a tightening in the pit of her stomach. What if Thomas refused her proposal? What if he would not countenance her unorthodox plan that he should become Kinrara's factor by day and her. . . . Her thoughts veered away from what the outside world might think of a man who kept house with a duchess who was not his wife.

It was just after noon when she passed the forbidding walls of Erchless Castle, a stronghold of the Chisholms in the heart of Strathglass. Thomas had told her once that close by, in Glen Moriston, was a cave nestled in the rocks where the Bonnie Prince himself had hidden out with seven men—three of them the fearsome Chisholms. This was prior to the prince's escape to France, disguised as a maid to a lady named Flora MacDonald. It had been in these very hills that Thomas's mother had starved to death, and his father succumbed to the effects of his imprisonment in the dungeon in Edinburgh Castle after the Rebellion of '45.

Jane shifted her weight on the sure-footed Highland mare and anxiously scanned the next hillside for a glimpse of a cottage or small farmhouse. With great anticipation, she crossed Struy Bridge and entered the tiny village of Struy itself.

Ahead of her was a collection of low-lying stone structures with sparsely thatched roofs greatly in need of repair. A filthy youngster, barefooted, thin as a rail post, and dressed in rags, stood in the middle of the dusty road and stared at Jane with vacant eyes. Jane was struck by the vision of hungry children living in a place of such heartbreaking beauty. It was for these people, Jane thought suddenly, as well as for Thomas himself, that he had fought so long and so hard to reclaim his patrimony. A working estate provided a way of life for an entire community. She glanced up the hill behind the village and glimpsed, through the trees, what she surmised was Struy House with its massive walls of rough Moray freestone. The looming structure appeared as unkempt as the village, and likewise deserted.

A wooden sign squeaking forlornly on a weathered post indicated that ale could be purchased in a dingy tavern called the Lovat Arms.

Jane dismounted and entered the gloomy, low-ceilinged chamber. The proprietor was asleep in a chair in the corner, his stained leather apron stretched tautly across his enormous belly. At the sound of her footsteps, he belched, fluttered his protruberant eyes, and sat up with a start.

"Zounds, man! Ye startled me!" he snorted.

"My apologies, sir," Jane said in her gruffest voice. "Can ye tell me where to find the cottage of Thomas Fraser?"

"Which Thomas Fraser?" he said, cocking his head toward her curiously. "There were two."

"Captain Thomas Fraser of Struy—late of the Seventy-first Fraser Highlanders. His family had the estate in this district, and now he raises sheep."

"Ah . . . *that* Thomas Fraser," her rotund informant exclaimed. "His cottage is just down the road from here and up Broch Lane."

"Thank ye, sir," Jane said, trying to mask her excitement. She turned to go.

"No point in thankin' me, laddie. Ye'll not find 'im there."

Jane stared at him dumbly.

"Where is he?" she asked, wondering if he had finally moved back into Struy House after all.

"Somewhere near Baltimore, I heard. America, dinna ye know? Left these parts . . . och . . . it must be about a year or so ago."

"W-what . . . ?" Jane stammered, her voice trailing off. She staggered back a few paces and sagged against a rough-hewn post that held up the roof.

"If ye know Captain Fraser, as it seems ye do . . . then ye know about the muddle over his godfather's will. Well, the judgment was finally rendered. The sale was ruled incomplete. It was offered to him for purchase, but he dinna have the siller, poor sod. He lost the estate."

"No . . . ye canna m-mean that—" Jane stuttered, "It canna be true . . . no!"

With an anguished cry, Jane stumbled out of the chamber and leapt on the gray pony tethered outside. The startled horse lurched forward as she gouged her heel against his flanks. The animal tore past the ragged child and down the deserted street at a dead run, quickly disappearing from view in a swirl of dust and drifting autumn leaves.

The cottage at the end of Broch Lane was a deserted hovel. It sat in a small clearing overgrown with brambles and thorns. Half of the thatched roof had fallen into the solitary dirt-floored chamber. One wall of the structure consisted of mere rubble, apparently scavenged for building material by the few remaining neighbors in the glen. An unshorn sheep chewed on a gorse bush outside, unruffled by Jane's sudden appearance.

Fighting back tears, she surveyed the desolate scene. The only door to the cottage was half off its hinges. A short-eared owl let loose a protesting hoot and flapped its wings, scurrying from its perch on a windowsill. Jane stepped inside the one-room hut Thomas had called home for three torturous years while he waited for his court case to be decided . . . while he waited for her to come to him.

The room bore no witness that he or anyone else had ever lived there. There was no furniture in the barren chamber, just a cracked, blackened pot near the hearth. Jane thought her heart would burst at the bleakness of it all, the poverty of spirit this existence must have inflicted on the man she loved so dearly. Her throat tightened as she ran her fingers over the windowsill, the stone wall, the rude hand-hewn mantel over the tiny fireplace. The sheer *loneliness* of it all! She was sickened by the thought of Thomas living within these four walls at the very moment she was dining on pheasant and champagne inside the silk-lined walls of her London and Edinburgh residences.

As she caressed the remnants of his life, her fingers grazed something stiff, a tattered piece of rolled parchment, wedged between the fireplace's beam and the jagged stones of the hearth. She caught her breath. Her fingers trembled as she sought to untie the knotted leather thong that bound it. Slowly, she unrolled it and stepped to the chamber's one small window. A narrow shaft of late afternoon sunlight slanted across the short missive.

> *Jenny:*
> *My heart is in the Highlands. I leave thee my love, and seek a new home.*
> **Thomas Fraser of Struy**
> 2 June 1788

Sinking to the sod floor, his note clutched in her hand, Jane gave vent to bitter tears for all the words not said, actions not taken.

Ye have a life waiting for ye in America? she'd asked him that snowy night in Edinburgh.

If I want it, he'd answered, the candlelight dancing on the wall of the small chamber atop Simon's townhouse. *Just as yer life is here—or in America. With me—or without me. However ye want it to be. . . .*

Oh, how very much she realized now she had wanted it to be with him . . . here . . . in the Highlands they both loved so much. He had waited nearly three years for her to come to him.

When she didn't and there was no possibility of recovering Struy House, or even surviving here, he'd charted the only course open to him.

I leave thee my love, and seek a new home.

A line of carriages filled the mud-choked roads from the Washington-Philadelphia Post Road leading to the entrance of Antrim Hall itself. Rain splattered the fur-trimmed muffs and beaver hats of the wedding guests, but no one seemed to mind. Arabella O'Brien Delaney Boyd was embarking on her third marriage in twenty-five years at eight o'clock on a Christmas Eve, and witnessing such an event was well worth any inconvenience.

Arabella's long-time servant trundled down the hallway and knocked sharply on Thomas Fraser's door. Mehitabel's dark brown eyes nearly popped out of her ebony, moon-shaped face.

"Captain Fraser . . . you gotta talk some sense into dat woman," she said in a singsong voice when he opened the door. "All dat girl ever say was she want to marry you, sir . . . and *now* she say she won't go through with it!"

Thomas quickly tucked his linen shirt into his breeches and followed the servant to Arabella's bedchamber.

"You're going to hate me if we do this!" cried the black-haired bride-to-be sprawled in her pale yellow gown across the massive bed, her elaborately coiffed head buried in her arms. "This is a terrible thing we're doing. You're going to feel trapped and henpecked and you'll go back to Scotland! I just know you will."

Mehitabel backed out of the room with a worried frown and closed the door.

"No . . . *no*, Arabella," Thomas said soothingly. He lowered his large frame on the bed and kissed her ear. "What's all this about, dearheart?" he whispered gently. "Ye're not going to abandon me at the altar, are ye now?"

"But I'm *pregnant*!" she wailed. "I'm forty-one years old, and I'm pregnant. 'Tis a flaming disgrace!"

"I've told ye from the moment we knew about the bairn that I couldna be happier! A babe comin' to us at our age! 'Tis some sort of miracle from God. I am proud to be yer husband, and the father of this bairn . . . truly I am, pet."

"You never would have married me if it weren't for the baby, though, would you?" she said reproachfully, leaning her elbow on the bed and looking up at him. "You'd have gone on forever, running Antrim Hall for my brother Beven and me, sneaking into the summerhouse to bed me until we were too old to—''

"I would have gladly married ye, minx, if ye'd told me of this a wee bit sooner,'' he laughed. " 'Tis yer own damned fault ye're facing the good reverend, so many months gone.''

"I thought I'd lose it, like all the others,'' she sighed. "And then, when I didn't, I thought you wouldn't make love to me if you knew . . . or you'd leave.''

"Arabella!'' Thomas interjected her with mock indignation. "Is that any way to describe yer faithful retainer—forever at yer service?''

"Well, ye might have,'' she said sulkily. "Only *you* could have done this,'' she added. "I've buried two husbands and kept myself cozy with a few lost souls over the years, but only *you*, Thomas Fraser, could make a baby with a woman of the ridiculous age of forty-one. I'll never forgive you!''

Thomas threw back his head and roared with laughter.

"Maybe I'll make *ten*!''

"Not if they make my tummy feel as wretched as this one does.''

She bit her lip, and cast her cobalt eyes fringed with long, dark lashes toward the noticeable bulge protruding beneath her skirts.

"Are ye feeling all right, pet?'' Thomas asked sharply, glancing at her with a worried frown.

"I *can't* get sick now!'' she groaned in a low voice that clearly indicated she felt unwell. "We deliberately scheduled this as an *evening* wedding!''

But sick, she was, and Thomas gently held her shoulders as she lost her last meal into a nearby basin.

"Poor, poor 'Bella,'' he said soothingly. "Ye'll feel much better now, pet.'' He eased her back down on the bed and patted her perspiring forehead with a damp cloth.

"Oh, Thomas,'' she sighed, looking exhausted and spent. "I wonder if it'll be a girl?'' She looked at him tenderly. "Would you like that . . . a little girl to replace your Louisa?''

He gazed at her somberly. They had no secrets between them. That was the source of their strength. When he had arrived at her door, threadbare and nearly starving fifteen months earlier, he had recounted to her exactly what had transpired since he'd last seen her after the war.

"I'm woefully homesick and sore of heart, dear friend,'' he had said that first night over a dinner of cold chicken and chilled wine served in the old summerhouse. "Sometimes, I canna believe I abandoned the fight and left the Highlands like so many before me," he had added morosely, shaking his head sadly, "but I had barely the siller for my passage, once my debts to the lawyers were paid. However," he had said, brightening, "I'm willing to work as a factor or plowman. Whatever. 'Tis entirely up to ye, if ye'll have me in yer employ."

Arabella's brother Beven had been less than enthusiastic when she decided to turn over the reins of running the plantation to Thomas. But to Thomas, the dissolute sod seemed relieved not to have to work so hard. It left the old boy more time to drink with his cronies in Annapolis.

Now that Thomas was to be Beven's brother-in-law, O'Brien was even less cordial. Antrim Hall was entailed by his father's will, which stipulated Beven would keep control of the plantation which he owned jointly with Arabella until it was inherited by either his own son—an unlikely eventuality, since he hadn't even a wife—or, by any male issue of Arabella's.

Thomas reached for Arabella's hand and kissed her palm.

"No child can ever be replaced, dearheart," Thomas said gently. "But this new one—lad or lassie—can bring light to our lives. I am honored to take ye as my wife, my beautiful 'Bella . . . and to call m'self father of yer bairn."

"*Our* bairn," she said smugly, patting her abdomen. "No one can doubt, Captain Fraser, that we did this together."

The staccato rhythm of a hammer striking lumber rang out across Kinrara Glen. Jane wiped her perspiring face in the warm May sun as she surveyed the progress of the carpenters and brick masons and felt a pleasurable glow at seeing how high the mansion's new walls had climbed. The burnished russet bricks marched up to the level of the second story. The graceful house, so long a part of her imagination, was slowly taking shape before her eyes.

The act of building a house, when so much else in Jane's life had been torn asunder, became her salvation in the months of anguish following her trip to Struy and the discovery that Thomas had departed for America. London and the gay society that had, in times past, filled the void in her life, was now without the slightest charm. Like an animal that must lick its wounds alone, Jane had spent her first winter in the Highlands in many a year, insulated from all the backstairs intrigues and rivalries that had been so much a part of her earlier life around the Court.

Even the furor caused by the mob storming the Bastille the previous July in Paris failed to ignite Jane's interest in the world outside Kinrara's boundaries. She sighed, sitting on a knoll that overlooked a sharp bend in the River Spey, and squinted into the sun. She had lost Thomas for good, but perhaps she had found herself. His note had bequeathed to her his love, and that love had pulled her through the misery of the previous year. She was proud of the house she was helping to build. She was proud of her children whose company she found delightful. She was proud of Thomas's long struggle to help his people, and she renewed her vow to help her own.

A feeling of satisfaction crept over her as she surveyed the crew of workmen swarming around the house. To promote local employment, she'd hired as many Spey Valley craftsmen as possible, importing from the south only those who had special skills of carving and fashioning masonry. When the house was finished, she would renovate the cottages and bothys that sprinkled the estate. Perhaps she would even try to persuade Alex, when next she saw him, to do the same with the loggers' cottages and spinning and weaving operations. Gazing toward the river, she caught sight of a dozen or so people tramping through the forest that flanked the Spey.

"Heigh-ho! Food to the rescue!" shouted her twenty-year-old son Lord Huntly, carrying one side of a large picnic hamper up the hill from the old cottages where the children and guests slept, dormitory-style.

Alex's natural son by Bathia Largue—now a commissioned officer in the Army and no longer called The Duke's George—held fast to the other wicker handle. The two brothers continued to look remarkably alike, a fact that still gave Jane pause. Even so, she was gratified to see her stepson was quite affectionate toward her, despite the fact she was hardly on speaking terms with his father. However, only one of the lads would eventually inherit his father's titles, along with the Gordons' vast lands and influence. An accident of birth . . . a piece of paper at the church registry . . . a judge's dyspepsia or pleasure on a given case. . . . On such slender strings hung a man's—or woman's—fortune.

Little Alexander trudged along beside his elder brothers, proud to be asked to bear a tartan blanket for the festivities. Thirteen-year-old Louisa, her glorious red tresses piled casually atop her head, transported a large jug of ale. Georgina, nearly nine, carried her mother's fan.

"William?" Susan called to a young man carrying several bottles of spirits, "would you be so kind as to pull on that far corner of the tartan rug?"

William Montague, the 5th Duke of Manchester, was the nineteen-year-old scion of Kimbolton Castle in the south near St. Neots. He had extraordinary good looks and an athletic body. The young blade was one of several visitors Lord Huntly had brought with him to the Highlands after the conclusion of his term at University. Jane had observed the admiration in Susan's eyes when the lass watched Montague and Huntly row their sleek barks in a race on Loch-an-Eilean. The young duke's broad shoulders and muscular arms were a rather stirring sight, even to a woman of Jane's mature years.

She nearly laughed out loud at herself. She didn't miss Alex's dark moods, or jealous rages, but on occasion, when she glimpsed a physique as intriguing as young Montague's, she realized she wasn't the dried-up matron of forty she suspected her children might consider her.

Jane appraised her middle daughter contentedly. Susan was young, of course, but Jane had every hope of marrying yet another of her five daughters to someone of note—and this young duke, she wagered, would do very well indeed.

The members of this casual party reclined on the tartan rug, sat on the grass, or perched on tree stumps, partaking of the simple repast. Jane had been delighted by the steady stream of friends and acquaintances hailing from as far away as London who were drawn to Kinrara by its renowned natural beauty and the news that the celebrated Duchess of Gordon was building her dream house.

"When do ye expect to start running yer sheep?" asked her stepson, his eyes squinting in the warm sunlight bathing their picnic area.

"In the spring, I should hope," she smiled.

"Shall we buy stock from the Grants, after the lambing?" Louisa asked, full of interest in the proposed project.

"You're planning to be a shepherdess, are you now?" Lord Huntly joked.

"Mama says she wants all her lasses to learn about sheep farming," Louisa retorted defensively. "Don't you, Mama?"

Jane glanced at her son, who exuded such confidence and pride at his place in the world. The future of the 5th Duke of Gordon was assured, his position secure both in the Highlands and at Court. Did it ever occur to him how different the situation was for his sisters?

"Aye . . ." Jane said, sipping on a tankard of ale the handsome Duke of Manchester had extended to her. " 'Tis good for lasses as well as lads to know a bit of farming and husbandry," she said, her voice full of meaning. "One never knows when ye'll be called upon to make yer own way in the world."

"Angus teaches us all manner of interesting things," Louisa continued with enthusiasm. "He's shown us which fields have the sweetest grass, and how to tell a lamb is sickly and should be culled out, and—"

"All right! All right!" Lord Huntly laughed, good-naturedly interrupting her. "I can see Mama will one day have an able estate factor in the fair Louisa!"

"But what about marriage?" teased the older George. "Do ye not intend to wed, miss?"

"Oh . . . I don't know," Louisa said, suddenly subdued. "It seems marriage is not such a welcome state, from what I've seen. . . ."

"Louisa!" Susan exclaimed, with a mortified glance in the direction of her hoped-for suitor William Montague, who was busy unpacking the wicker luncheon hamper.

"What I'm sure Louisa means, is that marriage is not the only source of pleasure in one's life," Jane said sardonically.

"What are you saying, Mama dear?" Susan replied tartly.

Jane cast a brief glance toward the good-looking young man who had so captured her daughter's fancy.

"I'm saying my experience has shown me, dearheart, that— whether one is male or female—there are *many* aspects to one's existence which afford one satisfaction. Marriage . . . music . . . good conversation . . . even *sheep farming*. Ye might remember that as ye go down life's path. . . ."

"Well, sheep may be interesting, and I love the country life," Susan said, smiling coquettishly at Montague, "but I do so look forward to the fall season, don't you, m'lord?"

"Oh, 'twill be capital fun to get back to London," the young duke replied, oblivious to the train of conversation. "Will His Grace come to Badenoch soon?"

Everyone but Jane engaged in speculation about whether the Duke of Gordon would appear in Badenoch this spring to indulge in his annual pastime of salmon fishing on the Spey. Alex and Jane had been giving each other a wide berth of late, and Jane was just as happy to keep it that way.

"If it pleases him to do so, I am sure he will," she answered calmly.

Jane felt very proprietary about Kinrara. Alex was master, of course, of his own estates in the region, but she had made it clear he was to come to this special place by invitation only. To date, she had made no such proposal, and, after their last unpleasant encounter, she doubted she ever would.

"Let's drink a toast!" Lord Huntly exclaimed, breaking into the conversation and raising his glass. "To Mama . . . the indomitable Mistress of Kinrara!"

Indomitable? Jane thought, a trifle irritated at her son's characterization of her.

"He makes me sound like a monument," she grumbled with as much good humor as she could muster.

She surveyed the circle of people who raised their glasses in tribute to her, including the numerous members of her brood. Perhaps a monument to survival is what I am, she speculated privately. Or perhaps the monument isn't me, but this new house, Kinrara.

There was no greater contrast to the climate of the Highlands of Scotland than the low-lying tidelands of Maryland in the month of May, thought Thomas, as he loosened the linen stock tied round his throat. Sweat trickled in rivulets down his back as he relaxed in his saddle, surveying the fields of wheat ripening in the rolling fields under a blistering sun. The air was still, heavy with moisture from the swamps nearby.

Suddenly, the thudding sound of pounding hoofbeats captured his attention. Galloping toward him with unaccustomed speed, his brother-in-law, Beven, whipped his horse mercilessly. His shouts were carried away by the wind. He reined in his horse and it clattered to a halt.

"Come quickly!" he gasped. " 'Tis 'Bella. . . . God, 'tis simply *awful, man*—"

"*What* is?" Thomas retorted, instinctively dreading his brother-in-law's words.

" 'Bella started her labor about two hours ago—"

"God's bones, lad!" Thomas exploded. "Why dinna ye call me?"

"She said to leave you to your work."

"Christ, man!" Thomas exclaimed, wheeling his horse around. "She's bleeding like a broken barrel," Beven exclaimed, his voice on the edge of hysteria. "Mehitabel said she suddenly started gushing blood—"

Thomas didn't wait for Beven to finish his description of Arabella's condition. Yanking his horse cruelly by the bit, he spurred his steed down the trail that ran alongside the fence. Thomas barely was able to collect himself as he urged his mount over a gate, cutting a swath sharp as an arrow through the budding wheat. He prayed this short cut would bring him to the house in time.

A thousand macabre images filled his thoughts. He'd seen poor and destitute women in the Highlands die from such violent hemorrhaging, their life's blood draining from their bodies in the time it took to saddle a horse and send for the physic. Arabella had suffered dreadfully with this pregnancy the entire nine months—due, the doctor told them, to her forty-one years and her history of miscarriages. Her feet and ankles had ballooned enormously in recent weeks, and her morning sickness never waned, even in her ninth month.

"I want this baby so much," she whimpered one night the previous week when she had had a particularly bad day. The infant was a good week or two overdue.

Thomas had placed his hand on the mound of her abdomen and chuckled when he felt the baby kick.

"I think ye shall get it, sooner than ye think," he'd laughed.

"We must discuss names . . . 'tis a disgrace we've let it go this long," she frowned. "If 'tis a girl, I'd like to call her Kathleen after my mother . . . that is, if you—"

"Kathleen Fraser," Thomas interrupted her, trying the sound of the name aloud. "Irish and Scots . . . 'tis a perfect blend. Kathleen it will be, if 'tis a lass."

"And if she's a *he*?" Arabella had said. "You shall decide."

"Oh, I dinna know . . ." he murmured, staring off into space. "I wouldna name the poor laddie Thomas . . . I know what 'tis like to have to live up to yer da who's the same name as ye . . . and I dinna have a brother or any family."

"What about your godfather, Simon?" she asked, curious that her husband rarely talked about his late guardian.

"No . . . I wouldna want that," he said shortly. He looked at her and smiled sadly. "I've so little family left at home . . . none, in fact, except Louisa . . . better that ye pick both names, dearheart."

"All right," she said, peering at him with uncharacteristic diffidence. "If 'tis a boy, I'll name him for a relative of Louisa's."

Thomas gave her a startled look.

"Maxwell," Arabella said firmly. "I would like a son named Maxwell Fraser. I owe you both that much."

He hadn't been able to speak because of the lump of emotion closing his throat.

Instead, he had lain down on the bed next to her bloated form and had taken her in his arms.

Thomas concentrated his thoughts on the task of forcing his horse to take the last quarter mile at a dead run. He thundered toward the front door of Antrim Hall, leaping from his mount even before it had skittered to a halt. He tossed the reins at a frightened groom and mounted the wide stairs, two at a time.

The sight that greeted him in the bedchamber he had shared with Arabella since their wedding was one that would haunt him for the rest of his days. A plump baby boy squalled in Mehitabel's arms, which were coated scarlet with Arabella's blood. The life force evident in the babe's piercing wails contrasted poignantly with the deathly silence of the chalk white figure lying on the bloodsoaked bed.

"He come so fast, Captain Fraser," Mehitabel blubbered, nearly incoherent after what she'd just witnessed, "I didn't know what . . . I didn't know that . . . I—"

"Ye've done the best ye knew how, Mehitabel," he said over the cries of his newborn son. "When it happens this way, there's nothing to be done. Wash him, please, and send for the—"

He bent low and pressed his ear to Arabella's lips. There was no movement of breath. Frantically, he searched for a pulse point, and when he found none, he cupped her swollen left breast in his hand, praying for a heartbeat. It was still. His wife's glorious black hair was matted with sweat, her dark lashes beaded with tears. Thomas sank to his knees, his shoulders wracked with sobs that made no sound. He wept for the love he had known in his life, love that never seemed to survive his loving in return.

32

November 1793

The Duchess of Gordon found it uncomfortably ironic that the broad lawns at Ayton House, where she and Alex had been married in 1767, provided the setting for their daughter, Lady Susan Gordon's wedding to the 5th Duke of Manchester. However, Jane's sister Katherine and John Fordyce had kindly offered their estate, and it certainly cut down on expenses when compared to holding such festivities in London.

Jane and Alex had hardly exchanged a word the entire day and the one unexpected bright note was the ardent attention paid Louisa by young Charles Cornwallis, Viscount Brome, the only son and heir of General Cornwallis, late of the unfortunate war in America—a national hero, despite his defeat.

Staring moodily at the bride and groom, Jane was startled to feel a hand gently take her elbow.

"Mama, may I have the honor of this dance?" Lord Huntly asked his mother gallantly during the reception which was sheltered beneath a cloth pavilion. " 'Tis the 'Babbity Bowser!' "

Jane smiled at her son gratefully, relieved to have an excuse to escape the mood of depression that came over her whenever she was in the presence of her mother or husband. As Jane and Huntly wove through the patterns of the rolicking dance, she tried to ignore her spouse who was lounging on the sidelines, wearing a faint scowl.

"You know, Mama, there is now real fear of a French invasion, and we must once again raise recruits," Lord Huntly said to her as the music ended.

"Aye, so I've heard," she replied, casting a glance at Viscount Brome who had elbowed his way to the front of a queue in order to secure a glass of punch for Louisa.

"Would you help with the recruiting?" Huntly blurted suddenly.

"For the Gordon Highlanders?" Jane asked, surprised. "Whatever for?"

"Because we must get a thousand lads to volunteer. The War

Office will be sending letters patent in January, and we're afraid that previous recruiting has bled the Highlands dry."

"Really, Huntly, my dear," she chastised her son mildly, "I dinna think yer da would take kindly to the idea."

" 'Twas *he* who suggested it," her son said, grinning mischievously. "You may not be the best of friends, but he still remembers your success in Seventy-five!"

Jane glanced in Alex's direction with surprise.

"Even so," she said quickly, "dinna ye think yer mother's a bit too advanced in years to be dancing jigs in village squares to fill the ranks?"

"Never, Mama, never," Huntly teased. His face grew serious. "At forty-three or *eighty*-three—you have that magic power. I know you'll think of something. We *must* fill the rolls. The Gordon honor is at stake!"

Jane gazed at her eldest son fondly. He tried so hard to please both Alex and her. Their rift had been perhaps hardest on him, she thought sadly. He tried to keep a boot in both camps, and it had long been a strain.

"Of course I'll help ye," she said, kissing him softly on the cheek. "Or, at least, I'll do what I can."

The effort to raise the Gordon Highlanders in the spring of 1794 took Jane and her son, the Marquess of Huntly, throughout the Highlands, from North Uist and the Isle of Barra to the shores of Aberdeen. At first, it was slow, discouraging work, reminding Jane of those weeks twenty years earlier when she helped recruit for the 71st Fraser Highlanders to fight in the American War for Independence. Huntly had adopted her idea to create a new Gordon tartan, taking the basic Black Watch pattern and overlaying it with thin yellow stripes both vertically and horizontally.

As Jane scanned the sparse number of spectators lurking in front of the jail in the old square at Elgin, she wondered if even purple peacock feathers would garner anyone's attention these days. The drum major in his spanking new kilt monotonously beat his drum to signal their arrival, but few seemed to take notice. One hulking young lad caught Jane's eye. He was staring at her, apparently not much impressed by their entourage.

"Ah, my lad," Jane hailed the youth, an outrageous idea forming just then in her head. "May I introduce m'self? I am Jane, Duchess of Gordon, and this is my son, the Marquess of Huntly, who'll command the brave Gordon Highlanders."

She flashed the lad her warmest smile. The local boy continued to stare at her rather stupidly.

"Have ye a mind to see the world?"

The feckless youth shook his head.

She held up the traditional King's Shilling, which sealed the bargain between recruit and the Crown when a lad agreed to join the ranks of the King's Army.

"Have ye a mind, then, to tell yer friends ye've kissed a *duchess*?" she asked slyly.

The lad's eyes widened, and a wolfish grin formed slowly on his features.

"Aye . . . that I do. I ken kiss *ye*, Duchess?" he said, leering appreciatively.

Jane could sense her son shifting uneasily in his saddle.

"But of course ye can, if ye accept the King's Shilling and enroll in the Gordon Highlanders today."

"Your Grace," Huntly said formally. "Really, do you—"

"Ye may kiss yer duchess, lad," Jane said in her most commanding voice, "*if* ye take the King's Shilling from my lips."

A gasp could be heard from the bystanders, and for a moment, she, too, wondered if she had gone too far. How humiliating it would be if the youth refused to accept the shilling from a forty-four-year-old woman who so seductively placed the coin firmly between her teeth and tilted her face to be kissed.

Jane's eyes bore into the lad's with deliberate, sexual intensity. As if in a trance, the youth leaned forward, wiped his mouth with the back of a dirty sleeve, and brushed his lips against hers. With her tongue, Jane pushed the coin from her lips to his. A cheer went up from the crowd, which had grown considerably larger as word of this transaction spread up and down the little town.

"Hear! Hear!" Lord Huntly exclaimed, both relieved and delighted to acquire such a brawny recruit. "The King's Shilling for a kiss from the Duchess of Gordon! A fair exchange if you were to be paid only *half* the price!"

In the next few days, their recruiting party traveled to other town squares—Forres, Barnhill, Buckie, and Keith, and even to remote glens and the Monaughty Forest—and everywhere, men came forward to take the King's Shilling for the price of a kiss.

Within two months, Huntly and the regiment were bound for Gibraltar, playing a waiting game with France's new *Directoires*. Jane's recently revived memory of recruiting on behalf of her brother so many years earlier was made all the more poignant on receipt of the news that Hamilton had died in India earlier that year.

Hamilton . . . Jane thought sadly, staring at the parchment from Ham's commander, which contained details of her brother's last hours. Hamilton, the tease, the perennial bachelor, the ambitious professional soldier. She and her brother had drifted apart after his return from the American War. Ham had rarely sought her company and seemed preoccupied solely with his advancement in the ranks. Now he was dead from some dreadful foreign malady.

It was with a heavy heart that Jane and her two youngest daughters returned from Inverness to London the following season of 1795. In order to raise their spirits, the trio stopped in Badenoch for the final inspection of Kinrara House. As their coach came around a bend, Jane caught her breath at the sight that greeted them.

Rising among the stately larch and pine trees loomed the well-proportioned residence whose bricks were now disguised with cream-colored plaster. The small, graceful manse stood as a welcoming beacon, harmonizing with one of the most beautiful settings in the world.

" 'Tis so perfect, Angus," she sighed to the Gordon factor who was confined to his cottage with a gnarling of joints that had shrunk his already stunted frame even further.

"Aye, Yer Grace," he agreed chuckling. "Ye've got yerself a fine, fair shieling. Now the question is, when are ye going to live in it?"

"Soon, Angus, soon," Jane laughed. "I've still two daughters to marry off, ye know . . . and to London I must go to do it, unless ye'll consent to marry one of them!"

"And forsake m'Flora? Never!" He smiled at the large-boned woman who hovered over him. "And, besides, I couldna afford 'em . . . I hear yer last two bairns also have a taste for dukes?"

"Not Louisa," Jane bantered back. "I'm thinking a future marquess would suit her just as well."

In London, Jane leased scaled-down apartments on Picadilly, wondering what direction her life would take, once the last two lasses were safely settled with husbands. She avidly followed accounts of General Napoléon Bonaparte, the French commander who put down a royalist insurrection in Paris, and worried incessantly over the fate of her son and the Gordon Highlanders. To keep occupied, she attended the opera in her private ground-floor box at the King's Theatre, and went to all manner of soirees and card parties. However, Jane and Prime Minister William Pitt had drifted apart since the overt troubles with Alex began, followed by her own preoccupation with building Kinrara House. When they did see each other, Jane simply didn't seem to spark to gossip and intrigue any longer, and she and Pitt found they had little else in common.

Jane did maintain her friendship with the prim and proper queen. She sympathized with the poor woman, who continued to fear that one day the king's strange malady would reappear.

Later that year, Jane received an invitation for Louisa and her to join in a house party at the family seat of the Cornwallises in Suffolk.

"Have ye been flirting more than usual, my dear?" she teased her daughter. "If ye have, it appears to have had a good effect."

Louisa had the decency to blush to the roots of her russet hair. Nearly nineteen, she was now in the full bloom of young womanhood. Her flawless skin, the wonderful natural rose color gracing her cheeks, and her loving spirit all conspired to draw others to her. She made her mother intensely proud.

In the back of her mind, however, Jane had always secreted away the uneasy thought that it was through Louisa that Alex might one day seek to punish his wife for the remarkably independent life she led. She feared that somehow the duke might eventually play this trump card, and reveal that he was not the lass's father. If he did, her daughter with the beautiful red hair would be ruined.

I must get her safely married, Jane vowed to herself, penning a favorable reply to her hosts in Suffolk.

The evening in mid-May selected for the formal engagement party of Louisa and Viscount Brome, the future Marquess of Cornwallis, proved to be warm and balmy. Jane surveyed the preparations in the Oriental Pavilion, the most popular section of Vauxhall. The pleasure gardens were awash with the golden glow cast by a hundred lanterns lighting the fantastical surroundings. Many guests arrived in elegant barges after being rowed from the City on the slow-moving Thames.

Jane had not consulted with Alex before making the arrangements for the party, and only under last-minute pressure from her sisters Eglantine and Catherine had she sent him an invitation.

" 'Tis his *daughter*!" Eglantine exclaimed. Jane looked away quickly and remained silent in the wake of her sister's mistaken pronouncement. "Louisa's marrying one of the leading peers in the land! Ye *must* invite Alex. 'Twill cause even *more* talk about your estrangement if he's not there."

Jane glanced down nervously at her mauve-colored gown, selected from the latest fashion of high-waisted, unboned creations dubbed empire. She appreciated the comfort and grace of the new designs, but worried that her ample bosom was indiscreetly displayed by the wickedly low-cut neckline that was key to the entire effect. The simplicity of these styles, Jane thought to herself, bordered on indecency.

Louisa looked breathtakingly beautiful in her pale green gown of transparent, diaphanous muslin gathered just below the bosom. Her deep burgundy tresses were piled in a deceptively simple style on her head and shot through with two green plumes.

Jane and Louisa and the assembled Gordons, Maxwells, and Cornwallises stood in an informal receiving line to greet the many guests. Alex was nowhere in sight. The Prince of Wales and the Duke of York arrived together—slightly tipsy, it appeared to Jane—but in fine humor. William Pitt merely nodded pleasantly and passed on down the line, but, much to her surprise, Richard Sheridan, whose comedies she admired despite his politics, bussed her effusively on the cheek.

"I shall write a play about you one day, madam!" teased the author of *The School for Scandal*. "*The Matchmaking Duchess*, I'll call it, and everyone shall know 'tis about you!"

Jane was pleased that the guests had gone to enormous lengths to dress for the occasion. The crowd virtually glittered in its finery. Even Louisa's intended groom wore the latest fashion—a dashingly cut tailcoat of dark green wool made to imitate a hunting jacket, with high black velvet collar and cuffs. He was shy and painfully thin, but Jane was relieved to observe his genuine devotion to Louisa.

Jane chuckled at the sight of all the unpowdered hair among the gentlemen. Prime Minister William Pitt had instituted a tax on powder to raise money for the war with France, and instantly, a custom of long standing had disappeared.

The viscount's father, the Marquess of Cornwallis, seemed to tower over everybody, including his rangy son. Jane had found the former commander to be pleasant in their dealings during her short acquaintance. However, this evening, she detected an unexplained reserve in his manner toward Louisa.

The small orchestra hired for the occasion began to play, and

Jane sighed with relief. The announcement of the official engagement would be made soon, and with that, Jane could relax.

Just at that moment, she caught sight of Alex, walking up from the dock toward the receiving line. As she watched him approach, she perceived there was the tiniest hesitation to his step, and she knew instantly that he had been drinking. Alex had always abhorred excessive imbibing and his inebriated state filled her with foreboding.

"Good evening, Lord Cornwallis," the Duke of Gordon said with a precision that would convince all, save one who knew him well, that he was sober as a judge. "I believe congratulations are in order . . ." He glanced grimly toward Jane. ". . . to my wife. It seems she has managed yet another sleight-of-hand, for which I must pay the bill."

"Good evening, Your Grace," Cornwallis said stiffly. Jane sensed that this soldier and statesman—a man of the world—could instantly detect a man in his cups, no matter how controlled he seemed.

Cornwallis studied his son's prospective father-in-law, seeming to mull something over in his mind. Finally, the former commander, whose life-and-death decision making had affected thousands of lives in the past, squared his shoulders.

"May I have a word with you both?" he asked pleasantly. "Shall we step into the pavilion for a moment?"

"Why of course, m'lord," Alex said, slightly slurring his words. "I had planned to ask you to do the same."

With a sinking heart, Jane accompanied the two men inside the ornate pagoda, its swooping roof suggesting an exotic Chinese temple. Wind chimes tinkled softly in the night air.

"I quite understand why my son should be so enamored of Lady Louisa," Lord Cornwallis began quietly. "She is one of the great beauties of England, I'll be bound."

"Thank ye, m'lord," Jane replied, wondering where this conference was leading.

Alex remained tight-lipped and silent.

"My son's enthusiasms took hold while I was abroad, and, naturally, I was delighted he seemed ready to settle down."

"Quite," Jane said with an uneasy glance in Alex's direction.

"However," Cornwallis said, pausing as if concentrating his thoughts on a difficult decision. "It has just come to my attention that there may be a matter of some concern regarding the parentage of my son's future wife."

Jane felt as if the room in which they were standing was

suddenly reeling. Had Alex secretly put out the true story of who had fathered Louisa, just to hurt both her and her daughter? Jane's heart pounded furiously, and for a moment, she thought she would faint.

Cornwallis looked directly at Alex and cleared his throat.

"It pains me to have to say this, Your Grace, but I am most mightily concerned with the taint of Gordon Madness so associated with your line."

Jane blinked and then stared in wonder at the look of utter shock that flooded Alex's face. He seemed to age before her eyes. His face turned gray and his eyes darted around the red-and-gilt room.

"I do not wish the Cornwallis family to risk such folly, sir," Cornwallis continued calmly. "If you'll take the trouble to look closely at my son, you'll see that our own blood is thin enough, as it is."

"If ye speak of the Duke of Gordon's brother George, or some distant cousins," Jane said with a rush, "I must respectfully remind ye, sir—"

"I speak of the Duke himself," Cornwallis countered, not unkindly. "I have it on good authority, sir, that you suffered a bout of madness in Sixty-four. A man, now in my employ, who was a stableboy to the physician Sir Algernon Dick of Prestonfield, confirms this unfortunate finding."

Alex remained silent, his eyes cast down. Jane knew that an old wound had been opened up, a wound so deep, the two of them had rarely spoken of it since their wedding day. Jane waited for Alex to defend himself, but he said nothing. Sir Algernon, who could vouch for Alex's stability, was long since in his grave.

"So, you see," Cornwallis said. "I must ask you not to make any announcement. Though there have been rumors of this engagement, we shall simply let the entire matter fade away quietly. You can rest assured as to my complete discretion on this unfortunate matter."

"That suits me admirably," Alex said bitterly. " 'Twas toward the same end of halting this engagement that I accepted my wife's *kind* invitation to attend tonight's festivities." He cast a twisted, triumphant glare in Jane's direction.

With a growing sense of horror, she realized that Alex had intended to hurt her through Louisa from the moment he had pleaded with her to come back to Fochabers—on his terms—and she had refused. This night, his eyes, staring at her so coldly, had become sunken hollows.

"Thank you for taking care of this matter for me, m'lord," Alex added, bowing with a kind of mocking courtesy. "You do me more of a favor than you shall ever know."

"Is yer objection to Louisa, m'lord, based solely on the fear of her transmitting madness to yer heirs?" Jane demanded boldly.

She was filled with barely controlled indignation. The fact that the man who had fathered her *other* six children would strike out so desperately at her seventh, merely to mortally wound his wife, had ignited in Jane a pure flame of righteous anger.

"That is my objection, yes," Cornwallis repeated with steely politeness. "I want healthy heirs to carry on my line."

"And if I could *prove* that ye had absolutely nothing to fear on that score, would ye accept Louisa for yer son . . . who loves her so deeply?"

"But—" Cornwallis said, puzzled, "as we've just seen, that is impossible."

"Why, not at all," she said in a low voice laced with bitterness. She was about to burn the last bridge of decency connecting Alex and her. "But let us be certain we completely understand each other. Ye swear ye'd have no objection to the match, but for the tainted Gordon blood?"

"I don't wish my son linked to a guttersnipe, Duchess," Cornwallis retorted, "but my objection rests on the issue of the Gordon Madness. Therefore, I see no reason to continue speaking together in this vein. . . ."

Jane flashed her most brilliant smile at the marquess, and turned her back on her husband.

"Then, my dear Lord Cornwallis," she said distinctly, her eyes flashing, "ye have absolutely nothing to fear . . . *for there's not a drop of Gordon blood in dear Louisa's veins!*"

There was stunned silence in the pavilion. Outside, Jane could hear the orchestra playing Handel. Time seemed suspended. Alex raised a trembling hand and touched his forehead. His shoulders sagged. He looked like an old man.

"Are you telling me, Duchess, that your husband, here, the Duke of Gordon, did not father your daughter, Louisa?"

"To be sure, he did *not*, m'lord!" she answered with ferocious candor.

"Your Grace?" Cornwallis said, looking at Alex closely.

The duke laughed bitterly.

"Louisa is not my child, as anyone with eyes can see. She's—"

"As ye are well aware," Jane interrupted quickly, "this sort of thing happens in the best of families . . . even among Royals. Louisa's father is someone ye know and respect highly, I believe, m'lord." Jane took a deep breath. "Louisa's father is Captain Thomas Fraser, son of Sir Thomas Fraser of Struy, though the sire was stripped of the title after the Forty-five. Captain Fraser served brilliantly under ye in all yer campaigns, I believe."

"That he did," Cornwallis replied, a look of utter amazement passing over his features. He rubbed his chin thoughtfully. "Is Thomas Fraser still alive?"

"Yes, I believe so," Jane answered with a catch in her voice. "He has emigrated to America and resides, I would wager, on a plantation called Antrim Hall in the American colony, Maryland."

Cornwallis turned to Alex.

"Is this fact of Louisa's parentage well known?" he asked.

The Duke of Gordon cast a glazed look on them both and shook his head in the negative.

"No one knows, m'lord," Jane said urgently, "except the adult parties directly involved. Louisa doesna know the truth, and, for her own peace of mind, never should . . . though sometimes," Jane said, half to herself, "I wonder if she dinna think something is . . ."

Cornwallis shifted his gaze from Jane to Alex and back again. Jane knew he was mulling over yet another momentous decision.

"My son is besotted with your daughter, m'lady. That is clearly obvious," he said, thinking aloud. "She's a charming lass, to be sure . . . and absolutely beautiful to behold . . ." Then the tall soldier, the one-time commanding general of legions of men, tossed his head back and laughed. "And I have to say—she certainly has *interesting bloodlines*! That's important to me. I've seen too many families ruined by weaklings and idiots. My son is a bit mild-mannered for my tastes, though I'm extremely fond of him. The Cornwallis line could use a little red pepper!" The marquess squinted at Jane's ample endowments as exhibited by her low cut gown. "Yes, Duchess. I think Lady Louisa *Gordon*," he emphasized with irony, "will make my son an eminently suitable wife."

Alex roused himself from his state of torpor.

"And you *believe* a woman who would say *anything* to further her bastard's prospects in such a dishonorable way?" Alex said, his face contorted with bitterness.

"My Lord Cornwallis can certainly ascertain whether or not I speak the truth!" she retorted caustically.

Cornwallis cast a look of mild disdain in Alex's direction.

"Now that I think on it, the lass looks a great deal like her father. . . ."

"There are probably a number of redheaded soldiers who have slept with my wife," Alex said coldly.

Jane heard her own sharp intake of breath. She shot Alex a poisonous glare.

"I can well understand my estranged husband's bitterness, my lord, but I have a proposal to make," Jane said with icy determination. "Why dinna ye write to Thomas Fraser directly, and explain these unusual circumstances. Ask for an honest reply. I do not doubt, sir, that ye would believe whatever answer he may give, since, in the past, I gather ye trusted him with some of the most important secrets of the American campaign."

"That I did, Your Grace," Cornwallis agreed. "A capital suggestion. I shall write immediately."

"What of those gathered here tonight?" she said, dreading the necessity of telling Louisa there could be no formal recognition of her betrothal. How could she possibly avoid her questions as to the reason for this postponement? "Must we wait until we hear from Captain Fraser?"

Lord Cornwallis, deep in thought, stared at Jane for a moment. Then he smiled.

"If you are willing to break off the engagement publicly, in the event Thomas Fraser refuses to confirm to me his parentage of Louisa, then, I am delighted to go forward with this evening's events, as planned."

"I would be most happy to accept the conditions ye impose, m'lord," replied the duchess with alacrity.

"As far as the actual marriage, however," he added sternly. "That must await the reply from Captain Fraser."

"Naturally, m'lord," Jane murmured demurely.

Alex stared at them both, his face mirroring a jumble of emotions—among them anger, remorse, and humiliation.

Lord Cornwallis extended his arm to Jane.

"Would you do me the honor, Your Grace?" he said, gripping her arm through the thin material on the sleeves of her mauve gown. "I think it's time we made an important announcement."

*　　*　　*

Thomas looked forward to the autumn months in Maryland when the stifling heat of summer tapered off and the nights, at last, were cool again.

He glanced down at the enormous ledger book laid open on the desk in the morning room. He stared at the entries made by Arabella during the years after the war, and sighed as he noted the next section of the book when his own bold hand recorded the ups and downs of Antrim Hall's fortunes in the five years since 'Bella had died. The plantation had turned a profit for three years now, though no thanks to his partner and brother-in-law, Beven O'Brien.

The sound of breaking glass interrupted his concentration and he heard the wails of his five-and-a-half-year-old young son, Maxwell.

"Damn your hide!" a voice exploded.

Thomas heard Max begin to shriek. He leapt up from his desk and dashed down the hallway and into the sitting room.

Beven froze as Thomas thundered into the room. O'Brien's hand was suspended above little Maxwell's bottom. A bottle of whiskey lay in pieces in front of the fireplace, its amber contents slowly seeping into the carpet. Another, almost empty, stood on a table next to Arabella's brother.

"Take yer hands off him, ye swine!" Thomas shouted threateningly. "Dinna ye dare to strike him, or I'll kill ye, scum!"

Max, free now of Beven's grasp, ran sobbing toward his father.

"He-he asked me to bring it to him o-off th-the s-shelf," Maxwell stuttered fearfully. "I'm sorry, F-Father . . . 'twas fearful heavy . . ."

" 'Tis all right, lad. 'Tis not a job for boys such as ye. Drinkin' like this is just for fools! Out with ye, laddie. Go see Mehitabel, now . . . I'm sure she'll give ye a wee treat for yer troubles."

When Max had disappeared through the door, Thomas turned to face Beven who sat slumped in a wing-backed chair.

"Ye are not to touch the lad ever again, do ye hear me," Thomas growled. "Never again."

"I'll not be bullied by you, Fraser, so mind what you say," Beven said sullenly, but made no menacing move.

"Ye're the bully!" Thomas said, trying to control his temper. In a cooler voice he said, "I'm just asking ye to remember Max is only a wee lad. If ye need more whiskey, which I doubt, ye can get it yerself!"

His anger rekindled as he stared down at his disheveled partner who hadn't done a lick of work around Antrim Hall in months.

"Look, Beven," Thomas said, sighing in frustration. "Why do ye drink away yer days? There's so much work to be done. Ye're sharing half the profits. Why canna ye do at least some of the work around here?"

"Because a gentleman doesn't concern himself with plowing fields and cutting wheat," Beven said snidely. "He gets hirelings to do it for him. That's what I've done. I've got my sister's stallion to pull my cart!" He laughed viciously. "Rather clever of me, wouldn't you say?"

Thomas grabbed his brother-in-law by his linen cravat and yanked him out of his chair.

"Ye'll not be talking to me that way, laddie," he rasped, "not if ye value yer stinkin' life!"

Thomas released his grip, pushing Beven roughly back into his chair. His brother-in-law glared at him malevolently.

"You'll not get far that way, my good man," Beven said disdainfully. "I own this place. If you murder me for it, you'll never get to taste its fruits, now will you?"

"Look," Thomas said, exasperated beyond anything he had endured since Arabella's death had thrown the two men into this miserable partnership. "There'll be no murder here. I have a vital interest in this place. Aye, ye're right—it supports me and my son. *Yer* nephew. And it may one day come to him . . ." Beven merely snorted and took a last gulp from his bottle. "So why can't we work together and cease this nonsense?"

"You're the one who's supposed to do the work, Fraser. I own the place."

"And if ye die without a son, Maxwell will inherit."

"That remains to be seen, doesn't it, Captain Fraser?"

Two days after their argument, a watermarked letter addressed to Thomas and stamped with an impressive red wax crest belonging to the Marquess of Cornwallis arrived at Antrim Hall. Thomas's hands trembled as he laid its opened contents on his desk. He stared out the window as the gold and red and tobacco-colored leaves of autumn drifted on the ground close to where Arabella's grave stood on the rise overlooking the summerhouse.

The news from his former Commander was too overwhelming to absorb all at once.

Louisa . . . Jenny. . . .

His fevered brain could only repeat their names.

33
April 1797

"The guest list is just as I want it, Alex," Jane said wearily, replacing her quill pen in its holder and looking up from her desk in the library. "I'm not changing a thing. After all, Charles and Louisa have been engaged for a year, and all London is clamoring to be invited, including the Prince of Wales."

Both Jane and Alex were loath to discuss the fact that Lord Cornwallis had apparently received a satisfactory reply from Thomas Fraser and had given his belated blessing to the forthcoming nuptials. Clearly, it was more important that the great soldier's moonstruck son marry a woman of healthy bloodstock than that she be strictly of legitimate birth. To a man such as Lord Charles Cornwallis, making a suitable match was not unlike breeding good horses.

But, as usual, Alex was now protesting the cost of hosting such an elaborate celebration. Only this time, his objections had taken on a particularly bitter tone.

"So I'm to pay three thousand pounds to dower off Fraser's bastard?" he growled to his wife who faced him across her desk in the library.

Jane clenched her fists against the smooth leather surface of the desk top and attempted to keep control of her temper.

"Ye'll keep a civil tongue in yer head!" she whispered fiercely, loath to be overheard by the staff outside the door. "Besides, ye're a fine one to complain of bastards, sir," she continued in a low voice. "What's this I hear of another babe by yet *another* sixteen-year-old ye've debauched? Ye've really gone too far this time, Alex. Isobel Williamson's father was in one of yer *regiments*! And now I'm told Jean Christie is also with child again. And to top it off," she added, her eyes flashing with anger and humiliation at what was common knowledge in the Highlands, "there's the baby Annie in the nursery at Gordon Castle. Seems no one is quite sure who *her* mother is. Canna ye learn to keep it in yer breeches for yer own honor's sake?"

Stonily, Alex looked past her at the Reynolds portrait of Jane, which hung in its new place of honor above the fireplace in the leased domicile on Picadilly. He had no ready explanation for the chaotic state of his existence. Nothing in his life made much sense anymore. There seemed to be no orderly pattern, no solidity in the center of his daily routine. For a while, he had retreated from the relationship with Jean Christie, and in the interval, he found himself bedding whatever comely servant in a skirt passed him in the passageway at Gordon Castle.

Now, he and Jean were together again; yet the same hollow feeling persisted. The woman's youthful allure and fecundity were soothing balm to his wounded ego, but the lass had little wit, and, at times, there seemed nothing much in life that interested her—but him. The only comfort was that his life, of late, had assumed some of Jean's placid calmness. Still, Jane had a point. All but two of the six little brass beds in the nursery at Gordon Castle would soon be filled with his bastards. 'Twould not advance his reputation in the straitlaced court of George III for such facts to be common knowledge in London. Worse yet, he might be snubbed at his club.

"So?" Jane broke into his reverie.

"What?" he answered, confused.

"So, the guest list is final, and the Bishops of Lichfield and Coventry will perform the service—agreed?"

"Aye . . . aye," Alex mumbled absently.

Good sense dictated that he and Jane proceed as if these were the normal nuptials of a much beloved daughter. To do otherwise would expose Alex himself to unbearable ridicule among his peers.

He studied the unlined face of his handsome wife. Her rose complexion was framed by a head of luxuriant chestnut hair lowered over the sheaf of papers on her desk. He was mindful, too, of her full, voluptuous breasts that rose above the scooped neckline of her yellow morning gown gathered just under her bosom. Sitting opposite him, she looked up from her papers, her chin tilted in characteristic defiance, as if waiting for another of his caustic comments.

"Ye have agreed to be in attendance, then? I can count on that?" she asked.

Alex took a long breath and then exhaled.

"Yes. I'll be there."

"Splendid," Jane replied, as if they'd merely agreed on the price of a bag of wool. Dipping her quill in the ink pot on her desk, she returned to her paperwork.

As he gazed at the top of her head, he was forced to admit that, at forty-seven, she had truly become a woman of substance, a woman to be reckoned with, a woman of unusual power and influence, operating in a world of powerful men. During the decade Jean Christie had been part of his life, his estranged wife had grown to be the person he had privately always known she was capable of becoming: autonomous . . . able to stand on her own . . . unafraid of hazarding an opinion or taking actions she felt were necessary. She was the only woman he knew who was willing to risk disapproval from the men in her life. From him, from William Pitt—even from the King and the Prince of Wales.

He realized with some consternation that she had not only played a significant role in the concerns of his hearth and home, but in the management of the vast Gordon estates; in the schools for the Highlanders she had instituted; in the woolen and weaving and logging industries she had helped to found to keep the tenants from emigrating during the period in which sheep raising had begun to gobble up the land; in her patronage of Robert Burns's poetry; and, perhaps most surprisingly of all, within the larger male-dominated arena of Parliament and the Court.

Before his very eyes, and without his having noticed the complete change in her, Jane, Duchess of Gordon, had evolved into an outspoken woman of the world, despite its being a world of men. He was forced to acknowledge that without his restrictive influence on her these past years, she had begun to act and make choices about herself and the children that shaped a future, separate from his. She had even broken society's most stringent rule for a titled noblewomen: she had borne a child by a man other than her husband, the duke. Yet she had escaped out-and-out censure. Louisa was about to wed the son of one of the most respected peers in the realm—and Lord Cornwallis obviously couldn't be happier. What's more, Jane had somehow convinced Alex himself to stand up publicly, as if he were truly the lass's father. To be sure, the Duchess of Gordon was a person to be reckoned with.

Boldly, Alex studied the face and figure of the woman who was legally still his wife. Now that Jane was of an age where there would be no more bairns, Alex realized his spouse had been liberated further from the constraints of her own sexuality. As his eyes took in her mature loveliness, he wondered with more than academic interest who might be meeting those strong physical yearnings of hers?

Watching her sort through the papers on her desk, he realized with a start that he had spent most of their marriage spurning her uniqueness and had done much to drive her from his life. *Why? Why had he done this*, he pondered, as a crushing sense of loss gnawed at his vitals. It was almost as if some force he couldn't control drove him to challenge her, to punish her for possessing that independence of character that he secretly admired; to doubt her loyalty when she was, or had been, in fact, loyal to him many times in spite of her own heart's desire.

He glanced down at her missing forefinger, unadorned by gloves or handkerchief or any other artful disguises. He marveled at her dexterity as she made notations with a quill pen. Once upon a time she had accused him of being unable ever to trust any woman. He sighed. Perhaps she was correct. Perhaps *he* was more seriously maimed in his way than she was in hers, with her stub of a finger.

Looking at her now, this woman of achievement and wit and grace, he tried to fathom how he had arrived at this chilly audience with his wife in a leased mansion in Picadilly on the eve of her daughter's marriage to the future Marquess of Cornwallis? How had the cobbled High Street in Edinburgh, famous in the days of their youth for pig races among the children, led them, after thirty years, to this day, a day in which they sat as strangers in a room that was silent, except for the scratching of Jane's pen?

Alex shifted in his chair, knowing he should depart, but feeling strangely reluctant to make his farewells.

"Where shall you go after the wedding?" he asked softly.

"Why, to Kinrara, of course, till after the autumn shoot," she answered absently, organizing the many lists of things she had to do before the nuptials. " 'Tis almost summer and I'm needed there, now that Angus isn't well. Alexander will be with ye at Gordon Castle and Georgina's been invited to visit friends in Bath."

"You'll be alone then . . . you'll have a good rest," Alex said, watching her carefully.

Jane looked up, puzzled by his friendly tone.

"Aye . . . I always feel Kinrara is a place of peace . . . a place to allow the well to fill up again."

"Sometime . . . I'd like to see what improvements you've made there," he ventured cautiously.

Jane stared at him oddly. Her face mirrored the rush of pity he suspected she was feeling toward him. *The great Duke of Gor-*

don seemed a forlorn figure to her, he supposed, *as if, despite his vast estates, he had nowhere to go.*

"Oh, ye'll see it one day . . ." She smiled vaguely. "If we can stop squabbling over this wedding, and behave like ladies and gentlemen," she teased almost affectionately, "perhaps I'll invite ye to shoot grouse some August."

"Our children love Kinrara best, don't they?" he said, a note of wistfulness surprising them both. " 'Tis much preferred by them to Gordon Castle."

" 'Tis a place where we can all just be ourselves," she said quietly, glancing at the clock on the mantelpiece. It was eleven . . . so much left to do before next week.

"Well, adieu, good wife," Alex said abruptly, unable to restrain his customary tinge of sarcasm. By now it was plain to both of them: she wished him to be gone.

"Farewell, Alex," she said evenly, as he strode toward the door. Then she added in a tone laced with kindness that took him completely off guard, "I think 'twill be better for all of us when Louisa is safely wed."

"Perhaps," he mused, his hand on the half-opened library door. He smiled enigmatically and departed.

It was the wedding of the season, almost everyone agreed. Some who attended opined it was even more grand than the Princess Royal's. The hum of guests milling downstairs in the large drawing room prompted Jane to hasten down the hallway to Louisa's chamber.

"The Bishop of Coventry's downstairs, darling," she said, entering the room, "and the footman just told me he saw the Bishop of Lichfield's coach coming around the corner. Are ye nearly dressed?"

Jane halted her progress abruptly and stared at the bride-to-be.

Louisa's arms were outstretched to facilitate Nancy Christie's challenging task of fastening scores of tiny pearl buttons decorating the tight sleeves of her pale silver batiste wedding gown. A swatch of the filmy material muted Louisa's glorious burgundy-colored locks, which were held in place by a rope of pearls intertwined with a crown of miniature white lilies.

Jane turned her head and blinked back tears.

"Oh, Mama," Louisa breathed, smiling through misty eyes as well. "Do you think he'll be pleased?"

"What a lucky lad awaits ye downstairs," Jane said softly, wiping her eyes on the back of her gloved hand.

She gently embraced her daughter so as not to crumple her gown.

"She's a Highland beauty, wouldna ye say, Nan?" Jane asked of her housekeeper and friend.

"Aye . . . Duchess, and a credit to her parents, to be sure," Nancy Christie added, her eyes full of meaning. "I'll just be going now, m'lady. There's a million things I must attend to."

The door shut quietly behind Nancy as Jane took Louisa's chilly hands between her own.

"Nervous?" Jane asked gently.

"A little," Louisa replied, nodding her head.

"Happy?"

"Oh, yes," she answered promptly, her eyes shining. "Charles is so . . . so . . ."

"Loving?" Jane asked hopefully.

"Yes! That's it exactly,' Louisa exclaimed. "He seems so happy just to be with me . . . it makes me feel—"

"Treasured? Cherished?"

"Aye, Mama," she whispered. "How did you know?"

"At one time in my life, I felt exactly like that," she replied lightly. "I'm so happy for ye, pet," she added, her eyes welling with joyful tears once again.

Louisa looked at her, puzzled, but she didn't pursue the topic.

"Charles is a bit intimidated by his father, of course," Louisa said, flicking a speck of imaginary dust from her sleeve, "and he seems so shy around crowds of people. But I think that *together*, we shall give each other courage. Do you think that's possible?"

"Aye, that I do," Jane smiled. "Sometimes the whole can be stronger than each of its parts." Jane bent forward and kissed her daughter lightly on both cheeks. "Ye have been a child of my heart, my darling, and, of all the lasses, I think ye have chosen a man who will appreciate that loving spirit ye possess."

"Thank you, Mama," Louisa whispered. "I love you so much."

Mother and daughter locked glances for a few moments, hardly conscious of the sounds of the string quartet which drifted up the staircase.

"Now, come, dearheart," Jane said briskly, forcing herself to attend to the pageant unfolding in the drawing room. "We canna keep *two* bishops waiting for long."

Jane left Louisa poised on the landing, out of view of the guests chattering excitedly in the drawing room, and descended down the staircase.

"Why, Duchess, how magnificent you look," boomed a familiar voice. Lord Cornwallis advanced to her side, resplendent in a glittering uniform unearthed, Jane wagered, from his seasoned campaign trunk.

"The lovely bride has no second thoughts, I take it?" he queried jovially.

"None whatsoever, m'lord," Jane said, smiling at the father of the groom. "In fact, I think we have quite a love match on our hands, as unfashionable as that may be these days."

"I can't tell you how delighted that makes me," the distinguished soldier said with sudden seriousness. Jane had come to realize that the gruff old campaigner was inordinately fond of his gentle son and had done everything within his power to provide the lad with a happy future.

"Their marriage makes me very happy as well, m'lord," Jane said sincerely. "I pray their joy in each other continues throughout their lives. And thank ye so much for . . . being so understanding of our family . . . situation," she declared hesitantly.

"And on that very subject," Cornwallis said, a mischievous twinkle glittering in his eyes. "I hope you, too, will be understanding of a rather impetuous action I have taken today."

"And pray, m'lord, what is that?" Jane asked.

"Part of its impetuousness is keeping it a surprise," he said, mysteriously. "Ah, the Bishops are giving us a sign."

And, with that, he retreated into the library to tell the groom the ceremony was about to begin.

The Bishops of Lichfield and Coventry, whose gold embroidered robes and mitered caps rivaled the elaborate gowns of the women in the room, stood before the fireplace, which was filled with spring flowers. Scattered around the large reception hall were numerous tall vases bursting with iris and daffodils and hollyhocks illuminated by the brilliant April sunshine pouring through the tall windows, which flanked the street. As the appointed moment approached, Cornwallis escorted his son to stand in front of the pair of bishops who had agreed, by special licence, to perform the ceremony in a private home. Viscount Brome fidgeted nervously with the lace cuffs of his coat, and then smiled rapturously at his bride who was just entering the room.

Alex escorted a radiant Louisa through the murmuring crowd and quickly deposited her next to the groom. Then he took his place beside Jane who had been brought to the front of the throng by her smiling son, Lord Huntly.

"Your servant, madam," her husband whispered in Jane's ear.

Alex was attired in rich, midnight blue velvet with an ivory satin waistcoat that matched the cream color of his silk hose, gartered at the knee with satin ribbons. Jane felt his eyes wander over her high-waisted gown of peach silk with its puffed sleeves that tapered, like long gloves, down to her wrist.

"Your feathers quite become you," he said softly, glancing at her hair, which was artfully arranged in curls piled in soft layers on her head. "Are you no longer the queen's partisan?"

" 'Tis my daughter's wedding," Jane responded tartly. "If I wish to wear peach plumes, I shall wear peach plumes."

"Well, I like them exceedingly," he said, chuckling. "Are we ready to commence this little pageant?" he added, extending his arm to Jane.

Jane nodded to the chief violinist leading the string quartet. Immediately the musicians began a short passage from Mozart's *Marriage of Figaro*, which had debuted a decade earlier in the Austrian opera and was a favorite of all Europe. Jane inclined her head toward faces she recognized from her vantage point on the right side of the room. She smiled warmly at Eglantine who looked vivacious as ever in a pale cerise creation. She caught the eye of their elder sister Catherine, slightly round-shouldered these days, who stood beside her stout husband, John Fordyce, and their numerous children.

Nearby, Lady Maxwell leaned on her silver-headed cane and positively beamed her approval. As far as Jane could tell, her mother took credit for the supreme achievement of yet another noble alliance. She'd heard Magdalene crow to her friends that she was mother-in-law to a duke, grandmama to a duke-to-be, and that so far, her tally of grandsons by marriage numbered two additional dukes, a baronet, and now, glory of glory, the future Marquess of Cornwallis.

"No telling what that darling Georgina will turn up when she comes of age," Lady Maxwell had been heard to brag.

Now, more than ever, local wags were wont to call Jane Maxwell Gordon 'The Matchmaking Duchess'. Well, so be it, she thought, trying to suppress a rueful smile as she exchanged glances with a flush-faced William Pitt, looking world-weary and slightly in his cups. The Prince of Wales had not yet arrived, but she assumed he'd appear in time for the sumptuous repast being laid out in a large room across the foyer.

Jane's hand rested lightly on Alex's sleeve. Suddenly she felt the muscles of his forearm clench. She turned her head in surprise and gasped involuntarily.

Standing against the windowed wall of the large chamber, but towering above most of the guests, stood a man dressed impeccably in a Fraser tartan kilt and black velvet jacket. White lace frothed at his throat and cuffs, which were in sharp contrast to the distinctive shade of his dark ruby hair, highlighted, now, by a sprinkling of silver. Unlike the pale faces of Londoners standing beside him who had survived yet another dank winter, his face was deeply tanned, except for the thin white scar, which had left its mark on his prominent cheekbone. He looked healthy and prosperous. Obviously, life in America had agreed with Captain Thomas Fraser, late of Struy.

Jane stared at Thomas in disbelief. He smiled warmly and then shifted his gaze toward his daughter who was just turning her profile to him as the Bishop of Lichfield began to address the wedding couple. From where Jane stood, Thomas's features seemed to soften and his eyes grew moist. Beside him stood a little lad in a matching Fraser kilt who looked to be six or seven years old. The boy held Thomas's hand tightly, obviously awed by the splendor of the scene.

Jane glanced at Alex whose face had by this time turned ashen. The arm she leaned on in an attempt to recover her own aplomb was trembling. She heard the wedding vows recited while caught up in a jumble of churning emotions. So this was Lord Cornwallis's little surprise! Thomas had returned. With a child. Had he discreetly left Arabella at their London lodgings while he watched his daughter Louisa plight her troth to the son of his respected commander? Jane's heart was beating so fast, she felt dizzy. She knew her face must be flushed and she sensed Lord Cornwallis staring at her with something of a knowing gleam in his eye.

Of course! Jane thought. *He had invited Thomas to the wedding after he had confirmed that his former intelligence officer was truly Louisa's father.* Cornwallis knew he could rely on Thomas's discretion, and he obviously admired the man. So, the general who had failed to defeat the rebellious army of the Americans had succeeded in bringing the three of them—Thomas and Alex and herself—together again after all these years. *Who would be forced to surrender this time?* she wondered, shivering slightly.

The Bishop of Lichfield gave the benediction, and the Bishop of Coventry blessed the young couple, declaring them legally wed. Louisa and Viscount Brome, who were exactly the same height, kissed each other tenderly and turned with glowing smiles to face the roomful of well-wishers. A number of guests rushed forward to congratulate the Gordon family while liveried servants walked through the crowd dispensing champagne from silver trays.

The next thing Jane knew, she was standing in a reception line between Louisa on her left and Alex on her right. It was agonizing to try to smile brightly and make appropriate comments, when all she could think of was that Thomas Fraser was in line to be presented to the bride and groom.

Alex's jaw twitched slightly and his mouth had flattened out into a thin line. His face grew even more grim as Captain Fraser approached to pay his respects. Thomas spoke first.

"May I extend my heartfelt congratulations on the marriage of Lady Louisa, sir," he said calmly.

Alex merely inclined his head stiffly. The little boy stared up at the two gentlemen uncertainly. Gently Thomas guided the lad a few steps closer to Jane.

"Duchess . . ." Thomas murmured in greeting.

"C-Captain Fraser," Jane managed to stammer. "We had no idea ye'd be returning from America . . ." Her voice trailed off.

"May I present my son?" he said softly, prompting the lad to step forward. "Max, this is Jane, Duchess of Gordon."

The little boy looked up at her with round blue eyes framed with jet black lashes the same shade as his hair. Gingerly, he took Jane's gloved right hand in his small one. He kissed it soundly as he had undoubtedly rehearsed under the watchful eye of his father.

"M'lady's finger seems so very stiff, Papa," he said with a child's innocent curiosity. "I hope you haven't hurt yourself?" he said to her, his eyes widening.

Thomas looked quickly at Jane, concerned for her feelings.

"I injured it once, laddie," she smiled down at Thomas's handsome son. " 'Twas a long time ago when I was a wee bit older than ye. Yer Papa was there when it happened, in fact. Ye must have him tell ye the story of how a naughty lass got into trouble."

"Does it still pain you, madam?" the little boy asked, furrowing his brow.

"No, dearheart," she said quietly. "Not anymore."

She turned to Louisa. "But ye must meet the bride, laddie. Louisa, pet, this is Captain Thomas Fraser, a friend of Lord

Cornwallis who's emigrated to America . . . and his son . . . Max, is it?''

''Maxwell, really,'' he said proudly, his piping voice clearly audible above the din. ''My Mama named me Maxwell and then she died.''

Alex flinched, but stared stonily ahead.

But Jane hardly noticed his discomfort. She shifted her gaze to stare at Thomas. She felt as if one of the crystal champagne glasses being served to her guests had snapped its stem with a loud crack.

Arabella was dead. Arabella of the fateful letter. Arabella of Antrim Hall. Arabella, wife of Thomas Fraser. The mother of this angelic little boy was dead. It hardly seemed possible that the woman she had hated with an anger stored in some deep recess of her soul had been in her grave these seven years. Deep inside herself, Jane had long stored resentment toward an unloving father, a nakedly ambitious mother, and an untrusting spouse—and, yes, resentment toward a young lover who chose adventure and revenge for past injustices to his family name rather than a life with her. For years, these shadowy passions and a lifetime of malice toward Arabella had formed a lead ball of hate in the pit of Jane's stomach. And now, Arabella was dead. The focus of all that rage and disappointment could no longer be called on, clung to, railed against, as a substitute for facing real conflicts with real people who still walked the earth.

She was dimly aware that Louisa was bending down to take Maxwell's hand. Her daughter smiled sympathetically at the child who'd lost his mother at such a young age.

''Maxwell's a family name of mine, too,'' Louisa said. ''I'm so glad you came to my wedding.''

Jane watched apprehensively as Thomas patted his son on the head and then took Louisa's hand and kissed it. The young woman glanced at the kilted stranger for a long moment, as if searching her memory. Her eyes drifted to his hair, startled to see a shade so near to that of her own striking mane.

''Ye made a beautiful bride, Lady Louisa,'' he said quickly. ''I wish ye many years of happiness.''

''Why, thank ye, Captain Fraser,'' she replied. ''Will you be in England long?'' she asked politely.

''For a while, I expect. I hope to show my son where I was born, and perhaps select a school for him.''

''How pleasant for you.'' She smiled graciously.

"How pleasant for *you*!" Alex whispered harshly in Jane's ear. "Your lover's named his *other* bastard after you!"

"Oh, do be still!" Jane hissed back.

Jane forced herself to turn to greet the next guest in line. When she looked back, Thomas and his son had been swallowed up in the crush of people crowding forward to congratulate the bride and groom.

It was more than an hour before the receiving line broke up. By that time, the two guests from America had disappeared. Jane deliberately kept her distance from Alex the rest of the afternoon, for his every glance in her direction seethed with repressed anger. She didn't have to avoid him for long. As soon as the duke had danced stiffly with the bride, he slipped away from the reception without bidding adieu to anyone in the room.

After Jane had seen the last guest to the door, she sagged tiredly against a pillar supporting the foyer. Slowly, she turned and mounted the staircase leading to her bedchamber on the second floor. She found herself pondering as she took each step why Arabella O'Brien Delaney Boyd Fraser, her sworn enemy, had chosen to name her son Maxwell.

"Wake up! Wake up, Jane!"

A single candle glowed in its holder beside the bed as Eglantine shook Jane's shoulders roughly.

"Jane . . . ye must stop them . . . 'tis *insane* at their age!"

Jane forced herself to open her eyes and sat bolt upright in bed.

"What is it?" she demanded. "I'm nearly dead with fatigue from the wedding, and ye come in here—"

"Well, either Alex or Thomas or *both* of them will be dead by dawn if ye dinna do something to stop it!" Eglantine exclaimed. "Alex has challenged Thomas to a duel! He found out from a groom where he's lodging and called him out!"

"What?" Jane protested, still half asleep. "Ye canna be serious. 'Tis some fool's play—"

"I *am* serious," Eglantine retorted. "Alex has called him out and Thomas has accepted the challenge!"

"Good God!" Jane cried, leaping out of bed in the direction of the tall armoire standing against the bedchamber's wall. "Where are they now?"

"I dinna know. One of the members of Alex's club who tried to dissuade the duke came by and roused Nancy Christie. She woke me just moments ago . . . and I came to ye, straightaway."

Jane was rummaging among her garments to find her riding habit.

"Did the messenger say where this lunacy will take place?"

"In the fields near Buckingham House, off Queen's Way, he said. At dawn's light."

Jane grabbed the candlestick off the bed table and peered at the clock on the mantel. It was four-thirty. Still an hour before the first streaks of dawn would steal through the willows, which graced the landscape near the ornate mansion King George III had purchased for Queen Charlotte in 1775.

However, the beauty of the setting was the last thought on Jane's mind as she urged the carriage driver to speed down the deserted streets, whose paving stones were bathed with heavy dew. She and Eglantine gazed out the window across a wide field toward a stand of trees where Jane's sister had been assured the duel would take place.

The carriage pulled to a halt in the grove of weeping willows, which stood shrouded in the early morning mists. The cold seeped quickly into the vehicle's interior and Eglantine's teeth began to chatter.

"God's eyeballs, but 'tis miserable out at this hour," she said, shivering.

Jane ignored her sister's plaintive remark and threw open the carriage door. She banged her riding crop on the top of the coach.

"Keep out of sight!" Jane commanded the driver and footman. She stood on the running board of the carriage and pointed in the direction she wanted the driver to go. With a jangling of harnesses and the creak of the wheels, the coach rolled deeper into the woods, pulled by a pair of dappled gray horses, whose nostrils billowed steam in the frigid morning air. "May I have yer pistol, please?" Jane asked of the coachman when the conveyance came to a halt.

"Your Grace, I don't think—"

"Give it to me, ye fool!" Jane demanded, stamping her riding boot on the soaking grass.

"Jane!" Eglantine cried with alarm, jumping down from the carriage. "Ye're not going to shoot Alex—"

"Dinna be daft!" Jane retorted with exasperation. "I came to prevent a murder, not to commit one! Is it loaded?" she asked.

"Yes, m'lady. You've merely to cock it."

"Excellent! Come on! Now, unharness one of the horses and put on the bridle and saddle I left on the floor of the carriage."

"Yes, Your Grace," said the coachman, shaking his head.

The two women huddled within a circle of weeping willows. The new spring leaves on the graceful branches were just starting to unfold, but the fog was so thick, the two sisters could hardly glimpse the top of the trees. The driver soon had Jane's saddle cinched around the horse's girth and he handed the reins to her without further comment. Before long, they heard other horses' hooves, and the shadowy outline of another carriage appeared in the mist. The small hackney trap was pulled by an old nag who had seen many years of service. It stopped not twenty feet from where Jane and Eglantine hid behind the grove of drooping willows.

"That must be Thomas," Eglantine whispered tremulously.

Jane peered through the swirling fog as a tall, familiar figure appeared out of the carriage. At the same instant, another carriage drew up. Because of the mist, the vehicle's gold embossed stag's head crest was barely visible. Five men emerged: the Duke of Gordon and four others whom Jane didn't recognize.

"No doubt the seconds and the surgeon—pressed into service," she whispered grimly.

Jane and Eglantine gazed silently at Alexander Gordon, whose black cape made him appear as sinister as a highwayman.

"Well, Fraser," Alex called belligerently, " 'tis been a long time since you insulted me on the High Street in Edinburgh—and you've been insulting me ever since."

" 'Tis not my intent to do ye harm, Yer Grace," Thomas replied quietly. "The words exchanged then were but the mouthings of children."

"Ah, but they set in motion what was to come, did they not, you scoundrel!"

" 'Tis a daft business, this," Thomas said wearily. "After all these years, there's no evil directed at either of us. Why not let—"

"My honor has been greatly compromised, Captain Fraser," Alex interrupted, snarling. "Ye've slept with my wife and now ye appear in London to rub my nose in it."

Thomas shook his head.

"I simply came to my daughter's nuptials at the invitation of her father-in-law, my former Commander. 'Twas nothing to do with yer honor, or any wish to besmirch it!"

" 'Tis of no consequence what you think about it now as you face my challenge, Fraser. State your weapon."

Thomas shrugged.

"Pistols."

"Ah . . . so I anticipated," Alex said. "Ambrose," he called to one of the shadowy figures who had stayed close to the duke's carriage, "present the arms for Captain Fraser's inspection. Unless you prefer your own?"

"I dinna sail from America prepared for a duel," Thomas said dryly. "But I must warn ye, m'lord. Arms were my profession for lo these many years. I ask ye once again to reconsider this folly."

"I wish to see you dead," Alex replied coldly. "And I intend to accomplish the deed myself."

"And ye wonder why ye lost the woman ye loved most in life!" Thomas retorted, his temper frayed to the breaking point. "Ye never understood Jane Maxwell . . . ye resented the fact that *I* did. So, I suppose ye'll have to try to kill me because of it. But if ye fail, my good man, then your death will break her heart another way!"

"Where's that horse!" whispered Jane, retreating farther into the grove of willows.

"What are ye going to do?" Eglantine croaked hoarsely, scurrying to keep up with her sister.

"I dinna know!" Jane cried, gesturing frantically to the coachman to assist her aboard her mount.

"Captain Fraser," said the man Alex had called Ambrose, a slightly stooped gentleman undoubtedly recruited from among the late-night habitués at White's. "These are a matched pair of pistols. As you have no second, these two men will each load one firearm, if 'tis agreeable with you?"

Thomas merely gave a short nod. Each man carefully placed a small square of loosely woven cloth over the muzzle of the gun's barrel. A single ball of lead was placed on it and an iron rod tapped the ammunition into place.

"Since both pistols belong to me, sir," Alex said tersely, "you may choose whichever one you wish."

Ambrose held a loaded firearm in each hand and offered them to Thomas. Without any deliberation, he selected the gun on his right.

"Now, gentlemen, to determine who will have first fire, I will toss a coin into the air. As the offended party, Your Grace," he said, nodding to the Duke of Gordon, " 'tis your choice to call the toss. These rules are acceptable to both of you?"

"These rules are *ridiculous*!" Jane hissed to her sister as she attempted to quiet her horse. " 'Tis simply civilized slaughter!"

"If His Grace calls the toss correctly, he will have the first fire," Ambrose intoned nervously. "If His Grace calls the toss incorrectly, Captain Fraser will have the first fire. Again, gentlemen, are the rules clearly understood?"

Both men nodded. Ambrose took a deep breath.

"I shall now toss the coin and allow it to fall to the ground where you may both examine which way it lands."

And with that, he dug into his pocket, and settled the coin on his thumb.

"Tails," Alex growled as the shilling sailed into the air, "for 'tis a dirty dog I challenge this morn."

All six men bent to see the result of the toss.

" 'Tis heads, m'lord," Ambrose announced. "Captain Fraser will have the first fire." Alex nodded, his jaw twitching slightly. "Your Grace," the duel master added resignedly, "will you take your ground?"

"With the greatest of pleasure," replied Alex between clenched teeth. He stalked through the verdant grass to a spot in the field where he was nearly obscured by the mist.

His fellow club member from White's followed him, and with his boot, scuffed a line in front of where Alex was standing, pistol at his side. Then Ambrose began to count off the distance which the rules ordained should exist between the two combatants.

"One, two, three, four . . ." he droned, until ten paces had been reached. Again, the doctor marked with the toe of his boot the place where Thomas was to stand.

"Captain Fraser, will you take your ground?"

"Aye," Thomas responded resignedly, walking slowly to the indicated spot.

Thomas and Alex faced each other in the wide field as a rosy blush of dawn appeared on the horizon.

"This is insanity, Yer Grace," Thomas shouted. "I beg ye—"

"Take your shot, sir," Alex retorted, "and then die a dog's death, you cuckolding rogue!"

At this, Thomas remained silent, his shoulders tense, his pistol at the ready.

"Your Grace, are you prepared to receive Captain Fraser's fire?"

Alex had paled, but his eyes stared at his adversary without flinching.

"I am," he replied coldly.

"Captain Fraser, cock your pistol, sir."

Ambrose held a lace-edged handkerchief above his head.

He took another deep breath, and in an unsteady voice, shouted into the dank air.

"Prepare to fire, Captain Fraser. One, two . . ."

Thomas slowly lifted his pistol from his side, and pointed it at the fog-shrouded figure in front of him. After a moment's hesitation, he swung his arm in an arc and held the gun above his head. He fired a shot harmlessly into the gray morning sky.

"The captain has refused to do you harm, Your Grace. Do you consider yourself satisfied by this act?"

"I do *not*!" Alex shouted, his voice trembling.

"Then, m'lord, cock your pistol, and prepare to fire."

Suddenly, the sound of thundering horse hooves startled the six men who stood poised in the damp field. Each looked around uncertainly.

A small figure in a green velvet cape rode into view and flung itself off its mount.

"Ye two prancing peacocks! *Stop this at once*!" Jane shouted furiously, standing in the direct line of fire between the two men she had loved.

"What the devil—" Alex bellowed. Then he cursed loudly as he recognized his wife.

"Jane . . . stand away, please! I beg ye!" Thomas shouted.

Ambrose, the two seconds and the surgeon gaped openmouthedly at the sight of the Duchess of Gordon withdrawing a pistol from beneath her cape. With a lightning motion, she pulled back its firing hammer.

"I will shoot *anyone* who comes near me or tries to kill anyone else standing in this field!" she cried.

Thomas took a step toward her.

"That means ye, Thomas Fraser! That means *all* of ye! I've had about as much of this nonsense as I'm going to stand!" she exclaimed.

"How did you get here?" Alex asked incredulously.

"In a carriage . . . how do ye suppose?" she snapped. "Word of such idiocy travels fast in London, Yer Grace," she added waspishly. "And ye, Captain Thomas Fraser," she cried, aiming her firearm directly at his chest. "How did ye propose to take care of little Maxwell Fraser if yer foolish gamble rendered ye dead?"

Thomas averted his eyes and stared at the ground.

"And I imagine the Duke of Gordon dinna give much thought to the future of Lord Huntly, when he demanded his so-called *satisfaction*," she said bitterly, turning to confront Alex. "And what of the lassies, and yer namesake, Alexander, or even the litter of wee bastards who lie in their cots at Gordon Castle. Would ye be *satisfied* to leave them fatherless, should yer fabled *archery* arm fail ye, and Thomas, here, be given another shot? No, to even *consider* ye might lose this contest wasna *manly* . . . not enough derring-do for ye!'' she said sarcastically. She took a step closer and waved her cocked pistol menacingly. ''Ye fools!'' she shouted angrily at both men. ''Between the two of ye, ye've sired at least *thirteen* bairns—and *not* all by *me*, as ye both are well aware!''

At this, Alex and Thomas exchanged uncertain glances. Alex allowed his pistol to fall to his side. Jane's voice rang out in the chill morning air.

''Those children need ye in their lives . . .'' she continued angrily. ''They need yer siller and yer guidance . . . and, yes, damn ye . . . they need yer *love*! Ye're *fifty-year-old men*! So think on *that* before ye decrepit old goats take up arms over the love ye claim ye bear Jane Maxwell!''

She nodded her head sharply to one of the astonished seconds.

''Ye there—Ambrose, is it?'' she said, squarely aiming her pistol at him.

''Douglas Cummings, Your Grace,'' he corrected her. ''He's Ambrose Leigh,'' he added, pointing at his companion.

''Well, come over here, Douglas, and help me mount my horse.''

Obediently, the middle-aged gentleman retrieved her mount and cupped his hands. Jane placed her muddy boot in his palms and easily swung herself on her charger. Once again, she aimed her firearm directly at her husband.

''Alex Gordon . . . repair to yer coach, if ye please.''

The duke opened his lips as if to protest, then thought better of it, and retreated to his carriage. The unneeded surgeon, the seconds, and Ambrose climbed in after him.

''And now ye, Thomas,'' she said quietly. ''Please ride safely back to yer lodgings . . . and say to Master Maxwell Fraser that the Duchess of Gordon very much enjoyed making his acquaintance.''

Thomas looked at her, shook his head slightly in disbelief, and strode to his hackney coach.

''When I discharge the bullet in this pistol,'' Jane shouted from her sidesaddle perch, ''ye're each to return to yer own warm beds.'' She yanked on the reins of her horse, prompting

her skittish mount to rear slightly. "Good night, Gentlemen!"
she cried loudly.

She raised her hand over her head, and pointed the muzzle of
her gun at the dawn-streaked sky. Suddenly, a sharp report rent
the air. Slowly, the two carriages rolled across the field in
opposite directions as the sun crested over the tops of the green
willow trees.

34

June 1797

In the days that followed, Jane was thankful to have received
no word of another duel between the two men whose quarrel
she'd interrupted in the swirling fog. Neither did she hear personally from either one of them. The meeting of the three of
them at the break of dawn in a field near Buckingham House
seemed a bizarre dream.

As soon as Jane had paid the bills from the wedding, she
departed alone for Kinrara. She could think of no way—other
than quizzing Lord Cornwallis, which was out of the question—of
discovering where Captain Fraser and his son might be lodging
while in London. Her only hope was to seek them in the Highlands.

And do what?

Jane stared out the coach window as the familiar scenery of
the Spey Valley rolled by. Thomas had finally made his choice
to build a life in America. Now he was widowed, but her
husband was still very much alive. She was a forty-seven-year-
old woman, the mother of seven children, estranged for nearly a
decade from one of the most powerful aristocrats in Scotland.
She lived on the slim proceeds of her sheep operation, supple-
mented by an allowance grudgingly granted her by the duke.

It occurred to her, as her eyes drank in the glorious moors
blanketed in soft, spring grasses and colorful wildflowers, that
she had spent the many years that Thomas had lived off and on
in America in a kind of tug-of-war. All these years, the glitter of
her life in the highest circles of London had been balanced by its
opposite: the simplicity of an existence in the Highlands, which

was dedicated to hard work, maintaining Kinrara, and to helping those who lived on Gordon lands to survive the rigors of climate and history. What had Thomas and her life to do with each other now—except for the fact that they had loved and lost each other time and again, over some thirty years? After halting their duel, she'd sent both men off in their carriages to their respective beds, and, perhaps, that was the best place for them.

'Tis almost comical, she thought, pulling on her gloves as the coach bumped along the familiar lane. Why had she rushed north from London? What did she hope to find? Wasn't she better off to accept what had always seemed to be the truth about her and Thomas: that God or the Fates or the Highland Fairies had decreed that their paths should be forever separate along life's highway?

A well-remembered turn in the road loomed ahead. Soon the chimneys of Kinrara House were visible above the larch and silver birch trees lining the gravel drive. Through the bright green leaves loomed the cream-colored walls and gray slate roof of the stately manse. Jane felt a surge of happiness every time she beheld the residence's classical lines and graceful proportions, which were in total harmony with its rustic setting.

The carriage passed into the wooded field near the various outbuildings dotting the grounds. Jane peered down the narrow lane on her left that led to Angus Grant's cottage. Flora had died the previous winter and Jane was anxious to see how the old man was doing, now that he was terribly crippled by rheumatism in all his joints.

A shaggy Highland pony was tethered outside the estate factor's door. As the coach clattered by, Jane caught a glimpse of the door opening. A tall figure ducked past the low frame.

Quickly, Jane knocked her fan against the ceiling of the carriage, ordering the horses to halt. She flung open the coach door, commanding the driver to proceed to the stables without her. Puzzled, he did as he was told, shrugging his shoulders at a duchess who would visit her factor before resting, after such a grueling journey from London on a quagmire of muddy roads soaked by a series of relentless spring showers.

But on this day, the warm sunshine was casting shafts of golden light through the tall trees as Jane trod swiftly along the spring moss lining the path to Angus's stone cottage. Then, she halted at the cottage gate, staring wordlessly at the man who had shut the door behind him and was walking steadily toward her. Without a thought for who might be watching, she bolted the last few steps separating her from Thomas and flung herself into his arms, feeling she would surely die if he didn't hold her.

At the sight of him, the burden of leaden disappointments that so long had seemed to weigh her down, simply melted and drained away. She was conscious only of the joy she felt to be embraced by him, to be engulfed by the blessed comfort of his being. Her tears felt sweet on her cheeks. Thomas had come back to Kinrara.

"Ye're not carrying a pistol today, are ye, hinny?" Thomas murmured into her hair, holding her gently.

"I found yer letter six years ago," she said softly, ignoring his jest. "I came to ye in Struy, but it was too late . . ."

"I know . . . I know," he soothed. "I've been back to that dreary, forsaken place and found the parchment gone. I guessed ye'd come to me. My heart broke that I wasna there to greet ye."

"Ye waited three years for me in such desolation," she whispered, painfully recalling his crumbling crofter's hut at the end of the weed-strewn lane. "Ye've always had to wait for me, Thomas . . . and I for ye. We've spent a lifetime like this!" His face swam before her as a fresh well of tears began to fill her eyes. She was swept along by an overwhelming urge to try to explain to him the opposing currents that had constituted her life all these years, a life she felt was beyond his comprehension.

"I simply couldn't come to ye after that night I left ye at Simon's. 'Twasna my feelings for Alex that stayed my hand, but the—"

"Yer children," he interrupted gently, holding her against the wide expanse of his chest and stroking her hair. "I dinna think I understood how ye must have been torn in two . . . wantin' to be with me and with yer babes also . . . till I had a bairn of my own . . . one I could hold and pet and comfort." He gently clasped her chin in his hands and kissed her softly on the lips. "They are flesh of one's flesh, and I doubt a person ever feels another bond like that in life."

Jane's face glowed with joy that he should understand so perfectly her life's dilemma. Miraculously, he seemed to grasp the awful fragmentation she had endured for what seemed forever.

"Ye even felt a bond with Louisa, dinna ye?" she murmured, standing away from him to meet his gaze. "After all these years, ye had to witness her safely wed, even if ye'd never laid eyes on her."

"Oh, I'd seen her," he said with a smile, which reflected both pride and pain. He took Jane's hand in his own and led her down a narrow path behind Angus's cottage, past the kitchen garden and the well. As they walked down a slope which angled toward the Spey, he told her of the day so many years earlier when he had seen the youthful Louisa at the Church Street Inn in Inverness.

"My beard then, and unkempt hair made me appear a wild man to her, I'll wager," he laughed ruefully, "though at the wedding, I feared for a moment she might dimly recall the meeting."

He related to Jane how he had overheard William Marshall tell Angus that the Duke had taken Jean Christie as his mistress and that the Gordon lasses were being sent to London to their mother.

"I thought then, perhaps ye'd come to me," he said without reproach. "I waited in the single-minded manner of a long-single man. But, of course, I couldna know, yet, that 'twasn't just the matter of Alex that held ye fast. When Struy House was finally beyond my grasp and ye hadna come after three years, I felt there was nothing left for me here. . . ."

They had reached the verdant banks of the river. A path of stones protruded above furiously tumbling water, which was being fed by a spring thaw of melting snow.

Before Jane could point out to Thomas how unfit her slippers were for such uncertain footing, he scooped her up in his arms and carried her across the rocks in the swift-flowing stream, heedless of the frigid water swirling around them. He set her down gently on the far bank and encircled her with his arms. She stared into his eyes, which looked greener than ever as the soft June sun slanted across his face.

"So ye went to America," she said, thinking silently of Arabella, who had been both loved and buried by this man standing before her. "Ye went to Antrim Hall."

"Aye," he answered heavily, clasping her hand once again and continuing along the lane that lead toward Loch-an-Eilean.

"And yer son . . . Maxwell . . . is Arabella's child?" she confirmed. "Ye two were married?"

"Aye, though she never saw the lad," he answered, staring ahead at a stand of pines clinging to a rocky rise on their right.

"Yet, before she died, she asked that he be named Maxwell," Jane said hesitantly. "Why?"

Thomas halted their progress and turned to look at her.

"In fact, she *insisted*, if it were a boy, that he be called after ye. Actually, 'twas very strange . . ." Thomas said pensively, "almost as if it were a kind of penance, I think, for having failed to post my letter to ye so long ago. She knew she could never undo that wrong, but she wanted to make some kind of outward gesture to me, and perhaps even to you, to somehow make amends.''

"Oh God, Thomas!" Jane blurted. "I've hated her for so long and blamed her for so long . . . 'tis hard to hear she must have loved ye as much as I did! I wanted her to remain the selfish vixen ye once considered her! We can be so disloyal to our own sex!''

Thomas framed Jane's face between his large palms, his eyes clear with hard-won understanding.

"Such wisdom often comes rather late to make good use of it,'' he agreed soberly. "I've been a lucky man, Jenny. 'Tis only recently I've seen that I've been granted so much in my life . . . when all I used to contemplate was how much I've lost.''

"Ye've suffered many losses, Thomas!'' she answered fiercely. "Dinna think ye havna . . . so have I, though ye've had far the worst of it. First yer family in the starving . . . then yer lands and titles lost . . . then me . . . then Arabella . . . and then ye nearly lost yer life *again,* accepting Alex's challenge for my sake.'' She stared up at him with ferocious intensity. "When I learned ye'd failed in yer fight over Simon's will and lost yer home, I wondered just how much loss ye could sustain without going mad.'' She grasped his hands tightly. "And now to learn of yer wife's death . . .'' She reached up and traced the scar that ran along his cheekbone. "With all my heart,'' she said, feeling a healing balm pour through her, "I'm sorry for your loss of Arabella.''

Thomas smiled sadly.

"I've been doubly blessed to love and be loved by two such women as ye,'' he said quietly. "In the end, 'twas my strange and curious life which taught me the truth of what good fortune has been mine all along. That knowledge quite makes up for the lack of a noble house and the honor of being called a lord.''

Jane kissed the backs of his hands and held them to her cheek for a long moment.

"How are ye managing with the little lad on yer own?'' she asked finally as they continued along the path.

"Maxwell, of course, never knew his mother, and so he had to make do with me and 'Bella's maid, Mehitabel.'' A slight scowl clouded his countenance. "'Bella's brother Beven has been the worst sort of . . . partner.''

"Why is that?'' Jane asked, glimpsing a patch of blue water between the trees.

" 'Tis simple," he said with a tinge of bitterness. "He's perpetually in his cups. Needless-to-say, he hasna taken well to my safeguarding Maxwell's half inheritance of Antrim Hall. In fact, Cornwallis's summons came at an extremely propitious moment, I must say," Thomas mused as his eyes scanned the curving bank of Loch-an-Eilean just coming into view. "I fear that Beven and I would have come to blows 'ere long. 'Tis just as well I stay away from Antrim Hall for a while. The factor I hired to look out for Maxwell's interests has been well paid to maintain the place while we're in Scotland."

"And how long will that be?" Jane asked, her breath catching in her throat.

Thomas didn't answer her immediately, for the two of them caught their first clear view of the tiny castle nestled on its island in the middle of the loch. The fortress's single tower glistened in the filtered sunlight. Tenacious vines clung to the lower walls and flowering clematis entwined the tower in a colorful, leafy net. Thomas halted on the path skirting the lake. He turned to face her, his hands firmly gripping her shoulders.

"I told myself I would depart as soon as I had shown Struy Village and my former home to Max. Then, I decided to pay a call on Angus Grant, merely dreaming of finding ye here, but not expecting it at all." He looked at her intently, as if searching for something he would discover in her expression. "Angus and Flora were as kind as parents to me when I struggled through my darkest days, living in that barren cottage in Struy, and coming here occasionally to visit them when I knew ye'd be in London or Fochabers. I wanted them to meet Max. Now I'm so sad for Angus. He seems lost without Flora."

"Aye . . ." she brooded. " 'Tis one reason I came from London as quickly as I could."

And ye, Thomas Fraser. I came because of ye, she thought.

"I must decide what to do about poor Angus." She shook her head as if to clear her mind of such a disturbing problem. "Where is the lad?" she asked, changing the subject once again. "Where is Master Max?"

"With some old friends in the wool trade up the road in Grantown-on-Spey. They have a son near his age. The lads get on famously and seemed so suited, I left him there for a few days. I merely came back today to say farewell to Angus. I had supposed ye'd stay in London till later in the summer . . ."

"Well, I dinna," Jane said abruptly.

So he had not come to Kinrara to find her, but had only come to say good-bye . . . and certainly not to her.

"Will ye be putting Max in school in England?" she asked, searching for a safe topic, while she attempted to cope with the familiar feeling of disappointment darkening her thoughts.

"Not if I canna find one that doesna beat the boys and call it 'discipline.' "

"Aye," she said, sighing. "I kept Huntly and Alexander with me as long as I could and tutored them myself. Lord Huntly was quite a lad by the time we sent him off to Eton . . . and he was all the better for it. I may not be so successful with the youngest. Keep yer boy with ye as long as ye can," she advised with a sad smile.

Thomas scanned her face once again, but she averted her eyes.

"I'd like to keep *ye* with me as long as I can . . ." he murmured, bending down to kiss her lips, at first softly, and then with growing intensity. His hands caressed her shoulders. "How long might that be, Jenny, lass?"

Her lips parted as a rush of emotions gripped her with as much tensile strength as his large hands, which were now pressing the length of his body against hers. His arms wrapped her in a tight embrace and he bent down and kissed her ravenously. Memories of numerous painful farewells pierced through the passionate haze which had started to envelop her. She pushed hard against his chest.

"*No!*" she gasped, her breathing ragged. "I canna bear ye to leave me again. Thomas! If I let ye touch me like this, and then tomorrow, ye go—" She stepped back several paces, swallowing tears, and shook her head fiercely. "We seem to make love every ten years or so!" she cried passionately, "and then we part. The next time 'twill be 1807—a new *century*!—and I'll be an old crone! I canna *bear* losing ye again, Thomas, so I—"

Suddenly, she bolted along the gravel shoreline, leaving Thomas staring at her retreating form.

"Jenny!" he shouted after her. "Jenny, come back!"

Jane ran blindly toward the stand of Caledonian pines that led away from the water's edge. The soles of her thin slippers were punctured by stones and she tripped repeatedly. She felt slightly foolish to be escaping from a man who, only a few short minutes earlier, had told her he would be leaving Scotland soon—and probably forever.

She stopped running and leaned heavily against a tree, trying

to catch her breath. She fought to regain some sense of composure. Thomas suddenly appeared behind her.

"Look at us, lassie!" he panted. "We can scarcely draw a breath! We're too old for such nonsense!" He gathered her resisting body against his and kissed the top of her head. "Ye're feeling sad because I told ye I'd planned to stay in Scotland only a short while, am I right?"

Unable to dissemble, she merely shook her head.

" 'Tis clear to me I'm not the only one who's suffered loss after loss, darling girl," he said softly, stroking her hair in a soothing, familiar fashion. "Ye've watched me go away many a time, havna ye, dearheart? I'm probably the only man ye'll ever know who's braved the treacherous Atlantic six times . . . but here I am . . . and 'twas always *ye* who brought me back."

"Not true," Jane mumbled into his neck. "This time ye came back for Louisa's sake."

"That was only one of the reasons, pet," Thomas said. He brushed his lips against hers once more. "Ye do know that I love ye still . . . love ye so very much?" he asked gently. "I think I need to tell ye that because ye have a certain look to ye, sometimes . . . a look that shutters yer eyes and shuts me out." He took her by both shoulders and shook her with infinite gentleness. "I love ye *still*, ye devilish wench! And I'm more than pleased to hear from Angus all the consternation ye've stirred up in Parliament and yer electioneering and backstairs maneuvering at Court, even if ye *did* keep old Geordie on his throne!"

He pulled away and stared at her, as if willing her to accept the truth of his words.

"I will always love ye, Jane Maxwell, until they bury me in the ground and use this kilt as my shroud."

For a moment, she stared at him silently and then flung her arms around his shoulders. She pulled his head down and pressed her cheek close to his. She luxuriated in the feel of his bronzed skin, in the slight stubble that had grown during his journey from Struy. She thought of what her life would have been like, had she always had the right to hold this man close to her all these years, to cosset him and cry on his shoulder when life's blows struck, to be angry with him and then make it up, to talk to him in the easy way they'd always shared, to be flesh of his flesh . . . to be Thomas's wife. She released her hold and searched his face, more dear to her now than ever before.

"Gods wounds! Dinna talk of shrouds and such!" she cried. "Dinna talk about death on such a day as this!"

"Then let's talk of life." He smiled down at her. "*Our* life. Will ye be staying the summer at Kinrara?" he asked, gazing at her steadily.

Nodding affirmatively, Jane knew instinctively that Angus had told him of her long estrangement from Alex and their separate living arrangements. She fought the impulse to let her mind speed ahead to wherever Thomas's question might be leading.

"I have an even better idea," she said quickly, leading him by the hand toward a small boat tethered to the branch of a tree which hung out over the water. "Let's not talk at all. Please step into this bateau, good sir," she said brusquely, pointing to the bow. "I shall row. I enjoy it."

Thomas fell silent as Jane pulled skillfully on the oars. As the boat pointed toward the small island studded with the flagstone castle, her mind drifted back to the many times she had rowed out here, seeking solace from the dreadful pain of Thomas's many departures . . . from the exhaustion of long years of conflict with Alex . . . from the disappointments and resentments she had felt that seemed, at times, too much to bear. Yet bear them she had, with the help of this place . . . the peace of this lair of the ferocious Wolf of Badenoch. Coming here had always made her feel closer to Thomas somehow. The sight of the vine-covered castle walls and the swans nesting in the reeds had often calmed her and stemmed her tears.

Jane pulled hard on the oars and headed for the old stone dock. She scanned the clusters of canary grass and yellow marsh marigolds nearby for a glimpse of the pair of swans that each year had made Loch-an-Eilean their home. She often wondered if it were the same pair Thomas and she had seen back in 1768, since she knew swans could live for thirty years or more in feathered monogamy, returning again and again to the same breeding grounds.

Thomas stepped from the bow of the little boat and secured the line to an iron ring embedded at the rim of the stone dock. Jane heard a loud rustling in the reeds. A large-breasted trumpeter emerged, honking at them angrily.

"They're still here . . ." Jane breathed as Thomas caught her hand and helped her ashore.

"They'll always come back to this spot, I expect," he whispered. "They, or their children." He scanned the overgrown courtyard and strode toward a small pine tree, which had struggled to take root in the thicket manteling the ground and stone outcrops. "Peel off a few branches, my love," he said with a wolfish grin, "unless ye'd prefer to be bedded right here on this stone dock . . ."

Jane's heart beat faster at his allusion to their making love.

"Why, ye're actually blushing!" he teased as she ducked her head to break off small fragrant pine boughs near the base of the tree.

"Ye're a confident jackal . . ." she tossed over her shoulder. "Cocky, aren't ye, that ye'll woo me so easily into yer lair?"

"Aye, that I am," he said, grinning. His face grew serious as he caught her hand, which clutched a small branch, and kissed it. "Angus told me ye and Alex had separated long ago. So, if ye'll have me, darling Jenny, I'd like to spend the summer with ye at Kinrara. I could take some of the burden off ye and Angus till ye can train a new factor."

Jane's mind whirled at a dizzying speed. Four months with Thomas by her side. Four months away from cares and worries and prying eyes and Alex's caustic jabs and the demands of being a duchess of the realm. Four months with Thomas . . . and then a lifetime without him.

Thomas took her other hand and held them both fast.

"We'll sleep night after night in each other's arms," he said, "and sometimes I'll woo ye not at all—just like old married folk!"

Jane leaned her weight against him and closed her eyes. He was really here. He wanted to stay. It wasn't a dream. They could live together at Kinrara as man and wife . . . at least for a while. Her breath caught in her throat. Could she ever acquire a talent for not looking forward and not looking back? Could she learn to live her life, one day at a time, enjoying the sweetness of each moment . . . the blessedness of having Thomas with her for a time? And could she possibly survive parting from him once again—probably for the last time—when the autumn leaves on the larches and birch settled on the rich, moist soil, and the lavender heather turned brown on the moors of Kinrara?

Her silence extended a moment longer. Then she spoke quietly.

" 'Tis the most wonderful proposal a lass could be offered," she said. "I'd be most pleased if ye'd stay the summer, Thomas. And I'd be pleased if ye'd let me serve as tutor to Max in exchange for yer acting as factor while ye're here. Dear God! Let us *please* be like old married folk!"

"But not today," he responded.

Her eyes widened. She looked at him questioningly. He laughed gave her a swift hug.

"I'll not treat ye like an old married woman *this* day, my Jenny of Monreith!" he exalted. "We've gathered branches enough, lass. Come on!"

Arms full of the pungent pine, they scampered like children up the moss-encrusted stairs that wound around the tower, up, up to the highest chamber. An empty bird's nest, large enough to house an osprey, rested on the wide ledge of the stone window. Jane and Thomas constructed a soft, fragrant pallet on the slate floor and stared at each other across its green expanse.

"I'm not a lass of seventeen—nor even twenty-five, my love," she said with uncharacteristic diffidence, referring to the previous times they had made love at Loch-an-Eilean. "I've birthed seven children, and I show it."

Thomas patted his midsection as he unstrapped the leather belt that held his kilt in place.

"Ye winna find the same bold stallion of memory here either, Jenny love . . . but an aging fool . . . a man who loves ye with all his heart and soul and poor, decrepit flesh. Come here, my dearest heart."

Silently, Jane stepped forward and allowed Thomas to undress her. His movements were deliberate and slow, relishing each moment as he removed the last vestments of Jane's clothing, except for her thin chemise.

" 'Tis so strange," he said, his eyes sweeping her body. "But when I see ye like this, I still feel like that eighteen-year-old stripling who first kissed ye in the hay byre behind Hyndford Close."

"Aye," she said, her voice crackling with emotion. " 'Tis the same for me." She kissed him softly on each cheek. "And now *ye*, Captain Fraser," she whispered. "I doubt yer flesh looks quite as decrepit as ye claim."

She tugged at his linen blouse. Her breath caught at the sight of his bare torso, still tightly muscled, despite the jagged scar indenting his upper arm and the other old wound, which slashed across his chest. The mat of russet hair nestling there, like that on his head, was now dusted with gray. Thomas was still a magnificent-looking man. An ache deep inside her started to expand in warm circles, sending tremors throughout the rest of her body. With a mischievous glance, she unwrapped his kilt from around his hips, which were still smooth and trim. Then, she removed her own chemise and allowed his eyes to feast on her naked form.

"It may be a fine, sunny day," he smiled at her as he

in the sight of her full breasts and slightly rounded belly, "but I would like it very much, lass, if ye'd wrap yer arms around me for warmth. I do believe the sight of my gooseflesh might soon disgust ye!" he laughed.

They both glanced toward the windows cut into the stone walls of the small chamber and shivered slightly as a chilly current of air blew into the room.

Together, they spread Thomas's kilt on the pine boughs, and stretched out on their makeshift bed. Enfolding each other in their arms, they sought warmth and comfort and an almost mystical closeness that they both had hungered for, for so long.

Jane nuzzled Thomas's neck, licking his ear like a proprietary cat. Soon, she was covering his upper body with excited little kisses. She could feel the strength of his desire for her against her thigh. He had become rigid as steel and she took inordinate pride in her power to arouse him to such a heated state.

"Ye always could do this to me, couldna, ye wench!" he whispered, as if reading her thoughts. "Since ye were a wee lass ye've known ye could bewitch me and reveled in it all yer life. Well," he added, gently kneading the small of her back with one hand, "so have I." Shifting his weight abruptly, he rolled her over on her back. His lips traveled sensuously along her collar bone, ultimately resting against the tiny mole nestled at the base of her neck. "Precious," he murmured against her flesh. "So precious."

Suddenly he was straddling her, parting her thighs with his knees. His arms flanked her sides as he supported his weight on his palms. He slowly brushed that bold and most vulnerable part of his body against the triangle of soft brown hair defining the space between her legs.

"I'll not dissemble," he said huskily, staring down at her. "I want ye, and I love ye, and I want ye to want me. 'Tis always been this way for me."

It all means something, a part of her mind sang as she reached up and pulled his weight down on her. All the love and caring and loyalty she'd carried for this man for an entire lifetime was well invested. All the pain and sorrow and loss and finding their way back through the confusion of their lives had led to these cherished moments at Loch-an-Eilean. *It all means something . . . still!*

There was a seasoned joy to their lovemaking on pine boughs in the tiny stone chamber above the lake. A lifetime of caring and concern shone in their eyes, speaking eloquently of the bond that they had forged between them in childhood and that they had managed to preserve and nourish, despite their long separations and their missteps along the way.

As Thomas entered her, Jane called to him fiercely, praised him, exhorted him, revealed to him all there was to know of her desires, her very essence. *'Twas like Robert Burn's poetry*, some sane part of her brain cried out. *And he knew her* . . . oh yes, this man *knew* her. Thomas knew her beginnings, knew her struggles, knew her diffidence as well as her bold ambition, her weaknesses, and her strengths. Thomas Fraser knew everything there was to know about her, good and bad, and *still* he loved her!

She was naked before him. Not merely in body, but her very soul was stripped of pretense and subterfuge, stripped of defenses and her lifelong need to control her world so she could protect herself from being hurt or abandoned. She could reveal to Thomas who she really was, including her flaws. And he accepted her—which only made her love for him multiply a thousandfold.

Their cries of release mingled in the crystalline air and an answering call of a proud trumpeter swan, gracefully carving furrows on the glassy surface of the loch, echoed their joy. Thomas and Jane seemed to be suspended in their tower room in a net of diamonds that sparkled on the blue water below their pine-strewn bower and shone in the clear, silvery sky overhead. A breeze whispering through their chamber cooled their bodies, slick with sweat, as they lay quietly in each other's arms. Each was reluctant to break the magical spell, which held them in its silence.

Thomas flung one end of his kilt around them both and held Jane against his chest. He tenderly coaxed a lock of her hair off her damp forehead and kissed the spot where it had lain. He clasped her right hand and brushed his lips gently against her injured finger.

"In so many ways, Jenny, love, ye're just the same—beautiful and so full of life," he said softly. "Ye're a wonder to behold." He leaned on one elbow and gazed through the narrow window opposite him, staring over the water at the protective circle of stately Caledonian pines holding Loch-an-Eilean in its embrace. "Dinna ye see," he mused aloud, "that we never, for one moment, lost what we had? Our sorrow was . . . that for such a long time, we couldna have it *together*."

"And now?" she whispered.

Thomas gazed down at her for a moment. His eyes spoke wordlessly of the futility of making any predictions about the future.

She smiled ruefully and tucked the top of her head under his chin.

"The summer . . ." she murmured, closing her eyes. " 'Tis like a gift from the Highland fairies. Ye're here at Kinrara for the whole, beautiful summer."

"Aye, Jenny, that I am," he said quietly.

The moment was sweet, indeed, she thought. She wouldn't look forward and she wouldn't look back.

" 'Tis enough," she said, smiling faintly, and tightened her arms around him.

Acknowledgments

When a writer embarks on a project of the scope and size of *Island of the Swans*, it is impossible to anticipate the scores of people who will make significant contributions to the finished work along the way.

Foremost on my list of people to thank are the staff and administration of the Henry E. Huntington Library and Art Gallery in San Marino, California. I was granted a Readership in Eighteenth-century Scottish and American History for a year, which stretched to nearly four. With this, came a desk in the library's magnificent Main Reading Room and the helpful assistance of such people in Readers' Services as Virginia Renner, Doris Smedes, Mary Jones, and Mary Wright, not to mention the cheerful support of the Huntington's former director Robert Middlekauff and assistance from able administrators Glenda Van der Zaag and Katherine Wilson. Thanks, too, to the head of the Department of Research Martin Ridge, to Diana Wilson, an art historian who led me to descriptions of the artist studio of Sir Joshua Reynolds, and to Robert Wark, Curator of the Huntington Art Collections. I am also grateful for the suggestions and encouragement offered by my fellow researchers and authors at the Huntington, among them, Marsha Fowler, Catherine Kelly, Karen Langlois, Karen Lystra, Barry Menikoff, Jeanne Perkins, Susan Puz, Elizabeth Talbot-Martin, Catherine Turney, Midge Sherwood, and Paul Zall. Any violations of the high standards of historical research embraced by these dear friends and staff are clearly my own responsibility.

In addition, I would like to thank the various anonymous librarians throughout Scotland who granted innumerable kindnesses to an American novelist dashing in and out of their quiet lairs over several years' research. Also, I greatly appreciated guidance from costume experts Helen Bennett of the National Museum of Antiquities of Scotland and Edward Maeder, curator of textiles and costumes at the Los Angeles County Museum of Art.

And then there is Major Robin McLaren, the present owner of Jane Maxwell's Highland home, Kinrara. He caught me looking longingly over the fence bordering the estate's parkland and invited me in for a drink. In his splendid paneled library, he shared part of the tale of the house's former mistress with me, gleaned from conversations with his late godfather and his own mother. Thanks to his wonderful hospitality, and that of his wife, Annie, I was treated to several stays in Kinrara House, sleeping in my heroine Jane's bedroom, which looks over the River Spey. Major McLaren himself rowed me out to the derelict castle of the Wolf of Badenoch on Loch-an-Eilean and permitted me to visit a variety of scenic spots Jane herself had once frequented.

Simon, the 17th Lord Lovat of Fraser, one of the great Highland chiefs and a Scottish hero of World War II, also extended extraordinary hospitality to me and my family over several years, never protesting when his ancestor Simon, Master of Lovat, began to figure as a faintly villainous force in the novel. To Lord Lovat and Lady Rose, I offer my deepest thanks.

Similarly, I am grateful to Sir George Gordon-Lennox and his wife for granting me several tours of Gordon Castle in Fochabers and filling my head with family lore. George Gordon, an historian in Aberdeen, made a major contribution to what is known about Jane Maxwell, 4th Duchess of Gordon, in his limited edition work, *The Last Dukes of Gordon and their Consorts, 1743–1864*.

Lorna Lumsden, of Abriachian, near Loch Ness, sheltered me on several research trips to the Highlands, generously offering her salty humor and lifelong knowledge of the area.

In America, I must thank my husband, journalist and screenwriter Anthony Pattison Cook, who accompanied me on many of my journeys and cast his professional eye on my manuscript many times during its preparation. My son, Jamie Ware Billett, grew to young adulthood during the period it took to complete this project and cheered me every step of the way, even to the extent of allowing me to dress him in his family tartan at a very young age.

I am deeply indebted to the work of pioneering historian, Gerda Lerner, Robinson-Edwards Professor of History at the University of Wisconsin, for her arresting book *The Majority Finds Its Past: Placing Women in History*. Her insistence that half of human history has yet to be written spurred me forward at a crucial period in the writing phase of this effort.

Another scholar, in her own way, is Ann Skipper, an instructress and member of the Royal Scottish Country Dance Society who introduced me practically and historically to Scottish country dancing and to Jane Maxwell's noteworthy talent for this lively pastime (still very much a part of Scottish and American social life—if you know where to look).

In the process of my refighting the American Revolution, Registered Guide Sonya O'Malley of Charleston, along with a number of other enthusiastic guides at Yorktown, Brandywine, Williamsburg, and Savannah made researching the saga of the kilted regiment known as the 71st Fraser Highlanders an utter delight. So did reading *The Fraser Highlanders* and interviewing its author, Colonel Ralph J. Harper.

Marilyn McCracken, a lover of Scotland herself and a superb copy editor, gave the manuscript meticulous attention before it ever reached a publisher, while Gayle Van Dyck proved an inspiring traveling companion and expert reader of eighteenth-century penmanship. Historical novelists Sue Gross and Elda Minger gave invaluable suggestions along the way. Thanks too, for the support of the women in the Los Angeles Women Writers' Computer Group, which I cofounded with writer Betsy James midway through this project.

And finally, I wish to express my deepest appreciation to my agent, Don Congdon; to my editor at Bantam Books, Beverly Lewis; to my late father, the novelist Harlan Ware; and to the late Jeanne Cagney, who gave me my first swan and convinced me that I could write a novel.

Ciji Ware

FIVE UNFORGETTABLE NOVELS
by
CELESTE DE BLASIS

☐ **THE NIGHT CHILD** (27744, $3.95)
The story of a proud, passionate woman and two very special kinds of love.

☐ **THE PROUD BREED** (27196, $4.95)
THE PROUD BREED vividly recreates California's exciting past, from the wild country to the pirated coast, from gambling dens to lavish ballrooms. Here is Celeste De Blasis' beloved bestselling novel: a world you will not want to leave, and will never forget.

☐ **WILD SWAN** (27260, $4.95)
Sweeping from England's West Country in the years of the Napoleonic wars, to the beauty of Maryland horse country, here is a novel richly spun of authentically detailed history and sumptuous romance.

☐ **SWAN'S CHANCE** (25692, $4.50)
SWAN'S CHANCE continues the magnificent saga begun in WILD SWAN: an unforgettable chronicle of a great dynasty.

☐ **SUFFER A SEA CHANGE** (27750, $3.95)
Her love, world and very future change under the light of an island sun as Jessica Banbridge comes to grips with the past and opens herself up to life.

Available wherever Bantam Books are sold or use this page to order.

- -